Empress of the Jade Realm

Fractured Empire Saga Book Four

Starr Z. Davies

Character Assassin Books

First published in the United States in 2022 by Character Assassin Books an imprint of Starr Z Davies, 1328 Lynn Avenue Altoona, WI 54720 USA. Email: starr@starrzdavies.com

Cover design and typography by Katrina Designs
Book layout and design by Starr Z Davies & Atticus software
Maps, glyphs, and illustrations relating to maps by Starr Z Davies & Inkarnate software

www.starrzdavies.com

Contents

For Mandukhai.
I hope I have done your spirit justice.

MONGOLIA 1450–1500

OIRAT
UYGHUR
TERRITORY
KHANGAI MOUNTA
ALTAI MOUNTAINS
ZAVKHAN RIVER
TIANSHAN MOUNTAINS
TURFAN
HAMI

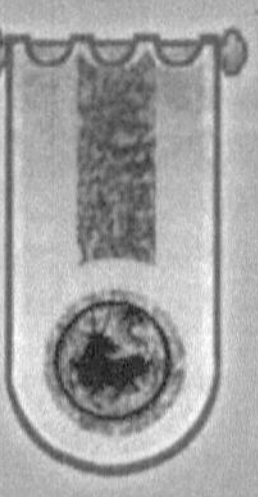

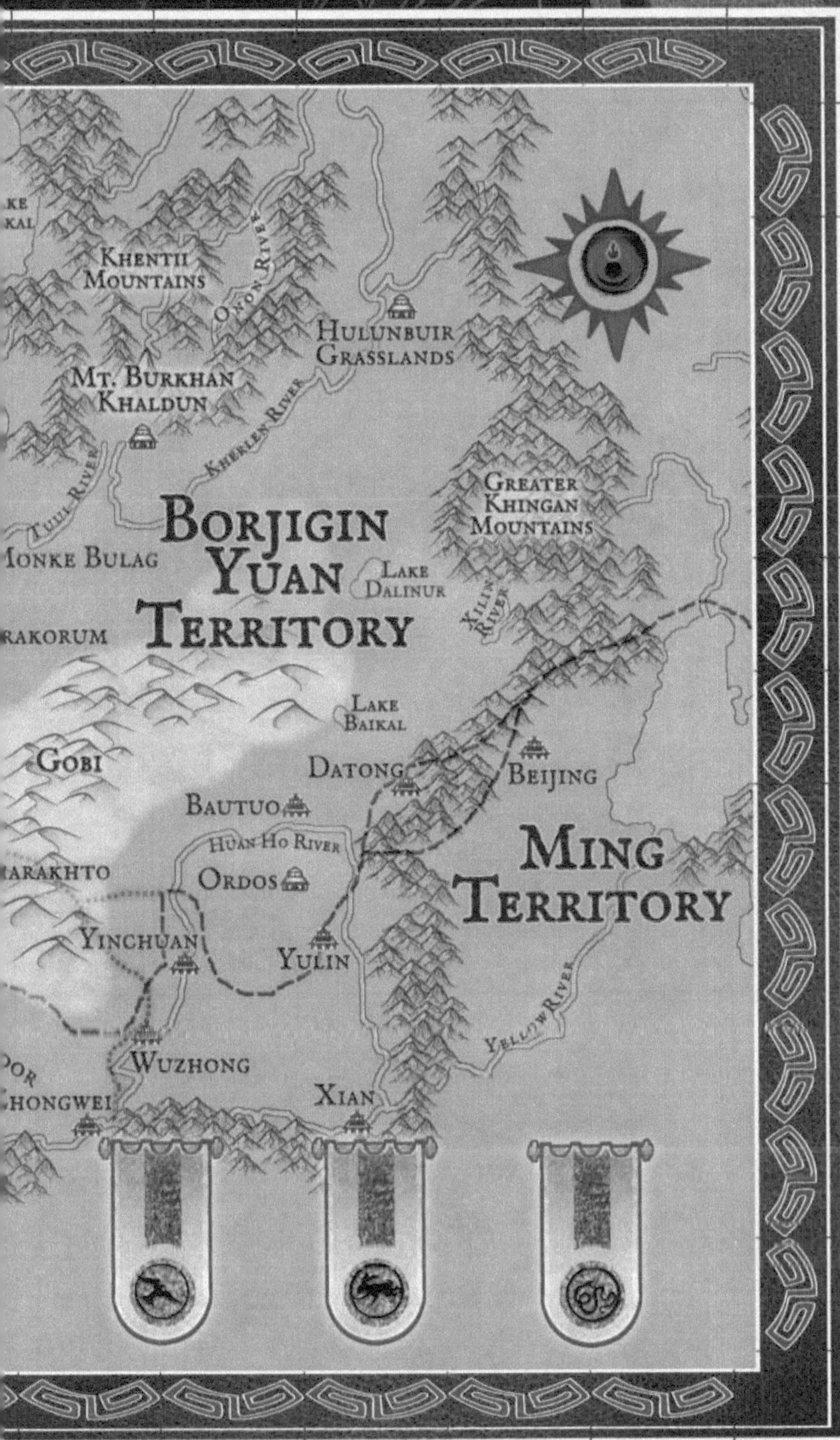
KHENTII MOUNTAINS
ONON RIVER
HULUNBUIR GRASSLANDS
MT. BURKHAN KHALDUN
KHERLEN RIVER
GREATER KHINGAN MOUNTAINS
TUUL RIVER
MONKE BULAG
BORJIGIN YUAN TERRITORY
LAKE DALINUR
XILIN RIVER
KARAKORUM
LAKE BAIKAL
GOBI
DATONG
BEIJING
BAUTUO
HUAN HO RIVER
MING TERRITORY
KARAKHTO
ORDOS
YINCHUAN
YULIN
YELLOW RIVER
DOR
WUZHONG
ZHONGWEI
XIAN
KE KAL

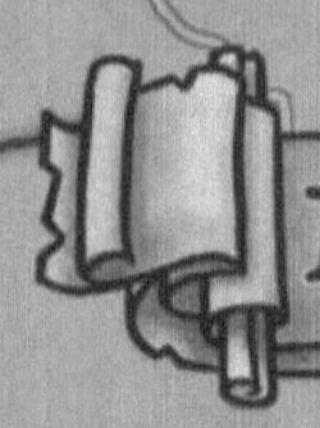

MONGOLIA 1450-1500

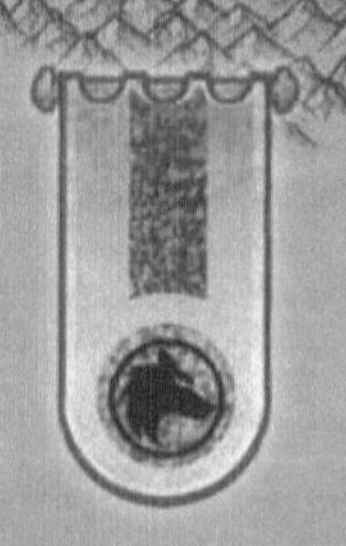

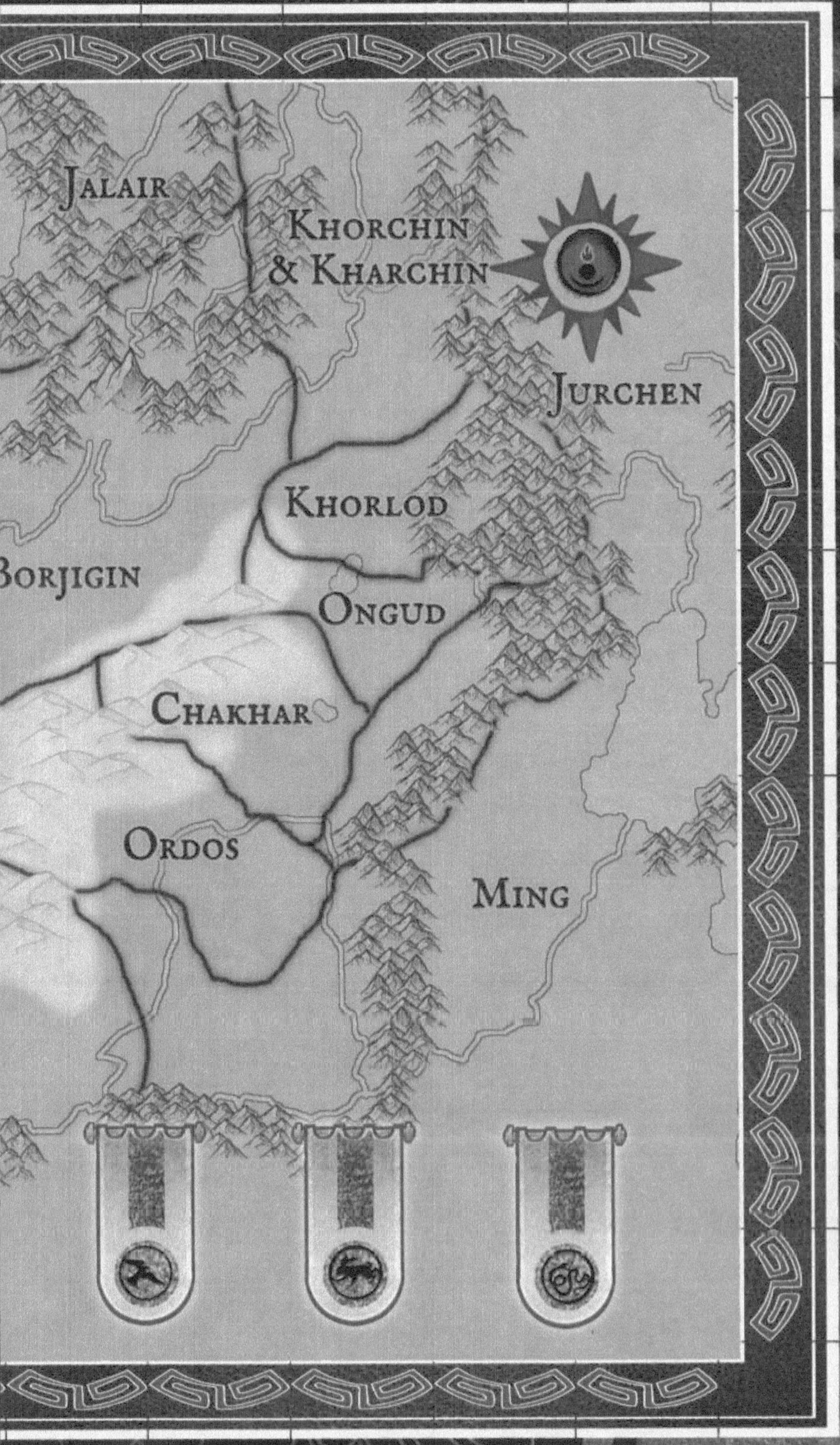

JALAIR
KHORCHIN & KHARCHIN
JURCHEN
KHORLOD
BORJIGIN
ONGUD
CHAKHAR
ORDOS
MING

SOUTHERN GOBI TERRITORIES
ONGI RIVER
LAKE BAIKAL
DATONG
BAUTUO
HUAN HO RIVER
ORDOS
YULIN
KHARAKHTO
YINCHUAN
WUZHONG
GANSU CORRIDOR
ZHONGWEI
XIAN

ROYAL LINEAGE
THROUGH 1480

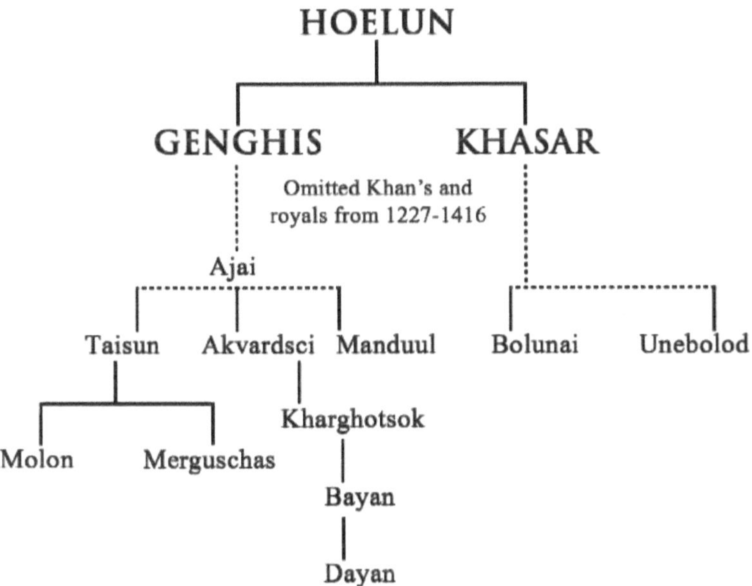

While there are certainly other royals before Ajai, for the purposes of this series, only those after him will be listed to avoid confusion. Esen is not listed on this chart because he does not descend from this royal tree.

Glossary & Pronunciation Guide

airag (eye-rahg) – alcoholic drink made from fermented mare's milk, typically milky in color

arban (ahr-bahn) – unit of ten Mongol warriors

Bankhar (bahn-khahr) – traditional sheepherding dog of the Mongolian steppe; 24-31 inches tall at the shoulder with typically dark brown hair

bariach (bar-ee-ach) – ancient art of bonesetting and therapeutic massage

Biyelgee (bey-eel-geeh) – traditional dance of celebration and community

black airag – stronger version of regular airag with a longer fermentation process, typically clear in color

boal (boh-ahl) – honey wine

bökh (boo-k) – Mongolian style of wrestling where only the feet are allowed to touch the ground or you lose

boqta (bohk-tah) – column-like headdress decorated with beads and silver; the taller the boqta, the more prominent the woman wearing it

buuz (boos) – meat stuffed dumplings

deel (deal) – robe-like wrap worn by the Mongol people, traditionally made of silk, velvet, or woolen felt with ties or silver buttons and belted at the waist with a belt; lined with sheep's wool or fur in the winter

ger (grr) – round, dome-like house made of Birchwood lattice and lathes, then covered in wool felt; known in America as a yurt

gonji (goonj) – a princess

jagun (jah-gahn) – unit of 100 Mongol warriors (or 10 arban)

jinong (gee-nong) – a prince

khatun (ka-toon) – an official title for a Mongol queen

kurultai (kuh-ruhl-tai) – a gathering of tribal lords where they elected the next Great Khan *mingghan* (min-ghahn) – unit of 1000 Mongol warriors (or 10 jagan)

Noyan (no-yawn) – exclusive title given to Mongol High Lords; an esteemeed position of honor

orlok (oor-lahk) – field commander of multiple tumens

paiza (pie-zah) – a golden medallion of safe passage, given only to high-ranking officials as a means of protection under the Great Khan

shanaavch (shah-navsh) – headdress made of long strings of beads and bells, typically silver, coral, or turquoise

sulde (sool-duh) – a banner made of colored horse-hair, typically arranged in a circle

toortsog (toort-sogh) – hat made of silk, sometimes with fur or felt lining and a knot of colored tails or feathers at the top; typically worn by noble men

tumed (too-med) – a Mongol province

tumen (tyoo-mehn) – regiment of 10,000 Mongol warriors

uni (oo-nee) – a pole made of birch; used as a support beam for the ceiling of a ger

CHARACTERS

Aglaqu[†] (ahg-la-coo) – Ordos Lord

Alag (al-lag) – Alyghuchid Lordling; Unige's heir

Alayitung[†] (al-eye-ih-toong) – Borjigin commander; Vice Chancellor

Albeq (al-bek) – Tabun khan

Altan (ahl-than) – Lady and commander of the Jalair; Hulun's daughter

Arqai[†] (ar-kai) – Ordos Lord

Arslan (ahr-slahn) – Mandukhai's night guard

Asha[†] (ah-shah) – Oirat Lord/Paisahan's son

Babaqai[†] (ba-ba-kai) – Togochi's second son with Jaghan

Babutai[†] (ba-boo-tigh) – Issama's second son with Siker

Bagasun[†] (ba-ga-soon) – Altan's oldest son

Bagatur[†] (ba-ga-toor) – Kharchin khan

Batsaihan (baht-sahi-han) – Odgerel's father

Bayan Bolkhu Mongke[†] (bay-yahn bohl-koo mohng-kay) – Borjigin prince; last true descendant of Genghis Khan

Belku[†] (bell-coo) – Chakhar Lord/heir

Berkedai (buhr-ke-dahee) – Khorchin commander; Bayan's guard

Bigirsen[†] (big-er-sehn) – Uyghur warlord; Manduul Khan's Vice Regent; orlok of the southern tumens of the Great Khan

Bolunai (boh-loo-nahee) – Khorchin khan; older brother of Unebolod; descendant of Khasar

Boke[†] (boh-kay) – Borjigin tribe; young leader of Manduul's royal guard

Boragan (bow-ra-gahn) – Ongud Lord; son of Korgiz khan

Borogchin[†] (boh-rohg-chin) – Borjigin princess; niece of Manduul Khan

Burani[†] (bur-ah-nee) – Issama's oldest son with Siker

Chakicha[†] (cha-key-cha) – Tabun Lord; son of Albeq khan

Chari[†] (cha-ree) – lesser Oirat Lord

Chenghua[†] (jen-gwa) – Ming Emperor

Chimgee (chim-jee) – Huoshai's mother

Dashai (dah-shy) – man who saves Bayan in the Gobi; serves in Issama's forces

Dayan Batu Khan[†] (day-ahn bah-too) – Bayan's long-lost son

Degghar (dehg-ghahr) – Chakhar man; Siker's father

Dochigen[†] (doh-chee-jen) – lesser Monochin tribal khan

Emeeltorson (em-eel-tor-sun) – Esige/Huoshai's oldest son

Enkh (enk) – Bayan's servant

Esen[†] (eh-sehn) – Oirat Lord and leader; Borjigin Butcher

Esige[†] (eh-seeg-hay) – Borjigin princess; niece of Manduul Khan

Ganzorig (gahn-zor-ig) – Bolunai's youngest son; promised to Odgerel

Genghis Khan[†] (jehn-giss) – First Great Khan of the Mongol Nation; died 1227

Geriel (jer-ee-el) – Togochi's second wife

Getei[†] (jet-ehee) – Ongud soothsaycr

Guden (goo-dehn) – Chakhar khan

Hulun (huh-loon) – Lord of the Jalair

Huoshai[†] (hwoh-shy) – Lord of the Urainkhai

Ibarai[†] (ee-bar-eye) – Ordos Lord/commander

Issama[†] (ee-sah-mah) – Bigirsen's Uyghur advisor

Jaghan (jahg-han) – Jalair tribe; Togochi's wife

Jangi[†] (jahn-jee) – Uyghur warrior; Nemeku's guard

Kelegei[†] (kell-eh-gay) – Erkegud tribal khan

Khadag[†] (kah-dahg) – Uyghur who rescues Batu from Issama

Khasar[†] (kah-sahr) – brother of Genghis; son of Hoelun

Khosolchi[†] (co-soy-chi) – Borjigin shaman; serves Manduul

Khutulun[†] (koo-too-loon) – daughter of Kaidu; warrior princess

Korgiz (koor-gihs) – Ongud khan

Legusi[†] (leg-oo-see) – Ordos khan

Mandukhai[†] (mahn-doo-khahee) – Ongud daughter of a lord; Manduul Khan's second wife

Manduul Khan[†] (mahn-dool) – Oirat-Borjigin ruler of Mongolia; descendent of Genghis Khan

Mendu[†] (mehn-doo) – Khorlod khan

Mingtau[†] (ming-taoo) – Chakhar elder/commander

Mogurkei[†] (mo-gur-kay) – Ordos Lord

Molon Khan[†] (moh-lohn) – 17-year-old Great Khan before Manduul; Manduul's nephew; killed in battle

Nahai[†] (na-hi) – Uyghur commander; Issama's right hand man

Nemeku[†] (ne-me-coo) – Bigirsen/Borogchin's son; Dayan's cousin

Nergui (nair-gooee) – Mandukhai's loyal Ongud guard; murdered by Bayan

Odgerel (ode-ger-el) – Khorchin woman; Unebolod's servant

Odsar (ohd-sahr) – Unebolod's dead wife

Ogedei[†] (oh-geh-day) – lesser Buryat tribal khan

Ong (ahng) – Dayan's servant

Ordag[†] (or-dayg) – lesser Asud khan

Orghana (org-ha-na) – Ordos Lady; Legusi's little sister

Ormeger[†] (or-mee-gr) – Urainkhai commander; Huoshai's cousin

Paisahan[†] (pie-sah-han) – Oirat khan

Qolotai[†] (co-lo-tie) – Issama's third wife

Qori[†] (kor-ee) – Ordos Lord

Samur[†] (sah-muhr) – great-great-grandmother of Bayan

Sarnai (sar-nigh) – Qori's wife

Satai[†] (sah-tie) – Lady of the Alaguchid tribe; wife of Unige

Sayiqan[†] (say-ih-khan) – Ordos Lord

Seguse[†] (seg-oo-say) – Uyghur warrior; Borogchin's spy/messenger

Siker[†] (see-kur) – daughter of Degghar; Chakhar girl; Bayan's lover

Soke[†] (soh-kay) – Khorchin commander

Sorkhogtani[†] (sor-kog-ta-nai) – Kublai Khan's mother

Taisun Khan[†] (tahee-soon) – Manduul's older half-brother; killed by Esen

Tayiqu[†] (tay-ick-oo) – Lady of the Urainkhai; Dayan's second wife

Tengghar (tayng-ghahr) – Khorchin lord; Bolunai's son; Unebolod's nephew

Toghon[†] (tohg-hone) – Oirat Lord/commander

Tolokan[†] (toh-low-can) – Urainkhai khan

Toregene[†] (tor-eh-jenay) – Ogedei Khan's wife; empress for five years

Torgus (tohr-gus) – Mandukhai's guard

Torobolod[†] (tow-row-boh-lod) – Mandukhai/Dayan's son

Toroltu[†] (tow-roll-too) – Mandukhai/Dayan's daughter

Torudur[†] (tor-oo-dur) – Togochi's eldest son

Tsetseg[†] (zeht-sehg) – Esen's daughter; Bayan's mother

Togochi[†] (toh-goh-chee) – lord and General of the Khorlod; Manduul's loyal sworn brother (no blood)

Tulugen[†] (too-loo-jen) – Three Guards Lord

Tuya (too-yah) – Mandukhai's Ongud servant

Uingen[†] (oo-in-jen) – Issama's first wife

Ulum[†] (oo-lum) – Ordos Lord

Ulusbolod[†] (oo-luss-boh-lod) – Mandukhai/Dayan's son

Unebolod[†] (oo-nuh-boh-lod) – lord of the Khorchin; Manduul's loyal sword brother (no blood); Orlok of the northern tumens of the Great Khan

Unige[†] (oo-nee-kay) – Alyghuchid Lord/leader; Borjigin loyalist; a member of Manduul Khan's council

Utagachi[†] (oo-ta-ga-chee) – Ordos Lord

Wang Yue[†] (wang-you) – Ming Commander

Yaqui[†] (ya-kwee) – Khorlod Lord/commander

Yeke[†] (yeh-keh) – Uyghur daughter of Bigirsen; Manduul Khan's first wife

Yungei (yoon-geh-hee) – Khorchin commander; Bayan's guard

[†] **Denotes real historical figures**

TRIBES

Alyghuchid (al-ee-goo-chid)) – tribe of the northern steppe

Asud (ah-sood) – lesser tribe of the eastern steppe

Borjigin (bohr-eh-gin) – tribe of the Great Khan Genghis

Chakhar (shah-kahr) – tribe of the southern steppe; Siker's tribe

Great Horde – tribe of the far northern steppe (Russian territory); formerly the Golden Horde

Erkegud (air-ke-goot) – lesser tribe of the Khorlod

Jalair (jah-laheer) – tribe of the northernmost steppe

Kharchin (car-chin) – subtribe of the Khorchin

Khorchin (koor-chin) – tribe of Genghis Khan's younger brother Khasar; Yuan Dynasty ally

Khorlod (koor-lahd) – tribe of the eastern steppe; Togochi's tribe

Oirat (ohee-raht) – collective of four major western tribes who oppose Borjigin rule; commonly called "Four Oirat"
Ongud (ahn-goot) – tribe of the southern steppe; Mandukhai's birth tribe
Ordos (or-dose) – tribe of the southern steppe
Tabun (tah-boon) – lesser tribe of the eastern steppe
Three Guards – collection of 3 smaller tribes in the south
Urainkhai (oo-ree-ahng-high) – southern tribe of the steppe
Uyghur (wee-ger) – tribe of the southwestern step; formerly Chagatai Khanate

LOCATIONS

Altai Mountains (all-tie) – mountain range cradling Oirat territory
Bautuo (bow-to-oh) – Ming/Mongol city north of the Huang Ho River
Datong (dah-tong) – Ming/Mongol city near the Great Wall
Gansu Corridor (gahn-soo) – corridor between the mountains and rivers leading into China
Greater Khingan Mountains (kin-gahn) – mountain range barring the eastern Mongol border
Hami (hah-mee) – oasis city in the Gobi connecting the far east to the far west
Huang Ho River (wang-ho) – Great Loop river, also known as the Yellow River
Hulunbuir (hoo-loon-boo-eer) – eastern Grasslands of the Khorchin & Kharchin tribes
Karakorum (ka-ra-core-um) – Mongolian sacred capital city
Khangai Mountains (khan-guy) – mountains west of Mongke Bulag
Kharakhoto (car-ah-coat-oh) – deserted Mongol city in the Gobi
Khentii Mountains (ken-tea) – dominant mountain range in the northern steppe
Kherlen River (curl-ehn) – river of the Mongol steppe
Kokegota (co-keg-oh-ta) – Ming-controlled city
Lake Dai (die) – Lake on the edge of the desert, surrounded by grasslands, future neighbor of Hohhot
Lake Dalinur (dah-lin-oor) – Large lake bordering the Gobi, Khorlod, and Ongud territory
Mongke Bulag (mohng-kay boo-lahg) – Manduul Khan's capital in the Orkhon Valley

Mt. Burkhan Khaldun (bur-khan cahll-dune) – sacred mountain of Genghis in the Khentii mountain range

Ongi River (on-jee) – Small riverbed feeding from Orkhan toward the Gobi

Orkhon Valley (ohrk-hohn) – lush river valley of the Mongol steppe

Tianshan Mountains (tee-ahn-shaan) – mountains dividing Oirat/Uyghur territories

Tohom (too-hom) – red, rocky cliffs at the edge of the Gobi

Turfan (tur-phahn) – city in the former Chagatai khanate

Tuul River (tool) – river branch heading east out of the Orkhon valley

Wuzhong (woo-zong) – Ming border city on the Huang Ho River

Xilin River (jgee-lyn) – river along the southeastern Mongolian territories

Yinchuan (yin-chwahn) – city bordering the Huang Ho River and Great Wall into the Ordos basin

Yulin (you-lin) – city along the Ming-Mongol border

Zavkhan River (zav-khan) – major river feeding Oirat territory from the Altai mountains

Zhongwei (zong-way) – Ming border city in the Gansu Corridor

MILITARY STRUCTURE

Arban = 10 men

Jagan = 100 men (10 arban)

Mingghan = 1000 men (10 jagan)

Tumen = 10000 men (10 mingghan)

Officer - man in command of a single jagan or arban

Commander - officer in charge of a single mingghan

General - commander in charge of a tumen

Orlok - field marshal in charge of multiple tumens; military strategist

May all beings rule through white virtue, living long lives
And become possessors of peace and happiness
With the spirits of the Khans descended from mighty Tengri blessing thor-
oughly.
May sickness, harsh winter, obstacles, and untimely death be removed and
pacified;
May merchandise spread, crops flourish and longevity increase;
May peaceful health and happiness prevail, and auspicious luck come like
rain.

~ Histories of Altan Tobchi

CHAPTER ONE

A Long Time Coming

T he summer sun burned hot and high in the sky. Not even the cool breeze blowing down off the Khentii Mountains relieved the infernal heat. Mandukhai sat on a cushioned chair beneath a white canopy, reviewing the day's reports while sipping honey wine chilled with snow from the mountains. Sweat beaded on her brow and she used a cloth to wipe it away before it could drop on the reports and smudge the ink. Not that wiping the sweat did much good. A minute later, more rose to the surface.

The hollow thumps of sword fighting from the practice yard ten yards away carried toward her. Mandukhai lowered the reports and watched the sparring match.

Unebolod had gathered a half dozen fighters to join him. The six men formed a ring around the small, wiry form of Dayan Khan. At thirteen, he was not yet as big as the men, but not a small boy any longer. The fighters danced around him like a pack of wolves preparing for the kill. Dayan watched each of them twisting to fend off blows when any of them lunged forward. But each strike still pushed him back.

Every day, Unebolod or Togochi would teach Dayan how to fight. Sometimes with bows or swords on horseback—which Dayan had fallen off of more than once, thankfully to no serious injury—and sometimes with swords one-on-one. Recently, Unebolod had begun surprising Dayan with an uneven match. And Unebolod never made it easy for Dayan, pushing him to become stronger, better.

But Dayan was still only a boy and sparring matches like this one today were hardly fair: six grown, experienced men against one boy. Dayan had yet to win a single match. She worried how this would impact his confidence.

One warrior struck out, catching Dayan's side. He cried out as the wooden practice sword hit him. Before he could recover, Unebolod used the moment of weakness to finish the fight. His movements were graceful, smooth. Mandukhai could not help admiring the way the sun shone off his muscular arms and shoulders in his sleeveless *deel*.

Dayan blocked Unebolod's blow, but the force of it was enough to make Dayan trip over his own feet. He fell on his back. In seconds, Unebolod had the practice sword poised over Dayan's throat.

Mandukhai grimaced as Dayan used his hand to knock the sword away.

"This was not a fair fight!" Dayan protested. His face turned red with anger as he pushed himself to his feet sullenly.

Unebolod's response was calm. "Learn to use all of your senses, Dayan. Men who wish to kill you will not fight fair. Especially once they have you alone. You need to learn how to defend yourself."

Dayan brushed the dirt off his deel gruffly. "But I won't be alone, will I? Boke and my guards will be there." His golden gaze darted to the guards waiting beside the sparring space as if to prove his point. He threw his wooden sword on the ground. "We are done."

Mandukhai sighed as Dayan stormed off. As Dayan had predicted, his guards closed in around him like a shield.

"My lady Khatun," Togochi said, drawing her back to her own task.

Togochi had returned late last night from a mission to bring his own Khorlod tribe fully under the banner of the Great Khan. The journey had been exhausting, so she had given him the night to recover before giving her his report. It would not change anything in one night.

Mandukhai wanted to console Dayan, but she knew that this was more important than soothing Dayan's moody angst. Hopefully he would grow out of that soon.

Unebolod strolled over to join them, his mouth set in a grim line. She knew he thought she was too soft on Dayan. He said nothing as he stopped at the edge of the canopy, leaning against the post with the casual grace of a wild cat.

"Togochi, I hope you had a good night of rest to recover," Mandukhai said.

Togochi rubbed his neck, chagrined. "I would like to say I did, but my wives were happy to see me return."

Mandukhai smiled. Jaghan had been sick with worry most of the time he had been gone. The women had tea every other day—a ritual Mandukhai was too busy for, but one she knew was necessary as well. The women needed to feel as if they had a voice with her.

Togochi cleared his throat and adopted a more serious expression. "It went well, Mandukhai. Mendu khan is a bit of an old soul, and stuck in the old ways. Between the young Khan's legitimacy and my position here, Mendu was more than willing to give his support. He says when you are ready to ride south, the Khorlod tribe will join your ranks."

Relief washed over Mandukhai. Togochi's position in the Great Khan's budding empire was one of the highest ranks a man could achieve—*orlok* of the northern *tumens*—and only a lesser khan had a higher position, and only over his own tribe. Mendu khan would have known that, if he had refused to follow Mandukhai and Dayan, Togochi could have killed him and taken over control of the tribe fully. Mandukhai aimed for as few deaths as possible. Killing khans and nobles would impose her strength, but it would also ruffle feathers. She hoped to make this reunification smooth and peaceful—and only fight when absolutely necessary.

She would have to fight one day against the Uyghur. Mandukhai had hoped that the Ming would, as Unebolod stated it, remove the Uyghur boot from their throats so she would not have to worry about it. If the Ming had killed Bigirsen for her, Mandukhai would have more easily unified the southern tribes. But nothing was ever so easy.

"That is a relief then." Mandukhai said sincerely. "Alayitung just sent a report this morning that one of the Oirat Lords attempted a revolt. Thankfully, it was put down almost as swiftly as it began. Chari now leads that branch of Oirat. Asha khan had the other Lord executed." She sighed, gazing at the reports in her lap. "Each of these deaths is necessary, I know, but it feels like such a waste."

Unebolod snorted. "That Lord was probably loyal to Bigirsen. We need to deal with him soon, Mandukhai. Before he gathers strength again."

"The Ordos Lords have abandoned him," Mandukhai replied. "That massacre at the red salt lake lost him all of his support in the south."

"But for how long?" Unebolod asked, crossing his arms over his barrel chest. Mandukhai tried not to stare. It would do neither of them any good.

"The Ming built a wall to block him out of Zhongwei and Wuzhong, but if he finds even an inch he will be like a dog with a bone. All it takes is one right move to position himself again. This fight against him has been a long time coming."

The bloodlust Unebolod had for Bigirsen was unhealthy. Mandukhai wanted the Uyghur warlord dead as well, but she had to be careful how she went about it. Bigirsen may have lost control of the southern tribes, but he could still be dangerous even with only the Uyghur. Her foothold over the Oirat was more important now than ever.

Unebolod had returned to her with the *sulde*, found in Bigirsen's camp, and told her all about the massacre. The women and children killed by the Ming. The loss had crippled the southern tribes, and Unebolod had pressed her to move in and assert the Great Khan's authority over the area before they recovered. She had refused. She would not use such a horrific tragedy to gain her own power. It was a move for the weak.

After the massacre, the south had become unmanageable terrain. The tribes constantly fought with each other with one clear purpose: kidnapping women and girls in an effort to rebuild. Females had become a commodity that the men constantly pillaged for. Another reason she had no desire to ride south yet. She would not put herself or any of the women under her protection in such a dangerous place. Not yet.

Mandukhai simply did not have enough warriors to launch the attack in the south. While she had garnered the loyalty of six subtribes—and the Oirat—six others remained between her and the south. And that did not include the twenty tribes and subtribes in the south. Instead, she had focused these past few years on teaching Dayan and making as many allies in the north as she could. It was tedious work—these lesser khans all seemed to want something from her—and she had only gathered oaths from three of them. *Four, now, with Mendu khan*, she thought.

She set her reports in her red lacquer box and closed the lid. "Bigirsen will have to wait a little longer, Unebolod. We are just far too outnumbered to run the risk."

Unebolod's jaw twitched. The two of them had this argument several times, and he had always insisted he could easily sweep Bigirsen off the map with their warriors, especially if he rode through Oirat territory to get to Bigirsen's men. But Bigirsen was not a fool. He kept his warriors on the move. They could not pinpoint his location since the massacre at the red salt lake.

"I agree with Mandukhai," Togochi said. "Until we know where he is and have more warriors to ensure victory, we cannot launch an attack. It would leave us vulnerable to the southern tribes. And if the Oirat are attempting revolts—even as brief as they are—we risk exposing ourselves to them as well, which would put us right back where we started."

Unebolod took an urgent step closer, waving his hand toward the gathering tent in the distance. "Put that boy in front of the *sulde,* and it will bring the rest of the eastern tribes to us," Unebolod said tersely. "Perhaps even some of the southern tribes."

Mandukhai raised a brow in his direction. *"That boy* needs more men behind him first. This is a matter of numbers, not blood. Right now, we don't even have half the tribes under our banner. Without securing the majority, we risk his life. I won't do it."

"You can't shield him forever," Unebolod retorted.

"Watch me!" Mandukhai surged to her feet and marched away.

Unebolod's impatience was precisely what had kept her from naming him Great Khan instantly after Manduul's death. He had displayed such impatience before, when Manduul had left him in charge as he rode off to fight with Bayan. With each passing year, she grew more certain that her vision with Genghis, where the horizon burned, would have certainly been their fate if Unebolod was in charge.

Mandukhai, however, took a more patient, practical approach. *Who is he to tell me I cannot shield Dayan forever? I can, and I will.*

The cloying scent of rosemary and sandalwood mingled inside the confines of Goram's *ger.* Dayan had little choice but to focus on his breathing to keep from gagging on the smell. This space always smelled of some floral or woodsy incense. Today, after Dayan stomped into the monk's ger for his meditation lesson with what Goram called "the look of a thunderhead cloud," Goram handpicked the rosemary and sandalwood. The scents were supposed to help Dayan feel grounded and calm while relieving stress and enhancing mental balance.

Dayan tugged at the collar of his deel from his place across from Goram on the rugs. He had dropped into his spot sullenly when Goram motioned to it, then adjusted the many colored belts around his waist.

"You need to learn how to focus your frustration and channel it into something more productive," Goram said, folding his legs as he joined Dayan on the rug.

The lines of age on the old monk's face fascinated Dayan. He didn't realize people could live so long. *How can Goram be so wrinkly? I hope I never get like that,* he thought as his nose wrinkled in disgust.

"I'm convinced he enjoys abusing me," Dayan grumbled, slouching and rubbing at his neck as he recalled how Unebolod had—once again—bested him. "It's hardly fair. He's ancient and experienced in battle. Besides, Mandukhai won't let me do anything."

Goram folded his hands over his knees patiently, giving Dayan a look that clearly said he expected Dayan to do the same. Dayan scowled and dropped his hands dramatically to his knees.

"Petulance will get you nothing," Goram said.

That's not helpful. Dayan rolled his eyes. He hated his body, all limbs and no muscle. Dayan was skinnier than other boys his age. And shorter, as well. But his limbs were disproportionally long, which often made those fights with Unebolod even worse. Dayan tripped over his own feet or miscalculated the swing of his sword far more often than not.

"It isn't like I will ever beat him, or ever need to," Dayan groused. "He serves me."

"Spoken as one who sees their power as absolute," Goram commented with a grin. Why was he grinning? It only made Dayan slump further down. "Sit up straight to properly balance the natural flow of your body. Close your eyes, Dayan."

Dayan grumbled under his breath but did as he was told—albeit with theatrical movements. If he was to feel miserable, he would make Goram miserable with him.

"There is a lot of negative energy flowing through you," Goram said.

Obviously, Dayan thought. But he knew better than to say such things to Goram. The monk was insufferably patient. He kept his eyes closed and awaited the instruction.

"Release your palms flat to the Eternal Blue Sky, Dayan," Goram instructed. "Open yourself to enlightenment and focus on your breathing. In. Out."

Dayan's boiling frustration diminished somewhat as he followed Goram's commands. He focused on the void of nothingness, allowing his energy to flow into it, through the earth, and away. Maybe, just maybe, if he could learn how to control his emotions, Dayan would beat Unebolod and show Mandukhai that he was not a little boy any longer. She had made him Great Khan when he was too young to know what that meant. He should have resented her for it, but her devotion, faith, and love had changed him. Dayan could never resent her. Without her, he had nothing.

Not that the other Lords fully supported him. And he had not been officially installed at *kurultai* yet, either. Those other men doubted him—even the ones who followed him. But he would show them all one day. It was a long time coming.

First, Dayan had to find some way to keep the Great Fist from squeezing at his heart and lungs as it so often did.

Issama politely sipped at his tea across from Ibarai. Issama had sent an offer of truce to Ibarai at the start of the summer. The Ordos in this area were constantly on the move and often came too close to Issama and his family for his comfort. He worried about the safety of his wives, Siker and Qolotai. Too many women had disappeared or been taken from their families these past years. But if Issama could offer something more to Ibarai, it would protect his wives and give him powerful allies—something he desperately needed. These alliances were a long time coming.

"I am dying to know what you have to offer that would make us forget what you did," Ibarai said, breaking the uncomfortable silence.

Issama had not been the one who killed the families at the red salt lake. Yes, he had selected the location for the camp, but these rest fell on the shoulders of one man. "Bigirsen was the one who had insisted the families remain with the Uyghur so he could monitor them—or control them. Perhaps I organized the campaign that drew too many of the men from the camp, but Bigirsen was the one who had insisted *all* the warriors be present when he finally broke through Yinchuan. Bigirsen was the one who had believed it would show his divine right to rule the Mongols." Issama set down his tea and eyed Ibarai intently. "We all lost too much. You can blame me for following his orders if you want, but we both know he would have taken my head if I hadn't. How could we have known what would happen?"

The massacre had been horrific, for certain. They had all lost everything. Bigirsen's entire family had been killed. Many of the Lords lost wives and children. The sheer number of deaths had been devastating.

"I lost a wife and daughter that day," Issama murmured, staring into the depths of his cup. He would play a victim in this until he gained what he came for. "I miss Uingen still, and Qolotai has not really recovered from the loss of our daughter."

The logical part of Issama knew his daughter was better off dead. Otherwise, someone would have kidnapped her for future mating. It was better that she died than live as a slave to some deviant man's will.

Issama would use the tragedy to shift all the blame. He came here with a rational purpose. To gain allies and funnel their rage where it belonged.

Against Bigirsen and Mandukhai.

"What do you propose, then?" Ibarai asked.

"Ordos independence, just like you have always wanted," Issama said, smothering a smirk. "The ability to choose your own rightful Khan, free of the Ming and Borjigin influence."

And if all went according to plan, they would choose him.

The *ger* was silent as the four children slept. Exhaustion crept up on Esige as she loosened her hair and let it fall around her shoulders. She and Huoshai had spent the better part of their day talking with Tulugen—a leader of the Three Guards tribes. Stories had swirled around Tulugen, about how he had gone to Bigirsen and how Bigirsen had nearly killed him with hot soup. Hearing the story now from Tulugen, it all made so much more sense.

Huoshai stepped up behind her and swept her hair away from her neck, nuzzling in and pressing his lips to her warm skin. She smiled softly and reached up to stroke his cheek.

"Do you think Tulugen will keep his word?" she whispered, afraid of waking the children. "His tribe is not exactly known for its loyalty."

Over the years, the Three Guards tribe had served whatever overlord offered them the most to gain. Mongols, Ming ... Bigirsen. Esige wanted to trust Tulugen, and felt they had truly bonded over their shared hatred for Bigirsen, but she knew his people had a reputation.

"This is not a trap, if that is what you are worried about," Huoshai said.

His breath rolled over her neck. He snaked his hands around her waist, holding her against him. Esige adored the way he showered her with affection in private, yet maintained a healthy respect for her in public. Somehow, she loved him even more now than she had the day she married him.

"The Three Guards may be swayed easily, but they can hold a grudge better than anyone else." Huoshai grinned, resting his chin on her shoulder. "Even you."

Esige laughed and swatted him off. "I don't know what you are talking about," she teased indignantly.

"The squirrel?" Huoshai replied, raising his brows as he leaned against the butcher block. "You still shake out your *deels* before putting them on."

"Perhaps if my husband didn't traumatize me, it would not have had such lasting effects," Esige retorted.

Huoshai chuckled and shook his head. "In all seriousness, I believe Tulugen meant every word. He is furious. That much was obvious."

Esige nodded. "Then we should send word to Mandukhai and leave in the spring to ride north and give Tulugen a chance to do as he promised." She glanced at the dark sky through the open smoke hole. "We should find Nemeku before we settle in for the night."

Huoshai grunted and popped a sweet curd in his mouth. "You mean *I* should. He should be back soon." As he headed for the door, Huoshai paused, kissing her on the cheek.

Esige smiled coyly at him. "Don't be too long."

"I wouldn't dream of keeping you waiting," Huoshai teased as he strode out into the dark.

Before turning in for the night, Esige strode toward the four slumbering children—three boys and a girl. As she leaned over to kiss each of their foreheads, Esige cradled her stomach. The fifth child would arrive soon, in the heart of winter.

Their faces were smooth. Esige could not remember the last time she felt such peace. Huoshai certainly made her feel safe, but Borogchin's death still scarred her heart. As long as Bigirsen drew breath, she could not know peace.

And he *would* die soon. It was a long time coming.

CHAPTER TWO

Hot Soup, Bitter Hate

KHERLEN RIVER – FALL 1478

Mandukhai paced the rug-covered wooden floor of the gathering tent. For seven years, she had waited for Bigirsen to fall. Seven years of impatience. After the Red Salt Lake massacre, Mandukhai had expected all the Mongols in the south to abandon Bigirsen. They had lost their wives and children because of him. Most of the tribes had abandoned him, but not all of them. A few of the smaller tribes in the south had kept their families in their own territories and hadn't lost everything as the others had.

The Three Guards tribes had remained loyal to him even after the massacre. Bigirsen used that tragedy to fuel their bloodlust. Too many of the southern Mongols still resisted Mandukhai and Dayan Khan's rule. Dayan was their Khan—the Whole Khan!—and he deserved their respect. *No, not deserve. It* belongs *to him!* she thought as she continued pacing the floor in front of the dais.

Copper pots burned low with flames, chasing away the cool fall air. Why could the Oirat see reason and submit to their Khan yet the southern tribes would not? Mandukhai had raised a Khan and held the rest of the Mongol Nation together during that time. The men respected her as much as they would a Great Khan and never questioned her commands. The *tumens* followed her and Dayan with all the loyalty and respect the two of them deserved. Yet they did not have the allegiance under the Great Khan's banner of even half the tribes. Too many remained independent.

Seven years had been too long.

"Please stop pacing like that," Dayan groaned. "You are making me anxious."

Mandukhai spun on her heel to face Dayan. The Little Khan, as the Ming called him. *He is not so little anymore*, Mandukhai thought.

At fifteen, Dayan Khan was still thin—as his father had been—but he resembled a man more than he ever had before. Today, as they waited for Esige and the assembly to join them, Dayan waited on his throne—Bayan's old throne—with his legs crossed and his palms resting on his knees. Dayan's eyes were closed, his face smooth, meditating as Goram had taught him. Proceedings had not even begun, and he was already stressed. Mandukhai still worried over his health, though Dayan had not been ill for years.

"Good," Mandukhai said, crossing her arms. "You should be anxious. Everything could be riding on this meeting. If we can get the Three Guards to turn against Bigirsen, it will be our gateway into the south. Without at least a few of the southern tribes behind us, we will never hold the majority vote and you could lose *kurultai*. We can only stall for so long. If we cannot complete the vision, Gen—"

"I know, I know." Dayan heaved out a sigh, then lifted his gaze to meet hers. Such piercing golden eyes! "If we don't complete Genghis' vision, then everything falls apart and we die."

Dayan rose and strode down the steps toward her. He certainly had gotten taller. And he was undoubtably stronger than she ever could have imagined he would be, thanks to Unebolod and Togochi's strict combat training. All traces of that weak and dying boy had vanished. When he stopped in front of her—now matched in height—his wolf-like eyes burrowed into her soul, as if he could see straight to her heart and understand her mind. On some level, she knew Dayan *could* understand her mind. She kept nothing from him—except her still-lingering feelings for Unebolod.

Since choosing Dayan, Unebolod had kept his distance and remained loyal to the Khan. He had shown very little suggestion that he still harbored feelings for her over the years. Yet, Mandukhai knew that if she could not stop loving him—despite their necessary distance—surely he had not stopped loving her.

As he had promised, Unebolod had not taken a wife. Did he wait for her? Perhaps he expected that, when Dayan came of age, he would release

Mandukhai from her oath and choose a different wife. A younger wife. Perhaps Unebolod still held on to hope.

Mandukhai could not. To do so would be too dangerous for her heart. Genghis had promised she would give her heart once to passion and once to compassion. Over the years, her passion remained with Unebolod. But now she was certain that the compassion belonged completely to Dayan. She loved them both in very different ways.

Dayan took Mandukhai's hand in his own, sliding his thumb over her skin. "If we are going to die, I can think of no better way to go."

"Dayan, we—"

He pressed a finger to her lips, silencing her protest. But the touch—the intimacy—made her insides churn. It was the first time he had done anything like that, and she could not handle it. Not when her thoughts were still consumed with Unebolod. Mandukhai drew back and pulled her hand out of his. The hurt look in his eyes forced her to avert her gaze.

Dayan turned his back to her and returned to his throne. He settled into his seat and folded his hands calmly in his lap. For a moment, as the sounds of the assembly outside approached, Dayan let his guard down, revealing his disappointment as she locked gazes with him. It broke her heart when he looked at her like that. But why was he disappointed with her? Because she withdrew?

Boots thumped up the steps outside onto the gathering tent's massive wagon, accompanied by a host of familiar voices. Dayan's youthful face smoothed out, adopting the outward calm confidence Mandukhai had not needed to teach him.

Unebolod had enjoyed his reunion with Esige when she had first arrived at the edge of the mobile capital. It had been three years since he had last seen her. Even then, with three children of her own, Esige had still resembled the girl he remembered. Now, two more children later, Esige looked so grown up it had shocked him at first. The girl's wild spirit had been tempered, but she remained as immovable as Mandukhai when she dug in her heels.

The men with him all waited for Esige to climb the steps to the wagon first. Unebolod found this a curious thing. Men never deferred to women in such a way. Men led. Women followed. But Esige, much like Mandukhai, assumed an air of command that the men clearly respected. He smiled to himself as he followed Togochi up the wooden steps. They creaked in protest. Had he ever had a daughter, Unebolod imagined she would be much like Esige—strong, proud, confident, fierce.

Before crossing the threshold into the gathering tent as Boke's men stood guard outside, Esige hesitated. Her spine stiffened. Her chin rose. Unebolod even thought he saw her steady her breathing. *She is worried even now, so close to Mandukhai, that she will fail*, he realized.

Esige glanced over her shoulder and flashed Unebolod a smile he could only describe as mischievous, revealing the girl he remembered. Then she entered the gathering tent with Huoshai close on her heels.

Even Huoshai had grown stronger over the years, and he had been impressive before. He carried himself as a tribal leader should. The muscles in his broad shoulders had grown as a testament to his experience with a bow. *He is not much younger now than I was when I met Mandukhai,* Unebolod mused. The thought saddened him. So long ago. So many years. And the distance between the two of them had grown insurmountable.

The only way Unebolod could ever be with Mandukhai now would be if Dayan died or released her before they officially married. *That won't be much longer now*, he thought as he stepped over the threshold into the gathering tent. Any day, if he was lucky.

Dayan Khan waited in his golden throne, adorned with jade and pearl embellishments that shined in the light from the wide smoke hole. He didn't flinch, didn't blink as the assembly approached. The boy differed greatly from his father in the way he carried himself. His eyes had a way of looking straight through a man.

At fifteen, Dayan showed few signs of weakness. Unebolod loathed the grudging respect the boy had drawn from him over the years. He did *not* want to respect Dayan. He wanted to hate him and everything he represented.

Their assembly kneeled before the Khan and Khatun, as custom dictated. Boke stood vigil off to the side of the Khan, inspecting each of them with a critical eye. The six of them waited in silence.

"Commander Tulugen," Mandukhai said. Her voice drew all eyes to her, but none of them stood without permission. "There is quite a rumor surrounding you."

Tulugen grimaced. "There is always some truth to rumors, my lady Khatun."

In his late twenties, Tulugen had taken command of a *tumen* of Three Guards warriors. Their tribe had been small but had spent much of its time along the Ming border resisting Ming invasion and fighting for whatever warlord had enough power to command. He had been a loyal man to Bigirsen for years. One poorly chosen act had broken that loyalty. Why Bigirsen had done it remained unclear.

"The Khan and I are interested to hear the truth and not the rumor so that we may better understand why you come to us today when you have spent so long resisting us," Mandukhai said with all the cool, even bearing of a queen.

Dayan waved, and the party climbed to their feet.

"Speak," Mandukhai commanded. "And do not lie. Your Great Khan does not take kindly to lies, and he will see straight into your soul."

Tulugen gazed at Dayan for several long moments. Unebolod found it amusing the way Tulugen began squirming under that penetrating stare. Mandukhai knew how to use Dayan's strengths against others. They operated as a unit almost effortlessly. He hated it, yet loved it.

"Of course, my lord Khan," Tulugen said at last. "I served Lord Bigirsen for several years, raiding and extorting the Ming as we could. My men traveled hard to catch up to Bigirsen's forces, what remained of them. I called to Bigirsen for Guest Rights. He welcomed me into his ger as he sat down to soup. The smell filled the air, and my stomach growled, thirsty for its tastiness after months of only curds and dried mutton. He did not offer, so I asked for a bowl.

"Bigirsen set down his bowl and rose to pour out one for me, with his back to me. As he handed me the bowl, there was a hint of madness in his eyes, but he smiled and made casual conversation. Since he picked up his bowl and drank without hesitation, I drank from mine as well."

Tulugen's jaw moved as if his tongue rolled around in his mouth. A bitter, angry heat filled his eyes and turned his neck red. "He had switched the cooled bowl I expected with the boiling hot soup, and when I took it in my mouth, it was like eating fire. But I could not spit it out."

Mandukhai nodded.

Unebolod had heard the rumors, and that it had spurred Tulugen to turn against Bigirsen. To spit out food was a grave insult, and unforgivable. Bigirsen must have given the boiling soup to Tulugen expecting him to spit it out so that Bigirsen could draw him out and kill him for the insult.

"He watched me as I held it in my mouth, waiting for me to spit the soup on the floor. It burned away the skin in my mouth. I knew that if I swallowed, my heart would burn, but if I spit it out, I would be shamed and probably killed. So I held it in my mouth as it cooled so it would not burn my heart, then I swallowed it down as he watched." Tulugen winced at the memory. "It was as simple as that, but I shall never forget my hate. There is no doubt in my mind that he did this on purpose. Bigirsen likely heard of my plan to disengage my men and return to our families to the east."

Silence fell over the gathering tent as everyone waited to see what Mandukhai or Dayan would say. Unebolod digested the story, much as he had in the past weeks since first hearing of it. Some versions said that the skin of Tulugen's palate fell off from the burns. Other versions claimed the soup had turned Tulugen's heart to fire. A few of the stories claimed Tulugen had superhuman strength to survive such a thing. Unebolod knew better than to put any stock into that claim.

Regardless of what the truth had been, the result had been to Mandukhai's benefit. Now, the power of the Three Guards was prepared to align with the Great Khan, with the Urainkhai at their side. They were prepared to join the Great Khan's fight—as long as it forced Bigirsen out of Mongol territory for good. Or killed him.

"And because you drank hot soup, you expect your Khan and Khatun to believe you are prepared to serve us?" Mandukhai asked sharply. Her eyebrows drew together furiously. "After seven years of resistance, we should believe you now?"

"I am here to support my Great Khan and his wise Khatun, however you see fit," Tulugen said carefully. "Should that mean I serve you in death, so be it. But I believe I would serve you better by helping you route the Uyghur scourge in our lands. Especially since I already have a man traveling with Bigirsen to track his movements. I believe you know him, my lady Khatun. Jangi served Lady Borogchin, and he continues to serve her son, Nemeku."

Esige stiffened as if someone had shoved a rod down her spine. Unebolod frowned.

Mandukhai's lips parted ever so slightly as her gaze flicked to Esige. "Where is Nemeku, Esige?"

The other woman moved her lips, but no words came out.

Mandukhai's turned her attention on Esige's husband. "Huoshai?"

The Urainkhai khan squared his shoulders, glancing at his wife for just a moment before he shattered their silence. "He ran off after Jangi was sent after Bigirsen."

All of Mandukhai's calm composure fractured. Unebolod could see how much she struggled to hold herself together. Not only could Nemeku die, but, with the right support, he could challenge Dayan. Support from his father. Did Nemeku know this when he left?

"He ran off?" Mandukhai's voice dropped to a heated growl. "Do you keep such loose reins on your household that the boy could run away?"

Esige shook her head and stepped forward, then froze at the withering glare Mandukhai threw at her. "We allow him to ride out, as a boy should, and he often does, but he always comes back by dinner. The night he ran off, the three of us," Esige motioned to herself, Huoshai, and Tulugen, "were discussing what happened to Tulugen, and what Bigirsen had done to Borogchin. It was a means of the three of us connecting, aligning our hatred toward Bigirsen. Nemeku was gone when we returned. We thought he just went riding but that night, when he didn't come back ... it's possible he overheard some of what we discussed."

Unebolod's stomach sank like a dead weight.

Mandukhai pressed her hand to her lips, and sorrow poured out of her drooping expression. "He means to kill his father," she mumbled.

Unebolod shared Mandukhai's conclusion. Nemeku had always spoken so dotingly of his mother. Now, knowing what had happened to her, he would surely seek vengeance. At twelve, he was just old enough to be confident in his abilities in that foolishly youthful way only boys were capable of.

But Bigirsen would not kill Nemeku when his son arrived. He would beat him into submission and use him against them. Such torture would be a fate worse than death.

"How long has Nemeku been gone, Esige?" Mandukhai asked.

"Nearly a year," Esige murmured. She sagged, but Unebolod watched as she seemed to collect herself and gather more steam to press on. "We sent men to track him, but they lost him somewhere west of Bautuo. We are fairly certain he followed Jangi, but we have not heard back from either of them yet."

"Fairly certain!" Mandukhai snapped.

Unebolod considered how he could intervene. This was not Esige's fault. Nemeku was a growing boy. "All the more reason to find Bigirsen and finish him," he interrupted. "We can get rid of our oldest enemy while rescuing Nemeku."

Mandukhai shot a scornful scowl in his direction. He knew she hated how often he brought up killing Bigirsen, but he could not let it go.

Bigirsen was a festering wound that would only get worse. The longer she waited to kill him, the more they risked Bigirsen rising to power again. Before she could speak, Dayan stood.

Dayan approached the edge of the dais. Everyone froze, watching the Khan. "Kneel." His gaze locked firmly on Tulugen, much as a mountain watched over its valley.

Tulugen stepped toward the edge of the dais and did as Dayan commanded. No one needed to ask what Dayan expected. Tulugen gave his oath to the Great Khan without hesitation as Mandukhai stepped up beside Dayan. When the oath was given, Dayan said nothing. He remained as still as a statue, staring at Tulugen as if he expected more. Unebolod frowned as he watched, casting a questioning glance at Togochi, who shrugged ever so slightly.

But Tulugen seemed to understand what Dayan Khan waited for. Tulugen repeated his oath, but this time, he directed it to Mandukhai. No one present displayed any shock that Tulugen gave the oath to Mandukhai as well. All of them had given an oath to the Khan *and* the Khatun. Of course, Unebolod understood that his duty first went to the Great Khan above all others. Above Mandukhai. So far, that had not been a problem. The two often acted as one mind.

Once the oaths were given, Dayan offered his hand, and Tulugen kissed the crescent moon ring.

Dayan returned to his seat. "Prepare your men, Huoshai and Tulugen," Dayan said. "In the spring, the Mongols will ride."

Mandukhai clearly struggled to hide her alarm. She often spoke for him and made these plans. Now, Dayan Khan was prepared for war.

Unebolod's mouth twitched as he fought off a smile. Perhaps the time had finally arrived. He had yearned for Bigirsen's blood for nearly twenty years.

The assembly broke off and Mandukhai spoke with Togochi, Huoshai, and Esige as they headed toward the exit. Unebolod watched them go. A family had formed, with Mandukhai at the heart of it. But Unebolod stood on the outside, kept at a distance. Mandukhai used him for her own political means, yet he often waited for those moments just so she would look at him again.

Tulugen paid final respects to the Khan before he also departed. Unebolod moved to follow—he wanted to find out what Tulugen knew of Bigirsen's plans—but a steady hand landed on his shoulder, pulling him to a halt. He glanced over to find Dayan standing at his shoulder, gazing at him with those golden eyes. Gazing *into* him. He suppressed a shudder.

"My lord Khan?" Unebolod said evenly.

"The sun and the moon will always dance on opposite ends of the sky," Dayan said. He removed his hand, tucking both of them together in the sleeves of his silk deel.

What does that mean? Unebolod wondered.

Dayan strode toward the exit, leaving Unebolod staring dumbfounded at his back.

War approached at last. There was no time to stand around musing over Dayan's cryptic words. Unebolod had work to do.

Dayan strode toward his ger, away from the gathering tent, with only Boke and a handful of his loyal guards to keep him company. None of them ever spoke to him unless he directed them to, which made them poor companions.

Mandukhai had disappeared into her own ger with Esige and Huoshai on her heels. He only had to approach and ask to enter. But Esige often made him uncomfortable, as if she blamed him for something he could not understand. Instead of joining them, he entered his own ger.

Dayan hated his ger. It was big and lonely. Only Mandukhai and Dayan's servants entered without summons. He loosened his multi-colored belts and sank down on the edge of the bed in a huff. His gaze swept the space. Rich with silk and jewels and unused armor. The sword and bow had only ever been used for ceremony. Mandukhai fought his battles for him. Dayan grew tired of being little more than a figurehead. Mandukhai respected men of action and courage, yet refused to allow him a chance to prove himself. He didn't doubt that she cared deeply for him, and had never felt used by her, but he found a difference between caring for someone and truly respecting them.

Angry, he kicked a bucket near the stove, spilling water out on the floor. His hands clenched into fists. Open. Closed. Open. Closed. He practiced his breathing as Goram taught. *Goram.* He missed the monk. Goram's death had been hard on Dayan. He had been one of the few people Dayan could vent to about almost anything. But a year ago, Goram had passed away peacefully from old age, leaving Dayan even lonelier than ever.

Nemeku was the only friend Dayan ever had, and he had not seen his cousin for nearly two years now. Nemeku had always been confident and spirited, just as quick with jokes as he was with bows. Hearing that Nemeku might have fallen into Bigirsen's hands did not settle well in Dayan's stomach. What would Bigirsen do to Nemeku? What if he never saw Nemeku again?

A pit filled his stomach, seemingly endless. Dayan pushed all of his fear and loneliness and disappointment into that endless pit and imagined it moving out through his feet and into the earth, as Goram had taught. But no amount of focused mental exercise could keep him from understanding what he was—what he would always be.

The second choice.

The Mongol Lords had wanted Unebolod.

If he trusted the rumors, Mandukhai had wanted Unebolod.

They had all settled for him. One of these days, he would have to prove that he was not second best. Genghis chose him. Tengri watched over him. Someday, he would make them all see it. *Dayan Khan is no longer a boy. He is a man. If Nemeku can prove himself, so can I!* But how, when Mandukhai guarded over him like a precious jewel?

Ong, his primary servant, entered the ger and murmured an apology for interrupting, then noticed the overturned bucket. "Another bucket, my lord Khan?"

"I tripped." Dayan tightened his belts. "Find a better place for them, Ong."

"Of course, my lord Khan." Ong bowed before he kneeled with rags to clean the mess, wringing them out in the now upturned bucket.

Ong was a dutiful servant and marshaled the rest with expert ease. But Dayan had not failed to notice that all of his servants were men. Every last one. Mandukhai refused to see him as a man, yet refused to allow him any female servants. What was she afraid he would do? Dayan had heard stories from others about his father, and the sort of scoundrel he had been.

But Dayan was nothing like his father. *One day, they will all see it.*

CHAPTER THREE

Into the Fold

KHORLOD TERRITORY – EARLY SUMMER 1479

For years, Mandukhai and Dayan had made their capital along the banks of the Kherlen River, moving as need dictated for herding. Most of her Mongols moved across the northern steppe to live their lives as they saw fit, but none were too far from her reach. Mandukhai had but to send a message, and her people would travel to her.

Just as the warriors had done.

Since the defeat of the Oirat, Mandukhai had reopen the long-lost yam stations of the old empire. These stations served as a wayside for messengers across her budding empire. After years of tireless work, a yam station now awaited every twenty to thirty miles along the primary routes. A messenger could swap horses, rest, or get food and drink, allowing them to pass messages at almost double the speed. Merchants who wished to cross her empire could travel safely along the yam roads without fear of ambush. The system reached from the westernmost point in Oirat territory, around the northern edges of the Gobi, all the way to the Urainkhai in the southeast, broken only through Ongud territory.

As soon as winter broke, Mandukhai sent messengers riders across the northern stretches of her empire to summon the *tumens* to her camp. By summer, she and her army rode south and swept across her lands to prepare for their final reunification strategy—and to deal once and for all with Bigirsen.

When she reached Khorlod territory, just south of the Khorchin grasslands, Mandukhai set up camp and arranged for a meeting with Mendu khan of the Khorlod. It was time to find out if he truly was prepared to follow the Khan and Khatun.

Mandukhai arranged a grand feast in Mendu's honor. A week after setting up camp, he arrived with a thousand of his own warriors—and a bonus entourage. Mandukhai waited in the gathering tent with Dayan. He said nothing and simply stared ahead, ready for the meeting.

Loyal Lords and Ladies lined the gathering tent. Altan, Unige and his fourteen-year-old son, Alag, Albeq and his son, Chakicha, Dochigen, Bagatur, Ordag. And of course, Unebolod and Togochi. It was an impressive gathering. Each of the leaders had sworn themselves to Mandukhai and Dayan. Not even Manduul had collected so many high-ranking leaders at once. Only the Oirat were missing, still under the leadership of Alayitung in their territory.

Mendu strode into the gathering tent, his dark gaze sweeping across the collection on either side of the aisle. A younger man Mandukhai did not recognize entered behind Mendu. She cocked her head as she examined him. The cut of his deel was fine, and the embroidering detailed, which placed him as a Lord. But Mandukhai could not recall the specific tribal style. Something about it tickled her memory. Who was this young man? He couldn't be more than five years older than Dayan.

Mendu and the young man kneeled at the bottom step.

"Mendu khan, thank you for meeting with us," Mandukhai said, using her sweetest tone.

"I gave my word to serve and follow with gers and blood," Mendu said evenly. "Lord Togochi has nearly outstripped me since he joined Manduul Khan—may the Khan rest well in the Eternal Blue Sky. Togochi's dedication to absolving our sins against Manduul's nephews years ago is something we should all strive toward."

Mandukhai smiled. "You will have your chance soon enough. But first, who is this young man you bring with you?"

The young Lord glanced sideways at Mendu, as if asking for guidance.

"You can speak for yourself," Mandukhai said, hoping it would ease his apparent tension.

He raised his gaze. A wild determination burned in his eyes as he stared at her. "Kelegei khan, my lady Khatun," he said. His voice was deeper than she had expected, but she supposed it matched his broad frame. "Of the Erkegud."

Suddenly Mandukhai realized why she had recognized the cut of his clothing. She had grown up close to the Erkegud tribe, which was closely aligned with the Khorlod. More than once, she had watched the old khan of the tribe ride into the Ongud camp to meet with Korgiz khan. But this young man was too young for her to know personally. He couldn't have been older than five when she rode off to marry Manduul.

"Kelegei khan?" she asked, suddenly realizing the significance of this moment.

Mendu had not only come to give his oath, but he had brought another into her fold as well.

"You can't have been khan for long," she said.

"Five years, my Khatun," Kelegei said, dipping his head in respect.

"Kelegei became khan as soon as he was old enough to lead," Mendu explained. "After his father was killed, his people followed me, and I raised him, taught him. I believe you understand something of that." He nodded to Dayan.

"How did your father die, Kelegei?" she asked.

Kelegei's determined gaze transformed to fire as he glared at her, but she knew his anger was not truly directed her way. She understood that look. "Mogurkei killed him on Bigirsen's orders." His voice burned with a heat that matched his gaze. "My father refused to give up his title to Bigirsen."

Mandukhai glanced at Unebolod and Togochi. They had all heard the stories of how Bigirsen had attempted stealing the title of khan from these lesser khans to undermine her own right to rule. Bigirsen may have given the order, and Mogurkei may have fired the arrow, but Mandukhai now realized she caused the Erkegud khan's death.

"I offer you my deepest condolences, Kelegei khan," she said sympathetically. "If there is anything I can do ..." Though Mandukhai already suspected what he wanted.

"Let me help you," Kelegei said fiercely. "I want to be there when Bigirsen dies."

"We do not yet have a plan to attack him," Mandukhai said.

"You will, though," Kelegei said with absolute certainty. "And my tribe is prepared to follow you into that fight, small as we may be. My Khan and Khatun, I and my people offer you salt, gers, horses, and blood from this day until our last. We are eternally in your service."

Mendu made a sound of agreement as he nodded sharply. Then he repeated the same oath, promising his own tribe eternally bound to the Great Khan.

Mandukhai's heart lifted. She needed this. Fifteen. This gave her fifteen tribes. An even split with the Ordos and Uyghur. Eighteen, once she could speak with the Ongud and Chakhar. Though four of those votes came from the Oirat, and Mandukhai could not be certain how the southern tribes would react to the legitimacy of Oirat votes after so many centuries of separation. The Three Guards would offset most of those votes, but if Mandukhai wanted to assure victory, she needed to acquire at least three more votes—and remove Bigirsen from any potential position of power. The votes of her own tribe and that of Dayan's mother had never been more important. They could be the deciding factor. They were so close to securing victory at official *kurultai*, and Mandukhai would not dare put Dayan up for the vote until she was certain of the success.

Once the *tumens* had rounded the eastern edge of the Gobi, Togochi had taken his warriors straight south to clear the way for the Great Khan's arrival. Unebolod remained with her and the Khan to help secure the eastern tribes he had previously allied with.

The *tumens* under Unebolod's command had spread out all across the east. Four *tumens* swept along Mongolia like a great wave from the Gobi's edge to the Greater Khingan Mountains, headed south, scooping up warriors and supplies. The few who resisted were overrun by thousands. Scouts and messengers rode east to west along hundreds of miles of lines like a swarm of flies, endlessly buzzing.

When at last they had reached the Ongud territory by mid-summer, Mandukhai felt as though she had returned home. While the Ongud spread out all across their eastern territory, her family had spent much of her younger years moving around the land near Lake Dalinur. The ground was hard, packed red rock, but the lake fed the area and made for ample grazing to support herds.

It was here, along the banks of the lake, that Mandukhai would meet with her tribal khan. She had blocks set around the wheels of the gathering tent wagon to keep it in place. Unebolod busied himself with preparing the campsite. Torgus stationed men around the gathering tent while Boke's men took their positions inside to protect their Khan and Khatun.

Mandukhai waited beside Dayan. He had not been so far south since he had been brought to her years ago.

"He will not show his face," Dayan said, rapping his fingers against the arm of his seat.

"He has no choice," Mandukhai reminded him. She had taught Dayan well. He understood the dangers of his position and who would oppose him.

Mandukhai was apprehensive about this meeting. Korgiz khan had died from a liver sickness made worse by a spring fever three years ago. His son, Boragan, had swiftly assumed command of the tribe. Rumor had it that Boragan was temperamental and often merciless. Had it not been Boke and Unebolod in charge of their camp and their safety, Mandukhai might have worried about Boragan's intentions. Sweeping across the steppe with her army had been effective up to now, but they had met little resistance. Most of the lesser khans in the east had already given their oaths to her. Resistance had been from smaller bands of independent families.

Boragan still might make a stand fiercely and to the bitter end. Mandukhai hoped to avoid destroying her own tribe. Most of the other tribes had fallen under her banner fairly effortlessly. Not all of them would come so easy. Boragan among them.

"He could just surprise us with an attack," Dayan said.

Mandukhai glanced at him, frowning. Dayan was right, of course. Boragan could easily choose to attack instead of seeking peace. "That's why I chose to have Unebolod with us and not Togochi. Boragan might be merciless, but he is not deaf. He would have heard the stories of the Steel Soldier. I do not believe even he is foolish enough to attack while we are under Unebolod's protection."

She needed Boragan's support. The Chakhar and Ongud would be the deciding factor in *kurultai*.

Dayan's jaw twitched, but he nodded. For a moment, Mandukhai thought Dayan might give a response. As voices rose outside the gathering tent, Dayan shifted in his seat, sitting straighter and assuming his practiced calm visage. She mirrored him, but instead of resting her palms on the arms of her seat, Mandukhai folded her hands into the sleeves of her deel.

"She invited me!" A male voice barked indignantly.

Mandukhai heard the low register of Unebolod's voice in response but could not make out his words.

After a few more terse words, Boragan khan stomped into the gathering tent with Unebolod close on his heels. Despite the obvious cloud of anger around Boragan, he still kneeled appropriately in front of his Khan and Khatun. Mandukhai let him wait on his knees a little longer than necessary to be sure he understood his position in this conversation. Dayan said nothing. He simply watched Boragan with his piercing golden eyes. All emotion washed away from his expression. How did he do that so easily at will when she knew he was distressed?

"Lord Boragan, I offer my condolences," Mandukhai said at last. "I knew your father well. He will be missed."

Boragan raised his gaze from the floor, but she did not permit him to rise. Not yet. "Will he?" Boragan asked. The bite in his tone drew a growl of disapproval from Unebolod. "May I rise?"

"Are your knees so weak?" she asked, not bothering to veil the implication that he might be weak.

Boragan's mouth twitched, but he did not respond. *He has some control over his temper*, Mandukhai thought.

"You may rise," she said.

Boragan placed a hand on the floor and was about to push himself to his feet.

Mandukhai leaned forward. "After you have given us your oath."

Boragan hesitated, glaring at her as if testing the sincerity of her statement. "You cannot force me to give the oath, just as you could not force my father," Boragan said at last.

"Your father helped raise me," Mandukhai said evenly. "And so I gave him the right to choose until need changed our circumstances." She raised her eyebrows pointedly. "Our circumstances have changed."

Boragan straightened as much as he could on his knees. If he rose without her permission, Unebolod, Boke, or any of her guards could kill him. Defiance radiated off of him in hot waves. Mandukhai fed that heat into her own determination.

"You understand, I assume, that I am your tribe daughter and have been made Khatun by your Great Khan, with the blessing of the Eternal Blue Sky," she said. "Whether or not you chose us, we have this right given to us by Manduul Khan and the High Heavens. Even you are helpless against that. I have no ill will toward my tribesmen and would rather you accept this new order and do your duty."

"If I don't?" Boragan asked, glancing at Unebolod from the corner of his eye.

"I think you already know the answer to that question." Mandukhai settled back again. "So, Lord Boragan, Ongud khan and tribe brother to the Khatun, will you give your oath and spare our kinsmen?"

His hand reached for the sword that should have been at his belt, which Unebolod had clearly forced him to relinquish outside. He brushed air and grimaced. What would he have done with his sword, anyway? If he had been bold enough to attack either of them, he would have been dead within two steps. One, judging by the glint in Unebolod's eyes.

"I remember you as a girl," Boragan said. He was only a few years older than her. "How you would ride with the boys. How you tried to join hunts. You used to stare down your mother in defiance. One time, I recall how you took your stepfather's bow when he broke yours. I don't know where you went with the bow, but when you came back with dirt on your face and fewer arrows, I saw how he beat you. How he told you that you were a Lady and should act like one if you ever wanted to be a good wife." His lips peeled back in an odd smile. "I don't think you received his message."

Dayan straightened at the insult, which drew Boragan's gaze. Within seconds, he was staring at the floor in shame, which appeared to satisfy Dayan.

Mandukhai knew the game this khan played. He sought to get under her skin, insult her, draw her out. While she and Dayan had not formally begun their marriage, she had bound herself to him years ago as a wife by title alone. Boragan insinuated that she was not a Lady or a good wife. But she had spent years beneath the thumb of men like Boragan. She would not lower herself to their standards.

"You insult my Khatun in front of me?" Dayan said evenly, but the coldness of his tone made even her skin crawl. "Her law is my law, and my law is her law. She *still* rides with the men, only instead of dirt on her face, she now wears the blood of those who would dare to oppose us. So I would advise, given your predicament, that you choose your next words carefully."

Mandukhai swelled with pride at Dayan's choice of defense, yet she also resented him for speaking up. Men like Boragan would never truly respect her if the Khan won her battles for her.

"More than one man has beaten me in my life," Mandukhai said, heat rising in her voice. "Do you know what it has taught me, Boragan?"

He stared blankly at her.

"Patience." Mandukhai leaned forward, gripping the arms of her throne. "What I learned is that those men who use their fists to get what they want often lose everything. All I have to do is wait. The mark of a strong woman is not in how she pours your tea. It is in her patience and perseverance. Your father did not recognize that, nor did my stepfather. But by the end of this, you will. Because I can already see how much smarter you are than either of them. Smart enough to come here to meet. Smart enough to know that you should stay on your knees until I permit you to stand." She sat back, analyzing him. "But are you smart enough to recognize when it is time to give an oath and when it is time to fight?"

Long, heavy silence settled over the gathering tent as they waited.

"Take your time, Boragan," Mandukhai said. "As I mentioned, I am a terribly patient woman."

Boragan weighed the couple before him. Mandukhai recognized the calculation in his eyes as he examined each of them, as well as the number of guards in the gathering tent. It took far too long for him to realize he was outnumbered and had little choice.

"My Khan, I give—" Boragan began.

"No," Dayan said.

Boragan frowned, clearly unsure of how to react. His gaze flitted anxiously between the two of them. Then he licked his lips and tried again. "My lord Khan—"

"Try again, Boragan," Mandukhai said patiently. "Whom do you kneel before?"

He choked, and his eyes popped wide in apparent shock, staring at Dayan as if asking whether she was serious.

"Take your time," she said, waving a hand at him.

Dayan did not indicate that he disagreed with her. He simply glared at the Ongud khan.

"My Khan and *Khatun*," Boragan said, placing sharp, sarcastic emphasis on her title. "I give you salt, gers, blood and horses, from this day until my last."

Mandukhai struggled to contain her joy. So many Lords gave this oath, but few meant as much as this. Mandukhai's tribe had finally come into the fold.

But this was far from over.

The tribes ahead would be the hardest of all to convince ... and it could end in war.

CHAPTER FOUR

A Deadly Pact

Dayan shifted in his saddle as he rode into the Chakhar camp beside Mandukhai. Today, he would meet Guden khan. Dayan had heard a lot about him from Mandukhai and dreaded this encounter. Guden was the one who had forced Dayan's father to marry his mother. Would Guden have marriage expectations regarding Dayan, as well? Dayan wasn't much younger than his father had been when he married Siker. Dayan glanced from the corner of his eyes at Mandukhai beside him. *She* certainly hadn't pushed the marriage issue.

They reached the Chakhar khan's ger and dismounted. Dayan ducked into the brightly lit ger behind Mandukhai. Three Lords and Lady Altan had come inside as a show of strength.

A single chair waited across the open space from Guden.

The old khan studied Dayan as Dayan folded his hands behind his back so Mandukhai could take the seat. Mandukhai would be better suited to handle this interaction than he would be anyway. Guden's forehead was almost as wrinkled as Goram's had been. How old was this khan? Standing behind him, a man roughly Unebolod's age observed them as well.

"I hear you bring the whole of the Mongol Nation into my territory," Guden said, addressing Dayan.

But Dayan knew his role. He stared at Guden with an emotionless face, allowing his eyes to do the work for him. Guden grimaced and shifted.

"We came to you before crossing the border, but we will be entering, yes," Mandukhai nodded. "The Khan and I believe we have neglected the southern tribes for too long."

"You cannot force me to give my oath," Guden said. "The Chakhar have survived better than most here since ..." His voice cracked and trailed off. Dayan knew what upset him though. The famous massacre at the red salt lake had been devastating to most of the southern tribes. "We don't need anyone forcing us into battle again."

"We did not come to fight you," she said. "We had hoped you would at last see reason. The Great Khan's mother is from your tribe. Even some Oirat followed him, despite his ties to them only being through his grandmother."

Guden glanced at Dayan only for a second before he shifted. Hot anger made his neck burn red. "Siker soiled her reputation when she followed Issama," he snapped. "And the Khan's father was weak and self-serving. He comes from bad blood."

Dayan clenched his jaw. He *hated* being compared to his father.

"He *comes* from the blood of Genghis," Mandukhai said forcefully. "I hope you understand he will take control of the whole nation, just as his name promises. That includes your people. And you."

Silence fell. Guden glared at Mandukhai as if waiting for her to break first. Dayan knew that would never happen. No one else moved. Finally, Guden sighed. "I will be dead soon. My son, Belku, will be khan of the Chakhar. Perhaps he should decide our future."

Belku, the man behind Guden, studied Dayan much the way a hungry predator might. *Don't flinch. Don't blink. Breathe. In. Out.* Dayan focused on keeping his thoughts empty, his expression neutral and unrelenting.

Guden appeared ready to snap at his son for an answer.

Belku nodded. "He isn't like his father," Belku said at last.

I could have told you that much, Dayan thought, but he didn't flinch.

Guden's brows shot up. "There is no way you can know—"

"Look at him, father." Belku waved toward Dayan. "It's plain as day. Bayan would have jumped in with some arrogant rebuttal by now."

Guden scowled, drawing his thick, gray, bushy brows together as he examined Dayan. Finally, he harrumphed and raised his chin stubbornly. "Bigirsen killed my oldest son when I refused him. Would you do the same?"

Mandukhai offered a kind smile that made warmth spread through Dayan's chest. "What would be the point? If we were to kill anyone here, it would be you. Clearly your son understands the value in this alliance."

Belku blanched.

Guden's beard quivered at the insult. "Fine. If you want our oath, you first take Bigirsen's head. I want him dead just as much as you, but I don't have the *tumens* you have. I can spare a thousand men when you find him to help bring him down. Kill him, and you have my oath. A fair trade."

"I will lead the *mingghan*," Belku announced, drawing a sharp glare from his father, but before Guden could interject, Belku stepped out and dropped to one knee. "I will see my brother avenged with my own eyes."

Guden hissed.

Mandukhai placed her hand on Belku's shoulder. "We accept. We will kill him together when the time is right. And then you both will swear your oaths to your Great Khan and Khatun."

"Agreed." Belku drew a knife and sliced his hand. "Blood for blood."

Dayan's stomach twisted as he watched the red droplets ooze from the cut. *I have to seal this to bind him*, he realized. Swallowed the lump in his throat, Dayan stepped forward and accepted Belku's knife. He thought for certain his hand trembled violently, but no one seemed to notice. A glance at Mandukhai revealed her anger that he was doing this at all. He quickly looked away. *A Khan's only oath is to protect his people*, she had taught him. But she had also taught him that sometimes, to get what they wanted, they needed to bend.

Before he could lose his nerve, Dayan cut his palm as well and shook with Belku.

The air in the sweat tent was thick and hot. A female servant ladled water over the scorching stones to increase the steam, and Issama noticed how thin her deel was, how it clung to her skin.

"Ulum warned me about you," Mogurkei said from across the tent, breaking the spell. He wore only a cloth around his waist, just as Issama did.

"And he already explained my offer, I assume?" Issama asked. He slid a scraper along his skin to force out the sweat and get it off his body.

"Yes. It's ambitious, and I highly doubt it will succeed. You are betting too much on the Oirat, but you lost their allegiance years ago. Just as you lost ours." Mogurkei scraped his skin as well, flicking the sweat at the stones. It hissed.

"I have friends still among the Oirat," Issama said calmly. At least he hoped he still had friends there. Issama had not heard from his Oirat contacts in some time. *I cannot let these Lords see my doubt.* Mogurkei commanded nearly twenty-thousand warriors. Issama needed this deal more than any of the others.

"She conquered them years ago!" Mogurkei barked.

"You can conquer a people, but you cannot conquer their spirit," Issama replied smoothly. "Once Bigirsen is dealt with, we will take back the Oirat and return to power."

"To what end? Mandukhai has already named a Great Khan," Mogurkei sneered as he said this. "He has the right."

"Why?" Issama asked his questions casually, watching the Ordos Lord across from him carefully. "Because he carries the diluted blood and bone of Genghis?" He scraped off more sweat and set the tool down, leaning closer. "Think about where this boy comes from. One grandfather, a weak-willed prince. The other, a madman. And his father! We all know the sort of prince he was."

Mogurkei snorted, and his face twitched in disgust. Issama understood why. Mogurkei had a daughter Bayan had seduced. She ended up with child and tried to hide it, but when it became obvious, the shame of it drove her to madness. She killed herself and the unborn child.

"Arrogant," Mogurkei grumbled.

"Yes. And self-serving. Entitled. Which of these men do you believe the boy Khan will become most like when a woman coddles him?" Issama slid his hands along his hair to push it back from his face. "He may bear the bones of Genghis, but his forefathers did as well. And they have brought nothing but ruin. Do not be fooled. He does not rule. *She* does. The strength of Genghis is dead. It's time we assert our independence."

Mogurkei spit at the stones. They hissed. "So, you propose we use our stronger numbers to defeat them?"

"Yes. But carefully. And once we succeed, we choose a Great Khan not based on his blood, but his skills. A rightful Khan with our best interests at heart, just we should have done centuries ago. We open vote at *kurultai* for *any* man strong enough to rule."

"You mean you," Mogurkei snorted.

"I mean any man."

"And what about Bigirsen?"

"They will kill him for us." Issama was certain of this. Mandukhai hated Bigirsen. It was only a matter of time. She just needed to know where he was, which Issama had already taken care of. He discovered she had someone searching for Bigirsen and had leaked the location of Bigirsen's camp carefully, to avoid implicating himself. She would hear word soon. "Once they kill him, we kill them. Dayan, Unebolod, and Togochi all must die. They hold too much sway over the tribes. Without their support, Mandukhai will lose everything."

Mogurkei studied Issama thoughtfully. "Bigirsen has his son back, you know. The one he had with that Borjigin whore."

Nemeku? Issama tensed. No. He had counted on Mandukhai controlling Nemeku. *Perhaps this works in my favor.* If he could get his hands on the boy before Mandukhai sent her men to kill Bigirsen, he would have an additional pawn to use on his board. "I will take care of that."

Mogurkei sloughed off more sweat as he considered his answer. Then the corner of his mouth curled up in a grin. "I want her for myself."

Issama's brows climbed in alarm. No one else had made the request, and Issama could only think of one reason to say no. Mandukhai's witchy ability to control men with the power between her legs. "She is dangerous, Lord Mogurkei."

"I will whip her into shape until she crawls on her knees, begging for mercy," Mogurkei said. "And I'll give her every inch of it." He grabbed his crotch to punctuate his point. Not that he needed to.

Issama dipped his head in agreement. "Very well. She is all yours."

If he could get all the Ordos Lords to agree to this, Mandukhai's forces would be outnumbered.

But Unebolod had to die *before* the battle.

CHAPTER FIVE

Buddhas and Knights

Mandukhai stood alone over the map table at the edge of the gathering tent, staring down at the markings. Togochi had reunited with her warriors here in this border camp. For the past week, he and Unebolod had spent hours staring at these very maps, debating the movements of the tribes, the weakest points in Ordos, how they would get their men across the Huang Ho River, and which cities they could not afford to leave at their backs.

She picked up an iron statue the size of her pinky finger and turned the small, squat warrior in her hand. One of these represented a *mingghan*—a thousand men—they had told her. Such a small thing for such a vast number. The little warrior reminded her of Buddha dressed as a Mongol Lord. A bizarre combination. The metal was cold in her palm. Her gaze swept over the map.

Another piece resembling a chess knight dotted the landscape of the Ordos basin. The knight, Togochi had said, represented a full *tumen*—ten thousand warriors. She returned the Buddha Lord to his place on the map, then folded her hands in to the sleeves of her deel. Four knights occupied strategic locations within the borders of the Ordos basin, along with another twenty-two Buddha Lords. *So many.* Another three knights spread across the land north of the river toward the west and south of the Gobi, surrounded by another ten Buddha Lords. One hundred two thousand Mongols who obeyed their Ordos Lords.

Mandukhai turned her gaze to the pieces representing her own forces. Fifty-five thousand men landlocked in Oirat territory. To reach those warriors, she either would have to cross the desert, cross Bigirsen's territory, or go all the way back around the Gobi, which would take at least a year.

Four knights surrounded her current location near Lake Dai—not including the Chakhar that Guden would not yet give to her. Another knight occupied Urainkhai territory to the east of the river, alongside five Buddha Lords representing the Three Guards tribes with Huoshai. One Buddha Lord slowly moved south on a scouting mission. Nine others spread out through Chakhar territory, prodding for potential gaps in Ordos borders.

They had left a trail of Buddah Lords behind, along their path through the eastern territories. A thousand men—totaling another thirteen thousand—distributed to enforce the Khatun's will in her wake. A whole *tumen* scattered across the empire. She had left far more men in Ongud territory than she wanted, but Boragan had insisted on keeping the bulk of his forces to reinforce the eastern border.

By Mandukhai's current estimation, she had sixty-five thousand to face off against over a hundred thousand. "We have left the south alone for too long," she murmured to herself.

Belku had warned Mandukhai about Issama as well, but his warning bore old worries and nothing new of significance. Mandukhai had too much to deal with to worry about Issama at this point. It satisfied her enough to know that he and Bigirsen had a falling out years ago. Bigirsen was her immediate threat. Bigirsen and the rebellious Ordos Lords.

A shadow fell across the table. Mandukhai spun around.

Unebolod's gaze locked on her own, and for a moment neither of them spoke. He had not complained—he never complained—about her choosing Dayan as Khan. But Mandukhai knew, deep down, that Unebolod resented her for it. They had shared intimate dreams of ruling this empire together. She had not upheld her end of the bargain. Yet Mandukhai knew she could not have created this growing empire without him.

"Once we receive word from the scouts, we can finalize our plans," Unebolod said as he stepped around her and edged toward the table at her side.

Mandukhai followed Unebolod's gaze toward the map, only to discover he did not study the knights and Buddha Lords. He stared at her hand on the edge of the table, so close to his own. Mandukhai yearned to reach toward him. Could a small touch be so terrible a thing?

Sometimes, the pull toward him was unbearable. If the same rules applied to Khatuns as Khans, she could have had both of them. But men would rip the empire apart fighting over the right to rule should anything ever happen to her. As tempting as it might have been to take two husbands, it could never work. Whose sons would rule next? How would either man know who had fathered her children? Unebolod would be a khan without actual power, much as he was now. The only difference would be that she could be with him again. It would not work, but that did not stop her from dreaming of it.

Her fingers edged toward his along the tabletop.

Unebolod jerked his hand back and strode around to the other side. The withdrawal created an endless pit of longing in her stomach. Mandukhai had not forgotten what his touch felt like, what his arms felt like when he held her. He had not done so for years. Nor should he. But that didn't stop her from wanting it. His retreat, the refusal to accept even the slightest intimate touch, contrasted starkly with the way Dayan had touched her lips months ago … and reminded her of how she had reacted much the same way to that intimacy. Mandukhai swallowed. It didn't mean anything. None of it did.

"I betrayed one Khan," he said, lowering his voice. Not that anyone else was in the gathering tent with them. The shame in his words made her heart ache. "I will not betray another. I am still serving my penance for the first."

"Are you Christian now?" Mandukhai asked, hoping to lighten the suddenly tense mood. "I did not think you had faith in anything."

"I have faith in one thing," he said. Unebolod looked up from the Buddhas and knights, and the way he stared at her made Mandukhai want to run into his arms.

Instead, she straightened her spine. "I would love to know what has finally drawn your fai—"

"Truth is a dangerous thing," Unebolod interrupted. "I would like to keep my faith to myself."

Mandukhai couldn't help her curiosity. Unebolod had been cynical for as long as she could remember. What had finally drawn him in?

The door to the gathering tent burst open. Mandukhai jumped at the sudden interruption, pressing a hand against her racing heart as she turned.

Togochi rushed toward them, oblivious to the tension that had grown thick in the space. "Jangi returns."

Mandukhai had sent word to Huoshai and Tulugen of Jangi's arrival. Jangi had been sent a two years ago to find Bigirsen. His return promised at least some level of success. Word had come far enough ahead of Jangi that Huoshai and Tulugen had time to make the trip from their own camps more than a day southeast.

The gathering tent was bursting with Lords and commanders eager for news regarding Bigirsen's status. *These men are all my own Buddha Lords*, she mused as the gathering tent filled. Each man present represented command of at least a thousand of her men, if not more. A handful of them were her knights—including the two who sat at the foot of the dais.

Unebolod and Togochi waited in the seats she and Dayan had placed near the dais, a special place of honor for her *orloks*.

Dayan waited beside Mandukhai as the last of the men filtered in and took their seats. The copper pots burned high with fires all along the aisle. The flames flickered light off the large gemstones hanging from the roof lathes, enhancing the light. As Mandukhai watched Dayan, the flames also danced in his golden eyes to supernatural effect.

Jangi entered at last, and all eyes were on the Uyghur warrior as he strode toward the head of the gathering tent, his gaze fixed dead ahead. Though exhaustion dulled his eyes, his expression bore a dangerous hope. When he reached the front of the dais, he kneeled as custom dictated.

"Rise, Jangi," Mandukhai said, a little disappointed that Nemeku was not in his company. What had happened to him? Did Jangi even find him? He had left to find Bigirsen before knowing of Nemeku's disappearance. That did not mean Jangi did not find the boy along the way, or in Bigirsen's camp. She would have to ask about Nemeku later. "Tell us everything."

Jangi launched into his story, explaining the purpose of his mission—to track down Bigirsen, then follow Bigirsen until he had isolated himself enough from his men to make him weak. Mandukhai knew all of this already, but she let him retell for those who did not know.

"He is in an isolated place," Jangi reported. "The Ming have pushed him back out of Gansu. The Ordos Lords seem to have abandoned him. Some of his own men have retreated deeper into Uyghur territory, possibly to gather reinforcements. He believes he is safe where he is. He knows you have moved away from your old lands, and I believe he assumes you are traveling in the east."

"Did you see him yourself?" Unebolod asked.

Mandukhai could not see his face from where he was seated, but she noticed the subtle way his left hand tightened into a fist.

Jangi reached into his deel, which made both Unebolod and Togochi tense. A moment later, Jangi pulled out a silver cup and took a step forward, placing it at the foot of the dais. "I did," he said as he stepped back.

Unebolod stood and picked up the cup, inspecting it, sniffing it. His eyes shined as his gaze shot toward her like an arrow, and he held the cup up in his hand. "I recognize this. The detail is a hunting lion. He has three others like it."

"Did you steal this cup from Bigirsen?" Mandukhai ask as she held out her hand.

Unebolod climbed the steps and offered it to her.

Mandukhai turned the cup in her hands, inspecting the ornate details and wide base. She had seen this cup, as well, when she had tea with Borogchin years ago. Her heart ached thinking of that poor girl's fate.

"I told him I was ill, and he offered me *airag* in the silver cup to help stave off illness," Jangi explained.

Mandukhai nodded. Silver had healing properties. Bigirsen had actually intended to help. Did he not remember who Jangi had been, or what he had done? It was Jangi who had ridden away with Nemeku years ago, just before Borogchin's husband had murdered her.

Jangi shrugging. "He did not seem to remember me after all these years."

"And he thought nothing of your arrival?" Mandukhai asked, setting the cup aside. "How do we know he is not baiting a trap to lure us in?"

If she sent an army in after Bigirsen and he knew she was coming, he would use any resources he had to kill her men. Jangi had no answer to her question.

"How far is he?" Togochi asked.

"Just south of Juyan Basin," Jangi answered. "Most of his men are dead or retreating to get more warriors for his next advance."

Unebolod straightened. Mandukhai could feel the anticipation rolling off of him. It was infectious, and she had to remind herself to remain calm.

"And Issama?" she asked, remembering Belku telling her that Issama had allied with the Ordos Lords against Bigirsen in the past.

Jangi shook his head. "Smoke in the wind. Some men say he returned to Turfan or Asku. A few claimed he has gone into Ordos to rally the *tumens* there."

Mandukhai's heart seized momentarily. With Issama potentially close, Mandukhai had to be certain she did not leave herself defenseless. He had not acted against her yet, but he had not given his oath either. Over the course of eight years, surely he could have found her done so, if that were his intent. Especially with Dayan's mother as his wife.

"Juyan Basin is not far," Unebolod said, turning to face her. His face lit up with enthusiasm. "We can reach him in a month, at most, if we move with stealth. Mandukhai Khatun, let me lead the men."

Mandukhai held up a hand to calm him. She had never witnessed such a thrill in him before. "Patience, Unebolod. We need to know how many men he has with him. It would also be prudent to remember that we have thousands of Ordos warriors between us. Last we heard, he has an alliance still with the Ordos khan, Legusi. I want Bigirsen dead, too, but we cannot be hasty."

Jangi said, "He has perhaps a thousand men nearby. As I mentioned, the rest have moved on."

Unebolod climbed a step, leaning closer to her and Dayan. "We have not been this close to him for years. *And* with the full force of your *tumens* at our backs when he is weak. He is only about five hundred miles away. With supplies and our best horses, we can reach him in as little as two weeks. Less if we move quickly, more if we move with careful stealth. He is within our grasp for the first time in decades. We cannot squander this chance."

Mandukhai did not react to Unebolod's eager petition to fight. She turned her attention back to Jangi. Something else drew her gaze past Jangi. Most of the men gathered shared in Unebolod's elation. They all had something to gain by destroying Bigirsen for good—and she had promised this chance to some of these Lords. But when so many were out for your blood, you would see them coming from afar. Bigirsen was not so foolish to be unprepared.

"Where is Nemeku?" she asked.

Jangi frowned. Everything about him tensed as his expression slipped into shock. Not the reaction she wanted.

"He left after you did," Mandukhai explained, hoping her voice didn't quiver enough for others to notice. "Did you not see him *once* on your journey? It has been two years since he ran off after his father!"

Jangi reflexively stepped backward, shaking his head. Shock and worry marred his weathered face. His gaze darted back and forth across the tiles as if attempting to calculate them. Then his gaze shot up to her own. "Bigirsen has him. He must!" Jangi closed his eyes and his brows knitted together, horror creasing the his forehead. "That was what he meant," he muttered to himself. "Please. I beg your forgiveness. I did not know Bigirsen meant Nemeku when I overheard. I thought he spoke of the Khan."

Everyone observed her response with bated breath.

Mandukhai flinched, then leaned forward. "What did he say?"

"I overheard him telling one of his men he would teach the boy he was his father's son." Jangi stiffened as if preparing for battle. "Shortly before that, he had been talking about our Khan's father, and I thought ... I just assumed he was referring to you, Dayan Khan."

Dayan did not blink at this news. He didn't even move. To him, she knew, Bayan had never been his father.

Mandukhai feared she might erupt with worry. It built inside of her, inflating her to the point of bursting. Bigirsen had Nemeku and intended to teach the boy where his loyalties belonged. What kind of pain had Bigirsen already inflicted on Nemeku? What sort of horror was the boy now living in? She had to rescue Nemeku ... before Bigirsen beat Nemeku into submission. Before he propped his son up as a contender to Dayan's title. Bigirsen could attempt destroying everything she had worked so hard for these past eight years.

"*Orlok*, it seems you will get your wish," Mandukhai said, raising her voice loudly and clearly. "Select your men. Rescue Nemeku. Kill Bigirsen. We can spare only one *tumen*."

Unebolod stood taller than ever before. Heat and excitement burned in his voice. "That is more than enough."

"I will give you a list of Lords who will accompany you. The rest of us will remain here and continue preparing for the invasion into Ordos," Mandukhai said. "Return quickly, Unebolod. We will need you when the time comes."

Unebolod placed his fist over his heart and bowed deeply. "I will make his death swift and bring you his head."

"You leave in two days at dawn," she said.

If any man could finally destroy Bigirsen, Mandukhai had faith that it would be Unebolod. And as he raised his gaze to meet hers, his eyes shone with the thrill of this battle. Unebolod had waited years for this. Now, at last, she had given him the men to kill Bigirsen. Hopefully it would not be a trap. But they had to rescue Nemeku before it was too late.

Unebolod was all the knight she needed to defeat her oldest enemy.

CHAPTER SIX

The Great Fist

Mandukhai rubbed sleep from her eyes once more as she sat in Dust's saddle on the hilltop. The wolf dawn retreated west—a blue haze that lightened as the sun rose. This morning, the wolf dawn raced away from deep shades of purple that broke over the red rocky cliffs and outlined them in a line of pink.

Tomorrow, Unebolod would take ten thousand of her warriors to kill Bigirsen. Removing Bigirsen presented her with two significant advantages. First, and most obvious, was that as long as he lived, the Ordos might never truly kneel to their rightful Great Khan. If she took Bigirsen's head, the Ordos would have nowhere to turn when she attacked. Not with the Ming hiding behind their wall.

The second advantage was over the flow of goods. Bigirsen still controlled the Silk Route from the far eastern edge of the Tianshan Mountains all the way to the Ming border. Once he was dead, she could take control of those goods. It would force the Ming to treat with her, or they risked losing access to all the goods and gold that flowed along that route. Bigirsen had held those goods hostage. Mandukhai, however, would use diplomacy.

Diplomacy and careful child rearing. She wouldn't make the same mistake as Genghis. He had been a visionary, but his fatal flaws were his expansionism and his parenting skills.

Mandukhai tipped her head back to the sky. "Tengri, guide us as we seek to restore our fractured empire."

Dust danced a step to the side, and Mandukhai glanced over as she heard hooves approach her hilltop lookout. Mandukhai gazed down at the base of the hill where Torgus and his men had dismounted to allow their horses a drink in a small stream.

"You should not be up here alone," Togochi said as he rode up beside her. "Even if your men are down there keeping guard. Arrows can fly anywhere." Togochi gazed at the purple sunrise a moment before turning his attention to her once more. "They are nearly ready to head west. Today, the men will gather the resources they need to cross the southern edge of the Gobi. Tomorrow, they ride out."

"I know." Mandukhai sighed. She did not like this plan.

Togochi hesitated, eyeing Mandukhai curiously. "What is it?"

"This stinks of a trap." Mandukhai rolled her shoulders back. "It creates an itch between my shoulders."

"I agree." Togochi exhaled in a huff of air. "But Unebolod is the most capable man we have to lead this mission. His plan is a good one, as usual. You need to trust his abilities. And if you allowed me to go with him—"

"I need you here, Togochi," Mandukhai said quickly. "You are *orlok* of my northern forces. And you have a duty to help me plan for our attack into Ordos."

Togochi scowled. "That's unfair. Don't throw duty in my face so recklessly. You know I respect you. But I also know you can plan this without me."

"I am worried about the Uyghur *and* the Ordos. Between you and Unebolod, I have every confidence we will finish this."

Togochi huffed, but said nothing more about it. For a moment, they sat in silence in their saddles watching the sunrise. After a few minutes, Togochi broke the comfortable silence. "The Khan has summoned you."

Mandukhai raised her brows. Curious. Dayan *never* summoned her. Usually it was the other way around. He had grown so much more headstrong in the last year.

Mandukhai whistled at the guards, who swiftly mounted their horses and met her at the base of the hill.

As the sun broke over the eastern horizon, the camp had become a flurry of activity. Thousands of gers dotted the dry, rocky winter ground in clumps. Women skimmed the surface of the mare's milk to dry out the top layer for curds the men would need, or they checked the status of the mutton strips left out to dry. Young children darted around underfoot in races and games with slings or toy bows, staying active to keep warm. Older children moved back and forth from the lake, collecting water in skins the men would take with them. Warriors checked mounts, fletched arrows, traded for fresh strings or fletching feathers, and exchanged comments about the coming ride in jests that made Mandukhai smile as she passed by on Dust's back.

The excitement of a coming battle created a stir among her people that Mandukhai found invigorating, but sad. How many of these men would die to restore the empire? How many of these women would become widows? While she knew it was necessary, and a part of life, Mandukhai did not want to be responsible for their deaths.

The gathering tent was hard to miss no matter where you were in the camp. The massive structure rose high above the rest of the gers, surrounded by the fluttering blue banners of the Great Khan, and the *sulde* of Genghis. Dayan had not officially been installed in Karakorum yet, but that day would be upon them soon enough.

Mandukhai dismounted beside the massive cart that carried the gathering tent and tethered Dust to it. Just as Genghis Khan had had a mobile command tent, so too did Dayan Khan. As she climbed the wooden steps, Mandukhai's gaze locked on the fluttering horsehair banner of Genghis. Issama had somehow stolen the banner from thousands of miles away. One of his spies had taken it and ridden south to bring it to him. *I will make him pay one of these days*, Mandukhai thought.

After Manduul's death, Issama had been bold enough to propose marriage in exchange for the title of Great Khan, as if he had actually believed she would have given it to him. When she had refused to answer him, he had stolen the sacred black banner, likely hoping she would not name another Khan without it. He had underestimated her, just as all men did. Mandukhai had the will of the High Heavens on her side.

She stepped over the threshold with Togochi following behind. The inside of this gathering space was much larger inside than it appeared on the outside. The cart had four double wheels on either side to support the massive structure, and it required a dozen yaks to pull when they were on the move.

Dayan straightened on his throne the moment she entered, raising his chin and squaring his shoulders as if preparing for a fight. Mandukhai approached, glancing at Unebolod, who waited patiently off to the side with his hands folded behind his back. Even he stood ramrod straight. Did he know what this was about?

Only Boke and the guards were in the tent with the four of them. Mandukhai raised her eyebrows curiously at Dayan.

"Have some scouts returned?" she asked as she climbed the dais steps.

Dayan held up a hand, freezing Mandukhai halfway up. She had never seen him in such a state before, as if he braced himself for some terrible news.

"What is wrong?" she asked, sincerely concerned as she glanced at Unebolod.

Dayan did not even flinch. His face remained a stony mask, but his jaw tensed ever so slightly. He set his hand back on the arm of the seat, wrapping his fingers tight around the ends until his knuckles turned white. Was he paler than usual?

"My *orloks* and I have spoken," Dayan said. His voice trembled a little, but gained confidence as he continued. "And we have come to an agreement."

Togochi stopped beside Unebolod. When Mandukhai glanced at Togochi, he averted his gaze to the floor.

"Oh?" Mandukhai folded her hands into the sleeves of her deel and put on an outward mask of calm. Inside, everything churned in a mass of acidic destruction. She trusted these three men more than any others in the whole empire. Had they betrayed her? *No. They would never.*

"I am Great Khan, and sixteen," Dayan said. Something in his voice chaffed at Mandukhai's skin, as if he braced for impact. Which meant he believed she would not agree to what he was about to say. "It is time for my men to see me lead."

Mandukhai's heart dropped so suddenly it made her dizzy. "You have been leading them for years."

"No. You have been." Dayan shifted slightly. Mandukhai saw the telltale signs of his anxiety by the way his fingertips pressed into the engraved wood. "It is time, Mandukhai. Genghis was my age when he first rode into battle."

A vision flashed into Mandukhai's mind of Dayan, helpless in the muddy banks of a river somewhere in the west as their enemies took his head. The horror of the vision made her breakfast climb her throat in revolt. It took several attempts to swallow it back down. Her heart thumped hard against her ribs.

"Dayan, you are not ready," Mandukhai said, shaking her head and blinking back the tears the vision had conjured. "See reason. This is no small skirmish. These men ride to war against thousands, against Bigirsen. Let our men handle this."

Dayan licked his lips but seemed to catch himself in the act, pressing his lips together for a moment before he spoke. "I do not come to this lightly.

But these are my men, and it is time that I show them the sort of Khan I will be. They will never truly respect me until I prove myself to them."

"You are chosen by the High Heavens, given this title by divine right!" Mandukhai climbed another step, edging close to him. "You have nothing to prove."

Dayan surged to his feet so suddenly Mandukhai froze once more. His movements were jerky. But he did not appear angry. Dayan's golden eyes pleaded with her. His shoulders sloped down almost desperately.

"I am Great Khan, Mandukhai," he said, shuffling closer to her. Mandukhai moved toward him as if some great force pushed them toward each other. "Everything that I am today, I owe to you. My parents abandoned me to die. You should have killed me or left me to die." For just a moment, his gaze flicked to Unebolod. "Instead, you healed my broken body." Dayan pressed his palm tenderly against her cheek, brushing away the tears she didn't realized had escaped. "You mended my shattered soul."

Mandukhai placed her hand over Dayan's. "We are so close, Dayan. Just let Unebolod handle this. He knows what he is doing."

"So do I."

She shook her head as if that could stop him. For the first time since she had chosen Dayan, Mandukhai felt powerless. He was Great Khan. If he insisted on going, she could not stop him.

"Mandukhai, you surrounded me with the best shaman, warriors, and scholars you could gather," Dayan continued. He jerked his hand away from hers. It left her suddenly cold. "My *orloks* have personally trained me to be the best bowman and swordsman I can be. I can ride a horse as well as you now, thanks to your care. They trust my skills. At some point, you will have to, as well. *Today*, you will have to. When my men ride out in the morning, their Khan rides with them."

Mandukhai's hands trembled, and she smoothed them over her hips to steady them. "Then I am coming, too."

"No." Dayan returned to his seat, and as he settled in it, his gaze locked on hers. His fingers fumbled with the white belt around his waist. He wore several belts, each a symbol for his position. The white represented his purity. "I need you here, leading, preparing."

"Preparing for what?" Mandukhai asked, resisting the urge to snap at him. She regretted the question before she had even finished asking. *What a stupid question!*

"Ordos. Then Karakorum."

Mandukhai gasped, glancing at Unebolod and Togochi for help. But Togochi kept his gaze locked on Dayan, his expression inscrutable. Unebolod's dark eyes met Mandukhai's, and he gave a slight nod, agreeing with Dayan. Mandukhai breathed deeply to center herself, then turned fierce eyes on Dayan.

"Dayan, I will not—"

"The Khan has spoken," Unebolod said.

Mandukhai's fingernails dug into her palms. Her chest heaved with angry breath. She turned abruptly and stormed over to Unebolod until the toes of their boots touched. "Was this your idea?"

So close to him, Mandukhai could feel the warmth of his body, the waves of heat rolling off of him. He met her gaze without flinching and gave away nothing in his eyes. But his lips parted ever so slightly.

"The Khan came to *us* last night," Togochi said. "We spent a great deal of time discussing this."

Mandukhai tore her gaze from Unebolod to glare at Togochi.

"Before you say anything else," Unebolod said, "Realize we outnumber you, and one of those votes is your Khan. He is stronger now, Mandukhai. It's time you see that for yourself. Dayan Khan is no longer a broken boy. He just wants to prove who he is."

Mandukhai's heart shattered all over again. These three men held her heart. Now, they smashed it together. If Dayan died, Genghis' line would fall for good. Dayan had no wives or children yet—except an informal marriage to her that he could easily walk away from still. Would he walk away if she refused him now?

"And just who is he?" she asked. Her voice shook, and she hated herself for showing such weakness right now.

"The Whole Khan," Togochi said. "As you promised."

"It is done," Dayan said.

Mandukhai spun around to confront him, to convince Dayan he was making a mistake, but he already rushed toward the exit like a rabbit desperate to escape a hunter. Dayan clearly was distressed about this. Perhaps where was a chance to change his mind. *I need to stop him.* Mandukhai took a step to follow.

Togochi placed a hand on her shoulder, halting her before she could hurry after Dayan. She shrugged him off. He deflated and shot an imploring gaze at Unebolod.

"He will die," Mandukhai said, her voice cracking over the words.

"He has made up his mind," Togochi said. "You cannot stop him."

Unebolod's hand brushed along her shoulder. "Don't let him leave with your anger in his memory. A thing like that can cloud a man's judgment."

"He's not a man," Mandukhai said miserably.

"He is," Unebolod insisted. "And I think he needs you to see it."

Mandukhai watched the door to the gathering tent as if it could summon Dayan back to her, but he did not appear. If her vision was to believed, this battle would be the end of him.

Dayan pushed through the door to his ger, struggling to breathe as if a Great Fist closed around his lungs. Before anyone could see his weakness, he slammed the door shut. He staggered to the side, eyes watering as the edges of his vision blurred. Desperate for air, Dayan leaned against the center pole near the smoke hole and yanked at his belts. Blue. Green. White. Red. Yellow. The yellow belt tangled on his hand. Dayan shook it violently in a moment of panic.

Unable to stop the Great Fist from tightening around his insides, Dayan stumbled around to his bed and collapsed awkwardly. Dark spots swam in his vision. He rested his hands against his knees and focused on his breathing like Goram had taught him. Dayan closed his eyes. In. Out. In. Out. Slowly, the Great Fist released its deadly grasp.

Mandukhai had always supported him, encouraged him, taught him patience and wisdom over impulsive acts. Dayan had not come to this decision lightly, and he had known she would not approve. Still, the boy in him had held on to the hope that Mandukhai would see reason, accept him as a man, and support him once more. Her refusal had not been a surprise, but it still had hurt.

The Great Fist that captured him had been much harder to control as a boy. Mandukhai had enlisted the monk Goram to help Dayan learn how to control his own emotions. She did not know that he still suffered from these sudden attacks. Dayan had no intention of telling her, either. It would be just one more thing for her to use as an excuse to shelter him.

Over the past two years, the attacks had worsened progressively—and only when he worried about disappointing or confronting her. They seemed directly connected to his need to please her or his fear of failing her—or being rejected by her. Dayan was concerned it would be yet another curse to create distance between them. Today had been the worst. Dayan had never come so close to blacking out before.

But he needed to do this. He had to leave to fight alongside the men. They would respect him more. And maybe, if Tengri blessed him at all, she would finally see him as the man he was and not a broken boy. His heartbeat steadied as he continued his breathing exercise.

Perhaps this distance will help cure me of these attacks, he thought, praying for some sort of mercy. As far as everyone else knew, their Great Khan was young, strong, and virile. Dayan would do everything in his power to keep it that way.

CHAPTER SEVEN

The Purpose of War

The last thing Mandukhai wanted to do was have tea with the Ladies as Dayan prepared to ride off to war. Yet this group of women had become a core of Mandukhai's court. She listened to their advice and considered their opinions in matters of State as wives of commanders and lesser khans. Sometimes, their opinions would be more of a hindrance than real wisdom, but every now and again, one of them would share a nugget of brilliance.

They rotated hosting responsibilities. This time, it should have been Mandukhai, but she had been so distracted that Jaghan had taken over preparations and invited the women to her ger. Mandukhai had been the last to arrive.

The usual women had already assumed positions around the ger and stood as she entered as a show of respect. Jaghan had been married to Togochi for over ten years and gave him four sons and two daughters in that time. She showed a little of her age around the corners of her eyes and mouth. Geriel was a young woman from the Chakhar tribe Togochi had taken as a second wife three years ago. Mandukhai was pleased with how well Geriel and Jaghan got along—as sisters, the way Mandukhai had wanted to get along with Yeke at first. Geriel was a pleasant woman with a fast smile and sharp wit.

Satai had joined Mandukhai in the summer and visited occasionally when her husband, Unige, did not need her nearby. Mandukhai had left Unige in charge of a series of yam stations between Lake Dalinur and Lake Dai.

Beside Satai, Odgerel held her teacup in one hand as her infant son nursed. Odgerel had resented Mandukhai for a time after the marriage to Boke, particularly after Mandukhai had bound herself to Dayan instead of Unebolod. However, once Odgerel stopped resisting and opened up to Boke, she saw the sort of man she had married. Honorable. Respectful. Loving. Now, Odgerel seemed happy with her marriage.

Altan leaned against the wall near the door with all the casual grace of a warrior. Despite having several children of her own, Altan had not relinquished control of the Jalair to any man—something Mandukhai admired about the woman. While she had four sons of her own now with her husband, Altan doted on her oldest so thoroughly Mandukhai could see the jealousy in the other boys even at such a young age.

Besides her regular circle of Ladies, Mandukhai noticed nearly a dozen more that had joined from tribes all around the northern and eastern tribes. Every one of them had married a Lord, commander, or general in the army. Some of them would say goodbye to their husbands in the morning. *Hopefully I will not make widows of them.*

Every one of these women had children of their own. Mandukhai had only the Khan she had raised. She had not even lain with a man since that night with Unebolod before the Oirat attack. Ever since, Mandukhai had held only one hand. She had only experienced affection from one person, and never intimately. How she ached to be held, kissed, enveloped in intimacy and love. But all she had was a boy.

And he was about to ride off to war.

Unebolod had no wife to attend these meetings, though Mandukhai had heard enough rumors over the years that he had not left his bed cold as hers had been. The news had hurt deeply, but she could not blame him. He was a man with needs. And if he refused a wife, he still had to satisfy those needs. She only wished it could be with her. She had wanted to know which women he had slept with. Either she could not uncover them, or he didn't want her to. Mandukhai suspected Unebolod tried to hide his women from her to avoid hurting her. Not that it did. No doubt some of those women hoped he might choose them as a wife.

In the morning, both Unebolod and Dayan would leave her behind and ride into battle. She could very well lose them both.

The women resumed their gossip as Mandukhai settled into her seat. Jaghan poured her a cup of salted tea and offered a sympathetic smile. Mandukhai did not want sympathy.

"How are you doing?" Jaghan whispered so as not to draw attention to them.

Mandukhai opened her mouth, prepared to say she was fine, but Jaghan was her oldest friend. She knew Mandukhai better than anyone, and lying to her would not help matters at all. Of all the women here, Jaghan understood what Mandukhai risked losing in this fight against Bigirsen.

"I think my body is on the verge of shattering," Mandukhai whispered back.

"Unebolod will allow nothing to happen to the Khan," Jaghan said, likely hoping that offered her some solace. It didn't.

Mandukhai stared into her teacup as a lump swelled in her throat. "He is not the only one I worry about losing," she croaked.

Jaghan offered a reassuring smile and patted her on the shoulder before taking her own seat beside Geriel.

"We are all sending off the men we love," Odgerel said in that sweet way she had perfected, speaking pleasantly while masking hidden resentment. Her dark eyes met Mandukhai's. Despite the honey-sweet smile on her face, her eyes told a different story. "Whether tomorrow or when you ride into Ordos. The difference is our men will sacrifice their lives to protect yours." That statement held more truth for Odgerel than any of these other women. Boke would die protecting Dayan without a second thought.

"Of course they will," Geriel replied patiently. "Because that is their duty. He is Khan of khans."

Mandukhai sipped the tea to mask the fear she knew etched over her face, then said, "He is not a man yet."

Altan snorted. Several of the women exchanged glances, raised brows, or small smiles. Mandukhai found this reaction annoying.

Odgerel shifted the infant slung across her chest. "Is that truly what you think? Have you not noticed?"

Mandukhai blinked. When she opened her mouth to retort, her gaze swept the ger, and she noted the way all the women seemed shocked. "What?"

A Khorlod woman whose name Mandukhai could not recall—Yaqui's wife?—spoke first. "I remember when Bayan first came to Mongke Bulag," she began. Speaking Bayan's name drew a few murmurs of shame, but no one interrupted. "He was fifteen. Handsome. Charming. All the unattached girls in the capital craved just a few moments of his attention. Even a few of the attached girls who had not yet married."

"Even a few of the married ones," Satai interrupted, drawing alarmed looks from everyone. Satai flushed, but shrugged. "I'm married, not blind."

Mandukhai didn't like where this conversation headed. "Bayan was an impulsive, foolish, reckless boy."

Satai nodded in agreement. "I don't think any of us will argue that point. But he also did not have the firm hand of a woman to raise him properly. To beat out those rough edges, teach him the importance of patience and wisdom and respect." Satai took a slow drink of her tea, watching Mandukhai pointedly over the edge of her teacup.

All the women were staring at Mandukhai as if waiting for her to put the pieces together. Mandukhai understood what they were trying to tell her, but she could not see it, not accept it. To her, Dayan was still the boy who held her hand when no one else dared. The boy who would not speak to anyone for months. He was not his father, and she saw that plainly. Dayan was what Bayan should have been—what he could have been with proper guidance.

Altan grumbled under her breath, then set down her teacup and stood abruptly. "I'm bored with this. You women waste too much time running in circles instead of charging straight in." Altan placed her hands on her hips and squared off in front of Mandukhai. "Dayan Khan is *not* a boy. He is a man. He is handsome and intelligent and strong, and he is drawing attention. We all see our Great Khan. But to him, none of that matters, because *you* don't see it. Mandukhai Khatun, he does not ride into battle for his men, no matter what he might have told you. He rides into battle for *you*."

Mandukhai flinched. "Me?"

"You are a wise woman," Altan said with a grimace. "You must know this. Dayan Khan has never cared what anyone thought of him, except for you. Girls flirt with him, make eyes at him, and he is either oblivious to it or he gave his heart away long ago, because he has never once shown any hint of interest in anyone."

Mandukhai flushed as all the women in the ger nodded in agreement, watching her expectantly. Dayan had never shown her such interest. And she had not entertained the idea. He was not old enough. Not ready.

They called him a man. Has he sneaked off already to lay with a woman? The prospect me her gut wrench. "What do you mean a man? What girls flirt with him?"

Altan rolled her eyes.

"All of them," Odgerel said. "All of them young enough to be unmarried and eager to be a Khan's wife, at least."

"Most men his age have already settled on a wife or had children," Satai said, nodding in agreement with Odgerel. "Don't worry too much. Our Khan of khans has not entertained the notion no matter how many girls would be willing."

Mandukhai's stomach twisted in knots. Was Dayan riding off to fight Bigirsen because of her? *He said he needs me here, preparing for Ordos... For Karakorum.* Mandukhai suddenly felt like a fool. If Dayan was trying to prove something to her, and he intended to end his road in Karakorum, then he also expected her to prepare the tribes for his final, official installment. And if he won this war against the Ordos and Bigirsen, the tribes would support him in a landslide victory. No one would ever question him again. He would prove himself to be the Whole Khan, as she had promised.

And then he would either choose her or free her.

Mandukhai set her cup down and stood on shaky legs, then smoothed out her silk deel. "Excuse me. My men ride to war in the morning, and I have work to do."

No one said a word as Mandukhai made her way to the exit. She hoped they could not see her trembling. Before she slipped out the door, Mandukhai saw the knowing smirk on Altan's face. It made the knots in her stomach tighten and twist violently.

She needed to speak with Dayan before he left.

Ong said nothing about Dayan's sudden change in plans, but Dayan could tell he had imposed on his head servant. Dayan left his ger to give the servants space to do their work. He didn't want to be under their feet as they packed prepared his belongings.

Dayan marched to the gathering tent where Unebolod and Togochi bent over a series of maps they had looted years ago. How many of them would now be outdated? His sudden appearance drew both of the *orloks'* gazes to him.

"My lord Khan, what brings you?" Unebolod asked, glancing past Dayan as Boke and the guards filtered in and took their usual positions.

"Unebolod, I think we are past the formalities, don't you?" Dayan asked as he joined them. "I expect to be included in planning, even if I trust the guidance of my *orloks*."

Unebolod nodded stiffly, turning his attention back to the maps. Togochi smirked at Dayan. A curious reaction.

"We were just reviewing Mandukhai's yam lines to finalize our supply routes for the incursion into Ordos," Unebolod explained, running a calloused finger over the parchment.

Dayan stopped beside the table, but instead of gratifying his curiosity about the route, he stared at Unebolod. For some reason, if Dayan stared at people long enough, it made them squirm. Everyone except Mandukhai. His silence drew their gazes to him again. Unebolod frowned, and for a moment, neither of them seemed to breathe.

"*Your* yam lines," Unebolod corrected, finally understanding what Dayan waited for.

Mandukhai had built Dayan an empire, patching it together over years of tireless work, holding it together with her patience and wisdom. Dayan adored her for it. She wanted him to be Great Khan. That meant these pieces of the empire were his as well. Dayan would be Great Khan. Yet no one ever referenced him in connection with the empire.

Unebolod had taught him how to fight, how to strategize battles. In many ways, Unebolod was more of a father than his own shameful father would ever have been. Unebolod had every reason to hate him, to want him dead. Instead, he had spent years preparing Dayan. Now, Dayan would show Mandukhai, show everyone, that he was worthy.

The first thing Dayan needed to do was get all the men to give over these bits of control Mandukhai had held. Or at least connect him to them as well. Dayan had no ill intentions toward her. He could never harm her. But she had known years ago, when she had chosen him for this, that one day she would have to step back and let him take the reins. He intended to share them with her, but his men would expect him to be in control. Not her.

"Show me." Dayan folded his hands into the sleeves of his deel and gazed at the maps.

Unebolod and Togochi explained everything in detail. What path they would take around the Gobi to reach Bigirsen's location and why it was the best course. Where the supply lines would be replenished and where they would need to be fortified going all the way back to Karakorum. How long it would be before they could accurately devise a strategy against the

Ordos. How many men would need to trail behind them with the supplies along the way across the Ordos basin.

Servants brought in drinks and food as they discussed their plans. Dayan drank the *airag* slower than the other two. He had never developed as strong a taste for it as most men, but he would need to develop a resistance to the intoxication. *Airag* was a staple of their diet while riding off to war.

As the evening approached, Dayan found himself disappointed Mandukhai had not come looking for him. Would she allow him to leave without saying goodbye?

Perhaps his disappointment showed, because Unebolod seemed to pick up on it, patting him on the back as he sometimes did after a good training day. Dayan did not know if he should love or hate this man. Different days drew out different emotions. Some days, Dayan loathed every breath Unebolod took. Other days, like today, the small acts of affection warmed Dayan. Did all boys feel this way under the gaze of their father? *He is not my father,* Dayan reminded himself. *He wants my title.*

Dayan had not been deaf to the rumors and stories as he grew up. He knew Unebolod had planned on becoming Great Khan and that he had not been happy when Dayan had first appeared in Mandukhai's camp.

"Togochi, enjoy your evening with your wives," Dayan said, dismissing the Khorlod Lord.

Togochi grinned. "I certainly would like to do that. I will see you two in the morning."

Togochi bid them goodnight and strode out the door with purpose. Dayan envied him. Togochi had not one, but two wives whom he adored, and they both adored him as well. It made that Great Fist threaten to grab hold of his lungs once more as Dayan thought about how much he longed for the same.

"You need to speak to her before you leave, Dayan," Unebolod said as he rolled up the maps and packed them into a leather bag he would attach to his mount. "If you leave these things unsaid, it will haunt your steps when you need to be focused."

Dayan pressed his hands against the tabletop, feeling the cool, smooth wood against his hot palms. He focused on his breathing, hoping to prevent the Great Fist from overpowering him. "If she wanted to speak, she would have done so by now."

Unebolod chuckled as he rolled up another map. "Sometimes I have to remind myself that you are still young."

Dayan pressed his fingertips into the tabletop. *Still young. What does that mean?*

Unebolod tucked the last map away in the saddlebag and hefted it over his shoulder. He faced Dayan. That scar on his face became a fissure in a great mountain as his expression hardened. "I have known her for a long time. Mandukhai is stubborn and proud. She will not come to you. Ever. If you wait for that day, you will become old and gray and turn to dust in the earth. Then she will stand over your grave and curse *you* for being too stubborn to speak first. That's the way of women, and she sets quite an example for other women to follow. Yet we men eagerly crave their attention."

The corner of Dayan's mouth twitched into a small smirk he quickly smothered. Mandukhai set quite an example for *everyone* to follow. Himself included.

"Such is the purpose of war," Dayan said. Men wanted to prove their manliness and strength to women to get their attention, which was why they rode off to war. To prove something. *Just as I am doing.*

Unebolod regarded him for a moment, then barked out a brief chuckle and nodded. "I suppose it is."

The two of them strode toward the exit together. A shadow fell over the opening as they neared the doorway. Unebolod edged himself subtly in front of Dayan in an obvious effort to guard him. Dayan appreciated Unebolod's dedication but resented the implication that he needed guarding.

Mandukhai crossed the threshold, halting as she saw the two of them. Everyone froze in place. Unebolod appeared shocked that she had come. Mandukhai's gaze lingered long enough on the *orlok* that the Great Fist squeezed Dayan's heart so tight it hurt.

Unebolod sidestepped her, glancing at Dayan and giving a small nod. But Dayan saw through the warrior. He saw the agony in Unebolod's eyes that his warrior's mask kept hidden.

"Sleep well, Dayan Khan," Unebolod said. "Khatun." He bowed slightly to her, then disappeared into the early evening beyond the gathering tent.

Mandukhai watched Unebolod go. Dayan deflated, fighting to adopt that cold face Unebolod had become such an expert with. When at last she turned her attention to him, the sorrow in her eyes was not well-masked. Dayan hated feeling inferior. Mandukhai cared deeply for Unebolod and often tried to hide it from Dayan. But he saw it in those small moments.

How could he ever compare to a man like Unebolod? Being Great Khan did not make Dayan worthy. Mandukhai only respected one thing.

"I don't want us to leave things as we did earlier," she said.

Dayan licked his dry lips. Would she take this moment to chastise him, dress him down for acting childish? He couldn't face it. Not before leaving. Instead, he grasped her hand. "Before you say anything, come with me."

CHAPTER EIGHT

Tale of a Khan and a Queen

Mandukhai stumbled along with Dayan, helpless to stop him as he dragged her with him. His hand was clammy, but his fingers held tight to hers as if he were afraid she would pull away. Mandukhai's curiosity had her wondering where he was taking her. An urgency seemed to hasten his strides through camp.

Then he stopped beside two horses. Dust, and one of his mares. Mandukhai frowned. This was what he wanted to show her?

"I don't understand," she said, edging toward Dust.

Dayan continued clinging to her hand. He turned to stand in front of her, grinning like a foolish boy. "I want one more race before I go."

A race? Mandukhai watched the excitement dance in his golden eyes. Once Dayan had been strong enough to ride, Mandukhai taught him how to race his mounts. How to stand in the saddle and guide the mount with his knees. How to get more speed without pushing the horse too far. Over the years, they had begun racing. Not that he had ever won. His skills had improved significantly, but Dust was faster than most of the horses in their herd.

Racing now seemed like a poor choice of time spent when two *tumens* of their men rode to battle in the morning. She had demanded on a second *tumen* when Dayan had insisted on going. It was excessive but would protect him better.

"Dayan, you leave first thing in the morning," Mandukhai said.

Dayan let go of her hand and leaped into his saddle, grinning down at her. "Then we had better not waste tonight."

Before she could protest further, Dayan kicked his mount into action. The mare snorted as she took off. Mandukhai had to scramble into Dust's saddle to avoid being left behind.

In just a few seconds, Mandukhai raced after Dayan, away from the camp and across the flat, red, rocky ground that led to the flaming cliffs. Wind whipped her hair, making her braid lash against her back. It was cold, freezing her cheeks and stinging in her eyes. She tightened her body near Dust's neck to remove some of the wind resistance.

Dayan glanced over his shoulder, a dumb, boyish grin plastered on his face. He whipped his mount to a faster pace as Mandukhai slowly closed the gap.

They passed brush, a few trees, hills, and shrubs in a blur of motion. Their guards would follow, but at the pace Dayan set, it seemed as if he tried to leave them behind. The sudden leap into action back in camp would have left the guards unprepared and scrambling for a mount to follow. Worried about danger, Mandukhai glanced back and saw the dark spots in the distance.

"Dayan, slow down," Mandukhai called to him. "Our guards are too far off." Without protection, anyone ambitious enough to attempt assassination could pick the two of them off easily. Mandukhai didn't even have her bow with her! Just the horn-handle knife she kept in her belt.

"Are you afraid of losing?" he called back.

Mandukhai grumbled. *Losing!* She had never lost a race to him, even when he had a head start.

Dayan whooped, the thrill of the race bleeding out in his excited tone. Mandukhai noted the subtle shift in his legs half a second before his mare shifted course and headed toward a rocky rise that looked over the Lake Dai valley. Mandukhai knew exactly where Dayan was headed, and she cut off his route deftly.

The rocky ledge was narrow, and their horses had to slow their pace to avoid slipping off the edge. Mandukhai adjusted her grip on Dust's reins so the stallion could use his powerful hindquarters to push up the steep slope. Dayan was behind her now, and his mare snorted as he forced her so close to Dust's rear her nose nearly touched Mandukhai's back. Loose rocks tumbled from the ledge, falling to the ground at the base of the cliff. Mandukhai held tight as Dust heaved up a steep incline, over a boulder.

They were high enough now that a fall would certainly seriously injure them, if not kill them. And their mounts would be useless. Mandukhai spared a worried glance at Dayan. If anything happened to him …

But Dayan set his face with determination. He handled his mount expertly.

The red, rocky path opened at the top of a wide cliff covered with brown grass. They had ridden a few miles from camp to reach this point. Dayan tried to edge his mare around Dust as they reached the top, but the mount didn't have the strength to scale the rocks for the maneuver. Instead, she snorted and waited her turn to climb safely.

Mandukhai reined in Dust atop the cliff, gazing out at the spectacular view. From here, she could see across the edge of the Gobi and down into Ordos territory.

They had come far from camp, but she could just make out the smoke from fires in the distance to the east. Atop the mountainous cliff, they would have a stunning view of the sunset.

"It is like we can see the universe from here," Dayan said as he reined in beside her.

Mandukhai spotted the dust clouds their guards kicked up as they raced toward the cliff. They would reach the ledge shortly, then set up a ring around the base of the cliff as Boke and Torgus would ride up.

"It is beautiful," Mandukhai agreed, watching the way the colors shifted as the sun sank toward the earth.

"Yet still not the most beautiful thing I've seen today," Dayan replied.

"Oh?" Mandukhai tore her gaze away from the stunning landscape, but her question died on her lips as she saw the way he stared at her. Mandukhai's stomach flipped end over end. *He has never shown interest in anyone except you.* Altan's words resurfaced. Mandukhai searched his face, unsure of what she sought.

She came to one logical conclusion. It hammered into her like a great weight, slamming down on her shoulders. Mandukhai had been his age when she married Manduul—a marriage of convenience thrust upon her without her opinion or consideration. While that marriage had brought her to where she was now, Mandukhai remembered how much she had wanted a choice in her own fate; how much she resented having it taken from her. She would not do that to Dayan. She could not.

Dayan dismounted and moved toward the edge, staring at the horizon as the sky blazed a brilliant shade of orange. Mandukhai jumped from the saddle and joined him. The beauty of the Eternal Blue Sky never ceased to amaze her. Mandukhai watched in silence as the sun dipped behind a cluster of trees, sending yellow rays across the length of the sky. Bitter wind whipped around them, but the exertion from the ride helped keep her warm.

"I know what you see when you look at me," Dayan said. The sorrow in his voice made her heart ache. "You see the small, frail, broken boy I was when I arrived in your care. And you see my father."

He was right. Mandukhai could not reconcile the man he was becoming with the boy she had cared for and raised. And he looked so much like his father that it was hard not to see Bayan. But even if she saw Bayan in his face, she did not see Bayan in his spirit.

"Dayan, I know our situation is unique, but you still have a choice."

"Please, Mandukhai. Just let me speak. This isn't easy for me."

She studied his profile. The lines of sadness on his face were out of place for his age. His golden gaze remained on the sunset as if in a contest to see which was brighter—the sun or his eyes.

"You're right, as you often are," he continued. "Our situation is unique. There is no precedent for it in any of the histories you have taught me. Men have inherited wives before, but this isn't the same. You chose a boy. You see a boy. And I hope, I pray to Tengri, that when this fight is over, you will see a man." He paused, raking his teeth over his lower lip, then stiffened his back.

Mandukhai reached for Dayan's hand, but he pulled it away, folding his fingers into his belt. Dayan had never withdrawn from her before. Both he and Unebolod had withdrawn from her touch in the same evening. What did that mean? Did it mean anything?

"I remember years ago, before you chose me," he admitted.

Dayan never talked about those early days. Mandukhai had often wondered how much he even remembered of the fight for succession at Mount Burkhan Khaldun. He had only been seven; still young enough to forget all of it.

"You told me a story that broke my heart," he continued. "The story of a young girl who dreamed of being a fierce warrior like Khutulun, of flying with eagles, riding fast horses, and fighting for the Mongol Nation to preserve what Genghis Khan built. The girl was married off to the Great Khan, a man of good intentions but weak ambitions, and she could not give her heart to him, no matter how hard she tried."

Mandukhai's breath caught, and she froze in place there on the edge of the cliff with Dayan. She remembered this story. She had told it to Dayan in her weak moments when she had struggled to accept that she could not have Unebolod. How that grief had torn her apart!

"But the girl became a queen and met a fierce, handsome warrior, and she fell in love." Dayan paused, taking careful, measured breaths that Mandukhai watched mist in the cool fall air. "Their love was powerful, but to save the Nation, she had to release him."

Mandukhai trembled, feeling suddenly bone cold in a way that had nothing to do with the air.

"You have sacrificed so much to restore the fractured Mongol empire," Dayan said, sorrow causing his voice to pitch deeper. "You have done well, Mandukhai. Genghis would be proud." Dayan remained as still as a statue as he stared at the horizon. "I will not be like Manduul, vying for a heart that can never be mine."

Mandukhai's heart seized as dread gripped her in its icy grasp. All the air in her lungs slowly dragged out. Tears blurred her vision. Altan was wrong. All the women were wrong. Dayan did not want her. He had locked his heart away to protect her. To protect himself. Dayan was about to release her. And for the first time, she feared the rejection, yet she couldn't say why.

"Dayan, please don't ..."

"I see the way you look at each other," Dayan said. She could hear the grief tearing through his voice. "I'm not a fool. You love Unebolod still. And he loves you. What am I compared to that? I have done my part to shelter your heart and soul, as I promised you the night you told me that story. But I am a poor replacement."

"No." She reached for his arm, clinging to it.

Dayan turned toward her, stepping closer. "I have done nothing to earn your respect, to be worthy of you. The way you look at me makes that abundantly obvious. But I will."

Mandukhai froze, gripping his arm. Wait, would he *not* release her? Mandukhai's head spun, unable to tell where the conversation was headed. At first, he had made it sound as if he would free her from the oath she gave at the shrine years ago, allow her to choose her own husband. Now, he wouldn't? Did she want him to?

"I ... I don't understand," she whispered.

"It is my turn to tell you a story," Dayan said. "The story of a baby, so unloved by his parents that they abandoned him to death. A boy who learned very young to trust no one, to depend on no one. But he could not care for himself, broken as he was."

Mandukhai's heart broke as she listened, locked in his gaze which blazed with life in the light of the setting sun.

"Just when this boy was certain he would never know love, never have anyone who cared for him, the High Heavens parted, and he found himself in the arms of a fierce and beautiful wolf mother. And for the first time, that boy felt loved, wanted, cared for. He learned to trust. He learned to love."

The wind ripped past them, swirling around the two of them in a furl of deels. Mandukhai should have shuddered from the sudden chill, but Dayan stood so close that she felt the heat of his body. She knew he had trusted no one when he first came to her, and she suspected he had waited for her to abandon him as everyone else had done. Dayan never spoke of this over the years. He had suffered so much for no good reason other than his parents' inability to accept responsibility.

"Mandukhai," Dayan said, cupping her face in his hand, "I have not paid my bride-service, but I intend to remedy that. I give you my word. I ride to war against Bigirsen, and I will either prove myself worthy by killing him, or I will fail and you are free to be with—" Dayan's voice broke, but he quickly recovered. "—with Unebolod. Both of us will return to you, but should something happen to me, I have already commanded my men to protect Unebolod at all costs. They know what I expect of them—to ensure at least one of us returns to you. Whether it is me or him, Mongolia will have a Great Khan worthy of our mighty Great Khatun."

Mandukhai's eyes widened. Was he talking about abdicating his right to Unebolod if he failed? She wanted to tell him this wasn't necessary, that he had nothing to prove to her, that Genghis had chosen him. But the power of speech completely evaded her. She was as mute as he had been when he first came into her care.

Dayan withdrew. Mandukhai's hand fell away numbly as she watched him gather his mount and head for the path back down. He paused at the edge of the path, glancing back at her as Boke started down ahead of him. When had Boke and Torgus arrived?

"I hope, should I crush your oldest enemy, you will finally see a man," Dayan said, then he left her there on the cliff with only Torgus and Dust for company.

Mandukhai remained on the cliff, watching Dayan and his guards ride into the sunset. It would be dark in a matter of minutes, but Mandukhai was in no hurry to return to camp.

Dayan felt as if he had just given up the world, but it was a promise that needed to be made. He could not leave without making his intentions clear. He would kill Bigirsen, or he would give her up. Because if he could not kill the Uyghur warlord, he was not worthy of her or this title she gave to him. Holding the crushing emotions in check, he hastened his return to camp.

The mare hardly skidded to a stop near his ger before Dayan jumped from the saddle and rushed inside. The haste drew a few odd looks from the commanders nearby, but he ignored them all, slamming his door closed behind him.

Dayan nearly fell apart the moment his door closed. Tears rolled down his cheeks, and he gasped for breath. He would be worthy of her. He had to be. Because if he failed in this, he would rather die. Dayan did not fear death. The King of the Underworld had been his shadow all of his life. Death was familiar to Dayan. He did not survive for himself. He survived for her. For the Nation.

He would either be worthy of all of it … or none.

A knock on the door caused Dayan's heart to leap in his chest.

"My lord Khan, are you alright in there?" Togochi called through the door. "I received a report that you returned to camp in a state of panic."

Dayan briskly swiped away his tears, hardened his expression, and shifted away from the door as he opened it.

Togochi's gaze swept over him the moment the door opened.

"I'm fine," Dayan said. "Just excited from the ride. Enjoy your night, Togochi."

Togochi's thick brows pulled together, apparently not buying the excuse, but he nodded. "Until the morning, Dayan Khan. The men look forward to riding with you."

As Togochi retreated, Dayan caught Boke staring at him as well. Neither of them believed he was alright, but no one would question him.

And if all went well, no one would question him again.

CHAPTER NINE

Leavetaking

Unebolod could not sleep most of the night. Last-minute concerns over preparations continually cropped up in his mind just as he would drift off—not to mention the excitement of finally moving toward a war against Bigirsen and the Uyghur threat. He had waited for this day since their last battle nearly twenty years ago, when Bigirsen had given him the scar on his face. The lack of war between he and Bigirsen had never truly been peace. They had held back because of the truce they both struck with Manduul. By the time Manduul died, Bigirsen had turned his attention away from them, and Mandukhai had been satisfied enough to allow the Ming to deal with Bigirsen.

The massacre at the red salt lake had changed Bigirsen's fortunes forever. The southern Mongol Lords who had followed Bigirsen for years had defected when their wives and children had been butchered—only a few Ordos tribes and the Three Guards had remained. That had been eight years ago. Unebolod knew Bigirsen well. The warlord would have retreated toward Uyghur territory to attempt regrouping before his next phase of attacks against the Ming. But without the full support of the southern Mongols, Bigirsen had done little more than raid the Ming borders in small-scale skirmishes. His power had diminished significantly. They should have killed him years ago. *I am more than happy to give him a send-off,* Unebolod thought as he stepped out of his ger. The prospect heated his blood with excitement.

The wolf dawn turned the black sky to lighter hues of blue that would gradually recede as the sun rose. There was so much to do. He checked his mounts first, securing his bow to the saddle hook. Two boxes of arrows were already fastened to the saddle, each holding sixty arrows. All was in order.

Boots crunched the packed dirt, advancing from the east. Unebolod turned to find Getei, the Ongud soothsayer, approaching. Unebolod grimaced, subconsciously fingering the yellow ribbon wrapped around his sword hilt. Over the years, this habit had browned the ribbon along the edges and left the ends frayed.

"You had better be approaching me with good news," Unebolod said gruffly. "I will not listen to ill omens, soothsayer. Not today."

Getei frowned as he halted a few feet away. The soothsayer's face showed his age with deep wrinkles, and his hair was now more silver than black. He wore it in a tight bun that pulled the skin on his face unnaturally.

"You chose this fate," Getei said.

Unebolod snorted. "I chose nothing. The fates play with my life. It has never been my own to determine. We have debated this many times, soothsayer. Your spirits pull at me like a bowman pulls at his string, and they direct me as if I am little more than an arrow for their own means. If you believe I chose any of this, you are not as all-seeing as you think."

The bitterness of these years bled through each word. Unebolod followed the will of the High Heavens because he had no alternative, not because he wanted to do so. He had not found his faith that night on Mount Burkhan Khaldun. He had submitted himself to his fate because he knew he had no power to stop it.

"You could have seized control eight years ago, Unebolod. Instead, you chose to follow her." Getei's smile was sad. "You still do not see it, though. Do you know what they say about hope, *orlok*?"

"That it is a tool for fools," Unebolod said. "Are you saying this is hopeless?"

"No." Getei edged a step closer. "Your Great Khan's fate is in your hands just as surely as my own. Tengri has faith in you. He chose you because there is no stronger man to protect the Khan. You do not hope to win this war. Deep down, you already know what will happen. That is not hope. That is faith."

Unebolod rubbed a thumb into the ache in his temple. "Then what are you talking about? Quit playing these games with me."

"Before this is done, you will face an impossible choice that will force you to confront your deeply seeded hope. And in that moment, you will finally see the truth and discover your faith." Getei patted Unebolod on the shoulder. "And you will make the right choice."

Unebolod shrugged off Getei's hand, leaning closer as he sneered. "You see, *that* is what I mean. It is not a choice if you already know the outcome. It is fate." He pushed past the soothsayer, eager to escape the conversation and not even caring where he ended up. "I've had enough. If I never hear one of your cryptic omens, it will be a welcome relief."

Unebolod stomped away, fuming. Getei always knew exactly what to say to get under his skin. Yet there was no good reason for it. Often, Unebolod did not understand the meaning of these conversations for some time—if at all. Perhaps that was the problem. Unebolod hated not knowing what it all meant, what it was all for. He loathed being told that something was inevitable. To him, the only thing that was inevitable was death. It claimed all who lived under the Eternal Blue Sky. Unebolod glanced at the sky as it slowly shifted toward lighter hues of blue. *Curse the Eternal Blue Sky, always lording over us, waiting for death to claim us. I follow your will because I have no other choice.*

The camp stirred with life as warriors woke and prepared to ride south. Soke approached Unebolod as they walked toward the edge of camp.

"The men will be ready within the hour," Soke reported. "We will then wait only for the Khan's command."

Unebolod nodded. "I will check his ger."

"The ger is already packed," Soke said. He squinted toward the eastern horizon. "I hear he didn't sleep last night."

"Did you?" Unebolod asked.

Soke grinned, understanding the implication.

The general had waited just as long for this day as Unebolod, but he would not be riding out with Unebolod. Mandukhai owed too many of the Mongol Lords and lesser khans a place of command on this mission for him to bring along Soke. At first, the news had disheartened Soke, but Unebolod had insisted he would be needed to help Mandukhai in the weeks to come.

"Hardly," Soke said. "I will go check with the officers."

"Remember, Soke," Unebolod said gravely. "Watch over her."

"I give you my word, Unebolod." Soke turned away, then paused. "You should say goodbye to her. Who knows what the future holds?"

With that said, Soke strode away. Unebolod's stomach churned at the thought of saying goodbye to Mandukhai. He had done it far too many times before. Instead, he approached the eastern horizon, where Soke's attention had been drawn.

The Khan's guards stood in a line near the edge of camp, facing a hill. Unebolod frowned as he approached, then spotted the shadowy figure standing on the hilltop. He paused beside Boke.

"What is he doing?" Unebolod asked, watching Dayan's figure outlined by the slowly growing dawn.

"It is not my place to question the Khan," Boke said. "But he has not moved for some time."

Curious, Unebolod passed the line of guards and climbed the hill. He could feel the eyes of the guards on his back. After all these years, they remained suspicious of his intentions around Dayan. Unebolod supposed that was fair. Everyone knew he had a connection to Mandukhai, and that he had wanted to be Great Khan. *That was a lifetime ago. I will never be Great Khan.*

Dayan didn't move as Unebolod drew up beside him. The boy's gaze remained fixed on the distance. Unebolod followed it, trying to understand what had Dayan so transfixed. But all he could see was the expanse of gentle hills and red, rocky earth. They remained silent for some time, watching the sun slowly rise over the lake's shallow basin.

Sometimes, Dayan acted as any other boy his age would act—cocky, confident, and often moody. However, Unebolod had noticed something different about Dayan a year ago, after the monk had died. The young Khan could fall into these almost trance-like meditative states where he would not speak for an hour or more, as if he observed the universe as it unfolded around him. Unebolod envied it a little. He felt it gave the Khan a supernatural authority. In those moments—moments such as this one—Unebolod understood why Genghis had chosen Dayan over him. Not that it hurt any less.

The sun broke over the horizon, throwing brilliant rays of light across the sky that sent the wolf dawn running. Unebolod flinched at the sudden brightness of the sun in his eyes and instead watched Dayan. The Khan didn't even blink, didn't flinch as he watched the dawn. His eyes darted back and forth as if searching for something.

Then Dayan smiled.

Unebolod frowned, turning his attention toward the horizon again. "What is it?"

Dayan closed his eyes, basking in the sunlight as it bathed and warmed their faces. "Destiny."

Unebolod raised an eyebrow and shielded his eyes as he gazed at the horizon again. How did one see destiny so definitively?

Time is wasting, Unebolod thought. "It's almost time to leave. You should say goodbye to Mandukhai before we go."

Dayan peeled his eyes open and gazed at Unebolod. The light of the sun made his golden eyes shine like jewels. "I said goodbye last night. It's your turn."

Unebolod shifted, averting his gaze to the ground as if ashamed. What was he ashamed of? "I don't think that's necessary."

"It is. She needs to hear it. So do you."

Unebolod swallowed a lump that swelled in this throat. She would be angry with him for taking Dayan's side, for encouraging the young Khan to leave on this campaign. But Dayan was not a boy anymore. And this was not a small skirmish. The Great Khan needed to lead his men in this war. Dayan was as ready as he would ever be.

Unebolod left Dayan standing on the hilltop and headed back into camp. Did Dayan know of his true feelings for Mandukhai? Surely he had heard that, at one time, there had been something between the two of them. The events surrounding Dayan's rise to power would have brought that forward. Dayan also had to know that, at one time, Unebolod had hoped to be Great Khan. *Hope is a tool for fools*, he reminded himself. He no longer harbored such hope. That title was never meant for him.

The camp had burst into a flurry of activity while he had stood with Dayan. Now everyone was up and moving. Warriors said farewell to their families and finished last-minute preparations for the long journey west. The warriors would only take what they could carry on this mission.

Unebolod gathered his mount, then found Mandukhai speaking with Taghan and Togochi. As he approached, Jaghan and Togochi excused themselves to give them privacy. Not that they could have privacy with so many men and women milling through the area.

Mandukhai met his gaze, the worry creasing the corners of her eyes. That timeless desire to pull her into his arms stiffened his spine as he resisted the urge.

"I worry over his mental state, Unebolod," Mandukhai said softly, glancing at the people going about their tasks around them. The two of them stood close, as if in the eye of a great storm. "I am placing his life in your hands. Bring him back to me."

All of his limbs had seized up at those words, turning him to stone. Even the act of nodding felt jerky, unnatural. "I will protect the Khan with my life."

Mandukhai's lips drew into a tight line.

"I give you my word," he said.

Mandukhai understood that his word was iron. His honor was the only thing he had left. Unebolod would do everything he could to keep Dayan alive, even if the Khan's death would open the door for him once more—a fate the High Heavens would always taunt him with and always deny him. No. He would protect Dayan, because that would be the only way forward.

"I will miss you, my fierce warrior," she said.

"There will be nothing to miss." Unebolod shuffled half a step closer, drawn to her. Even now, after eight years of separation, he could not distance himself from her completely.

"There will be everything to miss." Mandukhai reached up and brushed her finger along the scar on his face.

Unebolod flinched away, glancing around them. What was she doing touching him like that in front of everyone? The Khan would hear of it, and this would be a very, very long journey.

"Come back in your saddle, Unebolod," she said. Tears shimmered in her eyes, but they did not spill. Somehow, she controlled them by sheer force of will.

The words struck his heart. The alternative to coming back in the saddle was death. Her message was apparent. Even if they could not be together, she still loved him.

"As my Khatun commands," Unebolod said, forcing a playful smile. Though he spoke in jest, the words were sincere. He would do anything she asked of him. It had become his entire purpose for living. "I give you my most solemn oath that I will do as you request, so long as it does not interfere with my promise to protect him."

Mandukhai's smile was sad. "I would expect no less from you. May Lord Tengri watch over you."

Unebolod pulled back. It was time to go. He swung into the saddle but could not resist pausing to see her face one more time. Yes, he would do anything she asked of him. And if she expected him to return, he would. Because he knew where his faith lay. "I don't need Tengri. I have something more powerful."

Mandukhai stepped back to give his mount room to move. "What could be more powerful than the gods?"

The mare bobbed her head, eager to move. Unebolod pressed his knees in to keep the mount steady. For several glorious, painfully long seconds, he simply stared at Mandukhai. "Trust and truth," he said at last, remembering their first conversation a lifetime ago alongside the river near Mongke Bulag. He had warned her that trust and truth were the two most dangerous weapons to give another person.

Mandukhai smoothed her hands over her stomach. He knew that movement. Her stomach was just as much of a mess as his own, and she tried to calm it.

"And what truth is more powerful than the gods?" she asked.

Unebolod offered a sad smile. "Should I speak it here when you already know the answer?"

Mandukhai's gaze flitted around at the flurry of activity and people as if realizing for the first time that they were not alone. At last, she shook her head.

"We will see you in the Ordos basin, then, my lady Khatun," Unebolod said, steeling himself.

He turned his mare west, away from camp.

Away from her.

Mandukhai stood atop the deck of the gathering tent cart, watching the mass of horsemen ride away. Thousands of men, with those she held dearest leading the way. It would be the longest months of her life living without them. Dayan had not spent a day away from her side since he had first come to her as a broken boy. Even his hunting trips had been brief outings between sunrise and sunset.

The remains of the camp appeared barren. Patches of trampled grass and mud dotted the landscape as far as she could see. As with all things, these patches of earth would heal in time and leave no trace of the great gathering that had happened here. The agony in her own heart clouded her perception of just how vacant the camp became. Thousands had left.

But only two of them truly mattered to her.

Jaghan and Altan stood at Mandukhai's shoulders. Altan kept her arms crossed as she watched, leaning against the railing of the cart. Jaghan kept glancing at Togochi nearby, as if she expected him to run after Unebolod and Dayan. Twenty-thousand warriors flowed west like a great river, taking everything Mandukhai loved with them.

"Shall we drink now?" Altan asked, holding out a skin of *airag*. Her tone was completely deadpan.

"It's a bit early, don't you think?" Jaghan asked. But after a thought, she reached for the drink and took a generous gulp.

Mandukhai refrained. She feared that, if she started drinking now, she would not stop; that she might try to drown her dread in *airag*.

It would take at least a month for the men to finish this mission—if all went well and they moved with haste. They rode west, hoping to encounter only a few small clusters of Ordos families as they skirted the Gobi. Then they would sweep up toward Juyan Basin to finish Bigirsen for good.

Despite the people surrounding her, Mandukhai had never felt so alone.

CHAPTER TEN

Strategic Alterations

SOUTHERN GOBI EDGE – CHAKHAR TERRITORY – EARLY WINTER 1479

Dayan had not been so far south since Mandukhai had rescued him as a boy. For the first time, he saw the empire he ruled over, the people who trusted him to lead them. He rode past small Chakhar encampments of families where children stared at him with wide eyes. Men and women bowed to his banners as he passed, recognizing him as their Great Khan, though they had never laid eyes on him before. Or perhaps it was the *mingghan* of a thousand Chakhar warriors riding with him they recognized.

Dayan observed as much as he could along the ride. This was where his parents had met, where he had been born. Yet Dayan remembered nothing about it. Red sand kicked up in their wake, coating his face and mouth. He had to resist the urge to spit.

This place had once been home, but Dayan had left it behind years ago, before he could even remember. Home, for him, was in the north—or wherever Mandukhai lived. She was the only person to truly care for him in far deeper ways than either of his parents ever had. Dayan harbored no bitterness toward them. How could he? Dayan knew neither of them. It was hard to be bitter toward someone whom he did not know. He could not even make himself angry with them for abandoning him. That abandonment had brought him to Mandukhai.

Dayan shifted in his saddle. Unebolod set a pace that implied arriving at their destination too late would mean their lives. Dayan had no actual knowledge of what they headed into to say Unebolod was wrong, but he certainly chaffed in the saddle from such a brisk pace.

By the first nightfall, they had already crossed Chakhar territory and edged toward northern Ordos. Unebolod called the lines to a halt and dismounted. Scouts scoured the area for signs of danger, riding out miles in all directions. Dayan watched them go from atop his horse—a fine yellow-haired mare Mandukhai had selected for him from his herd. A dozen more horses trailed behind him, guided by Unebolod's men.

No, those are my men, he reminded himself. Dayan was Great Khan. These warriors were his to command. But inexperience made Dayan hesitant, so he allowed Unebolod to lead.

"Rest, Dayan," Unebolod said as he started a fire. "We ride out in the wolf dawn, deep into Ordos territory."

Dayan dismounted and settled on the ground near the fire as it roared to life. "Will we meet resistance?"

"There will always be resistance." Unebolod retrieved food and *airag* from his mount before settling at the campfire as well. He offered the drink to Dayan.

The Khan waved it off. He had never developed a taste for *airag* as all the other men had. He knew he should build a resistance to the intoxicant, as it was a staple in a traveling warrior's diet. Water could be scarce, but they could make *airag* as they rode. This, Mandukhai had once explained to him, was the reason warriors brought along more mares than stallions to battle. They offered more sustenance so the men could churn mare's milk into *airag*.

Neither of the men spoke as they waited for the commanders and scouts to join them at the campfire. Several other fires sprouted up across the rocky ground as the men attempted warding off the cold winter air for sleep. Dayan fell asleep there on the unforgiving ground, lulled into sleep by the mesmerizing dance of flames.

Issama stoked the fire in his stove, glancing at Siker as she barked commands at their two sons. The boys spent most of their time wrestling each other, picking fights with one another over pointless arguments. On the other side of the ger, Qolotai churned the bag of fermenting *airag*, ignoring the rest of them. She had only given him a daughter, who had died at the red salt lake eight years ago, along with his first wife, Uingen. Some days, Issama wished he still had that daughter to use as a bargaining chip with other Lords.

For three years after the massacre, Issama had followed Bigirsen's commands. More than once, he nearly lost his head when Bigirsen uncovered another plot against him. None of the evidence against Issama ever had been substantial enough to condemn him to death. After three years, Issama knew his luck had run out, so he hid from Bigirsen, attempting plots against him from a distance.

One of those plots had cost him several men, including his second-in-command, Nahai. That had been the most devastating loss of all. Bigirsen had captured Nahai on a scouting mission with a handful of Issama's remaining men. Bigirsen had tortured all of them to death, attempting to pry information about Issama's whereabouts and plans. A few of the men had broken under torture, forcing Issama to run four years ago. But Nahai—the only one who knew what Issama had planned—had remained loyal to his dying breath. He must have, or Issama would have been dragged into Bigirsen's camp and killed long ago.

I did not give Nahai nearly enough trust, he thought as Babutai, his younger son, punched his older brother in the nose. Burani dissolved into tears, clutching his nose.

Siker stomped over to the boys, thumping both of them on the ear. "I warned you not to push your brother."

Burani sniffled, stabbing an accusing finger at Babutai as he cried. "He said my nose was too big!" Now eight, Burani had lost his baby features, developing something that more resembled his father.

Without meaning to, Issama reached up and felt his own nose. Was it big?

Six-year-old Babutai stuck out his tongue at his older brother.

"Do that again and I will stab it with a hot poker to teach you a lesson, Babutai," Siker snapped.

Burani continued crying, and the sound grated on Issama's nerves. "You're acting like a girl," Issama said coldly.

"Maybe he is a girl," Babutai teased.

Siker smacked the boy in the back of the head. He winced, rubbing at his head and pouting.

"It hurts," Burani whimpered.

"So does life, but you don't see the rest of us crying," Issama replied sharply. "You will never grow strong if you let every little thing bring you to tears. And others will mock you for it. Sharpen your wit and dull your sensitivity or you will never survive this world."

Siker pulled Burani's hand away from his nose and sighed. It wasn't bleeding, at least. Issama knew from experience that she hated cleaning up blood.

"How much longer must we stay here, Issama?" she asked, nudging the boys to opposite sides of the ger.

Qolotai glanced at Burani and offered a sympathetic smile. Issama wanted to tell her to stop coddling the boys. It was the reason they were soft. But he let it go. For now.

"Just a few more days," he reassured her.

Once the Khan's *tumens* had moved south, Issama had deserted his efforts in the Ordos basin, worried that Mandukhai would kill him if she found him. Unebolod certainly would. Since then, he had tracked Bigirsen's movements. Juyan Basin was only a few hours' ride from Kharakhoto, and the natural walls of the abandoned city provided them shelter from passersby.

In a few more days, Issama would venture to Juyan Basin to scout Bigirsen's camp. Mogurkei had told him that Bigirsen had Nemeku back in his clutches. Issama would have to get the boy away before Mandukhai sent men to finish Bigirsen. That would be soon, if Issama trusted that his information had leaked to the man searching for Bigirsen.

Issama needed that boy as leverage against Mandukhai. He would have to sneak into the camp and rescue Nemeku.

In just a few days, Bigirsen would send some of his men back to Turfan or Asku for reinforcements.

It would be the perfect time to strike.

Winter had begun descending over the world like a cold blanket. Unebolod disliked winter. Besides the cold, the ice and snow made it easier to track the movements of his men.

Unebolod's mare bobbed her head as he squinted at the western horizon. A scout warned him of an Ordos camp along their route. Going around would take them almost a day out of the way. Going through could mean warning Bigirsen of their presence. With enough warning, Bigirsen could run before they caught up to him. Unebolod did not want to give him the chance.

His *tumens* waited a mile back as he studied the distant camp. Only a hundred people. Easy to defeat with so many men. He wanted to crash through the camp, show the Ordos tribes just where their allegiance had led them.

Unebolod turned his mare away and rode back to where everyone waited.

As he returned, he spotted Dayan sitting on a massive boulder with his eyes closed and face tilted toward the afternoon sunlight. *Is he meditating? Now?* This practice was one of the few things Mandukhai had taught Dayan that Unebolod hated. Meditation was a waste of time. Especially under the circumstances. They needed to move.

Belku, the Chakhar Lord and heir, was one among several of the Lords who Mandukhai had promised a hand in this attack on Bigirsen. The Uyghur warlord had made several enemies over the years. Unebolod had little patience for the Chakhar. They were foolhardy people, easily swayed by stronger men. But Dayan's mother was Chakhar, so the young Khan insisted on riding with Belku and his "tribe." This decision had obviously been more political than emotional. Yet this was the same tribe that had allegedly left Bayan on the battlefield against superior Ming forces ten years ago ... after promising their loyalty.

Unebolod wished he could avoid Belku, but the Lord sat in a circle with several other commanders.

Unebolod glanced at Dayan. He had promised Mandukhai to bring Dayan back alive, and he intended to do that—even if he had to declare war on the Chakhar should they turn against him.

"Well, *orlok*?" Belku asked. "What is your decision?"

"There are not so many," Unebolod said. He dismounted and strode toward them, guiding his mare along behind him. "If we act quickly and surround them, we can sweep them off the map before they send a warning to Bigirsen."

"We don't need to kill them," Dayan said, drawing all eyes toward where he perched on his boulder. "We can go around."

The men fell silent, watching Unebolod to see how he would react. He clenched his jaw and stalked closer to Dayan, lowering his voice. "We cannot leave an enemy at our backs."

"It would not be the first time," Dayan said. "Nor would it be the last. But I will not have my people butchered simply for being in our way."

"They are not your people," Unebolod said. "They have sworn no allegiance to you."

Dayan's golden eyes pierced straight through Unebolod. "All people under the Eternal Blue Sky are my people."

Those were Mandukhai's words spilling from his mouth. Unebolod wished she would have allowed him to teach Dayan more than just battle tactics and fighting. She was a brilliant woman, but some of her ideals were impractical when such division remained in the empire.

"Mandukhai chose me for this mission because I am the most experienced *orlok* she has, and my knowledge of Bigirsen goes far deeper than most men," Unebolod said, hoping to get Dayan to see reason. "Two *tumens* of our men cannot easily pass without leaving a trace behind, even if we swing wide. Their scouts will find our tracks and send word to Bigirsen. He will then do one of two things." Unebolod held up a finger. "If he does not have enough men to face us, he will turn and hide, and we will lose him again." He held up another finger. "If he *does* have enough men, he will set a trap and crush us. Is one small camp more valuable to you than finishing him?"

No one seemed to breathe as they waited for the Khan's answer. Every muscle in Unebolod's body tensed as he watched Dayan adopt that far-off gaze, considering the options. Then Dayan's shoulders sloped downward. He released a shaky sigh.

"Make your plans, *orlok*," Dayan said at last.

Unebolod grinned and clapped Dayan on the shoulder. "Good man."

The commanders gathered closer to Unebolod and Dayan as Unebolod shared his plan of attack. Dayan said nothing more, neither agreeing nor disagreeing, which suited Unebolod just fine.

LAKE DAI – EARLY WINTER 1479

Mandukhai brushed her fingertips over her armor. It stood on a wooden stand close to her door. They had replaced dented iron plates in the lamellar over the years with new ones. The leather was worn with scratches and gouges earned in battle. She remembered the first day she had put this armor on. The first war she had ridden into, taming the unruly Oirat and killing their leaders.

Dayan had ridden into that battle with her, as he had with every battle since. But when the Khan rode, a wall of dedicated guards surrounded him on all sides. His presence had always been for show, and he had rarely gotten any real fighting in himself. She had worked so hard to protect him for years. Now he rode off to fight without her.

Two days ago, she had received a message that Dayan and Unebolod had entered Ordos territory. Until a secure route could be established, she would hear nothing more from them. He could die, and she would not hear of it. This reminded her of when Manduul and Bayan would ride off to battle, disappearing for weeks at a time with no word. But neither of those men had endeared themselves to her heart.

Unebolod and Dayan owned her heart completely.

As a girl, Mandukhai had dreamed of being like Lady Khutulun, a fierce woman warrior just as capable at warfare as at politics. When Mandukhai had married Manduul, that dream had died. Now she had become something far more powerful. She had ridden into battle, like Khutulun, had led the Nation, just as Khutulun had helped guide her tribe. Would Mandukhai's people tell stories of her long after she passed, too?

No. If Mandukhai did not finish what she had started, she knew that history would forget her or write off the strength of women as leaders. She would be little more than a reminder of why women were too weak to rule. A stain on Mongol history. A woman who had tried and failed to lead. *I have to finish this*, she thought. She was leaving a legacy for all the women who would come after her. Mandukhai had a duty to ensure that the Mongols remembered how capable their women were.

A knock on the ger's door pulled Mandukhai from her deep thoughts. She opened it to find Torgus waiting.

"A scout from Datong has returned," he said. "And his report is not encouraging."

Mandukhai grabbed her *boqta* and strapped it on, then ducked out of the ger and strode toward the gathering tent with Torgus and her guards at her heels.

As the sun set over their camp, the bite of the winter wind ripped through Mandukhai's fur-lined deel along the short walk to the steps. She hated the necessity of these late-night meetings when she would much rather remain in the comfort of her ger.

Togochi hunched over the map table, along with Huoshai and two scouts. Their voices were clearly distressed, but she could not make out anything until she drew closer. Togochi shifted to the side to give her space around the table.

Mandukhai gazed down at the flattened parchment with inked-in markers. It was a scout map, created when the landscape had changed or became unfamiliar. They had used them as soon as they had entered this southern territory so that Mandukhai could be certain her information was current. She frowned at the long double lines on the scout's map. It stretched from the river, all around Datong, and continued east.

"What is this?" she asked, tracing her finger along the line.

"A wall," the scout said.

Mandukhai's gaze snapped up to him, hoping to see some sort of jest in his expression, but the seriousness etched on his face made her stomach twist. Togochi met her gaze as well and nodded solemnly.

"But this is Datong, is it not?" she asked, pointing at the sketched rectangles and roadways all packed together. "And our passage into Ordos."

"Yes, my lady Khatun," the scout said. "That is the city. And that," he stabbed a finger at the thick double lines, "is a wall."

Mandukhai's heart sank. Her body grew leaden. She attempted pushing past her shock. The men around the table just stared at her, waiting.

"I thought the wall was *behind* the city," she said at last. She knew there would be a wall along the Ming borders, but all of their records had indicated that wall was at least a mile or more behind Datong. These lines were in front of it.

"It is." The scout licked his lips anxiously and shifted from one foot to the other.

"The wall surrounds all the city now," Togochi explained, relieving the scout of some of his pressure. "The Ming are expanding it. Quickly."

Mandukhai straightened and glared at Huoshai. "How has no one noticed this? How have *you* not noticed this? A wall cannot just appear."

"And they have expanded it by miles," the scout said. "We still have men out there tracking the full length of it."

"Huoshai!" Mandukhai snapped. The Urainkhai territory stretched all along this expanse of double lines.

He shook his head. "We have kept our distance from the Ming. Our normal raiding locations are still accessible. The wall hasn't gone far enough to cut us off yet, so we didn't notice."

Anger rushed through Mandukhai, heating her from head to toe. She could feel the blood rushing to her face. "Didn't notice." She sneered. "You didn't notice a massive wall expanding along your borders?"

All of their plans had depended on crossing at Datong! No one in the area had seemed to take note of the Ming extending their wall? Her men were supposed to be the best scouts!

"Perhaps," she said, lowering her voice in anger, "you will also not notice when I have you whipped for your neglect. Or perhaps you will be oblivious as well if I have you trapped in a hole in the ground for a week!"

Huoshai blanched, dipping his head in shame.

"Mandukhai," Togochi said in soothing tones. "Punishing him will not solve anything. The wall is still there. He has been with us for some time. When would he have noticed it?"

Mandukhai glared at Togochi, her blood heating in anger. "We needed that river access. It's the narrowest, most shallow access point to the basin. Now the wall is in our way! How will we now get *forty thousand* men across the river?"

Unable to contain her anger, Mandukhai hammered a fist against the tabletop, making the little Buddha Lords and Knights dance across the maps. "This is no small thing! If that wall cuts us off from Ordos and resources, we are doomed before we even begin!" She drew in a ragged breath. She stabbed a finger at Huoshai as she glared at Togochi. "*His* neglect could have just cost us everything!"

How far did the wall go now? Would the Ming cut off the Mongols completely? *They need our horses!* Was their trade worth nothing anymore? She could not trust anyone to do anything right these days. What would Unebolod do? *He would go look at this wall for himself. If I want something done right, I have to do it myself.*

Mandukhai snatched the scout's map off the table and stormed toward the door. "I need to see this wall for myself."

"The wall is several days ride from here," Togochi said, rushing after her. "We have men out scouting. Let them do their job."

Mandukhai snorted, clenching a hand in a tight fist. "A lot of good they have been so far, not noticing a *massive wall* appearing!"

"At least wait until morning," Togochi pleaded. He picked up his step and stood in front of the door, blocking her way. "You cannot go now. It's nearly dark."

Mandukhai flipped a knife out of her sleeve and whipped it at the wooden floor, narrowly missing his foot. "Tell me one more time what I can and cannot do, Togochi."

He inhaled and raised his chin, but averted his gaze.

Mandukhai met each commander's gazes, and each of the men averted their eyes just as Togochi had done. No one would dare stop her.

She would see this wall for herself even if it took a month or more. She had nothing else to do here but wait for Dayan and Unebolod at the moment, anyway.

CHAPTER ELEVEN

Facing A Wall

Boke and his men surrounded Dayan in a ring, just as they always did when riding into battle. Their formation had become terribly efficient over the years. Today, as his *mingghans* moved into position with Unebolod, Dayan faced a wall of guards. While they could block arrows from reaching him, Dayan could not see more than a few feet in any direction. He charged into battle blindly, trusting his guards to guide the way safely. Just once, he wished they would actually give him a chance to fight.

Ogedei—one of the lesser khans only ten years older than Dayan—and Tulugen had each taken their two thousand men wide around the camp to form a ring, with a rear flank cutting off escape to the west and Unebolod charging straight ahead. Together, the seven *mingghans* of warriors would attack this camp as they would on a hunt. Their ring would squeeze more and more tightly into the borders.

Dayan stood in his stirrups to see over the heads of his guards and try to assess the terrain. It was hard to see anything clearly with heads, shields, and horses bobbing in his way. The ground didn't roll in gentle hills or slope in any direction as far as he could tell from the way his mare handled beneath him. No great red cliffs rose in the distance. Everything was red rocks, silt, and sky. The people in the camp must have either dug out a well for fresh water, or some small stream had to wind its way through the area somewhere. Dayan would have loved to splash in water. He missed the luxury of camp beside Lake Dai.

No survivors, Unebolod had instructed the men before they mounted. Dayan had wanted to refuse that order, but he understood the logic. A single survivor could warn Bigirsen. Dayan had given Mandukhai his word. He would either kill Bigirsen or lose everything. While he could handle facing Unebolod as Great Khan, he did not think he could handle Unebolod as Mandukhai's husband. He had to succeed.

And that meant killing every last person in this camp.

One small mercy was that, facing this wall of warriors as he did, Dayan would not have to witness much of the massacre. He wanted to fight, to prove himself, but he did not want to watch his men butcher women and children. What would Mandukhai think of this? She had such a big, warm heart, but when necessity called for it, Dayan had watched her give orders with cold, detached calculation. For Dayan, there was no greater necessity right now than killing Bigirsen.

An arrow with a red flag arced across the sky, and as it did, Dayan heard the great creak of thousands of bows and the thump of release. He held his breath and closed his eyes. It was not as if he could see anything. His mare followed the horses around her more than she followed his direction.

Horses squealed in the distance. Men shouted commands to mount and defend the camp. Some commands cut off as another volley of arrows flew into the camp.

Dayan opened his eyes, noting the ger roofs dotting the distance above the heads of his men. They were close now, and a cloud of red dust encircled the camp, rising into the sky. A whistling arrow cried out across the sky, and, as if of one mind, the *mingghans* reined in and slowed to a trot. Fast targets were harder to hit, but they would create dust clouds high in the sky that would warn anyone near enough to see.

Dayan slowed his mare behind his wall of guards. Despite the cold air, sweat beaded on his forehead and made the silk beneath his armor cling to his skin. He could hear his own ragged breaths accentuated in his ears like thunder. Dayan unhooked his bow and joined the next volley, praying to Tengri that his arrow would not hit one of his men with the blind shot.

Screams shattered the air. Men called for mercy. Women begged for their lives. Children cried. The noise assaulted Dayan's senses as he released his arrow. The string thrummed. The arrow arched up and out of his wall of guards. Dayan tracked it as far as he could, but it was impossible to track between his guards and the other arrows flying through the air. Horses trampled over bodies as the ring around the camp closed tighter.

Nearby, a woman stumbled and pitched forward as an arrow took her in the back of the neck. The ring or warriors closed tighter around camp.

An arrow zipped past Boke's helmet straight for Dayan. He barely had time to duck behind his shield to avoid the attack. It skipped off his helmet to no effect.

Dayan fought to steady his breathing, yanking his mare to a sudden stop. Without meaning to, he had reined in over the woman's body. Her cheek was pressed to the red sandy ground. His gaze remained locked on the woman, on her accusing eyes, glaring at him with hatred in death. She was young. Perhaps Esige's age. Then he recognized the arrow sticking out of the back of her neck.

His arrow.

Dayan sank back in his saddle. The world spun. Around him, the sounds of battle continued as if it were far away.

Fighting men in battle was one thing. Killing women and children was something else completely. The great fist seized Dayan's heart and lungs, squeezing as he gasped for breath. Dayan struggled to find focus, used his breathing tricks to regain control. Had time slowed down? His mind became a fuzzy, muddled mess.

A strap wound across the woman's back as she lay on her stomach. And then he heard the wails of an infant beneath her. The sound brought the chaos of the raid to sharp detail. Dead bodies trampled under hooves. Dayan's guards had not stopped when he did, and the back end of the wall of guards seemed to gain speed as they charged forward.

"Stop!" he called out.

But the command came too late for his guards to obey. Their horses stormed over the dead woman. The cries of the infant cut off abruptly. Dayan's vision narrowed. Vomit climbed up his throat. Breath evaded him. The guards regrouped and formed their ring around him again, a churning mass of bloodied black armor amidst the red earth.

What have I done? he thought as he struggled to remain in the saddle, fought for consciousness. But the great fist had him and refused to let go.

30 MILES WEST OF DATONG – CHAKHAR-URAINKHAI-MING BORDER – EARLY WINTER 1479

After riding south for five days alongside Mandukhai, Togochi witnessed the tan wall rising in the distance, a stark and oppressive backdrop amidst red, gold, and green foliage. So much of the old wall had been broken down in war over the years. But none of those walls had ever kept the Mongols out of Chin territory under the reign of Genghis or Kublai. Something about this wall felt different to Togochi as he crested another hill alongside Mandukhai. She reined Dust to a halt. Togochi stopped beside her, staring south. His jaw slackened and his thick eyebrows lifted. A glance at Mandukhai revealed her own shock, tempered by fury burning in her eyes.

The hills rolled in great waves in the distance, and the tan stone wall rode their backs east to west like the fins on a great serpent. Massive garrison watchtowers had been constructed at regular intervals, as far as he could see in either direction. The hills were tall, mountainous beasts, but nothing the Mongols could not overcome. Getting trebuchets up those hills and taking out those towers with any accuracy would prove extremely difficult.

"How long would it take for our trebuchets to break through that?" she asked softly, as if reading his mind.

The wall was so thick! How had the Ming set to building this so quickly? And why? Did they fear her power? Did they worry she would invade with Dayan and reclaim their lands? The very idea worried Togochi. If the Ming saw her army as such a threat that they felt it necessary to expand this wall, that certainly was a feat to be proud of. But Togochi worried this meant the Ming would soon prepare to invade Mongol territory. Once they finished with the Ordos, Mandukhai and Dayan would have to deal with the Ming before they destroyed her empire.

Togochi could only shake his head. "I'm afraid I have no suitable answer, Mandukhai. With incessant, concentrated volleys, we could probably break through in a few days. Maybe a week or more, depending on how deep it is. If we can get our hands on gunpowder, that would certainly help shorten the job."

Gunpowder. It had become a topic of extreme debate over the years. Unebolod had a strong distaste for gunpowder, which Togochi understood after what had happened to Unebolod's entire family. Yet Togochi grew more certain that they would need it if they ever wanted to defeat the Ming. They would need every tool they could get.

"We don't know their defenses, either," Mandukhai pointed out. "If they have cannons in those towers, we won't be able to get close enough with the trebuchets to do anything."

Togochi nodded, impressed by her deduction. His gaze swept the length of the wall in both directions. "We have to assume they have cannons. We could send a hundred men at the wall and see what happens, test their defenses."

Mandukhai grimaced. "No. I won't use men for fodder unnecessarily. We will have to find another way to cross the river."

The wall changed everything. Togochi and Unebolod had counted on the pass that angled through Datong, across the river, and into Ordos. It would allow them to sneak up behind the Ordos Lords.

She turned Dust away from the wall to head back to where their escort of warriors waited. "We need to send men to scout the progress on this wall, though. I can't have it screwing up any more of our plans."

"Agreed," Togochi said as he joined her. He glanced back over his shoulder, examining the beast-like wall again. At last, he shook his head. "Without Datong, we will need to take Bautuo."

He hated the words, but knew the necessity. Their original plan had been to use Datong as their crossing and avoid Bautuo altogether. The city was controlled by both Ming and Ordos Lords and had thousands of warriors hiding inside the walls. But there was a bridge near Bautuo that those Lords controlled. And it would be the only way to get their supplies safely across. Leaving an enemy at their back as they attempted crossing so close to the city could cost them far too much. The Ordos Lord in Bautuo could also send a warning to the other Ordos Lords. Or he could attack.

"Which Ordos Lord occupies the city?" Mandukhai asked, drawing Togochi from his thoughts.

"Lord Qori, I believe," Togochi replied. He shook his head in dismay. "He has a full *tumen* at his disposal. Between his men and the Ming in the city, we could face defeat."

Mandukhai fell silent. He knew better than to interrupt when her brows knitted together like that. She was calculating something, and if he interrupted her thoughts, she would give him a good tongue-lashing.

"Then we need to find a means for a peaceful resolution," Mandukhai said at last. "We need to find out what he wants, and if we can give it to him." She glanced at him, smirking slightly. "Everyone wants something for themselves."

Togochi didn't understand why that made her smile, but he knew the truth of her words well enough.

The two of them rode back down the hill, through the dense forest of trees, toward where their men waited. It would be a long ride back to Lake Dai.

SOUTH GOBI – ORDOS TERRITORY – EARLY WINTER 1479

Dayan hardly kept himself in the saddle long enough to ride away from the small camp. He stopped near enough that Unebolod would easily find him, but far enough that he felt he could breathe. Boke and the guards followed him, of course.

One hundred warriors. At least twice as many women and children. No one had survived the attack. Unebolod may have organized the strategy, but Dayan had been the one who agreed to it. He had challenged Unebolod and backed down. All of those people were dead because of him. That baby was dead because of him. *A Khan can never show weakness, or his enemies will close in and his warriors will doubt his ability to lead*. Mandukhai had taught him that years ago.

Dayan dismounted and let his mare forage as he focused on his breathing. Boke was used to Dayan's regular meditations, but something about the way Dayan sat on a red boulder must have garnered some sort of concern because the head of his guard frowned, watching him with deep lines creasing his mouth. Despite his obvious worry, Boke said nothing. He never questioned Dayan.

Unebolod continued his work back at the camp for now. According to him, the dead had to be dragged into the gers so they would not arouse suspicion if someone else came across the camp at a distance. They could not burn the camp, or the smoke would send warnings to anyone nearby. Unebolod had expressed hope that, by hiding the bodies in the gers instead of leaving them out to rot, they would have time to get closer to Bigirsen before anyone could send word to warn him. Dayan understood this plan, but he hated the idea of not properly caring for the dead. The sudden silence of the crying infant still haunted him.

One thing had become terribly apparent to Dayan in the massacre's aftermath. None of the men were ever under Dayan's command. They followed Unebolod's orders. It chaffed him that Unebolod commanded so much respect, even from Dayan himself—and that Unebolod had not even given Dayan command over a single *mingghan*. Surely he could be trusted with a thousand men. Men of lesser rank commanded more.

"We need to prepare to move out," Dayan commanded the men around him.

The warriors nodded, but they moved with no haste, checking horses and arrows, sharpening swords. He clenched his fist.

Once the camp was cleaned and Tulugen had returned with the warriors they had left behind, Unebolod rode out with his men trailing behind him like dogs eager to please their master on a hunt.

"Mount up!" Unebolod called.

Those who had remained near Dayan rushed into action, leaping into saddles even as they put their swords in their belts. Dayan clenched his jaw. Had he not just told them the same thing a little bit ago?

Dayan stood and climbed into the saddle, remaining near the rear of the *tumens. They jump into action for him, but not me. That has to stop.*

They rode west, deeper along the edge of the rocky Gobi terrain, toward Juyan Basin, until the sun set. Discomfort and exhaustion weighed Dayan down. He had not complained, but Unebolod must have sensed Dayan's desire to stop, because he called for camp. The commanders joined Dayan and Unebolod around a small, low fire, rubbing their hands together to warm them.

Airag flowed freely, and everyone seemed in good spirits except for Dayan. He watched as the commanders deferred to Unebolod in all things, hardly sparing a glance for their Khan. They asked how many fires to build and how large, organized hunting parties based on Unebolod's commands, and waited for him to give perimeter orders for watch before riding away.

Dayan feared he was losing their respect. *You speak the language of reason, Dayan,* Mandukhai had told him once, *but to be a Great Khan, you will also need to speak the language of authority. Men follow strong, decisive, intelligent leaders. If you falter, even in a small thing, you will lose their respect.* And he had faltered. He had faced off against Unebolod before that attack, and when Unebolod challenged him with reason, Dayan gave in. He was handing these men over to Unebolod willingly. If this continued, would they turn against him in favor of Unebolod? *I came on this campaign to prove myself.*

Irritated, Dayan leaned forward, holding a hunk of dripping, greasy mutton from one of the camp's sheep in one hand and resting his elbow on his knee. The men sat on the ground so that he could have the only boulder around. A few of the commanders sat on saddles resting on the ground. His movement caught the attention of several of the men, who turned their gazes on him.

Dayan used the one tool he knew he had. For whatever reason, if he stared at men long enough, he could cause discomfort. He adopted this penetrating stare until everyone around the fire fell silent.

Unebolod lounged back on a fur he slept on at night. Dayan's stare drew him upright, and Unebolod cocked his head as he waited.

"Unebolod, when will I be given men to command?" Dayan asked at last, focusing all of his attention on the *orlok*.

Unebolod appeared amused by the question, which only fanned the flames of Dayan's irritation. "My lord Khan, you command *all* of them."

Again, Dayan allowed his silence to cause unrest among the men. He remained still until everyone squirmed. Unebolod, though, never squirmed. The *orlok's* body tensed, but he did not squirm. He didn't even flinch as they stared each other down.

Dayan knew he had two options. Walk away from this and let tempers cool—which would make him look weak and cede more power to Unebolod. Or he could assert himself. *Men respect strength, and if you show weakness, they will never forget it*, Mandukhai had taught him. They had already seen him weak over the years. He needed to change their perception of him.

"Leave us," Dayan ordered the commanders without averting his gaze from Unebolod.

For a moment, no one moved. Then the campfire became a flurry of activity as men rose, gathered their belongings, and moved off to find a different campfire to keep them warm. Soon, only Dayan and Unebolod remained.

"You see?" Unebolod said, grinning and waving toward the empty space around them. "Even if I had told them to stay, they would have left. Because their Khan commanded it."

"Don't patronize me," Dayan said coldly. "I know how the structure works. I also know that the men respect leaders who guide them to victory."

"And you will."

Dayan squeezed the meat in his hand so hard it squished between his fingers, dripping into the frozen ground at his feet. "No. You will. Because you are commanding them and not giving your Great Khan the lead."

Unebolod leaned forward, and his dark eyes narrowed. The campfire flickered over his features in a haunting, shadowy manner that made Dayan's stomach squirm. "I am your *orlok*. My job is to marshal your *tumens* to victory. In *your* name. What sort of command are you looking for, boy?"

Boy! Dayan threw the ruined meat at the fire. The fat made the flames blaze for a moment, and Dayan saw the worry in Unebolod's eyes for just a second before the flames returned to normal.

"You will not speak to me like this again, Unebolod. I am your Khan, and you will never call me boy again or I will have my guards rip out your guts and feed them to the birds."

"'Too frightened to do it yourself?" Unebolod teased, smirking once more.

Dayan surged to his feet, grasping his sword. Unebolod froze, watching Dayan's hand. The grin slid from his face. *He fears me. He knows I can kill him and no one else will question me.* Mandukhai would, though. The men respected Unebolod, and if Dayan wanted to defeat Bigirsen, he needed Unebolod's help. Dayan practiced his breathing, then relaxed his grip on the sword.

"You *are* too frightened," Unebolod said, as if shocked by this.

Dayan shook his head. "He will win who knows when to fight and when to not fight."

The surrounding air thickened despite the winter cold. Neither man moved, weighing the implication of the words. He remembered that exact phrase from a lesson on the art of war years ago. Knowing when to pick a fight and when to walk away was a key to success. This was not the place for a fight.

At last, Unebolod nodded. "Flex your muscles all you want, Dayan Khan. Show the men you know when to pick a fight and when to show mercy."

"We should not have killed everyone," Dayan said, praying Unebolod could not see how badly his hands were shaking. He released his sword and tucked his hands into the sleeves of his deel.

"We had no choice."

"You have made your point, but you are wrong." Dayan straightened his back. "Those were my people. We will not kill women and children again.

There has to be a better way. There is a better way." Already, ideas were spinning in his mind like knucklebones waiting to rest. "Tomorrow, you will give me command of a thousand of my men. Officially."

Unebolod leaned back again and shook his head. "No."

Dayan tightened his hands into fists inside his sleeves.

"They are all your men, Dayan Khan. Tomorrow, you will command both the *tumens*."

Panic gripped Dayan's chest. A shock ripped through him. All twenty thousand men? He had not commanded so many before. Mandukhai had always been with him to take charge. She would not be there to speak for him this time. Could he lead as she would? Was he even capable of it? A thousand man he was certain he was capable of. This was much different.

"You want command?" Unebolod asked, though it didn't sound like much of a question. He waved his hand toward the mass of men scattered across the terrain. "Good luck. Lead them all."

I wanted to prove myself, he thought. But Unebolod's words smacked of a challenge, like he thought Dayan couldn't handle the task. Can *I handle it?* Whether he could no longer mattered. He would not back away now.

"Fine. All of them." Dayan swallowed the lump in his throat. "We will do this together."

"I think you made yourself perfectly clear, Dayan Khan," Unebolod said, leaning back on his furs. "I can advise as an *orlok* would. But the rest is on you."

Dayan's jaw twitched. He wished he had some quick-witted comeback for the obvious jab, but nothing came to the surface. Frustrated with this turn of events, Dayan strode away from the fire. He would do this because he had to. And the first step would be using the same skills Mandukhai had given him. Compassion for his people, but steel when necessary. There would be no more unnecessary killing. Everyone would have a chance to surrender and accept their Khan.

Did Unebolod know of the promise he had made to Mandukhai? Was Unebolod setting him up for failure? *Keep your friends close, but your enemies closer.* Was Unebolod his enemy?

CHAPTER TWELVE

Grasping at Legacies

Mandukhai carefully picked her path through the rolling hills and forests along the wall. Togochi rode beside her. Most of their ride had been in silence as they were both lost in their own thoughts.

For nearly a week, they traveled the length of the wall, seeking an end or weak points. The wall continued for miles where no wall had been before. Their most recent maps had marked the wall several miles to the south, traveling east. This new beast meandered like a giant snake through the landscape, without end.

The nearest crossing for her *tumens* would leave Bautuo at their back—dangerously close to the *tumen* of Ordos and who knew how many Ming. There could be no sneaking into the Ordos basin for a surprise attack, as Unebolod had planned. They had intended to pinch off the resisting Ordos tribes. Half of their men would cross in the south and sweep a wide net across the land toward the north as the other half closed in from the north similarly. The strategy was risky because it forced the Ordos to either submit or retreat west—toward Bigirsen's territory. But she had trusted Unebolod's decisions in such things. With any luck, Bigirsen would not be a threat much longer.

However, the wall changed everything. The old plan might never work. The farthest south they could cross was still near Bautuo—too near to not be noticed with so many men and horses. And it didn't solve the problem with supply lines.

"We need to take this information back to camp and regroup," Togochi said after they had ridden nearly a hundred miles of wall. "We cannot do anything until we receive word from Unebolod, anyway. Without the men he and Dayan took with them, someone will resist our attacks in the Ordos basin."

Mandukhai grimaced, her gut churning, but she nodded in agreement. She already knew what she had to do. Somehow, she had to discern what Qori, the Ordos Lord in Bautuo, wanted most. And then she would have to deliver it.

The week-long ride back to camp had not been idle. Mandukhai's mind would not silence. And one question continually poked at her, insisting on an answer. What would Genghis do?

Even with Togochi beside her, Mandukhai had never felt so alone.

Fifteen years of companionship. Fifteen years of making friends, building trust, creating a family even though she had no children of her own. Thirty-one and childless as a queen. What sort of failure had she been in that regard? If she had just married Unebolod, she would have a ger full of children by now.

But would she still have this empire if she had chosen Unebolod? Surely the two of them could accomplish it. They *had* accomplished this together. Her fearlessness and strategy, combined with his battle skills and military experience, had brought this empire together. And still he was not Great Khan, nor her husband. She could never repay the debt she owed him.

Mandukhai had dedicated her life to Genghis' vision, and when this battle against Bigirsen and the Ordos was over, that vision would be nearly complete. Would Dayan then free her?

Did she want him to?

The longer the men were gone, the more Mandukhai worried over whether she would ever see Dayan's face again. The longer he was gone, the more she missed him. How he held her hand and offered reassurance without words. The way just having him beside her had given her endless strength. That devilish grin he wore every time they raced their horses.

It occurred to Mandukhai that she had spent only a few weeks with Unebolod, and years waiting for him. Now, it seemed the other way around. She had spent years with Dayan, and only weeks waiting for him.

And the weeks were far too painful.

GOBI DESERT – ORDOS TERRITORY – EARLY WINTER 1479

Dayan rode west with his men. *His* men. The strategy had been simple, and Dayan hated himself for not thinking of it sooner. Mandukhai would have. He had broken the *tumens* in wings. There would be no way for so many to pass through Ordos territory without sending warnings. Stealth was not on their side on this mission. And he would not kill women and children again.

Instead, Dayan split the forces apart as they continued west, sending them as far north as the men could travel safely, and far south, deep in Ordos territory on the plateau outside of the basin. Scouts rode ahead to seek any who might try to escape to send a warning to Bigirsen. Most of the warriors rode through the south, then west, where there would be more camps and potential resistance. They would sweep across all the Ordos camps this side of the Huang Ho River and offer a choice. Fight and die, or submit to their Khan. He would not leave enemies at his back, and he would not kill without giving Mongols a chance to swear their oaths to him. Everyone deserved a choice.

After defeating the largest group of Ordos warriors they had encountered—nearly a full *tumen* spread across the northwest—Dayan took up residence in the defeated Ordos Lord's ger. He waited for the men to bring the Lord to him. The air inside was thick, and Dayan had to focus on keeping his breathing even. How did the man live like this? He sat on the edge of the bed but quickly became restless and stood once more, pacing the floor. Unebolod had insisted Dayan take over the Lord's ger as his own.

"If you have taken over his ger, it demonstrates your power over him," Unebolod had pointed out.

Dayan had not disagreed. It seemed like a tactic Mandukhai would use. Now, with Boke and the guards outside the door, Dayan paced the floor impatiently. As voices arose from outside, Dayan stopped and settled himself in what was clearly this Lord's seat. He imagined this man probably gave orders from this very chair.

The door opened, and Boke entered first, followed closely by a man near to Unebolod's age. The thick, bushy eyebrows made his massive forehead appear even larger.

"I have come on my own," the Lord snapped, tugging at Unebolod's grip on his arms.

Unebolod snorted and nudged the man further into the ger. "Lord Ulum, my lord Khan." Everything about Unebolod screamed dogged loyalty. It might have duped others, but it didn't deceive Dayan. Unebolod's loyalty was to Mandukhai, not to him. He would be a fool to think otherwise.

Dayan said nothing. He folded his hands together in his lap and used his golden gaze to bore into Ulum until he squirmed where he stood.

"You come on your own," Dayan said, keeping his voice cold, as Unebolod often did. "After your men attacked mine? That is hardly willingly."

Ulum scowled. "My men were defending the camp. Yours would do the same."

Dayan studied Ulum. The cut of his clothing indicated his rank among the Ordos Lords well enough. Ulum was the highest-ranked Lord they had encountered outside of the Ordos basin. Bringing him to his knees would be a big victory for Dayan.

"My men think I should kill you," Dayan said at last.

Ulum tensed but said nothing.

"However, I, like my Khatun, believe that a man should have a chance to recognize his position in this realm." Dayan narrowed his eyes and thinned his lips, putting on a show for this Lord as well as his own men. They seemed to enjoy watching him make others squirm. "It is easy for one man to overrun and kill another. It takes much more strength for one man to make friends of his foes. The fate of your people rests on your shoulders, Lord Ulum."

Ulum glanced at Unebolod and the sword on the *orlok's* hip. His jaw twitched. After a moment, he raised his chin proudly and met Dayan's gaze. A second later, he was clearly unnerved as he broke the gaze. He opened his mouth, but Dayan held up a hand.

"Before you speak, you should know, Ulum, that we are riding out against Bigirsen," Dayan said. "I will expect you to fight with my men and not against them. We will expect you to help us kill Bigirsen. If you do not, no oath you make today will matter."

Ulum's jaw slackened slightly as his eyes widened. For a moment, Ulum seemed to calculate something. Dayan wanted to ask what he was thinking, but it would make him appear weaker.

"You cannot defeat him…" Ulum sounded uncertain, though. Did he truly believe what he said?

"He has committed many crimes against the realm, and murdered a Borjigin princess, *my* cousin," Dayan said coldly. "I can, and I will, defeat him. Swiftly, and without mercy. I will not give him the same choice before you. But if you try my patience much longer, it will not end well. Make your choice now, Ulum. Give your oath to me or become an enemy of the realm along with Bigirsen."

Sweat beaded on Ulum's forehead. He studied Dayan curiously, as if weighing the strength of the Khan. A moment later, Ulum's lips twitched and he sank to both knees. "I offer my rightful Khan salt, gers, horses, and blood from this breath until my last, under the Eternal Blue Sky." He straightened his back proudly. "Should I fail to keep my word, may my limbs and my soul be severed from my body for eternity."

The oath officially bound Ulum's eternal soul to Dayan. To break the oath would not only be justification for execution, but it would condemn his soul forever. No man would risk that.

Dayan stood and crossed the short distance between them. He held out his hand. Ulum kissed the crescent moon ring. When it was done, Dayan pulled Ulum to his feet and they marched out the door together.

The air outside was refreshing after the stifling air of the ger. Ulum's commanders had been collected outside, all kneeling with guards behind each. When Dayan exited the ger, Ulum's men paled, and their gazes flicked to their leader.

Dayan gazed sideways at Ulum. The Lord swallowed before speaking. "It is finished! Give your oaths to the rightful Khan, as I have, or these men will kill you for treason."

The other commanders' and officers' eyes bulged. A few jaws slackened, but a minute later, they spoke the oath together.

After the success of unifying Ulum's men behind him, Dayan felt a little lighter. Without Mandukhai's help, Dayan had managed to draw an oath from one of the highest-ranked Ordos Lords. It bolstered his confidence as they continued their campaign westward.

Some nights, Unebolod called their *tumens* to a halt outside encampments that submitted to their Khan. Families insisted on giving up their homes for the evening so that their Khan and his generals could have a proper night of sleep. Dayan knew he could not refuse these offers. It would be an insult to the families, and Mandukhai had always insisted that he be careful not to insult those who followed him. *Bitter men have vengeful hearts*, she had told him frequently. Still, he was uncomfortable on those nights sleeping in another man's bed, knowing that man slept on a floor or out in the bitter cold to offer him the luxury.

Along the way, Dayan also continued to establish yam stations and expand the routes through the empire. Gers were constructed around makeshift stables along yam lines. A few of those gers would belong to the families maintaining the station, but most of them would remain vacant, waiting for the messengers who passed through. On those nights, Dayan slept easier. The bed was not his; it was everyone's. Oddly, it made him feel closer to the men who served him. He slept as they slept.

On the nights when they slept under the sky, the men grumbled about the cold. Dayan thrived on it. The freezing air filled his lungs, opened them wide enough to make up for the effects of the horse illness he hid from everyone. On those nights, Dayan did not have to sneak the herbs that fought off the breathing fits.

No one knew of Dayan's illness. Not even Mandukhai. She assumed he had recovered from the illness as he had aged. He had suffered from it for as long as he could remember, but thanks to the herbs, he could hide it. Getei had come along on the campaign—at the shaman's insistence—to tend to the Khan's health, he had said. Sometimes, Dayan wondered if Getei knew Dayan still suffered from the affliction. If he did, Getei said nothing.

The reactions had been much stronger when he had been younger, sometimes seizing his breath until he passed out. Now it was more of a nuisance, but the crisp winter air cleared it from his lungs so that he did not even need to take his herbs most nights.

The *tumens* swept along southern Mongolia like a great wave, scooping up warriors who shifted their alliances to their Khan, seizing supplies. Thousands overran the few who resisted. Scouts and messengers rode north to south along hundreds of miles of lines, like a swarm of flies, endlessly buzzing. The unending motion fascinated Dayan.

On the nights where riding had not been too hard, or mornings they had rested well, Unebolod woke Dayan at the wolf dawn to train him with a sword. Combat on horseback was one thing, but if Dayan found himself unseated, he needed to be prepared to defend himself. These lessons felt much more brutal than they had ever been before, as if Unebolod punished him simply for breathing. Perhaps he did.

But Dayan learned from Unebolod. He would not fail Mandukhai, and he refused to feel inferior to men like Unebolod any longer.

Unebolod rode in relative silence as their *tumens* continued westward. His plan had backfired spectacularly. He had assumed Dayan would refuse taking full command of twenty thousand men. When that had not happened, Unebolod was certain Dayan's inexperience would cause him to crumble apart or come crawling back to Unebolod, admitting just how wrong he had been.

But once more, the young Khan surprised him in a way that drew even more grudging respect from him.

Dayan Khan had assumed command with a natural ease that Unebolod would have envied were he not so experienced himself.

Dayan watched the horizon endlessly as they continued west. He did not change the current strategy of sweeping like a blanket across the Ordos plains, smothering any potential opposition. He even managed to maintain the lines of warriors with some ease. Messengers carried the Khan's commands up and down the *tumens*. The men immediately took to Dayan's command.

Even more irritating had been the Khan's ability to know exactly when he should take control or delegate tasks elsewhere. He knew instinctively when to ask Unebolod for advice and when he should not. By the time they neared the Juyan Lake Basin territory, everyone had begun speaking of their Great Khan riding with the spirit of Genghis.

All Dayan Khan needed was a large victory to shift the fortunes of fate his way, and his legacy would be secured.

JUYAN BASIN – ORDOS TERRITORY – EARLY WINTER 1479

Before Issama had left for Juyan Basin, Siker had strongly voiced her dislike for his plan. According to her, it was too risky. Burn the woman, but she was never satisfied. She wanted him to act, and so he did.

He had as many of the Ordos Lords waiting for his signal as he could gather before Mandukhai had invaded the south. No one had sent him word for some time on Mandukhai's progress into their territory, which made him wonder just what she was up to and where she was. Time ran dry on him.

Once Issama rescued Nemeku from Bigirsen, he would send word to the Ordos Lords who had aligned with him. Ulum and Mogurkei would then launch their attack against the Uyghur border, cutting Bigirsen off from any reinforcements. Issama could then sweep in and take control of the Uyghur with Nemeku in Siker's care. With any luck, Mandukhai would already have men riding in to kill Bigirsen. She must have heard by now where Bigirsen had made camp for the winter. Issama had leaked that information carefully to one of her men.

Once she removed Bigirsen from the playing field, the Ordos Lords would turn their attention to Mandukhai's weakened *tumens*—hopefully removing Dayan, Unebolod, and Togochi from power in the process. Once they captured Dayan, Issama could use both Dayan and Nemeku as leverage against Mandukhai. Whether he ended up as Great Khan at the end, he could not be certain, but if he conquered Mandukhai and captured both potential heirs, the Ordos Lords, at least, would not question his strength. And strength won *kurultai*.

If the Ordos Lords killed Dayan, Issama would still have Nemeku, who had the strongest claim to the title.

Siker's issue was not with the plan to capture or kill her estranged son. Issama had learned years ago that she had written Dayan off. It was cold how easily she had cut him out of her heart. Siker's real problem stemmed from Issama's plan to infiltrate Bigirsen's camp to rescue Nemeku completely alone. Hopefully, she would forgive him when he returned with the boy.

And if Tengri graced him at all, Nemeku would not resist too much.

Issama had only a handful of Uyghur men following him, and he had sent them with Siker and his sons toward Hami. It was the safest place for his family to lie low as his plan launched into action.

Then Issama rode north. Alone.

Bringing others along risked someone tracking him before he reached the basin where Bigirsen had set up his own base for the winter. Issama had waited nearly a week after his family was gone before he headed north. That should have given Bigirsen enough time to get reports that Issama had gone east. Assuming Bigirsen was watching for him at all.

The basin was only a day's ride from Kharakhoto. Issama crossed the rocky terrain, dotted with shrubs and patches of grass. Gulls flew overhead in great swarms, squawking at him for trespassing. The lands around the basin offered an oasis in the Gobi, but the water was undrinkable. A man could cross the desert, come across the lake, and drink his fill but still die of thirst.

As the sun set, Issama dismounted and walked through the dead patch of grass. The water was undrinkable, but it still created a lush landscape for the desert. The land sloped down closer to Juyan Lake, creating a bowl of life around the lake's edges. Reeds grew as tall as a man along the northern banks even in the cold winter.

Issama approached along a patch of tall, dead grass and reeds to mask his movements. The horse remained tethered to a boulder far enough away from the edge of the basin that no one would spot it without looking. Not that he believed for a moment Bigirsen would set up camp without scouts. But after years in Bigirsen's camps, Issama knew how he operated, how he set up his scouts, and how far out they would be from camp. He used this information to help him get as close to camp as possible.

As he neared the edge of the basin, Issama crawled along on his stomach to watch the movements in the camp and get a handle on the size. The sun burned his face despite the frigid winter wind. Snow melted beneath him, soaking into his clothes. Snow didn't stay on the ground for very long here. It fell and melted within hours.

The camp below spread out all around the basin. Issama squinted, focusing first on counting the number of men below. More than once, he lost count and had to start over, but eventually came to the conclusion that only about a thousand men protected the camp. A thousand men were easier to slip past than a full *tumen*. Issama patterned out their movements, seeking weak points in patrols or residents. He could predict the flow of people to and from gers, along the water, toward the herds of sheep and cattle. He observed as the men switched guard, timing out how long each man was left on watch before his shift changed.

Families and warriors moved around the camp in easily recognizable patterns of relaxed, everyday life. Issama had to be certain they would not catch him, and he would not enter camp until after dark. Certainly not before he knew exactly where Bigirsen would be.

Bigirsen's ger was hard to miss. While it was not larger than any of the others, as Manduul's had been, the blue crescent-moon and star banners fluttering high above the domed ger were unmistakable. A dozen guards watched over the door of a ger beside Bigirsen's. A young woman left Bigirsen's ger with a bag, walked to the other ger, and the guards inspected the contents. Issama could only think of one reason the guards would be so concerned. Nemeku must have been in there.

The sun fell below the edge of the basin. Bitter icy wind blew over Issama's back. His bones were stone cold from lying so still on the ground for so long. He pressed his fur-lined hat tighter to his head, as if that would ward off the cold, then rubbed his hands together to try warming his frosty fingers.

Bigirsen emerged from the guarded ger. He stretched his back and rolled his neck. The young woman stiffened when he appeared. Bigirsen stepped close to her, brushing his fingers along her jaw, and said something in her ear. Then his hand slid down her body in a very familiar way. The entire encounter she had remained stiff, obviously terrified of him, but she tipped her head back and he kissed her. Was that Orghana? Issama heard rumors from the Ordos Lords that Legusi khan had given his sister to Bigirsen. The poor girl.

The massacre at the red salt lake had cost Bigirsen more than Issama. All of his wives had died. Legusi's sister had only recently come of age for marriage. It made sense that the spineless Ordos khan would give his sister to Bigirsen.

Orghana ducked into the ger as Bigirsen strode away toward his own.

As Issama waited for dark, moving his body and rubbing his limbs so the cold did not set in, he thought about what he might say to Mandukhai once her precious *orloks* were out of the picture.

I don't need to convince her to give up her power to me. I only need to kill Unebolod and Togochi, and eliminate Dayan from a position of power.

And if that failed, he would threaten Nemeku's life if she did not back down.

If only he knew what the other Ordos Lords were up to now.

CHAPTER THIRTEEN

The Value in Anything

Unebolod nudged a pile of rubble with the toe of his boot, examining the sand-covered remains of what had once been a thriving city along the Silk Route, before the Ming had stormed in and destroyed the Mongols and diverted the shallow river. One hundred years could wreck terrible destruction on a place.

Dayan had climbed the rampart walls surrounding Kharakhoto. Unebolod gazed toward the silhouette of the young Khan, wondering what he saw in the world beyond.

Genghis had conquered Kharakhoto so long ago. It had lain at a crossroads between Karakorum, Xanadu, and Hami. Stories of the wealth that had once flowed through this city seemed unbelievable to Unebolod as he stood in the remains. Precious metals and jewels. Silk and spices. Porcelain and weapons and horses and camels. Now, nothing remained.

Like most Mongol cities, there were no permanent structures within the walls. The outer walls of Kharakhoto ran well over a thousand feet in all directions, forming a great square wall with pointed towers along it. On a modest level, it reminded Unebolod of the walls of Karakorum. But a century of abandonment had left everything coated in sand that had blown in from the desert. The sand now climbed up the inner and outer walls like ever-shifting hills.

He crouched beside the remains of a firepit as the warriors rode into the walls and set up camp. Wayward merchants traveling the Route would still take up residence in this place, using the walls as a barrier against raiders and the desert. It provided some protection, if no real shelter. Unebolod held his hand over the ash. Heat seeped off of it. He frowned and turned his hand, rubbing his fingers together.

"You found something," Kelegei said, standing at Unebolod's shoulder. The young lesser khan had a level head for his age.

Unebolod nodded. "Someone has been here recently. This ash is still warm."

"The men found markings on the ground as well," Kelegei said. "Rings as if gers had been here recently. And tracks all over the place. Someone lived here."

"Recently." Unebolod stood and smoothed out the folds in his fur-lined deel. He hated this infernal sunlight. The wind remained bitterly cold, but the sun blazed unforgiving. It created an odd mixture of hot and cold simultaneously. "Tell Boke we need to keep the Khan off the wall."

Kelegei rushed off to send word.

Unebolod called commands to a few of his own men, and the group of them moved around the perimeter of the walls, searching for anything that might be a danger to the Khan.

Only tales remained of the last battle that had been fought in Kharakho-to. General Kharabatur had thousands of men in this city, surrounded by superior Ming forces. The Ming had diverted the only water source away from the fortress and laid siege to the walls. When Kharabatur had realized what would happen to his family, he had killed his wife and children out of mercy, then killed himself. Another version of the story claimed Kharabatur had created a breach in the northern wall and fled the Ming.

Unebolod stopped at the northern wall, in front of the massive, carved-out gap through all twelve feet of wall. This was where he and his men had entered. Could Kharabatur truly have killed his family only to flee? It was the act of a coward. Unebolod preferred to believe that the famous Black Hero would not have ended his days as a coward. It did not bode well for Unebolod's own fate. If the Black Hero died a coward, would the Steel Soldier as well?

"I sent scouts to the basin," Dayan said.

Unebolod turned to find Dayan standing only two feet behind him. The men made some noise as they set up camp for the night, but surely not enough for Unebolod not to hear Dayan's approach. *Sometimes he terrifies me*, Unebolod thought. But he would keep that secret to himself.

"Tulugen has led the way with strict orders to bring back reports and not attack," Dayan continued.

"We should prepare tonight," Unebolod said. "Tomorrow, we ride out to claim Bigirsen's head."

Dayan shook his head. "It would be pointless to make plans when we don't yet know the circumstances. Our time could be better spent."

"Oh?" The comment caught Unebolod's attention. What did Dayan think would better serve them?

"If the dawn brings the battle, with dusk we should be vigorous with our training," Dayan said, glancing at Unebolod's sword.

Unebolod could not hide his alarm at this. Dayan *hated* training. He constantly complained about it like a petulant child—just as his father often had. On this journey, they had no sparring weapons and had to use their actual swords against one another. Dayan complained about it at first. Though throughout this journey, something had changed in the young Khan. Dayan had become more confident and assertive. A determination burned in his eyes.

"We should rest for the ride ahead," Unebolod said. "If you want to train, I am happy to oblige, but if you wear yourself out tonight, you will have nothing left to give."

"Much like a racehorse," Dayan said.

Unebolod nodded.

"Well, this racehorse is much younger than you," Dayan said, and the corner of his mouth turned up in a rare, teasing grin. "So we shall see."

Unebolod hardly thought now was the best time to exhaust themselves in a sparring match, but if the Khan determined it would happen, he was helpless to stop it.

Dayan marched toward the center of Kharakhoto with his guards trailing behind him like tall shadows. Unebolod glanced toward the sunset, shielding his eyes from the blazing, round yellow sun as it sank toward the walls. The sky burned red with no clouds to offer any forgiveness, and the sunset made the distant walls and spires appear black—giving Kharakhoto its namesake of the Black City. They had a couple of hours before they needed to sleep.

Grumbling, not looking forward to the match, Unebolod followed Dayan to an open, sandy space near the center of the city. Red rocks crunched under Unebolod's boots, and occasionally, red sand shifted beneath his feet. The ground was unsteady here. Rocky in one step and sandy in another.

Boke's men formed a ring roughly fifteen steps across. Dayan stood near the center, sword held defensively in front of him. Unebolod strode into the ring a few steps away. He rested his hand on the hilt of his own sword, but did not draw. Unebolod's fingers brushed the yellow ribbon.

He called me old. His mouth twitched. Unebolod was not old. He was only in his thirties, and still stronger than most men.

A glance at Dayan's feet revealed the slight tip forward toward his toes. He would try to sprint the distance and take Unebolod by surprise. Unebolod pressed the balls of his feet into the sandy earth for a firm, steady stance. Still, he did not move.

The two of them sparring was not unusual, but this night it caught attention. Before either of them made their first move, more than a dozen commanders had gathered, with at least twice as many warriors. Unebolod would walk a dangerous line. The men had begun to respect their Khan. One poor sparring match could undo that—and cost Unebolod dearly as well. Dayan had not shown himself to be a man of wrath, but any man could be pushed too far under pressure. Unebolod would have to be certain not to let Dayan win easily, but not make a complete fool of the boy, either.

The sun stretched Dayan's shadow long across the ground. Unebolod noticed the subtle shift in the elongated boot shadow before Dayan took his first step. The young Khan rushed forward, holding his sword in a defensive position in front of him in case Unebolod swung. Unebolod remained calm, his hand on his hilt, unmoving as the boy closed the distance.

Dayan's eyes swept Unebolod, seeking signs of movement from his feet all the way to his eyes. At the last moment, Dayan shifted feet as he swung the sword out toward Unebolod's armored chest. Unebolod swung his body to the opposite side, out of the way, as Dayan spun around on his heel for a second rapid attack. Unebolod drew his sword with lightning-quick speed, slicing toward Dayan's exposed back. But Dayan raised his sword over his shoulder to block, pushing out as he turned to face Unebolod again.

In seconds, the two were locked in combat. Sweat trickled down Unebolod's back and forehead as he raised his sword against Dayan's lowered defenses. Dayan spun around to block, forcing the swords to glide off each other. Back and forth, blow to block. Their feet danced, kicking up sand that coated Unebolod's mouth. Dayan swung the sword down at Unebolod's neck, and he raised his own to block. The offending sword pushed closer to his skin. Unebolod pressed his free hand against the flat of his blade and forced it out.

Dayan stumbled back.

"Use all of your assets," Unebolod lectured. "Not just speed and strength. Every sense is your ally."

Dayan recovered his footing, gritting his teeth.

Unebolod swung his own blade up. It sliced across Dayan's golden-plate chest armor. The sound pierced the sky and echoed off the walls. It set Unebolod's teeth on edge. But the boy recovered quickly, jabbing the tip of his blade forward to force Unebolod back a step.

"Desperation forces you to make mistakes," Unebolod said. "Breathe, focus on everything."

The dance resumed as the gathering crowd swelled.

Something about the determination in Dayan's eyes unnerved Unebolod. This was not a fight the boy intended to lose, which worried Unebolod. If he beat Dayan, would the Khan punish him?

The attacks intensified, each blow pushing harder, becoming more desperate despite Unebolod's warnings to breathe and focus. Unebolod scrambled back a few steps. The two circled each other.

"You are too desperate to win," Unebolod said.

"Am I?" Nothing about Dayan's voice sounded joking anymore. This fight held some significance for the boy that Unebolod did not fully understand. Something had changed from when they started.

Dayan lunged forward, and Unebolod shifted to defend. By the time he realized the move was a feign to cause his misstep, it was too late. Dayan spun toward Unebolod's exposed back and struck the armor hard enough to force Unebolod forward. He stumbled and fell.

The moment he hit the ground, Unebolod rolled onto his back and raised his sword across his body. Dayan grinned as he heaved the sword directly across Unebolod's chest. Unebolod's sword was barely on time to block the sharp blade from a cut that surely would have been dangerous—if not deadly. This was no mere sparring match.

Unebolod kicked out, forcing Dayan's feet out from under him. As the Khan fell on his back, Unebolod scrambled toward him. Their swords skittered across the ground. Unebolod blinked sweat from his eyes as he pinned the boy to the sandy ground.

"Settle down," Unebolod growled.

Sweat dripped from his temples. Dayan grimaced as the drops hit his face. Sweat rolled down his own temples toward the sand beneath him.

Dayan reached up and grabbed hold of the shoulders of Unebolod's armor. "I am not a weak child. Better that you see that today than tomorrow."

Before Unebolod could respond, Dayan jerked him downward. Their foreheads hammered together, leaving Unebolod momentarily dazed. It was just long enough for Dayan to kick him off. Dayan rolled to his feet before Unebolod's back hit the sand. It kicked up around him, coating his mouth. Unebolod coughed.

A blade pressed against his neck at the shoulder joint, firm and unrelenting. Dayan's grin was cocky. "I win."

"I'm not dead. You've won nothing."

Dayan's eyes widened. If the Khan wanted to make this a proper fight, Unebolod would not give up easily. He knew his next move would cut him, but it would not be a deadly cut if he moved fast enough. The muscles in his arms twitched and ached from the fight. He thrust a fist into Dayan's forearm. The blade nicked his neck, but it threw Dayan off balance. Unebolod then kicked at the boy's legs to force Dayan back and give himself space.

As the Khan stumbled and caught himself, Unebolod rolled to his feet, scooping up his sword. The two circled each other within arm's reach.

"If you want a proper fight, you had better be prepared to finish it," Unebolod said. "Bigirsen will not show you mercy. He will riddle your body with arrows and take your head for sport. There is no value in anything until it is finished."

Dayan swiped his arm across his forehead. "So said Genghis."

Unebolod nodded ever so slightly.

Dayan lunged forward. Their swords glanced off each other, ringing in the air. Both men stepped back to reassess. "You don't fight for me," Dayan said.

This time, Unebolod made the first move. The blades locked against each other. Unebolod's muscles twitched. "I gave my oath and served you for years," Unebolod growled. "My word is iron."

They both stumbled back as they pushed away, dancing around each other. "You gave her your word. Not me." Dayan thumped his chest. *"I am your Khan."*

The cheers from the gathered warriors kept their conversation from reaching anyone else. All the men must be watching now. *Tumens* of them. Unebolod spared a cautious glance around and noted that men even cheered from atop the distant walls. *I cannot win this one*, he realized.

Dayan thrust the sword straight out. It glanced across Unebolod's side, skimming across the edge of his armor. Surely Dayan wasn't foolish enough to kill his best general on the eve of their most important battle.

Unebolod swung his sword up toward the boy's neck. Dayan raised his arm, but the blade sliced through the leather gauntlet on Dayan's arm. The boy's eyes widened in alarm and he stepped back, hugging the injured arm close. It was not a serious wound, but it would slow him down for the moment.

"I see the way you look at her," Dayan said. Was that pain in his voice? "And I know how she feels about you, even if she never says a word of it. The truth is plainly obvious."

Unebolod's heart sank into his stomach. So that was what this fight was about. He stepped back away from the jealous, enraged boy. He knew what those emotions could do to a man. Sweat rolled down his back.

"You won't release her," Unebolod murmured, his words swallowed by the roar of the crowd.

Dayan edged closer, holding his sword at his side for a swing in any direction. He had planned this. A fight between them, out here where she could not witness it. The roar of the crowd at his back. Dayan had never intended to release Mandukhai from her oath to him. *Hope is a tool for fools, and I am the biggest of them all.*

Unebolod had lost this fight before it had even started. He placed his sword on the ground and sank to his knees. The men needed to see their Khan win. Dayan needed this victory. Unebolod's pride would never recover.

"I do as my Great Khan commands," Unebolod said. The words dragged out of him, as if compelled by some otherworldly force.

Dayan shuffled closer, placing the blade on Unebolod's shoulder so the sharp edge faced his neck. "Yield."

Unebolod bowed his head. "I am at your mercy."

"Then be thankful I am not as merciless as men like Bigirsen." Dayan removed the blade and stepped back. "When this journey reaches its end, she will have a man worthy of her."

Unebolod raised his gaze.

Dayan's face had lined with hard edges, and his golden eyes glowed in the setting rays of the sun with supernatural light. It was fearsome to behold. Unebolod suppressed a shudder.

"If we defeat him, she will see that I am just as worthy as anyone else," Dayan continued. "And you will never look at her as you do again."

The words hurt more than the nick on Unebolod's neck. He could neither let go nor control where his eyes strayed. He would rather die than never look at her.

"If Bigirsen escapes and we lose, I will know that I am not worthy of her and release her to better men." Dayan stared pointedly down at him. In that moment, for the first time, Dayan in no way resembled his father. He appeared much stronger, fearless. "I will defeat Bigirsen, or die trying."

Unebolod flinched. Under no circumstances could he return to Mandukhai with the body of this boy. While it seemed as if Dayan presented an option, it was nothing of the sort. Unebolod had promised Mandukhai that Dayan would return—which meant Unebolod would have to do everything in his power to ensure that happened. Dayan would defeat Bigirsen, because Unebolod would stop at nothing to keep his promise to her.

Dayan winced. "There is no value in anything until it is finished," he said as he turned away, cradling his arm against his chest. Getei rushed forward with his pack of medicines to tend to Dayan.

The crowd disbursed, chatting enthusiastically about the strength of their young Khan.

"You had him," Kelegei said as stopped beside Unebolod and placed a hand on his shoulder.

Unebolod shook his head. "Sometimes victory lies in defeat."

Beside Kelegei, Ulum harrumphed and nodded.

Kelegei snorted. He stepped back as Unebolod shifted to stand. "Says who?"

"Me." Unebolod collected his sword and stalked away.

Issama waited for nightfall so he could sneak into Bigirsen's camp. When the watch was at its weakest point, he would slip in, kill the guards posted outside of Nemeku's ger, then convince Nemeku he was there to rescue him and return him to Mandukhai safely. Not that he would keep his word, but he needed the boy to come without a fight.

As the sun set, Issama felt a tremor in the earth. Worried that Bigirsen had reinforcements arriving, he pressed his numbing, gloved hands against the earth. The familiar rumble of distant hooves made his forearms vibrate just enough to confirm his fear. Issama scrambled back away from the edge of the basin to where he left his horse.

Crouching beside his mount in the willowy reeds, Issama spotted the shadowy figures of riders from the south. *Reinforcements?* He could either sleep out in the open and try sneaking in after these new men had settled—which risked frostbite—or he would have to come back tomorrow night and try again. Nemeku wasn't going anywhere in a day.

He rubbed his hands together and squinted at the riders. They moved with caution and great care, picking their path with purpose. It was hard to make them out in the dark. But there were not nearly enough to be reinforcements. Seven men. Perhaps as many as ten. He had a hard time telling in the dark.

He breathed into his gloved hands to attempt warming them. He needed fire if he could not enter camp tonight. Which meant he would have to return to his camp in Kharakhoto.

Issama waited until the men moved further away, their backs to him, before mounting. He turned his mare away from the basin. For the first quarter of a mile, he picked his path carefully, vigilant for other riders. Once certain they were not following him, he rode as hard as he dared toward the abandoned city. Something was happening, and he would have to return another night for Nemeku.

The ride to Kharakhoto was frigid. Chilly wind whipped his face, stinging his eyes. It was nearly dawn by the time Issama was within a mile of the abandoned city. He jerked his mount to a halt. Scouts circled the walls of Kharakhoto a mile out.

Someone else had made camp in the walls. He grabbed his bow, prepared to fire if he was spotted. Then he dared to edge his mount as close to the scouts as he could without being noticed—an arduous task in such barren land.

Dozens of them milled around in the dark all around the outer walls. Issama tried distinguishing whom they served. Each man seemed to be from a different tribe. But the moment Issama spotted a Khorchin among them, he knew with absolute certainty who slept inside those walls.

The scout belonged to Unebolod—to Mandukhai.

Issama glanced back toward the basin, now miles in the distance. Jangi had received Issama's cryptic message about Bigirsen's location and, as

Issama had predicted, Mandukhai had immediately sent thousands of men to hunt and kill Bigirsen. Most likely, those had been spies approaching Bigirsen's camp were there to confirm the camp location and size. Tomorrow, they would attack.

Issama edged his mare backward to avoid detection. The pieces of Issama's plan were moving into place. If Bigirsen died tomorrow, Issama would have a head start on the Khan's men if he headed straight for Hami, then deep into Uyghur territory to claim Bigirsen's vacant space of ruling the tribe. Then Issama would send word to his Ordos allies, return with the full force of the Uyghur, and together with the Ordos, they would finally remove Mandukhai, Unebolod, Dayan, and Togochi from power.

But doing this meant abandoning Nemeku to Unebolod's men. Irritated that this part of his plan had gone horribly wrong, Issama ground his teeth until his head ached. If he sneaked into camp tomorrow to rescue Nemeku before Unebolod's men arrived to kill Bigirsen, and Mandukhai knew Nemeku was in the camp before, Unebolod would send men to track Issama. He would be questioned—or killed if they had learned anything of his plans. Clearly, Mandukhai had sent plenty of men to deal with Bigirsen. Unebolod no doubt led the mission. She would trust no one else to kill Bigirsen. Some part of Issama was sorely tempted to sneak into Kharakhoto before the wolf dawn to kill Unebolod while he slept. Surely it wouldn't be too hard to find the Khorchin khan.

Without realizing it, Issama had circled wide around the perimeter of scouts, seeking gaps to enter without notice. But they had done their job well. The only way he could sneak in would be to climb one of the mounds of shifting sand along the wall. It would be hard to climb, and even harder to escape if he was discovered and chased. He could not take his mare into the walls.

Near the southwestern corner of the wall, Issama's breath caught as he recognized the cut of the scout's deel. *Ordos men!* The other scouts had been from tribes he knew followed Mandukhai now. But this one ... Which Ordos Lord did this scout serve? *I cannot dare to hope it's one of my allies.* Yet he did.

Issama licked his chapped lips and rode at a slow canter toward the Ordos scout. If he was wrong and this was not one of his allies, he would have to kill the man and flee. But if he was right, he had his way into camp.

The scout spotted him within a hundred yards. Issama raised both hands into the air to show he was no threat, but he dared not say anything until he was close enough to see this man clearly.

As he closed the gap, he noted the way the scout held his bow, ready to fire in a heartbeat.

"Which Ordos Lord do you serve?" Issama asked, keeping his voice low so it didn't carry on the breeze.

"Ulum."

Fortune smiles upon me. Ulum was certainly one of the Lords Issama had allied with. Issama smiled. "And who does Lord Ulum ride with?"

The scout narrowed his eyes as he examined Issama. "You are Lord Issama?"

Issama tensed, still holding his hands up. The truth could get him killed. He counted on Ulum still serving him, and making his men aware of that as well. "I am."

For a moment, either man moved. Issama worried he had overplayed his hand as the scout continued pointing his arrow at Issama's chest. The seconds ticked by painfully slow until, at last, the scout lowered his bow.

"We ride with the Khan and his *orlok*, Lord Unebolod."

Adrenaline pumped through Issama's veins, creating a sensation of euphoria. *Both the boy Khan and Unebolod? The High Heavens shine upon me.* He fought to control his delight. "I need to speak with Ulum tonight."

The scout shook his head. "You should go, Lord Issama. Lord Ulum will expect you to keep your end. He has things currently under control, and the ear of the Khan himself." He glanced nervously around, but no one else was near. Still, he lowered his voice and leaned closer. "Tomorrow the lines will weaken on both sides."

The lines will weaken on both sides. Issama nodded, understanding this meaning clearly. Tomorrow, the Khan intended on killing Bigirsen. Then, Ulum would weaken the Khan's lines as well. All of Issama's careful planning was coming to pass.

Once Bigirsen was dead, the Uyghur would be without a leader. He wanted to believe Ulum had everything under control, but often found it difficult to trust others. Would Ulum double-cross the Khan ... or him?

I need those Uyghur men. More than Nemeku. I need control of the Uyghur.

"Let your Lord know I am headed to get the reinforcements," Issama said. "I will be back by spring."

The scout nodded and turned away.

His next course decided, Issama turned his mare west. He would take control once and for all. And Bigirsen would not stop him this time. First, he needed to reach Hami and reconnect with Siker.

CHAPTER FOURTEEN

No Arrows Need Fly

The journey back to Mandukhai's Lake Dai camp had begun as a disheartened one. The Ming had worked tirelessly to build a wall that would keep the Mongols out. It was a testament to the divisive nature of Bigirsen's attacks—or perhaps Ming fears of the "Little King," as they called Dayan. Mandukhai had no intention of conquering the Ming. Mongols had struggled enough over the years to hold *themselves* together. For centuries, the tribes had allowed inner struggles for power that had divided alliances.

Most of the southern tribes had been content to live off black market trade with the Ming, or to raid caravans full of goods. Mandukhai knew she could not ignore the Ming threat forever, but until she united all the tribes beneath the Great Khan's banner, she could not strike deals with the Ming. Her primary goal was to unite and preserve the empire for generations to come. Everything else was secondary.

To create a lasting legacy, she would have to build the government Genghis had failed to secure; something that would last the test of time. To do that, she would have to restructure the tribes, blend them together in a massive pot, and erase old tribal lines for good. No small task.

The wall had also induced great frustration in her. Once Mandukhai rebuilt the government, she would have to open trade with the Ming—or conquer them. With a wall in the way, she had few bargaining tools to work with. The Ming could attack from the comfort of their own defenses.

By the time Mandukhai reached her camp two weeks later, she realized she had been looking at this wall the wrong way.

With a quick command, Mandukhai summoned her generals to the gathering tent. In little time, she had all seven men—and Lady Altan and Esige—gathered at the base of the dais on their usual benches. Each of these leaders commanded thousands under Togochi's leadership as *orlok*.

Mandukhai sat on her throne holding a cup of *boal*—honey wine—in her hand as a surge of triumph pulsed through her. Bagatur approached with a small stack of papers. Mandukhai accepted them, but did not look at them just yet. She wanted to share this news with her generals immediately.

Togochi took the lead in the conversation, explaining to the generals what the two of them had observed of the wall on their journey. By the time he finished, stunned, disheartened silence settled in the gathering tent.

"So the rumors of the great wall are true," Soke said, a deep frown creasing the corners of his down-turned mouth as he broke the silence.

"Yes," Togochi said. "They have been working on this for years right under our noses." He glanced accusingly at Huoshai. "It stretches for miles where it had not been before."

Huoshai stiffened and raised his chin but said nothing.

"Then we have no choice but to cross at Bautuo," Albeq said. "We must take the city and use it for our supply lines into the Ordos basin, then pray that the Ming don't attack our backs like they did to Bigirsen."

The comment drew mutters and grumbles. Soke nearly spit on the floor in disgust.

Mandukhai watched them all calmly.

"Walls work both ways, Lord Albeq," Mandukhai said, rapping her fingertips on the arm of her seat. "They keep us out, but they also keep the Ming in. Tengri has blessed us."

"I fail to see how this is a blessing," Huoshai grumbled.

Mandukhai took a deliberate drink, savoring the sweetness of the *boal* before swallowing. Making these men wait for her to speak always gave her a small thrill. For years, she had waited for them to finish before speaking. Having the roles reversed certainly felt liberating.

"Initially, I also thought the new wall disheartening, my Lords," she began slowly. "As you know. But after weeks of careful consideration, I have discerned two points from this." Each of the men shifted forward as if eager to hear her words, and she suppressed a smirk. "Expanding the wall tells us that the Ming do not have enough soldiers to defend the borders or engage us in battle. Their emperor has proven weak and ineffectual, and to our knowledge, he does not have a legitimate heir. So for the time being, that wall reinforces the fact that the Ming either have no interest or no ability to properly launch an attack against us."

Togochi leaned his arm against his knee and raised his brows at her deduction. Had he considered it and failed to mention it?

"Assuming you are correct, what is the second point?" Soke asked.

"They fear our Great Khan," Mandukhai said, this time allowing the corner of her mouth to tip up into another smirk.

"So you have heard the rumors?" Bagatur asked. He had been at Mount Burkhan Khaldun. He had ridden away along with everyone else. He had held out against her for far too long. She trusted his oath, but not always his intentions.

Mandukhai took a drink to cover her confusion at Bagatur's question. Slowly, she lowered the cup and motioned for him to continue. "Pretend I have not."

Bagatur apologized, then nodded at the stack of papers he had given to her. "The messages from Lord Unebolod and Dayan Khan," he said quickly, motioning with urgency at the papers.

Her heart skipped. Had she missed so many messages during her absence? *Hopefully I have not missed anything too critical.*

Mandukhai read the first report, a transcribed message from Unebolod explaining their first victory and the changes Dayan implemented afterward. The next described the process for opening yam lines as they continued west. She shuffled through each, her heart thumping a little harder with each message. Instead of passing through Ordos territory quietly and eliminating any threats at their backs, Dayan had used his position to subjugate those willing to give him their oath. Heat rose in her cheeks as a surge of pride rushed through her body. Mandukhai absently finished the rest of her *boal.*

The Great Khan commands an additional tumen and moves toward Kharakhoto, the last message read. It included a map of the yam lines established throughout the northwestern Ordos territory.

"When did these begin arriving?" Mandukhai asked. She hated how breathless she sounded. Was this path of victory truly Dayan's doing, or did Unebolod guide his hand?

"The first came just after you left to see the wall, within an hour of your departure," Soke said. "We had several of them all transcribed from verbal messages for you."

Mandukhai had been away just shy of four weeks. "And what are the men saying?"

Esige beamed as she shifted toward the edge of her seat. "They say that the sky father blesses our Great Khan, and that he has the vision of Genghis, to put it simply. Mandukhai, they say *you* have given us back our strength. And with Dayan Khan, we will return to our former glory." Esige's eyes shined with pride and excitement as she relayed the rumors. If anyone had ever believed in Mandukhai, it had been Esige.

"When did the last message arrive?" Mandukhai asked. Could it be true? Dare she hope that the empire would come together?

"Yesterday, during the wolf dawn," Mendu said. The Khorlod khan had been left in charge during her absence, with Esige overseeing everything as well.

Mandukhai's entire body heated. She set down her empty cup. Was this excitement or fear? Would this new-found glory of Dayan's push her out of her position? By now, the *tumens* would have reached Kharakhoto at the very least, and at best, attacked Bigirsen.

Sudden inspiration struck Mandukhai. She would use these subjugated Ordos Lords against Legusi khan. The Ordos Lords were to serve their tribal khan, but they had given their oaths to Mandukhai and Dayan above Legusi. She could use that as leverage against Legusi, making certain he knew his alliances were weakened or broken and he was alone.

"I know what must be done," Mandukhai said at last. "Ordag, fetch my scribe and the fastest yam rider."

The young man jumped to his feet, bowed, and rushed out the door.

Togochi straightened his back. "You have that look on your face. What are you thinking, Mandukhai?"

"I have two messengers to send," she began. It took great effort to remain casual as the excitement pumped through her veins and made her bones itch to move. "First to Dayan Khan and his men. If they have defeated Bigirsen, which they should any day now if the messages are to be believed, and the Great Khan has swept smaller Ordos encampments into his ranks, we face a unique opportunity. He can absorb the Ordos tribes outside of the basin and join us, then we can use those Lords who used to follow Legusi to weaken his position. With any luck, he will fold under the pressure before an arrow need fly."

Togochi shifted, a grin breaking across his face. Mandukhai knew her plan was a good one. Nearly half the might of the Ordos lived outside of the basin. If Dayan continued absorbing them, Mandukhai's sixty-five thousand would become nearly one hundred thousand.

"But can we trust them to fight for their Khan and Khatun against their own tribe?" Togochi asked.

"Once they kneel to their Khan, they are no longer Ordos. They are Borjigin," Mandukhai said. "We will distribute them accordingly."

"We still have no way to cross the river," Togochi pointed out. "Nor access near Bautuo. Not to mention how hard it has been to move our supplies along the lines this winter already."

Mandukhai chewed her lip for a moment. It was harder to move goods along her yam lines in the winter. Carts moved much slower.

Suddenly she sat up straighter in her seat, eyes widening. "Albeq, how long until the thaw comes?"

The old Tabun khan frowned, creating deep wrinkles in his forehead. Beside him, Altan smirked.

"It's hard to say," Albeq said at last. "Three, maybe four months."

"Long enough for the Great Khan to return," Altan pointed out as she leaned forward, resting her arms on her knees. Mandukhai could see the same light in the other woman's eyes. She understood.

"Long enough for our *tumens* to cross the frozen river," Mandukhai said.

The Lords around her absorbed this in stunned silence. It took several seconds for understanding to hit them, and it changed the mood in the room.

Mandukhai pressed her back into the seat to keep from bouncing with giddiness. Once Dayan returned to her, they would have just enough time to cross the frozen river and force the Ordos tribes to their knees.

"You said there were two messages," Altan said, drawing Mandukhai out of her moment of delight.

"Yes. The second will be to Lord Qori, in Bautuo," Mandukhai said.

This drew a few murmurs from the Lords. Mendu shifted in his seat. He had been remarkably silent throughout this meeting. Mandukhai wondered what he thought of her plans.

"Speak up, Lord Mendu," Mandukhai said. "I have yet to master the art of reading minds."

"That is up for debate," Mendu commented with a worried smile. "My Khatun, you know Qori leads a full *tumen* of Ordos warriors and has power over the Ming who claim to control the city. If he knows what you plan to do ... He is a man of greed and luxury, which makes him easily bought by the Ming or anyone else who seeks to control the city."

Mandukhai grinned. "By your own mouth, he is easily swayed. If he enjoys his life in Bautuo, I will let him keep it. In exchange for his vow and his men. With any luck, no arrows need fly before the Khan returns."

Mendu opened his mouth to protest, but Mandukhai held up a hand to stop him. "Men like Qori are much easier to handle than men like Legusi. Their wants are easy to fulfill."

"Only as long as you can continue fulfilling them," Mendu pointed out. "And when your resources run dry, he will turn to the next seller."

While Mendu spoke the truth, Mandukhai knew something deep in her bones. Something she could not actually prove to any of these men at this moment.

By the time Qori sought a new seller to cater to him, it would be too late.

Mandukhai intended to have control of everything before that happened.

Tayiqu sat primly on the floor in front of Esige's bed, patiently allowing Esige to comb out the knots with little more than a wince when her hair was pulled too hard. Tayiqu was only eleven now and had come into Esige and Huoshai's care when her father had died in the struggle against Huoshai's father during the transition. Tayiqu's mother, overcome with grief, had taken her life. Huoshai was the closest blood relative to the girl willing to take her in. His cousin and most trusted ally, Ormeger, had said his wife had refused to care for the girl.

Esige had swiftly stepped in. The thick layers of shame Esige had laid over Ormeger's wife caused tension for nearly a year, but Esige regretted nothing. The shame of refusing a girl simply because she was a girl and not a boy! What would have happened to Esige if the same had been done to her?

Tayiqu had only been two at the time and hadn't understood what was happening around her. In the course of a year, Esige had been thrust head-first into motherhood, caring for a six-year-old, two-year-old, and infant all at once.

At last, the knots had all been worked out of the girl's hair. Esige began weaving it into braids, which Tayiqu hated.

"Stop," the girl begged, pulling her head away.

Esige tightened her hold on the girl's hair to keep her from escaping. "If you do not want braids, quit knotting it up."

"You could shave it off," Emeeltorson teased, running his hand over his bald little eight-year-old head. Esige adored her oldest son, but he certainly enjoyed digging at his cousin's nerves. *He will be nine soon*, Esige thought, remembering his birth, how he had nearly been born in the saddle while the bitter winter winds had frozen her in place. His name meant "saddleborn."

His comment brought a wave of voracious laughter from his little brothers and sister. Tayiqu lunged for him, but yelped as Esige's grip on her hair yanked her back. Emeeltorson laughed as he dove away.

"Stop," Esige said softly, but firmly.

The two of them knew well enough to listen to her commands. Emeeltorson shifted his backside backward across the rugs to put more distance between himself and Tayiqu, but he said nothing else. After a few painful minutes of silence, he clearly couldn't take it anymore and opened his mouth to say something Esige was sure she would have to punish him for.

The door opened and Huoshai ducked in. Emeeltorson's mouth snapped shut and he looked at the rug as if interested in the patterns. When Esige saw the flush of anger on Huoshai's face, she understood the boy's sudden silence.

Esige tied a ribbon around Tayiqu's finished braid, then stood to help Huoshai out of his fur-lined coat. "Snowing again," she noted as she shook the wet snow out of the coat.

"Yes. Which means our supply lines are delayed. Again." Huoshai slipped off his boots.

Over the past month, Huoshai had been at the receiving end of a fair amount of criticism. It had begun with Mandukhai's anger about the wall. Esige hated how Mandukhai had shamed him in front of everyone, threatening to whip him or force him into a hole. She could not have reasonably expected Huoshai to know everything that happened all along his borders. Urainkhai territory stretched the southern length of the Mongol empire right along the Ming border from the Khingan Mountains to the Huang-Ho River. Hundreds of miles.

Huoshai had to save face, forcing him to question the scouts responsible for watching the border. Two of them, he had believed, *might* have been spies for the Ming, which made Huoshai question the trustworthiness of all of the border scouts. He had killed all of them to root out the problem, unwilling to take any risks. That night, he had sat in silence in the ger with Esige's arms around him for long hours.

As if the issue with the wall had not been bad enough, Huoshai had also been put in charge of the southeastern supply lines. His task was to keep them moving fluidly between the main camp near Lake Dai and their origins around the eastern part of the empire. Esige had taken on some of the burden for him and had grown quite adept at managing the lines, but as winter settled over the routes, it had become increasingly difficult to maintain those lines. Supplies dwindled. Whether or not intended, Togochi's comment about their supply lines upon Mandukhai's return had turned several heads in Huoshai's direction.

I am failing him, Esige thought as she moved his boots aside.

"We will get through this," Esige said far more confidently than she felt. "Just as we have always done. The end is near. I can just feel it."

Huoshai stalked past Esige without his usual kiss on the cheek and headed straight for the jug of *airag*. Her heart sank into her toes. Was he angry with her?

"I will fix this," Esige reassured him.

"Just leave it alone," Huoshai muttered.

Esige glided toward him, stepping over a puzzle box one of the children had left out. "There has to be a way to secure the lines even through the winter storms. If we—"

"I said leave it alone, Esige!" Huoshai roared, spinning around to glare at her. "I don't need your optimism feeding me false hope."

Esige planted her hands on her hips and scowled at him, aware that the children had frozen in their hand-slapping game to watch them. "Hope is only false when you let go of it, and I refuse to let go of it. If you are angry with me, tell me plainly why. If you are not angry with me, don't take it out on me. I will not tolerate it in my ger!"

The seconds seemed to stretch on in utter stillness. The children remained frozen, watching their parents. Huoshai stared at Esige. She refused to budge. Finally, she waved toward the door, clearly indicating he could take his anger elsewhere.

Huoshai's shoulders sagged. His hands fell limply at his sides. "I'm sorry. But what happens if we run out of food?"

"There are plenty of animals around the camps."

"What happens if we run out of supplies to make more arrows?"

Esige raised her eyebrows at him. Did he truly believe that would ever happen? "You heard what Mandukhai said. With any luck, no arrows will fly before the Khan's return. That gives us plenty of time."

The children lost interest and returned to their game. Esige stepped toward her husband and slid her arms around his waist. Huoshai curled around her, warm and familiar. The two of them fell into comforting silence.

Huoshai broke the silence, quietly giving voice to something she knew he had bottled up long ago. "I lost Nemeku," Huoshai muttered so the children wouldn't hear. They had asked about Nemeku so often Esige had run out of excuses for his absence.

"No. I already told you. That blame lies completely on me. I told her I could care for him. When he needed me most, I failed him. That isn't your fault." Esige leaned her head against his shoulder and closed her eyes.

Losing Nemeku had devastated Esige. When he first had disappeared, she had expected him to return. When no one could find him, she had put the pieces together and knew her mistake. Nemeku had always worshiped his mother's memory. Learning the truth of what had happened had been too much for his young heart to handle. No doubt it had filled him with a fury he had needed to satiate. And Esige had not been there to help calm the storm.

For all she knew, he could be dead at his father's hands.

Esige had begged to be part of the mission to kill Bigirsen, but Mandukhai had firmly put her foot down against it and refused to be moved. How could Mandukhai have allowed Dayan to go, and not her? Esige wanted to be there. She wanted to rip out his beating heart and shove it down his throat. She wanted to see the light leave his eyes.

None of that would happen now.

If Bigirsen has killed Nemeku, I will place a curse on his head so foul that every rebirth will lead him through a lifetime of torture, Esige thought with furious resolve. *And he will beg to never be born again, but he will. Endlessly. In agony.*

CHAPTER FIFTEEN

Into the Lion's Mouth

Dayan had been twitchy all night. He tossed and turned, dozing in brief increments before waking to that restless snake writhing in the pit of his stomach. Before the wolf dawn, he could no longer lie still. Dayan rose and tiptoed his way to the ramparts along the wall again, facing east. He sat with his legs crossed beneath him and rested his palms upright on his knees. The Great Fist threatened to capture him, and today, of all days, he could not afford to let this demon seize him.

Today, the summation of his entire life would be decided.

Mandukhai had raised him and put her faith in him before he had even understood the depth of what she had intended. All he had wanted since the age of ten or eleven was to prove himself worthy of her faith. If he could not defeat Bigirsen, Dayan knew in his heart of hearts that he would have failed her in the worst sort of way. A Khan who led his men into battle was expected. A Khan who could not defeat his oldest enemy was worthless.

If he lost today, he would either live to watch her become another man's wife, or he would die. For him, death was preferable.

The sparring match with Unebolod last night had seemed like a good way to warm up for the coming day. It also would have given him a chance to show Unebolod he was not a helpless child before they rode against Bigirsen. But his jealousy had taken over somewhere along the way.

Dayan closed his eyes and focused on his breathing. He understood how much Unebolod stood to gain if some accident befell Dayan in battle today. It would be all too easy for a stray arrow to kill Dayan. A man who wanted power was dangerous enough. A man who fought for the love of a woman was far worse. Unebolod was both.

Tengri, Lord of the High Heavens and father of the Eternal Blue Sky, if I truly am a worthy heir of Genghis, let today be my proof, he prayed. *Send me a sign no one could ignore. Offer me guidance to succeed.*

"My lord Khan."

A familiar voice pulled Dayan from his inner reflection. He cracked his eyes open just enough to see Getei fumbling with the layers of his shaman robes.

"Why do you disturb my meditation, Getei?" Dayan asked.

The shaman produced flint and a fan of ginseng. "Apologies, my lord Khan. I had hoped you would allow me to aid in your communion with the spirits."

Without Goram to guide him, Dayan knew he needed all the help he could get. Dayan nodded once. It could hurt nothing. Getei struck the flint and lit the edges of the fan, then waved the smoke close to Dayan's face. The scent was strong and oddly pungent. Dayan breathed it in, using his measured breaths to regulate his own body like the monk had taught him. He closed his eyes.

The effects of the ginseng worked quicker than Dayan had expected. His body relaxed. His breaths became even. The snake writhing in his stomach slowed, then stopped altogether. A few minutes into his reflection, once more using his mind to speak to the spirits of the Khans before him, Dayan felt as if his body slid down a slope. He snapped his eyes open and stood at the peak of Mount Burkhan Khaldun hundreds of miles to the north of his actual location. In front of him, the entire Mongol empire was visible as if he stood over a vast map.

Banners fluttered in the wind. Multicolored pennants bearing the crests of a dozen various tribes. Drums beat somewhere in the distance and echoed off the mountains like thunder. Hundreds of thousands of horses raced across the Mongol steppe, riderless and free. Armies converged and split, ebbing and flowing in mesmerizing patterns.

A monolith towered from the south, surrounded by stones, blue flags, and a yellow ribbon. Dayan squinted to read the name inscribed on the stone but could distinguish none of the letters. He was certain of one thing ... it was not his own.

Dayan raised his arm toward the Eternal Blue Sky as if he expected to touch it. In his hand, a wolf-head sword appeared, pointed at the cloudless sky. The swirling mass of armies once more converged together. All colors of banner merged as well, becoming one. A blue banner as light as the sky rippled above his head, bearing the crest of Genghis. Dayan's heart pounded with excitement as Oirat kneeled before him in the Zhavkhan valley; as the Uyghur crumbled to the earth like shattered stones; as all tribes became one.

Only one person dared to approach him. Mandukhai, years younger, as he remembered her when he had first come into her care. But instead of bearing the burden of a mountain on her shoulders, her steps were light, as if gravity had no hold over her. As everyone else bowed at his feet across the empire, she did not. Dayan reached his free hand out. He waited, breathless, for her to reach back as pride shined in her dark eyes.

The thunder of hooves snapped Dayan out of his trance. He blinked a few times before realizing he sat on the rampart. The horses approached from the north. He bolted to his feet, running along the wall to get a better view. Somewhere within Kharakhoto, he heard men calling to him to get down off the wall. He ignored them all, bolstered by the strange vision.

Boke joined him on the wall, watching the riders approach.

"It's Jangi and Tulugen," Dayan said the moment he recognized the two men leading the charge. "They have found him!"

As the scouts rode through the opening in the northern wall, Dayan and Boke rushed for a dune pressed against the wall. Dayan did not care about propriety at the moment. He slid down on his backside with all the dignity he could maintain while sliding down a mound of sand. Boke grumbled and followed him. Dayan reached the bottom on his feet and ran.

Unebolod, Ulum, and Belku had greeted the returning riders first. A crowd had quickly gathered, but they parted for Dayan as he joined the men.

"Bigirsen is there," Unebolod reported the moment Dayan stepped beside him. "With hardly enough men to protect himself."

"And Nemeku?" Dayan asked. "Mandukhai will want to know what has happened to him."

Jangi massaged his shoulder as he responded. "We did not see him, but there was a ger heavily guarded. It's possible he could be in there."

Dayan nodded, glancing at the sky. The sun had begun to rise. "If we ride now, when will we arrive?"

"At a full pace around the dunes, three or four hours," Tulugen reported.

Dayan maintained a cool expression, but inside he was jumping up and down like an overly excited boy. "Unebolod, order the men to mount. We ride immediately. Be sure everyone understands Bigirsen is to be captured, but not killed. I will deal with him myself."

Unebolod flinched in a rare show of alarm. "You cannot show him mercy."

"We will show no one in that camp mercy," Dayan agreed. "But Bigirsen's life is mine, and I want him to know it before he dies. Nemeku is to be spared, unharmed. Mandukhai will not forgive any man who harms him."

"He poses a danger to your title," Unebolod pointed out.

Jangi rested his hand casually on his sword. The man had spent years protecting Nemeku. Dayan had spent years seeing Nemeku as a cousin. He would not kill him.

"He is no danger to me," Dayan said confidently. "Nemeku is my cousin and son of a Borjigin princess. He will be treated with the respect he deserves."

Unebolod bowed. "As you wish." Then he excused himself to ready the men to ride.

Chakicha, the Tabun commander, edged closer to Dayan. "Be careful, my lord Khan," he said under his breath. "You allow too many lions into your ger and may wake to find them all at your throat."

"A Khan does not fear a lion," Dayan said confidently. "He tames a lion or kills it and wears its fur in the winter." Dayan turned his burning gaze on Chakicha. "I am Khan of khans, wolf of the Borjigin, divine representative of the Eternal Blue Sky. I tame dragons and lions alike." With that said, he stalked away.

Chakicha shrank back from Dayan as he passed, bowing to the Khan.

This morning, Dayan awake with a fear that he would fail this mission. But the High Heavens sent him a sign. He would conquer the tribes and turn the Uyghur into dust.

Then Mandukhai would see him for the man he was.

JUYAN BASIN – MID-WINTER 1479

Unebolod had organized the men into three wings—right, left, and center—with a full *tumen* each. He mistrusted the Ordos now riding with the Khan, so he had reorganized the *tumens* so that the Ordos warriors were spread out and not fighting together as much as possible—much as Genghis had once done. It would be too easy for them to turn against him and Dayan if they rode as one unit. Some Ordos commanders had complained about the new assignments—and demotions—until Dayan had stepped in and proclaimed them all one tribe. He also promised that any of the men who proved their value and loyalty in this fight would be recognized, whether they be from Ordos, Chakhar, Three Guards, or any other tribe. Unebolod hated how easily a few words from the boy had soothed ruffled feathers.

The *tumens* spread out long and wide across the southern Gobi, with the right and left wings pulling ahead to form the horns of the attack on either side. Bigirsen could attempt fleeing, though Unebolod did not think Bigirsen had such cowardice in him. The man was more likely to die fighting than to flee for his life. He was too proud and stubborn to give up. Even if he fled, they would force him to ride north, deeper into the Gobi toward the Singing Sands. He would not make it out alive with the Khan's men on his heels.

Unebolod had not felt such invigoration before battle since the last time he had ridden against Bigirsen, before Manduul had become Great Khan. That fight had been cut short. Bigirsen had pulled back to regroup, then requested a private meeting with Manduul. Unebolod had not had his chance to fight the Uyghur warlord again. He was certain Bigirsen had made peace with Manduul because he had known, deep down, that he could not have beaten Unebolod on the battlefield. Unebolod had nearly run him over with a fraction of the men he had today.

This time will be different, Unebolod thought as he rode across the desert with the rest of the men.

Unebolod had thirty thousand men at his command. Bigirsen only had a thousand. And this time, Unebolod knew for certain the Khan would not back down as Manduul had done. Dayan had something to prove, and to the boy's estimation, that meant taking Bigirsen's head himself.

Mongol warriors did not need to stop in a charge such as this. They had food warming under the saddle that they could pull out and eat at their leisure, as well as enough *airag* to sustain them for weeks. The mounts could be switched on the go as well. This allowed them to cover more miles in a single day. The thirty miles between Kharakhoto and Juyan Basin were nothing to them.

To avoid exhausting their mounts before battle, Unebolod had insisted they ride at a moderate pace to the basin instead of racing there. It would also give them the benefit of arriving at night, when the camp guard was weakest. Every advantage was worthwhile to ensure they won the day. Dayan had not liked the slower pace, but he had seen reason and agreed. He wanted Bigirsen's head and wouldn't risk losing.

The sun rose high into the sky. Despite the stiff wind of winter whipping at his face, Unebolod sweated under the unforgiving heat. Only the Gobi could make a man sweat while simultaneously making him bone cold.

When the sun dipped beyond the western horizon, all the sweat turned to ice against his skin. He shuddered at the sudden frigid cold. The moon shone bright in the black sky, surrounded by thousands of stars, not long after the sun disappeared completely.

Scouts swarmed back and forth from their destination to the advancing lines. The camp was quiet, lit only by a few campfires and torches. Bigirsen had retired to his ger. They had killed a few of Bigirsen's scouts to avoid detection. Messengers carried orders along the wings as they approached their destination.

Unebolod itched to watch Bigirsen die. His sword had waited years for this day. If the warlord paid any attention at all, he would feel the ground tremble as thousands of hooves raced closer. Bigirsen would have a chance to flee. Unebolod grinned, eager to be the one to kill Bigirsen's horse and bring him down. His adrenaline pumped in rhythm with the pounding hooves. Soon, they would plunge into the basin, sweep across the camp, and destroy the Uyghur boot on their throats for good.

Near the crest of the basin, Dayan jerked his mare to a halt. It happened almost instantly. All of his guards followed his lead, as did the rest of the center *tumen*. Bannermen waited beside the young Khan, showing the blue banners. One of Unebolod's Khorchin warriors held the *sulde* of Genghis.

Unebolod stopped with the rest of them, watching as the left and right wings also drew to a halt. Thirty thousand of the Khan's warriors formed a bowl around the upper edges of the basin.

Below, Bigirsen's men scrambled to their mounts. They had noticed the rumble in the earth and raised the alarm.

Unebolod trotted to Dayan's side and gazed at the burst of activity below. "Dayan, we need to attack now, before they build up their defense."

"Which ger is Nemeku in?" Dayan asked Jangi, ignoring him.

Unebolod clenched his jaw to keep from lecturing Dayan right here and now. This was hardly the time to worry about Nemeku.

Jangi pointed with his lance toward the domed home beside Bigirsen's obvious ger—marked with fluttering banners in the center of camp. The guards at the door of the ger Jangi indicated shifted anxiously in the torchlight, as if uncertain if they should remain in position or prepare for the attack. It had to be the right place.

"Send word along the lines," Dayan ordered the messengers. "That ger is to remain untouched. The men can take what they want and burn the rest."

Unebolod shuddered at the coldness, the detachment in Dayan's command. "My lord Khan, we should attack," he repeated.

"We will." Dayan unhooked his bow and grabbed an arrow from the quiver.

Unebolod noticed the tip of the arrow and raised his brows. What was Dayan up to? They had a plan. Form the horn and sweep in without mercy. *If he thinks he can frighten Bigirsen, he does not know the man he is up against,* Unebolod thought.

Dayan raised the bow high and released. The arrow screamed through the air, followed by the siren's call of a thousand other whistling arrows from their warriors. In an instant, Unebolod understood Dayan's decision. Their horses snorted and danced at the noise. Unebolod's own ears hurt. The sheer volume of the sound as it echoed off the basin was enough to burst any man's eardrums.

The whistling arrows had forced horses, oxen, and sheep into a panic in the camp. They scrambled in every direction, snorting or bleating or bucking in fright. Uyghur warriors chased their horses in a feeble attempt to mount.

Torches sprang to life around thousands of gers. Women screamed. Children shrieked and cried. Sheep protested as they trotted as fast as their legs could carry them in a chaotic mass. A few camels grunted.

A ring of fire sprang to life around the camp as the Khan's men nocked flaming arrows. A moment later, the flames streaked across the sky toward camp. Some struck earth. Some hit people milling in a chaotic mass in the camp, their terrified, flaming bodies running. The rest struck gers. In a matter of minutes, flames licked at the walls of the homes. The Uyghur camp had descended into utter chaos.

Unebolod's chest clenched as he watched. More than anything else, he wanted to charge into battle and find Bigirsen. He *needed* to do this. Hatred and anger burned in his heart, heating his frozen bones. It pulsed in his ears.

What remained of Bigirsen's army had finally mounted, preparing for their own attack. Women scrambled to put out fires with the meager water supply on hand.

A glance at Dayan revealed a whole new beast. Distant flames flickered in his eyes, making the golden color seem to glow in the dark with a menacing light. His back was perfectly straight, and he held a bow in one hand and the reins in the other as he watched. His face bore no expression at all. With a small flick of his wrist to signal the men, the charge down the basin began.

Unebolod whooped with glee alongside the rest of the men as their horses thundered down the basin. Arrows fired in all directions. The man riding beside him was caught in the shoulder and thrown off his mount. Unebolod did not have to check to know what had happened. The charge would trample over him before anyone stopped. Such was the way.

He glanced back only for a moment. Just long enough to see Dayan Khan in his saddle, surrounded by his banners and guards on the rim of the basin where he watched and waited for a signal that Bigirsen was cornered or captured. Unebolod had insisted Dayan protect himself at least until they located Bigirsen.

Arrow after arrow, Unebolod released without mercy, not caring if it was a man, woman, or child. Dayan's orders had been clear. The men could take whatever they wanted. The rest would die. None of the men or boys in Bigirsen's camp could be allowed to survive—except Nemeku.

Unebolod's path was clear in his mind. He knew where Bigirsen's ger was, and he used arrows for as long as he could in the charge before drawing his sword and leaning into his mare's neck to become a smaller target.

A Uyghur warrior cut a path ahead of him. Unebolod grinned, dodging a Uyghur sword aimed at his arm. The man behind him finished the Uyghur with a slice across the neck that sent a spray of blood in his wake. Unebolod dodged around the gers, punching through makeshift barricades of hen cages or stools. All around him, homes blazed, sending the stench of burning wool high into the night sky.

The Uyghur banner snapped angrily in the wind. Unebolod was so close now. His palms sweat. His breathing evened out.

A sword sliced into Unebolod's arm. Unebolod cursed and turned his attention ahead again, just as a sword sliced down at his neck. A Uyghur warrior attacked on horseback, his face covered by a long iron-linked shield. Unebolod raised his sword to block the blow, nearly unseated by the strength of the attack. As they fought for the upper hand, the edges of the swords ground against each other. The swords slipped off each other. The two men circled away, then charged at each other again. Arrows rained down around them, glancing off their armor. Unebolod tried to see the man's eyes as their swords struck again. The vibration from the impact jolted up his arm. A second attack followed with lightning-quick speed. Unebolod blocked again, surprised by this warrior's strength.

Just past the Uyghur's shoulder, Unebolod spotted Bigirsen rushing out of his ger with his helmet on his head. He leaped onto a horse.

I cannot let him get away, Unebolod thought. He yanked his knife from his belt with his free hand and slammed it into the warrior's leg. The man screamed in pain as Unebolod twisted the knife and ripped it out. It served as enough distraction for Unebolod to push past him.

Bigirsen had mounted and now raced away from the camp, followed by a dozen of his guards. The red tassel on his helmet gave him away among a crowd of Uyghur warriors. Unebolod raced after him.

Bigirsen would not escape this night alive.

CHAPTER SIXTEEN

Out of the Lion's Mouth

Togochi eyed the other tribal Lords as they made their way out of the gathering tent once the meeting had been dismissed. He remained rooted in place. Worry burrowed under his skin, and he had tried his best to hide it in front of the other Lords. They had received a response to the message Mandukhai had sent to Lord Qori, the current Ordos Lord in Bautuo. His proposal was laughable, but not nearly as much as Mandukhai's willingness to agree to the terms.

He glanced at Esige and Huoshai, seated across the aisle from him. Huoshai's brows had pulled tight together. He stared at the floor, deep in thought. Beside him, Esige eyed Mandukhai with that glimmer of curiosity that told Togochi he would get no support from her.

The moment the doors closed, Togochi began pacing. He couldn't stop moving now that he had started, as if his feet propelled him onward of their own volition.

Mandukhai sat in her throne, hands folded demurely in her lap as she watched Togochi. *Good*, he thought. *She should know I don't like this plan.*

He started toward the door, prepared to storm out and make Mandukhai come talk to him, but ten steps from the door he turned around and marched up the aisle toward the dais. Torgus tensed. *Are my steps so aggressive?* Togochi could only imagine what he must look like right now.

He could feel the fear in his bones. It made him tremble like some terrible flu.

Before he reached the steps, Togochi spun on his heel and marched back toward the door again.

Mandukhai, Esige, and Huoshai ignored his obvious agitation and turned to each other to converse. *Do they not care at all what I think?* he wondered, affronted that they brushed him off when he was in this state.

"Mother, let me come with you," Esige said.

"It may not be safe, Esige," Mandukhai said.

The patience in her tone grated on Togochi's last nerve. He whirled back around, throwing his hands in the air. "Of course it isn't safe! Which is exactly why you shouldn't go, either, Mandukhai. Let me go in your place."

"It has to be me," Mandukhai replied calmly.

"It could be a trap."

"I know." Mandukhai rose and glided down the dais steps toward him, stopping a few feet away. "Togochi, this has to be done. He wants to meet, and I cannot ride in with a large guard or it could alert others to my arrival. Soke will be with me, as will Torgus. We need Lord Qori, and he is offering me a chance to win him. I cannot send someone else in my place or I risk insulting him and losing this opportunity." She placed a reassuring hand on his arm. "We cannot hope for our supplies to cross the river without Lord Qori's support. Even if it is only for him to turn his back and ignore our presence."

The nerves in Togochi's gut coiled tight. "At least let me come along. If Unebolod and Dayan return and you are dead or captured, I will die next."

Mandukhai's eyes shined with regret, and he knew what she would say before she said it. "No, Togochi. I need you here. You and Esige can manage the *tumens* and families while I am away. And should something happen to me—"

Togochi's muscles tensed instinctively. *Dayan will kill me.*

"—you will under no circumstances use the *tumens* to attack Bautuo on a rescue mission," she finished.

All of his muscles suddenly went limp. His fingers numbed. Shock ripped through his core. "You can't be serious."

"You are to take the *tumens* to the Khan to regroup. He can decide the best course of action with the full force of the empire at his back."

Togochi shook his head stiffly.

Esige and Huoshai had risen and approached the two of them. "Mother, we cannot—"

"*No one* is to come for me without the Khan," Mandukhai said. Fury burned in her dark eyes as her hand fell away and she edged back to look at all three of them, clearly daring them to challenge her. "I need you to swear it. Even if Lord Qori betrays me and sends me back one finger at a time. You *will not* come for me before regrouping with Dayan Khan."

Huoshai dipped his head to his chest and muttered his agreement. Esige's reaction mirrored what Togochi felt inside. She turned wide eyes on her husband, jaw slack.

"I need you to swear it," Mandukhai said. She met Esige's gaze firmly.

Esige's hands clenched into fists at her sides. Togochi stood at Mandukhai's shoulder, shaking his head, willing Esige to refuse. Someone besides him had to see reason.

"I will not come," Esige said through her teeth. "I swear it. But make no mistake. If he harms you in any way, I will one day cut off his hands and make him eat them before I rip out his heart."

Mandukhai smiled as she stepped forward and stroked Esige's cheek tenderly. "I would expect no less from you." She turned to face Togochi, raising her brows expectantly.

He took a step back. "No." She opened her mouth, but he couldn't let her speak first. Her logic could silence his protests. "You cannot ask me to do this. You can't ask me to abandon you, abandon my oaths. Mandukhai, we need you to finish this."

This is madness!

"You need Dayan Khan to finish this," Mandukhai said with a serenity that drove Togochi mad. "And we need Lord Qori to cross the river. Your oaths are foremost to the empire and Great Khan. I cannot risk my best *orlok* on this mission."

"Just yourself," Togochi snapped. "And Unebolod is your best *orlok*."

"He isn't here."

"If he was, I can guarantee he would not allow you to leave him behind." How could he get her to see reason? Once Mandukhai decided something, talking her out of it was like trying to talk the mountains into crumbling to dust. He knew he would lose this fight, but he couldn't help himself.

"Then it's a good thing he is not here."

Togochi trembled, but he was uncertain if it was fear or rage or defeat causing the reaction. He slumped, knowing there would be no way to get out of this. "Fine."

"I need your word, Togochi."

He hated the way she looked at him like a wounded animal.

"You have my word. I will join the Great Khan." If he was going to give his word, Togochi would be certain she understood exactly what he would do. "Then I will come back with the full force of the empire and tear Bautuo to the ground."

JUYAN BASIN – MID-WINTER 1479

From where Dayan sat in his saddle, he could see the whole of Bigirsen's camp burning. The flames grew taller, lighting up the night. A smoky haze hung over everything as felt burned like tinder. The screams of children and wails of women pierced the air. Dayan closed himself off from emotion, gazing at the massacre as if another person possessed him. Otherwise, he risked his sorrow swallowing him whole. These were Uyghur. Men who opposed him. Women who supported these men. Children who would grow to hate him.

Watching the tides of horsemen crash through the camp, Dayan found himself disappointed with the lack of resistance. Bigirsen did not have nearly enough men to oppose such an attack. At first, Uyghur warriors had fired arrows in his direction, but as the attack closed in on camp, only a handful of Uyghur men cared about the Khan any longer—and those men who had tried to rush up the southern tip of the basin were put down like rabid dogs before they could break out of the camp perimeter.

Boke rolled his shoulders, watching stoically beside him. Dayan knew the *mingghan* that remained behind with him itched to join this fight. It was a battle most of these men had yearned to fight for years. With nearly thirty thousand men already attacking the camp, Dayan had every confidence the warriors could destroy any resistance.

Dayan only sought one man in the chaotic, burning mass below.

A cluster of horsemen burst out of the northern edge of the camp before the Khan's *tumens* could close the gap. A quick estimate accounted for fewer than a hundred men. The moment they were free of the Khan's men, the Uyghur cowards broke off into two groups. One headed northwest. The other due north. And at the head of the northbound group, Dayan spotted the red horsehair helmet marking out Bigirsen.

Dayan pointed. "There."

Without another command, he wheeled his mare around and raced north around the edge of the battle. The rest of his men could handle those in the camp. He would chase down Bigirsen himself. This was it. He would kill Bigirsen or die trying. He would not give up the chase until he caught his prey.

As Dayan's *mingghan* rounded the northern edge of the camp, he spotted another thousand of his men breaking out of the camp in pursuit of Bigirsen. And at the head of the group, Unebolod rode hard, whipping his mount for more speed. The ground trembled as thousands of hooves hammered against the earth, unforgiving and determined.

The gap between Bigirsen's men and his own closed slowly. By some unspoken understanding, Dayan and Unebolod formed flanking wings around the Uyghur. Arrows crossed the night sky, invisible once released. Dayan could only tell if their aim was true when a horse squealed or if a Uyghur was thrown from his saddle. They trampled the bodies without mercy, without pause.

As the Uyghur attempted firing back, Boke signaled. The Khan's guards closed around him like a wall. Arrows thumped into shields or sank into the ground. Two warriors riding with Dayan fell from their saddles.

Unebolod shouted a command to his men. In seconds, his warriors had flaming arrows arching across the night sky. The flames startled some of the Uyghur horses, causing them to change course suddenly and crash into one another. A few reared back, bucking riders from saddles.

Dayan's gaze was locked on Bigirsen's red horsehair tassel on the top of his helmet. Bigiren's mount reared back, but the warlord remained in the saddle. The pause was enough to allow a hundred of Dayan and Unebolod's men to close in a ring around him. Unebolod commanded the rest to finish the Uyghur who continued to escape.

Several of the Khan's warriors jumped from their saddles and rushed to Bigirsen's mount as the horse spun in a panicked circle. They ripped Bigirsen from the saddle, dozens of hands grabbing at him as he struggled against their grip. They dragged him across the ground. He kicked and protested the whole way. Before they could reach Dayan, Unebolod called them to a stop.

"Remove his helmet!" Unebolod called out.

Dayan glared at Unebolod. What sort of game was he playing at?

The men hesitated, watching Dayan. He nodded. They pinned Bigirsen down on his knees and yanked off the helmet.

Unebolod cursed out a string or profanities that made Dayan's cheeks heat.

This man was not Bigirsen.

"Where is Lord Bigirsen?" Boke snapped.

The Uyghur spit at the ground, which earned him a punch in the skull.

Dayan didn't need an answer. He already knew. "This way!" he called out as he turned his mare west. "Kill him."

Dayan didn't wait to see his command carried out. The men who had captured the false Bigirsen did their job. The rest followed Dayan as he raced his mare west. Bigirsen had put his helmet on the wrong man to distract them and give himself a chance to escape. *The coward.*

Scouts raced back toward the camp to gather more men. The warriors who rode off to finish the escaping Uyghur wheeled around to regroup with Dayan.

Sweat coated Dayan's forehead. Bigirsen could not escape! Dayan would chase him to the ends of the earth if necessary. He would not quit until he had Bigirsen's head in a sack.

Unebolod raced alongside Dayan. Neither spoke. Unebolod did not even question Dayan's certainty that they were headed in the right direction. Dust from the desert kicked up the further they rode from the basin. Dayan had to breathe through his nose and mouth in turns to keep the sand from clogging his nose or coating his mouth. The muscles in his body ached from a full day of riding.

Dayan had been on hunts before, and he imagined Bigirsen as a sheep and he the wolf chomping for a meal of mutton. This hunt would not differ from any other. In the end, the hunter would catch the prey. The wolf would catch the sheep.

Two thousand warriors swelled into nearly five thousand as more warriors from the camp raced to join their Khan and *orlok*. Soon, the only sounds were those of the hooves pounding against the desert rocks. Dayan leaned as close to his mare as he dared to reduce wind resistance and hopefully increase speed—having a fit of horse illness right now would be dreadful. He sent scouts ahead to find Bigirsen's trail, but the Khan and his men were too close behind for the scouts to get more than a mile ahead.

The wolf dawn caused the sky to shift to lighter hues of blue. All night, they chased down Bigirsen. The scouts reported they were on his trail, but it was not until Dayan could feel the sun against his back that the first sighting of Uyghur warriors came back. The news restored energy to the men who drooped from exhaustion.

Dayan's armor grew heavier the longer he stood in the stirrups. To ease some of the pressure, he rode in the saddle and stood in turns. It offered only a little relief. Exhaustion pressed down on him so firmly that even his adrenaline could not chase it away. Many of the men were used to riding like this. Mandukhai had never allowed him to do it. But Dayan also realized he could not show his weakness now, when Bigirsen was so close at hand.

Just when Dayan was not sure he could ride any longer, he spotted the Uyghur riders. The wings of the Khan's men spread wide and closed in on the sides in horn formation. Dayan rode at the center beside Unebolod. Arrows thumped into shields as the Uyghur attempted to discourage pursuit, as if they actually believed that would stop anything. One arrow punched through the shoulder of Unebolod's armor. Dayan ducked, as if the arrow would hit him instead. He watched Unebolod grab the arrow, twist it, and yank it out without slowing his horse or flinching. Instead, his face became a mask of determination. The silk under his armor would act as a temporary patch until they could get him treated.

Suddenly, the Uyghur wheeled around and launched a suicide charge. All but one rider, who raced onward.

Unebolod fired as if the injury had been nothing. His arrow flew over the Uyghur and sank into the haunches of the single rider's mount. Following his lead, several more arrows feathered the horse until it bucked forward, forcing the rider off its back. The furthest flanks of the Khan's warriors closed around the lone rider.

Dayan pulled out his sword and crashed through the line of Uyghur warriors. His blade sliced through men. Blood coated his face and armor, bathing his horse in red. He did not slow. Not as a sword sliced into his armor at his side. Not as a blade cut through the silk under the lamellar armor at his shoulder. The pain from the injuries kept him alert, a dull throbbing masked by his desire to reach Bigirsen.

As his warriors finished off the handful of Uyghur warriors, Dayan stopped his mare and dismounted.

Five men pinned Bigirsen on his knees—two on each arm and one holding a length of black and silver braid back so his neck was exposed. They had already removed his helmet, not eager to make the same mistake twice.

Dayan had never witnessed so much hate burning in any man before. Bigirsen's black eyes may as well have been windows into the pits of the underworld. It occurred to Dayan that he had never actually seen or met

Bigirsen before. As Dayan approached, sword in his hand dripping blood at his side, Bigirsen bared a hideous row of blackened teeth in a feral snarl.

Dayan stopped in front of Bigirsen, realizing that the man's gaze was not on him. The hate directed over his shoulder. A moment later, Unebolod stepped up beside Dayan. *It's Unebolod he hates,* Dayan realized. That knowledge bothered Dayan ... and threatened him.

Because if Bigirsen saw Unebolod as the threat, then where would the men's loyalty truly fall after this day? Would this victory be Dayan's ... or Unebolod's?

Sweat and blood mingled on Unebolod's face. The arrow had made it hard for his arm to function properly, and it sent fresh waves of searing agony through him every time he moved it. But he would not show weakness at this moment. Not with Bigirsen on his knees in front of him. His adrenaline, the pure elation of knowing Bigirsen was already defeated, sent waves of euphoria through Unebolod's body. Decades of waiting, and the moment was finally here.

Every one of Unebolod's senses had come alive as he dismounted and strode up beside Dayan. The boy had proven himself quite capable today. Once more, Unebolod hated the grudging respect he had developed for Dayan Khan. Even now, facing down a warlord who had conquered more than half of the Mongol tribes, Dayan didn't flinch as his father would have.

I cannot believe this day has finally come, Unebolod thought. It filled his chest with a lightness he had not experienced in years. At last, he would see vindication for Bigirsen's crimes.

"You are nothing to me, boy," Bigirsen growled.

Dayan remained statue still, staring at Bigirsen with unnerving golden eyes, all-knowing in his gaze.

Unebolod stalked toward Bigirsen. Dayan had called the kill for himself, but that didn't mean Unebolod could not enjoy the moment. He crouched in front of Bigirsen, smirking viciously at the Uyghur scum who had dared try to conquer *their* Mongol Nation.

"How does that scar feel, Unebolod?" Bigirsen asked. His voice burned with a rage and hate that matched his dark eyes.

Unebolod casually reached out and pulled the cloth of Bigirsen's belt toward him. He wiped the blood and sweat off his face first. It was an obvious show of power at this moment. Unebolod dipped his face away from Bigirsen, exposing his neck for an attack that would not come. In this moment, he wanted Bigirsen to be certain just how inevitable his fate was, and how helpless he was as well.

"The scar is my most prized possession," Unebolod said as he used the belt to clean his sword. "It reminds me of a debt to be paid."

As he dropped the belt, Unebolod noticed the bleeding wound in Bigirsen's leg. Unebolod's muscles tensed. He gave that wound to a Uyghur warrior earlier. *I was fighting Bigirsen back there, not some random warrior.* It made sense. That warrior had been stronger than he had expected, and more skilled as well. Bigirsen had tried to kill him earlier and fled when it didn't work.

Unebolod placed the edge of his sword under Bigirsen's chin, pressing the edge just enough for Bigirsen to feel the pressure, but not enough to break the skin. "It's time to pay that debt."

Bigirsen glanced past Unebolod at Dayan. Did he believe the Khan would spare him? Bigirsen was not such a fool.

"If I die tonight, I will die happy," Unebolod said. "Because not only have I defeated you at last, but you will already be dead. Tengri will welcome me with open arms for driving a rat like you from our Great Khan's empire."

A hand fell on his shoulder. Unebolod glanced back to see Dayan. Unebolod shifted out of the way as he stood, then took a step back to give Dayan space. Would he truly do this? Dayan had never seemed the type to take a man's head himself, nor to kill a man in cold blood like this.

Bigirsen's rigid muscles twitched. His fevered stare locked on the young Khan. The corded tension in his neck and the throbbing vein clearly displayed Bigirsen's animosity toward the two of them.

"I wish I could have killed your father myself," Bigirsen said to Dayan. Heat poured from his every word. "But I still experience intense satisfaction knowing I sent the very man who drove a wedge between your father and his uncle. Your father was a spineless, arrogant idiot, and so gullible."

Dayan didn't flinch. "I have no father but the Great Khan Genghis."

Bigirsen snorted in derision. "Issama did not even have to try hard to befriend your father. That entire brainless court welcomed him. Including your precious Mandukhai."

Dayan's hand clenched into a fist at his side and his jaw twitched. "Bigirsen, Lord of the Uyghur, you are guilty of treason against the Great Khan and Khatun of the Mongol Empire."

"I never should have listened to Issama," Bigirsen continued, as if Dayan had not spoken at all. "When Manduul died, I should have killed that woman ... or taken her into my harem."

Unebolod wished Dayan would get on with this already. He was on the verge of killing Bigirsen himself. Not only had this outsider tried controlling the Mongols, but now he threatened Mandukhai.

"Manduul told me once that she is quite wild in bed," Bigirsen said.

"Your punishment is death," Dayan continued, his voice hollow of emotion. "And your head will be my wedding gift to the Khatun."

"You would know, wouldn't you, Unebolod?" Bigirsen asked, still ignoring Dayan. The pointed gaze Bigirsen bestowed on Unebolod made Unebolod wonder just how much Bigirsen knew.

The question stirred immediate tension among the surrounding men. Rumors of Unebolod and Mandukhai having an intimate relationship before she had made her vow to Dayan had not been proven. But at this moment, when Dayan was filled with vengeance, it seemed like a poor time to remind the Khan that the woman he intended to marry had slept with his most trusted *orlok*.

Dayan's shoulders lifted, drawing so tight Unebolod could see the tension even under layers of armor.

Bigirsen smirked, knowing he had kicked a hornet's nest in his last act. "You would not even be Khan, boy, if Issama hadn't poisoned Manduul Khan's spawn—if it was indeed his at all." He shot a knowing glance at Unebolod. The corner of his lip twitched up mockingly before he turned his attention back to Dayan. "You're welcome, by the way." He bowed his head as much as he could with a man holding his braid taut.

Poisoned Manduul's... Unebolod's heart tumbled as Bigirsen's meaning hit him. His breaths quickened. His vision reddened with rage. Issama was Altan—the man who had hired that serving girl to poisoned Mandukhai and caused the miscarriage years ago. Togochi could never find Altan because they had been looking for the wrong person.

I am assuming Bigirsen speaks the truth. But as much as Unebolod wanted to deny it, the cold logic of Bigirsen's words felt indisputable. They sank into Unebolod's bones. As did something else Bigirsen had said ... if it was Manduul's at all. *Bigirsen couldn't have known about my affair with Mandukhai. Togochi was not even certain the extent of it.*

If she had not miscarried that child—*his* child—she never would have had the vision of Genghis. She never would have hunted down Dayan. They would have had a child and a marriage and a life together.

Unebolod's mind spun out of control. The world around him tilted as the gravity of everything spun around him. It took everything in him not to show just how unsteady he felt. The harder he tried to grasp at his thoughts, the more they ran through his fingers like mist. *Issama was Altan. He must have been.*

Dayan stepped around Bigirsen to his side.

I need answers. Whose idea was it to poison her? Where is Issama? What else had he done under our noses?

The men holding Bigirsen stretched his arms out at each side as far as they could go. Ulum used Bigirsen's long hair to yank his head back and expose his throat.

"Be careful who you trust around your woman, Dayan Khan," Bigirsen said. "Some of them already have a reputation for stealing a Khan's wife."

Fury burned white-hot in Unebolod's veins. His vision pulsed with red. Without thinking, he rammed his fist into Bigirsen's jaw hard enough to hear it crack.

"Unebolod, step back now," Dayan commanded, his voice cold, angry.

"Covering for something, Unebolod?" Bigirsen taunted. He spit a thick wad of blood on the ground.

Unebolod stumbled back a step, too numb with shock and grief to move further. He squeezed his eyes closed to fight for control, ready to plunge his own sword into Bigirsen's body. *Answers. Get answers before it's too late.*

"That who—" Bigirsen's deep voice cut off with a gurgle.

Unebolod snapped his eyes open, and it was too late to stop Dayan. The corner of Dayan's mouth twitched in disgust as he finished slicing the blade slowly across Bigirsen's throat, pressing it as deep as he could by pushing the heel of his palm against the opposite edge of the blade. Blood poured from the deep cut in Bigirsen's throat, as well as from his mouth.

There would be no more questions. Bigirsen was already dead. Unebolod watched, too stunned and confused to move as the light left Bigirsen's black eyes.

"Take his head and put it in a sack," Dayan ordered as he turned his back on the body and marched to his mount, blood dripping from his sword. "Leave the body for the crows."

Blood pooled on the rocky earth beneath Bigirsen's body. Unebolod thought he would feel more satisfaction seeing the light leave Bigirsen's eyes. Instead, coldness spread through his limbs.

Bigirsen and Issama had conspired against Manduul the entire time.

And Issama had played them all like a horse-head fiddle.

CHAPTER SEVENTEEN

Spoils of War

Dayan, Unebolod, and the rest of their men returned to the remains of Bigirsen's camp shortly before the sun reached its zenith. Bigirsen's head had been placed in a sack and tied to Boke's horse for the time being. Most of the fires had been extinguished. A few gers still threw pillars of smoke into the sky, but the blazing inferno they had created was tamed. The men worked on pulling bodies into a massive pile away from the lake so the decomposition of the dead could not infect the water. The animals or birds could eat the dead. Already, a murder of crows circled above.

As Dayan rode through the scorched camp, the men called out to each other, tossing jokes as the cries of women were suddenly cut off as they died—an odd mixture of amusement and cries of death. Inside a few of the intact gers, Dayan heard the all-too-familiar grunts and cries of sex. Death or submission. Those were the only choices offered to these women.

It tore at Dayan's heart knowing that he had given these men permission to take what they wanted and kill the rest. His deep respect for Mandukhai made him wonder if this way of taking women without giving them a choice was right at all. He could not imagine doing it to Mandukhai—or any woman.

Yet he also knew that these were Uyghur women who had supported their husbands against he and Mandukhai. Bitterness could burrow deep and resurface at the most inopportune time. Dayan could not take that chance. This was the way of life. These were the spoils of war. And men who were denied their share would turn against him. *I have given them permission. They expect these spoils as rewards. I cannot stop them or it makes me look weak.* He tried to block out the sounds.

Dayan stopped outside the guarded ger. A ring of his own men surrounded it now. He dismounted and frowned at the guards.

"He is not a prisoner," Dayan said.

"He is feral, my lord Khan," the guard beside the door said. "He killed two of your men."

Dayan frowned at the closed door. *Nemeku did that? Why?*

Unebolod strode past and opened the door, hand on his sword as he entered. Something in the *orlok* had changed when Bigirsen died. Dayan had expected him to be celebrating, relieved, but he had grown more distant. Unebolod had not said a word since Dayan cut Bigirsen's throat. Dayan glanced at his hands as if expecting to see the blood there. It was not the first man he had killed, but it was the first he had executed. Just remembering the blood and the way the light had left Bigirsen's eyes made Dayan tremble. He clenched his hands into fists as the Great Fist threatened to close around his chest.

At some point, he knew he would have to speak to Unebolod about what Bigirsen had said. Had Unebolod been sleeping with Mandukhai? Was he still? Picturing the two of them together in that way made everything inside of his shrivel up. *Not now.* Right now, he had more immediate matters to attend.

Dayan ducked into the ger. The light inside was dim, and he had to blink to adjust his vision. The floor had one rug, a bucket, and a small mattress on the ground. Otherwise, the space lay wide open.

Most distressing of all was unfamiliar huddled form on the far side of the ger. *Is that Nemeku?* Dayan fought off a wave of shock.

Nemeku crouched low to the ground, arms around his knees, and his long hair hung limp around his swollen face, bruised, bloody. Last time Dayan had seen Nemeku, he was barely eleven—tough despite his age, and stronger than Dayan had been at the time. He had been a boy. This hunched form was no longer a boy, but burgeoning into a man. While he was only fourteen, Nemeku was nearly Dayan's size, and solid despite his damaged condition.

Dayan swallowed the lump in his throat.

Nemeku's gaze slid past Unebold—who he snarled at—and fell on Dayan. Instantly, Nemeku sprang into action, lunging at him. Startled, Dayan stumbled back a step. Nemeku was taller than Dayan had expected, and at least as big as him, if not bigger.

Unebolod seized Nemeku's arm, twisting it around behind his back. The boy raked his free hand across Unebolod's face, digging in his nails. Unebolod did little more than grunt before capturing the other arm and pinning that back as well.

The guards had not exaggerated. Nemeku appeared as feral as a wild dog. His eyes narrowed suspiciously at Dayan, pupils dilated. He bared his teeth at Dayan as well, as if he intended to take a bite right out of him.

"Nemeku, did my men do this to you?" Dayan asked. If any of his men had disobeyed his command not to harm Nemeku, he would kill them.

"This is clearly his father's handiwork," Unebolod muttered.

Nemeku tugged at Unebolod's grip, but he couldn't break it, no matter how he bucked. Unebolod nodded toward Dayan, but his gaze slid past Dayan to something else. *The door? Does he want me to leave him alone with Nemeku?*

"Please, don't hurt him," a small female voice said from behind Dayan.

Alarmed, Dayan turned on his heel.

A young woman who couldn't have been any older than himself cowered in the shadows near the door, hugging herself. *Oh, that's what Unebolod was trying to tell me.* He had spotted the girl and was warning Dayan.

Like Nemeku, her eye was swollen. Dayan shuffled toward her, holding his hands up for her to see. His shadow shifted off of her. Sunlight streamed down on her face and accentuated the angry red marks on her throat. *What was Bigirsen doing in here?* Dayan wondered, disgusted with the condition of these two.

"Touch her, and I'll kill you all," Nemeku growled.

Dayan glanced at Nemeku only for a moment. "It's okay." Dayan held out one hand toward her.

She shrank back against the wall.

"I won't hurt you," Dayan reassured her. "I am Dayan Khan. You are under my protection now."

Her gaze flitted to Nemeku, and tears welled in her eyes. "It isn't his fault."

"I know." Dayan pointed at her neck. "Who did that to you?"

A young woman like her would have made any of his men thrilled today. Did they leave those marks on her? There were some base desires in men that he just couldn't understand.

"His father," she said. Her mouth curled back in disgust.

Bigirsen had done this to both of them? *No wonder so many people hate him. He has no respect for anyone else*, Dayan thought, then corrected himself. Had. He *had* no respect for anyone else. Bigirsen was dead now. *I won, but it still feels like I lost.*

Would Mandukhai be proud of his victory? If not, it had all been for nothing. And he would have nightmares for no reason.

"When the fighting started, and the guards abandoned the doors, I realized no one was attacking here," she said. "So I hid in here with him." She cast a sympathetic look at Nemeku. Dayan recognized something else in her eyes. A look he knew all too well because he wore it far too often. Affection. Longing.

Dayan crouched in front of her, leaving a safe distance between them so he didn't startle her or further enrage Nemeku. "He is my cousin, and the son of a Borjigin Princess. I will allow no one to harm him."

She cast a scowl over his shoulder at Unebolod.

"He is only protecting me," Dayan reassured her. "What is your name?"

"Orghana."

Dayan smiled. "Named after a heroic princess. Your family honors you. I'm surprised to find such a name among the Uyghur."

Nemeku spit in Dayan's direction. "Pitiful excuse for a Khan!"

Unebolod made a sound of warning in his throat, but Dayan shook his head. They both knew Mandukhai would be furious if anything happened to Nemeku.

"I'm not Uyghur," she whispered.

Dayan returned his attention to Orghana sharply. "So you were married? I'm sorry."

Orghana shook her head, and for just a moment, she looked like a Mongol princess. Was she angry that his men had killed her husband? Did she not believe he was sorry?

"I'm not," she said with fevered anger. Her hand drifted to her throat, and she tenderly brushed her fingers over the marks on her neck. "I hated my husband. He was a horrible man. My brother, Legusi, gave me to him as a show of loyalty."

"*Lord* Legusi?" Unebolod said. "Khan of the Ordos tribes?"

Dayan stood and stepped back, staring down at Orghana as a new sense of elation warmed him. His heart leaped into his throat. Today, he had killed Bigirsen and captured the sister of the very man he would ride against next? He tipped his head back and gazed at the smoke-hole in the ger's roof.

Unebolod inched closer, still holding Nemeku, who had settled down somewhat. "Dayan—"

"I know." Dayan waved the comment off. "Tengri smiles on this day."

Orghana bestowed a gaze of abject affection on Nemeku. "Please, my lord Khan, let me care for Nemeku. I can calm him down."

Dayan nodded. "I will come back with dinner. You will both be safe here."

"Thank you," Orghana whimpered, pressing herself to the dirt to prostrate herself at his feet.

Dayan turned and marched toward the door, motioning for Unebolod to follow. The *orlok* refused to release Nemeku until he stepped outside. The moment he let go, Nemeku ran to Orghana, throwing himself over her like a protective shield.

Unebolod closed the door as Dayan instructed the men to guard the door. No one was to enter this ger without him present. As he strode away, looking for something to eat, Unebolod matched his stride.

"She will be a useful tool in the fight to come," Unebolod said. "What will Legusi give to protect his sister?"

"Not as much as we might hope," Dayan said. "He gave her to Bigirsen, knowing full well what sort of man he was. I'm not sure she is as powerful a bargaining chip as you think."

Unebolod grunted after a moment of consideration. "All the same, if you offer an alliance in exchange for her hand, it might make all of this much easier."

Dayan chuckled and shook his head. Unebolod didn't understand him at all. "I'm not interested in her." The very idea of taking another woman as a wife had never entered his mind. To Dayan, no other woman could compare to Mandukhai.

"You can have multiple wives, Dayan," Unebolod said. "It is normal for a man to have as many as four. Especially one in your position. If you choose the right women, like Orghana, it can smooth out ruffled feathers and further instill peace. Such is the purpose of a Khan's wives."

"Says the man without a wife." Dayan stopped suddenly, turning to face Unebolod. He had to know the truth of Bigirsen's words. It had already wormed into his stomach and eaten at his insides. Knowing they cared for each other was one thing. Knowing they had acted on those feelings was something else entirely. "Is it true?"

Unebolod flinched. "What?"

"Did you share your bed with her? Do you still?" Dayan's voice broke over the last question. He held his breath as he waited for an answer.

Unebolod stared at him with that stony, emotionless face. But Dayan didn't back down. Unebolod swallowed hard enough to make a sound. "This is hardly the place for this conversation," Unebolod said at last, lowering his voice and glancing at the men milling around them.

Dayan's gaze swept the open space. Dozens of his men worked to dig for loot or move bodies. Many of them glanced at the Khan and *orlok* curiously but dipped their gazes away the moment they noticed Dayan staring. Unebolod was right. Because if he called him out in the open, he would have no choice but to punish him in front of everyone. Privacy gave him more control over the consequences.

"Follow me," Dayan ordered, then turned and headed for one of the nearby gers.

Dayan ducked inside, startling warrior and his captive woman tangled around each other. As far as he could tell, they were fully clothed still. Both of them froze as they saw him, followed a second later by Unebolod.

"Out," Unebolod snapped.

The two scrambled to obey. As they left, Dayan opened the smoke hole to let in light. Unebolod closed the door, then turned to him with his hands folded behind his back.

"Well?" Dayan asked.

Unebolod took a deep breath and let it out in a huff. "It was a long time ago. Before you."

The Great Fist closed around Dayan's chest and squeezed tight. He grabbed the support post in the ger to keep upright as his vision darkened. Now was *not* the time to show weakness. Dayan could hear his heart pounding all the way into his ears.

"After Manduul?" Dayan asked, hardly able to get the words out.

"Once." Unebolod straightened, as if preparing for Dayan to lash out at him. "And before."

Dayan smothered a groan. It hadn't just been once. If it had only been once, Dayan could have excused it as a fluke, a moment of weakness. But they had both gone back for more, which suggested it had meant something to them. And when she was married to Manduul ... Would she betray him if he forced her to stay with him? Dayan knew she loved Unebolod, even if she would never say as much. He could not force her to be with him if she wanted to be with someone else. Dayan just didn't have the strength for it. How long would she stay faithful to him before turning to Unebolod? The very thought crushed his soul.

Unebolod seemed to understand at least some of what Dayan worried over, because he said, "She never loved Manduul, Dayan."

"I know that."

"He was not good to her in the beginning. I don't have the heart to tell you the things he did to her. But a thing like that never leaves you." Unebolod sighed and rubbed his forehead. "She wouldn't do the same to you. She loves you."

"How do you know that?" Dayan said, and he hated how small and weak his voice sounded.

"How do you not?"

The questions brought with it an uneasy silence that made the air grow so thick Dayan couldn't breathe. Mandukhai had not loved Manduul. Dayan could accept that. And he knew that she loved him, but perhaps not in the right way. Even if he could trust her not to approach Unebolod in desperation, the *orlok* had given Manduul Khan his word. And then took his wife.

"You betrayed him. You betrayed your Khan for her." Dayan trembled all over and prayed Unebolod could not tell. "Why didn't you just take her when you had a chance, before she could promise herself to me?"

Unebolod's upper lip twitched. "Could you just take her?" He shook his head, and the movement seemed stiff. "She was not a prize or the spoils of war. She was a queen. Besides, she made herself perfectly clear. For me to be Great Khan, I would have had to raise you as my son, and when you came of age, she expected me to abdicate the title to you. And our sons would have had no claim over you and your line. They would have lived their lives in your shadow. She would accept nothing less."

"But you could have had *her*," Dayan said. "Would that have been such a terrible sacrifice? The title for her?"

"Would you give it up for her?"

"Yes." Dayan didn't even hesitate.

Unebolod's jaw slackened only a little, but the alarm Dayan's response caused was written all over his stunned face. "It was not the loss of the title that bothered me most."

"What was it then?"

Unebolod fell silent. For some reason, the *orlok* would not answer.

Sudden fear surged in Dayan. Unebolod would do anything for her—and that had to include killing him. "Why am I still alive?" The question came out far more vicious than he had intended.

Unebolod's answer cut deeply.

"I ask myself that every day."

The Great Fist refused to let up on his heart or lungs. Dayan struggled for every breath. A thousand needles prickled his skin. His heart tightened so painfully he feared it would explode from the pressure. He gripped the center post tight enough to turn his knuckles white. He fumbled at his belt and pulled out his hunting knife. Unebolod flinched, but didn't back away. Dayan tossed it at Unebolod's feet.

Unebolod stared at the knife, blinking dumbly at it. "What should I do with that? Kill you?"

"I can't live with your shadow constantly casting over me," Dayan grumbled.

Unebolod snorted. "Welcome to my entire life. I won't kill you. I gave my word, and my word is iron."

"Just as you gave Manduul your word?" Dayan snapped. He began feeling lightheaded. "How long before you betray me as you betrayed him?"

"I have suffered for it!" Unebolod roared.

Dayan flinched. He had never heard such anger from Unebolod directed his way before.

"The High Heavens saw fit to subject me to a lifetime of torture! Did I betray Manduul's trust? Yes. Worse yet, I don't regret a moment of it," Unebolod said. "And for that, Fate has played a cruel trick on me, offering me the love of a woman I can never have while forcing me to watch her with someone else—while forcing me to serve him! *Twice*!" He nudged the knife toward Dayan with the toe of his boot, a clear sign he would not pick it up. "I will play my part. I will do my duty. And then I will die." Unebolod's face reddened as he ranted. "And if all I leave behind is an empire in your name, then I have at least left behind an empire!"

Dayan winced, but the Great Fist let up a little. His heart still ached from the pressure, but it no longer felt ready to explode. "You don't have to leave nothing behind. You can show your loyalty by taking a different wife. One that will help bring us peace."

Unebolod's brows shot up his wide forehead. "Orghana? You aren't serious! I gave Mandukhai my word. I won't do it."

Dayan tensed. "What word was that?"

Unebolod's lips parted as if he realized he had said too much. For a moment, the two of them just stared at each other. As the silence stretched, Dayan grew more certain Unebolod had no intention of answering him.

"Tell me now, *orlok*, or I will find someone else to serve in your place."

Unebolod growled. "You are becoming quite full of yourself."

"I am becoming the Great Khan I was meant to be, and I won't ask a third time."

Unebolod squared his shoulders and straightened his back, glancing around the ger as if he could find escape, as if he forgot it was at his back. "That I would not take another wife."

"You won't get *her*."

"I know that."

"Yet still, you refuse."

Unebolod's lips thinned in a tight line, and he nodded.

"I see. So your word is only worthwhile if you give it to her." Dayan strode forward and snatched his knife off the floor, pointing it at Unebolod's cheek. "I have done what I promised her. When we return, she will have a man worthy of her. If I have my way, that will not be you. And once she is with me, the slightest hint that you have touched her or looked at her the wrong way and your life is forfeit. Because your word to her may be worthwhile, but your word to me is clearly flexible."

Dayan stalked out, quivering, though he couldn't be certain if it was rage or fear that caused such a deep reaction. In no uncertain terms, he had just staked his claim on Mandukhai, as if he could simply plant his flag on her heart. Yet he knew it would never be so simple. She would not refuse him. Her oath forbade it. But that did not mean she would remain faithful if she still desired someone else. She had already betrayed one husband for Unebolod. And Unebolod had already betrayed one Khan for her.

The reality, Dayan knew, was much harder to face.

He would either have to give her a choice and risk losing her for good.

Or he had to kill Unebolod—and she might never forgive him.

Unebolod couldn't move for several minutes after Dayan left. There would be no more secret glances. He could never touch Mandukhai again, or Dayan would kill him. He firmly believed that. After watching the coldness in the Khan during the battle and the execution of Bigirsen, Unebolod did not doubt Dayan for a moment. After all, he had done all of this for Mandukhai. Dayan would not risk losing her. He had made himself very clear.

Dayan would do anything for her, and everything to keep her. It was exactly what she deserved—a man willing to fight for her, to stand up for her, to listen to her. Dayan, even at such a young age, was everything Unebolod had never been for her.

The finality of Dayan's warning broke through the cracks Unebolod had worked so hard to hide. The moment he was alone, Unebolod stood, rooted in place, as tears rolled unchecked down his cheeks.

Mandukhai had never been his.

And she never would be.

Yet he still could not let go.

CHAPTER EIGHTEEN

Feeding A Starving Wolf

BAUTUO – MID-WINTER 1479

Mandukhai tugged at her plain, fur-lined coat to bring it close to her neck. Bitter winter wind bit into her back as she rode through the city gates of Bautuo with only Soke and Torgus to accompany her. She had even left Dust behind, riding a chestnut mare from her herd. The pale white stallion had become recognizable, and she needed to blend in.

Soke led the way as they rode single file through the crowded city streets. Torgus brought up the rear, leading a packhorse. Citizens glanced at them occasionally, but the trio had dressed in common clothing and hidden anything on the packhorse that might draw attention to them. To anyone else, they were passersby who didn't deserve a second glance.

The city was bursting with activity as everyone went about their daily tasks. Shutters on stone homes were closed against the winter winds. Smoke pumped out of brick chimney stacks into the air, giving everything a scent of dried burning dung mingled with wood-smoke. The roads were narrow, packed with dirt damp from recent snow melts and buckets of dumped refuse. Children played out in the open, while others huddled near doorways with their bodies curled against the wind.

Ming and Mongol blended together in a manner Mandukhai had never believed possible. Some were even hard to distinguish from one another as they mixed the style of their clothing in an odd ethnic blend of unity. They traded goods and services before her eyes, shared polite words, and seemed friendly. All she had ever known of the Ming were soldiers and courtesans acting superior to her own people. Somehow, the people of Bautuo found peace with one another.

They passed a forge with fires burning so hot she could feel their heat from outside despite the frigid winter wind. The ting of hammers reverberated from within. *I could do so much with these resources!* This realization gave Mandukhai a healthy new respect for what Lord Qori had managed here.

A merchant with a dirty, wrinkled face jumped at Mandukhai's mare, thrusting his wares at her—bracelets of silver and gold, likely stolen, judging by his appearance. Torgus nudged his mount forward to force the merchant back. But Mandukhai's heart wept for the man. She produced a coin, asking for one of the silver bracelets. He expressed his gratitude, bowing repeatedly as he backed up again. His eyes darted to Torgus, then to Soke as he bit the coin to determine its authenticity.

Torgus made a sound of disgust as they continued. She knew that he, like many of her warriors, felt cities and walls went against everything true Mongols lived for—the open steppe, freedom, prosperity, strength. Cities had walls and permanence that held back Mongols and made them weak. Genghis had expressed similar beliefs centuries ago, claiming these cities and walls were the very reason no one could truly stand up to his army. But she could not lead as Genghis had. She would not conquer the world. She only wanted to bring all the tribes together under one banner, as they had been so long ago.

The closer they rode to the center of the city where Lord Qori took up residence in a small palace, the fewer people crowded the streets. Stone homes were closed to the cold, but Mandukhai could hear voices from within. The homes were larger here, and some had gated entrances.

"I don't like this," Soke muttered ahead of Mandukhai. "It feels like a trap." He subtly adjusted his grip on the reins so it would be easier to draw his sword or bow at a moment's notice.

Mandukhai ignored him. She shared the sentiment, and it made her stomach twist in knots, but she would not share her fear with anyone else. This needed to be done. The results of this meeting would solidify the Ordos intentions one way or another—as well as their fate. *Does Lord Qori realize his actions will determine not only his fate, but that of all the Ordos subtribes?*

They approached the walls of the small palace—a wide, two-story building made of wood and stone. The large gate was open, and ten Mongol warriors blocked the path within. Soke edged closer to them and pulled a paper from his own fur-lined coat, offering it to one warrior. "Lord Qori sent for us."

The warrior took the paper and examined it, then eyed the three of them with intense distrust. Another stepped forward and glanced at the paper, then whispered something to the first, who grimaced. The way he examined Mandukhai made her uncomfortable, but she only raised her chin. With a gruff command to his men, he waved Mandukhai's party through the gates. The guards stepped out of the way to give the three of them space to pass.

The palace embraced an open courtyard, and the roof swept downward over a long balcony and terrace around the space. A light dusting of snow covered the ground. Mandukhai reined to a halt near a fountain in the center of the courtyard. She dismounted, then stepped toward the fountain, inactive for the winter. A stone crane stood on thin legs, wings spread outward and beak open. No doubt water spilled from the beak when the fountain was functioning. Instead, the water had frozen solid in the fountain's base.

Several servants bustle around them to gather the horses to take them to the stable. Mandukhai ignored them as she studied the crane.

"It's beautiful, isn't it?" A man asked from across the courtyard. His boots crunched the ground as he approached.

Mandukhai glanced at him when he stopped beside her. He was close to her own age, dressed in a strange mix of Mongol and Ming style just as many of the citizens of Bautuo had done. The colors on his deel were brilliant in the dull light of the winter sun. He wore his hair back in a topknot. A band of leather stitched with Mongol runes was wrapped around his forehead.

"Lord Qori, I assume," she said, turning her attention back to the crane. "It is well-crafted stone. How do those thin legs hold up so much stone?"

"How do the thin legs of a real crane hold it up?" he asked. "Even the most delicate of creatures is strong and graceful." He turned to her. "Not unlike yourself. Please come inside. It's cold out here and I prefer the warmth of the hearth fires."

Mandukhai turned to Soke, who had come up behind her. He wore his sword on his hip now, and his hard gaze almost dared Qori to try harming her. She inwardly sighed and waved toward Torgus and the packhorse. "Where shall my man take my things?"

"I will have my servants bring them to your rooms," Qori replied. "But I would prefer not to stand in clear view of the open gates for too long. Please. Come inside. Your men can accompany you."

Soke and Torgus trailed along on Mandukhai's heels as she walked beside Qori toward the open door, glowing with life from lights within.

The inside of the main space had several benches and chairs of polished dark wood. The entire set matched. High backs of ornate, boxy design and carved cranes. Clawed feet on the legs and sweeping arms. In the center of the space, a table with matching feet and trim with carved cranes held a tea set. Steam rose from the pot. On the far wall, a brick fireplace blazed with life. The dark wood mantel shined in the flickering flames. Mandukhai examined the wood panel walls around the fireplace. Did he not worry those wooden walls would catch fire?

Qori motioned for Mandukhai to sit. She chose a bench where Torgus and Soke could sit beside her on either side. Qori eased into his own chair. The moment he did, the doors to the next room opened. Soke and Torgus both tensed, hands falling to their weapons.

A team of servants rushed into the room, setting out a small feast on the table.

Qori chuckled. "I see you don't trust me."

"I have no opinion either way," Mandukhai replied. "You have given me no reason to either trust or distrust you. My men, on the other hand, trust no one."

A pretty woman in silk just as fine as Qori's glided into the room. Her face was plump and round, and her hair was swept up in an intricate series of braids that wrapped in a loose bun. Jewels crowned her hair, accented by a comb of jade. She immediately began pouring tea.

"My wife, Sarnai," Qori said. He beamed at his wife with open admiration.

Mandukhai felt a flash of jealousy. She wanted a husband to look at her like that. "Thank you for welcoming me into your home, Lady Sarnai."

"I have been looking forward to meeting you, Khatun," Sarnai said as she offered a cup of tea to Mandukhai.

Would they poison the tea? It would be the easiest way to deal with Mandukhai. But if she refused the tea when she had been invited into their home, it would be an insult. She slid her hand around the cup with a murmur of thanks but did not take a drink. Sarnai poured a cup for Soke, but he politely declined. It would not be an insult for him to refuse since he was simply a guard, as far as Qori knew. In truth, Soke was one of the highest-ranked men in her army. Sarnai frowned, then offered to Torgus, who shook his head. Slightly distressed, Sarnai held the cup to her husband. Qori accepted with a thankful smile.

"Please help yourselves to the food as well," Qori said. "We have plenty more where that came from."

Mandukhai glanced at the fruits, a rarity among Mongols, especially at this time of year. A steaming wooden bowl of rice rested at the center of a series of other foods—smoked bluegill, steamed crab, grilled prawns, steamed green beans. Her mouth watered just smelling the food. How could he acquire such things in the heart of winter? *Mendu warned me Qori is a man of luxury. What kind of information did he have to give in exchange for this feast? And how long before he shares my presence? Has he already?*

This visit was a game. Mandukhai had played this game of politics more than enough times with other men. She had but to appease Qori, make him relax around her, and then she could move in for the kill. Such a battle would not be won over a single meal. It would take time.

This also meant she had to drink the tea and take the risk that they had poisoned her. If she showed her fear, Qori might doubt her strength. Mandukhai watched Sarnai settle in a chair beside her husband, folding her hands in her lap. She would not eat before he did. Mandukhai took a drink of the tea, just enough to appease them.

"It's a bad time of year to make a trip to Bautuo," Qori said as he ate without shame. "This winter has been harsh."

"You seem to have managed fine," Mandukhai said as she reached for a plum. They could not easily poison a whole plum. "I admit I am impressed with the wealth you have acquired here. It cannot be easy to rule a city like Bautuo with so many Ming within the walls."

"As long as I leave them to their daily lives, they are content," Qori replied, then stuffed a hunk of crab meat into his mouth and chewed loudly. "My wife is fascinated with you."

"I don't see why."

Sarnai shifted in her chair, adding some rice and smoked bluegill to a small wooden bowl. "You have become quite legendary, my lady Khatun," she said. The awe dripped from her voice. "A woman trusted and adored not only by her late husband, but by the men who follow her still. You lead the nation! Not many women could dare to aspire to your level."

"Do you?" Mandukhai asked, eyeing Sarnai curiously. Perhaps the way across the river was not with Qori, but with his wife.

Sarnai flushed as she settled back with her bowl. "No. I could never. Even managing my husband's household is almost more than I can handle."

"Nonsense," Qori said around a mouthful of crab meat. "She is being modest. Sarnai is a force in her own right."

Soke and Torgus both relaxed enough to dig into the offered food, though neither was shy about watching not only the couple hosting them, but the guard beside the closed door to the courtyard.

The feast carried on with small talk for so long Mandukhai found her mind drifting far away, tired of their conversation. Sarnai gave Mandukhai a tour once they finished their meal, showing her the bathhouse, then the kitchen where servants kept busy cleaning from their meal. With a few sharp commands from Sarnai, the servants leaped into action to obey. Clearly this woman was more adept at commanding the household than she gave herself credit for.

At last, Sarnai escorted Mandukhai, Soke, and Torgus to their rooms.

Mandukhai's room occupied much of the second floor of the west wing of the U-shaped home. It was much larger than Mandukhai had expected, with an outer chamber she knew Torgus and Soke would take turns sleeping in to protect her.

Thickly quilted silk blankets and furs covered a massive bed with a downy mattress inside the innermost chamber. A fire already burned in the fireplace on the far wall, and the lantern on the bedside table added light to a dark corner. Mandukhai's bags from the packhorse sat on a bench at the foot of the bed.

"Feel free to use the bathhouse," Sarnai said from the doorway between Mandukhai's sleeping chambers and the outer chambers. "The water is fresh and easily heated to your liking. I can have my personal female servants help you wash in rosewater."

"Where will my men be sleeping?" Mandukhai asked as she pressed her palm against the soft mattress. It was like a cloud!

"We have prepared another suite beside yours for your men," Sarnai replied.

Sarnai edged into the room, hands folded in the sleeves of her deel. Sincere respect shined in her eyes and softened the lines of her face. "You are safe here, Mandukhai Khatun. My husband is no fool. He knows you have more men than him, and near to here. He also knows you would never come with so few guards of your own unless you were confident in their skills."

If only the words offered comfort. But Mandukhai could not let her guard down.

Sarnai chewed her lip, eyeing Torgus as he inspected every nook and cranny of the chambers for hidden danger. "My lady Khatun, is it true you charged across a battlefield with nothing but a sword and no helmet to protect your head, ahead of the rest of your men, when you tamed the Oirat?" Sarnai asked reverently.

"I did nothing more than any other warrior would have done when faced with probable victory," Mandukhai replied.

"I look forward to getting to know you," Sarnai said. "For now, I will leave you to get settled." Then she slipped out and closed the door.

The moment Sarnai was gone and the doors of the outer chamber were firmly closed, Soke strode into the bedchamber and leaned against the doorframe. "We will take turns sleeping in the outer chamber," he said, nodding toward Torgus. "The other will remain on guard outside the door. I don't trust these people."

Mandukhai nodded. She could argue with him, but knew that Khorchin stubbornness would make any argument as useful as arguing with a wall. "Get rest tonight, Soke. I have a task for you while we are here. It will keep the two of you busy, and there may be times you have no choice but to trust I am safe here alone."

"Alone!" Soke's arms dropped to his sides.

Mandukhai held up a hand to silence him. "Patience, Soke. It will only be during the day for brief periods of time, as need dictates. You hold a position of respect. Qori's Ordos men will listen to you."

"Only if I tell them who I am," Soke interrupted.

"And you will. Because you have the power to do here what neither Torgus nor myself can do."

"Which is?"

"During our stay, you will take at least an hour each day infiltrating Qori's inner circle," Mandukhai replied calmly. "Meet his top-ranked men as quickly as possible. Tell stories about the divine right of the Khan and myself, in whatever way you see fit. Your words need to come from your own heart to make them believe you." She drew in a deep breath. "To believe in your absolute faith. Be certain to share any morsel of truth in how you doubted us at first, and why you believe in us now, that we are guided by the spirit of Genghis. You can sell the two of us to these men far better than I can."

If he could convince the men of this, Dayan's bloodline would only seal their resolve that the Mongol Empire could be restored under the young Khan's rule—and under her own.

"We need an escape plan, Mandukhai," Soke said, glancing over his shoulder at the closed door of the outer chamber. He lowered his voice. "If this goes wrong, we need to know exactly how we plan to get out of this place alive."

As much as she hoped it would not come to fleeing, Mandukhai knew Soke spoke the truth. "Which will be another part of your job. As well as Torgus. Scout the palace, the city, the outer walls. I am counting on the two of you to learn as much as you can about this city's defenses and plan our way out."

That seemed to satisfy Soke. He relaxed against the doorframe, then slid into the outer chamber.

"Torgus, you take first watch so Soke can rest," Mandukhai said. "He seems too tense."

Torgus nodded and left her alone, sliding the inner door closed behind him.

Mandukhai sagged as she let out a slow breath. She needed rest, but first, she would see about this bathhouse.

The next morning, Sarnai appeared in the open corridor the moment Mandukhai stepped out of her chambers. The two of them walked the grounds as they chatted. Sarnai took her through the garden, which Torgus examined with expert eyes before allowing Mandukhai to dismiss him. He would not leave her until he was certain no danger lingered in the foliage.

Sarnai asked questions about Mandukhai's marriage to Manduul—had she been happy with him? How had Mandukhai managed to gain enough respect from the Great Khan for him to leave her control of the entire nation? Mandukhai had done her best to answer questions as amicably as possible. She did not dare mention how Manduul had treated her in the beginning, or how weak he had been, how many mistakes he had made. Instead, she poured out only affection for her late husband.

"I have heard that you were quite close with Unebolod *Noyan* at one point, before you named Dayan Khan," Sarnai said as she settled on a stone bench beside a frozen koi pond. "My husband was convinced you would name him Great Khan after your late husband passed."

Mandukhai sighed and gazed at the frozen pond, a distant look in her eyes. "I nearly did. He is a good man. One of the best I have ever known. But I made a sacred vow when my husband died. I promised the Lords that I would do what was best for the Mongol Nation, and all the people within it. Naturally, when an heir of Genghis emerged, my path was chosen for me."

Sarnai fidgeted with the hem of her sleeves. "Sure, but were you in love?"

"What does love have to do with it?" Mandukhai asked. "I gave my heart and soul to the Nation, not a man."

For several minutes, the two women sat in silence. Mandukhai held her fur coat close to her body as she watched the gentle breeze make the long branches of the willow tree sway. Periodically, a branch would dip down and slide across the surface of the ice.

On the second day, Mandukhai had seen little of Lord Qori, as if he avoided her. Torgus and Soke worried over the increased activity around the palace grounds. Soke was convinced they were up to something, and Mandukhai had to admit the activity did seem unusual. Especially when she came across Sarnai leaning close to one of her servants in an urgent, hushed conversation.

"Is everything alright, Lady Sarnai?" Mandukhai asked sweetly as she strolled up to the two women shamelessly.

Sarnai stiffened, spinning to stare at Mandukhai like a deer caught by a hunter. She flicked her wrist, and the servant hustled past Mandukhai, her head dipped down. "It's fine. Just some trouble with one of our fish shipments." Sarnai plastered an innocent smile on her face. "I would love if you could join me for lunch."

"I would be delighted," Mandukhai said. "Will your husband be joining us?"

Sarnai started toward the central room where they ate their meals. Mandukhai fell into stride alongside the other woman effortlessly. "Sadly no. I do apologize for his absence, but he was called away this morning by some of the city leaders on some urgent city matters. I'm afraid I don't pay much attention to what he does."

Mandukhai did not believe for a moment that Sarnai did not know exactly what her husband did at all times. The woman came across as highly intelligent. But this mysterious disappearance of Qori would only further arouse suspicion in Soke and Torgus.

"Where are your guards, my lady?" Sarnai asked pleasantly.

"I have reassured them I feel perfectly safe here, and so I sent them to train to work off some of their energy." Mandukhai cocked her head slightly at Sarnai. "You know men when they have pent-up energy. It does no one any good." She released a lilting laugh. "I'm sure Soke has already found a few of your husband's men to relieve of coins. He does like to gamble."

If Soke had not yet penetrated the inner circle, the prospect of winning some of the Khan's gold should get him in the door the moment Sarnai shared the gossip.

The two women settled in the central room. Sarnai gave a few sharp commands to the servants, and in minutes they had a small lunch feast spread before them.

"How long have you and your husband been married?" Mandukhai asked as she nodded politely to the servant pouring her tea.

"Nearly fifteen years," Sarnai said.

"And you have no children?"

"We do. They spend most of their time in the city with friends, or hunting," Sarnai said. "They are on a hunting trip right now with some of Qori's officers."

Mandukhai wondered at the timing. He sent his sons away when she came to visit. Was he worried what she would do, or that they would get in the way and let a secret slip?

"Any other wives?" Mandukhai asked

A haunted expression crossed Sarnai's face and she quickly averted her gaze to her food. "She died. E-eight years ago."

Sudden understanding slammed into Mandukhai and she frowned. "Oh. I'm sorry. Were you ... were you there? When the Ming attacked?"

Sarnai nodded. "It was the most horrible thing I have ever experienced. I thought—thought I would die. My husband was furious. He took his men and what remained of our people and came north. He was so angry with the Ming that ... well..." She waved around the room.

Mandukhai nodded. Qori had turned his vengeance on the city of Bautuo. He had stolen this stronghold from the Ming. "Well, he seems to have everything under control now." How could Qori work alongside the Ming after what had happened at the red salt lake?

"These walls protected us when the tribes began turning against one another," Sarnai said. "He saved so many of us by taking this city."

"A commendable act." Mandukhai reached over and gave Sarnai's hand a reassuring squeeze.

The other woman looked up and offered a timid smile. "I would love to hear more of your story. I heard you gave a sacred oath at the Shrine of the First Queen when you named Dayan Khan. That you bound yourself to him. He must be a man now. Have you...?"

Mandukhai couldn't help blushing. "Our relationship is strong." There was no way she would tell this woman that she and Dayan had not been officially married or shared a bed. Not when she needed these people to follow their legitimacy.

For the next hour, Mandukhai shared stories about Dayan—making him as extraordinary as she could without lying outright. A lie would undo their progress. Instead, she carefully stepped around the truth to paint the picture as she wanted it to be painted, even sharing her vision of a united Mongol Nation, a restoration of their former glory. No doubt every word she spoke would be relayed to Qori that night.

By her third night in the palace—with too much time alone with her own thoughts—Mandukhai's agitation over the status of Dayan's mission burrowed into her mind. Was he still alive? Had he killed Bigirsen? So far from Lake Dai and her own court, Mandukhai felt blind to the world.

Soke stood inside the closed door to her inner chamber as she paced in distress. Mandukhai told Soke about her fear, and he shared her concern, not only over Dayan's fate, but over Unebolod's as well.

"Do you trust him?" Soke asked. He stood with all the casual grace of a predator prepared to kill anything that looked at her the wrong way.

"Who?" Mandukhai hoped Soke couldn't see her trembling.

"Dayan, of course."

"Yes."

"Then relax." Soke said it so plainly it only irritated Mandukhai even more. "He will return to you."

"You don't know that."

"I do."

"How?" Mandukhai snapped. She hadn't meant to be sharp with him, but her nerves were coiled so tight all the time. Dayan had been gone months now. A lot could have happened in that time. A lot could have changed.

"Because you do," Soke said. "And because I know Unebolod. He will do everything in his power to bring the Great Khan back alive. Even if it means abandoning the mission."

Mandukhai swallowed the thick lump that formed in her throat. She wished she could share in his confidence.

"Maybe this distance will be good for the two of you," Soke said with all the diplomacy of a punch to the head. "People grow and change."

Mandukhai gaped at him.

"And what if he has grown too much or changed too much?" Mandukhai asked. She hadn't meant to say it aloud, but now she could not take it back.

The inevitable loomed on the horizon. Either Dayan would set her free to choose, or she would have to accept a more intimate relationship with him. Could she accept Dayan as her husband and share his bed? The very thought twisted her stomach. Dayan was handsome, for certain. All the women noticed that. Sometimes, Mandukhai swore she heard them whispering about it as well. But to her, he was still the broken boy she had rescued from certain death. Over the years, Mandukhai had done her best to avoid seeing him as a son, knowing that one day she might have to accept him as her husband, but that did not stop her from seeing him as a boy.

Soke shifted feet. "On a sling, there is the strap and the stick. No matter how much the strap stretches away from the stick, it always bounces back."

The analogy broke through Mandukhai's melancholy, and she laughed. "Are you saying we are little more than a sling?"

"I am saying that as long as he breathes, he will always come back to you."

Mandukhai bit her lip and raised her brows. "Are we still speaking of Dayan?"

Soke shrugged. "Maybe. Maybe not." Soke was one of the few who knew something of the depth of feelings she and Unebolod had shared. He probably knew more about Unebolod's current feelings than she did. *Does that mean he still waits for me?* It was unfair of her to even expect it.

As she often did when worried about their survival, Mandukhai remembered the promise Dayan had made before he had left. If he failed to kill

Bigirsen, he would free her to choose. If he defeated Bigirsen, he had hoped she would see him as worthy.

But if she got to choose, what choice would she really make?

"We are wasting time here, Mandukhai," Soke said. "Lord Qori is dragging his feet in the mud, sending his wife to host you instead of himself. I have a way out."

"I have not been wasting time," Mandukhai replied, settling on the edge of her bed. "Do your wives talk to you about rumors they hear?"

He grimaced, but nodded.

"These past two days, I have been carefully feeding Lady Sarnai the information her husband needs to hear," Mandukhai said. "If you want to hunt with predators, you must first feed the starving wolf. I have done just that. And tomorrow, I will tame him as well. We are nearly there, Soke. He will bow to me as the others have."

"And if he doesn't?"

"Did you not just say we have a way out?" she asked, smirking. "Have you done as I have asked among his men?"

"The best I can. But if I'm being honest, I don't know if this will work. They seemed to believe me, but at the same time, they really enjoy the riches they have gained under Lord Qori's guidance. I'm not sure they would turn on him."

"They don't need to betray him. Only convince him. I have faith, Soke," Mandukhai said, hoping her tone conveyed conviction. She had to believe this to be true, or everything could fall apart. "Genghis has blessed us. The High Heavens guide us. The spirits would not send us this far only to have us fail."

The knock at the outer door and call for dinner startled the two of them from their conversation. Soke's hand fell on his sword before he relaxed.

"Where is Torgus?" she asked.

"He should be posted outside," Soke said, but the edge in his tone made it clear he worried something was about to go horribly wrong.

CHAPTER NINETEEN

Invisible Scars

The argument with Unebolod had left Dayan shaken and riddled with doubt. When he left the ger, he had climbed to the edge of the basin and sat in mediation with his guards around him until he felt the sun setting at his back. Mediation gave him the ability to focus his thoughts, center his emotions, and remove the nagging sensations that ate away at him. Today, even after lengthy meditation, he still worried over the problem of Unebolod's devotion to Mandukhai.

Dayan's father had been killed for cavorting with Manduul Khan's first wife, yet Unebolod still lived. Which meant he knew how to hide his betrayal. While Dayan's marriage to Mandukhai remained informal, like a promise he could choose when he came of age—as he was now—she was still bound to him until that day. Did that make Unebolod guilty as his father had been? From his own lips, he had admitted bedding her when she was still married to Manduul. Dayan could not hold him accountable for doing so *after* Manduul had died, before she had made her promise at the Shrine of the First Queen. Could he hold him accountable for stealing a dead man's wife? Would she resent him if he did?

Dayan strode toward Nemeku's ger as the sun set, with his guards always on his heels. Outside the door, he stopped and removed his sword from the belt, handing it to the guard outside the door.

"My lord Khan," Boke said, shifting the wicker basket of food and drink they had scavenged from a ger. "Why do you disarm yourself?"

Dayan removed his knife as well, offering it to the guard. "Bigirsen has abused Nemeku for who knows how long. Perhaps nearly two years. Perhaps less. For whatever reason, Nemeku sees me as a threat. I will not enter armed and let him think I mean him harm."

Jangi jogged over, bowing deeply to Dayan as he huffed for breath. How far had the man run to get here? Jangi had been a loyal guard to Nemeku until Nemeku had run off.

"I would like to see him, if that's alright with you," Jangi said.

Dayan motioned for his guards to remain outside, then reached for the basket Boke held. "No weapons. He is not himself, Jangi. Prepare yourself for that."

Jangi quickly disarmed himself to follow Dayan inside.

The air inside was thick with the stench of urine. Dayan gagged and ordered the door left open to get fresh air inside. Jangi opened the smoke hole in the roof.

Nemeku sat on the edge of the mattress beside Orghana, leaning against her. Orghana's arms wrapped tightly around him as she rubbed his back. Offering her to Unebolod had been an impulsive, petulant decision born of jealousy. Dayan saw that clearly now and was thankful for Unebolod's refusal.

Dayan shuffled closer slowly so as not to startle either of them. Nemeku raised tremulous dark eyes to him. Lines of sorrow creased his forehead and squeezed at his eyes. So much agony for someone so young. Dayan's heart broke for his poor cousin. *How could a father break a son in such a way? How could a father abandon a son?* he wondered. Dayan swore to himself that he would never do either to his sons—if he ever had any.

He set the basket of food down on the rug at Nemeku's feet, then sat on his heels.

Tears streaked Nemeku's swollen, dirty face, leaving several clean lines in the dirt. He rested his head on Orghana's shoulder. She stroked his loose, stringy hair with so much affection Dayan actually felt a flash of envy.

"I'm sorry ..." Nemeku's voice sounded too small and weak for a fourteen-year-old who had always been so strong for as long as Dayan could remember. "I don't ... He ..."

"Shh." Orghana swept a few locks of his hair away from his face, then held his head tight to her shoulder.

"I'm not angry with you, Nemeku," Dayan said. "Your father ..."

Nemeku's entire body tensed. He jerked away from Orghana. The battle for control of himself was written all over his face as it shifted from grief to fury to hate to love to contempt. Some of that seemed directed at Dayan.

"What did he do to you, Nemeku?" Dayan's voice hitched with sorrow. He reached out for his cousin.

Nemeku swatted Dayan's hand away and slammed the heel of his palm against Dayan's chest. Dayan stumbled back on his backside, blinking in stunned alarm at Nemeku. Orghana wrapped him up in her arms again, whispering soothing sounds in his ear.

Jangi edged closer, helping Dayan sit back upright. "Nemeku, do you remember me?" he asked.

"Oh, I know you. Jangi the traitor." Nemeku bared his teeth as he snarled out the words with a hate that startled Dayan.

"He saved your life, Nemeku," Dayan said.

"He left my mother to die!" Nemeku shouted.

"Your father killed her, Nemeku, not Jangi," Dayan said calmly, hoping to smooth out Nemeku's frayed nerves.

"Lies," Nemeku hissed. "Lies created by your whore so she could steal me away from my family!"

Heat rose in Dayan's neck. *Did he just call Mandukhai a whore? Calm breaths*, he thought, trying to focus so that his anger didn't overstretch where it needn't be. "Is that what he told you as he beat you? That Mandukhai stole you? That he didn't kill your mother?"

Jangi's hands clenched into fists at his sides. Dayan gave a subtle shake of his head. Showing Nemeku anger right now would only make matters worse.

Nemeku's frantic gaze darted from Dayan to Jangi to the ger around him, like he expected his father to manifest from the shadows.

"My lord Khan, can I speak to you?" Orghana asked, dipping her head and averting her gaze.

"Speak."

"Alone?" She raised her brows, indicating away from Nemeku.

Dayan stood and nodded, offering a hand to help her off the mattress. Nemeku snatched Dayan's arm as Orghana's soft, smooth hand slid into Dayan's. Fury burned in his dark eyes, as dangerous as a battlefield full of enemies.

"If you hurt her, I will rip your throat out with my teeth," Nemeku said. Judging by the dangerous edge in his tone, Dayan did not doubt his sincerity for a moment. He didn't want to think about what that would feel like either.

Dayan patted Nemeku's hand. "She is safe with us, cousin."

Orghana stood and guided Dayan to the other side of the ger. Nemeku spit at Dayan's back. "You are not my cousin!"

Those five words crushed Dayan. Nemeku was the closest thing to family Dayan had, aside from Esige, and the only male relative he had left. Jangi attempted soothing Nemeku as the boy glared at Dayan.

Orghana stood with her back to Nemeku. Once away from Nemeku on the other side of the ger, Orghana released the flow of tears as if a dam had broken. She did not make a sound aside from an occasional sniffle, and wiped away her tears as quickly as she could once they fell.

"Bigirsen came in here every day, at least twice a day, and tortured him in your name and Mandukhai's," Orghana said, her voice thick with grief. "At first, he kept Nemeku tied to the center post with a sack over his head when he was gone, until Nemeku brought the roof down on his own head trying to escape. That ..." Her voice broke. She pulled in a breath that audibly shuddered. "That was when he started beating him. Whenever Bigirsen was not in the ger with Nemeku, he kept that horrible sack over Nemeku's head. Whenever Nemeku tried to escape, Bigirsen beat him until his fists bled. When he stopped trying to escape ..." Orghana worked her jaw as if trying to fight the words out, finally just shaking her head in defeat.

Dayan gave her arm a reassuring brush that drew a vicious growl from Nemeku. The level of brutality Bigirsen showed his son, his own flesh and blood, filled Dayan with an anger that made him happy he had killed the man.

"I never saw what happened while he was in here," Orghana said, her voice little more than a whisper. "At first, he would send me in to clean and dress the wounds once he was done. He told me he had no choice. Nemeku had been conditioned against him and he had to break his son of the lies to strengthen him."

"So he could challenge me." Mandukhai had warned Dayan this was a possibility. Nemeku was the closest to a Borjigin prince aside from himself. But Nemeku's claim was weak with a Uyghur father.

Orghana nodded. "I think so. Bigirsen ranted often about how he would remove the bastard son of a disgraced prince and replace him with a rightful heir."

Dayan flinched. To have his parentage laid so bare without a second thought had not been something he expected.

"I mean nothing by it, my lord Khan," Orghana said quickly, obviously worried that he would punish her.

"They aren't your words, are they?"

She quickly and vehemently shook her head.

Dayan glanced over at Nemeku, whose eyes could have been arrows trained directly on his heart. Jangi offered soft assurances and a skin of *airag*, but Nemeku only had eyes for Dayan.

"Bigirsen has trained him to hate me," Dayan said. His voice cracked with sorrow.

Orghana sniffled and swiped away the last of her tears, and a fire burned in her dark eyes. "My lord Khan, if you let me help make him better, I will be in your debt. Nemeku was such a sweet boy when he first arrived. Spare him."

"I can have my shaman, Getei, help," Dayan offered. "Maybe he knows a bit about how to break this conditioning. Nemeku is my cousin. I want to see him better as much as you."

Her hand fell on his arm, drawing Dayan's full attention to her. "Let me help him, and I will serve you faithfully in any way you see fit."

Dayan's cheeks heated. The implication was clear enough. He casually stepped away from her. "The way I see it," he said, then cleared his throat, "your husband is dead. As his only son, you are Nemeku's responsibility now."

Orghana gasped. Once more, tears shimmered in her eyes. When a man died, his wives became the responsibility of his sons. And if a wife was not the son's mother, as Orghana obviously was not, then he could marry her or give her away in marriage to another. Dayan had just given Nemeku the right to choose what happened to her. Something told Dayan he already knew what that choice would be.

"Thank you!" Orghana cried, dropping to her knees and seizing his hand to kiss it. "You truly are a great Khan!"

Nemeku tensed on the other side of the ger, prepared to strike. But as Orghana leaped to her feet and rushed toward him, Nemeku relaxed. They fell into each other's arms and a burst of jealousy rushed through Dayan.

Mandukhai would never hold him like that.

BAUTUO – MID-WINTER 1479

Mandukhai sat at the vanity in her room, fixing up her hair and jewels for the inevitable meeting with Lord Qori. Soke joined her from the doorway to her inner chamber as Torgus stood guard at the outer chamber door. Soke and Torgus had taken turns over the past few days meeting with the Mongols in Bautuo, assessing the Ming numbers, and probing the city walls for signs of weakness in case they had to fight their way out. The prospect of fighting to escape did not settle well in Mandukhai's gut. She needed these people and this city to launch her campaign in the Ordos basin successfully.

Bautuo's outer wall was only a few miles from the bridge across the river. Even if the bulk of her forces crossed the frozen river, she needed that bridge open for supply lines. Fighting her way out of the city would ensure Lord Qori would not allow her access.

"We cannot fight our way out, Soke," Mandukhai said as she fastened a jade pin in her hair. The mirror in this room had a reflective, smooth surface of polished silver. "We need that bridge."

"We need to consider the possibility that we will have no other choice," Soke insisted.

"You are right. We have no other choice. I know the plan was to leave tonight, but I will not leave until I have Lord Qori on my side, whatever that requires."

Soke opened his mouth to argue, but whatever he had been prepared to say, he must have thought better. Mandukhai noticed the way his grip tightened on his sword.

"He cannot avoid me all day," Mandukhai said calmly. She glanced at Soke over her shoulder. "I will extract an agreement from him."

Soke marched toward the vanity and leaned closer, lowering his voice. "I am worried he has sent word to Lord Legusi that you are here, and he is delaying so you do not leave. He is just as likely to have sent word to the Ming emperor. And you have even admitted that something is going on around this place. They are hiding something."

Mandukhai had also considered the possibility that Qori had sent word to the Ming emperor, but it was a risk she had to take. Even if the Ming or Legusi captured her, they would not have hold over the kingdom. However, she did know that something was happening around the Bautuo palace.

Soke straightened and grimaced. "I know that look. Let me speak plainly, as Unebolod and Togochi would. If you are captured, Unebolod, Togochi, and the Great Khan will throw everything they have at whomever holds you. It could destroy everything."

"I prepared for this already," Mandukhai said. She stood and placed a hand on Soke's arm. "Please do not think this means I don't listen or respect your opinions, but I knew what I was walking into. Now I need you to have faith in me. Please."

The muscles in Soke's arm twitched. His shoulders sagged. He nodded. Not that arguing with her would help him.

Mandukhai had waited well into the afternoon for Lord Qori to either make an appearance or summon her to meet. Her patience now wore thin. She would have to hunt him down, instead.

A gentle, familiar knock on the door silenced the three of them.

Torgus slid the door open, hand on his sword.

Lady Sarnai waited with her hands folded in her sleeves. "My Khatun, I would love it if you could join me for afternoon tea."

Soke shot an I-told-you-so glare at Mandukhai. *He thinks Qori is biding his time. If he is right, I need to act now.*

"Where is your husband?" Mandukhai asked. She laced her tone with all the sweet innocence she could muster. "I would love to speak with him."

"He is in a meeting in the central room," Sarnai said. "He wanted me to reassure you he will meet with you this evening, though."

The moment she said the word "meeting," Soke pivoted on his heel and marched toward the door. Mandukhai thanked Sarnai for the invitation and politely declined as she followed Soke. Torgus trailed Mandukhai like a shadow.

Sarnai rushed after them until her stride matched Mandukhai's. At the brisk pace around the courtyard, Sarnai nearly had to jog to keep up with them. Mandukhai's gaze swept the courtyard as they made their way to the central room in the north building. Servants bustled about, feeding and grooming half a dozen new mounts. From this distance, Mandukhai could not discern the saddle styles. Only that they were not Mongol.

Soke led the way, hand on his sword, ready for a fight.

"Mandukhai Khatun, I must insist you join me for tea," Sarnai said as she labored to keep pace.

Why? Mandukhai wondered. "I will not be drinking your tea today, Lady Sarnai, but thank you."

The door to the central room was closed, and warm light glowed through the white screens. A mixture of Ming and Mongol men guarded the door. The Ming stepped forward defensively as Soke marched toward them. The Mongols hesitated, casting anxious glances at Sarnai. The Ming rested their hands on their sword hilts.

Sarnai jumped forward, holding up a hand, speaking swiftly in the Ming tongue. Mandukhai eyed the woman curiously. She was certainly more than she pretended to be. Whatever she said, the Ming glanced at Mandukhai, then stepped out of the way and released their swords.

Soke brushed past them and slid the door open as if they owned this palace, instead of Qori. He marched in first, with Mandukhai on his heels and Torgus bringing up the rear.

The central room was a wide, warm space. Sage and burning wood filled the air as the fireplace lit the space. Two Ming men in fine silk sat at a richly engraved table. At the head of the table, Qori surged to his feet, startled by Mandukhai's sudden appearance. The Ming men twisted in their seats to see who had interrupted. Their gazes swept right past Mandukhai and landed on Soke. She clenched her hands into fists until her nails bit into her palms.

Qori recovered from his alarm with a charming smile as he motioned toward her. "Ah, here she is now. Lady Mandukhai, we were just speaking of you."

The Ming lords gaped at her.

"Were you?" Mandukhai glided fearlessly toward the table. "I would love to hear what you have to tell these Ming lords about me."

"Nothing anyone else has not already heard," Qori replied smoothly. His gaze flicked to Sarnai, who flushed and dipped her chin to her chest. Whatever he had instructed her to do, Qori likely would give her an earful about later ... or perhaps worse.

Mandukhai strode around the table, past the two Ming lords who continued gaping at her brazen interruption. She pulled out a chair directly beside Lord Qori. "And it is Mandukhai Khatun, not Lady Mandukhai. It would be best if everyone acknowledged my position. Surely I outrank all of you." She settled in the seat. "Please, Lord Qori, carry on regaling tales of me to these men." Mandukhai poured herself a cup of wine and waited.

Qori flushed a light shade of pink as he settled in his seat beside her.

Soke took a seat at the table, beside Mandukhai, without waiting for an invitation. She smiled inwardly at his assertiveness. Unebolod would be proud.

Torgus moved into position behind Mandukhai and stood as still as a statue as he watched the men.

"It's alright, my love," Qori reassured Sarnai. "You can leave us."

"Surely you can allow your wife to stay for such a feast," Mandukhai said, waving a hand at the food on the table. "Even the most delicate of creatures is strong and graceful." Qori had used those exact words to describe the crane fountain outside, and she delighted in turning his own words against him. "Have a seat, Lady Sarnai. I insist."

Trapped between her husband and the Khatun, Sarnai froze in place, eyes wide and face pale. *What is she so afraid of?* Mandukhai wondered.

Soke poured himself a drink and took a sip, then grunted in disgust. Wine was clearly not to his taste.

Qori gave his wife a small, sharp nod. Sarnai glided toward the table and settled into a seat at the far corner, away from the others. It irritated Mandukhai that a woman should feel so small among men.

"Introduce me to your guests, Lord Qori," Mandukhai said as she piled food shamelessly on her plate.

He cleared his throat and gave the introductions. The two Ming lords were former leaders of Bautuo, now under Qori's thumb. Mandukhai had heard the tale from Sarnai about how Qori had conquered the city and forced these lords into his service.

"We have come to a mutual understanding with one another," Qori said as he finished introductions. "I keep the city safe, and their men obey *my* commands in exchange for their lives."

"That hardly sounds like a relationship born of mutual respect," Mandukhai said, smiling sweetly at each of them. "Do they speak Mongol?"

"I insist on it in my home."

"Good. That will make this much easier."

"What?" Qori asked.

Mandukhai ignored him. "Carry on. I would love to hear what tales you tell these Ming lords of my presence." She bit into a dumpling, not bothering to appear like a delicate flower in front of these men as she ate. Soke smirked slightly as he bit off a chunk of prawn.

The two Ming lords, however, picked delicately at their food. Mandukhai could sense their discomfort. She reveled in it.

Qori cleared his throat. "I was just explaining to them how the two of us might come to some sort of accord. A mutually beneficial relationship. They are quite worried about the *tumens* you have camped at Lake Dai."

"Among other places," Mandukhai said around a mouthful of food. "Any day now I should receive word that the Great Khan has executed Bigirsen for treason against the empire."

The lump in Qori's throat bobbed as he swallowed.

"Good riddance," the older Ming lord muttered in Mongol.

Mandukhai allowed a small smile of satisfaction as she sipped her wine. Bigirsen had been a nuisance to the Ming as much as he had been to her over the years. Perhaps more so. She drew her father's horn-handled knife from her belt and began carving up an apple. The appearance of the weapon made all three men, as well as Sarnai, tense.

"Surely you have also told them the stories of Dayan Khan's divine legitimacy," Mandukhai said casually as she sliced the fruit. "We have not had a Khan as powerful in a long time. Perhaps since Genghis and his sons. Or since his grandson, Kublai."

Just the mention of Kublai made both Ming lords stiffen, their eyes wide. Nearly two hundred years ago, Kublai Khan had been one of the most aggressive Khans to venture into Chinese territory. He had conquered the Song Dynasty and reigned from the ocean in the east to the sea in the far west. Where Genghis had worried the world, Kublai had been much worse for the Chinese leaders.

Once more, Qori cleared his throat. "I have not."

"It is a good thing to have you all here. We can get straight down to business." Mandukhai held a slice of apple out to Qori, pressed against the blade of her knife.

Qori moved slowly, like a body through water, as he accepted the slice. *Is he trembling?* Mandukhai wondered as she thought she saw a tremor in his hand.

"And what business would that be?" the younger Ming lord asked.

"You want to keep your city safe. We want to cross the river without threat of an army at our back." She bit a slice off her knife and continued carving.

The Ming eyed the way she ate off her knife—surely a violation to their delicate sensibilities—then they glanced at each other in discomfort.

"Is that all you want?" Qori asked. "You could have said so when you arrived. I would have agreed already."

"Would you have?" Mandukhai set down the core of the apple, wiping the juices off on a cotton napkin. "I think I should be perfectly clear with you, gentlemen, so that you don't misunderstand my intention."

Soke pushed back his chair, scraping the legs across the wooden floor loudly. Everyone jumped. He stood, drawing all gazes to him. His hand rested casually on his sword, shifting it so he could step away from the table and chairs. Without a command, Soke marched toward the door, sliding it closed, then posted himself there.

There could no longer be any doubt that these men were worried. The Ming lords shook as they surged to their feet, then froze in place. Their faces paled considerably. Sarnai pressed her back into her seat, eyes wide as she placed a worried hand over her mouth. Qori bristled, then surged to his feet and opened his mouth to shout for his guards.

"Rethink that, Lord Qori," Mandukhai said calmly from her chair. "I am not here to kill anyone. I am here to assert the Great Khan's divine power. To restore that which has been broken for far too long. To mend our invisible scars."

"Your man is threatening us," Qori snapped, wagging his finger in Soke's direction.

"He is protecting me from those guards you have stationed outside the door," Mandukhai replied smoothly. "Soke will kill no one unless they attack me first. So I suggest settling back down so we can finish this."

Qori crossed his arms. "What is there to finish? I already told you that your army could use the bridge."

"I apologize if I was unclear before," Mandukhai said. She lived for these little moments when she could flex her power over men who thought themselves superior. When she could show them that they were never truly in control, even when they were certain they were. "I cannot leave an opposing army at my back. There is only one way for me to be certain your men will not close in behind my *tumens*."

Qori's arms fell slack at his sides as the realization struck him. "I am an Ordos Lord."

"I am Khatun of all Mongols, no matter tribal affiliation." Mandukhai set her wine down and shifted to see Qori more clearly. "You say these Ming Lords follow you, but I'm afraid, for their own benefit, it would be best if they prove that to me."

"How?"

Mandukhai pushed her chair back, making it scrape across the floor. "They will join you when you kneel to me. They will be held accountable to their oaths as any other Mongol would."

At this, two Ming lords began speaking at once, insisting they would not give an oath to a Mongol woman.

"And if they betray me or my people in any way, they will die for their treason," she continued.

"She cannot rule me!" the older lord snapped.

Mandukhai whipped her knife in his direction. It sunk into the wood near his shoulder. She turned a furious glare at him. "I did not miss."

He paled, but anger still burned in his eyes.

"This is not a negotiation for them," Mandukhai said.

Qori's chin trembled in outrage. "They are good men. Loyal to me."

"Then this should not be a problem."

"What makes you think *I* will give you my oath?" he asked.

"I control the wealth flowing from the west along what remains of the Silk Road," Mandukhai replied patiently. "You stand to become a very wealthy man."

Greed flashed in Qori's eyes.

"Or a dead one," she said. "You choose. Now. And know this. We will either conquer or kill Lord Legusi if he does not agree to kneel to his rightful Khan and Khatun."

Qori sank into his seat. "He is not your problem."

Mandukhai hated the momentary confusion that flitted across her face. It meant he knew something she did not, and she did not like giving anyone the upper hand on her. "Who is?"

He poured himself another cup of wine and took a drink. She wanted to smack the cup from his hand and strangle the truth from his lips. *He is toying with* me *now*, she thought.

At last, he settled back in his chair again, facing her with seriousness that created wrinkles in his forehead. "Legusi khan has spent years struggling to get out from under Bigirsen's thumb. If you kill Bigirsen, Legusi is likely to fall at your feet in gratitude. But Lord Mogurkei has struck a deal with the Uyghur. I suspect Lord Ibarai has as well."

"Once Bigirsen is dead, that deal will be worthless," Mandukhai said. She raked her brain to remember which part of the Ordos territory Mogurkei reigned over. Should they target him first, then? Or was it better to sweep in after Legusi and use him to bring Mogurkei to heel? *I need to speak with Togochi and Unebolod about this.*

"Bigirsen has not been in control of anything for a long time," Qori snorted. "He was turned into a puppet years ago."

Mandukhai's gut twisted. Who could pull Bigirsen's strings? "By whom?"

"Lord Issama." Qori's declaration only amplified the worry burrowing into her soul. "You sent the Great Khan in to kill Bigirsen?"

She nodded stiffly, feeling the muscles in her neck resist movement.

"Then Issama has decided the time is right."

Could she trust anything Qori was telling her? Or was he using these men to sew doubt in her own mind?

"I will take your oaths now, Lord Qori."

"If your husband is working toward restoring the fractured Mongol empire, I would be a fool to stand in your way," Qori said.

Husband. Qori assumed she and Dayan were already married. She could not afford to correct him.

Qori carried on, oblivious to her alarm. "Especially with so many already under his banner. The Ordos can only resist for so long, and I will not lose men to suffer the inevitable defeat. But I will give my oath to the Great Khan."

Mandukhai knew better. If she accepted his word on this, he could still turn against her when her back was turned. She stood and folded her hands into the sleeves of her deel. "You will give it to me."

His jaw twitched. Probably, he considered his odds if he refused. His gaze slid past her to where Torgus loomed behind her. At last, Qori snapped his fingers and motioned sharply for the Ming to join him.

The two men stood rooted in place. The older lord shook his head stubbornly. Soke subtly loosened his sword from his belt.

"You both know defiance will not be tolerated," Qori told the two Ming lords. "Or do I need my guards to bring in Hou as a reminder."

The way the two paled stoked Mandukhai's curiosity about Hou. They shuffled around the table, arms tight to their sides.

When Qori dropped to his knees, the Ming lords clenched their jaws so tight it made their jowls stick out. Neither man dropped to their knees, glaring at Mandukhai in open defiance.

"There is room for two more alongside Hou," Qori said. His fingers ran along his belt.

Both lords immediately dropped to their knees and pressed their faces to the floor.

What did he do to Hou that scares them so much? she wondered.

Before Qori could utter a word, the Ming both uttered the same vow or loyalty in haste, as if afraid that saying the words too slow would mean instant death. Their vows were not quite the same as a Mongol oath, but it still carried a weight of sacred connection from what she could tell.

As they finished, Qori seemed satisfied, giving them a nod of approval—not that either could see it with their faces pressed to the hardwood floor.

"I give you my word, Mandukhai Khatun, that I will follow and obey your commands from this day until my last," Qori said. "And should I break my word, may the Eternal Blue Sky condemn me forever to the pits of the underworld."

"And you will support Dayan Khan at *kurultai*," she added.

"I will, upon my eternal soul, follow you until Dayan Khan calls for *kurultai*, at which I will give my full oath to the rightful Great Khan."

Mandukhai nodded.

Qori kissed her ring, then rose and stepped back, nudging each of the Ming Lords with the toe of his boot. Though their oaths had sounded binding, Mandukhai mistrusted the Ming. It would be much easier to kill them now and avoid future complication, but Mandukhai had a better idea.

"If these men betray their oaths, you will send me their heads," she declared. "If you don't, I will send for yours. They are under your command, Lord Qori, and so they are your responsibility. I will hold you accountable."

She settled back in her chair and pulled it back to the table. "Good. Now that's over. Let's celebrate over a feast, and you can tell me everything you know about what the Ordos and Uyghur Lords have been doing behind our backs."

CHAPTER TWENTY

Bones of Winter

Two days after killing Bigirsen, Dayan had ordered the men to break camp and head southeast again. Their mission had been a success, and he sat proudly in his saddle each day, often glancing at the blood-stained sack tied to Boke's horse. He would bring the head back to Mandukhai as the bride-price ... but would she accept it?

When he slept, nightmares plagued his sleep. Bigirsen's head spoke to him, taunting him, calling him Little Khan, Puppet Khan, telling him that his own men did not follow him, but instead followed a woman and her lover. No one had wanted him. And Bigirsen's voice would morph into his father's. Or, at least, he assumed it was his father. Dayan had never heard Bayan's voice. His father came to him, sneering arrogantly, calling him a bastard cripple. The face that showed so much scorn and so little love was his own, and not his father's.

Sometimes, his mother would come to his defense, but even her defense was weak and scathing, belittling. She had no face; only black eyes and moving lips. She was a woman he had never known. Or, at least, a woman he could not remember. She and his father would coax him with ugly words, offer him knives to cut his own throat and save everyone the trouble.

In one dream, his mother tenderly tied him to a tree so that his father, Bigirsen, and Unebolod could use him for target practice. The four of them laughed as if puncturing him with arrows was the most entertaining thing under the Eternal Blue Sky. When they were finished, blood dripped from his wounds, but the pain was all in his heart, an intense aching as if the Great Fist would at last claim him. His chin hung to his chest. Arrows feathered his torso. His hair hung limp around his shoulders.

And then Mandukhai appeared before him, dissolving the arrows with a touch, healing his wounds with a swipe of her hand over each puncture. She raised his chin, stroked his cheek affectionately. All the pain in his heart melted away, replaced by absolute adoration. His blood pumped with excitement as he leaned closer to her, eager to steal that first kiss.

Mandukhai's hand plunged into his chest and ripped out his heart. Blood oozed between her fingers and down her forearm as she held it up for him to see.

"Our hearts are not our own to give, Dayan Khan," she said, and her voice was like a terrible song in his ears. A siren's call that would lure him to his doom. "They belong to Tengri and the Great Khan Genghis. We are servants to their will."

He watched as she observed the rapid thumping of his heartbeat in her hand. And then she squeezed.

Dayan woke in an icy sweat, gasping for breath as his heart raced faster than it ever had before. Faster and harder than a herd of Mongol horses racing across the steppe. The pain overwhelmed him, and he pressed his hand against his chest as if he could slow the beating by touch alone. His breaths came in freezing, quick gasps. He closed his eyes and focused on his breathing, centering himself as Goram had taught him.

All around Dayan, men snorted in their sleep. The sound formed a strange, musical rhythm. Snorting out and in together, punctuated by the occasional crunch of movement as someone rolled or by the sniff of horses grazing nearby.

The speed of his heartbeat gradually steadied, though it still thumped hard against his ribs. Dayan rubbed his chest and sat up. His armor stuck to the earth as he moved, peeling away with the popping noise he had become familiar with on his journey. Most of the men rolled around in their sleep. Dayan had found he hardly moved at all. He slept as he would when he died, laid out on his back with his hands folded over his chest inside his sleeves. And he never moved from that position throughout the night.

He was always the last to sleep and the first to rise. In the two weeks since they left Bigirsen's camp to travel east again, Dayan had grown used to the way he rose before anyone else. His guards had as well. Those on shift early in the morning no longer said anything as he rose and stretched his aching muscles.

He tiptoed around the disorganized mass of bodies littering the ground, careful not to kick or step on anyone. His two guards on night watch followed him like shadows at a respectful distance.

The warriors scattered across the ground reminded him of the aftermath of a battle. Bodies lay everywhere as far as he could see. The difference was that these men still breathed. They had only lost a few men in the fight against Bigirsen. None of the Uyghur had survived, save a few women some men had taken as wives or lovers for the rest of their trip. Dayan had allowed it as long as the women didn't slow them down or show any signs of defiance.

Bigirsen's head remained in a felt sack and tied to Boke's horse day and night. While Dayan doubted Mandukhai would want to see it for herself, he would not miss the chance to present it to her. Thinking of her, Dayan rubbed at his chest. His heart no longer beat quite so hard.

Dayan spotted a lone figure sitting up amidst a field of slumbering men. He made his way toward his cousin to see how Nemeku was faring. Orghana and Getei worked with Nemeku day and night, as much as they could from saddles, to help him practice breathing exercises, as well as focus on the memories he knew to be real versus those his father had tried to force on him. It had been rough for the first week. Getei insisted Dayan keep his distance from Nemeku until they had a breakthrough. Unebolod insisted Nemeku have a few men guarding him—both for his protection as well as Dayan's.

After the first week, Nemeku's temperament had softened. He still sometimes cast angry glares at Dayan, but the two had managed to sit around the same fire, share food, and even most recently, talk. Dayan felt like he had started getting his cousin back. He didn't realize how much he had missed Nemeku until they began talking honestly and openly with one another. By the time they returned to Mandukhai, Nemeku would be himself once more.

"You are awake early," Nemeku said, sitting on the ground beside a slumbering Orghana. She always remained at his side now, like an extension of him.

"I always am," Dayan said, stopping in front of his cousin. "How are you feeling today?"

"Bitter."

Dayan snorted. That seemed an understatement, considering all Nemeku had been through.

Nemeku's gaze flicked across the field of bodies. Dayan followed it and noted Jangi sleeping nearby. He had insisted on being in charge of Nemeku's guards.

"He is loyal to you," Dayan said. "I won't pretend to understand what you've been through, but you are my cousin, as was your mother. I have little by way of blood."

"Nor do I." Nemeku glanced at Orghana. "She told me what you did, giving her to my care." The affection on Nemeku's face burned Dayan's chest. "She was the only light I've had for so long now. And he knew it. He beat her for defending me, even made me watch him rough her up once just to prove his power over us. When he realized she cared more for me than him..." Nemeku stroked her matted hair, shaking his head sadly. "My father grew mad these past few months. When he saw the dust from your army, he raged and asked what it was, as if I would know." Nemeku's grin bore a vicious, devious light. "I wanted to please him, but I also wanted to drive a knife through his heart for what he did to my mother, and to Orghana. So I told him it was probably the dust of his own vast herd."

Dayan blinked in alarm. Nemeku, despite the feral nature of his hate toward Dayan at the time, had delayed Bigirsen's response? "I know it isn't much, and you don't have to look, but if you want me to bring the sack...so you can say your final farewell?"

Nemeku chortled. "No. Salt will grow where he died, such was his bitterness. He hollowed what he born, rooted out what had grown, and bit what had gone out. He has laid down his black head."

The words were laced with a deeply seeded loathing Dayan could commiserate with, even if he didn't fully understand it. Both of their fathers had done them wrong, but Dayan had been abandoned and rescued. Nemeku had suffered torture at his father's own hands. Bigirsen had transformed his son, and perhaps not in the way he had desired. Nemeku's words made that clear enough. The malediction placed not only over his father, but over himself, was a final curse on his father's head. Bigirsen hollowed him out, ripped out Nemeku's roots, and beat him when he had broken already. A black head was an omen of darkness and a restless afterlife.

"We have one other problem between us," Dayan said, wincing as he uttered the words. He hated where these words would take him. Before he continued, Dayan glanced at the guards around them, then checked to be sure Orghana slept. Still, he lowered his voice to a whisper. "You are a danger, a replacement, to my title."

Nemeku shook his head, hugging his knees against his chest. "I bear no envy for you, cousin, nor desire for what is yours. I want only one thing." He glanced at Orghana to make clear what he meant. Not that Dayan needed an explanation.

"I believe you." Dayan's stomach twisted in knots. It didn't matter if *he* believed Nemeku. Everyone needed to believe it. "But there cannot be any doubt. When you are strong enough again, you will challenge me."

Nemeku gaped at him and hissed, "I will not."

"Then I will have to challenge you, but if you force me to do so, I will have no choice but to kill you, and that is the last thing I want. I already have to deal with Unebolod, and I'm not looking forward to that at all."

"Why him?" Nemeku asked.

Dayan ignored the question. He just didn't have the strength to explain right now, so he carried on as if he hadn't heard the question, still whispering so no one else might hear them. "If you challenge me, you can submit once we have put on a good show."

Silence smothered their conversation like a heavy woolen blanket.

Doubt was a dangerous weapon. Dayan had no brothers. The closest thing he had known were Togochi's sons, but they were several years younger and could not understand him like Nemeku, who was only two years younger. Fighting each other for this title was not something Dayan desired, but until he beat Nemeku, the men might always wonder. That doubt had to be smothered more thoroughly than this silence now between them.

At last, Nemeku nodded. "I will make a show of it then, so there will never again be doubt."

Dayan offered a weak, yet grateful, smile. "I wish you and Orghana happiness. But I would advise waiting for the moon to cycle around again before you share a bed."

"We may not have one to share until then anyway," Nemeku said with a teasing grin. But a determined couple would find ways. "What about you and Mandukhai?"

Over the past few days, Dayan confided in Nemeku, sharing his worry about her rejection, that she would only ever see him as the broken boy she had saved from certain death. Nemeku had pushed him to be more assertive with her when they returned to her camp. Dayan had not told

Nemeku what he knew of her feelings for Unebolod—nor Unebolod's feelings for her. It was too painful to speak the words aloud.

Instead of answering, Dayan straightened his shoulders. "I should go check the men on watch."

Before he could see the look on Nemeku's face, Dayan turned and strode away.

The wolf dawn approached as he neared the edge of the camp. Some warriors stirred. A couple of men grunted in a conjugal embrace with their new women out in the open where everyone could see them. It made Dayan ache. Heat flooded his face. Thankfully, he was quickly distracted by the sound of bells approaching.

A messenger found them along the yam lines. Dayan ran toward the sound, hand on his sword, both for defense and to hold it steady. It had to be from Mandukhai. Did she know yet what he had done? Would she be proud of him? Would it change anything?

The messenger dismounted and kneeled to Dayan as the early morning guards protected their Khan. Dayan snatched the letter from the rider's hands impatiently and didn't bother looking at the dragon seal before ripping it open.

Mandukhai had arranged a meeting with Lord Qori in Bautuo and was confident she would soon be able to acquire safe passage for their supply lines across the bride. He skimmed the rest of the letter to find out how she intended to accomplish the task, but she gave no details. Only promises that she was confident she would succeed, and that she wanted him to return to Lake Dai so that they could charge across the Huang-Ho River together. Had she succeeded already? Was she safe?

As much as he wanted to return to her, Dayan had other plans. While Mandukhai's strategy had merit, Dayan would not leave any pathways for the Ordos tribes to escape to the west and reunite with any remaining Uyghur to regroup.

He intended to change their previous strategy of regrouping to attack. But first, he needed to speak to Unebolod.

"Is anything wrong, my lord Khan?" Lord Ulum asked as he glanced at the message. "Can I be of help?"

"No." Dayan rolled the message in his fist. "Fetch me paper and ink," Dayan commanded one of his guards. "And someone find Unebolod and summon him to me." Dayan turned to Ulum. "I appreciate your loyalty these past weeks, Lord Ulum. It has not gone unnoticed. But harder days still lie ahead of us."

Please forgive me, Mandukhai, he thought as he held her message in his hand. Hopefully, she would understand.

Mandukhai's return from Bautuo had been greeted with joyous celebration. Togochi had latched to her side for days after her return, citing the need to finalize their plans now that she had secured Bautuo. She had understood the sentiment, but recognized his clingy behavior for what it was. He hadn't thought she would return alive.

The new year came and went with little ceremony. Mandukhai wore the customary white for five days to show the purity and promise of the new year, but even that reminded her of Dayan. Of the white belt he wore. Did he wear it still? The white belt was a symbol to show he had not yet taken a wife, but a lot could happen when he was away from her for so long. Boys could be reckless and foolish.

Soke had worked with Mandukhai for weeks, organizing his men for the journey south. While she prepared to cross near Bautuo, Soke had taken five thousand men to rendezvous with the remaining three thousand Three Guards warriors. By the time Dayan returned, Soke's men would wait on the eastern banks of the Huang-Ho River for the message to cross the frozen river near to where Ibarai's scattered families camped. She had watched the mass of warriors ride away only two days before.

Dayan and Unebolod had been gone for months, through the worst of winter. She yearned to see them both again.

The families waiting with her had spread out across the snow-covered grasslands for better herding and grazing. When Mandukhai stood atop any hill, she could see gers dotting the horizon in all directions. Not all families were so far south. Some remained in the north, guarding their borders and maintaining their lands. Holy men performed hundreds of marriages throughout the winter months. Come summer, the strength of the nation would grow with new alliances and children.

Mandukhai stood atop one such hill today, staring west as if she could see her men in the distance. They would not return for at least two weeks, and she eagerly waited for some word from either of them.

As she watched, Mandukhai spotted a cloud of dust trailing westward, and she dared to hope. Her mount raced down the hill toward the gathering tent nearly a mile away. By the time she reached the steps, the messenger had arrived.

"From my lord Khan," he said with reverence as he kneeled and offered her the parchment.

He lives! That news alone was worth more than anything the page could contain. Dayan had survived the fight. She would see his youthful face soon.

Mandukhai snatched the parchment, sealed twice. Once with the crescent moon of the Yuan, and once with the bull of the Khorchin. Her heart leaped with joy. They both lived!

The message was much longer than Mandukhai had expected, and quite detailed. She turned from the messenger and climbed the stairs, entering the gathering tent as she read the news.

I have proven my worth. I have taken the head of your oldest enemy to bring to you as proof. His life is ended, his herds divided among our loyal men, his son rescued from his lies.

Mandukhai pressed a hand against her aching heart. Nemeku! They had Nemeku! She sank down into her seat as she continued.

But a wind blows from Burkhan Khaldun, and it carries with it the will of Tengri. I'm afraid my journey will take me farther from you before I can return. Unebolod and I have discussed and outlined the strategy for the taming of Ordos. While your plan is good, Tengri guides me in this, and as a single united front, we will not find victory.

The words sent a ripple of shock down Mandukhai's spine. Dayan had never refused her plans before and had only changed them on her once ... when he had insisted on hunting Bigirsen himself. She read the words again, hoping that she had simply misunderstood, but Dayan's intention was clear. He would not be coming back to her yet. Neither of them would be.

Togochi strolled in, bowing to her before taking his usual seat near the foot of the dais. "You received word. What is wrong?" Worry tinged his voice. "Is the Khan alive?"

The question startled her. Mandukhai looked up, only then realizing that she was crying. Mandukhai briskly wiped the tears away and raised her chin.

"Yes, he is well," she said, hoping to mask the disappointment worming into her stomach. "Bigirsen is dead. But they are riding south and east instead of returning to Lake Dai." Mandukhai shuffled through the pages, skimming the plan. "He and Unebolod intend to sweep up the Ordos outside of the plateau as they did on the way to Juyan Basin. It seems his plan is to swell the numbers and stretch the lines from Yinchuan to Bautuo, then close in on the Ordos like a net, trapping them between our forces and the Ming."

Togochi stroked his chin as he considered the strategy. At last, Togochi grunted. "It's quite clever, Mandukhai. You should be proud of him for devising such a plan."

"Of course I'm proud of him!"

Mandukhai continued reading. A final note from Unebolod stopped her heart. Mandukhai paled as she read the words over and over to be sure she read them correctly. *The truth is unveiled. Issama was the Altan we hunted fourteen years ago. The man who poisoned your child. Men report seeing his family moving east toward Hami. We don't know for certain where he is now.*

Issama was the man Altan. The mysterious man responsible for her poisoning and for the death of her child with Unebolod. This aligned with what Lord Qori had told her. If Issama had been pulling Bigirsen's strings for so long, this news made perfect sense. He had asked for her hand after killing her child? *He has been out for the title since the beginning!* Mandukhai clenched this note in her fist. Her jaw pulsed with anger.

Togochi cocked his head. "What is wrong?"

"Nothing." Mandukhai was not sure why she lied to him. "I'm just eager to get this over with and angry about what Bigirsen did to Nemeku." After all these years. After all the meals and drinks she shared with Issama. All the council meetings and respectful deference he had shown her. Mandukhai struggled to control her ragged breathing.

Togochi raised his brows but did not question the obvious lie. "If Dayan and Unebolod succeed with the outer Ordos as they did along the northern path, we could end up with an extra two *tumens* before we even cross the Huang Ho River—more than enough men to press our way south. It will force Lord Legusi to submit to the Khan and Khatun, push the Ordos into the arms of the Ming and out of our land, or they die—whether by our might or by the Ming. That wall had been a curse, but perhaps it's a blessing."

Mandukhai nodded, forcing herself back into the moment. She could deliberate how to kill Issama later. But without knowing where he was, she would be aiming at an invisible target. Before she went to Bautuo, she had sent a message to General Alayitung and Lord Asha in Oirat territory, telling them to move into Hami the moment they received word of Bigirsen's death. She would capture the city before anyone else could. If Issama headed that way as well, perhaps Alayitung and Asha would deal with Issama for her. She *would* find him and kill him somehow. Right now, she had another foe to conquer.

Togochi was right about Dayan's plan. It was a good one—better than their previous plan. She was not upset that Dayan had proven his ability to lead. She was upset about what it meant. He was no longer the boy she remembered—the boy who never would have told her no. Dayan was now a man capable of leading as she had wanted—and marrying who he wanted.

This new strategy also meant Dayan and Unebolod would not return to her. She wanted to keep Dayan close and safe. She wanted to see Unebolod's stony face again. Their absence had been agonizing. Once Unebolod returned, she could speak with him about Issama.

"What shall we do while they launch this grand campaign, Togochi?" Mandukhai asked, holding out the plans to him—all except the private letters from Dayan and Unebolod. Those were hers alone.

Togochi climbed the steps to accept the plans. His eyes skimmed the pages, and his brows climbed farther up his wide forehead. "This is quite detailed. He really put a lot of consideration into this. Did you see who they rescued from Bigirsen?"

"Yes, Nemeku." Mandukhai waved impatiently, waiting for him to answer her question.

"No. I mean, yes, but they also have Lord Legusi's sister." He shuffled the pages, chewing on his bottom lip as he studied them.

Legusi, khan of the Ordos tribes. What sort of leverage would that be for them to use against the Ordos khan?

Togochi shook his head. "I would like a little more time to review their plan. But I think our best course of action would be to rally all the additional warriors we can, extend our reach across the north as far as we dare, and prepare for the river crossing. This should not change anything about the deal you made with Lord Qori. We can still use the bridge and cross our warriors as planned."

Mandukhai skimmed the first page from Dayan again. He had Bigirsen's head … which meant once he returned to her—as a man—his hope that she accept him as her husband would no longer be a thing of the future. *I have proven my worth,* he had written.

Yet it was not his worth that she doubted.

It was her own ability to accept the inevitable.

Togochi remained in the gathering tent late into the night, pouring over the new plans Dayan and Unebolod had sent as he stood at the map table. Things were finally coming together. Dayan already had an additional *tumen* of Ordos with his twenty thousand. Mandukhai had secured the oath of Lord Qori. Even if Qori didn't join the fight, at least his ten thousand would stay out of it. The Uyghur were now out of the picture. That left sixty-four thousand Ordos inside the basin, with Mandukhai's combined forty-five thousand around the north and east, if Dayan could sweep up the last of the Ordos outside the basin, they would have a total of ninety-five thousand warriors.

What kept Togochi awake all night was the warning Mandukhai had received from Lord Qori. He warned her about other Ordos Lords striking up deals with Issama—Mogurkei among them. Twenty thousand of the Ordos remaining outside the basin followed Mogurkei. Would Lord Ulum remain loyal to Dayan in a fight against Mogurkei's warriors? Or would Ulum turn against the Khan, leaving Dayan and Unebolod outnumbered and without reinforcements?

Togochi rubbed his burning eyes. Sleep threatened to pull him under, but he fought it off. There had to be some way to determine the answer to his question.

I need to send word to Dayan and Unebolod. But would his warning reach them before they reached Mogurkei? He considered waking Mandukhai to have her send the message, but he didn't want to waste time. He would sent the message immediately and let her know in the morning.

CHAPTER TWENTY-ONE

The Challenger

Issama was near utter exhaustion by the time he spotted the walls of Hami shimmering like a mirage. The journey from Juyan Basin had been far too long and treacherous. Water had been sparse, offered only by occasional springs as he crossed the rocky wasteland. Thankfully, his journey had not taken him across sand. He was certain his mount would not have handled the shifting grains under hooves. A camel would have been better for the journey, but Issama had been in dire straits. Trading at any of the small outposts along the route would have brought attention to his presence, and instinct warned him to remain inconspicuous. The fortune of having a mare and not a stallion sustained him when his food supply ran out, though he was tired of milk.

Throughout the journey, Issama had wondered what happened to Bigirsen's camp—and to Nemeku. He could assume that Bigirsen was dead but needed some way to confirm this. Hopefully, he could find answers in the city.

Hami burst with life. Women shielded their faces with thin silks and laces that wrapped around their heads to ward off the sun. Even in winter, the rays of the sun could be brutal against the skin. A few women dared to make eye contact, as if prepared to offer him a warm bed and even warmer company, but upon seeing the state of him, they all thought better of it and turned their attention to the next man. Was he really in such a state that even whores would assume he had no coins to exchange? He must appear a dreadful beggar.

The bazaar offered a variety of spices, trinkets, jewels, and cloth from around the world. Merchants came from thousands of miles to cross this oasis before entering the desert. Issama kept his head down as he passed a handful of Mongol men laughing and gambling with skins of *airag* in their hands. If Mandukhai had sent men to kill Bigirsen, would he be next? Issama was not about to take chances and risk exposing himself to men who might be loyal to her.

The stench of sweat mingled with the smell of freshly baked breads. Issama's mouth watered as he passed a stall selling hard, crusted bread and fresh cheese. He had coins to exchange for food, but those coins might be better spent elsewhere. He would have no way of knowing the extent of his situation until he found Siker.

Would she hold this failure against him? He had promised her comfort and assured her he would always hold a powerful enough position for her to never worry for the rest of her days. That promise had been made years ago, when they had first married. Issama had fought to uphold his end of their deal. But since Manduul's death, everything had slowly unraveled. It was like trying to catch smoke with his bare hands. Capturing Nemeku had been his last chance to prove he was not utterly worthless. *Now what can I do? Hopefully Ulum has Unebolod right where we need him.*

Issama hated placing all of his plans—his future—in the hands of another man. But under the circumstances, he had little choice. The Ordos would need to keep their word. *Maybe I can find someone to seek out Ulum or Morgurkei and find out what is happening.* But would he have enough wealth to exchange for the information?

Issama squeezed down a narrow alleyway, leading his mount by the reins. Years ago, before everything had fallen apart, Issama and Siker had claimed a couple pieces of property around Hami. The larger, more grandiose home was likely watched. He could check that later. Hopefully, Siker would not have been foolish enough to go there without him. He counted on her being wise enough to wait for him in their hovel near a back alley. Just before Bigirsen began hunting him down, Issama had hidden away a small fortune in the hovel and secured it with traps that only he and Siker knew how to disarm. He had expected to need to buy his safety from Bigirsen.

Instead he would need to buy his way into the palace—and into Mandukhai's good graces if the Ordos did not hold up their end of the deal.

Issama had done his part. Bigirsen most likely was dead at Unebolod's hands. It was their turn to act.

Uyghur and Ming had heavily contested Hami territory for years. Now, with the Ming forces retreating behind their growing wall and Bigirsen most likely dead, Hami would have no leader. The Oirat were not far off, and Mongols often traveled to Hami to trade horses for other goods at extortionist prices. A single Mongol horse could cost as much as a wagon full of silk or tea. The finer the mount, the more the Mongols demanded. Issama knew Mandukhai was to blame. She had stolen the Oirat lands from his control years ago and her appointed Oirat leader kept a heavy rein on the trade. How long before she sent her army to capture Hami? Perhaps that would be their next move. He didn't know if the Khan's men followed him this way.

Issama coughed as he inhaled the bitter taste of stale, urine-soaked air. He covered his mouth with his sleeve. Perhaps, if he handled things delicately, he could take control of Hami before Mandukhai's army arrived. How far behind him would they be? It could cost him a small fortune, but thankfully he had one hidden right here.

The street at the other end of the alley opened to a busy, but not bursting, residential neighborhood. Outside of the sandstone hovels, old men sat on wooden benches, watching passersby with narrowed eyes. Meat hung from open windows to dry. Small potted herbal plants dotted the landscape. Issama nodded politely to an elderly man with a face so scrunched and wrinkled it was a wonder he could see at all. The old man studied him a moment before giving a small, polite bow of his head as well.

Shouts from inside another hovel broke the clatter of hooves and chatter of people in the street. Inside, a women dressed her child down for some misdeed.

When he reached the hovel, Issama hobbled his mare and pulled the valuable saddle and weapons off her back. Then he stood, frozen in front of the door. He had not entered this place in three years. Would Siker be waiting? The weight in his arms threatened to make his knees buckle, and Issama edged toward the door. He would have to open it carefully or risk the arrow trap he had set.

Before he could reach out, the door burst open. Siker drew up short, startled by his presence with a hand pressed against her heart. For a moment, they stood, staring at one other. He waited for her to say something, anything that might show him how she felt about his appearance. Slowly, she eased the saddle from his arms and set it inside the door, then took his weapons and placed them against the saddle. His heart hammered, worried that she would push him out. After all he had lost, the one thing he knew he could not handle losing was her. How had he grown to love her so much?

Tears shimmered in her eyes, but still she did not reach for him. He didn't dare reach for her first.

"I thought you died," she said at last, her voice trembling.

"Why?" Issama had not been so far behind schedule she should be worried he would not return.

Siker snatched his arm and pulled him over the threshold, throwing her arms around his neck. Her body trembled against his own. He snaked his arms around her, stroking her back. They held each other for a moment before he spotted Qolotai entering from another room further back in the hovel. She dropped the clay pot on the rug, momentarily frozen in place as the pot rolled on its side, spilling *airag* on the floor. A moment later, she broke from her spell and shoved the door closed behind him. Then Qolotai joined the embrace.

The reaction from Qolotai surprised Issama. He had always assumed she simply tolerated him. To be welcomed by both wives with so much affection relieved him.

Siker pulled away. Qolotai followed Siker's lead, lingering between them and the door. Siker sniffled and swiped her cheeks.

"Bigirsen is dead," Siker said, still shaking. "The Khan rode into the basin and cut off his head. Word has been all over Hami. They killed everyone in his camp, then burned the rest."

Issama's knees finally gave out. Qolotai caught him and eased him onto a stool near the door, then rushed off to get him something to eat and drink. *At long last!* The first piece of his plan had been completed. With Bigirsen out of the way, it opened new opportunities for Issama.

"Who is in charge here now?" he asked, angry at how violently his hand shook as he reached for the *airag* Qolotai had retrieved. She kneeled in front of him to help lift the cup and give him food.

Siker shook her head. "No one yet. It has only been a few days. When we heard, and we knew you had gone to confront him, we just assumed you were there when it happened."

The *airag* rolled down his throat, offering cool relief to his parched body. "We will have to buy our way into the palace quickly, then. If we move fast enough, I can have control of this place before the Khan arrives."

Siker shook her head. "He isn't headed this way. After they took Bigirsen's head, they turned south. All paths to the Ordos basin are closing."

Issama's stomach dropped. "He's cutting us off. First the Oirat, now the Ordos." *Have the Ordos Lords betrayed me?*

"And he has closed the Silk Road to any who will not pay him tribute," Siker added. "I hear merchants returning, complaining of his exorbitant tax."

Issama growled, which chaffed at his raw throat. "They are feeding his army."

Siker shifted, exchanging an anxious glance with Qolotai.

Issama gritted his teeth. "What is it?"

She licked her lips. "The rumors are spreading."

"What rumors?"

Qolotai drew back, leaving the *airag* and bread at his feet. She put space between the two of them, glancing at Siker nervously.

"That the spirit of Genghis rides with Dayan Khan," Siker said at last, wringing her hands together.

Time seemed to stop. Issama's head spun. He pressed his back against the cold sandstone wall. Both women froze in place, watching him with anxious eyes. After all this time, after all this work, Issama faced perhaps his greatest challenge yet—overthrowing a boy the people saw as divine. He closed his eyes and took deep, measured breaths. Was it even possible anymore? If he could not count on the Ordos, he would have to change his plans.

"Issama," Siker said, her voice timider than he had ever heard it before. "I do not think we have enough to buy our way into power here. It would cost us everything we own. Perhaps more."

He understood the implication well enough. *If the boy Khan garnered enough respect, men will flock to him like a Christian to the Virgin Mary,* he thought sarcastically. People adored their useless idols, gravitating toward them as if it could save them. He cursed under his breath and peeled his eyes open. If Dayan had so much power now, opposing him without the support of the Ordos would cost Issama—and possibly his family—their lives.

"We can use your position to elbow our way into the boy's graces," Issama said. Hopefully, Mandukhai and Dayan did not know anything of what he had done over the years. There was no reason to believe they knew the truth. Issama had been careful to cover his tracks for more than ten years. He needed their ignorance to save the lives of his family. "You are his mother, after all. I will take Hami in the name of the Khan, with his mother at my side." With any luck, Mandukhai and Dayan would be ignorant to his misdeeds, accept his position in Hami, and even allow him to keep it. Then he could rebuild his strength.

Issama reached for her.

Siker tensed and retreated a step back. "He will not show me mercy. Not after being raised in *her* care."

"You are his mother," Issama snapped. "He would not exist without you!"

"He's done just fine so far without me."

Issama frowned. "You are afraid he will reject you." He scoffed and shook his head. "You don't need to worry, Siker. From what I hear, the boy has a tender heart."

"The boy did." Siker nodded, folding her hands into the sleeves of her deel. "But he is not a boy any longer, Issama. And I chose you over his father and him. How do you think he would ever forgive me?"

Issama caught the hem of her deel and pulled her into his lap, then wrapped his arms around her. "All of that was Bayan's fault. Explain that to him. Bayan left you with no choices, Siker."

"You want me to beg my son for your life," she said. Her entire body was rigid in his arms.

"*If* the time comes, I want you to beg your son for all of our lives."

Somehow, no matter what Issama planned, there was always a challenger to the place that should be his.

Dayan had quickly learned the reason the Ordos tribes controlled so much of the south was simply because so much of the land was barren and deadly. Unprepared for such a long campaign, he had needed fresh mounts and food for his *tumens*. The size has grown to nearly thirty-five-thousand, and it had forced him to promote men to command the ever swelling ranks.

He had sent Ogedei, Dochigen, and Tulugen south with a full *tumen* and nearly half again as many of the absorbed Ordos. They now traveled around the sand and salt desert to close in from the far south where another five-thousand Ordos lived, scattered across the plateau. The rest of Dayan's men swung north around the same desert and swept across the wasteland like a net, scooping up wayward families or smaller Ordos forces. Soon enough, they would reach Mogurkei's camp.

But the need for food had turned their attention to the Silk Road. Control of the road was always troublesome. Between the Uyghur to the west and the Ming to the east, Mongols could not control any portion of the road for long. Unebolod had insisted they had no other choice but to raid the caravans along the road.

Dayan sat atop his yellow mare, watching as a hundred of his men set the trap for a merchant caravan. They used the land to their advantage, hiding the bulk of their forces a mile off the road. Only a hundred of his men waited on the ridges on either side of the road. The moment the caravan entered the depression, the warriors closed around it with expert ease. On Dayan's order, no one was to be killed unless they struck first. He had a simple goal in mind. Supplies for his army.

Once the caravan was stopped and secured, he rode down with his guards and Unebolod. The banners fluttered around him so that all knew who rode in. Dayan's only job was to sit in his saddle near the wagons and camels and watch the man in charge with his unnerving golden eyes.

Unebolod rode a few steps close to a man in dirty robes. The man bore a scowl on his face that seemed permanently etched in it. His gaze was locked on Unebolod, but he didn't touch the weapon on his hip.

"You travel the Great Khan's road," Unebolod said. "To pass through his land, you must pay him tribute."

The man sputtered. "Humble apologies, but we have little to offer the Khan of khans."

Dayan squared his shoulders and hardened his gaze on the man. The subtle motion caught the merchant's attention, and his eyes widened as he stared at Dayan.

"Khan of khans—"

Unebolod cut the merchant off with a backhand that sent him sprawling. He jumped from the saddle and loomed over the merchant. "You do not address the Great Khan unless the Great Khan so requests it."

The merchant threw himself on his hands and knees, pressing his face to the dirt as apologies rushed from his lips.

"To travel the Khan's road, you must pay him a tribute," Unebolod said, then motioned for the men to loot the carts. "He requires a third."

The merchant lifted wide eyes to Unebolod. "A third! But we shall have nothing for profit once taxes are paid all along the road."

"That is not the Great Khan's problem."

Dayan's stomach twisted with regret. He did not want to leave these merchants destitute. They would not travel his road again if he did, and he would not profit from future trade. Mandukhai stressed the importance of balancing their economy in the new empire. If he ruined their chances now, she would be angry with him for quite some time.

Once they had taken their third, they escorted the merchant up the road to safety, then returned to their own camp to celebrate.

Dayan did not feel celebratory as he dismounted and strode away from the cluster of commanders around a campfire. He left administration of the loot to Unebolod and sat on a boulder away from the bulk of his officers to be alone for a few minutes. The *airag* burned as he drank, but he had been forced to develop a taste for it on campaign. *Airag* was easier to make than water was to come by. The tea looted from the merchants was useless without water.

Nemeku marched toward him, hand on the sword he had been given—his father's sword, though Nemeku had ripped off the horsehairs and replaced them with his own. It had been a minor act of defiance.

Boke and the guards lingered nearby, as always. A dozen warriors trailed behind Nemeku, including Ulum, which drew Boke's attention and put the rest of the guards on alert. Nemeku's mother had been a Borjigin princess, just as Esige was. While Nemeku himself was not Borjigin like Dayan, that bloodline could open the door for Nemeku to challenge Dayan and take over with the right Lords behind him. Dayan found it curious that Ulum aligned himself with Nemeku in this.

Orghana tugged at Nemeku's hand, pulling him away and pleading with him.

Dayan's stomach twisted. He knew this moment would come. He had ordered it. Nothing Orghana said would change anything.

"Dayan Khan," Nemeku said, speaking loud and clear so that any who were nearby would hear him. "Son of Bayan and Siker, blood of my blood, I challenge your right to the title, as is my right as the son of a Borjigin princess."

Boke growled before Nemeku even finished speaking. Dayan held up a held up a hand to silence the guard. "I have given you Guest Rights, Nemeku."

"I understand," Nemeku said with a nod. "Defeat me in combat and I will give my oath and never challenge your right again."

"My lord Khan—" Boke once more was cut off.

"I accept." Dayan spoke before anyone could interrupt, before Unebolod or any of his generals heard and stopped him. "At sunset today. You understand, cousin, that I cannot submit to you. Either you will submit to me, or you will kill me. Such is the way."

"Please, I beg you, Nemeku, don't do this," Orghana petitioned, stepping between them. "If you kill him, his guards will kill you."

Nemeku swallowed. "I accept the terms."

Dayan stood and held out a hand to Nemeku. "My men will honor the outcome of the challenge. If you defeat me, they will follow you as they have followed me."

Word spread like fire through the camp, as it often did. Dayan had spent the rest of the evening keeping a careful distance from everyone—particularly Unebolod. Several times, the *orlok* had come looking for him, and Dayan would duck away before Unebolod could find him. Not that he was a coward or afraid of Unebolod. But he had no desire to listen to the older man lecture him.

The outcome was already decided. He and Nemeku both understood this. No one else, not even Orghana, knew the truth.

As sunset arrived, Dayan strode toward the makeshift ring that had formed. Thousands of men crowded the landscape, making the depression in the rocky terrain perfect for this fight. If they spread out far enough, most of the men could see.

Nemeku stepped out of a pathway of bodies wearing full armor, across the shallow valley.

Boke held out Dayan's shield. "I will ask again, my lord Khan. Let me fight for you. I will end this quickly."

Dayan patted Boke's shoulder, then accepted the shield. He had grown used to the weight of the metal reinforced disk.

Unebolod stomped toward Dayan with all the generals trailing behind him like shadows.

"This is foolish, Dayan," Unebolod snapped. "No one would follow him even if he won. He is more Uyghur than Borjigin. This is his father's doing."

Dayan pulled his sword from his belt and tested the weight in one hand. "No. This is inevitable, and we both know it."

"End him swiftly then," Belku said.

"I will not."

"You must," Unebolod said sharply. "He has challenged your legitimacy. You cannot let that go unpunished."

Dayan's temper flared, and he turned hard, sharp eyes on all of his generals. "You do not command the Great Khan! I command you. And you will honor the outcome of this no matter what it is."

They cowered back. Dayan stared at Unebolod. "If I die, she is yours."

"If you die, she will kill me herself," Unebolod snapped. "Remember to use *all* your senses." Then he stomped off to the side for a better view, crossing his arms over his broad chest.

"This is an unnecessary risk," Kelegei grumbled.

Dayan shifted his shoulders to adjust the armor, then turned toward Nemeku across the shallow valley. "If I defeated Unebolod, I can defeat Nemeku," he said confidently.

Kelegei choked and stepped closer. "You didn't beat him. He let you win. Did you not see that?"

Dayan hesitated. No, he distinctly remembered winning that fight.

"Way to make him doubt himself right before he fights to the death," Boke grumbled under his breath.

Did Unebolod let him win? And if so, why?

I cannot let this cloud my mind right now, Dayan thought as he strode down the shale slope to the valley floor.

Nemeku met him in the center of the wide open space.

"Let's make this a good show," Dayan said.

The corner of Nemeku's mouth turned upward. "Who said anything about a show?"

The question caught Dayan off guard. Would this be a sincere fight? His heart hammered and perspiration beaded under his helmet. The two of them circled each other, watching how the other moved with their shields raised in front of them. Nemeku had learned how to fight from Huoshai, who was a great fighter, but everyone knew his strength was with the bow. Dayan had learned from Unebolod, who was the best at everything. Even if Nemeku meant this as a serious contest, Dayan had better training and more battle experience. He also had the spirit of the Eternal Blue Sky on his side.

Nemeku's boots tipped forward as he shuffled experimentally toward Dayan's exposed side. Dayan responded by dropping the shield to block, then swinging his sword out and up toward Nemeku's face. Dust kicked up under their feet as they both staggered back and circled each other again. A stubborn determination set between Nemeku's brows and his dark eyes burned with concentration. *He is thinking too much*, Dayan realized.

Dayan lunged forward, hammering blow after blow against Nemeku's shield. Nemeku planted his feet in the slippery shale and dug in his heels. With two mighty thrusts of his shield, he pushed Dayan off balance. As Dayan struggled to regain his footing, Nemeku heaved his sword down. Dayan hardly got his shield up before the blow struck, forcing him to his knees. *He is stronger than he looks.*

The crowd of thousands gathered in the massive ring roared as they watched the contest. Most of the men followed Dayan and expected him to win. *He* had expected to win. Now, with Nemeku pressing him to his knees, Dayan wondered if Nemeku had tricked him. Just how much like his father was Nemeku?

Dayan thrust his sword up behind Nemeku's shield and encountered some resistance. Nemeku jerked the shield back, yanking the sword from Dayan's hand. *I've made a terrible mistake.*

The rim of Nemeku's shield hit the ground and rolled away, spinning like a top as it settled. Another barrage of attacks hammered against Dayan's shield and he ducked behind it, reaching desperately for his sword. Nemeku's sword grazed the metal plate covering Dayan's shoulder, driving it away from his neck. As he stretched for his sword, Dayan realized he faced a terrible choice. He could either drop the shield to get his sword, or continue hiding behind it without a weapon. Neither option boded well for him.

"Get up!" Nemeku roared. His voice carried around the valley as he grabbed the shield and yanked it away, forcing Dayan out from behind it.

Use all the senses. Dayan closed his eyes and listened. The subtle shift of shale beneath them gave away Nemeku's next move. Dayan's eyes snapped open. Nemeku plunged his sword straight toward Dayan's chest. Ready, Dayan rolled aside, snatching his sword in his hand again as he bounced back to his feet. Nemeku's sword skidded across the shale with a painfully loud shriek.

He tried to kill me, Dayan realized as he raised his sword.

The two circled each other once more, shieldless. "We had a deal," Dayan growled.

"No, we didn't," Nemeku snapped. "You gave an order and expected me to obey. I never agreed to let you win."

"You said you didn't want this," Dayan replied, watching how Nemeku's body tensed, listening to his movements and the wind, seeking signs of attack.

Nemeku was barely two years younger than Dayan. He was nearly fifteen now and had not been a weak boy as Dayan had. Nemeku had fought and wrestled and rode when Dayan could hardly walk without crumbling from exhaustion. They had been like brothers in those early years. How had it come to this?

The subtle shift in Nemeku's stance gave away his move a fraction of a second before he lunged forward, attacking with all the power his arms had in them. Dayan raised his sword to block. The hilts locked for a moment. Dayan pressed harder, hoping to throw Nemeku off balance as their swords ground against each other. A gloved fist blindsided Dayan, and he stumbled to the side, ears ringing. Nemeku's sword hacked at the armor covering Dayan's back.

Dayan spun in a rage, swinging the sword as a distraction as his fist connected with Nemeku's jaw and knocked the helmet off his head. The blades glanced off each other. Nemeku followed through quickly, slicing Dayan's side. Dayan gritted his teeth so he didn't scream as the sword sliced through the silk at the seam of his armor. He stumbled back, clutching his side with his free hand, glaring at Nemeku. His cousin rubbed his jaw and spit blood on the ground.

"So much for a friendly fight," Dayan snapped. "You were my blood."

"I still am!" Nemeku snarled as he plunged forward.

Their swords hacked at each other, block, grind, swing, glance, swing, grind, block. Their feet tested each other as they both tried to catch the other and trip them on their back. The cut in Dayan's side burned white hot, fueling his rage. The rest of the world fell away. All Dayan could see was Nemeku. All he could hear was the shuffling of their feet on the shale, the grinding of their weapons against each other, the growls of combat. All he could smell was sweat, blood, and dust. The cut on his side had become inflamed, searing up his entire side and into his arm. His cheekbone was swollen from a punch to the face.

"I wonder," Nemeku grunted as he held his sword at his side to prepare for the next attack. Blood trickled from the corner of his mouth and his eyebrow. An ugly bruise already formed around his eye. "Do you think Mandukhai would accept me as a husband in your place?"

Dayan's skin mottled and the grip on his sword was white knuckled and shaking. His nostrils flared. He peeled back his lips in a furious sneer. All the muscles in his body screamed in rage, eager to finish this. Instead of plunging forward, he planted his feet like a bull and rolled his shoulders. His pulse increased, drumming in his ears. Pain from his wounds vanished in a rush. This was no longer just a matter of his pride. If Nemeku thought Dayan would let him touch her ...

A mocking smile twitched at the corner of Nemeku's lips.

Dayan howled and surged forward, swinging his sword with abandon, battering at Nemeku's blade repeatedly as he released a fierce battle cry. The bloodlust had taken over. Dayan no longer had control. His emotions took charge.

The swords vibrated against each other continually. A twist of Dayan's blade forced both weapons from their hands, but Dayan had already planted a foot behind Nemeku's. The moment the weapons were gone, Dayan swept Nemeku's leg out from under him.

Nemeku's back slammed into the ground. Dayan didn't hesitate. He pounced on Nemeku like a hungry wolf, slamming a fist against Nemeku's jaw. His other fist found a kidney. Pure rage pumped through Dayan's veins, unlike anything he had ever felt before.

"I submit!" Nemeku shrieked.

The words drifted into Dayan's ears as if through water. His fingers grasped Nemeku's hair at the scalp hard enough to make Nemeku cry out.

"Dayan, I submit! You win!" Nemeku squirmed and bucked under him, clawing at his arm. Terror shined in his dark eyes.

Dayan snarled.

"I submit," Nemeku whimpered as Dayan punched him in the side again.

The roar of the distant crowd shattered the heart-pounding silence in Dayan's ears. His name echoed off the shallow valley walls, hammering back against him.

Orghana cried and shrieked for mercy as several men held her back from charging for Nemeku.

"Finish him!" A familiar voice of Belku hollered from the distance.

Nemeku's fearful gaze locked on Dayan. He loosened his grip on Nemeku's hair, panting hard as sweat rolled down his face in waves.

"I didn't mean it," Nemeku whimpered. "I didn't mean it."

Dayan sat back, still straddled over his foe, and dropped his arms at his sides. "You didn't mean it," he mumbled, as if seeking the meaning.

Nemeku calmed as he realized Dayan had finally stopped. "You wanted a show," Nemeku said at last, a tremor in his voice.

Dayan suddenly understood. Nemeku had riled him up so that their fight had been real. But what if he had lost, as he nearly had a few times? "You are insane."

Nemeku laughed, a desperate sound that cracked the tension between them. "I don't think *you* can call *me* that."

Dayan patted Nemeku on the face and climbed off. He held out a hand to help Nemeku up. His cousin took the hand, but didn't stand. Instead, he rolled to his knees, holding tight to Dayan's hand.

"Dayan Khan, I relinquish all rights to titles unless the Great Khan gives me those titles," Nemeku said. Though both of them were panting, dripping sweat, and exhausted, Nemeku raised his voice loud enough that some men nearby must have heard. "I offer you salt, gers, horses, and, when necessary, blood from this day until the end of my days."

The ring had tightened around them as the warriors drew closer. Jangi held Orghana back as Dayan and Nemeku finished. Hundreds now clustered around, cheering as if a new day had dawned.

"Rise then, *Lord* Nemeku," Dayan said, pulling his cousin to his feet. "You have earned the right to your title, but you and your children will never be Borjigin heirs. You will be treated as you are, a Mongol Lord and cousin to your Great Khan, and from this moment forward, you will be shown all the respect your position entitles you to. You are my blood."

Nemeku gave his thanks and winced as he bowed. At that moment Orghana broke free from Jangi's grip and raced to Nemeku, inspecting his injuries with quick, experience eyes, before throwing her arms around him and helping him limp away.

Dayan picked up his sword and shield, fighting off a scream as the cut on his side reminded him of its existence. Men closed in around him as he strode with the straightest back he could manage, away from the valley.

"You fight like your father," a warrior said, patting Dayan on the back as if that were a great compliment.

Dayan winced. Under the circumstances, those words offered Dayan no comfort at all. He had been ready to kill Nemeku. He had become ugly, wild, and impulsive. If that was the sort of man his father had been, that was the last man he wanted to be like.

Dayan knew he would have to allow Getei to see to his wounds right away. Then he would spend the night in meditation, praying that the High Heavens could forgive him for becoming such a gruesome beast.

CHAPTER TWENTY-TWO

To Bait A Queen

LAKE DAI – LATE WINTER 1480

Jaghan stood beside Mandukhai outside the gathering tent. The other woman's eyes had grown at least double as she gazed upon the carts laden with finely woven silk clothing. It was a rather substantial fortune in silk alone.

Mandukhai, however, did not show her awe as she gazed at the line of carts fading toward the south.

The Ming knew Mandukhai had a growing army on their threshold. They would have had to be blind not to notice. It had only been a matter of time before they realized just how large her Mongol force had become. And without Bigirsen to control the southern Mongols or a sufficient Ming military presence, she suspected they sweated her being there.

Years ago, before she named Dayan Great Khan, the Ming had attempted enticing her with a comfortable, pampered life. She had received an offer to join the Ming royal court, learn how to write Chinese, and otherwise live in a way they deemed civilized. But Mandukhai had grown on the steppe, living the life of a nomad, and she had learned to write in her own Mongol language. She had immediately recognized the offer for what it was. Prison.

Sure, she could have lived how she liked and never worried about ruling a nation. But she knew in her heart she never could have lived such a sedentary life. Those years with Manduul remaining fixed in place had been the most grueling years of her life. If she had submitted to the Ming, she would have also given over the Mongol Nation.

It had never been a choice. Such a life was not meant for her wild heart.

Now, with her army so close to their borders, the Ming were restless. They could not stand against her, and she knew it. Instead, they sent her bait.

"How many?" she asked Togochi, eyeing the line of carts.

He shook his head, momentarily too stunned to speak. At last, he licked his lips and shook his head. "I don't have an official count, but it appears to be over fifty carts."

The Ming ambassador continued bowing at the base of the gathering tent cart—albeit at the edge of a blade. He had resented bowing to a Mongol, let alone a woman. Mandukhai now ignored him like the ant he was. He would learn respect one way or another.

"This is more silk than I have seen in my life," Jaghan murmured.

After a small motion of approval from Mandukhai, Jaghan descended the steps of the gathering tent cart and approached the nearest wagon, running her long fingers over a fine pink dress—of Ming style, Mandukhai noted.

A crowd had gathered to stare at the wealth of silk in admiration. Women murmured appreciatively at the stacks of colorful dresses. Men conversed about reinforcing battle armor. Mandukhai knew she could not send this wealth away now that the people had laid eyes upon it.

Torgus continued standing over the Ming ambassador, holding the sword at the man's neck and watching Mandukhai for any indication that he should kill the tiny man.

"You will return to your emperor to deliver my message," Mandukhai said, speaking loud and clear so everyone around her could hear. "I accept his tribute, though I am uncertain how he will top such wealth in his next payment."

The ambassador choked on her words, raising his head to gaze at her. "This is not tribute! He offers you this in exchange for—"

The rest cut off as Torgus smashed his foot down on the ambassador's back, slamming his face into the dirt.

"You may not speak to the Great Khatun, Mandukhai the Wise, without her permission," Torgus said.

"*Orlok*, see that someone safely escorts the ambassador to Ming territory," Mandukhai ordered. "He is not to be harmed. I want to be certain his emperor gets the message."

"Your will, my lady Khatun," Togochi said formally, putting on a show for the ambassador.

She turned and headed into the gathering tent alone.

It was a risky move to challenge the Ming emperor in such a way, claiming this was due tribute to a Khan he did not submit to. But the emperor had cast his bones and revealed the truth. He feared her presence, and he needed horses, which she controlled. The black market horses had likely drained the empire's coffers. She smiled to herself. The Ming would be no threat for some time.

HAMI – LATE WINTER 1480

Issama swiped sweat from his forehead as he waited in the shadows of an alley for the Mongols to reach him. These three Mongol men had control of the doors leading into the Hami palace. If Issama wanted in, he needed these men on his side. He only hoped his relationship with the Oirat remained beneficial.

Down the street, the afternoon market was relatively empty. Since news of Bigirsen's death and the destruction of his army, many people had deserted the markets for safer territory. Surely a war would break out over control of Hami, as these people were accustomed to. He licked his lips as he watched a woman barter for a loaf of day-old bread. Bitter, salty sweat from his upper lip coated his tongue. Issama winced. Hami was one of those rare places that could freeze at night and turn blazing hot under the sun, even in winter.

The Mongol men spotted him and glanced around the market before slipping around the corner to join him. They had agreed to this meeting, as long as he showed up with the silver Issama had promised them. One of them—a man with a round belly from too much *airag*—reached for the leather sack in Issama's hand. Issama immediately placed his free hand on his sword and turned his hip away. The leather sack contained all the silver he could scrounge up—every sliver he possessed. It was a hefty price to get in the door, and Issama worried these men would betray him. A last resort would be to kill them and sneak into the palace to seize control before anyone could stop him. But he needed men to do that. Men he didn't have.

"We have a deal?" Issama asked. "I give you this silver, and when I am ready, you open this door and help me get inside."

"We can keep our end," the fatter man said. "Can you keep yours? How can you kill Lord General Alayitung from the palace? He is with Asha khan deep in Oirat territory."

Asha khan was the son of the late Paisahan, and has been controlled by Mandukhai's Lord General for years. Not all of the Oirat were pleased with the arrangement.

"I have my ways," Issama replied. "But unless I have control of this city, Asha will never control your tribe again. Get me in when I come, and I will see that Lord Alayitung is replaced with your khan's heir, Lord Asha."

Issama understood their Oirat weakness. Mandukhai had conquered them and put her own Borjigin man in charge of the Oirat tribes. If Issama could get in her good graces with this city, he could finish what he started and restore Asha to power. Then, with the power of the Ordos and Oirat behind him, Issama still had a chance to seize everything.

Round Belly reached for the sack again, grunting in agreement. "Tomorrow at sunset."

The stove in Dayan's command tent blazed with heat to ward off the deadly cold of desert nights. He stood at the edge of the map table, thumbs hooked in his belt and expression impassive as the commanders talked.

Thus far, the absorbing of the Ordos camps had gone smoothly—too smoothly, according to some. Each time another camp submitted to Dayan's men, Unebolod would distribute the Ordos warriors across the different *mingghans* so that they were not all together. By Dayan's estimation, they now had as many Ordos warriors as he had his own men. *They are all my men now*, Dayan reminded himself.

"What can we expect from the terrain around Mogurkei's main camp?" Unebolod asked Ulum. "Is there anything useful to battle?"

"Nothing he would not already know of," Ulum replied. He motioned toward the map, pointing at a path through a rocky crag. "This is the best point of approach. He will have scouts all along it, but we can easily deal with those men before they can warn him. Then Mogurkei won't see us coming until it's too late."

Dayan examined the area around the crag. Perhaps Ulum was right, but it also served as a funnel. An ambush should Mogurkei be ready for them. There would be no escaping. It would be a death trap.

The rumbling sigh that rolled out of Unebolod indicated he saw the same problem. He wouldn't lead the men into the crag.

"If I may offer an alternative to attack," Ulum said.

Dayan met the Ordos Lord's gaze and nodded once.

"Allow me to meet with Mogurkei," Ulum offered. "I can ease his tension and perhaps bring him in without needing to attack."

Belku snorted and rolled his eyes. The distrust he had for the Ordos had caused trouble for Dayan several times these past weeks. Dayan had warned him against punishing the Ordos for trivial matters. In one instance, Belku had beaten an Ordos warrior nearly to death for failing to break camp quickly enough.

Dayan shot a warning glare at Belku. The Chakhar Lord grimaced and averted his gaze in shame.

"Do you think you can succeed?" Dayan asked.

"If not, he is likely to kill me as a traitor, in which case you will have your answer," Ulum replied. Something about his tone was far too casual for such a statement.

"Then you have permission," Dayan said.

Ulum smiled.

"Take Kelegei and Chakicha with you," Dayan added. "It will be good for Mogurkei to see that I have rewarded you with trust in our inner circle for giving your oath."

Kelegei frowned. Chakicha shifted from one foot to the other as if eager to leave that moment.

Dayan only hoped this gamble paid off. If Mogurkei killed them instead, Dayan would lose two of his tribal leaders.

HAMI – LATE WINTER 1480

The air had already grown bitter cold before the sun fully set over the city. Issama crouched in the shadows across the wide street from the palace, waiting for his escorts. If Round Belly did not keep his word, Issama would have to fight his way in. That was unlikely to end well unless he had any luck on his side. Lately, luck had not been his companion.

The wide paved street had few pedestrians or carts so close to the palace. Everyone avoided this part of town as if it had become infested with some form of a plague. Any man bold enough to seize control would have to wage war on this palace to do so.

Issama hoped for an easier resolution. If he could just march through the doors with an escort, battle would be unnecessary.

He glanced up and down the street again. Nothing moved but his own shadow. Round Belly was nowhere to be seen—nor were his friends. *They have stolen my silver and left me*, he thought bitterly.

The clatter of hooves on the paved street drew Issama's attention away from the palace. His heart sank.

Riding toward the palace, wearing full battle gear and surrounded by half a dozen fluttering banners, Lord Alayitung led an escort of a hundred men.

And at his side, Lord Asha sat tall and proud.

Round Belly knew they were coming and had either deceived Issama to steal his silver, or he avoided Issama knowing that today would be a lost cause.

If I had my network of spies, I would had known they were coming before I paid those men a sliver of silver

WESTERN ORDOS PLATEAU – LATE WINTER 1480

Unebolod hated this entire plan. Sitting out in the open with Mogurkei aware of their position. Sending a lesser khan and the Tabun heir to help smooth the transition of power. Waiting. He loathed waiting.

His boots scuffed the dirt as he paced outside of the command tent. When he left on this mission to kill Bigirsen, Unebolod had been overflowing with excitement. The men had obeyed his commands without question. Now, they all cast their gazes toward Dayan, waiting for him to confirm Unebolod's orders. It had not yet been an issue, but it could end up costing them precious moments to react in an emergency. *Dayan needs to clarify that the men have to follow my orders*, he thought, unknowingly clenching his jaw.

A scout arrived just an hour ago, citing the approach of at least a hundred riders. Unebolod had set up a wall of warriors around their camp in case anyone attacked. Perhaps these riders were a distraction from the real approaching force of Ordos. *Have I become so paranoid in my older age?*

From within the command tent, Unebolod heard the muffled voices of Dayan and Getei. The Khan and the shaman spent hours in there together each day as they waited for Ulum and the commanders to return. *More meditation probably*. Unebolod did not understand why Dayan wasted his time with it.

A group of men approached the tent on horseback. Boke and the Khan's guards created a line of weapons that forced the riders to dismount.

Unebolod eyed each of the men. Kelegei, Chakicha, and Ulum among them. But a dozen Ordos men accompanied them. Unebolod stopped pacing and knocked on the tent door, then waited with his hand on his sword.

Dayan followed Getei outside. The Khan's piercing eyes landed immediately on the Ordos Lord in the center of the pack. Was that Mogurkei? Unebolod could not remember how old Mogurkei was. This man had to be close to his own age, if not a little older. His braided beard was laced with silver hairs and his dark eyes had hard edges around them. Mogurkei's frame was beastly large.

A small crowd gathered behind the lines of Dayan's guards. Ordos and the Khan's own men blended together. Dayan approached the new arrivals, stopping just out of reach of any sword as if by instinct. The many colored belts at the Khan's waist fluttered on the chilly breeze.

Kelegei, Chakicha, and Ulum immediately kneeled with their heads bowed. Dayan waited with his hand resting casually on his sword for the rest of the new arrivals to do so as well. They would not, until Mogurkei did first.

Unebolod's muscles tightened, prepared to strike out should anything happen.

Mogurkei's hard gaze swept the Khan. Then he raised his chin proudly. Would he refuse now, surrounded by Dayan's men? Surely he could not be such a fool. Perhaps only a few seconds had passed, but it felt like minutes before Mogurkei eased himself gracefully to his knees. The rest of his men followed his lead.

"My lord Khan," Mogurkei said as he bowed close to the ground. "Lord Ulum and your commanders have spoken high praises. I have heard the rumors that you ride with the spirit of Genghis." He raised his gaze. "Now that I have seen you, I also see the truth of these rumors. Only a fool would stand against someone with such a spirit at his disposal. I hope you can accept my humblest apologies if I have caused you trouble in the past. I can assure you those days are behind me."

Unebolod narrowed his eyes. He didn't like this. It reeked of a plot. But he wouldn't move. Not unless Mogurkei refused to give his vow.

"I did not request your presence for apologies," Dayan said. "You can reassure me with your oath of fealty. I will accept nothing less from you or your men."

"Of course," Mogurkei said a little too quickly for Unebolod's liking. "I offer my rightful Khan salt, gers, horses, and blood from this breath until my last, under the Eternal Blue Sky."

Something about this created an itch between Unebolod's shoulder blades, a discomfort he could not place. He watched Dayan's reaction, the calculating way the Khan eyed the Ordos men as they all gave their oaths. When it was done and Mogurkei had kissed Dayan's ring, Dayan pulled the Lord to his feet. The way Dayan clung to Mogurkei's arm even after the man had risen, how he pulled him closer, set Unebolod's teeth on edge.

"Send word to your men further south that they are to report to my commanders," Dayan said. Something dangerous lingered in the young Khan's eyes.

"I am already a step ahead of you," Mogurkei replied. "I heard of your approach and warned my men to use caution. They know what to do when your men arrive."

"To surrender to the Khan's men," Unebolod clarified. He didn't appreciate the way Mogurkei said any of that. On the surface it sounded like an agreement with Dayan's command, but beneath that, Unebolod sensed a lurking danger.

Weeks bled away. Mandukhai loathed every moment of each day that Dayan and Unebolod continued their trek slowly toward the Huang Ho River. Every time she heard the bells of a yam rider approaching, she met him eagerly, devouring every word they sent her way. Togochi had sent them a warning about Lord Mogurkei, but Mandukhai did now know if they had received it yet.

The most recent message from Unebolod caused some alarm at first. Mandukhai read Unebolod's tight script, sensing his frustration with each short, sharp slice of his writing. Nemeku had challenged Dayan's right. Mandukhai pressed a hand to her lips, unable to breathe as she read the rest of the message. It was not until she saw the results of the contest that she could draw another breath. Dayan won and handled himself admirably under the circumstances—though Unebolod's words hinted he did not agree. Dayan showed Nemeku mercy and removed Nemeku's right to be an heir. The news told her he had grown wiser. Some men believed mercy was weakness. Mandukhai believed it showed strength.

The message also reported the *tumens* continuing to grow the closer they drew to the Ordos basin. Just as she felt pride at Dayan's judgment, the prospect of seeing them again bubbled to the surface.

By the time you receive this, our forces should be near enough to close the bow formation around the plateau in just two more weeks. His last words warmed her insides.

Two weeks, and she would see them both again.

As she folded up the message and tucked it safely away with the rest, a guard entered the gathering tent and reported another caravan of carts had entered her camp. She headed outside and recognized the curtained Ming box almost immediately. This time, the emperor had sent a noble instead of an ambassador.

Her warriors stopped the caravan, examining the contents as she watched from the gathering tent cart, her hands wrapped around the railing. Catcalls from her warriors sounded along the line.

Togochi led the wheeled litter toward Mandukhai from the rear of the line, holding the reins of the horses pulling the litter along until they reached the edge of the gathering tent cart.

"What have they brought this time, Togochi?" Mandukhai asked.

"Grains, spices, wines, fruits, and other delicacies," he said.

The discomfort on his face drew a frown from her. "And?"

"And women for the Great Khan's harem," Togochi said.

Mandukhai grimaced. That explained the way her men were acting. She flicked her wrist. Torgus tugged the curtains aside and dragged the Ming Lord out of the litter. He was younger than she had expected, and far too thin. But a fire burned in his eyes that she knew was dangerous. Torgus used the lord's arm to control him, forcing him to his knees in front of her.

His young, angry eyes burned as he glared at her.

"Another suitable tribute from your emperor," Mandukhai said. "With these carts, we shall feed our men through the winter again. The women are of little use. Mongol men have no need for weak Ming dolls."

The Ming Lord sneered, but quickly composed himself. The snarl that had curled his nose and wrinkled his forehead smoothed away so swiftly, as if washed away by a great tide. "And what of them men he sent?"

Torgus raised his foot to press a boot into the young lord's back, but Mandukhai raised a hand to stop him. "We shall not be such barbarians that we treat a man clearly of noble birth like a commoner."

The catcalls stopped as a line of more than a dozen beautiful young Ming women—all apparently between fifteen and eighteen—kneeled in the dirt behind the lord. Mandukhai spotted the shock on their faces as they saw men kneeling to a woman.

"These women are not suitable for the Great Khan," Mandukhai said. "But I do owe Lord Qori a gift. Perhaps he will find use for them. What is your name?"

"Lei Wei, Lord of—"

"I don't care." Mandukhai waved the rest off. "What men do you speak of? Have you slipped soldiers into our midst?"

His jaw twitched. "No. The emperor sends male escorts for the queen."

Mandukhai blinked in alarm. Male escorts? She had not known such a thing even existed!

"We have sterilized them for—"

"Take them all back," Mandukhai commanded. "I have no need for your pleasure men. Leave the women. My men deserve a reward, and I'm certain Lord Qori will appreciate the gift."

"The Son of Heaven has commanded I not return unless I succeed," Lei Wei said.

"Then he shows his true face," Mandukhai said, raising a brow at him. "For he sends a Lord of no consequence to pay tribute to his superior."

"This is not tribute," Lei Wei snapped, sitting back on his heels and staring at her in open defiance. "These are merely samplings of what is coming when you kneel before him."

Hundreds of her men had crowded around to observe, probably hoping they could get their hands on a concubine. At Lei Wei's confession that the women and goods were meant to force Mandukhai to the kneel, every man and woman within earshot laughed in hearty amusement.

Mandukhai simply gestured toward them. "You can hear just what we think of this proposal. Your emperor is weak. We will leave him in peace ... for now. Should he come to his senses, I would be willing to open the Silk Road to his lands again. For a price."

Lei Wei raised his voice in protest, but the laughter of Mandukhai's men swallowed his words.

The emperor thought he could bait her, a queen, with silk and food while offering women to a Khan too young to know what to do with any of them. *Does he know what to do with women now?* She knew the nature of men on campaign, how they chose women to satiate their appetites. As Great Khan, Dayan would have first pick of any of the women. Would he give in to the temptation? She shook her head as she turned to head into the gathering tent. She had no room for doubt now.

CHAPTER TWENTY-THREE

Women and Warriors

Dayan's forces took over a small fishing village along the Huang Ho River for the evening. After aligning Mogurkei under his banner, Dayan had commanded Mogurkei's men further south to join them. The Ordos warriors were expected alongside Mogurkei at dawn. Then they could cross the frozen river and begin the campaign within the basin.

The homes in the village were logged with thatched roofs. Only a few stone structures marked out what had once been wealthy establishments. Now, those structures were battered and in disrepair.

Dayan followed his generals and *orlok* into one such stone building after they promised him a hearty meal and full appetite when he left. He had to admit he was starving for a proper meal. Ulum had insisted the establishment was one of his favorites to frequent.

What greeted Dayan inside did not promise a hearty meal. The lobby reeked of incense and alcohol so pungently that it slammed into his lungs. Most of Dayan's guards had taken up positions around the building. Only Boke had accompanied him inside—along with the commanders and generals—but something about Boke's expression made Dayan uneasy. Boke fought to smother amusement.

The moment the last of his generals were through the door and it closed behind them, a swarm of beautiful women flowed into the outer chamber from deeper inside. Dayan turned, but the women had surrounded them, blocking the door. Dayan tensed. Boke chuckled.

The women wore little more than sheer fabrics that hung loosely from their bodies, exposing far more than Dayan was prepared to see. Their hair was drawn back elegantly with coral decorations dangling and chiming to each fluid movement. The collection was a strange mixture of Ming, Mongol, and Hindu.

While he understood why some of his men needed release, Dayan had no interest in it himself. Panic clenched his chest and his gaze darted to the door as a young woman slid her hand along his arm. Dayan cast a pleading gaze in Boke's direction, but the guard simply crossed his arms with a crooked grin on his face. Dayan swallowed a lump that lodged in his throat. His heart hammered against his ribs. *I need to get out of here.*

One by one, his generals and commanders disappeared deeper into the building with at least one woman, if not more.

Chakicha encouraged Dayan to choose a few of the women. "It could be good for you to relieve some of that tension. A few of these women should do the trick."

More than one? The idea of one woman was bad enough, but Chakicha made it sound like Dayan needed an entire herd of them. Dayan's pulse thumped in his ears. He knew his face must have turned a brilliant shade of crimson.

Ulum nodded in agreement as his hands roamed over the chest of one woman. "Yes, I will even pay," Ulum added. "A special gift for my Khan."

Ulum nodded toward a young woman beside Dayan—the one with her hands all over Dayan's arm and chest. He wanted to push her away, but was frozen in terror. "That one can be whatever you need her to be. Gentle. Simple. Rough. Bendy. Have you ever been with a woman? Better to get the first one out of your system so you don't disappoint the Khatun when you do finally take her to bed."

Dayan had never suffered such humiliation. *My face will catch fire any second*, he thought. The idea of sticking his cock anywhere Ulum had already been—and apparently more than once—made his gut twist. He worried he might throw up. Was this a test of his manhood? What would these men think if he refused?

She leaned close, pressing her body against his chest. Her thigh slid along his own. Her hot breath rolled down his neck, making his head swim. The momentary distraction made him ignorant of where her hand had drifted until she pressed the heel of her palm against his crotch gently, enticing. Dayan jumped and stepped back as he nudged her away from him.

"I'm not interested," he said, but his voice shook in a way that gave away his inexperience with all of this. "As Great Khan, until I have sons, I cannot be so careless. Besides, I would rather not pay for it."

Ulum and Chakicha grinned at one another. "That will change one day," Ulum said.

Dayan shook his head. He could not imagine that ever changing. "Enjoy your night."

The two men shrugged as Dayan turned to head out the door. The very idea of lying with any woman other than Mandukhai did not appeal to him at all.

As he opened the door, Dayan was startled when he glimpsed Unebolod. The *orlok* disappeared into a room with more than one woman. Before he vanished, Unebolod noticed Dayan's face. The *orlok* grimaced but said nothing more. What would he say, anyway? Without a wife, Unebolod would need to find some way to release the tension. Dayan supposed he couldn't blame him, even if Dayan was not interested in the women himself.

Boke sighed in dismay as he followed Dayan out the door, but he did not complain. Clearly he had been hoping to partake as well, but if Dayan was not in the building, Boke could not stay or he risked punishment for abandonment.

Dismayed at losing out on an actual meal, Dayan sank down at a fire with some warriors and shared their roasted meat, listening to their tales of battle. But he could not stop thinking about Mandukhai. She distracted his attention until, worried he would offend someone when they realized he was not paying attention, Dayan excused himself from the fire and wandered the streets with his guards trailing in his shadow.

The river was east of the village. Tomorrow, he would take his men across the ice. And soon, he would see Mandukhai again. In just a few days, his *tumens* would meet Mandukhai's own forces. Would she be among the warriors? He hated holding on to hope, yet could not help fantasizing about their reunion. Would she finally see him as a man, or would he be forever cursed to appear as nothing more than a boy to her?

Months had passed since he left her at Lake Dai. Dayan had changed during his time away. Had she changed as well?

Dayan's wandering had brought him to a small hut where Nemeku and Orghana had rented a room for the evening. Maybe talking to his cousin would help.

He knocked on the door and entered, bowing respectfully to the family before wandering to the closed door of Nemeku's room. He rapped twice. Whispers and shuffling feet sounded from the other side of the door. A moment later, Nemeku opened it a crack and peeked out. Upon seeing Dayan, he opened the door a little more. Dayan could only glimpse the nearby wall through the gap.

Nemeku's hair hung loose, and he had clearly wrapped his deel around his body in haste. A flash of jealous raced through Dayan as he realized what he had interrupted. With his blessing, the two were free to marry at their will. All they had to do was declare it so, and it was done. Dayan wanted what they had and feared he would never find it.

"Is everything alright?" Nemeku asked, frowning at Dayan.

What must I look like? Dayan wondered. "Um. Yeah. I just ... sorry. I didn't realize ..."

Nemeku's frown shifted slightly into a hint of a smile. "I waited a full moon cycle, like you said."

Is he worried I'm mad at him? Dayan nodded. "Okay. Good. I'll just ... leave you to it."

Dayan turned and marched stiffly toward the door to leave the hut. He heard the door to the room close and latch somewhere behind him.

As he stepped outside, Dayan breathed in the frosty night air. *Well, that settles it. Nemeku is just shy of fifteen and already married and sleeping with Orghana. I am officially a lost cause.* Deep down, Dayan feared Mandukhai would never accept him. If she shared his bed, it would most likely be out of obligation, which may well drive her right back into the arms of Unebolod as it had when she was married to Manduul. He would never have anything like what Esige and Huoshai or Nemeku and Orghana had.

The bells of a yam rider drew Dayan's attention from his inner reflections. He paused. Boke and the guards closed around him in the middle of the street. Out in the open, he was an easy target for an expert archer. Though considering the small fortune his men were paying out in this village tonight, he doubted anyone would want to kill the man who brought them such wealth.

The rider dismounted and bowed to Boke, holding out a message. Tulugen, Dochigen, and Ogedei's men had finished absorbing the five thousand warriors in the far south. They had all surrendered as Mogurkei had promised they would. Their fourteen-thousand warriors would cross the frozen river in the morning.

It begins, Dayan thought.

Tonight, his men could enjoy themselves. Because it might be the last night for a long time any of them would have a chance.

Tomorrow, they would cross the frozen Huang Ho River.

HAMI – LATE WINTER 1480

Issama huddled near the wall of a sandstone hut near the bazaar on the east side of Hami. Merchants operated booths overflowing with fruits, fresh breads, cloth, spices—anything one would desire could be found in any of the six markets around the small city. It was also where warriors patrolled the streets and purchased their own goods.

Alayitung's takeover of Hami had been unchallenged. He and Lord Asha rode into town with thousands of men, right up to the palace and through the doors, claiming Hami in the name of Dayan Khan and Mandukhai Khatun. No one had controlled the city since Bigirsen's death, and the men guarding the palace had been Oirat. The guards had remained because they didn't know what else to do. Issama had hoped to capitalize on that uncertainty. But now it was too late.

What remained of Bigirsen's loyal men around the palace—and the city—were rounded up by Alayitung's men and killed without mercy. Like himself, any remaining Uyghur had learned in less than a day to remain hidden to avoid their own executions. Issama spent a fair amount of time searching for those hidden Uyghur, with little results.

Over the last two weeks, he had kept to the shadows of the city, observing the way the Khan's men patrolled the streets or left on missions. Issama was careful not to visit the same bazaar two days in a row, but just as careful to be sure he did not repeat any sort of pattern as he rotated around the six locations. He also listened to the Mongol men who visited the bazaar for signs of disgruntlement with the current leadership. No matter how powerful a Khan or his leaders were, there would always be men who found some dissatisfaction with how things operated. In Issama's experience, those were the places in between when he could swoop in on weakness to better position himself.

Not that he was sure what that position was at first. Any attempt to take control of the city now would be in opposition to Dayan Khan. His original plan had also included putting the Oirat khan, Asha, in charge again. But now Asha helped Mandukhai's General control the city. *Perhaps he just needs allies to help him overthrow her control*, Issama thought. His only choices now were to help Asha free the Oirat from Borjigin control, giving Issama control of Hami ... or he could abandon this mission and crawl to Mandukhai and try to elbow his way into her court. He had little faith that option would bear any fruit unless Dayan truly wanted his mother in his life. Would he, at this point? Had Siker been right?

Issama leaned against the wall of a home near the bazaar and bit into a wedge of Hami melon. The soft tissue of the fruit was easy to chew, and the flavor did not overwhelm his senses. He swiped his sleeve across his chin to catch stray juice.

There had to be Uyghur left in the city. *Perhaps I can sneak into the palace and convince Asha to help. We can throw off the yoke of the Khan, kill General Alayitung, and take control of the Oirat and Hami.* Mandukhai would then be cut off from economic wealth. It would only be a matter of time before her forces turned against her.

As he debated the merits of his options, Issama spotted Uyghur warriors. Alive. Free. He sat up straighter against the wall, sweeping his eyes across the bazaar to see if anyone noticed the clear Uyghur cut of the men's deels. A small cluster of three Oirat guards chatted with a young woman running a bread booth, their backs to the Uyghur. If they turned and spotted those Uyghur men, they would be facing execution like all the others Issama had watched Asha and Alayitung's men kill.

Issama licked his lips, easing off the ground and wrapping the cloth tighter around his head and neck to keep his face hidden. The hot woolen deel he wore was unbearable under the unrelenting sun, but now he was thankful for the drab clothing. It made him invisible in the crowd. He shuffled toward the Uyghur, skirting around the far edge of the bazaar to avoid catching the eyes of the Mongol guards.

As he drew within just a few feet of the Uyghur men, Issama raised his head just enough for them to see his face. They had fallen silent when they noticed his approach. Upon seeing his face, their eyes widened. Issama nodded toward an alleyway and ducked out of sight swiftly.

Issama walked slowly enough for the men to follow him, putting distance between them and the bazaar to avoid the Oirat guards. At last, he stopped in the shadows of the awning on an abandoned home.

"Lord Issama?" one man asked. His gaze swept over Issama critically. He sneered in disgust. "You look like a beggar." He fanned the air between them. "Smell like one, too."

"Better than wearing Uyghur clothing in the middle of a city occupied by the Great Khan's men," Issama snapped. "General Alayitung is killing any Uyghur they uncover."

The man, at least ten years older than Issama, scoffed and spit at the ground. "And they call the Uyghur usurpers. Yet this boy Khan has taken control of the Oirat, killing any who oppose him, and now sets up his men in one of *our* strongholds. We intend to remove them all."

Issama had to fight off the urge to roll his eyes. "And how would you do that?"

"Count his men. Storm the palace," the younger man said.

Issama shook his head. "You wouldn't get close enough to put a dent in their forces. I have been watching for weeks. General Alayitung and Lord Asha have thousands of men here, and the heaviest concentration of them is in and around the palace. Here is what you will do." Issama had to take command of these men before one of them could challenge him. "Find any other Uyghur lurking in the shadows in this city. We will meet at the pass through the Tianshan Mountains ten miles west of Hami and regroup together. The two of you won't make a difference alone. But if I can gather enough men, I can devise a strategy for retaking the city, then we can send for reinforcements from Turfan."

The older man scowled. "Who put you in charge?"

"Shall I make you a list?" Issama snapped. "You will do as I command, or I will call those Mongol guards over to kill you as I disappear. No one will ever find me. Now, will you take your chances with me, or the guards?"

The younger man nudged the older man's arm and nodded away from the alley. "Come on. I know where Dashai is holed up."

Issama watched the two melt into the crowd, adjusting their deels to hide the Uyghur cut along the collar. If the two of them lurked in the city, perhaps more of Bigirsen's men had survived. Issama could collect the stragglers, reforge his forces, and regain his power. If he could get enough men, he might just be able to convince Asha to turn against Alayitung. Between the Uyghur and Oirat in the city, Alayitung's own men would be outnumbered.

Then Issama would have the power of the Oirat, Uyghur, and Ordos at his disposal.

CHAPTER TWENTY-FOUR

Thin Ice

Dayan hardly slept all night. He had lain awake in one of the log homes with only Boke and the guards around. After hours of sleeping and waking repeatedly, Dayan gave up hope he would rest at all.

Anticipation for the impending fight coiled his nerves tight. While it was hardly his first time in battle, this felt different. The scale of what they attempted was much larger than anything Dayan had ever done before. It was not the only anxiety pressing down on his chest. Soon he would see Mandukhai again. The prospect of seeing her, facing potential rejection, burdened him more than the coming fight. *I cannot let this distract me*, he thought as he stepped over Boke's snoring body on the floor and edged toward the door.

The wintry morning air burned into his lungs as he stepped outside. Two of his guards shifted to attention the moment he emerged, hands on their swords. He reached down reflexively for his own before remembering he had not yet slid it into his belts. Instead, his fingers slid across the white belt. How much longer would he have to wear the white? Would Mandukhai ever be interested in him the way she so obviously was interested in Unebolod?

His jealousy lured him toward killing the *orlok*, but he knew that would solve nothing. If anything, she would resent him for it. *If Unebolod would just go away, she might move on.* Sadly, he knew that was not an option, either. They needed Unebolod's skill on the battlefield, at least until the reunification was complete. That could be days ... or years.

I have to let her choose, he realized as he leaned against the wooden doorframe.

For all his bravado when he warned off Unebolod, Dayan knew deep down that unless he let her choose, she would never be his. He wanted her to choose him, but the way she looked at him left little confidence that would ever happen. If she chose Unebolod, Dayan worried it would destroy him. All of his strength, his purpose, his motivation stemmed from Mandukhai. Without her, he would be little more than a Great Khan without a soul, which could very well drive him to destroy everything they had worked so hard to build. He closed his eyes and drew in a deep breath of the frosty morning air, then let it out slowly. He would rather die and leave everything in their hands than destroy everything she built. He could think of no greater insult to her.

Boots thumped against the wooden planks of the small porch as his two guards stepped away from him.

Dayan's eyes snapped open as he heard what caught their attention. The bells. Dayan gazed south, expecting the messenger to arrive from Tulugen's position further along the riverbank. But as it drew near, he realized it came from the north. Dayan's heart leaped. He stepped up beside his guards, gazing into the darkened street.

A minute later, the messenger approached, escorted by two of the Khan's men. The rider dismounted and withdrew a parchment. He approached the small porch and kneeled, holding the parchment up for the Khan.

Dayan snatched it, holding his breath. He deflated when he saw Togochi's crest of a hawk in flight. It was not from Mandukhai. More likely, these were orders sent from Lake Dai. He broke the seal. His gaze swept the message.

Everything inside of him turned to stone, as if he had become part of the earth. Dayan could not blink, could not move, could not breathe. He read the message once more, hoping he had misunderstood some part of it. Mandukhai had forged an alliance with Lord Qori in Bautuo successfully. *Lord Mogurkei works for Issama. We do not know the extent of their alliance, but you cannot trust him. His oath is meaningless. Take only his head.*

Mogurkei was to return in the morning with the rest of his men. If Togochi was so certain of Mogurkei's treachery, what would happen? Dayan quickly calculated the numbers. He had over three full *tumens*.

Mogurkei only commanded one, perhaps two, if Dayan counted some of the lesser Ordos tribes scattered across the southern steppe. *Can I count Ulum's* tumen? *Can I trust him as well, or is he working with Mogurkei and Issama, too?* Dayan had to assume the worst. That meant he had only two *tumens* against their three combined.

He gave me his oath, Dayan thought. He subconsciously clenched the message in his fist. But *did* Mogurkei? Dayan struggled to recall the Lord's exact words. *No*, Dayan realized, *he gave his oath to the rightful Khan. In his mind, that could be anyone*. Did that mean Mogurkei thought Issama was the rightful Khan? Or perhaps Legusi ...

"I am already a step ahead of you," Mogurkei had said. "I heard of your approach and warned my men to use caution. They know what to do when your men arrive."

Dayan's head spun. This was all a trap into which he had naively fallen.

"My lord Khan, are you alright?" one of his guards asked, placing a supporting hand on Dayan's arm.

Dayan broke from his spell and shrugged the guard off. "Messenger, I'm afraid you will not get rest here. I need you to travel south as quickly as you can and find Lords Tulugen, Ogedei, and Dochigen. Tell them this. 'The Ordos men are not to be trusted.' Go. Ride with the wind at your back."

The messenger jumped to his feet and rushed to his horse. In seconds, he galloped away as fast as his mount could carry him.

Dayan turned to the men who had escorted the rider to him. "Find *orlok* Unebolod now. Wake everyone. Mogurkei is coming with an army. We need to be ready."

The two men ran off into the night.

Then Dayan felt it. The rumble in the wood beneath his boots. Horses on the move. *We are too late!*

Dayan darted into the hut and snatched Boke's horn off the floorboards, then rushed back outside to belt out three sharp, quick blasts. As he did, the sound echoed across the village.

In seconds, the village erupted in a flurry of motion as men scrambled into action.

Heavy clouds covered the entire sky as Mandukhai rode toward bridge across the Huang Ho River, only a few miles south of Bautuo. Over the course of the evening, Mandukhai sent scouts to check the ice and be certain it would hold under the weight of thousands of men and horses. Only so many could cross the bridge. She would not be funneled into the Ordos basin, where a trap could be waiting.

True to his word, Lord Qori waited beside the bridge entrance with a small retinue of guards. Mandukhai trotted toward him with her own guards, along with Togochi.

"My lady Khatun," Qori said, bowing from his saddle just enough to show deference. "The bridge guards know they are to allow your carts back and forth across the bridge indefinitely. I came personally to see that you have no trouble with your crossing." He glanced past her. The line of carts dwindled into the distance, but few warriors rode with her. "Where are your men?"

"The bridge is not for our army," Mandukhai replied. "It is for our supply lines. I trust there will not be an issue with anyone raiding our resources in your territory. The supply lines will have their own guards."

Qori frowned.

Did he assume I would send all thirty-two thousand of my men across one bridge? What waits on the other side? Mandukhai squinted across the river but could not make out anything beyond the clusters of trees.

"Your strategy is intriguing, my lady Khatun," Qori said. "I commend your *orlok* for his tactical skills."

"I do not bother myself with fools," she said sharply.

Togochi chuckled softly. The idea had been hers, supported by his concern for sending everyone across at one point. The conclusion had been a joint effort between the two of them. At the moment, her *tumens* lined the edges of the Huang Ho River from this bridge toward the east, then south where Soke had his men ready to cross as well, alongside Huoshai, Esige, and what remained of the Three Guards. Spreading out reduced the risk of the ice cracking beneath all their weight, avoiding areas where the scouts had found weak spots. It also allowed them to close in around any potential waiting ambushes on the other side.

"I don't imagine you do," Qori said, nodding appreciatively. "I will ensure your supply lines are untouched with my own men if need be. But if you lose this fight and Legusi comes to me demanding answers, I will firmly deny any part in this."

The only way Qori could affirm his denial would be to have someone else take the fall for his men helping her supply lines. Mandukhai suspected he already had more than one man lined up for that horrible fate.

"I will not lose, so you have nothing to worry about," she said confidently. "I ride with the blessing of the High Heavens and the spirit of Genghis, in the name of our Great Khan, Dayan."

"Before you go. My wife has a gift for you." Qori reached into his deel. As he did, Mandukhai heard the creak of armor behind her as her guards tensed. She didn't flinch as Qori pulled out a set of gloves and offered them to her.

Torgus took the gloves instead, inspecting them as Qori watched in amusement. Satisfied that they were not somehow a trick to harm or kill her, Torgus handed them over. Mandukhai raised her brows at Torgus with delight. Did he expect to find a scorpion hiding within them, waiting for her hands? She slid the new gloves on in place of her old ones. The outsides were smooth, supple sheepskin, but the inside had been lined with a thin layer of soft, woven fur, likely from the sheep that had provided the skin. They instantly warmed her chilly hands. As she closed her grip around Dust's reins, it alarmed Mandukhai how much she could still feel along her fingertips.

"May your horse never fall and your arrows never break," Qori said.

"I will see you soon, Lord Qori, and your Great Khan will be with me ready for your oath," Mandukhai said, inclining her head respectfully.

"I look forward to it."

Mandukhai turned Dust and rode toward the bridge where the carts burdened with materials for gers already crossed. The gathering tent cart had been too wide to cross the bridge, so Mandukhai had ordered it dismantled in parts to be reconstructed when they made camp.

The sun had only just risen, but Mandukhai was certain they would see little of its rays this day, if the cloud cover gave any sign. As she crossed the bridge with her entourage, Mandukhai took in the long, wide expanse of the river. It certainly was magnificent from this point of view. Were it not frozen, this crossing would have taken much longer.

They had left the families of her warriors back at the Lake Dai camp, bringing only the supplies they needed until they could secure a safe place to camp within the basin. The families were distant and safe from the coming fight. She would not risk another massacre like that at the red salt lake, where Bigirsen's men had lost everything and everyone they cared about.

Togochi stopped beside Mandukhai. He squinted east along the river. In the distance, she could make out a mass of men guiding their horses across the ice.

"It rained last night," Togochi said.

Mandukhai's heart sank. "I thought you said the ice was safe to cross? Togochi, we already have thousands making their way across the ice all along the river."

"The ice should be fine," he reassured her, but she didn't feel very reassured. "It's thick enough to cross, but slicker than usual. I already sent word to warn the men to cross with caution. The wrong slip could make a horse lame. Not to mention the dangers of creating pits with hooves on the riverbank where the land is softer from the rain. I cannot say how long the ice will keep up under the weight of our entire army, though. Hopefully, spreading them out thin will allow it to hold."

Mandukhai clenched her jaw. It seemed something always barred her passage, whether it be Lords, warriors, a wall, or nature itself. *Genghis would not let it stop him.* She trusted Togochi's judgment. He knew what was at stake.

Mandukhai did a quick calculation in her head. She had over three *tumens* of warriors to cross. And that did not include the backup mounts. She could not cross without extra horses to replenish her forces after battle. How much of that weight could the ice handle before it finally gave out?

They were pushing their luck. Rain meant spring was right around the corner. The ice may not be as thick as they hoped. And even if she got her men across, how would they get back? Would one bridge still be enough?

Mandukhai eyed the carts laden with supplies. Conquering the Ordos tribes would be no simple task. They had grown strong over the years, and spread out all over the Ordos basin. She had to close in on them and leave them nowhere to go. That would take time. According to Qori, Legusi might be quick to fold, but a few of the Ordos Lords would hold out—possibly in favor of whatever Issama might have promised them. Ibarai, in particular, may prove a problem according to Qori.

But Mandukhai would not judge Ibarai too quickly. Cautiously, for certain, but not without merit. After all, Qori could not be certain if Issama and Ibarai worked together or not.

Mandukhai watched her warriors from the bridge. Even from so far, she could hear the ice protest under the weight. Each pop worried her. Each crack that webbed outward made her heart skip. Each step a mount took that slipped on the slick surface made her breath catch. As she watched, a few horses slipped and were recovered by warriors. The mounts limped to the other side when this happened. Hopefully none of them would be beyond healing.

Mandukhai clenched her jaw and refused to blink with each crack of the ice or slip of hooves. *Please just make it to the other side*, she thought, tightening her grip on the reins. Her heart hammered against her ribs. Could her guards hear it? Could Togochi? Certainly, the way it pulsed in her ears, it must be as loud as war drums.

Thousands of horsemen crossed the frozen water, trailing far into the distance until she could no longer see the lines. She imagined each of them wearing the same cold warrior's mask that Unebolod so regularly wore. Were the men even scared? Did they feel fear? Mandukhai had been in her fair share of battles, but this was different, a foe she could not defeat or talk into submission. The ice could break, plunging her *tumens* into the icy river as the current swept them under. They would drown or freeze to death before anyone could rescue them.

Only a few more yards, she reassured herself. At some point, she had slowly continued along the bridge, matching the pace of the men crossing. The other side could not draw closer fast enough. More pops of cracking ice broke the rhythmic beating of her heart in a macabre melody of fear. If fear had a song, this would surely be it.

Dust's hooves sank into the muddy, half-frozen shoreline as he stepped off the bridge. With a mighty heave of his muscles, he leaped safely to the other side. Mandukhai released the breath she had been holding in with a great huff of relief.

All along the river, thousands of men crested the other side with her, cheering and whooping victoriously.

They made it.

Mandukhai breathed a sigh of relief. Her *tumens* had reached the other side. By the end of the day, she would have full reports on the mounts and men potentially hurt during the crossing from all along the lines.

Now she had to turn her attention to finding a place to make camp, set up the gathering tent once more, and plan for the attack on Lord Aglaqu's five thousand. With Aglaqu, Mandukhai could also gain the support of Lord Utagachi. They were lesser Lords among the Ordos, but closest to Bautuo. According to Lord Qori, both men were reasonable under the right circumstances.

She had to create those circumstances.

Meanwhile, Huoshai and Soke would lead two *tumens* against a small cluster of Ordos along the eastern riverbank and Lord Arqai, then meet with her as they rode against Ibarai. By then, Dayan and Unebolod would be close.

And only Legusi would remain.

CHAPTER TWENTY-FIVE

Oathbreakers

FISHING VILLAGE – WEST OF THE HUANG HO RIVER – LATE WINTER 1480

Dayan snatched his weapons from the hut and raced toward the stable where his horse had been sheltered for the night. Boke and the rest of his guards marched alongside him. No one asked questions.

Unebolod and a handful of his men burst out from behind a building on horseback so suddenly Boke nearly fired at the *orlok*.

"We found the Khan!" Unebolod called.

A horn sounded once, then repeated across the village.

Dayan reined in before Unebolod.

"What is happening?" Unebolod asked. "I sent scouts out to find out."

"Mogurkei is attacking," Dayan said. "We need to get out of the village and into the field before the Ordos trap us against the river."

Unebolod nodded once in agreement and began barking out commands.

Belku rode over to join them, pressing his palm against a bandage on his neck.

"What happened to you?" Dayan asked, frowning at the Chakhar Lord.

"Whore tried to kill me in my sleep," Belku muttered.

Unebolod scowled, his jaw tightening. "You too...?"

Dayan's stomach dropped. Would he be dead if he had gone with one of those women? *Ulum betrayed us.* He was the one who insisted they go to the whorehouse. He was the one who tried to convince Dayan to go with one of the women.

"Where is Chakicha?" he asked.

"Here!" The Tabun Lord galloped toward them. An ugly gash on his face from nails was all the confirmation Dayan needed. "I checked the whorehouse before I came. Five of our commanders are dead. A couple more wounded but not seriously."

"Chakicha, take Belku with you and go find Ulum," Dayan said as anger burned in him. "Kill him on sight."

The two nodded and raced away together.

"Unebolod, send someone to find Nemeku and Orghana," Dayan commanded. "Get them across the river now."

The *orlok* didn't question him. In seconds, another warrior rode toward the hut where Nemeku and Orghana spent the night together.

Dayan kicked his mare into action. The others joined him as they raced along the narrow streets toward the edge of the village.

The farther they rode, the more distinct the sounds of battle became in the distance.

An arrow skipped off the armor covering Dayan's shoulder from the shadows of a side street. Before he could react, Boke fired at the attacker. A moment later, they heard the thump of the attacker's body as he fell out of the shadows. Boke's arrow had lodged through his eye.

Dayan's focus narrowed on his attacker. He instantly recognized the Ordos cut of the man's clothing, certain he was one of Ulum's men.

"Dayan, we need to get you to safety!" Unebolod called from behind the tight ring of Boke's men.

"I will not hide!" Dayan called back.

Yet every instinct told him to run. If the Ordos turned against him, they outnumbered his men three to one. He would be spread too thin along miles of the Huang Ho River. *I cannot run away like my father would have done.*

Unebolod shouted something unintelligible—a curse on Dayan's stubborn pride, he was sure—but moments later the *orlok* had already launched into action, sending one of his men to rally the *mingghan* commanders to gather their forces at the edge of the village.

The entire village and surrounding landscape had erupted into burning chaos. Warriors fought against each other. Horses bolted in every direction without riders to guide them. Villagers raced into hiding places, uncertain who to trust.

As Dayan crested a hill just outside of town, he jerked his mare to a halt and gaped at the devastation. The village had been too small to sleep more than the generals and commanders of Dayan's *tumen*. The rest of the warriors had slept out in the open field among the horses. Now, thousands of men churned in a mass on the field below, fighting every man bold enough to come near. His original *tumen* had been mixed with Ordos absorbed over the winter months, and now they all fought against one another, unable to tell friend from foe.

"We have to stop this before our own men kill each other," Dayan commanded.

Unebolod raised his horn to his lips and belted out a series of patterned blasts of noise. Dayan recognized the commands to fall back and regroup immediately. It was an old horn command—one that the Ordos still training in new formations would not recognize. Dayan understood well, though. They had to stick with their old horn commands to avoid giving away their strategy to the Ordos they had absorbed.

As Unebolod blew the horn again, the chaos below broke apart. Thousands of men raced toward the bottom of the hill, but their attackers followed close on their heels. Unebolod cursed under his breath.

Dayan grumbled as well and snatched Boke's horn away. He called out the tones for return fire upon retreat. The warriors who had joined Dayan from the village immediately launched their arrows across the dark sky. He could not watch as his men were killed with their backs turned. The second he finished sounding the command, the men below also twisted in the stirrups and fired behind them.

But the Ordos men did not relent. For the moment, Dayan's men were matched evenly.

At the center of the Ordos lines, Ulum led the charge. *Oathbreakers. They are all dead men now.*

Unebolod called to his men and kicked his mare down the hill, leaving the Khan behind with his guards. He despised being taken by surprise like this. Planning a battle was easy. Reacting to an attack was much harder. Most of these men had been asleep when this attack had started—as he had been until he felt the movements of the woman in his bed. Thankfully,

Unebolod slept light or she would have cut his throat. Instead, he had been forced to cut hers.

How many men had they already lost? As his mare thundered down the hill, he tried to calculate what remained. One full *tumen* each.

Unebolod's second *tumen* had been sent further south to scoop up the rest of Mogurkei's men. If the Ordos Lords had betrayed them, Unebolod could only pray his southern *tumen* survived. If they faced a similar fight, they were likely outnumbered two to one. Maybe they could regroup if Unebolod could hold the line long enough.

But first, he had to get these men organized for the attack.

As he closed the gap and approached the rear line, Unebolod heard the blasts from the hilltop. Dayan called them into arrowtip formation. In seconds, the Khan's warriors responded, turning their mounts and forming an arrowtip. Unebolod did not even break stride on his mount as he joined the mass racing toward the Ordos traitors. The thrill of battle heated his blood. He fired arrow after arrow above the heads of his men and into the unruly lines of Ordos charging at them.

"Kill all Ordos!" he shouted. "Kill the oathbreakers!" The command repeated outward like a ripple on the breeze.

Heartbeats passed. Unebolod depleted his quiver of arrows. Then he heard the crash and squeal of horses charging into one another and getting cut down. The hollers of men in the thick of combat became a deafening thunder in his ears on all sides. Unebolod hooked his bow on the saddle and drew his sword as the lines began to break. Ulum was out there somewhere. Unebolod would find him and slice his guts open for this.

Above the thunder of battle, the horns called for the ripples in water attack. A moment later, the men surrounding him formed a ring pressing outward in all directions. The Khan's knowledge of the old formations surprised Unebolod. He found himself a little pleased that the boy had been paying attention to his lessons for so long. *Perhaps there is hope for him yet.*

Unebolod joined the formation without hesitation, cutting down any Ordos traitors to cross his path. A sword sliced across his leg, but with adrenaline pumping through his veins, Unebolod hardly noticed the pain. He swung his sword for another attack and happened to catch an arrow headed straight for his head, shattering the shaft. He ducked his head away from the wooden splinters. A sword sliced across the top of his hand. Without a second of hesitation, he ripped a strip of cloth from his belt to wrap around the hand, then brought his sword around just in time to slice across the face of an oncoming attacker. Blood spattered over his armor.

Another series of blasts sounded from above. Spinning top mixed with ripples in the water. Unebolod grinned, turning his mare to charge around the ring in a churning mass with the rest of the Khan's warriors. He raised his own horn to repeat the orders in case any of the men missed it. Six thousand of his men pressed the ring outward as they angled their mounts to follow the orders.

All around them, the Ordos *tumen* mirrored their maneuver. Unebolod caught glimpses of Ordos warriors riding in the opposite direction in a ring, as well. As Unebolod's men pressed outward, the Ordos warriors pressed in at Ulum's command.

And Unebolod realized the Khan's mistake. Unless the High Heavens truly blessed the Khan's decisions, Unebolod and the men inside this chaotic ring could not break formation. If they collapsed into another formation, the Ordos would fall around them and pick them all off. Six thousand men trapped inside a ring of nearly three times as many enemies.

The mare danced beneath Dayan as he watched the battle from the hilltop as his warriors moved through the formations he called. As the men began pressing outward, a surge of hope rushed through him. *We can win this.*

Beside him, Boke frowned at the battle below. Every other minute, he heard the other man grumble about oathbreakers and disgrace. He glanced at Boke. The man was right. Dayan knew with absolute certainty that he would have to root out the men who organized this and kill them for treason. He could not let them live. He could not let Ulum live. *Where is Mogurkei?*

Dayan turned his attention back to the battlefield, and his heart sank. The ring of his warriors slowly pressed inward under Ordos pressure. And he saw his mistake. Those men, *his* men, were trapped inside the ring of superior numbers.

And Unebolod was in the center of it all.

Before he could sound a horn, distant dust caught his attention. Dayan squinted into the growing daylight. The horde of warriors raced in bow formation toward the ring.

"Who is that?" Dayan asked, squinting toward the men in the center of the charge.

Boke raised his hands to his eyes to narrow his focus, then leaned forward in the saddle. "Chakicha, Belku, Jangi, and ... Lord Nemeku. They lead the rest of your men."

Nemeku! Dayan could let nothing happen to his cousin. Nemeku was not yet fifteen, hardly old enough for such a battle.

Dayan kicked his mare. She leaped forward and raced down the hill toward the fight.

No matter how hard Unebolod's men fought, they could not relieve the pressure of the crushing force of Ordos warriors pushing the ring inward. Horses and men fell in the fray, making footing for hooves uneven and treacherous. In a matter of minutes, the men racing beside him had drawn so close their legs bumped. But there was nowhere to go.

The press reminded Unebolod of that cavernous tunnel beneath Hulunbuir. Panic clenched his lungs and turned his mind to mud. The horses had stopped moving with nowhere to go but into each other. The air thickened in his lungs. The stench of death permeated everything around him. For the first time in his life, Unebolod feared his own death. It clouded his judgment and made his thoughts sluggish. The men around him were now so tight together that he could no longer move his legs. The mare bucked her head, but even she could find nowhere to go.

An arrow zipped past his head, narrowly missing before hammering into the warrior behind him with a squelch he heard even over the cries of men and whinnies of the horses. Unebolod glanced over his shoulder. The dead warrior lay at an odd angle in his saddle, having nowhere to fall. His body half lay across the horse to his left, further hindering the warrior on the mount. The air tasted metallic, the taste of death itself.

Come back in your saddle. The memory of Mandukhai's voice drifted through the haze. She had spoken those words before he left with Dayan on this campaign. He had been so confident he would return to her.

I'm sorry, Mandukhai, he thought as another warrior fell against him from an arrow in his throat. But he could not accept his death here and now. Even if he did not survive this attack, he had to ensure Dayan Khan would return to her. He couldn't leave her with nothing.

Unebolod drew back his bow, unable to wield his sword against any foes in this crushing press. Twenty arrows left. Not nearly enough. Not on his own.

"Concentrate your arrows!" Unebolod hollered, hoping at least the men around him would hear and the order would ripple outward from there.

He released the first arrow over the heads of his men. All around him, warriors slumped in their saddles. Unebolod drew back another arrow and released it in the same place as the last. Thankfully, the surviving warriors near him understood. The moment he saw their own arrows firing into one spot, he quickened his own volley.

The horses edged forward. Through the screams of men and horses, over the whistling of arrows and clash of steel, he heard Ulum's distant call of warning to his own men. Unebolod stood in his stirrups to get a better look.

An arrow punched through his armor, lodging in his shoulder. He grimaced. Burning pain seared through his arm as he drew back another arrow and fired. Ten more.

The purpose of the call was lost on him, but the Ordos relieved some of the pressure on his ring of warriors, averting their attention outside the circle. Unebolod cursed aloud when he heard the horns blasting out commands.

Arrowtip split formation.

Dayan Khan was riding into the battle.

And they would both die.

As Dayan raced his yellow mare toward the battle, he became certain of two things. They would lose more than half their men. And Unebolod or Nemeku would die. Dayan could not face Mandukhai with the weight of that failure on his shoulders, even with Bigirsen's head in a bag. He would rather die trying to save them than have her always blame him for their deaths.

But he would not go down without a fight.

As Dayan's *mingghan* galloped closer to the fray, his golden gaze swept the battlefield. If he could get Nemeku to concentrate his forces and break apart the ring of Ordos warriors, they had a chance to escape even if they lost this battle.

Dayan raised the horn once more, blasting out the call for arrowtip split formation. Already, Ulum's men noticed the warriors rushing toward them, and it distracted them from their concentrated massacre on the men trapped in their ring. Dayan held his breath as he watched Nemeku at the head of two thousand men, praying for a sign that he understood the call. Nemeku was not yet trained in battle as Dayan had been.

At Nemeku's side, Belku steered his mount toward Dayan's men. Dayan breathed a sigh of relief as Nemeku and the rest of the warriors followed him. It had only taken a few seconds for the formation to change, but those seconds had seemed much longer.

Arrows flew in every direction now as the Ordos warriors fired at the men inside the circle and at those charging toward them. Within fifty yards of the battlefield, Nemeku, Belku, and the rest all joined Dayan's men, ready to rescue the trapped men. Boke grinned from ear to ear, firing at such rapid speed his motion was a blur.

Dayan could not smile. Not until they broke that ring and freed his men trapped inside.

"Spears!" he shouted at the last moment.

The command carried swiftly along the outer flanks. Warriors lowered their spears, piercing the Ordos ring, trampling the men in their way. Instead of driving straight through and risking injury to his men, the arrow formation split, as he had commanded, and sent a wave of the Khan's horsemen crashing through the Ordos, opening a gap. Dayan charged in with his men. Despite the certain death they all faced, his nerves remained calm. He abandoned his arrows in favor of his sword for better, quicker kills in close combat. Blood covered his armor, but he hardly noticed. Dayan had one clear focus. Get Unebolod and Nemeku safely away from the battle.

And kill Ulum.

His hands were steady; his senses alert to everything around him. Some great spirit possessed him. Dayan could sense everything even if he could see almost nothing through the mass of horses and warriors.

The warriors trapped inside the ring boiled outward. One voice bellowed above the thunder of hooves. Unebolod called for his men to escape the ring and circle around both outer edges of the Ordos.

Between Dayan's warriors charging through the Ordos lines and Unebolod's men forcing stragglers back, the battle almost seemed won.

Dayan spotted Ulum and turned his mount toward the Ordos oathbreaker, sword in hand. Seventy yards. He leaned close to his mount, racing through the battle with singular focus. In this void where only Ulum existed, Dayan heard a warning, but it was an intangible thing. Distant. Sharp. Unintelligible.

Instincts kicked in, and Dayan cut down anyone in his path like a man possessed. *I will kill you and add your head to the bag*, he thought as he glared at Ulum—fifty yards.

A horse cut in front of his path. Someone seized Dayan's reins, jerking his yellow mare around. Dayan swung his sword instinctively at the arm, only to have it met by matching steel. He gritted his teeth and glared at the man who had stopped him in his tracks.

Through the haze of his own bloodlust, Dayan recognized Unebolod, covered in blood with an arrow sticking out of his chest.

"Now!" Unebolod commanded.

But Dayan had not heard what he said before that. *Now what?*

He followed the sound of distant thunder and whoops of warriors.

Thousands of Ordos poured over the hills from the south, racing toward the battlefield. And at the center ... *Mogurkei!* Dayan sheathed his sword and grabbed his bow from the hook.

"Stop!" Unebolod snapped. "We can't defeat them here. We need to pull back and regroup with Mandukhai before we punish them."

Dayan howled in frustration and rage. "I can't leave them at our backs! The rest of the Ordos will hear of this. We will never win!"

"She could be facing the same trouble as us," Unebolod snapped. "Will you risk *her* life for this suicide mission?"

Fury burned hot in Dayan's veins. He wanted to smite the Ordos from the face of the earth.

"The Khan is injured," Boke shouted as he joined them.

Dayan blinked at Boke. He felt no injury. He felt nothing at all but rage. But he saw the blood seeping from his side, the arrow shaft broken in his shoulder.

A horn sounded for retreat. Dayan glanced around for the source before realizing it had come from his own horn. He had accepted defeat. He had to. Injured, he could not win. And if Unebolod was even a little right, he could not risk Mandukhai's life.

When this was over, the Ordos tribes would be no more. Dayan would break them apart to be absorbed into other tribes firmly under his command. The name Ordos would become a forgotten memory.

What remained of his *tumen* raced back toward the hill, with Mogurkei and Ulum leading the Ordos hot on their heels.

Chapter Twenty-Six

Conversation Before Knives

Esige was overjoyed to no longer manage the supply lines. While she had been adept at the task, it bored her to tears. Mandukhai's orders to cross the river further south near Soke's warriors had been a welcome relief. She had sent an offering to Lord Arqai—one of the southern Ordos Lords—two days ago. He responded positively and agreed to meet them. Huoshai had wanted Esige to remain safe on the other side of the river. She had put an end to that nonsense immediately. There would have been nothing he could say or do to make her stay behind while he gained all the glory.

Besides, she thought as she rode beside her husband, *Mandukhai sent me to tame the Ordos here. If we can do that without losing men, she will be thrilled.* It was a half-lie, and Esige knew it. Mandukhai had not specifically sent Esige, but Soke and Huoshai, along with the Three Guards. Regardless, for Esige, failure was not an option. She would make Mandukhai proud.

"This is your worst idea ever," Huoshai grumbled from his saddle as he rode alongside her toward the Ordos camp. He had not meant for her to hear, as low as his voice had been, but Esige had the ears of a rabbit.

"Peace before war," Esige said patiently from her own saddle. "Conversation before knives. It worked with Qori. It could work here as well."

"Could." Huoshai snorted. "Was this her idea or yours?" His jaw twitched.

Esige knew he meant well. Huoshai wanted to protect her and he would be helpless today. But she needed to do this. "Does it matter?"

"Following the Khatun's orders differs greatly from following yours," Huoshai replied. He glanced back at their honor guard. A hundred warriors hand-picked by Soke and Huoshai's cousin Ormeger.

"I beg to differ," Esige replied, smirking playfully at him. "Tengri help you if you don't follow my orders just as quickly."

Huoshai met her eyes, and his hard expression cracked into a faint smirk.

As the massive Ordos camp came into view, Huoshai's smirk faded. Esige tensed as well. Gers dotted the dry, brittle ground as far as she could see. At the edge of camp, Arqai had set up a tent for them to meet. She eyed the fluttering Ordos banners as they approached. Her stomach did flips.

As they neared the tent, Esige wondered if this had been a mistake. Arqai had a full *tumen* at his disposal. Not all of them were here, but certainly a fair number of them were based on the size of the camp. Esige tightened her grip on the reins to steady her shaking hands.

Before they were within two hundred yards of the camp, a line of warriors raced out to greet them. According to Lord Qori, Arqai was a reasonable man, and he bowed to the whims of his wives and children. Esige had sent them a wagon of silk, foods, and finely crafted toys from the wagons the Ming had sent to Mandukhai. With that wagon, Esige had promised more should they agree to meet and discuss supporting the Great Khan. It was a massive gamble that could go terribly wrong. While she had more, she could not spend it so recklessly.

A line of warriors intercepted their party, leading them toward the tent. Their honor guard accompanied them as well.

Women, old men, and children watched the massive processional with curious eyes. *I could save these people a lot of heartache if I pull this off. If I don't, I likely won't live long enough for it to matter to me.*

When they reached Lord Arqai's tent, one guard motioned for them to dismount. Esige did so first, followed by Huoshai. When they began taking weapons, Huoshai protested.

"Peace before war," she said, placing a soothing hand on his arm.

Huoshai stiffened as he handed over his sword and knife.

None of their guards would enter the tent with the two of them. Ten of Huoshai's men assumed positions near the entrance beside Arqai's guards. No doubt they would be tensely listening for signs of trouble within.

Esige ducked into the tent behind her husband—Lord Arqai likely would not understand if she entered first. The moment she stepped through, Esige's gaze swept the inside of the tent. It was open, sparse, with only a single rug under Lord Arqai's seat. A guard was stationed on either side of the doorway, watching the two of them. Esige waited off to the side as Huoshai took the lead. *Remember what we rehearsed*, she thought, folding her hands together to avoid wringing them.

Lord Arqai was younger than Esige had expected. Not quite as young as she and Huoshai, but he couldn't be much older than Mandukhai. No silver yet touched his dark forelock or beard.

"I trust you have kept your end of the deal and not told any of the other Ordos Lords we are meeting," Huoshai said without missing a beat once greetings were over. "Not all of them will get such an offer."

"I could guess who that might be," Arqai replied.

Huoshai waited for Arqai to say more, perhaps even reveal names. Esige's intense curiosity took over, but she remained silent. After a minute, it became apparent Arqai would say nothing more.

"When was the last time you were free of Uyghur or Ming control?" Huoshai asked casually.

Arqai sank deeper into his seat and sighed. "Personally? Never. But my tribe has flourished in the basin under both."

"Have you?" Huoshai asked. "How many did you lose when Bigirsen enraged the Ming and they sent their army to the red salt lake?"

This created an instant tension in the air. Not only between Huoshai and Arqai, but among the two Ordos guards beside the door. Arqai spit on the floor and sneered. "The act of a coward."

"I don't disagree," Huoshai said. He hesitated a moment, cocking his head. "Unless... Are we speaking of Bigirsen or the Ming?"

Esige fought off a smirk. *Well played, my love.*

"We don't just have goods at our disposal," Huoshai continued. "We have women."

Arqai's gaze darted to Esige. "Like this one?"

"No. None of them are like this one." Huoshai grinned at Esige.

She took her cue and stepped up beside her husband, sliding her arm through his to be sure Arqai understood where she belonged. "Lord Arqai, I understand you were one of the unlucky ones who lost everything when the Ming attacked. I'm happy that you have found new wives to give you new children. But as a mother, I also understand that nothing can ever replace what you have lost."

Sorrow creased the corner of Arqai's eyes. "No. And it was difficult to start over. We told Bigirsen to leave the Ming be, but he was determined to prove his divine right to rule us all. He still is, but I won't follow him."

"He won't be a problem for you any longer," Huoshai reassured Arqai. "Unebolod Noyan and Dayan Khan took his head."

Noyan. Gooseflesh rose on Esige's skin. Mandukhai had given Unebolod the title of Noyan—High Lord—when he returned to her with the missing *sulde*. No one else in the empire ranked above Unebolod any longer, except for the Khan and Khatun.

Arqai's eyebrows shot up his forehead. "Are you sure of this?"

"We have not seen the head yet, but have no reason to doubt our Khan's word," Esige replied. She couldn't wait to see Bigirsen's head. She wanted to gouge out his eyes, beat his head into the earth with a blacksmith hammer, bathe her hands in his brain matter, watch whatever remained burn to ash. Another part of her wanted to peel away all the muscles and flesh until only the skull remained, then keep it as a prize.

Arqai sank back in his seat as the weight of this revelation sank in. After a moment, he let out a long sigh and nodded to himself. "Your Khan and Khatun want to conquer us."

"Conquer is a poor choice of words," Esige replied.

"It's more like reclaiming what once belonged to the Great Khans of old," Huoshai said, finishing Esige's sentence. "To men like Genghis and Mongke and Kublai."

"Well, he must have the spirit of Genghis if he managed to do what none of us could," Arqai said. "We have all wanted Bigirsen dead for some time, but no one could pull it off." He rubbed his fingers along his beard. "Issama was right."

Esige tensed. She had heard Issama had been behind more than one plot over the years, and possibly still had several others in the works. None of it could be proven yet, though. Could Arqai be the key? "Right about what?"

"He said Dayan Khan and Mandukhai Khatun would kill Bigirsen the moment they found him," Arqai said. "He also warned me that Bigirsen's death would lead the Khan to his own downfall."

Esige nervously brushed her fingers over the knife she had stitched into her deel to avoid detection. Was this it? The moment Arqai refused them and killed them? *I won't go down without taking him with me.*

"How is that?" Huoshai asked. His tone shifted to something sharper, more demanding and dangerous.

Arqai huffed, crossing his arms over his broad chest. A faint smirk tugged at the corner of his mouth. Esige only noticed it because of the way his skin folded in the corners.

Esige parted her lips slightly, then whispered to her husband without moving her lips. "He's betrayed us."

Huoshai tensed, instinctively reaching for his sword.

"Months ago, before your men invaded our territory, Lord Issama made his way through the camps making deals with each of us. He promised us Bigirsen's death at the Khan's hands. He promised us freedom from those who have tried to oppress us for centuries." Arqai stood slowly, looming like a giant in the ger. "He promised us the right to choose the rightful Khan for ourselves. Ordos independence."

Huoshai shuffled a step in front of Esige. "I told you this was a terrible idea," he muttered under his breath.

"Now?" she hissed. She resented him for stepping in front of her, but then realized he had done it to conceal her hand so she could retrieve her knife.

Arqai eyes narrowed as he watched the two of them.

"We tried conversation," Huoshai muttered.

Time for knives.

Arqai grimaced. Esige knew he had noticed their whispered conversation, even if he could not make out exactly what they had said.

"Mandukhai has been holding our cocks for far too long," Arqai said sharply as his face reddened. "It's time to cut the woman loose."

Esige pulled at the thread stitched around her hidden knife to free it. The cold handle pressed against her fingertips as it came loose. A guard grasped her by the back of the neck, tugging her back. Esige yelped, reaching desperately for Huoshai and sliding the knife subtly into his hand.

"Give me her and we have a deal," Arqai said. His greedy, hungry gaze devoured every inch of Esige. She wanted to gouge out his eyes.

Huoshai moved in a blur. One moment, he stood two steps in front of her as the guard held her now also by the arm. The next, Huoshai stood beside Arqai, the Lord's arm twisted around beside him and Esige's blade against the pulse of his lifeblood in his neck.

"She is my wife," Huoshai growled. "Take another man's wife and he has every lawful right to kill you. Order your men to release her or I will assume you are taking her and cut your throat."

"What makes you think you would make it out of this tent alive when you are surrounded by my men?" Arqai snarled.

Esige could hear the scuffle outside. Huoshai clearly heard it as well. "We are on the edge of your camp, and my honor guard has already overpowered your men. They could not react before we disappear. And you would already be dead."

Arqai sneered but nodded to his guard. The hands gripping Esige released. She slammed her heel down on her captor's instep, then spun around and punched him in the jaw.

"Touch me again and I will do much worse," Esige snarled.

Arqai chuckled. "She's spirited. I like her."

Huoshai pressed the blade tighter to Arqai's throat.

The Ordos Lord held up his hands. "Not what I meant."

Esige planted her hands on her hips as she stalked toward Arqai. "I have stood on a battlefield between charging lines of horsemen. With the power of my will alone, I stopped a battle. You do not scare me, Lord Arqai. If anything, you should be scared of me." She stopped toe-to-toe with him, glaring at him as Huoshai continued holding the knife to Arqai's neck.

The two guards were tense, ready to strike. But they knew Huoshai had Arqai in a killing stroke. One false step and Arqai would be dead.

Shadows fall across the door as Arqai's men and Huoshai's guards jostled to see what caused the commotion.

"If you think my husband will not kill you, I would advise you to reconsider," Esige said. "He killed his own father for defying the will of Genghis. You are nothing by comparison. And if you think *I* am terrifying—as you should—I am nothing compared to what Mandukhai Khatun will have in store should you resist our rightful lord, Dayan Khan." Esige cocked her head. "Would you defy the will of Genghis?"

Arqai gulped.

"Would you defy the Khan who bears his bones?" Esige asked.

He shook his head slightly to avoid cutting his neck on the blade.

Huoshai eased his grip, then let go as he stepped back. The moment he did, the two guards posted inside the door surged forward. Huoshai's men blocked the doorway from the rest of Arqai's guards.

"Stop!" Arqai commanded.

They froze in their tracks, bodies tense. Esige turned in a slow circle, challenging any of them to step forward. The moment the guard who had grabbed her met her gaze, he immediately averted his eyes to the floor.

Esige took a step back. "Now is the time for wisdom and unity, Lord Arqai. Not further division. Only a fool would ignore the divine right of our Great Khan. Kneel and swear yourself to them. And if your men even think about touching me, my husband, or any of our men, I have plenty more blades where that one came from." She hoped he didn't call her bluff. "And I *never* miss a target."

Arqai eased himself to his knees. "Be aware, my Lady, that I do this under duress. What value is an oath under such conditions?"

"One of two things will happen, Lord Arqai," Huoshai said. "Either you will break your oath and we will come back to wipe out your entire camp…"

"*Or* you will see the true value of your choice here today," Esige finished, "and be grateful you made this choice as your fellow Ordos Lords lay dying."

Arqai's lips thinned.

Esige held her breath, waiting for the words. It was not long before she received her reward.

"You have my vow," Arqai said. "I will travel with you to the Khan and Khatun and personally deliver my oath to them. I will serve our rightful Khan faithfully. Until I can give the oath in person, you and your men are safe from my own, upon my Eternal Soul."

After crossing the river, Mandukhai had taken some of her horsemen to the nearest Ordos camp. All along the river, Mandukhai's warriors had followed her generals and commanders into these strategic attacks. The groups nearest to the river were certain to spot her army crossing, so she had to deal with them before they could send warning deeper into the Ordos basin.

Mandukhai oversaw only one of these attacks, fighting alongside her men, forcing the Ordos commanders to their knees in front of her. They were given the same choice Dayan had given those outside of the basin. Kneel to their Khatun, give their oath to follow her and the Khan … or die. None resisted her.

Soon, they would close in on Ibarai's *tumen* with her Three Guards, Urainkhai, and the remaining Khorchin closing off escape.

Now, Mandukhai stood inside her command tent, pacing as she waited for some word from the west. From Dayan and Unebolod. It had only been a few days since she had crossed the river, but surely Dayan's fastest riders could have gotten her some word by now. Instead, she did not know when to expect them. Had their own crossing been a success? She hated waiting in this mud-infested place.

"I think you worry enough for all of us," Altan commented. The other woman, the General of the Jalair warriors, leaned casually against the center post of the command tent, slicing off bits of apple she munched on casually. "You will pace yourself into a muddy grave."

Mandukhai huffed and stopped, planting her hands on her hips. "Why haven't we heard from them yet?"

Altan shrugged as if it didn't matter. "It's a long way from there to here."

"We have word from the Urainkhai," Mandukhai pointed out.

"It's not as far." Altan pushed off the post and stalked toward Mandukhai. Her movements were graceful, like a tiger. She placed a hard hand on Mandukhai's shoulder. "Have a little faith in them. Dayan Khan is a clever man. Unebolod is a skilled leader. Between the two of them, I have no doubt they will be fine. We need to focus on the next round of attacks."

Mandukhai grimaced. She hated when Altan was right, mostly because, of all women, Altan was nearly a mirror of herself. Perhaps even stronger. "It would help if we knew which camp Lord Legusi is in. If we can get him to bend the knee, this will end much faster."

Altan drew back and studied the map. Several painfully long minutes passed as the two women considered their next course. Until word came in from the scouts, they could do little more than guess.

"Mandukhai," Altan said at last, shattering the silence. "What will you do once you have the Ordos under your control? The Uyghur are dead or scattered, with no one to lead them. Your vision will be complete."

Mandukhai wished it were that simple, but she knew it would not be. Her goal was not to conquer the tribes. She needed to unite them in a government they would continue long after her own death. No simple task. Not even Genghis had done this. And there was still Issama to deal with. Would he lead the Uyghur? Did he already?

"Ruling the world from horseback is easy," Mandukhai said. "It's dismounting and governing that is hard. This is not about controlling the tribes. It's about building something that lasts beyond us. There is no value in anything until it is finished."

"So said Genghis," Togochi commented as he strode into the command tent. "The scouts we sent to Ibarai's camp should be back soon. No word from Unebolod yet, I assume?"

Altan groaned. "Great. Now she will start pacing again."

Mandukhai fired a glare at the other woman. "No. We have to assume they successfully crossed until we receive word otherwise."

Togochi clasped his hands behind his back and stood straighter. "I think we should send scouts in their direction to be certain. We cannot afford any assumptions with the Ordos."

Mandukhai hated how right he was. The Ordos simply had too many warriors. "Fine. But only two. We need our scouts here."

Togochi nodded.

She had to hold on to the hope that Dayan's crossing had been as uneventful as her own. They already had several thousand Ordos under Unebolod's command. They could handle a few small camps with so many warriors.

Return to Hulunbuir

10 MILES NORTH OF THE FISHING VILLAGE – HUANG HO RIVER – LATE WINTER 1480

Unebolod continuously checked over his shoulder for signs of the pursuing Ordos warriors as he and Dayan rode north. Ulum, Mogurkei, and their warriors chased Dayan's men for several miles before Unebolod sent a detachment of men to divert them away from the Khan. Their lines spread long and thin toward the river now, but Unebolod knew they had little choice. They might have to race across the frozen river. Doing so with thousands in one place would break the ice.

When he was not looking over his shoulder, Unebolod watched Dayan ride at breakneck speed. Dayan only slowed if Nemeku fell behind. Clearly the Khan worried about his younger cousin.

Nemeku had resisted racing away from the village. He put up quite a fight about abandoning Orghana. It was not until Jangi said he would ride back and ensure her safety that Nemeku finally calmed down.

Unebolod, however, worried about the Khan. Dayan appeared completely unaware of the gashes in his arm or side, or the amount of blood he had already lost. It coated the neck and side of Dayan's yellow mare. Unlike the Khan, Unebolod felt each cut with every jarring motion of his mount. He had even attempted wrapping a tourniquet around his leg to stop the blood-flow. They were not in good shape and could not ride like this much longer.

Once a scout reported they had lost the Ordos for now, Unebolod insisted they stop and tend to the Khan's wounds. Dayan cast him a resentful glare, but as Dayan dismounted and gazed west, Unebolod saw the fear the young Khan tried to hide.

"Start sending our men across," Unebolod commanded Belku. "Send as many scouts as we can spare south to find out what happened to Tulugen, Dochigen, and Ogedei."

The Chakhar Lord bowed and darted off to organize the men, favoring his right leg.

Unebolod cast a worried glance at Nemeku, who remained in his saddle, too stunned to move.

Boke appeared with Getei, nudging the dumbfounded shaman toward Dayan. The shaman had been trying to gather supplies and men in the fishing village during the battle, before eventually joining them in retreat.

"I'm fine," Dayan insisted.

Getei took one look at the Khan and shook his head. "You lost a lot of blood and need silver and rest. Sadly, you will only get one of those things for now." He immediately set to work unbuckling Dayan's armor to get closer to the wound in his side.

Dayan swatted Getei away. "I said I'm fine. Leave the armor alone."

Unebolod limped toward the two, painfully aware of the severity of his own injury. Each step was like fire from his thigh to his temple. Sweat beaded on his forehead. "Dayan, I know you feel fine, but if I return you to Mandukhai with such an injury left untreated, she will string us both up and flog us for sport."

A phantom of a smirk played across Dayan's lips, and for a moment, that fear in his eyes disappeared. It made Unebolod's heart ache. There was no doubt Dayan loved her.

"Fine, but be quick about it. Then see to the *orlok*. He isn't much better off." Dayan's knowing gaze swept over Unebolod.

Under the circumstances, Unebolod knew he didn't have a leg to stand on. Especially not with one already injured.

Something haunted crossed Dayan's face. He cleared his throat, gazing toward the western horizon as the sun rose at his back. "We should have stayed and fought. I had Ulum in my sight."

"If we stayed, you would be dead," Unebolod said with certainty. "It was a losing battle. I hate retreating, but I know a lost cause when I see one."

Fury flashed in Dayan's eyes as he glared at Unebolod. "And I should trust your word on it?"

Unebolod flinched, clenching his jaw so tight it ached. He waved a hand toward the west. "They had us outnumbered and outmaneuvered. Even if you killed Ulum, his men would have killed you."

"Don't pretend you wouldn't like that!" Dayan snapped. "Having me out of the way is a best-case scenario for you. For all I know, you had a hand in this."

The men milling around them, preparing to cross the river, froze and stared at them. Unebolod glanced at them. Anger burned in his veins. It certainly was true that he stood to gain a lot by Dayan's death, but that did not mean Unebolod wanted it. Mandukhai would never forgive him for that failure.

"I have never *once* betrayed my oaths to you," Unebolod hissed.

"To her."

"To *you*!" Unebolod roared. "If I had a hand in that attack, I can guarantee I would not have rescued you from your suicide mission! I *would* have left you to die. If you cannot accept that I have been loyal to you, then take my head now and spare me your jealous, self-righteous blame."

Dayan's pale face turned a light shade of pink.

Unebolod heaved angry breaths, hands clenched in fists, all too aware of how Boke loomed near him. No one along the river moved.

"Get across that ice!" Unebolod shouted at the men. "Now!"

That broke the tense silence and men scrambled into action.

Getei finished tending to Dayan's wounds, helping the young Khan to his feet. Unebolod sank to the ground, relieved to take his weight off his leg. If Dayan wanted to kill him, so be it. *Not like I can stop him.*

Unebolod reveled in the cold mud beneath him as it helped cool his burning hot skin. By the time Getei tended to him, most of their warriors were across the ice. A few had raced away along the riverbank to send word to the rest to cross as well. With any luck, they could escape further pursuit on the other side and reach Mandukhai in a few days—less if they made quick time of it. *When this is over, I am going to return to my homeland in Hulunbuir and retire.*

"She has earned the right to choose her own destiny," Dayan said, standing over Unebolod as Getei tended to Unebolod's wounds. Dayan's voice was timid, small. It reminded Unebolod of the boy Dayan had once been.

The words sank in, and Unebolod stared at Dayan in stunned silence.

Hope bloomed in Unebolod's chest. Yet fear took root as well. Would she choose him after all this time? Mandukhai had become more than a queen. She was a symbol, much as Genghis had been. If she turned away from Dayan to choose him, what would that make others think? No matter how much he wanted to hope, Unebolod knew, deep down, that Mandukhai would not risk the Nation. Their love was a lost cause. *Hope is a tool for fools.* He had to admit he respected Dayan's decision. Dayan risked losing her by allowing her this choice. That could not be easy for him.

Dayan said nothing before gathering his horse's reins and leading her further from the frozen river to where chutes of grass poked out of the dead, muddy earth. Unebolod twisted around to watch the boy as Getei finished dressing the wound in his leg.

Nemeku had hardly moved at all since they stopped, still in his saddle, almost too stunned to blink. Unebolod felt bad for the boy. He remembered watching men get butchered at the same age. It changed him.

With any luck, Orghana would be waiting with Jangi across the river already. She could help Nemeku snap out of it. Just as Odsar, Unebolod's long-dead wife, had helped Unebolod cope with witnessing his father and oldest brothers butchered at Esen's command. *That was a lifetime ago,* he thought.

Boke spoke with the rest of the Khan's guards near the riverbank, giving their orders as he watched Dayan with one eye.

"Boke," Unebolod called. "Have your men get Lord Nemeku across the river."

Boke scowled, glancing at Dayan.

"I can manage watching over him for a few minutes," Unebolod snapped. "Do as I commanded you."

Without a word, Boke waved a few of his men toward Nemeku's horse. The guards began the descent down the muddy riverbank. Ice cracked under their weight, but it held. *It won't hold the Ordos if they chase us down.*

Unebolod watched until Nemeku reached the other side.

Getei stuffed a bandage back into his pack as a breeze blew past them, shaking the branches of the bare trees. The shaman suddenly stiffened. His hands trembled. Perhaps from the cold.

"So this is it," Getei muttered. "It is time to find our faith." He surged to his feet and spun toward Dayan.

Something about Getei's behavior set Unebolod's teeth on edge. *What does he sense now?*

"Dayan!" Getei shouted, waving his arms frantically.

Dayan turned, frowning at the shaman.

In a heartbeat, Unebolod surged to his feet, ignoring the searing hot pain in his leg. Before he could take half a step, an arrow punched straight through Dayan's right shoulder, in through the back and out the front. Had he not turned when he did, the arrow would have pierced his heart. Unebolod raced for his horse as the earth rumbled.

Getei ran to Dayan faster than Unebolod had ever seen him move. The shaman's urgency made Unebolod's heart leap into his chest.

Then Getei darted around Dayan. An arrow struck through Getei's neck as Unebolod mounted his mare. The shaman fell face-first in the mud, instantly killed by the arrow. But if he had not been there, that arrow would have been in Dayan's neck instead.

Dayan leaped into the saddle, wincing only slightly as he wheeled the mare around toward the river. Another arrow zipped past Dayan's head.

Unebolod raced toward the Khan. Everyone else had crossed the river. Boke and his men had not returned yet from escorting Nemeku.

There was only Dayan and Unebolod left.

The two men raced toward each other. Dayan didn't bother with the arrow in his shoulder. There would be no time to remove it now.

Unebolod reached the lip of the hill where Dayan had been. His gaze swept the plains beyond.

A thousand Ordos warriors rode toward the two of them at full charge. Among them, he spotted the yellow crest on Ulum's helmet.

Unebolod cursed. The Ordos closed the gap far too fast.

"Go!" he shouted at Dayan, whipping the Khan's mount into action. "Get across the river now!"

Dayan did not protest this time. He leaned close to his mare's neck as he rode toward the ice. Unebolod reached for arrows in the box attached to his saddle, then cursed aloud when he came up empty.

The two of them raced side-by-side to the riverbank with nothing to guard their backs. The horses slowed in the mud as they descended the riverbank.

Across the river, Boke sped toward them. *He has arrows to cover our escape!* It would not be enough to kill all the Ordos warriors, even if every shot killed an enemy. But it was better than nothing at all.

"Return volley!" Unebolod shouted. "Protect the Khan!"

The Khan's warriors began firing what arrows they had remaining across the river toward the oncoming Ordos as Unebolod and Dayan descended the sloping riverbank.

Unebolod glanced at Dayan, who no longer rode with confidence. Dayan sagged in the saddle, having lost too much blood already.

The muddy slope made for unsteady footing for their horses. Unebolod prayed for something to protect the two of them.

Dayan's yellow mare squealed and pitched forward. Dayan fell from the saddle face-first into the mud near the ice-covered river's edge.

Unebolod's heart hammered against his ribs. Was Dayan dead? *She has earned the right to choose.* Dayan's words echoed in Unebolod's head. If Dayan died here, Mandukhai would be his. But she would never forgive him for not trying to save Dayan.

What do you think of my loyalty now, boy? Unebolod thought bitterly as he leaped from his own saddle, gripping the reins so his own mare didn't bolt. The Khan's yellow mare struggled to stand on the ice, and the way she favored her front leg made it clear she was lame. The ice cracked, threatening to give out. It wouldn't handle the weight of the charging horsemen. *If we can reach the other side, we might escape.*

Unebolod yanked Dayan out of the mud on the river's edge and hoisted him into his own saddle. For a moment, he considered climbing on behind Dayan, but the extra weight would slow them down. *You will face an impossible choice, confront your deeply seeded hope, and make the right choice. You will find your faith.* Getei's warning before they left Lake Dai rose to the surface. Unebolod let out a slow breath. Getei knew all along. He had insisted on coming on this campaign. He had warned Unebolod.

This was never a choice, he thought bitterly. *It was my fate, all along.*

He had promised her he would protect Dayan. Unless the ice broke, the Ordos would continue their charge across the river and they would not escape. He had to make sure the ice broke to protect Dayan. Unebolod quickly untied his bag of caltrops from the back of his saddle.

"Chuh!" He smacked the mare on the hindquarters. Unebolod's mare lurched forward, slipping on the ice as she made her way toward the far riverbank. Boke edged his way down the far side of the river's edge, slipping and sliding on the muddy slope. "Boke, get him out of here. Make sure he reaches Mandukhai safely."

Boke reached the eastern edge of the river at last and crept toward the mare, reaching for the reins. "*Orlok—*"

"Go!" Unebolod climbed the western riverbank, then ran along the river's edge, dropping all the caltrops along the way. "Return volley only until he is secure. Don't waste arrows. Get him to safety. I will try to catch up."

Unebolod yanked his sword from his belt.

As the Khan's guards thundered away, arrows fired across the river toward the oncoming storm of Ordos warriors. They did not have enough arrows to make a stand and secure Dayan's safety.

Unebolod turned to face the oncoming storm with nothing more than a sword and the knife in his boot. He took a deep breath, then released it slowly. He could not stop all the Ordos, but with any luck, he would slow them down.

Unebolod knew one thing for certain.

He had to break the ice.

He edged from the middle of the river toward the western shore. It brought him closer to the Ordos, but he had to weaken the ice on their side, or they might still reach Dayan. With a mighty thrust, he rammed the tip of his sword into the ice. It cracked around the steel blade. He tried to twist it, to little effect.

Once the mass of horsemen a hundred yards east of the river enveloped Dayan, the return volley stopped. Hooves from the approaching Ordos army made the ground tremble.

Unebolod stomped the ice with all his might. Agony throbbed in his injured leg. He gritted his teeth and stomped again. The cracks grew, webbing out away from the wound he created. Unebolod clutched his hilt and tore the sword up. The yellow ribbon brushed his hand. The ice had dented the edge of the blade. Unebolod grimaced, edging backward across the frozen river toward the eastern shore, away from the oncoming army.

Ordos arrows soared toward him. Some missed, a few thumped into his armor along his chest or arms. They stuck in the armor but didn't break the skin thanks to his layers of silk. Unebolod swung his sword down, shattering the shafts.

Everything slowed. His heartbeat. His breathing. His mind.

Unebolod glaring death at Ulum as the Lord crested the far riverbank at the head of the charge. If he was to die today, he would take Ulum with him.

As the first few horses stampeded onto the ice, the webs raced outward in all directions. A few slabs of ice broke off. A horse squealed and pitched forward as its leg plunged through the hole. The rider tumbled from the saddle, crushed under the weight of the horse. Another rider could not avoid collision fast enough on the ice. His horse slipped of the ice, tripped on the fallen horse, and took down several other riders as if skidded sideways and fell. In seconds, the crossing descended into chaos. Ulum attempted commanding his men to halt.

Bows lifted.

Unebolod's boots squished in the mud on the eastern riverbank. He met Ulum's gaze and grinned. Then he thrust his sword into the ice once more. A few arrows skipped off his armor. One knocked his helmet askew.

The cracks expanded. More riders lost control of their mounts. Ulum's horse squealed as it lost its footing on the slippery, shifting slabs of ice. Ulum tumbled from the saddle and slid on the ice. He scrambled to reach the safety of the eastern riverbank.

Unebolod edged up the eastern riverbank, knowing he had done all the damage he could do, not daring to turn his back on these men.

The riders on the ice broke into panic as more of the ice broke. More of the riders and their mounts plunged into the icy depths. Ulum shouted for the men trapped on the ice to reach the eastern bank. But it was too late to rally the warriors. Some turned back toward the far shore, a few rushed toward Unebolod's side of the river. And still a handful of dim warriors on the western edge tested their luck on the ice.

Unebolod had stopped the Ordos advance.

Only a dozen men had made it to his side of the river. Ulum among them. None of them with a horse. Unebolod continued backing away, holding his damaged sword in defense. Arrows soared toward him from the far side of the river. Unebolod turned his back and ducked, knowing he could not avoid them all, but not willing to take one to the face. Not until he finished these men.

As the twelve men on his side of the river formed a ring around him, the arrows stopped flying. Unebolod glanced around, watching each of his foes like a hawk watches a mouse, seeking the best time to swoop in for the kill.

"Stand down, Unebolod," Ulum said.

"You have committed treason against your Great Khan," Unebolod said, struggling for each breath. One of those arrows must have punctured his lungs. He rose cautiously, both to avoid further injury, and to observe the men surrounding him. "There is only one punishment for treason."

The twelve men all drew swords. Meanwhile, a detachment of Ordos warriors on the other side of the wide river rode off. Most likely, they sought a safer place to cross.

Unebolod wiped mud from his face, far too aware of the tremble in his hand. How did Dayan calm his nerves so easily? Was it the meditation? Unebolod could use his trick right now.

"You will die here," Ulum said.

Unebolod smirked. "So will you."

"Arrogant to the end."

"I know my worth. Do you?" Unebolod raised his sword. He could not attack first.

Boots squished in the mud behind him. Unebolod didn't bother turning around. He flipped his grip on his hilt and rammed the blade beside him, as if sheathing it. Instead, the sword met bone as he struck his attacker. He twisted and yanked it out. The warrior fell behind him.

"You have enough arrows in you to stock a warrior," Ulum jested.

"Proof that your men are terrible shots." He laughed, but it sent a surge of pain and breathlessness through him.

"Perhaps we can just wait you out," Ulum said. "You will die soon enough."

"You first." Unebolod knew he should wait for them to attack, he but had to finish them before he died so they could not chase down the Khan. He rushed toward Ulum, and the ring closed tighter around him.

Ulum raised his sword to lunge forward. Unebolod spun to the side, missing the blade, pushing the Ordos Lord off balance as Unebolod slid his sword through the man beside him.

In seconds, everything descended into chaos. Unebolod moved on instinct, paying attention with all of his senses as he had taught Dayan to do. He killed by cutting throats, slicing hamstrings. He predicted attacks based on the sounds of boots around him and the slowing thump of his own heart. Every shuffle of his feet or movement of his arms became harder to manage. His limbs grew heavy. But several of the traitors lay dead or dying around him.

Only three remained. Including Ulum. The three men circled Unebolod, probing for signs of weakness. How they could miss the lead in every movement he did not understand.

"You just won't die," Ulum noted.

Unebolod swallowed the blood that climbed up his throat. It had to be filling his lungs by now. Several fresh cuts marred his body. But no one had managed more than a surface wound. Most of the damage had been done by that last volley of arrows.

"You lack skill," Unebolod managed to say. He had wanted to say more, but worried he could not keep from spitting up blood. Sweat poured down his face, stinging his eyes, yet coldness grasped his bones.

The other two men closed in on either side slowly, stepping cautiously over the bodies of their fallen comrades. In unison, the two lunged for him. One swung at his head. The other lunged for his heart. Unebolod dropped to his knees and ducked. Momentum carried the two forward. The head of one rolled across the ground to Ulum's feet. The other staggered backward, clutching the sword jutting out of his chest. Then he tumbled back.

Unebolod wanted to poke at Ulum, but feared it would give away his weakness. He hardly had the strength left to raise his head. The roar of the men trapped on the far shore thundered in his ears. He had almost forgotten about them. Even if he killed these men, the rest would likely fire a thousand arrows at him.

He sank back on his haunches, eyes dancing victoriously at his foe.

Ulum sauntered toward him. Yet there was caution in each step.

Unebolod spit a wad of blood on the Lord's boots. He wheezed for breath. "No one will remember you."

Ulum kicked Unebolod's sword. He was too weak to hold on. It skittered across the ground. The other man smirked and crouched in front of him.

"I think you will die first," Ulum said. All the arrogance of ignorance rolled off every word. "And then everyone will remember me. I will be the man who killed the invincible Steel Soldier."

Unebolod subtly slid his fingers along his boot, fumbling. He coughed up more blood. It spattered across Ulum's face. The other man wiped it from his eyes, grimacing.

At that moment, Unebolod felt the warm handle of his knife.

Ulum adjusted his grip on his sword, preparing for the killing blow. "Issama sends his—"

Unebolod reacted instinctively. He yanked the knife from his boot and drove it up through the commander's chin, using all the strength he had left in him to be certain it went into Ulum's brain. Hearing Issama's name sent a wave of wrath through Unebolod.

Even as he gave a final push to be sure he completed the job, and Ulum's lifeless eyes stared at him in shock, he heard the whistle of a thousand arrows over the slow thump-thump of his heart. Now that he had killed all twelve Ordos, the warriors on the other side of the river had no reason to hold back.

Exhausted, accepting the inevitable, Unebolod closed his eyes and lay back on the ground. He had kept his promise.

Dayna Khan still lived.

"Unebolod..." A familiar voice called to him, coaxing and gentle. A warm hand brushed across his face.

Unebolod opened his eyes. Long, dark hair fell straight as an arrow around a face he had not seen in years. Still as young and beautiful as ever.

"Odsar..."

His wife leaned closer and kissed his forehead. "You have done well, my mighty orphan."

His heart ached. She had often called him that to tease him when she thought he was being too tough. "She needs me. There is more to be done."

"You have done all you can do. It's time to let go."

Mandukhai... Tears welled in his eyes as he lay on the ground. "No."

"She was not meant for you in that life. Wait for her here. With me." Odsar smiled. It lit up her face. A brilliant light emitted from her. "It's time to let go."

Unebolod closed his eyes, hoping this would be a dream. *Wake up.*

"Unebolod, the High Heavens praise you. The spirits bless you. Come to us."

He opened his eyes again. Odsar now stood beside him, holding the hands of two young boys—his sons. Sons he never knew. One had died in childbirth, taking Odsar with him. The other was Mandukhai's child, stolen too soon. The tears blurred his vision. If he accepted this death, he would never be with Mandukhai again, but he would be with his family. *I was never with her to begin with.*

He pushed himself to his feet, following his wife and children.

In the distance, the red-tiled roof of the Khorchin palace glowed in the bright light. In the doorway, the silhouettes of his entire family waited. Unebolod was home again, in the grasslands of Hulunbuir.

Chapter Twenty-Eight

Reclaiming Old Ties

Issama stoked the ger stove to spread more heat through the space as he waited for the men to arrive. Siker, Qolotai, and his two sons remained behind in Hami, hidden in their little hovel to keep them safe.

Alag, the older Uyghur man Issama met in the bazaar, had promised to meet him here with the full force of what remained of Bigirsen's men. Apparently, the Great Khan had not caught and killed everyone. A few remained. Enough for Issama to use for his own devices, with any luck.

And Issama had a plan he intended to put into action this very day. One that would steal some of Mandukhai's power away.

The clomp of hooves against the hard ground drew Issama toward the door. He stepped outside and was momentarily stunned by the number of men dismounting outside the ger. His breath caught in his throat. *There must be at least a thousand!* he thought as his gaze swept the open space. They would not all fit inside the ger.

Excitement raced through his veins, heating his skin despite the winter chill in the air. He had not dared to hope for so many. Issama could do so much damage with this many men at his disposal.

Alag hobbled his mount and approached Issama. Only ten of the men trailed along with Alag. The rest tended to the horses, shifting in obvious anxiety.

"You could have warned me you would bring so many," Issama said. "Asha and Alayitung will notice this many men riding all in the same direction." He glanced past the warriors as if he would see the oncoming Borjigin and Oirat attackers. They were alone. For now.

Alag shrugged. "You wanted men. This is what we have. We didn't all ride out at once."

Issama gazed once more at the mass of warriors behind these ten men. Ten miles could cast a long shadow. Surely Asha or Alayitung had noticed something. They were not safe here. "Those men need to move into the pass, so no one from Hami spots them. If Alayitung hears we have an army amassing, he will send out his own to crush us before we even start."

One leader, a man in his mid-thirties and a set of shoulders that would make an ox envious, headed back toward the waiting warriors to give the command. Issama motioned the rest of the leaders into the ger, waiting by the door as each man ducked inside. By the time the big man returned to the ger, the horde of warriors had mounted again and rode northwest toward the pass through the mountains.

Issama closed the door behind himself. All ten men had made themselves comfortable in his ger, lounging on the bed, on benches, and even on a collection of pillows Issama had left on the floor.

"So how do we retake Hami?" Alag asked, crossing his arms over his chest.

No delays with this one, Issama noted. Before answering, he made his way to his skin of *airag* and took a drink before passing it around the ger. He pointed at ox-shoulders. "I recognize you."

The man had just settled on a rug and taken the offered *airag* in hand. He froze as he was put on the spot, glancing at the others. All eyes fell on him.

"Dashai," the ox man said. "I was a *jagan* officer under your command. I was part of the group you sent into the Gobi to hunt down Bayan *Jinong*."

Issama had never bothered getting to know the *jagan* officers. There were just too many of them. But he remembered this one now. The corner of Issama's mouth twitched up. "Ah. Yes. You were the one who found him and reported it to your commander. I owe you gratitude. Without you, he might still be alive."

Dashai bowed slightly.

"I am certain you have heard numerous rumors about my past," Issama said, raising his voice clearly so all could hear. He needed the loyalty of these men, who clearly controlled what remained of the ragtag Uyghur army.

They needed to understand him and what his ultimate goals would be. "I started out just like many of you likely did. With nothing and no one. But I quickly rose through the Uyghur ranks, and do you know why?" He paused for effect. A few of the men even shook their heads. "Because no one could match my strategy, and the men in charge noticed. Bigirsen was not wrong to put his faith in my abilities. But his fatal flaws were his pride and vanity. His vision was weak. His execution pitiful. He lacked finesse."

"What makes you any better than him?" Alag asked.

Issama smiled to himself. He had hoped for this question. "Where he used brute strength to force himself into position, I used subtlety. A poke here and a nudge there. Lords prefer feeling secure in their control. If you try to rip that control from them, as Bigirsen had done, they will resent you. To this day, I still have allies among the Ordos and Oirat because I allow those Lords to think they are in control." Issama sighed for dramatic effect. "Sadly they have not truly had any control for a long time. Gentlemen, I have been working tediously for years on Uyghur supremacy. And we are nearly there."

Silence settled in the ger. Men exchanged uncertain and anxious glances. Several shifted uncomfortably in place. No one dared to speak first. Issama folded his hands into the sleeves of his deel and waited patiently.

At long last, Dashai broke the silence. "Most of us were only officers. Alag had the highest rank. And he only commanded a *mingghan*. What good are any of us? All of our generals are dead."

Issama raised his brows. "Only officers?" He strode toward Dashai slowly, each step measured. "And I was merely a destitute orphan. Yet here I stand. I served as officer, commander, general ... *orlok*." He placed strong emphasis on the last, leaning close to Dashai. "You are only limited by your ambition. Do you lack ambition, Dashai?" As he asked the question, Issama turned slowly, casting a penetrating stare took each of these men in. "We have lost more than we can ever recover under Bigirsen's reign. But he is no longer a problem. His impulsive, greedy recklessness will no longer hold us back."

Issama resumed pacing in a circle around the ger, hands folded patiently behind his back. "Right now, we have one major advantage at our disposal. Dayan Khan is young. He believes he has us defeated with Bigirsen's death. That we are weak and unable to resist his reign. But he underestimates the Uyghur. I think it's time we showed him just who the Uyghur are. And it begins right here, in this ger."

A few of the men sat straighter. A couple nodded.

"Lord Asha and General Alayitung are Dayan Khan's men, and right now they control Hami," Issama continued. "They believe they have taken what belongs to their Khan. I disagree. They have taken what has always belonged to *us*. Hami has been our stronghold for decades. But we cannot storm the gates of the palace. Even with a thousand Uyghur warriors, they outnumber us."

Everyone listened to him curiously. Issama drank it all in. This was it. History would mark the beginning of his reign on this day.

"As we speak, I have Ordos allies positioned alongside the Khan and his woman, Mandukhai," Issama said, pressing forward what he had their full attention. "Once we reclaim Hami, they are prepared to turn against the Khan. You see, men, Dayan and Mandukhai's power is an illusion."

"If we cannot storm the palace, how do you expect to retake the city?" Dashai asked, drawing a few nods of curiosity from the others.

"We divert General Alayitung's attention elsewhere," Issama answered.

Again, he waited to see if the others would understand. Instead, he was greeted by deep silence that only comes from ignorance. Issama sighed inwardly. *This is not the group of leaders I would have chosen if I had any say in the matter*. But he knew this was all he had.

"As I said before, I still have allies among the Oirat," Issama explained, irritated that not a single one of them seemed to put the pieces together. "Just north of the mountains at our backs is a small camp of Oirat protecting the pass. But the man in charge there is an old friend. I have already sent word to him, and he has responded in kind. His Oirat are prepared to join us. We will send the bulk of our forces through the pass to stir up trouble among the Oirat. My Oirat friend will send word to Alayitung that they are facing an uprising.

Issama resumed his measured pacing. "Alayitung will believe the city is secure and take most of his men with him to stamp out the uprising. The rest of us will then slip into the palace and retake the city. If Asha stays behind, I will persuade him as I have done with so many other Lords."

Each of the men listened with keen interest now. Except for one.

A man perhaps a couple of years younger than Issama pressed his lips together in a tight line, making the skin around the edges turn white. His skeptical gaze remained locked on Issama.

"You seem uncertain," Issama noted, standing in front of the other man. "Speak."

The man licked his lips nervously and took a deep breath. "I have seen Lord Asha with the Khan's men. I don't think he will be swayed so easily. He has grown rich under General Alayitung's hand."

Issama crouched. "Tell me, then, why you are here. Is your Uyghur pride not stronger than your desires for wealth?"

The man opened his mouth, but Issama held up a hand. He crouched in front of the man.

"Before you answer, look around you. Every one of these men has served the Uyghur not because they had to, but because of their pride in our tribe's power. We want wealth, but not at the expense of our pride." Issama rose, spinning in place to eye each of the men. "If you all swear to serve me and follow my orders to the letter, I can promise you this. Not only will we all become wealthy men, but we will see a resurgence of Uyghur power. Serve me now, and you will all become generals or *orloks* under my reign."

Quiet laughter rolled from a man in the back of the ger, soft at first, but growing in mirth and volume with each moment that passed. Everyone stared at the offender in anger. Issama stalked toward the man, towering over him as he sat.

"Did I say something you find amusing, officer?" Issama asked as he folded his hands together behind his back.

"Oh." The man wiped tears from his eyes as he reined in his amusement. "For a second there, it sounded like you expect to win and become Great Khan."

This statement drew a few tense chuckles from some others.

"I do," Issama replied without missing a beat.

The man froze, staring dumbfounded at Issama. "You plan on retaking Hami, conquering the Oirat—"

"Reclaiming, but yes."

The man hesitated a moment. "—and then becoming Great Khan over this young Khan people are calling the reincarnation of Genghis?"

Issama snorted. "He is not the reincarnation of Genghis. But yes. I have more allies among the Oirat than you might think, and there are nearly five full *tumens* in their territory. Not to mention my allies among the Ordos. Once we control the Oirat and Hami, we can regroup with the Ordos, and our power will be stronger than his. Dayan Khan will either accept me as his superior, or he will die. I have a feeling he will see reason when he is reunited with his mother. My wife. After all, what boy doesn't love his mother?"

The last part, Issama knew was a stretch. Siker seemed convinced Dayan had no interest in her as a mother. *She might have a point.* But he couldn't allow his men to know that.

The man blinked slowly. "You're serious."

Issama nodded. "I am. Lady Siker is my wife, and the Khan's mother. I have possession of her, body and soul, and he will do just about anything to save his mother." Hopefully they would not see through the obvious lie.

"And what of Mandukhai Khatun?" Dashai asked. "I hear she is like a dragon. If you want to control Dayan Khan, you will need to either control her or remove her."

"Yes, I have heard he will do just about anything for her," Issama noted. "And I will deal with that in my own time. Alag, you will take two-thirds of our men through the pass into Oirat territory, being the most senior commander among these men. Choose six to bring along to command. The other three will remain here with me and the final third of our forces. Once Alayitung has left Hami, we will close in and retake control."

The eleven of them spent the next hour discussing strategies before Alag left with his chosen men. By nightfall, they would be in the mountain pass. Within a week, Alayitung would vacate Hami, leaving Lord Asha in charge. And if Asha went in the General's place, Issama would slip in and kill Alayitung himself.

While this motley group of inexperienced officers was hardly what Issama would have selected if given a choice, he had to take what he could get. Hopefully, they could deliver.

Chapter Twenty-Nine

Mud and Blood

Northeaster Ordos Basin – Late Winter 1480

Togochi's boots squelched in the muddy ground as he stepped off the gathering tent cart. The surrounding camp bustled with activity, trampling trenches on the sodden ground as everything melted. Spring would arrive soon. Too soon. *At least the men are all across the river*, he thought.

They still had no word from Dayan or Unebolod. Had they crossed? What delayed them? Each day that passed, a deeper sense of dread filled his gut. Not that he could ever show that worry to Mandukhai. Since crossing the river, the rims around her eyes had darkened. She was clearly not sleeping well enough, worried about the two men she loved more than any other.

Togochi clasped his hands behind his back and arched as he stretched them behind him. A satisfying series of pops moved up his spine.

The delayed response from the Khan could not bode well for them. Togochi knew this from experience. Nothing good ever came from delays. He hid that from Mandukhai, though. She could only handle so much.

They had other concerns to deal with. Such as the Ordos Lord sitting in their gathering tent. Huoshai had escorted Lord Arqai to meet with Mandukhai, taking the long way around to avoid Lord Ibarai's scouts. Arqai turned out to be a surly man hardly eager to participate in any of Mandukhai's plans. Knowing what they did about Mogurkei's and

Issama's dealings, Togochi loathed having Arqai in their camp. He didn't trust the Lord in the slightest.

But Arqai had bent his knee to Mandukhai and recited his oath perfectly, naming Mandukhai and Dayan specifically. Breaking that oath damned him to death. Would he really be so foolish?

Togochi glanced back at the closed red doors of the gathering tent. Arqai was still in there with Mandukhai, Huoshai, and all of Mandukhai's guards.

Altan stepped up beside Togochi as he started away from the massive cart. "I don't trust him," she said.

"Nor do I. Oath or no oath. But Mandukhai insists we treat him as equal now that he gave the official oath. What can we do?"

"Seduce him and slice his throat," Altan said casually.

Togochi raised his brows at her.

She smirked. "I'm kidding. Mandukhai would skin me alive if I tried. Not to mention my husband's reaction. Actually, come to think of it, he might approve."

Togochi shook his head, eyes locked on his own ger, where Jaghan and Geriel now camped with his children. "We ride against Ibarai in a day. I suggest getting rest." He glanced sideways and noted her mischievous grin. "In your own bed."

"I thought you were the fun one," Altan pouted. She adopted a seriousness. "Your plan is good, Togochi. We will have Ibarai kneeling or bleeding out soon."

Togochi grunted in agreement. They had not choice but to defeat Ibarai. He had one of the largest armies inside the basin, aside from Legusi. And he stood between them and Legusi's camp.

Togochi bid Altan goodnight outside his door. Before ducking inside, he gazed at the orange glow of the sunset. *I hope you get back soon, Unebolod.*

The void floated around Dayan's consciousness, holding him tight and removing all pain. Something tethered around his waist. For a moment, he reverted to that helpless boy Mandukhai had tied to the saddle in his first battle. The memory was scattered, just like his own understanding of the world around him.

Dayan's helmet knocked against something solid, and his lungs tightened. He struggled to pull in a breath, to open his eyes, to remember what happened to him. Thunder rumbled in his ears, accompanied by the loud thump of his own heartbeat. He squeezed his eyes, then snapped them open.

Sand and desert rock raced past him in a blur that made his stomach twist into knots. Vomit climbed up his throat, and he closed his eyes again, trying to block out the dizzying sight. No matter how hard he tried, the lump of vomit attempted rising. He pressed his hands against something smooth and soft. It flexed beneath his fingers repeatedly.

Dayan focused his attention away from his current situation to recover before he puked his guts out where he sat. Horses snorted for breath all around him. He became dimly aware that he was riding.

That was the moment the memory hammered to the front of his mind, like a forge hammer against hot steel. Unebolod hoisting him into the saddle. Boke taking him away and leaving Unebolod behind.

"Stop," he said, but in his condition, his voice was too weak to be heard over the thunder of hooves all around him.

Dayan sat up in the saddle, opening his eyes cautiously. Rocks and tufts of desert grass breezed past as the horses churned up the ground in their haste. He tried shifting his left arm, but it refused to move more than a few inches. Dayan took a few measured breaths to gather strength, then yanked his reins. His stomach lurched. The horse stopped so suddenly he nearly tumbled out of his saddle, caught by the rope tethering him in place.

Boke reached for the horse's harness. Dayan feebly pulled the reins again, making the horse turn its head away.

All around him, the riders ceased, forming a protective ring around their Khan.

"We have to ..." Dayan struggled to get out each word. "... to go back."

"My lord Khan, we will be overrun," Boke said, edging cautiously closer to Dayan's horse.

Dayan shook his head, unable to find his voice again. At that moment, his strength gave out. The rope gave way, unable to hold him as his weight shifted completely against it. He slid from the saddle. His left shoulder slammed into the hard ground, causing blinding pain to shoot throughout his entire body. He screamed out, but the vomit he had struggled so hard to hold down swallowed the sound in seconds.

"Get the Khan on his horse now!" Belku commanded from somewhere nearby.

Dayan blinked dark spots from his vision as several warriors surrounded him. He rolled toward his back, but someone stopped him.

"Don't roll over," one man said.

Dayan was too disoriented to associate a name with the face. "We have ... Unebolod ..."

"Get that arrow out of his back," Belku said, kneeling in front of Dayan. For a moment, Dayan could see nothing but Belku's hard face.

"He said he would catch up," Boke said.

"Without a horse?" Dayan asked, his voice weakening.

"Going back will only get you killed," Boke said. "I have strict orders to ensure that at least one of you makes it back to Mandukhai Khatun alive."

The implication of Boke's words hammered against Dayan's already throbbing skull. Unebolod was dead.

No. Dayan squeezed his eyes shut. *Unebolod cannot be dead. He can't.* "She has to choose," he whimpered pitifully.

White hot pain lanced outward from his shoulder blade. Dayan arched his back reflexively. Several hands pinned him on his side. His own vomit stared back at him, making his stomach churn again. His vision darkened.

Dayan groaned and opened his eyes again as several men lifted him onto a litter created with branches and a horse blanket. Then they were moving again. The litter bounced over each bump, making his wounds scream out. *Unebolod ... Mandukhai has to choose. She has to. I can't let him die.* But weakened as he was, Dayan could provide no protests aloud.

Fever dreams plagued Dayan's sleep. Unebolod's body exploding, then covering Dayan's own until he was no longer himself, but a newer, stronger, younger version of Unebolod. His generals and commanders mocking him as he attempted firing a bow with only one arm, calling him lame. Then they put him out of his misery like a lame horse. Mandukhai brought him back to life only to beg for answers about Unebolod, then blamed him, cursed him, and abandoned him with words to punch his fate home: "Even your parents didn't want you. Why should I?"

Dayan cried, begged on his knees, pleaded with every breath he had for her to stay, but she faded into the darkness, and her voice echoed in the surrounding air. "I would never choose a weak boy like you."

Agony ripped at Dayan's chest as he woke. A mask of gray clouds matching his dark mood covered the sun. Tears rolled down his temples. Every breath was a struggle. The pain from his wounds was nothing compared to the pain in his heart.

It took several minutes to calm himself enough to stuff the pain into his emotional void. He reached a dirty, trembling hand to wipe the tears from his face, then swiped his sleeve over his nose.

He was no longer bumping over the ground. Instead, the litter rested on a bed of horse blankets. Men moved around him in thick rings, each carrying out some unknown duty.

"We were worried we lost you," Orghana said, kneeling beside his litter. She dipped a cloth in a bucket of water beside her and wrung it out. "You are lucky to be alive. Between the wound in your shoulder and the one on your side, you should have bled out."

Dayan closed his eyes. He didn't feel lucky. "Where is he?" He dared a look around.

"Nemeku is on watch," Orghana said, glancing at the men around them. "They sent scouts to find out about the other men. Only Chakicha and Kelegei have regrouped with us so far. We still don't know what happened to the men in the south."

"Not them," Dayan said, and his voice cracked over each word. "Unebolod."

Orghana paled, wiping sweat from his brow with the cool, damp cloth. Her lips pressed together, making the rim around the ruby red color a pale white.

When it became apparent she had no intention of answering him, Dayan attempted sitting upright. Despite the void around his pain, he still became lightheaded and fell back.

"Don't move. You need rest," she said. "Drink this." She held up a skin of water.

Dayan took a greedy gulp.

He could not leave Unebolod behind. Mandukhai would never forgive him. It was bad enough the *orlok* was likely dead. If Dayan returned to Mandukhai without a body, it was as good as killing him with his own hands. If he ever hoped she might forgive him and move on, he knew he couldn't go back empty-handed.

"Boke," he said, but his voice quivered. He cleared his throat, pulled in a breath, and focused on calling out as loud as he could. "Boke!"

Orghana sat back on her heels, avoiding the gazes of everyone around them.

Boke kneeled beside the litter. "I am relieved to see you awake."

"We have to go back," Dayan said.

Boke's face fell. "My lord Khan, if we go back …"

"I'm not asking, Boke!" The heat in Dayan's voice drew the gazes of several men around them. Orghana's face reddened. "If he is alive, we will save him. If he isn't …" Dayan swallowed the lump that leaped into his throat. "… then we need to give him a proper burial. I won't leave his body for predators and birds to pick apart."

The hate in Mandukhai's voice from the nightmare resurfaced, along with her blame. Grief gripped Dayan and he could not stop a few rogue tears from escaping.

Jangi loomed behind Orghana. "The Khan needs rest," he said. "We won't be going anywhere for a while. It can't hurt to send a few men to find the *orlok*."

"It could lead the Ordos traitors right to us," Boke argued.

Dayan turned the fury burning inside of him on Boke. The guard met his gaze, but quickly shrank back, heat rising to his face.

"If my men are so dim-witted that a handful of them cannot avoid the oathbreakers, they deserve their fate," Dayan said. The coldness in his tone startled even him. "We camp here for the night. That should give the men plenty of time to find him and bring him back. The *orlok* is going home with us."

"Our scouts need rest," Boke said.

Dayan snatched Boke's collar so quickly Boke didn't even have time to react before Dayan yanked him closer. Dayan's lips curled back in a fierce snarl. "Question my commands again and your head will be in that bag with Bigirsen's."

He released his grip, and Boke stood, straightening his deel. He murmured his apology before stalking off to carry out the orders.

Dayan's anger was misdirected. He knew that. He just could not cope with the look on Mandukhai's face if he did not at least return the body. He would rather die.

Nightmares made Dayan's rest quite restless. Mixed with his inability to change position without further injuring himself, Dayan had a pitiful evening of sleep. All he could think about was Unebolod. He had wanted the other man dead, but now that it might be a reality, he regretted the hate he cast at the *orlok*. Could he really blame Unebolod for loving Mandukhai? Dayan had met a lot of women, but none of them compared to her. It only made sense that Unebolod would love her, too. Was love a justification for wanting a man dead?

Or maybe Dayan never really wanted Unebolod dead. He just wanted Unebolod to let go of whatever hold he had on Mandukhai. Now, Dayan would return to her with a body. The odds of Unebolod surviving over a thousand riders with nothing but his sword were impossible. If Dayan hadn't fallen out of the saddle on the riverbank, Unebolod never would have died. They would have made it across the river, and likely would be with her as early as tomorrow morning. Both of them. Then she could have make her choice and Dayan would know for certain, at last, if she truly wanted him. Now he would never know. She would stay with him because she had no other options. As far as Dayan knew, he would always be her second choice.

I should have settled this before we left, he thought as he stared at the haze of the wolf dawn. *But I let my arrogance and pride keep me from doing what I knew needed to be done. I should have let her choose already.*

Dayan drew in a deep breath and let it out slowly, focusing on centering himself as Goram the monk had taught him.

"He was like a father to you, wasn't he?" Orghana whispered.

Dayan rolled his head to the side. Orghana had spent the night between him and Nemeku. Now, she lay on her side with Nemeku's body curled up against her back, his arm holding her tight against his chest. Seeing the two of them so close sent a pang of longing through him. Such closeness was all he wanted, but he was cursed to never have it. He returned his gaze to the sky.

"Sure," Dayan whispered, and sarcasm bled into each word. "If your father slept with the woman you love and drove a wedge between you." Suddenly, he realized maybe Orghana and Nemeku *did* understand. How long had they had feelings for each other while she was Bigirsen's wife? *The difference is that Mandukhai obviously loves Unebolod, or at least did, and Orghana never loved Bigirsen.* His heart sank. In this scenario, *he* was Bigirsen. That realization further crushed his soul.

Orghana placed her hand on his arm. "You can care about him, grieve him, and still resent him. If emotions were easy to handle, we would all be better off. Love and hate are not so different. Both are full of passion. Both can lift us to new heights and destroy us utterly. But what matters is how quickly we get back on the horse and continue riding."

Dayan forced a smile for her. He knew she was only trying to help, but it did little good. "Nemeku is lucky to have you."

"And we are both lucky to have you," she said. She moved her hand to stroke his cheek. "My sweet Khan. You feel more deeply than people realize. The men revere you. They see you as a strong, cold warrior. But I see through that. She will, too."

Tears pricked the corners of Dayan's eyes. "She has never seen a warrior. She only sees a boy."

"Then she is blind." Orghana pulled her hand back, resting it instead on Nemeku's arm. "If she truly had feelings for the *orlok*, make sure you give her time to grieve. Then she will see how much you have grown."

Dayan wanted to escape this conversation. He tested his luck sitting up. For a moment, everything darkened and spun around him, but the dizziness passed quickly. He got his feet under himself, but every muscle in his body protested as he attempted standing.

"Be careful," Orghana said. "You will tear your wound open again."

Dayan ignored Orghana, fighting against his protesting muscles. The muscles in his back twitched. His calves strained to hold his weight. But he was on his feet.

Before he could take a step, he heard the commotion that stirred several others awake. Dayan's heart leaped into his throat. He followed the direction of the sound to the northwestern edge of camp. Each step threatened to give out, but he forced himself onward.

By the time he arrived at the far edge of camp, hundreds of the men were awake and following him. Everyone had anxiously awaited the *orlok's* return.

Dayan nudged his way past a cluster of men. His lungs collapsed in on themselves.

Twenty men had gone out to find the *orlok*. Only six returned. *So few. Were they followed?* Blood stained the gray coat of one mount, led by the reins along with the others. Sagging over the saddle of the horse leaned a massive body covered in arrows. Dayan focused on each step, edging closer to confirm what he already knew to be true.

"My lord Khan," the lead rider said, dismounting while holding tight to the reins of the packhorse. If it could be called a packhorse. "We found him on the edge of the riverbank, surrounded by bodies. He broke the ice and killed Ulum. We found the Ordos Lord's body beside his. A few Ordos were still on the western riverbank, firing at us as we dragged his body away. We are all that survived."

"Their families will no doubt be rewarded for their sacrifice," Belku reassured the lead scout.

Everything inside of Dayan numbed as he gazed at the unmistakable face of Unebolod. He was covered in blood, and dozens of arrows peppered his body.

"Get him down," he said, but the voice that came out of him was distant, not his own.

More than a dozen men stepped forward to do the honors. Sober silence filled the air, punctuated only by the stamping of impatient horse hooves and ragged breathing of men around him.

They laid Unebolod on the ground with great care and stepped back as Dayan edged closer. Dayan eased himself to a knee, startled to find Orghana there at his side to help ease him down. Dark pools of lifeless eyes gazed at the brightening sky. Despite the grim circumstances of his death, Unebolod appeared almost peaceful.

So this is it, Dayan thought as he reached out to close Unebolod's eyes. His hand remained remarkably steady. He would return the body to Mandukhai.

"Remove the arrows and wrap the body," Dayan commanded. Orghana helped steady him as he stood again. "He comes back with us and will be honored as a hero." It was the least he could do. Unebolod gave his life to save Dayan.

If only Dayan deserved the sacrifice.

As Dayan turned to walk away, he noticed the sword hilt peeking out from between the saddle and horse blanket. The yellow ribbon fluttered, stained with blood and mud. He edged closer, running his fingers along the hilt. Then he carefully slid Unebolod's sword out from where it was wedged and slipped it into his own belt on the opposite hip from his own sword.

Dayan crossed the camp and left the men to deal with Unebolod's body. He headed toward his own makeshift bed, fingering the yellow ribbon on the hilt.

Yellow. The color of religion and joy. Yet Unebolod had little faith in the gods for as long as Dayan could remember. And his life was hardly filled with joy. So why had the *orlok* tied this yellow ribbon to his sword? Dayan had asked him a few times over the years, but Unebolod either changed the subject or simply fell silent. When he was eleven, Dayan had tied one to his own sword, but Unebolod had ripped it off, told him didn't understand anything, and stormed away. The fury in that moment had terrified Dayan so thoroughly that he had not tried it again.

Dayan looked down at the ribbon, surprised by the tears that dripped off the tip of his nose.

Whether or not Unebolod was his rival, he *had* been like a father. More of a father than Dayan's own had ever been. Everything Dayan knew about fighting, shooting bows, and battle strategy had come from Unebolod.

The Great Fist tightened around his heart and lungs. He should be happy to have Unebolod out of the way, but he had never felt more miserable and lost.

CHAPTER THIRTY

Diversions

Winter wouldn't last much longer. Issama could feel the way the heat of the sun intensified each day. Issama had men planted all around Hami. Each location had been strategic, and he was careful to place few enough men to go unnoticed, but enough in each place to bring his plans together fully. With any luck, the moment Alayitung left to retake the Oirat, Issama could sweep in to take control.

Issama watched the main road with two of his men—all of them wearing local garb to better blend in with the crowd. None of them would be easily spotted, and they spaced themselves out around the street to avoid the suspicious eyes of Asha's men. This main road through the small, dusty city would be the best way for Alayitung to leave quickly and pursue the men Issama had sent into Oirat territory.

Just this morning, Issama received a message that his men were in position just north of the pass. Alayitung would receive a false report about an Oirat uprising. If he ignored the danger, he risked Mandukhai's wrath later. A chill ran down Issama's spine just considering Mandukhai as a threat. He had always respected her intelligence, but ever since she took control of the Mongols, he grew more and more certain he had underestimated her. It had been a costly mistake he could not afford to repeat. But until he received reports from the Ordos Lords, he had to trust in his plan.

Issama had to take control of Hami swiftly. He needed this oasis to funnel supplies to his men when he turned his attention to Mandukhai's *tumens*. It also gave him a foothold on the Oirat.

Hopefully the Ordos Lords keep their end of this bargain, he thought. It made him uncomfortable that so much of his plan depended on the obedience of men like Ulum and Mogurkei. He hated having so little control over what happened to the Khan's forces. If his plan failed, he was a dead man. *The quicker I finish here in Hami, all the sooner I can get to those Lords before they change their minds.*

Issama wiped sweat from his brow with his sleeve and sank back into the cooler shadows of a building along the wide road. It was approaching midday. If he was wrong about Alayitung's response, this plan to take Hami could fall apart before it began. Maybe he had underestimated Alayitung, too. All morning, messengers rode in and out of the small palace. Perhaps Alayitung would only send orders to the men he already had in Oirat territory to end the uprising. How would he react when he learned it was a ruse?

Just as Issama doubted his plans would come together, the palace gates opened and a stream of Oirat and Borjigin riders poured out. At the head of the group, General Alayitung rode his mount, surrounded by blue and yellow banners. Issama sneered at the arrogance of the Borjigin General in his rich armor and vainglorious superiority. *I wish I could see his face when he realizes I have bested him*, he thought.

The stream of horsemen continued for several minutes before the line dwindled and the gates once more closed.

Tonight, Issama would make his move on the palace. But first, Alayitung needed to ride far enough away from Hami that he could not return in time to stop Issama.

Dust snorted and dragged his hoof across the rocky earth. Mandukhai patted his neck absently as she gazed south, toward Ibarai's Ordos camp. She and Togochi had determined it would be best to attack Ibarai's camp at night when he had fewer men on watch and the dust from her army would be harder to spot in the dark. Even if she outnumbered the men in the camp, she could not take chances.

Nearly a week had passed since the river crossing. Mandukhai's scouts had returned with word that the Khan and his men were headed in their direction. His forces further south regrouped with Dayan after the Ordos who followed him had turned against him and attacked. All Mandukhai knew was that they had suffered severe losses. But they lived. Dayan and Unebolod were on their way to her. Just knowing that allowed her to focus more on the battle ahead. They could deal with the losses later.

The news forced her to reconsider the oaths Arqai and Qori had given her. Mandukhai recalled their words, certain that if they betrayed their oaths, it would be the end of them. They had firmly bound themselves to her by name. Qori, for certain, had rested his eternal soul on his oath. Mandukhai trusted he would not break his word. Arqai, on the other hand, had been much more glib with his words. His eternal soul was not dependent on his loyalty—only his life. *Must I make them all promise on their eternal souls to trust them?* Mandukhai hated the prospect of asking anyone to re-swear themselves to her. It would make her appear weak. *I will not be so forgiving with the rest of these Lords. Their oaths must be eternally binding.*

Mandukhai had Lord Ibarai pinched into his camp. Arqai's men, now under Soke and Huoshai's command, closed off the southern route of escape. Albeq, Bagatur, and her Three Guards warriors circled around the western flank. Ordag and Altan commanded the eastern flank. Mandukhai and Togochi commanded the north. Altogether, her force of over forty-thousand would cut off any chance of escape. They outnumbered Ibarai four to one.

A single arrow soared silently through the air, sinking into the mud fifty yards ahead of her waiting forces. Mandukhai eyed the red ribbon attached, signaling that her men were in place. The bulk of her forces waited in rings, hundreds of yards out from the massive camp. But each of the four wings had sent a thousand warriors forward to create a tighter circle and draw the warriors out so that woman and children would not be harmed. They had wrapped the horse hooves in felt to reduce the noise. Her men had been commanded to move forward at a casual pace to make any movement of earth feel normal. With any luck, no one would notice. If they did, it could be dismissed as their own herds moving.

Togochi shifted in his saddle beside Mandukhai. She nodded.

Togochi waved his hand, giving the signal to his men. Bowmen lit their arrows and raised their bows into the night sky. In a matter of moments, the wider ring of her warriors surrounding the Ordos camp stretched as far as she could see in either direction, lit by flaming arrowheads. Arrows flew, streaking fire across the sky toward the camp.

Mandukhai would have to show her strength over Ibarai quickly to avoid any further uprisings like the Khan had faced. They could not afford to lose any ground. *This would be so much easier if the Ordos Lords would just bend the knee to their Great Khan*, she thought as the flaming arrows soared through the night sky silently.

Togochi's strategy was brilliant. Light fires to draw the warriors out of the camp, leaving the women and children safely in their gers. Mandukhai had no desire to see women or children killed over the stubborn pride of the Ordos Lords. It was not their fault, and they would still serve the future of the Mongol Empire.

The fires were only meant to catch attention, not reveal the forces waiting close to the camp. Before the light from the flames could reach her tighter ring of warriors, the flames on the arrows dimmed, then blinked out, plunging the sky into darkness once more.

As predicted, the Ordos warriors launched into action. Shouted commands echoed across the night sky.

Dust snorted. Mandukhai absently patted his neck. Only the shouts from the camp or the occasional snort of horses and jingle of armor penetrated the darkness.

All around the camp, more campfires sprang to life. Mounted Ordos warriors surged past the campfires, racing out in all directions to find the source of attack.

Too late, they realized their mistake.

Even from four hundred yards away, Mandukhai could hear the creak of bowstrings and thump of release crack across the dark. Her inner ring of warriors released their first volley at the oncoming Ordos men. The sound repeated seconds later, punctuated by cries of death as the arrows met their mark.

The first wave of Ordos had been destroyed before they even realized Mandukhai's men were waiting so close to their camp. Their commanders rallied several thousand Ordos men into action, and they pressed outward toward the awaiting forces. Her men held fast to their positions. They fired arrows into the charging Ordos, but did not race forward. The Ordos returned fire. Only a few men fell. Once the charging Ordos drew close enough to her inner ring of warriors, a horn sounded and her men wheeled around to pull back and fake retreat. Togochi wanted them to not expect the second wave of warriors hiding in the dark.

"Hold!" Altan bellowed from further down the line.

Mandukhai didn't blink. She didn't dare. For all the fighting she had done, the fear of death still surfaced each time she faced down her foes. If she blinked, she might miss something important.

Her advance warriors jumped the line of caltrops, having measured exactly where the spikes were in the dark. They then joined the ranks of waiting men.

The Ordos drew closer.

A hundred yards.

Suddenly, their horses squealed and pitched forward. Men and mounts alike were trampled by the warriors riding behind them. A few more mounts went down.

Mandukhai took a deep breath to steel her writhing nerves.

Togochi had ordered all the Ordos scouts and watchmen killed quickly and quietly as soon as their camp had gone silent for the night. The moment they had removed the threat of being spotted, Togochi's men set to work placing layers of caltrops in a ring around the camp. Her warriors knew where it was to jump it. The Ordos did not. The strategy proved useful. They must have lost close to a thousand warriors under hooves.

Fifty yards.

Mandukhai watched as another volley of arrows arched inward, crossing paths with the Ordos arrows flying toward her own forces. Some of them struck midair and broke apart. She raised her shield overhead as arrows rained down on her. Most of them skipped off the shield. A couple punctured the first layer of metal. She lowered the shield as Togochi sounded the command for lancers.

Ten yards.

By the time the Ordos noticed the gleaming tips in the distant firelight it was too late. Horses continued the charge, slamming the long lances into their necks before tumbling. Some lances pierced armor and threw Ordos warriors out of the saddle. Her warriors already began shifting formation, prepared for the oncoming horses and tumbling bodies.

Mandukhai steadied her nerves and drew her sword as Dust pushed forward toward the oncoming Ordos. As horses moved in a swirling mass all around her, Mandukhai could no longer see the length of the battlefield. All of her focus turned toward the enemies at her sides. She focused all of her attention on everything Unebolod, Togochi, and Altan had taught her about sword fighting on horseback. Her swings arced across armor, sometimes meeting flesh, other times scratching over the plates. But always, she kept it moving, never stabbing, always swiping, careful to avoid pressing too deep into flesh where the blade could get caught on bones.

Torgus and her guards remained close to her sides. Mandukhai felt a little safer with her men around her, knowing they would give their lives to protect her.

Dirt kicked up from the ground, turning the fires in the distance into a haze of red and brown. It distorted everything around Mandukhai. She could only see a few feet in any direction. The only way to tell which direction she faced was by the location of the fires.

HAMI – LATE WINTER 1480

Word spread quickly through Issama's men stationed all around the palace once Alayitung had ridden out of the city. They all knew their roles. Kill Alayitung's palace guards. Don the guard clothing. Assume the guard positions. Secure the palace grounds. Anyone not guarding the gates would slip in and help take out as many of the remaining enemies as they could find. There was no sure way to know how many men remained inside the thick palace walls, but Issama thought it safe to assume that most of the men were either placed around the city or had left with Alayitung. The courtyard in front of the palace revealed little activity.

Once the sun set and the sky had gone black, Issama met with his Oirat compatriots at a door along the south wall. They were not expecting him, so he would have to hustle.

Issama shuffled toward the massive sandstone wall, keeping his face covered until he drew close. The two Oirat guards stiffened and placed hands on their swords upon his approach.

"I paid you quite handsomely for this door to be opened at my will," Issama said, keeping his voice low so no one else who might be near could hear.

"That was before Lord Asha took control of the city," Round Belly said.

Issama stopped four feet away. Far enough that they could not reach him quickly if they struck. Close enough that he could kill them both if need be. "I thought General Alayitung was in control. And he rode out this afternoon." Issama smirked. "I wonder what drew him away."

The second guard gaped at him as he suddenly realized what had happened. "You drew him out."

"I told you I would get into that palace, and now I am prepared to put Lord Asha firmly in control of the Silk Road, just as I promised," Issama said. It was a lie. Issama would not leave Asha in control without his own protections in the city first. "But if we are to succeed, we need to do so before Alayitung realizes what I have done and returns. The only thing standing in my way is you."

The two exchanged uneasy glances. Issama held his breath and kept his expression neutral. They could not know he planned on removing Asha if the man did not bend to his will.

They scanned the surrounding streets.

Round Belly leaned toward Issama as his companion opened the door a crack. "This has become more dangerous than it was when you first paid us. I expect another payment in the morning."

Issama forced himself to smile as he nodded in agreement. They would be dead before morning.

Issama passed through the ten-foot-thick wall, climbing the stairs to the courtyard above. Once in the courtyard, he stuck close to the cold sandstone as he made his way around the massive, open space. He knew his way around the palace, having occupied it with Bigirsen several times over the years. He would have to slip around the guard quarters and watchtowers to avoid detection. Even if his men had secured the gates, they would not have secured the interior of the palace.

The palace rested on a massive hilltop, surrounded by walls. Each of the guard gates around the lower levels led to a staircase that opened near watchtowers. Those towers had an expansive view of all of Hami and the surrounding landscape. No buildings were allowed within fifty yards of the palace walls so that all approaching enemies could be easily spotted. The palace had been built years ago by Uyghur ancestors. Copious amounts of wealth had flowed through this city over the centuries, and from the palace, the man who ruled could see it all.

Issama crouched beside the wall, peering around the corner toward the nearest watchtower. Men paced inside. He observed the front of the palace.

The building was squat, with sloping roofs, blue-white mandala designs, and massive red lacquered pillars. It was a grand place for such a small city.

No one moved near the palace doors. Issama glanced over his shoulder, scanned the courtyard, and darted toward the doors. Before slipping in, he peered around the corner. Two men guarded the inside door. Issama pressed his hand to a shuttered window and eased the shutters open. Peering over the lip of the sill, he saw no one inside. Issama slipped through the open window into the palace.

This room was near the king's quarters. With any luck, he would find Asha there, sound asleep. Then Issama could appeal to Asha's Oirat pride. And if that failed, Issama would have the upper hand to kill the young Oirat khan.

Issama stuck to the shadows, checking open doorways before passing. In no time, he faced the massive red doors with their giant golden lion knockers. He licked his lips and edged into the room as silently as he could.

As Issama eased the door closed, someone pressed a sword against his neck. Issama tensed, daring a glance from the corner of his eyes at the assailant.

"You are not as quiet as you think." Asha stood against the wall, holding his sword in a steady hand. "The Great Khan will pay handsomely for your head."

Issama sighed in mock relief. "Asha khan, you are just the man I was hoping to speak with."

"Is that why you were sneaking into my chambers in the dead of night?" Asha asked, clearly not buying into Issama's act.

"Would your guards have let me walk in?"

Asha paused, narrowing his eyes suspiciously. "What is it you want, Issama?" he asked at last.

"Would you please remove your sword? I have no intention of harming you." Another lie. Issama would kill Asha if he had to.

Asha chewed the inside of his lip, then stepped back and lowered the sword, but he didn't slide it into his belt. Anger burned in his tone. "My father trusted you, and it led him to his death."

"From what I hear, you killed him."

Asha froze for only a moment, then turned and strode across the room. He was in his late twenties now, and he moved with the grace of a true predator, confident and smooth with each stride. His bare feet didn't make a sound against the white tiles.

Asha poured two cups of honey wine, holding one out to Issama. A dangerous glint sparked in his eyes and his jaw twitched. "I had no choice. If I didn't kill my father, Mandukhai would have killed me, too."

Issama crossed the room, wishing he moved as gracefully as Asha. He accepted the offered wine.

"A woman made you tremble?" Issama asked, sinking into one of the cushioned chairs with the drink.

Asha grimaced as he dropped into his own chair. His brows knitted together as he glared into his cup. "Have you faced her in battle? She is like a dragon."

Issama suppressed the urge to snort. "She is a woman. Her power is false. You and I are the ones who hold true power."

"I suppose, now that Unebolod is dead, that may be true."

Issama choked on his wine, nearly spitting it out of his nose. "What?" he asked, gasping for air.

Asha took a casual drink, as if his news was old. That fury simmered beneath the surface no matter how casual he tried to act. "We intercepted the message just today," Asha said with a shrug. "It worked Alayitung up into quite a frenzy, between that and the Oirat uprising. I offered to go take care of the Oirat myself, but I think he didn't trust me."

"Unebolod? You are certain?" Hope bloomed in Issama's chest. With Unebolod out of the way, this could all be much simpler. Dayan was only a boy still. Only Togochi would stand between Issama taking Mandukhai down at last. Once the Ordos attacked her and he secured Hami, the end would come. Mandukhai would fall.

Asha nodded. "Killed by Ulum. Mandukhai will be furious." He snorted as he stared into the depths of his cup. "I would hate to be the Ordos right now."

Issama took a slow drink to collect his thoughts. *Ulum truly had everything under control, just as his man promised me. Perhaps I am in a better position than I thought before.*

The death of Unebolod could be Issama's greatest stroke of fortune yet. Now, with the Khan's mother as his wife, Issama would have an even stronger position in court. What would Mandukhai give to have Siker brought safely to her? What would Dayan give? Issama had far more control now than he ever had before. And from what he had gathered, Dayan had yet to have any sons.

Perhaps Issama had only to use his leverage with the Ordos Lords to get them to bend the knee to him. Then he could march into Mandukhai's court with the Ordos Lords at his back and Siker at his side and take Mandukhai's power away.

And Unebolod would not be there to protect her anymore. *Togochi still will be.*

Issama finished his drink in a gulp and set it on the table beside him. "Lord Asha, how would you like to rule your people properly again, without a Borjigin spy overseeing your every move?"

Asha hesitated with his cup halfway to his mouth, frowning. "That sounds like treason."

"Only if we fail." Excitement pulsed through Issama. A sensation he had not felt in years. Not quite like this. It was intoxicating, far beyond anything the wine could offer. "Send word to your loyal Lords immediately. We can throw off the yoke of this woman. You can once more rule over the Oirat."

Asha narrowed his eyes, lowering the cup. "What do you get out of this, Issama?"

"My wife is the Great Khan's mother." Issama hoped Asha understood. Asha had to harbor some resentment toward Mandukhai after everything she had taken from him. He certainly had seemed angry with her a minute ago.

"He is not a boy any longer," Asha said slowly. Issama could see the wheels turning in Asha's head as he pieced together their chances.

"Do you love your mother any less? Would you hurt the man she loved out of spite? Or would you learn to welcome him?"

Asha snorted. "You think he will learn to love you like a father, and you can just take control? He carries the spirit of Genghis at his beck and call."

The calls of fighting resounded from outside. Issama's men had penetrated the palace walls. In the halls and the courtyard beyond the windows, Issama heard the unmistakable clash of steel against steel, and the snap of bowstrings. The sounds grew louder, closer. For a moment, Issama's head swam with heady excitement.

Then he saw the corner of Asha's mouth curled upward as he eyed Issama. "That message we intercepted relaying Unebolod's death was meant for you."

The message had been meant for him, which meant Asha knew what he had planned. Did Alayitung? "What have you done, Asha?" Issama asked, surging to his feet.

Asha rose, lifting his sword again. "You offer me empty promises. I already control Hami, Issama. And the Oirat. Your plot is doomed to fail. I want no part in it. I like my life as it is."

The doors to the chamber burst open. Asha's guards stormed in, seizing Issama and dragging him out of the room.

No. He could not lose like this.

A horn sounded. Mandukhai attempted discerning the message of the blasts from the Ordos commanders but could not figure it out. The Ordos began a retreat toward their camp.

Mandukhai's men pursued until they reached the field of caltrops, now covered by the bodies of dead horses and men. The Ordos rode over the top of them carelessly.

"What is happening?" Mandukhai asked Togochi as he rode toward her. Blood dripped from a cut on his face.

"Regrouping?" he offered.

Burning pain in Mandukhai's arm drew her gaze downward. Blood stained her sleeve. She prodded a finger into the hole in the cloth to inspect the wound, wincing at the intensified pain. But it wasn't deep enough to worry about. Little more than a surface wound.

"Mandukhai!" Altan called as she galloped toward the Khatun, waving toward the Ordos.

Mandukhai raised her gaze.

The Ordos had gathered together in a cluster from all sides of the battlefield, converging on one point. Facing her.

"Hold the lines!" Mandukhai commanded. Hopefully, the men she had encircling the camp would not leave any gaps for anyone to escape. Even one Ordos warrior could warn the rest of the Ordos camps all across the basin.

Her command called out down the line in both directions.

"They are converging on you," Togochi noted. "You should go. We will finish this."

"I will not run."

"He is right, Mandukhai," Altan said. "This cannot be good."

Mandukhai clenched her jaw, staring at the Ordos behind their wall of dead bodies.

A few of the men at the head of the Ordos group conversed, waving their hands toward her line. Clearly, they were not all in agreement about whatever they discussed.

"I don't like this," Altan muttered.

Mandukhai didn't like it either, but she would not attack. Not yet. Her curiosity got the better of her. As the Ordos commanders argued, the rest of their warriors waited anxiously for their orders. At least five thousand Ordos remained, if not more. They eyed Mandukhai's forces with obvious dread. Instead of pulling further back, as Togochi suggested, Mandukhai nudged Dust forward at a casual trot.

"Mandukhai!" Togochi called, reaching out as if he could stop her.

Altan grumbled under her breath before following Mandukhai. Torgus and the rest of the queen's guard also closed in around her.

Mandukhai stopped a few feet from the wall of bodies. Her banners snapped in the breeze behind her loud enough that she could not hear what the Ordos commanders argued about.

One Ordo commander threw down his sword at the feet of his companions. Their faces turned so red Mandukhai could even see it in the dim, distant campfire lights.

Mandukhai held her breath. *He is prepared to surrender!* This was her moment to end this. She cleared her throat and raised her voice high enough for them all to hear.

"Surrender and submit to the will of your Khan and Khatun," she called. "And I may be inclined to show mercy." But could she trust any of these men? Dayan had trusted his Ordos commanders, and they had turned against him. "I will not make this offer again."

The swordless Lord marched forward. The other four men exchanged incensed looks before dropping their weapons to follow the Lord. Their hesitation and insolence was obvious to everyone.

"Lord Ibarai," Togochi said to the swordless leader.

This is him? Mandukhai thought, her gaze sweeping over him critically. Ibarai was an older man in his late forties with as much gray in his hair as black, hanging in long, thin braids around his round, wrinkled face. *Why do his commanders defy him so openly?*

"We surrender and submit, as requested," Ibarai said.

"Why surrender now?"

"We are surrounded and outnumbered," Ibarai said. "I could fight to the end and kill all of my men or spare their lives by accepting your superiority and that this is the will of the High Heavens."

Mandukhai flicked her wrist. Dozens of her own warriors dismounted and cleared out the path of bodies and caltrops in her way. Mandukhai kept a cautious eye on the Ordos men as she waited. Once a path was opened, she dismounted and stalked toward Ibarai. Torgus loomed behind her like a deadly shadow.

"Your fellow Ordos Lords have done the same, then turned against their Great Khan," Mandukhai announced. "I have a hard time trusting anything that comes from the mouths of traitors."

Ibarai's chin trembled in indignation. His angry gaze swept over the guards trailing behind her. He licked his lips, and his Adam's apple bobbed. His jaw twitched.

A moment later, Ibarai dropped to his knees, then pressed his face to the bloody, dirty ground. The other four men exchanged bewildered glances. They kneeled as well, but did not bow prostrate on the ground as Ibarai did.

"If I must give my life to amend for the sins of my tribesmen, I will," Ibarai said, still facing the ground. "As long as it spares my men and their families."

He thinks we will kill everyone, Mandukhai realized. She could use this to her advantage. "A noble act," Mandukhai said. "But unnecessary. You may live as long as you swear the oath to me upon your eternal soul. However," her gaze flicked past him to the other four commanders, "I *do* worry about these four. Their hesitation and open defiance cannot go unpunished."

As if reading her mind, Torgus and the queen's guards strode forward, seizing all four commanders and dragging them forward.

"Please, I beg you, spare them," Ibarai said in a rush, daring to raise his eyes. "They are good men."

"They are open traitors. I cannot risk their enmity turning others against the Khan or myself. They have sealed their own fates. Let this be a lesson for you. Never misunderstand what will happen to traitors against the Great Khan and his empire." Mandukhai nodded to her men.

The guards moved in unison, yanking on the commanders' braided hair and sliding swords across exposed throats. Ibarai's skin turned sickly white.

"Now, Lord Ibarai," Mandukhai continued, unable to watch as blood poured from the wounds. Her guards dropped the lifeless bodies to the ground. "You were saying?"

"I will be of service to my Khatun and Khan," Ibarai said in a rush. "I know the locations of the larger Ordos camps, as well as Lord Legusi's own camp. I know how many warriors are in each camp, and how far apart they are. I know who has struck deals against your eminence and the Great Khan. This information I offer for the lives of my men."

Mandukhai edged closer, eyeing the lines of Ordos horsemen behind Ibarai. Some of them watched in utter shock, some in horror, a few with clear resentment on their faces. Mandukhai would have to create a task force of trusted men to weed out potential traitors hidden in the mass of Ordos men.

"That is a good start," Mandukhai said. "But I think you know what you must do right now to save yourself and your men." She stopped so close to him the toes of her boots nearly kissed his forehead.

"Upon my eternal soul, I give my oath to you, Mandukhai Khatun, to follow you and Dayan Khan with salt, gers, horses, and blood from this day until my last," Ibarai said. "By order of the High Heavens, I will serve the house of the Great Khan and atone for the sins of my tribesmen."

Mandukhai tipped Ibarai's face up with the toe of her boot, then held out her hand to him. Ibarai sat up enough to kiss the ring on her finger.

This was not a glorious victory, but it was a victory nonetheless.

"Disarm them all," Mandukhai commanded, waving toward the waiting Ordos warriors. "Lord Ibarai must prove his value and credibility before I return weapons to his men."

Torgus pulled Ibarai to his feet and turned him to face the waiting Ordos warriors. *Seven thousand?* she wondered.

"Dismount and disarm!" Ibarai called out.

The command was met with some hesitation and grumbles.

Mandukhai turned to Togochi. "See that any man who refuses to disarm is killed for insubordination."

Altan strode toward Mandukhai, holding Dust's reins in her hand.

"Your will, Mandukhai Khatun," Togochi replied.

Mandukhai did not wait to see how the order would be carried out. She climbed into her saddle and rode alongside Altan toward the Ordos camp. Her guards formed a protective ring around them, clearing the path.

All across the battlefield, Mandukhai heard the creak of saddles and clang of metal on steel and stone as Ibarai's warriors dismounted and piled their swords, bows, and knives.

"I remember when *you* envied *me*," Altan noted as they rode together. "Seems hard to believe now. I can command ten thousand, but this..." She swept her hand across the horizon. "This is the stuff of legends. You have put the legacy of Khutulun to shame, Mandukhai."

Mandukhai appreciated the sentiment, but she did not want to be a legend. She simply wanted to do her duty, have a family, and die in her sleep.

Was that too much to ask?

CHAPTER THIRTY-ONE

Shrouded in Steel

ORDOS BASIN – LATE WINTER 1480

Dayan rode in front of the cart carrying Unebolod's body in stony silence. He had ordered the cart emptied and packed with a bed of snow to help preserve the body. Thankfully, in the cold winter, the body would not bloat or rot as quickly. The bed of snow helped slow the process. He did not want to return with a man Mandukhai would no longer recognize. It would be hard enough to confess the truth—that Unebolod's death was his fault. *She will never forgive me.*

During the trip toward her camp, he put on a hard face for the men. Losing the *orlok* had been devastating to morale. Many considered Unebolod invincible, indestructible. That this fight for reunification could bring down the strongest of them struck a cruel blow.

Dayan tried not to look back at the cart, to see the pale, ghostly face of the man who had helped raise him. If he looked back, it might break him in front of the men.

The fight between them before that last attack now felt petty to Dayan. How could he have doubted Unebolod's loyalty? *I nearly branded him a traitor in front of everyone,* Dayan thought, swallowing the lump of grief in his throat. Unebolod had been the closest thing he ever had to a father. Did all men reach a point where they doubted or challenged their father? Tears stung his eyes.

You can feel weak on the inside, but you cannot show it to the men or they will doubt your ability to lead, Mandukhai had taught him.

He blinked back the tears and clenched his jaw. *I will not show them this weakness, Mandukhai.*

Nemeku followed alongside Dayan for most of the trip, and Orghana spent much of her time tending to both Nemeku and Dayan's mental state. Dayan wanted her to go away, leave him alone, but he could say nothing.

Boke and the rest of Dayan's guards now escorted the cart like an honor guard.

Unebolod had not been the only casualty in the attack. Tulugen and Dochigen had returned with only half of their men and Ogedei's saddled mount, which carried only Ogedei's belongings. Mogurkei's men had killed him in the attack. Ulum was dead, killed by Unebolod, but Mogurkei remained out there with more than two *tumens* of warriors.

Belku took command of what remained of Dayan's *tumens*, forcing back any small Ordos camps in their way. It had tempted Dayan to command killing them all, but he would not make such a decision while burdened with grief. For now, pushing these families deeper into the Ordos basin was satisfactory. They would face him soon enough. They all would.

When the head scouts returned on the sixth morning and reported the Khatun's camp was within miles, Dayan's heart grew heavy.

By the end of this day, he would lose her forever.

The air in the dungeon was stale. Issama could taste urine with each inhalation. His cell had little more than straw on the floor and a bucket for a commode. No windows to shed light in the room. A lamp on the wall outside his cell was the only light he had in this dank, dark pit. He couldn't be certain how long he had been in the cell. A week, at least. Perhaps longer. Twice a day—or what he assumed was twice a day—guards walked up and down the rows of cells. One brought food and water. The other carried the keys and always remained closer to the far wall. Too far away for Issama to have any chance of grabbing the man or the keys. The first two days, Issama had attempted talking his way out of the cell, but quickly had learned his lesson the first time the door was opened as they teased that he had persuaded him, then set about kicking him until his ribs were blue and purple and it had been hard to breathe.

How long would they leave him to rot in this prison? Until the Khan made his way to Hami? Until Issama died?

There had to be a way out. Surely some of his men had survived. Someone must have planned his rescue. *The arrogance that I did not even plan for this possibility.*

The unkempt beard on his face itched, but he resisted the urge to scratch, worried he might dig too hard and draw blood like last time.

The familiar jingle of keys and scuff of boots against the stone floor told him it was time to eat. Issama, like all the prisoners, shuffled toward the iron bars. Two cells down, a metal cup clattered against the floor. The prisoner cried out, then begged for another cup of water. The guards chuckled and moved on.

When they reached his cell, Issama shrank back half a step and waited for them to offer the cup through the bars. He knew their moods could be touchy. Sometimes the cup would "slip" from their hands, and they refused to refill it. Issama dipped his head and held out his hands. If they thought he was being aggressive, they would enter the cell and beat him. If they thought he was too passive, they would drop his cup. He licked his dry lips, glancing at the keys hanging from the far guard. If only he could get ahold of those.

The guard dropped the cup in Issama's hands and Issama had to hurry to wrap his fingers around it before it could fall. Some of the water sloshed out onto the floor, but not all of it. He drank with greed, the warm water coating his insides in bliss. Before Issama could finish his drink and hand the cup back, the guard threw a small lump of crusty bread into the cell. Issama's heart sank as it soared toward his bucket of urine. Thankfully, the guard was not a great shot. The bread missed by about an inch and rolled across the straw on the floor.

Issama offered the cup back, glancing at the key guard once more. He recognized the eyes that peered out of the helmet. Issama bit his tongue to smother a cry of alarm climbing his throat. *How had Dashai become the key guard? What took him so long? Maybe this is my chance,* Issama thought, afraid to hope for release.

The water guard reached for the cup in Issama's hand. *If I am wrong, this will hurt a lot.* But what other choice did he have? Issama had to get out of here. As the guard's fat hand wrapped around the cup, Issama struck like a viper, snatching the man's arm with his free hand and yanking him toward the bars.

The water guard's head slammed against the bars, but it didn't knock him out. Momentarily dazed, he blinked and shook his head.

Dashai slammed a knife into the back of the guard's neck, then ripped it out. The other prisoners began calling out, raising a commotion.

"Hurry, before anyone else comes," Issama hissed.

Dashai grimaced, tucking the knife away and fumbling with the keys to find the right one for Issama's cell.

Issama stepped back, shifting from one foot to the other impatiently as Dashai tried and failed repeatedly. The other prisoners rattled their cell doors, calling to be released.

At last, Dashai opened the door. Issama bolted out, afraid it might close and lock him in again.

"Get the rest of these men out," Issama ordered.

"We don't have time."

"We will need every man we can get." Issama moved deeper into the dungeon toward the next cell. Some of them would have to be fodder for escape.

Dashai grumbled, but moved to unlock the next door. "Go out the back way. We have a couple men posing as guards there who will help you out of the palace. Go north and find a place to hide until we can regroup out where we met before. I have some men creating a diversion along the south wall so no one will see you leave through the north."

Issama joined the rest of the prisoners, ushering everyone toward the door while glancing back over his shoulder at the staircase leading deeper into the palace. A part of him wanted to barge into Asha's rooms and slit that miserable runt's throat. But first, he needed to regroup.

Without a doubt, Asha was firmly under Mandukhai's spell. That woman must have been a witch the way she commanded men, and they obeyed.

Issama slipped out into the night along the north wall as the two guards posted there watched his escape.

Lay low. Asha would likely turn Hami upside down to unearth Issama. But Issama knew how to hide, and he had to be sure his family was safe. He would not leave his wives and sons behind. They could hide in his hovel until Asha gave up searching.

Mandukhai stood over the map in the gathering tent with Togochi and nearly a dozen other commanders. After capturing Ibarai's camp, Mandukhai ordered gers and the Great Khan's gathering tent brought to her. It had taken several days to organize and deliver.

The death toll on her own forces had been small, but no less significant. Albeq had taken an arrow through the throat, killing the Tabun khan. Albeq had been an old man compared to the rest of her commanders, nearly twice her age. His reactions had been too slow to save him. Thankfully, Bagatur had been close enough to rally Albeq's men. When his son Chakicha returned with Dayan, he would be raised into his father's position and given time for his grief.

As they waited for Dayan and Unebolod to return, Mandukhai and Togochi spent their days in meetings with Ibarai, questioning him and sending scouts to verify his information to adjust their strategy. Lord Ibarai seemed more than eager to comply with all of their requests. Arqai had been less kindly about helping, but he still obeyed. Mandukhai was sure to keep Arqai, Ibarai, and their commanders away from each other to avoid a disaster like the attack on Dayan's men.

Ibarai's information mirrored some of what Lord Qori had told Mandukhai already. Legusi hated Bigirsen. He would likely fold willingly. According to Ibarai, Legusi commanded eighteen thousand men along the southern tip in the Ordos basin. Another ten thousand under Lord Sayiqan's command would be near enough to the western border for Mogurkei to align with before she could reach either of them.

Mandukhai had poured over the map marking out the locations of Lord Sayiqan and the possible rally point for Mogurkei. According to Arqai, Mogurkei would be foolish enough to resist her forces even if she absorbed Legusi, Sayiqan, and the other two remaining Ordos Lords. Ibarai also advised that, if he could send a message to Legusi, Utagachi, and Aglaqu, he might be able to convince them to stand down. She could not take that chance. Surprise was her greatest ally until all of her forces were reunited.

Last night, Togochi had planned a surprise attack when they received word that the Khan was within a day's ride from them. All plans of attacking were immediately halted.

Today, Dayan would return. As would Unebolod. While Togochi had spent years devising brilliant strategies and advising Mandukhai, she knew he would rather defer to Unebolod's more strategic mind. Unebolod could take on a thousand men with only a few—odds they would need if they were to turn their attention back on Mogurkei and finish this for good.

Altan lounged in a chair she had dragged over to the table. The skin of *airag* in her hand only enhanced her careless attitude. It grated on Mandukhai's nerves that this woman would act so blasé about such important matters, yet in the heat of battle, few could match Altan's skills.

"So we wait for the Khan and *orlok* to return and converge our forces," Togochi said, breaking the silence that settled over them as they assessed how many men Legusi had at his command.

"Perhaps we should call in more of the men we left across the eastern steppe," Huoshai said. "It couldn't hurt. If we need to patrol the men and women in the east, we have bigger problems."

Mandukhai chewed her lip, then shook her head. "Those men also protect us from any Ming who might try sneaking up behind us from Beijing. We need them out there."

A call from outside the gathering tent drew all of their eyes toward the door. Mandukhai held her breath, waiting to hear it again to be certain she heard it right.

"The Khan has returned!" someone outside shouted. "He approaches!"

Dayan! Mandukhai wanted to run out to greet Dayan and Unebolod, but a queen could not run like a child. Instead, she moved the marker for Dayan's men into her camp. As she did this, the rest of her companions made their way to the door. Togochi hung back and matched her stride.

Mandukhai stepped out onto the deck of the massive cart holding the gathering tent and wrapped her hands around the rails. For a moment, all she saw was Dayan. His stony face that would have given Unebolod competition. The rich furs and gleaming armor he had not left with. He looked so much older than he had when he had left just months ago. Stronger. His gaze met hers, but she could read nothing of his emotions. Was he happy to see her?

Mandukhai scanned the party, pleased to see Nemeku riding alongside Dayan—alarmed by how much older he was. Quite a handsome young man. Before she could marvel at how much older he looked, Mandukhai frowned at the apparent grief on Nemeku's face. Was he angry about his father's death? Did he grieve the man who had killed his own mother?

She scanned the riders, seeking out Unebolod. *Where is he?*

Togochi gasped beside her. Mandukhai glanced at him, at the way the color drained from his face. And just past him, Esige pressed her hands over her mouth as tears welled in her eyes.

Suddenly, everyone was looking at *her*. Why?

She moved toward the steps to descend as Dayan dismounted. Her gaze slid past him to the cart surrounded by guards. They dismounted, giving her a clear view of the bed of the cart from where she stood on the deck. Her vision narrowed on Unebolod's sallow face and sunken cheeks. Her head suddenly became stuffed with wool. Her body, too heavy to hold up any longer. A scream climbed up her throat, but as she opened her mouth to release it, the sound lodged in her throat, choking her, suffocating her.

Somehow, she had descended the steps. Dayan strode toward her. Mandukhai was only dimly aware of his presence. She tried to pull in breaths to no avail. Then her knees gave out.

Before Mandukhai fell to the ground, a muscular arm slid around her waist, holding her upright and practically carrying her unmoving feet up the steps of the gathering tent cart and inside.

Voices rose around her. A hurricane of sound muffled by the thumping of her heart and the wool in her ears. Mandukhai sank back, only then realizing she was sitting on her throne. A flurry of activity began all around her in the gathering tent.

Unebolod was dead.

Mandukhai drew in a breath that caught in her throat. Tears blurred her vision and rolled unchecked down her face. They dripped on her trembling hands. *It can't be. This is a terrible vision. Someone will wake me up.*

Half a sob choked out before it was cut off. A lump the size of the moon had grown in her throat. *Wake me up. Wake me up!*

Living without Unebolod as her husband had been impossibly difficult. Every day she had wanted to give in, to go to him, to revoke her vow and her life. But she couldn't. And she had taken some solace from the fact that at least he was still at her side. It had been agony, but this was a whole other kind of anguish.

Esige crouched in front of Mandukhai, taking her hands. Mandukhai could not look at Esige, though, because if she saw the grief on Esige's face, it would make this real. And she could not handle this being real.

Someone loomed over Esige's shoulder. The motion drew Mandukhai's eyes up, hoping beyond hope it would be Unebolod.

Togochi met her gaze. His own eyes reddened. His jaw set in obvious grief. "Mandukhai, how are you feeling?"

How am I feeling? Anger burned through her. How could Togochi ask such a stupid question? He flinched, and she wondered just how angry she must appear.

Esige leaned closer, gripping Mandukhai's hands in her own clammy hands—or perhaps the clamminess was Mandukhai's. Esige wrapped her arms around Mandukhai's waist and pressed her cheek against Mandukhai's stomach. Mandukhai couldn't move to hold the girl. She couldn't move at all.

"Leave us," a hard voice commanded.

Mandukhai looked up, expecting to see Unebolod. Instead, her gaze caught Dayan's. He quickly looked away, still giving nothing away.

Boke led the Khan's guards through the door, carrying a litter holding the body. They had placed a shroud over Unebolod's face. Mandukhai stared at the body, unable to think, unable to feel. The moment they placed the body on the floor in the center of the tent, everyone moved toward the exit.

Dayan stood with his back to Mandukhai, thumbs hooked on his belt as he watched the others leave. She wanted to call them all back. She wanted to be alone.

Esige paused in the door, tears streaming down her cheeks, meeting Mandukhai's gaze. Then she ducked outside where Huoshai's arm wrapped around her instantly. The guards at the door closed it with a thump that made Mandukhai jump, sealing her in the tomb with only Dayan and Unebolod.

For several minutes, Dayan remained statue still, facing Unebolod with his back to her. Mandukhai herself was frozen in shock. He seemed to be staring at the body. The air around them grew thick, stifling, and she could swear she smelled the body. *The body ... Unebolod's body ...* Mandukhai struggled not to vomit on her own feet.

The silence stretched on forever. Mandukhai could not avert her eyes from the body on the floor. Shrouded as Unebolod was now, Mandukhai could tell herself it was someone else. She would trade anyone to have him back. That stoic face. The way his eyes shined when he looked at her. How he rode in the saddle and fired his bow. The feel of his hands against her skin. Mandukhai couldn't hold it back any longer. The dam broke. She buckled over in her seat and released a wail that hurt even *her* ears.

Dayan crossed the floor in just a few strides, wrapping his arms around her. He stroked her back. She reached out, clinging to him, pulling on the fur cloak around his shoulders, tightening the soft fur in her fists so hard it hurt her hands. Mandukhai sobbed against his chest, and he said nothing at all. He only held her, lending his strength.

As Mandukhai's sobs eventually subsided and she regained enough control to not be a snotty mess, she pulled back. The second she met Dayan's golden gaze, he turned his head away.

"What...?" Mandukhai swallowed, surprised at how foreign her own voice sounded in her ears. How raw. "What happened to him?"

Dayan withdrew from her arms. Mandukhai tried to hold on to him, to keep him close, but he seemed determined to put space between them.

As he shuffled backward, Mandukhai's eyes locked on him so she wouldn't have to see the body behind him. She slouched in the chair, unable to summon any strength to sit any taller.

Dayan cleared his throat and bowed his head, kneeling in front of her. As he spoke, his own voice sounded as hollow and distant as her own. "Unebolod died a hero's death. We were crossing the river with at least a thousand Ordos on our heels when my horse's hoof caught in the mud and pitched forward. Unebolod—" Dayan's voice cracked. "He set me on his horse and sent me safely to the other side while he bought me time to escape." Dayan's voice grew thick with grief. "I'm sorry, Mandukhai. His death was my fault. I know what he meant to you." Dayan pressed his face to the floor at her feet.

In that moment, Mandukhai realized there was one person she would not exchange to have Unebolod back. One person she *couldn't* trade. Dayan was her everything now. Perhaps he always had been. She had chosen him years ago.

Mandukhai was uncertain what to make of this news. She could not blame Dayan. Unebolod had done exactly what she had asked. She would have cried all over again, but could no longer summon the tears. But where had everyone else been during all of this? Where had *Boke* been? Unebolod's job was to marshal the *tumens*. Boke's job was to protect the Khan.

Dayan pulled further back and stood. Mandukhai tried to catch his eye, but he avoided her. "Take all the time you need," he murmured. "The gathering tent is yours. No one will disturb you."

Before Mandukhai could find the words to protest, Dayan turned and strode out—and his stride reminded Mandukhai so much of Unebolod that it broke her heart all over again.

The door closed behind him. Muffled voices sounded from outside.

Mandukhai trembled violently as she stood and shuffled toward the shrouded body on the floor. When she reached the edge of the litter, Mandukhai hesitated. Could she handle saying goodbye to the man who had consumed her for sixteen years? She sank to her knees beside his body and reached a trembling hand toward the edge of the shroud. Could she handle seeing his face?

Mandukhai closed her eyes as she pulled the cloth away. After a moment to attempt—and fail—at centering herself, Mandukhai slowly opened her eyes. Oh, how they burned!

Unebolod's skin bore the paleness of the moon in death, but his strong features remained. Mandukhai traced a finger along the scar Bigirsen had given him, from his eyebrow down his cheek.

"I told you to come back in your saddle," she whispered, unable to speak any louder. "You gave me your most solemn oath. Yet here you are, deliberately disobeying my command. Why did you have to be so stubborn?" She leaned closer, pressing an ear to his chest in the vain hope that they were all wrong and his heart still beat. But nothing came from within. No heartbeat. No breaths. No denying the truth.

Mandukhai sat on her heels, her palm against his cold cheek. His face seemed so peaceful, and she recalled what he had said before he left on this campaign with Dayan. *I will protect the Khan with my life.* She stroked stray hairs away from his face. He had kept his word.

Something else he had said that day struck Mandukhai. Something she had not fully understood before, but it made perfect sense now. She had blessed his path, and he told her he had something stronger than Tengri to believe in. *Trust and truth.* Unebolod had harbored so much resentment toward the gods. He had placed all of his faith in her.

This realization brought a fresh wave of tears to her eyes. She sniffled and swiped a tear away, then leaned closer to him. Her lips brushed his cold forehead. "I will fight until my last breath to make sure you didn't die for nothing," she whispered. "I give *you* my most solemn oath. I will finish what we have started."

Unable to remain with his body any longer, Mandukhai pulled the shroud back over his face as her eyes blurred with tears. For a few moments, she sat there, drawing in careful breaths and releasing them slowly, measuring each one to regain control of her emotions.

Once she was in control, Mandukhai stood and turned toward the door. When Manduul had sentenced Bayan for treason, he had lost himself in his grief. It had disgusted her that, in such a critical moment, he had given up and submitted to his own weakness. She could not afford to do the same, or Unebolod's death would be for nothing. The nation still needed her.

Dayan still needed her.

Mandukhai would take this veil of grief and transform it. She would become shrouded in steel. For the sake of everyone.

CHAPTER THIRTY-TWO

Not Strong Enough

Esige's overwhelming relief at seeing Nemeku alive and seemingly well had swiftly been replaced by utter devastation when her gaze fell on Unebolod's body. The shock rocked her to her core and made her knees so weak she could hardly stand without Huoshai's arm snaking around her waist.

As Dayan helped Mandukhai into the gathering tent, Esige's gaze locked on Unebolod. Huoshai pulled her closer. She leaned gratefully against his chest, trembling. His lips pressed close to her ear. "She needs you."

What about what I need? Esige swiftly squashed the rebellious thought. Huoshai was right. She followed them into the gathering tent, using Huoshai for support until she drew near the dais where Mandukhai sat in stunned silence. Her vacant gaze fixed on some mysterious distance as tears rolled down her pale cheeks. Esige pulled away from Huoshai and kneeled in front of Mandukhai, holding her hands, but received little more response than Mandukhai averting her gaze away from Esige.

Togochi loomed behind Esige, asking how Mandukhai was feeling. Esige wanted to slap him. *How do you think she is feeling, you idiot?* But her anger was misplaced. Togochi meant well. He just didn't know how to respond to the situation.

Esige leaned toward Mandukhai, desperate to share in this grief, to hold Mandukhai and be held by her. But as Esige's arms wound around her, Mandukhai didn't move. Esige tightened her grip, but it garnered no response.

And then Dayan kicked everyone out of the gathering tent.

Huoshai placed a hand on Esige's shoulder. She drew reluctantly away from Mandukhai and allowed him to help her to her feet and guide her out. At the door, Esige stepped to the side to allow the guards to enter with the shrouded body. She wanted to reach out, touch Unebolod, feel some form of life still in him. Tears streamed down her face as she tried to meet Mandukhai's gaze. *Please see me. I need you!*

Huoshai ushered her gently out the door. A moment later, the red doors of the gathering tent closed with a final thud.

"Let's get you home," Huoshai murmured in her ear, assisting her toward the steps.

The moment Esige's feet hit solid ground, a wail of grief split the air from inside like a crack of thunder. Esige's knees shook. She instinctively turned to go back inside.

Huoshai tightened his hold on her. "Dayan is there. They need this moment. You can see her later."

Esige shook her head but knew she didn't have the strength to fight him. Unebolod was dead. He had been her sole father-figure. He had taught her everything she knew about fighting, about defending herself, about honor and pride. She wanted to be in that gathering tent with Mandukhai, grieving, wailing alongside her, clinging to her, sharing this burden so it didn't swallow them both. She *needed* it.

"Esige?"

She turned away from the gathering tent, trying to block out the sounds of grief from within that carved into her heart with each rise and fall in pitch.

A young man stood before her. One she recognized despite how much he had clearly grown since she last saw him.

Nemeku's voice had changed, too. He sounded older, no longer like a child.

"I'm sorry," Nemeku croaked. "I should never have left. I heard what he did to my mother and I just ..." Despite how much older he looked, something about him reminded her of the boy he had been.

A fresh wave of tears blurred her vision. All of her anger burst from her. Esige strode toward Nemeku, only a few feet away. He let go of the hand he had been holding—a girl Esige didn't recognize—and looked ready to embrace her.

Esige pulled Nemeku close, giving him the hug he obviously wanted, but it was not the comfort she needed. He had turned out to be a reckless, impulsive child and run away from her. He had abandoned her without a word instead of coming to her to ask her questions about his mother or sharing in his hatred of his father.

The anger and disappointment in his actions overwhelmed Esige. She jerked away from him and slapped him as hard as she could. Tears welled in his eyes as he stumbled back, watching her with like a hurt little calf. He tenderly touched his cheek, now red with the mark from her hand.

"Hey!" The girl beside him edged forward, placing herself between them. She nudged Esige away with the tips of her fingers.

Esige analyzed her. Young. Close to Nemeku's age. Thin and lithe as a willow branch. *I can break her in half.*

"Stay out of this, girl," Esige hissed.

The girl bristled. "I will not! He has been through enough."

Huoshai edged close to Esige, reaching for her hand. She jerked away.

Nemeku straightened. He tried glaring at Esige, but the wounded child inside shined clearly in his dark eyes. He slid his arm around the girl, pulling her back beside him.

Suddenly, everything became very clear. Nemeku had run off to kill his father, but along the way, this girl had seduced her way into his heart. Esige clenched her fists at her sides, ready to punch the girl.

"Stop," Nemeku said more forcefully. "She's my wife."

Wife! There was no way Esige would allow this. He was Esige's responsibility, her nephew. He had run off and thought he could just marry whomever he wanted? Did he think that was how the world worked? Esige snorted. "No she isn't."

Nemeku straightened. How had he grown so tall? The hurt look dissolved into defiance. "Yes, she is. We already have Dayan Khan's blessing."

Dayan! Esige's nails bit into her palms, drawing blood. "And what about my—"

"It's done, Esige," Nemeku said.

The meaning of his words snapped into place. The Great Khan had given his blessing and they had already shared a bed. Tears sprang to her eyes. Huoshai seized the moment, closing in on her and forcing her hand open to take his.

"If you want to be angry with anyone, be angry with me," Nemeku said. "I was the one who ran off. She was no better off than my mother had been. Forced into marriage to him. Abused by him. Dayan rescued her, just as you wanted to do for your sister."

She had been Bigirsen's widow? Esige's eyes widened. Her stomach dropped. Nemeku had married his dead father's wife? It was not unheard of, but the truth of it startled Esige.

Nemeku took advantage of Esige's speechless vulnerability, stepping toward her urgently to make his case. "Orghana took care of me, did what she could to protect me. I owe her everything. I would have surely died without her." He turned his gaze to the girl—his wife—and Esige would have been a stubborn old fool to not notice the love they shared.

"Well then," Huoshai interrupted. "We had better get you two set up with a ger."

Esige wanted to fight this, but she knew it was pointless. As Nemeku said, it was already done. He had left her a reckless, wild boy and come back to her a man.

At least he came back to me, she thought. Overcome, Esige rushed to Nemeku. He flinched back, but she pulled him into her arms and held him tight. He returned the hug eagerly.

Togochi had not felt such deep grief in his life. Not even after Manduul had passed away. He wanted to be angry, to kill every last Ordos Lord, oath or no oath. But that would solve nothing except his own thirst for vengeance, and he knew it. Instead, Togochi spent his night wallowing in despair over Unebolod's death.

At some point in the evening, Jaghan and Geriel gathered the children and took them to Geriel's ger. Then Jaghan spent the rest of the night tending to his wounded soul with soothing words when needed, silence when necessary, and controlled amounts of *airag*. Were it not for her, Togochi was certain he would have drowned his grief until he blacked out.

All night, Togochi tossed and turned, unable to find his own rest as the weight of everything crushed him beneath it. Togochi had always accepted his responsibilities and kept to his word, but he always had Unebolod to fall back on. Unebolod had been the one who planned the brilliant strategies, had known where the next moves would come from before they happened, had kept the men in line just by passing among them. His mere presence had been all the men required. Unebolod had walked taller than any of them ever could.

Taller than *he* ever could.

And Unebolod had done it while in agony over losing everything he wanted.

How did you do it, brother? How can I possibly carry all this weight like you did?

Mandukhai would need support and understanding to get through this. Togochi had to be certain Dayan understood just what that meant, just now much she and Unebolod had cared for one another. The truth might break the poor boy. Which meant Togochi had to hold up both Mandukhai and Dayan while planning the final phase of their plan against the oathbreaking Ordos.

Togochi sat on the edge of his bed, pressing the heels of his palms into his eyes. *First, I just have to get through this day*, he thought.

Dayan spent most of the night walking through the camp. Boke trailed along at his shoulder—a shadow always there, never giving him space. The rest of his guards had been given the night to rest. But Dayan was incapable of rest on the best of nights.

The look on Mandukhai's face when she had seen Unebolod's body would haunt him for the rest of his life. The way her expression had shifted from happy—excited, even—to confused, to vacant. And then her face had turned ghostly white and crumpled completely. Small lines had formed at the corners of her mouth and eyes. Pure agony had dulled in her dark eyes. Unebolod had meant more to her than Dayan had expected. He knew he could never compete. Not even with the memory of Unebolod.

As Dayan walked the camp, he fought to erase that image, knowing full well he never could. He focused on the surrounding camp. Most of the women wore Ordos clothing. Whenever an Ordos man bowed out of his way—unarmed—Dayan cast a disdainful, mistrusting glare in their direction. Boke's hand would tighten on the hilt of his sword. After what Ulum and Mogurkei had done, Dayan was uncertain he could ever trust another Ordos man.

Thousands of gers dotted the landscape in the Ordos basin. Most of them were Ordos Mandukhai and Togochi had conquered. Some were his own followers. Dayan did his best to avoid his men as much as possible. He could not avoid them forever, but tonight he needed space.

It was not until Boke struggled to stifle a yawn that Dayan made his way to his ger. He placed his hand on Boke's arm.

"Find someone else to take watch and get some rest, Boke," Dayan said.

Boke glanced warily at the men around them—though none of these were Ordos. "I would rather keep watch."

"Go see your wife. I'm sure she must be dying to see you." Dayan did not know if Odgerel was in the camp or not, but Boke deserved the night off, and the reunion.

Boke grimaced and nodded.

Dayan slipped inside and closed the door. He lay in bed to sleep, but it evaded him. Every time he closed his eyes, he saw Mandukhai's grief all over again. She had cried for so long in his arms. Dayan had not seen her cry so much since he first arrived in her care, and that memory was broken, distorted by time. Had her tears been for Unebolod then, as well? Had Dayan's arrival in her life caused her this grief? He squeezed his eyes closed and pinched the bridge of his nose to fight off the welling tears.

Have I not done enough yet to be worthy? Dayan thought bitterly. *I wiped out Uyghur power, killed Bigirsen, expanded our yam lines across the empire. What more can I possibly do?* The next logical step was to wipe out the Ordos as he had the Uyghur. Mogurkei was still out there.

During his musings, Dayan drifted off to sleep, only to wake from a nightmare that fled the moment his eyes opened. His heart hammered in his chest. Dayan sat up, rubbing at his ribs, then took slow, even breaths as Goram taught him. How he wished his monk could be with him now! He could use Goram's wisdom to help guide him through this battlefield of emotion.

Today, they would bury Unebolod in a stone grave. Dayan knew Mandukhai needed him—and he would be there, as he always had been—but at this moment, he just didn't have the strength to give. *At least I won't have to give the speech*, he thought with some relief. The honor had been given to Togochi and Mandukhai.

He rose and used a bucket of water and cloth to clean himself off, wiping away dried blood, wary of his healing wounds. It was the first bath he had since Unebolod died. Dayan changed into a white deel embroidered with elaborate swirls of blue—a union of purity and the eternal blue sky—then bound his many colored belts around his waist.

Dayan opened the door to the ger for some fresh air. The wolf dawn was well underway, and already the camp stirred with life. He stepped out long enough to glance at Mandukhai's ger beside his own. The smoke hole was open to the sky above, and smoke pumped out the stack, but no sound penetrated beyond the felt walls. For a moment, he considered going to knock on her door, but fear planted his feet to the earth. Mandukhai wouldn't need him or want him. Not today, of all days. Instead, he sighed and rubbed his neck.

Togochi strolled over, offering a slight bow. "My lord Khan, you are up early." Togochi's face was pale and his eyes bloodshot. Dark rings circled his eyes. The downward slope of his shoulders made it apparent he had not had a good night either. And why would he? Togochi was like a brother to Unebolod. This loss was hard on him as well.

"I always am," Dayan said.

Togochi's lips thinned. "This will be a hard day for all of us."

Dayan glanced at Mandukhai's ger again.

"They were close," Togochi said, and looked prepared to say more, but Dayan couldn't stomach it.

"I'm well aware of how close they were," Dayan said sharply.

Togochi's bushy brows climbed his forehead, then he nodded toward Dayan's ger. "Can we speak in private?"

Dayan knew there was no point in refusing. It would only raise more questions and perhaps resentment. He could not afford to have Togochi resent him as well. Where Unebolod had been like a father to him, Togochi was much like an uncle. Dayan stepped into his ger.

Togochi joined him, closing the door behind them. The other man shifted from one foot to the other, clearly uncomfortable.

"Just say it, Togochi. I'm too exhausted to play games." Dayan sank down on the edge of the bed. "If this is about Mandukhai and Unebolod, he confessed everything to me already."

Togochi stood a few feet away, arms folded behind his back. "Then I suppose you know more for certain than I ever did. None of this will be easy to hear, I'm sure."

"It can't be much worse than what he already said," Dayan grumbled. "He all but wished me dead, but wouldn't kill me."

Togochi jerked his head up. "I suppose that shouldn't shock me. He felt the same way about Manduul. Unebolod spent his life in the shadow of Great Khans. Esen, who butchered most of his family. Manduul, who stole the title he had intended claiming." Togochi's shoulders tensed, as if bracing himself for impact. "You, for stealing Mandukhai."

Dayan snorted. "I stole nothing. I didn't ask for any of this." He waved his hand around them as if that explained his meaning. "I gave him a chance to kill me, to drive a knife through my heart like he wanted and take her and the title. But he wouldn't do it."

"Of course he wouldn't!" Togochi snapped. "Because what good would it do him? She would never have forgiven him. Even if she never found out it was him, she likely made him swear an oath to protect you. If there is one thing he never, ever gave ground on, it was that—"

"His word was iron. Yes. I've heard it a thousand times." Dayan rolled his eyes. "But his word was not quite strong enough to keep for Manduul."

Togochi sighed, then strolled over and sat beside Dayan. "Their past is complicated, and there is no doubt in my mind they loved each other fiercely. I'm sure some part of him hoped you would release her one day."

Silence fell over them as those words fully sank in. Unebolod had never married because he hoped Dayan would release her one day. He had waited for Mandukhai. Because she was worth waiting for.

"She never wanted me," Dayan moaned pitifully. "If I gave her a choice—"

"She made her choice years ago," Togochi said, placing a hand on Dayan's shoulder. "She may have loved Unebolod, but she chose you."

Dayan scrubbed a hand over his face, then threw the hand up in defeat. "Because of some cryptic message from Genghis! If she never had that vision, we both know I wouldn't be here. She would have chosen him."

"Maybe." Togochi shrugged. "But how you came together is irrelevant. The fact is, she could have married him then and still named you. But she didn't. She believes in you. She believes in the hope you embody to everyone. And she believes you will restore Genghis' legacy—together. She chose you, knowing full well what she was committing herself to."

Dayan snorted. "Compassion. I am her act of goodwill."

Togochi stood and marched toward the door. He paused and stared back at Dayan. "Call it what you want, but she loves you. I have seen the way she looks at you. Even if she hasn't realized it yet, she will. Because those feelings are there. While you two were gone, she worried more about you than him. And not because she thought you needed her worry, before you say that much, but because she loves you. She made her choice years ago."

Before Dayan could argue, Togochi opened the door and strode outside.

Soon, the sun would rise, and Dayan would have to be the rock for everyone. His gaze fell on Unebolod's sword propped beside his ... on the yellow ribbon stained with dirt and blood.

Dayan stood and marched over, removing the ribbon and dipping it in the bucket of water.

All the camp awoke early in the morning. Mandukhai had dressed in robes of white and blue. Tuya fastened her hair up and placed the *boqta* on Mandukhai's head. Today, she was Khatun, a woman and not a warrior. A queen, not a lover. Today, Mandukhai would bury the man who stole her heart. Nothing could have prepared her for this day. Unebolod had always seemed invincible.

At last, Mandukhai stepped outside to wait at the gathering tent with the rest of the funeral procession. Though she kept her face devoid of emotion and her shoulders squared, every part of her body felt weighed down by some great force. Only one loss could devastate her any more than this one. But Unebolod gave his life to save Dayan, and Mandukhai was eternally grateful for his dedication to the young Khan. Unebolod had every reason to turn his back on Dayan and leave him to die. Instead, he had stood his ground and kept his promise.

Togochi and his wives all stood at the bottom of the gathering tent steps. Even Togochi's older sons—now eleven and thirteen—joined the processional.

The group gathered was larger than even Manduul's funeral processional had been. Generals, Lords, and commanders from all the tribes following Mandukhai waited. And behind them all, hundreds of warriors awaited as well. Thousands. Huoshai stood close to Esige, his arm around her and rubbing her back as she leaned her head against his shoulder. Mandukhai glided over toward the couple and stroked Esige's grief-stricken face, then kissed her forehead.

The action drew Dayan's attention toward her for only a moment as he stood at the front of the mass closest to the stairs. Dayan kept his back straight and chin high. The moment Mandukhai met his eyes, he turned his attention back to the door of the gathering tent. She stepped up beside him. Had he grown taller? Dayan had been eye level with her before he left. Now he towered several inches over her. She remembered how his father had shot up several inches around this same age.

Khosoichi led a group of Khorchin men out of the gathering tent. Soke carried the body, now wrapped in white silk, out the door head-first, along with several of Unebolod's other tribesmen. Khosoichi fanned juniper and perfume in the air ahead of them as they descended the steps and loaded the body into the waiting cart. The inside of the wrap around Unebolod's body would be blue on top and green on the bottom, representing the sky father and earth mother. This would better allow him to move on to the spirit world and be welcomed into the High Heavens.

Mandukhai wished they had time to plan a better funeral for Unebolod, but she knew they had little time to delay before the remaining Ordos attacked. They had to move on quickly. Unebolod had already been dead for more than a week. They could not delay any longer.

Unebolod's horse pulled the cart, the final act of his favorite mare. As the cart lumbered forward, the rest of the funeral procession—thousands of men—walked behind.

The walk up the hill a mile from the camp was silent. A few sniffled behind them. The walk seemed to go on forever as they meandered up the hill. Mandukhai's hands trembled, and she repeatedly rubbed them together as covertly as she could. Now and then, she glanced from the corner of her eye at Dayan. His gaze remained stony, fixed on the horizon ahead. Not for the first time, she wondered what he was thinking about.

When they at last reached the hilltop, Soke and the Khorchin men stepped forward once more. All of them had their sleeves rolled inward instead of out like normal. This inversion served to communicate with the world of the dead, showing that they brought one who should be honored and welcomed. They slid the body out of the cart and onto their shoulders, carrying Unebolod to his grave. They then placed his body on the western edge of the shallow grave, head facing north to never lose his way.

Khosoichi stepped forward, sprinkling mare's milk over the grave as he raised his voice in blessings for the voyage into the afterlife. Mandukhai blinked back tears, a lump swelling in her throat. Khosoichi finished the blessing ceremony by burning and fanning juniper needles over the grave. He scattered grains on the earth to please the mountain spirit.

The seconds ticked by like minutes. Mandukhai's knees grew weak as she waited, eyes fixed on the white-wrapped body.

Dayan rubbed Mandukhai's arm. She jumped. It was not until then that she realized everyone waited on her. She squared her shoulders, cleared her throat, and edged toward the shroud. It was customary for the wife to say a few words, but since Unebolod had no wife, the honor had been given to Mandukhai as the queen.

"Unebolod was one of the most honorable men I have ever known," she said, mustering all of her strength to lift her voice so those around her could hear. It was forbidden to turn around and face the crowd during such a funeral, as it could anger the spirits to look back when she should look forward. "But that is no surprise to anyone who knew him. Outwardly, he was stoic, calculating, and very matter-of-fact. But inside, he was a man of passion and dedication. When he gave himself to a cause, he gave himself wholly, never once turning back. The empire will be lesser without him in it. But we will continue to honor his memory and finish what he has started. We will make certain that his death was not for nothing."

These were not the words her heart wanted to speak. Mandukhai wanted to confess the truth, admit how passionately she had loved him until his final breath. How she loved him still. And how she would see Issama burn for stealing their child away. But they were dangerous words. Instead, Mandukhai held them in her heart, a final promise to the man she had loved for so long.

She edged backward until she stood beside Dayan again.

Togochi, as Unebolod's oldest and dearest friend, stepped forward to finish the ceremony. It should have been Dayan sending Unebolod off, but he had insisted on giving the honor to Togochi instead.

Togochi bowed his head a moment and swiped a palm over his cheeks. Then his voice lifted on the breeze.

"Unebolod, brother, it was an honor to have spent my life at your side. If I had to do it over again, there is no greater man I could choose to walk beside." Togochi stiffened his back, bracing himself. "Unebolod spent his life serving the noble line of Genghis Khan. While his ambition is known to all, his dedication to the preservation of our empire always came before his own personal desires. He challenged warlords determined to prove themselves superior. He brought together tribes that had been foes." He paused, glancing at the blue morning sky above. His voice trembled. "I heard he once said that when our bones become dust, the only thing that matters is what we build and leave behind. Unebolod, you helped our Khan build a great empire. We will remember your work for centuries. And there could be no greater praise or honor than that."

Togochi trundled backward, surrounded by his wives offering him support. His sons shuffled a step closer to him as well but didn't offer further consolation. Mandukhai offered Togochi a weak smile, but her heart wasn't in it. She glanced once more at Dayan, but he didn't move or seem to have blinked at all.

As Soke and the Khorchin men stepped forward to lower Unebolod into his shallow grave, Mandukhai could no longer fight the tears. She blinked, hoping to force them back. Instead, they rolled down her cheeks.

Once Unebolod was in the ground, Dayan stepped forward, drawing his sword. Mandukhai tensed. What was he about to do? Then she saw the yellow ribbon fluttering from the hilt, bright and clean like new. Unebolod's sword. Dayan kneeled beside the grave, placing the weapon over the body. He removed the ribbon and tied it to his own hilt. Mandukhai thought she saw his lips move, but heard nothing.

As Dayan joined Mandukhai again, backing into his place, she reached for his hand, seeking the comfort as much as offering it to him. This must have been hard on him. Dayan accepted Mandukhai's hand, but with gloves on to protect their hands from the cold, she could not feel his skin. And he offered no squeezes of comfort.

Khorchin men placed stones over the grave, covering Unebolod's body. He would return to the earth mother. As his body was covered, everyone around the grave sank to a knee—a sign of respect and honor. Mandukhai could only glance around without looking behind her, but the sentiments seemed shared by everyone. Hundreds—thousands!—of men kneeled at Unebolod's graveside. Mandukhai had never seen such dedication in her life. As Dayan kneeled, he pulled Mandukhai down, yet also steadied her so she did not fall. Everyone remained this way until the body was covered in stones.

The funeral processional began the walk around the grave—three times south to west to north to east and back around again to show their honor and grief. Dozens of tribal Lords and commanders joined Mandukhai, Dayan, and Togochi leading the procession. Esige trailed behind Mandukhai, and the sound of Esige's grief was limited to sniffles and sobs she attempted stifling.

As they completed the last circle, Soke and the Khorchin men overturned the cart—someone would retrieve it later once the spirits cleansed it—and Dayan led the processional back toward camp along a different path—following the same path back was a bad omen.

Mandukhai watched the procession continue climbing the hill as thousands still made their way up to pay final respect to Unebolod and place a stone on his cairn. It would take all day for everyone to make the pilgrimage.

Two massive ceremonial fires burned at the edge of camp. When Mandukhai and Dayan returned at the head of the processional, everyone passed through the cleansing fires to ward off evil spirits.

The moment the ceremony ended, Dayan withdrew from Mandukhai. She retreated to her ger without a word, and hardly a glance in his direction. Dayan didn't mind too much. He didn't want her mourning the man she loved by making any mistakes with him. As if that were even a possibility.

While others ate and drank to celebrate Unebolod's life, Dayan headed into the freshly cleansed gathering tent. His fingers absently stroked the yellow ribbon on the hilt of his sword. He had promised Unebolod he would do what he could to respect and protect Mandukhai, that he would give her the freedom to find joy in this life. That he would carry on Unebolod's faith in her just as he carried the ribbon in Unebolod's honor. It was the least he could have offered standing at the man's grave.

Dayan now stood over the maps marked with pieces for *mingghans* and *tumens*. Still so many Ordos out there—nearly sixty thousand. Dayan wanted to punish them all. He wanted to wipe them off the face of the earth. They were oathbreakers, and a Khan could not leave their offense unpunished. *When I am done with them, there will be no more Ordos tribes,* he thought, clenching one piece in his fist so tight it bit into his skin.

But how? How could he eliminate them without tarnishing his own name?

What would Unebolod do?

CHAPTER THIRTY-THREE

Abandoned

SOUTH OF HAMI – SPRING 1480

I ssama paced his ger, waiting for more men to join him. Lord Asha had sent scouts looking in all directions for Issama's camp, but Issama had spent the first week since his escape hiding in the hovel in the city itself with his family. Once Lord Asha's men had given up on finding him a week later, Issama took Siker, Qolotai, and his sons and left the city under the veil of darkness. According to Dashai, what remained of Issama's men were to meet him outside the city to the south.

Few men had met him since the attack on the palace. How many had he lost? Did any more men remain?

"You could send word to your allies in the Oirat territory," Siker offered. She had taken to chewing on her fingernails since his escape from prison. He found the habit disgusting.

"Please stop biting those things," Issama snapped. "I don't have anyone to send. If I do, General Alayitung will intercept them before they get far." This only reminded Issama that he did not know what was happening among the Oirat anymore. Were his men there alive? Hopefully, he had not been abandoned here.

All of my plans, no matter how carefully laid, fall apart! he thought, growling under his breath. *Why does* everything *turn to dust?* Issama stopped pacing and punched the center post in the ger. The roof shook over their heads.

Siker clicked her tongue in irritation, then glided toward him. Issama had not realized how tightly his muscles had coiled until she ran her hand over his shoulders. Siker pressed a kiss against his neck. "We will get through this. Together."

Issama pulled her into his arms and pressed his forehead against hers. Together. If he had to hide outside the city as a herder until he heard from his men among the Oirat, he would. For a little while, at least.

ORDOS BASIN – SPRING 1480

Dayan had called all the lesser khans, Lords, and commanders together first thing in the morning, knowing he could not delay his plans against Legusi khan any longer. He had to make an example of the Ordos for their betrayal. And it had to be in front of his entire court.

As Belku entered, he gave Dayan a small nod. *It has started. I cannot stop this now.*

He glanced beside him, where Mandukhai perched on her throne. The two had hardly spoken to each other since Dayan's return, and he became more certain he had lost her when Unebolod died—or perhaps more accurately, he had never had her to begin with. But he could not linger on this any longer when the Ordos were on the move. *I have to destroy them.*

Before leaving on the campaign against Bigirsen, Dayan had allowed Mandukhai to do most of the talking. She had always been better at this than him. But if he was to be Great Khan—with or without her as his wife—he had to take control. Now.

Mandukhai sat in her throne beside Dayan, hands resting primly in her lap. Part of her burst with curiosity. Why had he summoned everyone? Though she had commanded all of these gathered men for years now, she had never seen so many of them in one place. The gathering tent was bursting at the seams.

Those given closer preference to the Khan stood nearest. No one sat except she and Dayan. All others stood, packed in shoulder-to-shoulder.

A path from the doorway to the dais was the only open space, and even that was hardly wide enough for three men to walk abreast.

"We are all mourning the loss of Lord Unebolod," Dayan said clearly.

The whispers in the tent fell silent. Several people bowed their heads. Mandukhai among them. She knew with certainty that she would never get over losing Unebolod.

Dayan pressed on. "But we cannot forget *why* he died." The dangerous tone in his voice gave her chills. "I tried to give the Ordos tribes a chance. I allowed them to swear an oath of fealty and join my empire just as all of you have done. I attempted uniting our people under the many-colored banner of Genghis." Dayan's jaw twitch. His voice heated, rising in fury. "But they have broken their oaths, betrayed their Great Khan and Khatun, and murdered not only Lord Unebolod Noyan, but Lord Ogedei and thousands of men! *My* men!"

A murmur of anger rippled through the gathering tent. The chills in her flesh intensified, making her flesh rise in bumps as she eyed him. Without a doubt, the man sitting beside her had come a far cry from the weak boy he had once been. This man exuded power like an aura bending around him.

"I will *not* make the same mistake twice," Dayan said, silencing the murmurs of anger from the gathered men. "Boke, bring in Lords Arqai and Ibarai."

Mandukhai tensed beside him. Her eyes widened as she watched the guards drag the two Ordos Lords into the gathering tent, bound at the wrists. A pulse of fear surged through her. What would he do to these men? Would he kill them for payback?

"Dayan," Mandukhai hissed, leaning toward him so no one else could hear. "They have proven their loyalty."

"So did Ulum before he killed Unebolod," Dayan said coldly.

"Dayan—"

"Don't question me, Mandukhai!" Dayan snapped, his neck heating as he glared at her.

Mandukhai instinctively shrank away from him. His outburst drew all eyes toward the two of them. They had always been a united front in these gatherings—often with her as the mouthpiece and him as the looming presence. They never disagreed so publicly, and he had *never* shouted at her.

"I know what I'm doing," he added sharply. "I learned from you, after all."

I don't like this side of you, she thought. It reminded her of Manduul, and not in any good way. Mandukhai clenched her jaw tight, but glared at him all the same. What could she do? He was Great Khan, not her. No matter how much respect she had from these men, they would listen to him first. *Have I created another monster?*

Dayan grimaced, and she thought she saw a flicker of regret in his eyes, but he turned his attention to the Ordos Lords kneeling at the base of the dais.

"Arqai, Ibarai," Dayan said, leaning back in his throne and staring down his nose in disgust at the Ordos Lords. "Do you know what your fellow Ordos Lords have done?"

"Y-yes, my lord Khan, but only from your men," Ibarai said. He pressed his face to the floor, hands clasped together.

Arqai clenched his jaw and hardened his own gaze as he gave a curt nod. *There is defiance in that one still*, Mandukhai thought. She feared what Dayan would do if he saw the same. The sweet boy who left her months ago had not returned.

"Let me confirm the rumors," Dayan said. "Lord Mogurkei swore to join me, his rightful Great Khan, but instead of joining me, he turned his army against my own. Lord Ulum bent the knee to me as his Great Khan. He gave his oath to serve me and helped my men kill Bigirsen. Then, while my army slept, he mounted his warriors and attacked my camp. He broke his oath, betrayed his Great Khan, and murdered Lord Unebolod *Noyan*!"

A roar arose from among the gathered men. Ibarai trembled on the floor. *He assumes Dayan will kill him. Will he?* Mandukhai didn't know for certain herself what Dayan had in store for these men. Arqai averted his defiant gaze to the floor.

"Tell me, Arqai!" Dayan shouted above the din. His elevated voice slowly silenced the crowd. "How am I ever to trust a single word that comes from the mouths of any Ordos Lords? Choose your words carefully, for they could be your last."

All eyes fell on Arqai. Mandukhai trembled in rage. Perhaps there was defiance in Arqai's eyes, but he had given the oath on his everlasting soul. By reacting with vengeance in his heart, Dayan made himself seem to be coming undone. Would the rest of the men following them assume the same? *Please don't do this. We will lose men if we start killing those who give the oath!*

"You cannot, my lord Khan," Arqai said at last.

Dayan's lips thinned. "So what value do you have to me if I cannot trust your word?"

"My men—"

"*My* men, Lord Arqai!" Dayan snapped. "You bent the knee. You gave your oath, and the moment you did, those men were no longer yours. As we speak, they are being reorganized to serve the rest of my *tumens*, men I *can* trust."

Mandukhai's palms sweated as she clenched them so tight in her lap that the nails bit into her skin. How could this man be the same sweet boy she had raised? Dayan terrified even her. What must the others think of him?

At last, that defiance in Arqai's eyes winked out and the flush in his face drained into a pale white. His gaze darted around as he kneeled in front of the dais, bound and under guard. No one would come to his defense. Certainly not with Dayan in such a rage. Arqai must have realized how thin a blade he walked upon, because his shoulders sagged.

"I can help you bring Legusi peacefully," Arqai said at last.

"Do you think I care about peace with the Ordos any longer?" Dayan growled, leaning forward with his arms on his knees.

The question, though he asked it quietly, had reached all edges of the gathering tent. Almost as one, the collected Lords and commanders shifted and tensed. Even Mandukhai moved in her seat. Somehow, she had to stop this. Their men had grown used to Mandukhai's years of seeking peace. Now, faced with a newly ascending Great Khan, they were no longer certain of their futures. Would they turn against Dayan if he decided to destroy the Ordos and declare war?

"My lord Khan," Arqai said, a tremble in his voice. "I will help however I can. How can I prove myself?"

"As you said, Arqai, you cannot. For now, you will remain isolated from all of your men until I have decided how you may be of service—or if you have any value to me at all." Dayan flicked his fingers as he sank back into his seat again.

Two of the guards stepped forward, hauling Arqai to his feet and escorting him forcefully from the gathering tent. All eyes watched the Ordos Lord as he left.

Dayan turned his attention to Ibarai, who remained prone on the floor, waiting for the Great Khan to speak to him. "Ibarai," Dayan said. His hard voice shattered the silence. Everyone waited to see what he would do next. "Arqai, at least, gave his oath with little resistance. You attacked the Khatun and her men. I no longer have any tolerance for any form of resistance or defiance."

Sweat beaded on Mandukhai's forehead, thankfully covered by her headdress so no one else would notice. *Dayan is going to kill him!* She felt it certainly. *I have to do something.* But what could she do? Dayan was Khan, and though Mandukhai held power, she knew that if he wanted Ibarai dead, there was nothing she could do to stop it.

"Why should I trust you now?" Dayan asked Ibarai. "What do you have to say for yourself?"

Ibarai sat up on his heels. His bound hands hung limp in front of him, and his eyes were terrified. "My lord Khan, we attacked because we did not know what was happening. Mandukhai Khatun's forces came at us at night. Once I realized who we were fighting, I surrendered. I know what happens to traitors of the Great Khan. My commanders who refused to submit paid the price. I will tell you what I told Mandukhai Khatun that day. If I must give my life to amend for the sins of my tribesmen, I will. As long as it spares my men and their families."

Mandukhai released a slow, steadying breath. She had to act now before it was too late. Hoping no one could see her trembling, she leaned closer to Dayan.

Dayan's muscles tensed as he glanced at her.

Mandukhai licked her lips. "I have agreed to show him mercy for valuable information about some of the other Ordos Lords."

Dayan shifted subtly away from her. The move clenched her heart. Was he beyond her reason now? Was it too late? She watched as he swallowed, then eyed Ibarai.

"You have already shared information about the other Ordos Lords with Mandukhai Khatun," Dayan said. "So what more could you offer me?"

No, he is twisting my words!

Ibarai adjusted himself slightly. The guards behind him tensed, ready for anything.

"I can tell you where many of the western Ordos Lords are receiving support."

Dayan cocked his head curiously at this statement, his golden eyes as sharp as an eagle on the hunt. "A ploy, I'm sure, to get me into position to die. Just as Ulum attempted hiring a whore for me whom he had no doubt paid to drive a dagger through my heart."

Mandukhai gasped before she could stop herself. Ulum had given Dayan a woman? *Did he sleep with this whore?* Her stomach twisted in knots as she considered Dayan with another woman.

Dayan carried on, oblivious to her alarm. "Lucky for me, I had no interest in his used women. Though some of them did manage to injure my *orlok* and commanders, and even killed a few just before the attack."

Unebolod had been with those women? The twisting in her stomach became a writhing pit of snakes. She knew Unebolod had slept with other women over the years since she tied herself to Dayan, but he had always kept it from her. She could always deny the truth of it without any confirmation. But she had no reason to doubt Dayan. In his anger, he didn't even seem to notice that he had implicated Unebolod's sexual exploits.

"Please, I beg you," Ibarai sniveled. "Lord Issama has been making deals with the Ordos Lords for at least ten years. Some of them are still loyal to him. I can give you a list of names. I can tell you where he most likely is!"

Issama! If Ibarai could help them find and kill Issama, it was worth his life. She needed to know where Issama was so she could kill him. He had poisoned her and killed her child. She would make him pay.

Mandukhai placed a clammy hand on Dayan's arm. He dragged his gaze to her. Mandukhai said nothing, but poured all of her pleading from her gaze. She needed this information. Hopefully Dayan was not so far gone that he would deny her this.

Dayan's jaw twitched. Slowly, he slid his glare toward Ibarai. "Give the names to *orlok* Togochi and Lord Nemeku. Show them where you think Issama is. We will see if your information is worthwhile. We are done here ... for now."

Mandukhai sagged slightly in relief, easing her grip on Dayan's arm.

"Thank you!" Ibarai exclaimed.

"My mercy is hanging on by a thread, Ibarai," Dayan said. "Don't test your luck, or your sons will be the first to die."

The coldness of Dayan's threat sent a tremor of fear through Mandukhai.

The guards pulled Ibarai out of the gathering tent. Nemeku followed on their heels, standing tall and important. *He is so tall and grown up!* Mandukhai wanted to trust Nemeku, but she was still unsure what sort of damage his father had done to him.

Dayan dismissed everyone else and sat back, studying all of them as they left. Mandukhai wondered what he was calculating as he glared at the dwindling gathering. His shoulders remained tense until the last person left the tent. The moment they were alone with only the guards posted at the door, he sagged.

Mandukhai cocked her head. All of the wrath he exuded vanished. Dayan rubbed his forehead.

She rubbed her palms against her deel, then gripped the cool arms of the throne for a moment.

Anger pulsed through her. That display had been destructive and she would have to spend days undoing the damage. Mandukhai surged to her feet and faced Dayan.

"What was that all about?" she demanded, planting her hands on her hips.

"I have to show them my strength," Dayan grumbled. "You taught me that. If I show weakness, they will see it, exploit it, and question everything I do. How would you have me deal with the Ordos? If I had my way, I would wipe them all off the map! How are you *not* angrier?" He surged to his feet, flushed with anger once more.

Mandukhai flinched back half a step, but she noted the haunted look in his eyes. *He left me a timid boy and came back a haunted man.* Her face fell, all anger and indignation melting off.

"Oh Dayan. What happened to you out there?" She edged closer, pressing her now cooled palm against his cheek. "Of course I am angry about what they did, but we are not yet in a position to threaten these men. They gave their oaths, and until they give us a reason to doubt them, we cannot punish them. Otherwise, where does it stop? Perhaps the commanders who had been with you should have done more, so they deserve punishment as well. Or perhaps we should punish Boke for not protecting you and putting Unebolod in a position to make that terrible choice?"

"No, that—"

"So where will the Khan's wrath end?" she asked, stroking his cheek tenderly.

Dayan stared at her. His brows sagged as something inside of him altered. He slumped. "Now isn't the time for coddling." He eased her hand away from his face. "I was serious, Mandukhai. How can we ever trust the Ordos? And with Mogurkei gaining men from those I lost, it's only a matter of time before he makes a move. We have to do something drastic. Something he *expects* from an inexperienced young Khan."

Something Mogurkei expects... Mandukhai mulled this over for a moment, then realized what Dayan had done. *Oh you beautiful, brilliant boy!*

It had been an act. All of it. Dayan's unhinged behavior, his wrath, his outburst at her. He *wanted* word to reach Mogurkei.

"We have to make Mogurkei think he has won," Mandukhai said, and her smile transformed into a sly grin. "By making your actions seem rash, angry, and impulsive, and by casting a shadow of doubt in the men you should trust, you are giving Mogurkei a false sense of security that he might win. You always were a clever boy."

Dayan groaned. "Please stop calling me a boy. Is that still all you see?"

Mandukhai narrowed her eyes and studied him—really studied him. Though he was slim like his father had been, he was strong, tall... formidable. Reflecting on how he had acted in front of everyone, how he had commanded the room, she now saw something in him she had never noticed before. Dayan had grown. She had not created another monster. Dayan was becoming the man she had promised everyone he would be. Her cheeks flushed.

Finally, she shook her head. "No."

His lips parted, then pressed closed again. "The men will talk. Belku already has orders to spread rumors among the Ordos here that I am losing myself in my grief. When that happens, the Ordos will question their choice to follow me. I expect some of them will defect."

"What?" Mandukhai's eyes widened. "No. Dayan, we need every man we have."

"If we want Mogurkei to believe I am losing power, we need someone to turn against me, abandon me," Dayan insisted. "Then he will think we are weak enough to move in and we can finish this. With any luck, it will also weed out rebels in our camp. As I see it, either Huoshai or Togochi have to blame me for what happened to Unebolod. I need it to be someone everyone sees as loyal."

Mandukhai scoffed. This plan was brilliant—and deeply dangerous. "No one will ever believe it. Especially not Mogurkei." Then her eyes widened. *Esige!* "Unless ..."

Esige and Dayan had never really gotten along well, and she had adored Unebolod. If they played this right, Esige could turn all of her anger and blame for what happened to Unebolod on Dayan and Mandukhai. It would not be the first time Mandukhai had failed to protect someone Esige loved. Mandukhai's face lit up and she placed an excited hand on his arm.

"Esige. She will blame us for Unebolod's death." Mandukhai choked over the name but pressed on. "He was like a father to her, and she adored him for years. She also could resent me for not protecting her sister. Of anyone, she has the most reason to turn away from us. My actions cost her two people she loved dearly."

Dayan nodded slowly as he put the pieces of her plan together in his own head. She could almost see the light come on inside his head. "... And the Urainkhai will abandon their Great Khan. They can use that to draw out the men who might oppose us. We need to make a show of this in front of Arqai. There is a defiance burning in him, and if he is with them, not only will it give their story more credence, but it will test Arqai's oath as well."

"Let's talk Esige and Huoshai." Exhilaration bubbled up from deep within, a sensation of delight she had not felt in years. Without thinking, Mandukhai kissed his cheek, then marched toward the door.

Esige hated this plan! To leave the camp and make a show of her anger regarding Unebolod's death felt like sullying his memory. To top it off, she hated leaving Mandukhai so soon after Unebolod's death. She wanted to help Mandukhai through her grief. She wanted to stay here and help finish this fight. If there was any truth to the rumors about Issama's plot against Mandukhai all these years, she wanted to be part of his downfall. Esige already felt cheated out of being there when they killed Bigirsen.

Just as much as all of that, Esige hated Arqai, and Mandukhai and Dayan made it sound like they wanted her to take Arqai along. He had leered at her far too many times. Though Huoshai had put any ideas Arqai might have about stealing her in check, Esige didn't trust Arqai. His eyes were pits of darkness she couldn't read, like a void of black. Just thinking about it made her skin crawl.

Esige crossed her arms and tapped her foot against the rugs in her ger. "This is a terrible idea."

Huoshai had listened to the entire plan in rapt silence, while Esige had questioned every aspect incessantly. He seemed keen to carry this out. Normally, Esige would be eager to use her spy skills, but she missed Mandukhai. She also worried she might throw knives into Arqai's eyes if he couldn't keep them to himself.

Mandukhai stood beside Dayan near the door, a united front. Her own arms were crossed. "I am so glad you trust my judgment after all these years."

"Your track record isn't exactly perfect," Esige snorted. Mandukhai had chosen Dayan over Unebolod, after all. Something Esige still was not convinced had been the right decision. "No one will ever believe we abandoned you."

"Yes, they will," Mandukhai said. "Because you will make them believe it. Only you can pull this off, Esige."

Sometimes I hate how well she knows me, Esige thought. One of Esige's honed skills, aside from spying, was her power to manipulate people. Huoshai once told Esige she could talk the feathers off an eagle.

"Just to be clear," Huoshai said slowly. "We are making a show of abandoning you because Esige blames you for Unebolod's death and what happened to Borogchin. And we are to use that to meet in 'secret' with these other Ordos Lords so we can probe for information and get close to Mogurkei?"

Dayan grimaced, and for a moment Esige noticed he looked much older than he should. Did he blame himself for Unebolod's death? *He should. Were it not for him, Unebolod would have been Great Khan a long time ago, and he never would have died for him or fallen into such an obvious trap.* Esige couldn't help the bitterness she felt toward Dayan. Everything she had ever wanted as a child had vanished the moment Dayan appeared in her life.

"Yes," Dayan said. Esige heard the tension he tried to cover. He couldn't hide anything from her. "Find out which of these Lords truly rides against us. And when you know Mogurkei's location, you will send it to us and we will finish him."

Huoshai rubbed his chin thoughtfully. Esige choked as she noticed how impressed her husband seemed to be with this plan.

"Sounds fun," Huoshai said, grinning.

Esige threw up her hands. "I don't know why I even try anymore! I don't want to bury anyone else."

"Then you had better be convincing," Mandukhai said. "Trust me, Esige. This will work."

Esige huffed, staring at the ceiling. "No. It won't. Because Mogurkei is the reason Unebolod is dead. Not you. Not Dayan. Even if I can convince the Ordos that I blame Dayan, they won't believe I don't also blame Mogurkei."

"They will believe you," Dayan said confidently. "Because you don't blame Mogurkei. He isn't the one who attacked and killed Unebolod. You blame me. You blame Ulum. You don't hold Mogurkei accountable. As far as you are concerned, you have no real evidence he was even there when Unebolod died."

Esige pursed her lips. "Fine," she groaned at last. "But I want Nemeku to come with us."

Dayan shook his head. "Nemeku is an adult, and he can make his own choice."

She bristled. "Your will," she growled in agreement. "If this will work, we need to make a show of us fighting soon. Then it will connect more directly to my grief. And to be clear, that part is still very fresh. I don't like using his death like this."

"We agree," Dayan said. "On both counts."

Esige supposed this plan would be more exciting than going over supply line numbers day and night. And they were right. She could easily convince the Ordos Lords that she hated Dayan and blamed him for everything. *The best lies stem from the truth*, she thought.

"Get out of my ger," Esige hissed.

Mandukhai blanched, obviously not understanding that Esige was putting on this show that they so desperately wanted.

"I said get out!" Esige roared.

Dayan laid a hand on Mandukhai's arm and guided her out the door, leaving it open behind them as they ducked outside.

Without even trying, Esige summoned tears. "This is your fault!" she said, allowing her grief to pour out. She ducked out after them, waving angry hands away from her doorway. "Good riddance. He was the only father I had, and now he's gone because of you!" She stabbed a finger at Dayan.

He swallowed.

"Esige..." Mandukhai edged closer, but Dayan grabbed her and held her back.

"First my sister ..." Esige shook her head, her voice trembling. "Now Unebolod. You are cursed. If you cannot protect those closest to you, I don't want to be in your inner circle any longer."

Mandukhai's chin trembled. Dayan whispered something in her ear, and the two headed away. Dayan glared at Esige over his shoulder.

She simply planted her feet and crossed her arms over her chest, glaring after him. Nearby, Arqai stood in his own doorway under guard, watching the scene unfold.

Waiting is the Hardest Part

Mandukhai had returned to her ger after the "confrontation" with Esige. After a quick dinner, Mandukhai received a summons to meet with Dayan and a handful of the other Lords in the gathering tent to plan their next phase. Being summoned was a new sensation to her. For the first time since her marriage to Manduul, Mandukhai scrambled to catch up to the men. It meant Dayan was becoming stronger and more capable, but she worried he might be moving into that position of power too quickly. He had only returned to camp two days ago.

When she entered, everyone else had already gathered. Chakicha, Albeq khan's son and heir, stood in front of Dayan, his hands clenched in fists and his face red in anger.

Mandukhai raised a questioning brow at Dayan, but could not decipher what his small head shake meant. She settled into her throne beside Dayan, waiting to find out why Chakicha was so angry.

Chakicha only cast Mandukhai a cursory glance before returning his anger to Dayan. "I have a right to justice!"

Ah. Now I understand. Mandukhai wondered how long Dayan had allowed Chakicha to rage at him already.

"He killed my father," Chakicha snapped. "I want Ibarai's head. Why are you protecting him?" Albeq had died fighting Ibarai's men.

Dayan tensed slightly, his fingers digging into the arm of this seat. He often did this when he was angry or felt backed into a corner.

Mandukhai placed her hand gently over his as she straightened. "Cha-kicha, we are sorry for your loss. Albeq was an old friend, and loyal to the

Mongol Nation. His loss certainly was a hardship for all of us. But he died in battle, as men often do—"

"Against Ibarai's men!" Chakicha argued.

"It does not warrant execution," she continued patiently.

Chakicha sneered. For a moment, he appeared on the verge of spitting on the floor. Mandukhai tensed. If he did, the guards would drag him out and execute him for showing hostility toward the Great Khan.

He swallowed hard, licked his lips, and said, "Mogurkei and Ulum were responsible for Unebolod's death in battle. Will you spare Mogurkei's life when you have him in your grasp as well?"

Mandukhai's grip on Dayan's hand tightened as she fought off her own anger. "This is not the same. Ibarai surrendered the moment he realized who he was fighting. Mogurkei defied his oath and turned his forces against the Great Khan."

The vein in Chakicha's neck pulsed with wild life. He clenched his hands into fists at his sides. "I want his head," he said through gritted teeth.

"This is the grief talking, Chakicha," Dayan said, breaking his silence. "We fought beside one another. I feel as if I have formed a bond of brotherhood with you, so I don't take your loss lightly." Dayan sighed, as if his next words were hard to admit. "But Mandukhai is right. These two situations are not the same. It may be a fine line, but there is a difference. Take some time to grieve and get adjusted to being the tribal khan." He leaned forward. "If Ibarai outlives his usefulness or betrays his oath, I will give you his head myself. Upon my eternal soul, if he betrays us in any way, you will have your wish."

Mandukhai clenched her jaw as Dayan gave Chakicha his vow. *Did he have to act so reluctant to agree with me?* They had to seem a united front. Instead of debating, Mandukhai gave a tight nod, then withdrew her hand from Dayan's. He deflated slightly, glancing at his lonely hand.

The vow appeased Chakicha's anger. He bowed and gave his thanks before marching out of the gathering tent.

Mandukhai leaned closer to Dayan and whispered, "Do you have any idea what you have just done?"

He matched her hushed tone as the gathered Lords murmured among one another. "Yes. I gave him exactly what he deserves." He turned his golden eyes on her. She saw something in them she had not seen before. Defiance daring her to challenge him. "I meant every word. The Ordos Lords are lucky for the mercy I have given them. It will not go any further."

Mandukhai wanted to protest, but something about the way Dayan's gaze bored into her made her swallow her arguments. So much intensity, defiance, coldness, warmth … and something else she could not put her finger on.

The door to the gathering tent opened and Nemeku strode in, a young woman on his heels. Though Mandukhai had seen him since his return to their camp, she had not had time to really take him in. Nemeku was eleven the last time she saw him nearly four years ago. While he had grown tall and had the same broad shoulders of his father, there was a grace to the way he moved as well, a gentleness in his angular face. The lack of facial hair confirmed that, though he acted like and carried himself as a man, Nemeku was still a boy.

Nemeku stopped near the bottom of the dais, kneeling and offering something to Togochi. The *orlok* took the paper and glanced at it, then offered it to Dayan.

Mandukhai leaned closer as Dayan read, curious about the message. He held it guarded, as if he didn't even trust her with the news. Then the corner of his mouth twitched up in a grin.

"While some of us would like more time to grieve, we need to take action swiftly," Dayan announced, tucking the paper in his deel and not sharing with her.

She slumped a little. Why was he keeping it from her?

"Word has reached the remaining Ordos Lords that Bigirsen is dead," Dayan continued. "This means we are presented with a unique opportunity to seize control if we don't delay. Two of the Lords in the northern basin are weak and without stewardship. I am sending some of you after them. If we are lucky, we will cut Issama off from any potential alliances he might have forged before he can collect."

Mandukhai could not say she disagreed with his logic. But she also had a debt to settle with Issama. Would it not be better to cut the head off the snake than try to cut it off from its holes?

Commander Bagatur harrumphed. "What if any of these Lords ask for Dayan Khan to rule them? What if they offer to bend the knee and give their oaths?"

A dark cloud seemed to pass over Dayan's youthful face, making him appear ten years older. "Mogurkei did the same. He gave his oath. He broke his vow, likely on some convoluted idea that Issama offered him a richer future. How are we to trust any of these men who have followed Issama in the past?"

"So they die even if they beg?" Altan asked, raising her brows and appearing impressed with the cold calculation from Dayan.

Dayan's mouth twitched. Mandukhai placed a hand on his forearm. Before he could respond, she spoke up. "No. We will kill no one who gives their oath to the Great Khan. We are attempting to reunite the Mongols, not conquer them. However, they will be disarmed, down to their last man. Until we can be certain of their trust, they will not be allowed weapons."

"Like you did to the Oirat," Altan said, nodding.

"And the Ordos men here," Mandukhai said. "Ibarai and Arqai's men have not been allowed weapons yet, but they have been instrumental to the security of our camp and the movement of our supplies from Lake Dai. And Arqai's information has helped us identify Ordos scouting paths and avoid them."

"Why not just take out the scouts?" Belku asked.

"Because if you had scouts out, and they did not report back, how long would you wait before preparing your men?" Dayan asked.

Belku grimaced and said nothing more.

"Kelegei and Bagatur will head west to find these two Lords," Dayan commanded. Togochi nodded in approval of Dayan's plan. The two men bowed and marched out together. "Altan and Ordag, you will head south and see if you can contact Legusi. I will give you details on your mission in the morning before you leave."

Ordag and Altan also bowed and headed toward the exit.

Mandukhai's gaze fell on Orghana. Legusi's little sister, according to Dayan. She had wormed her way into Nemeku's heart easily, from what Mandukhai heard. Has this been Legusi's plan all along? Maybe her older brother was playing a much longer game, planting his sister where she could get close to Dayan's family. Or perhaps Bigirsen's hand was in this, even in death. The girl blinked slowly, unable to meet Mandukhai's gaze.

"What do you know of your brother to share with the court, Orghana?" Mandukhai asked. The question made Altan stop and turn back.

Orghana shook her head, shuffling half a step closer to Nemeku. "Nothing. My brother sent me off to marry Bigirsen as a sign of his loyalty. But Legusi was always scared of Bigirsen more than he was loyal." She chewed her lip and dropped her gaze to the floor.

Nemeku slid his arm around her and pulled her close. He glared at Mandukhai. "She is a victim in all of this, Mandukhai. Not a spy."

Mandukhai felt for Nemeku, but she also worried for him. They knew nothing about Orghana, and she certainly had latched onto *him* quite firmly. "Nemeku, your mother was a spy married to your father. I have no reason to believe this would be any different."

"She isn't you," he snapped.

"Watch yourself, boy," Soke growled.

Togochi frowned at Nemeku as well. Jaghan and Geriel appeared scandalized by Nemeku's outburst. Mandukhai composed herself.

Nemeku's face reddened. For a moment, he simply glared at Mandukhai. Esige had told Mandukhai all about how Bigirsen and beaten Nemeku and attempted conditioning him against the two of them. That Orghana was the only one who could control that temper Bigirsen had created did not settle well with Mandukhai. For all she knew, Bigirsen and Orghana could have planned it that way. Orghana would be the salve, whispering in Nemeku's ear to tame his wild rage to her own ends while Bigirsen broke Nemeku to make it all possible. But to what end? So Bigirsen could install his son—a boy he could control—as Great Khan instead of Dayan? *I would not put it past Bigirsen*, Mandukhai decided.

Mandukhai opened her mouth to question Orghana, but Nemeku cut her off before she could speak. "Mandukhai, can the two of us please speak to you alone?"

"Not a chance," Altan and Jaghan said in unison. They exchanged bemused glances.

Nemeku's shoulders tensed, and his grip on Orghana tightened. "So it's like this then. Only my aunt and the Khan trust me anymore. Now that I'm not a little boy you can manipulate, you don't trust me at all."

Hearing the anger and pain in his tone broke Mandukhai's heart. "Nemeku, your father spent his life attempting to undermine everything the Khans did. I hope you can understand that we just need more time to be certain your father has not done some irreversible damage."

"I am not my father!" Nemeku snapped.

"Nemeku—" Togochi said, but Mandukhai ignored him.

"You challenged Dayan's right to the title," Mandukhai replied as patiently as she could, remembering the message Unebolod had sent her about the altercation. "And you attacked him more than once, from what I hear."

Beside her, Dayan shifted forward, but Nemeku pressed on before Dayan could speak.

"I also saved his life," Nemeku snapped. "More than once. But that counts for nothing, it seems. And for your knowledge, he told me to challenge him. He told me that my presence could undermine him. I tried to refuse, but he insisted. If you blame anyone for that, blame him. Did he not tell you any of that?"

Mandukhai felt her cheeks flush in embarrassment. Why had Dayan not told her what they had planned?

"It's true," Dayan murmured to her shyly.

"He almost killed you," Orghana whispered to Nemeku.

He flinched. "But he didn't." He turned his stubborn gaze on Mandukhai. "He is strong, intelligent, and capable. But you can't see it."

Dayan squirmed in his throne. "Nemeku," he hissed. But his tone was more embarrassed than angry.

"I *do* see it!" Mandukhai said.

"No, you don't!" Nemeku scoffed, and a hint of disgust played across his face. "You still see that little boy who needs to be rescued. What scares you is that he *doesn't* need you anymore. He can do all of this," he waved around the gathering tent, "without you. And that terrifies you. What makes you any better than my father?"

"Nemeku, stop," Dayan said, but it was not a command. It was more like one boy pleading with another to stop defending him.

Mandukhai paled. Her heart clenched. She wanted to deny his accusation, but could she? Leaving Dayan in charge *did* terrify her. Not because she wanted to hold on to her power, but because she wanted to ensure she secured a legacy in his name. Yet Nemeku was right. Dayan had proven himself more than once. He could secure his own legacy now. *I am afraid he doesn't need me anymore ... or want me.* It had nothing to do with the power and everything to do with losing every chance at happiness. Unebolod was dead. Dayan was all she had left.

Nemeku nodded, as if her silence only proved his point. "You see it, too. I gave Dayan Khan my oath, and I will keep it to my dying breath. Even if that means I have to protect him from you."

Dayan's entire body had gone rigid. Only a handful of people remained in the gathering tent, and they had all fallen silent as if everyone were afraid a breath would bring attention to them.

Soke edged toward Nemeku. Mandukhai shook her head.

Nemeku glared at Soke, challenging him as Nemeku reached for his sword. "Hey, don't kill me, okay."

Soke's brows drew together curiously, but his gaze remained on Nemeku's sword as the boy drew it.

Nemeku set the blade on the steps of the dais, then turned his glare at Mandukhai. The pain in his eyes made a lump swell in her throat. She had not meant to hurt him. She only wanted to protect Dayan. *Maybe he is right. The problem is me.*

"I am no better to you than any of the Ordos Lords," Nemeku said. "So, like them, I don't deserve a blade until I have earned that trust. But I will watch you just as sharply as you watch me. Remember that."

Mandukhai swallowed. "Nemeku—"

"Pick up your blade," Dayan said.

Nemeku shook his head. "No." He glared at Dayan. "You are only half of a whole. You can either become whole yourself, or I will wait for the other half to accept me and my wife. Until then, leave Orghana and I in peace."

Mandukhai licked her lips as she watched the exchange.

No one spoke as the couple marched out. For at least a minute, silence settled in the gathering tent.

Dayan remained rooted in place, watching with a stony expression as the others followed Nemeku out, bowing to Dayan quickly before slipping out the door. At last, he stood.

Mandukhai surged to her feet, taking his hand to stop him from leaving. "Dayan, what he said ..."

"Forget it. It's fine." He pulled away from her and jogged down the steps toward Togochi as the *orlok* made his way to the door. "Togochi," Dayan called as he caught up. "Walk with me. I have a special task for you."

Togochi matched Dayan's stride.

Mandukhai remained rooted in place, watching Dayan lumber out the door. For years, Dayan had been a sweet, soft, pliable boy. Since his return from campaign, that boy had vanished. Or had he always been this way and the distance had opened her eyes to the truth? Perhaps Soke had been right, and the distance had done them good.

"Now that is a man I could get behind," Altan said, startling Mandukhai out of her thoughts.

Mandukhai's heart nearly burst in alarm. She yelped, pressing a palm against her chest. She had not been aware that anyone else remained in the gathering tent with her.

"Or under," Altan said, grinning from ear to ear.

"Who?" Mandukhai asked, lamely attempting to recover.

Altan just laughed at her. Mandukhai was clearly flustered, and Altan could tell. There was no hiding it.

"I warned you about him," Altan said. "Months ago, before he left to kill Bigirsen. He was a handsome young man then. But now ..." Altan emitted a low whistle.

"This is hardly appropriate," Mandukhai snapped.

"I think it's about time someone broke that stallion in," Altan continued, ignoring Mandukhai's comment altogether.

Mandukhai rolled her eyes and huffed as she stormed toward the exit. The reaction only made Altan chuckle.

She loved Dayan, without a doubt. But she also had loved Unebolod, and they had only put his body to rest two days ago. She still could not accept that he was gone.

Though Mandukhai attempted reining in her unruly emotions, she could not stop her skin from prickling each time Dayan popped into her mind.

Sunset approached. Mandukhai shielded her eyes as she took a moment to gaze west. Jaghan stepped up beside her, matching her stride.

"Don't let Nemeku get to you," Jaghan said. "He has gone through a lot, and he is still so young. No one believes you are grabbing for power. You have made yourself clear for years. This is all for Dayan, and he knows it."

Mandukhai wished she shared Jaghan's certainty. "Does he? There is some truth to what Nemeku said, Jaghan. I am afraid that Dayan doesn't need me."

"He certainly does," Jaghan insisted.

Mandukhai could not share her sentiment. "He is young and strong and could have any woman he wanted. I am old. Why would he ever want me?"

Jaghan snorted. "You are not old. He loves you."

"He did," Mandukhai corrected. "But I made him wait, and I'm afraid he grew tired of waiting."

"Did Unebolod ever grow tired of waiting? Did he give up?"

Mandukhai rolled her eyes. "How will I ever know?"

"You know." Jaghan gave Mandukhai a knowing smile. "I wish you could see what I see. But I assure you, that young man will wait until his last breath. I don't know how you wrapped two such men around your fingers, but you did."

They rounded a ger and Mandukhai spotted Dayan striding alongside Togochi. His movements were fluid, cat-like, confident. She could not help staring, seeing what Altan had been talking about.

Jaghan placed a hand on Mandukhai's shoulder and gave it a reassuring squeeze. "Waiting is the hardest part."

Mandukhai wished she shared that feeling. The hardest part for her was when she stopped waiting and accepted the inevitable.

CHAPTER THIRTY-FIVE

The Bride Price

Dayan gazed at the brilliant hues of red and orange on the horizon. He and Togochi strolled along the thoroughfare between gers, headed toward Dayan's ger. Men and women moved about their evening tasks, giving a wide berth to their Great Khan as they bowed to him.

"I have a special assignment for you, Togochi," Dayan said, breaking the comfortable silence between them. "We can hunt down these Lords still loyal to Issama, but as long as he lives, we can never truly trust them, no matter what oaths they give. They need to see our power as superior."

"Agreed." Togochi nodded, keeping his gaze fixed ahead of them, flitting from one person to the next as if inspecting each for signs of danger.

"Good. Because I need you to take a special force to kill him. Only two hundred men, so you can travel faster."

Togochi missed a step, then paused, forcing Dayan to stop as well. "Once we trap Legusi and Mogurkei, I assume?"

Dayan folded his hands together behind his back, which he found made him look taller, more confident. "No. Tomorrow."

Togochi gaped, momentarily stunned into silence. At last, he found his voice. "As your *orlok*—the most senior you have right now—I would like to advise you against this. We are weeks away from absorbing the Ordos. You will need me in the days to come, and when we meet Legusi and face off against Mogurkei, you will need me at your side to help you organize your *tumens*. This is my job, my lord Khan, and if anything happened to you or the Khatun while I am away, I would lose all honor and the nation would be with no one to lead them. This is not the best time to split our strength."

Dayan listened with calm patience. Togochi was right. He was the most senior military officer now, with Unebolod dead. But he was also the only man Dayan could trust undoubtably not to betray him or Mandukhai. Dayan wanted to trust others, but he just couldn't bring himself to do it. Not from the men he still had available.

"You have already set us up for success, and we will have Soke with us as well," Dayan replied. "Mandukhai trusts his ability to adjust our strategy if need be. He did learn from Unebolod, after all. Besides, if all goes well, you will be back before anything happens." Dayan resumed their walk, forcing Togochi to keep up. "You know as well as I do that even if we capture these rogue Lords, as long as Issama breathes, they could still turn against us at any moment. Boke brought me a message this morning from Lord Asha in Hami. Issama snuck into the palace and attempted coercing him into turning against us. Asha put him in prison, but somehow Issama escaped."

Togochi nodded. "Then he could be anywhere."

Dayan reached into his deel and produced the map Asha had sent with the message. "No. We know exactly where he is. This information confirms what Ibarai told Nemeku about Issama."

"The information Nemeku gave you before that meeting," Togochi said, understanding the connection as he unfolded the paper and paused to examine the map.

"Yes. If we delay, Issama could disappear again."

"Then send Asha to deal with him," Togochi said. "He is already within miles."

"I need someone I trust explicitly to handle this," Dayan said. "That only leaves me with you."

"I'm honored," Togochi muttered sarcastically.

Boots scuffed the muddy path behind them. Dayan recognized the confident stride and the way the soles of the boots swept across the ground, almost like a whisper. A moment later, Mandukhai stood beside them, frowning at Togochi.

"What is that?" she asked, nodding at the map.

"Issama's location," Dayan said. "Togochi is going to finish him."

Mandukhai gasped, leaning over the map to see it as well. Her eyes shined as her gaze shot up to meet Dayan's. "Was this Ibarai's information? How do we know we can trust it?"

"Lord Asha sent it." Dayan quickly filled Mandukhai in on the details.

Togochi folded the map and tucked it safely in his own deel. "I still think now is a bad time."

Mandukhai slid her arm around Dayan's. A shock of heat raced through him from the simple gesture.

"Dayan is right," Mandukhai said, stunning both men. "We need to deal with him while we know where he is. Issama is slippery. He will sneak away if we wait."

"Sure, but..." Togochi's gaze flicked from one to the other, as if waiting for one of them to come to their senses.

Dayan took some solace from the knowledge that Mandukhai was on his side in this. He worried she would disagree with him for the same reasons Togochi had already mentioned.

"Mandukhai—"

"Issama was Altan, Togochi," Mandukhai said. The hard edge in her voice stunned Dayan. He had no idea what this meant. Altan was the female Jalair general. How could she be Issama or Issama be her? "The one who hired the serving girl who poisoned my tea fifteen years ago."

Dayan didn't understand, but Togochi seemed to. His eyes widened and his arms dropped to his sides. "What ... how do you know that?"

Mandukhai hugged Dayan's arm tighter, and he placed his free hand over her arm for some reassurance, though he was not sure what was happening.

"Unebolod sent me a message, months ago, when they sent us word of Bigirsen's death. He said Bigirsen confessed Issama had poisoned Manduul's seed."

"I remember that," Dayan said. He hadn't known Bigirsen was talking about Mandukhai, specifically.

Mandukhai pressed on. "You never found Altan because you were searching for the wrong man."

Togochi's face hung slack. His shoulders slumped. Then his neck slowly turned a shade of red that bled all the way up into his face. "All that time ..."

Dayan had never heard so much anger from Togochi. While serious, Togochi had always been the optimist, upbeat in even the darkest times. But this anger in Togochi stunned Dayan.

Togochi clenched his hand into a fist. He glared at the ground, his gaze darting back and forth in some mysterious calculation as his hulking mass drew in angry, ragged breaths.

Mandukhai slowly reached out toward him until her hand rested on Togochi's arm. Dayan saw his own concern reflecting in her eyes.

"It was him," Togochi said, his voice hollow. Then a heat bubble to the surface. "It all makes so much terrible sense now."

"What does?" Mandukhai asked.

Dayan remained still, afraid they would discover he still stood there. He needed to understand what was happening.

"All of it!" Togochi snapped. "He was Bigirsen's man from the start. Bigirsen sent him to Mongke Bulag. Within weeks, Issama had Manduul's ear and Bayan's trust. He was the one who hatched the plan in the south, remember? Then after he left to return to Mongke Bulag, the Ming started attacking and almost killed Bayan. Issama was also the one with the Oirat connections, reassuring Manduul that they would not attack him—and they didn't, did they?" Togochi was raging now, his words tumbling out as he paced back and forth. "No. Instead, they waited until *after* Manduul died."

"I remember," Mandukhai whispered. Her entire body tensed beside Dayan. What had happened when they attacked? Mandukhai had only given Dayan the basic details of what the Oirat had done years ago. Never anything too specific.

Togochi remained oblivious to Mandukhai's sudden tension as he carried on. He anxiously grabbed his hair at the scalp, tugging at it. "High Heavens. I bet he never went on that hunting trip! Do you remember that morning Manduul called in Yungci and I and sent us to question Bayan, but Issama had gone hunting?" Togochi's eyes were as wide as cups, like a man possessed. "The snake! I would bet my entire fortune he never went hunting. I would stake my life that he went to tell Bayan ... *After* he told Manduul what Bayan had done. He set the whole stinking thing up. He must have! He had Bayan's trust and knew exactly how to spook him. Let me tell you, I remember the dumb look on Bayan's face to this day. Issama said something to spook him. I can't think of any other reason Bayan would have attacked us."

Mandukhai's jaw slowly slackened the more Togochi raged. Her head shook ever so slightly. "But they found the herbs Bayan used on Manduul in Bayan's ger."

"Sure. And just as conveniently, Siker just went along with Issama because she was told to? Does that seem like Siker to you?"

Dayan swallowed. While neither of these people were his parents, as far as his upbringing was concerned, it unnerved him to hear Mandukhai and

Togochi talking like this about the people who had given him life. Were they such terrible people? Would he become like them?

"So you are assuming Issama and Siker formed an alliance?" Mandukhai asked.

Togochi threw up his hands. "Why not? You and Unebolod did. And Siker certainly wasn't happy about Bayan's relationship with Yeke."

Dayan's head hurt trying to follow this conversation. He knew who these people were from stories, but he did not know what these two were talking about. Alliances?

Dayan had enough of this. He hated being left out of the conversation, completely clueless. "The past is the past and we need to look toward the future. Togochi, select your men—any men you want as long as I have not already given them other assignments. Finish Issama, then come back as quickly as you can."

"Togochi, bring me his heart," Mandukhai said.

Dayan blinked, once more alarmed by Mandukhai's coldness.

"He killed my child and stole my heart," she said. "I want his heart in my hands."

Child. Dayan was not sure why it had taken him so long to connect that Manduul's spawn had been Mandukhai's child. He had always known Mandukhai had a past before he came into her life, but he had never given it much thought. It made sense, he supposed. She and Manduul had been married for years. If Issama had killed her child, he deserved a fate worse than death.

"Make him suffer," Dayan said. "Make him feel pain until he begs for death." His hand pressed more firmly over Mandukhai's.

Togochi grinned, but this differed from the jovial grin the *orlok* usually wore. There was a hatred and menace in the way his lips curled up. "With pleasure." Then Togochi spun on his heel and began marching away.

"Togochi!" Mandukhai called. "Remember that Siker is the Great Khan's mother. Treat her as such."

Togochi spun around and paused, bowing to her, before resuming his determined pace.

Mandukhai remained beside Dayan as they watched the *orlok* disappear into the crowd. As if by some unspoken agreement, they remained there, watching the sun dip beyond the horizon.

The prospect of killing Issama made Mandukhai's steps a little lighter as she followed Dayan toward his ger. Or maybe it was the way he held her hand as he pulled her along. His energy was infectious.

Instead of going into the ger, Dayan stopped outside his door. He paused beside a tall wicker basket.

"What is that?" she asked.

"I told you when I left I would bring you Bigirsen's head as a bride price," Dayan said.

Flies buzzed up and out when he lifted the lid, grinning proudly. Mandukhai gagged on the stench of death and stepped backward, waving flies away from her face. All her delight dissolved as she pulled her hand out of his.

The boyish grin slid off his face. Dayan frowned, glancing into the basket before replacing the lid. He gave a half-hearted shrug, but she could see how her reaction had hurt him. "It's in a bag, too. We can do whatever you wish with it."

Mandukhai crossed her arms over her chest, hugging herself. "I think we should give it to Esige. She has been after Bigirsen since he stole her sister away. It might help ease some of her pain."

Dayan's shoulder sagged. "Oh. Okay. Well ... I wanted to show you. Because..." He rubbed his neck, like he often had when he'd been anxious as a child. All the energy that had swarmed around him a minute ago vanished.

Mandukhai's heart ached. She attempted reaching out to him, but Dayan already turned his back and headed into his ger.

"Dayan, wait," Mandukhai called, rushing after him

When she reached the threshold, Mandukhai hesitated, staring down at the crossing. She had entered his ger plenty of times over the years, but this felt different. Something between them had changed and crossing his threshold could further solidify the one thing she had been so worried about for so long. A deeper relationship with him.

Dayan watched her from beside his stove. Or rather, his gaze fell to the threshold she stared at. As she looked up, the pain on his face broke her heart.

It's just a threshold, she told herself, then stepped over and entered before she could lose her nerve.

"I did not mean to diminish your gift," Mandukhai said quickly. "I know how much this meant to you."

"Do you?" Dayan squared his shoulders. "It's alright, Mandukhai. I think, deep down, I always knew I would have to give you a choice. You took a monumental risk on me years ago, and you put everything on hold for me. Freeing you from your oath is the least I can do."

Mandukhai's heart plummeted. *Now? Now he is freeing me? Now that the only other man I ever loved is dead?* And then something far more terrible occurred to her. *He no longer wants me.* Why would he want Mandukhai, who was as old as his father, when he could have someone much younger and more supple to his needs?

"I paid my bride price, a debt for everything you have given up for me," Dayan said. "Though it feels insufficient."

Mandukhai edged closer, trembling.

"Now you are free to choose whomever you want. Or no one at all, if you prefer it that way. I'm just sorry I couldn't free you in time."

Mandukhai had not been this devastated since she had given up Unebolod years ago. Any chance of happiness blew away like smoke in the wind. Tears blurred her vision. "Dayan, please ..."

"He told me everything," Dayan said, fidgeting with the sleeve of his deel.

A sob caught in Mandukhai's throat. She reached out, grasping his sleeve and pulling him toward her.

He avoided her gaze, his eyes darting to look everywhere but at her. Pain created creases along his brow and turned down the corners of his mouth. "Mandukhai, you are free to choose."

She swallowed several times to fight down the lump in her throat. "Dayan, I made my choice years ago."

"I want that to be true more than anything, but this is different," Dayan said, shaking his head.

Mandukhai brushed a hand along his cheek, cradling his face in her hand and tilting his gaze to hers. His golden eyes penetrated her soul, piercing and vulnerable at the same time. His Adam's apple bobbed. He pulled her against him, but even that gesture seemed more anxious than excited.

The vulnerable boy was still in there, but Mandukhai didn't see that boy on the outside any longer. Dayan had a strong jaw, stoic yet smooth face, and broad shoulders that dwarfed her own. Altan was right. Dayan had changed into a handsome, powerful warrior when she hadn't been looking.

His fingertips grazed her face, as if feeling her skin for the first time. His touch trembled. Something in his eyes transformed. A spark ignited, making his golden gaze burn with life. His touch left a trail of tingles on her skin. Mandukhai's face heated. Her heart beat faster.

They drew together, breaths mingling, enhancing the heat on her skin. Yet he did not kiss her. Mandukhai's disappointment made her stomach churn.

To Mandukhai's knowledge, Dayan had never kissed anyone else before. Like her, he was likely scared to take that step.

Summoning her courage, Mandukhai slowly tipped her lips toward his, inviting him in, but he remained frozen in place, eyes burning into her, burrowing into the very fibers of her soul. She closed her eyes and made the first move, brushing her lips over his.

Dayan's breath caught. For a moment, he didn't respond at all. Then his lips melted against hers. His hand slid along the back of her neck and tangled in her hair. Mandukhai's head spun. Her heart thudded in her chest. The churning in her stomach became a burning heat she had not felt in years. Hungry for more, Mandukhai's tongue darted out, testing his lips.

Dayan pulled back and pressed his forehead against hers, cradling her head in his hand. "I have been waiting so long to do that," he whispered.

She wanted more. Mandukhai tilted her head to steal another kiss.

But Dayan tore further back and shook his head. "Not like this. Not now. I know you loved him." He kissed her forehead. "When this happens, I need to know I'm not your second choice."

No! Mandukhai wanted to tell Dayan he was not her second choice—he was her only choice. But that would help no one. Did it matter who she loved more in what way? The fact was, she loved him, and she wasn't getting any younger.

She found her voice, and it sounded more desperate than she liked. "I already told you—"

Dayan withdrew, leaving her cold and very exposed. "Please don't make this harder. This is the hardest thing I've ever done. There is a difference between choosing me as Khan and choosing me as someone you love—"

"I do love you!"

"As a husband."

Mandukhai had never felt so bone cold before. So alone.

"Take the time you need to mourn him," Dayan said. "And if you are ever ready to move on and choose me—really choose me—my door is open."

Mandukhai wanted to reach out to Dayan, pull him close, reassure him. But she knew he was right. She needed to mourn Unebolod properly before she could really move on. She was weak, eager for love, and Dayan easily could have taken advantage of that. But he deserved better. They both did.

All she could do was nod in response.

Mandukhai stepped outside, gliding toward her own ger. Her fingers brushed her lips. The last person to kiss her like that had been Unebolod. And that had been ten years ago.

Pain lanced through her chest. *We buried him only two days ago and already I am kissing someone else. I'm a terrible person.*

Esige finished packing up their ger and checked the cart to be sure everything was secure. Already, haphazard lines of Urainkhai warriors and families snaked their way southeast along with some of Arqai's Ordos warriors.

She had made a show of leaving, throwing heartfelt accusations toward Mandukhai about Borogchin and Unebolod. The words had clearly hurt Mandukhai, even if she knew they were meant as a show. In all lies there is a nugget of truth. She hated leaving Mandukhai's camp but knew her role in finishing this conquest would rest on her ability to draw these disloyal Ordos Lords out.

Huoshai stepped up beside Esige and slid his arm around her shoulders, holding her against him. She loved the solid comfort of his body. Nothing could touch her while he held her.

Nearby, Arqai waited impatiently on his mount. Esige could feel his dark eyes burrowing into her.

"I think I have only ever hated two men more than him," Esige muttered to her husband, glancing past his shoulder toward Arqai.

The Ordos Lord smirked at her.

She shivered.

"He knows I will kill him if he tries anything," Huoshai said. He meant well, but the words offered no reassurance.

A young rider raced toward them, dismounting in a rush. "Lady Esige, I have a gift for you from the Khan and Khatun. A peace offering to show how sorry they are and that they want you to stay."

Esige straightened, pulling away from Huoshai as she edged toward the rider's mount. The boy unfastened a tall wicker basket from his saddle and awkwardly placed it on the ground in front of her. Esige gagged on the stench from whatever was inside.

"No peace offering could ever smell so foul," Esige said, wrinkling her nose.

Huoshai edged closer. "What is it?" He gagged.

She shrugged.

Arqai edged his mount closer to them so he could get a look as well.

Esige lifted the lid on the basket and gagged again. Flies buzzed out in a rush. Her heart fluttered. Mandukhai would not send her anything so foul without reason, and a dark pulse of excitement raced through her as Esige reached into the basket and pulled out the sack stained with dried blood.

Huoshai choked, stepping back. "Don't take it out."

"What kind of peace offering is that?" Arqai asked.

Esige grinned, suddenly no longer queasy. She ignored her husband as he shuffled backward. She kneeled on the damp ground and set the bag in front of her reverently. Then she untied it and rolled the sides of the back away.

Bigirsen's skin had drained of all color. His formerly strong cheeks were sunken in decomposition. His dark eyes had become pearl-like stones with a milky onyx heart. The jaw hung loose, as if still in shock. Black hair threaded with silver hung limp from his chin and scalp.

Someone behind her vomited. Esige's stomach remained remarkably calm.

"Please leave that behind for the animals," Huoshai groaned.

Esige pulled her knife from her belt and rammed it through one eye. The orb burst, oozing fluid along the decaying cheeks. Disappointment settled in her stomach. She wanted to gouge out his eyes, but if she did that again, she would destroy the second. Esige wiped off the knife before returning it to her belt, then rolled the sack back up over Bigirsen's head.

"Please?" Huoshai pleaded.

"Tell them I appreciate the sentiment," Esige told the boy, who had turned away, ghostly pale. "But this changes nothing."

Esige grinned as she stood and hoisted the bag, then spun around to face her husband.

Huoshai's shoulders sagged.

Arqai's face was sickly green, and he wiped his sleeve across his mouth.

Esige sauntered past both of them, smirking at Arqai. "This is what happens to men who cross me."

CHAPTER THIRTY-SIX

Hunting A Snake

The only difference between winter and spring this close to the desert was the heat. As spring came into full swing, the coolness of night burned away faster with the sunrise. Issama waited for his men to arrive, hidden in his desert valley near enough to Hami that he could watch for signs of trouble, yet far enough that they would not easily spot him. Lord Asha had stopped searching for him not long after his escape. It was some relief that the Oirat khan had never found him. Asha had been made rich by Mandukhai's administration and turned his back on the Uyghur—Issama foremost. It grated on his nerves. Had he and the Uyghur become so weak?

Few of his men had found him here, despite carefully spreading word. Issama did not know what happened to the men he sent into Oirat territory. He had heard nothing more from them. Had Alayitung's men killed them ... or converted them? If that was the case, he would not be safe here for much longer.

A few times, he sent Siker or Qolotai into the market for supplies and information, but they rarely heard more than a few rumors. Nothing substantial he could use. The Khan had set up a camp somewhere in the Ordos basin—which meant he intended to fight Lord Legusi. It also meant Issama did not have to worry about Dayan or Mandukhai for a while. So far, the Ordos had upheld their promises. If Issama could not return to them soon, he could lose his foothold over the Lords.

A few of Issama's followers camped with him, but not nearly enough men to launch any kind of attack. He didn't even have enough to post regular guards around their small camp. Once Issama was certain he had all of his men from Hami, he would pack up his family and remaining followers and head into Ordos territory to secure his place.

It would not be long.

Togochi stood beside his mount and held the reins as she drank from the shallow stream his men had come across. Finding water this close to the desert often proved a challenge, and he had called them to a halt to give their mounts time to rest and drink.

Nothing existed in the barren landscape. The Ordos families that would have been along his route had fled months ago—likely to a more secure location among other Ordos tribes. They had to know that, after the murder of Unebolod, the Khan would come for them. It had tempted Togochi to ride out against the Ordos himself and kill as many as he could before they killed him. But it would solve nothing. Unebolod had given his life to save Dayan Khan—something that surprised Togochi. He knew Unebolod better than most, and he had seen the depth of Unebolod's love for Mandukhai. If Dayan had died instead, by Mandukhai's own oath, she would then be bound to Unebolod and his descendants.

Unebolod's devotion to Mandukhai and her vision, in the end, had been absolute. He had given his life to protect the Khan so that Dayan and Mandukhai could finish what they had started. Togochi knew that riding off to his own death would dishonor Unebolod's memory.

Yet here I am, in this wasteland, hundreds of miles from both of them, Togochi thought.

Togochi understood the importance of this mission—and he would see it successful—but it did not make the assignment any easier. He wanted to be with Mandukhai and Dayan when they met Legusi or Mogurkei, whether it be on the battlefield or in the gathering tent. Instead, he would be six hundred miles away, killing the snake that continued to poison everything they achieved. It was a place of honor to cut the head off the snake, having Dayan Khan's absolute trust, but Togochi couldn't stop himself from feeling somewhat resentful.

"Time to ride!" Togochi called, glancing at the setting sun burning on the horizon. He wiped sweat from his forehead, adjusted his helmet, and mounted his mare.

The horses swiftly churned up the rocky earth beneath their hooves, racing across the southern edge of the desert.

Dayan had established yam lines on this route during his campaign against Bigirsen. Those same routes gave Togochi a quick and easy path to follow. If they needed fresh mounts, they could exchange the weakest at the yam stations. They rode hard and fast across from the northern Ordos territory, only stopping for the night when they reached a station with enough space for the men to sleep, or when they had secure, safe crevices to hide in. An army of two hundred men was just small enough not to attract attention. A wise decision on Dayan's part.

Just over two weeks after leaving the Khan's camp, Togochi reached the yam station nearest to Hami.

"Dochigen," Togochi called after leaving his mount in the care of the station owner.

The commander jogged over. *"Orlok."*

"Go to Hami and let Lord Asha know we are here," Togochi said. "He is to remain where he is and send no one out toward Issama. We will deal with him ourselves. I will not have Asha startling Issama away before we get to him."

Dochigen nodded and headed to retrieve a fresh mount.

Togochi pressed his knuckles into his back and stretched. Tonight, he would get rest. Tomorrow, they would hunt the snake.

Issama sharpened his sword. He grew impatient with all of this waiting, and he could tell that Siker had grown weary of it as well. During the hot days, she snapped at the littlest things—Issama moving something into the wrong place; the boys getting too dirty; Qolotai never doing what Siker wanted her to do. Never mind that she never actually told Qolotai what it was she wanted. His other wife began distancing herself from Siker and the boys. At night, all of Siker's irritation would melt away as she curled up next to him.

Every night.

If Issama hadn't known better, he would think Siker was cutting the other woman out of their lives completely. Yet he could not, for the life of him, figure out what Siker thought she had to gain by isolating his other wife.

One cool night, Qolotai ran out the door crying when Siker told her she was utterly useless at everything. The insult was uncalled for. Issama headed toward the door to console Qolotai, but Siker appeared in his way, slithering her arms around his waist.

"Let her go," Siker murmured. She kissed his neck. "I don't know what you see in her. She is too soft."

Issama eased her arms off of him. "I would think you might understand the pain she suffers, having lost a child of your own."

Siker snorted and rolled her eyes. "I didn't lose him. I left him. And he is alive out there."

"All the more reason for you to pity her," he said. "At least *your* children all still draw breath." Qolotai had lost her only child in the red lake massacre.

He pushed Siker aside, irritated with how cold she had become.

"Issama, wait," Siker pleaded, seizing his arm. "I'm sorry. You know I love you, and I don't mean to hurt you. But ... we are running low on food, and we have little left to barter for more. She is another mouth to feed, and she is not contributing anything."

Issama's heart lurched. They would run out of food? "How low?"

Siker bit her lip, and tears welled in her eyes, making them seem to sparkle. He hated how much he loved the way her eyes looked when she cried.

"A few weeks, at most."

A few weeks. He knew they ran low on anything worth trading for food or clothing. *I swore I would never be poor again*, he thought. Issama had worked so hard to gain his wealth. This last year had cost him nearly everything. He would not lose another wife. "I hunt meat we can cure," he said. "But I won't abandon her to die."

"And if it comes down to her or your sons?" Siker asked sharply.

Issama glanced at the two boys playing knucklebones in their space on the far side of the ger. For the first time, he noticed how thin their faces were. *I am failing them*. He stiffened his back. "It won't." Issama wouldn't let it come to that. He would hunt for food. If matters took a turn for the worst, he would send Siker and the boys to Mandukhai. She likely would not accept him, but Siker was Dayan's mother. Issama's sons were Dayan's half-brothers. Mandukhai might hate him, but she would not hold his faults against his sons.

Just considering that made his skin crawl, begging that woman for anything! She was the reason he had lost everything.

For two days, Togochi and his two hundred men waited for Dochigen to return from Hami. It left Togochi with far too much time to think. To worry. Had Asha decided to betray them? What if Dochigen didn't come back? *If Dochigen doesn't return by morning, I will ride against Issama and end this quickly.*

He tried to pass time planning their attack, but until he understood more about the size of Issama's camp, he could not make proper plans. If the High Heavens smiled on him, Issama would not have nearly enough men to resist a quick attack. If Dochigen didn't return, Togochi would send out his men to close around Issama's camp in the morning. He could not fail Dayan. *But there are so many ifs*, he thought.

If Issama orchestrated Manduul and Bayan's falling out, Mandukhai's miscarriage, and the Ordos attack that ended Unebolod's life, Togochi had a score to settle. He had never truly hated anyone in his life. Togochi had disliked a fair number of people, but hate was so powerful he could never hold on to it.

Issama, however, was the exception.

By mid-day, Dochigen returned to the yam station east of Hami, grinning broadly. He dismounted and marched straight up to Togochi, who leaned against the frame of the door to the ger he shared with a dozen of his men.

"Did you enjoy your trip?" Togochi asked, noting the grin on Dochigen's face. What had he been doing in the city for so long?

"Immensely," Dochigen said. He reached into his deel and pulled out a detailed map of the area. "This is an updated map, courtesy of Lord Asha. He claims Issama has been hiding in this desert valley here for weeks with only a handful of men. The rest were killed during the attempted seizure of Hami, or they fled north into Oirat territory and deserted him. He is weaker than we expected."

Togochi examined the map. An "X" on the map marked out the yam station they currently called home. Not twenty miles almost directly west,

Asha circled a small section of the map and made notations about the number of people there. Fewer than a dozen, including Issama's family.

Something about this reeked of a trap. It could not be this easy. Asha had been loyal to the Khan and obedient with Lord Alayitung, according to the reports Mandukhai had received over the years. But it was still hard, after centuries of bitter feuds, to trust the Oirat completely. And Issama was far too clever to not have men hiding somewhere in case of an ambush.

The valley where Issama's camp nestled would be out of sight of Hami, yet close enough for Issama to sneak into the city for supplies. *Or he could sneak in to plot against Dayan*, Togochi thought. He grimaced.

"Do you believe Asha?" Togochi asked.

Dochigen's brows shot up his wide forehead. "Why wouldn't we? He has served the Khan and Khatun for ten years now."

"Issama is patient with his plans," Togochi noted, thinking of everything the Uyghur had done over the years.

Even weeks after learning the truth, he still burned with so much hate when he thought about Issama. It hurt even more that he had trusted Issama for so long. *I should have known better*, he thought for what must have been the thousandth time. *I just need to end this so I can get back to the Khan ... back to my wives*. Togochi called his commanders around him.

Within an hour, they had their plan in place and mounted. Two scouts had been sent ahead to verify Asha's information. A dozen of his warriors would ride around the valley to cut off the only route Issama had to escape. Togochi would lead the rest right into Issama's camp. If Issama truly had so few men, there would be no chance for resistance.

Siker sat beside the ger door, darning a hole in one of Issama's deels. He played knucklebones with the boys, trying to distract himself from his own worries. Hunting had gone well enough for the day. He managed to bring home a couple of small marmots Qolotai skinned to roast or dry. It wasn't much, but it would hold them over for a couple of days so he could hunt for more game.

Suddenly, Siker raised her head toward the open door, gazing outside. "Issama, why is the ground shaking?"

Issama paused as he reached for the scattered knucklebones. As he felt the rumbling in the earth, Siker dropped her work on the ground and darted out the door. Hope bloomed in his chest. Was this it? Had his prayers been answered and his men returned? He rubbed a palm over each of his boy's bald heads as he scrambled to his feet, grinning. In seconds, he was outside.

Siker already had his horse ready. He leaned over and kissed her cheek. "Our fortunes are returning," he said. "It must be my men."

He leaped into the saddle and turned east, riding out of the camp to greet his men.

A cloud of dust rolled behind the small force riding his way. He grinned, whipping his mare for more speed as he raced toward them.

By the time he recognized the man riding at the center of the line half a mile from his camp, it was too late.

Togochi! Panic gripped Issama. He considered fleeing, then thought of what Siker had told him. They were almost out of food. Maybe, if he played this right, he could convince Togochi to help them.

"Togochi!" Issama called out, waving his hand. "Thank the High Heavens!"

Togochi released an arrow. Issama's heart sank into his stomach.

The arrow pierced Issama's raised hand. He shouted in pain as agony ripped through his palm and down his arm. Everything inside of him lurched as reality slammed down against him. There would be no rescue. No begging.

They sent Togochi to kill him.

Before he could recover, another arrow pierced his unarmored stomach with enough force to throw him from the saddle. Searing hot agony and wet warmth spread outward. Issama's vision momentarily darkened when his head slammed into the ground. He blinked a few times and rolled over, but the pain overwhelmed him. He cried out, kicking his legs feebly.

He knew his death was coming, yet he was helpless to do anything about it. *I won't die like this!*

Another arrow punched through his shoulder. Issama could do little more than whimper, unable to catch his breath.

A stream of horses raced around him—straight toward the camp. *Siker! The boys!*

"No!" Issama reached pathetically toward camp as if the action would stop the warriors in their tracks.

A few horses stopped, forming a ring around him.

Issama closed his eyes against the blinding sun, focusing on his breaths and fighting against the agonizing pain.

Togochi's boots thumped against the rocky earth nearby. He stalked toward Issama. "At last we meet, Altan." He sneered as if in greeting.

Issama frowned, inhaling quick breaths to fight off the pain screaming in his body. Every movement was agony. Altan? Had Togochi gone mad?

Then understanding hit him. Mandukhai knew the truth. That Issama had tricked that serving girl to poison her years ago. He had given that girl the wrong name to avoid ever being connected. How did they find out?

"She sent you to kill me," Issama said through gritted teeth.

"No. He did."

Once more, confusion muddled Issama's mind.

"Dayan?" he asked.

"You won't even both *trying* to deny you killed that baby?" Togochi asked. Issama heard the pure hatred dripping from every syllable.

Togochi pulled a rope from his belt and began wrapping it around Issama's ankles without mercy. Each jerk of the rope around Issama's ankles sent a fresh wave of agony up his spine. When he finished the knot, Togochi marched to his mare, holding the other end of the rope.

Issama's heart sank as the brutal truth sank in. He drew breath now, but he was already dead. *I have to talk my way out of this!* "Kill me now and the Khan dies."

Togochi snorted and tied the rope to the back of his saddle, then climbed back on without another word.

Togochi and his men rode toward Issama's camp, dragging Issama screaming behind them.

Every scream, whimper, and moan Issama emitted on the way into camp fueled Togochi's anger. Mandukhai wanted Issama's heart, and Togochi grew more certain by the second that he would take great delight in carving it out of Issama's chest. Perhaps before the other man even died.

When they reached camp, Togochi's men had already seized control. Only a handful of Uyghur warriors had been there to protect the camp, just as Asha had predicted. All the Uyghur men were dead. Togochi didn't trust that more Uyghur or Ordos men would not ride in from the other end of the valley, so he sent men out to secure the valley and the camp.

Issama's wives and children had been sequestered inside their ger. Every man had strict orders not to harm any of them without Togochi's verbal confirmation. Mandukhai wanted Siker returned to Dayan unharmed. For now, he would assume that extended to the children who might also be Dayan's half-brothers.

Issama had lost consciousness on the ride back to camp, leaving a trail of blood in his wake along the sandy ground. The arrows that had been jutting out of his flesh had broken off somewhere along the way, leaving shafts, arrow tips, and splinters buried beneath Issama's skin.

Hate pulsed through Togochi as he crouched beside Issama in the open space near Issama's ger. Togochi needed him awake. Mercilessly, he drove his thumb deep into the shoulder wound.

Issama's eyes shot open as he screamed. Wild eyes darted in every direction before falling on Togochi.

"I know everything, Issama," Togochi said. The coldness in his tone alarmed him. He had never been so detached before.

"No ..." Issama's eyes drifted closed.

Togochi slapped him hard enough to draw blood at the corner of Issama's mouth.

Issama jolted, then screamed. Despite his pain, a sneer curled back his lips. "There ... is no way ... you know everything."

"Bigirsen told Unebolod what you did to Manduul's child before the Khan took his head," Togochi hissed. "It doesn't take much to put the rest together."

With some satisfaction, he yanked his thumb from the wound, hooking the tip under Issama's flesh to inflict more pain as he pulled it out. Issama howled, then whimpered as tears rolled down his temples. Togochi wiped the blood off his thumb on Issama's deel.

Issama cackled with frenzied laughter that turned Togochi's hot blood cold. "Manduul's ... child ..." He continued laughing, a high-pitched sound of madness. Just as suddenly, Issama stopped laughing, turning vicious, dark eyes on Togochi. "He never had a child. Never would have. That child wasn't his ..."

Togochi blinked.

"You already knew that though," Issama panted. "Couldn't be his ... I saw to that."

Togochi did know, or at least highly suspected, that Mandukhai's child was Unebolod's and not Manduul's. Unebolod's grief when she lost the child, the way he separated himself from everyone, could only have meant one thing. None of that mattered now.

"I did ... everyone ... a favor ..." Issama said, struggling for breath. His skin paled and sweat beaded on his forehead.

Togochi pressed a knee into the ground beside Issama. He would die soon from his wounds. Togochi would let him bleed out slowly. He deserved far worse. "You poisoned Manduul and framed Bayan. Which means you were also responsible for Yeke's death. Does Siker know all of this? Does she know the sort of man she married?"

Togochi glanced at the ger. The door remained firmly closed, but he could hear Siker's protests inside as she shouted at Togochi's men.

Issama trembled and the mad fury in his eyes suddenly turned desperate. "Kill me, but spare my wives and sons."

"Did Siker know what you did to them? To everyone? What did you hope to gain by hurting everyone?"

"Everything," Issama murmured. Issama reached up, his hand shaking violently as he grabbed desperately at Togochi's arm. "Everything!" He squeezed his eyes closed and fought off some emotion Togochi didn't care enough to identify.

Cold to the bone, Togochi swatted Issama's hand away. "Don't touch me, snake. Who else is working with you?"

Issama relaxed, and for a moment he almost looked peaceful, which only stoked Togochi's hatred. He had no right to look peaceful after all he had done! And clearly he had no intention of answering Togochi's question.

"I see it now," Issama murmured weakly. "The error in my choices. I could have done better, but the heir of Genghis is strong, just like his mother." He gasped, his breath rattling. "I was born to nothing." Blood trickled from the corner of Issama's mouth. "But I will die the Great Khan's father." Issama cracked his eyes open, challenging Togochi. He growled. "Finish it, Togochi."

The challenge fueled Togochi's hatred. He wanted to draw out Issama's life as long as possible just so he could teach Issama a new form of torture. But he had something far more powerful at his disposal.

Issama clung to his false beliefs in these final moments.

Togochi would tear them away.

"You are not his father," Togochi growled. "Unebolod and Bayan were his fathers, and you killed them both. You will die as you were born." He stood, looming over Issama's prone form. "As nothing."

Togochi rose and turned toward the ger where Siker waited with Issama's sons under guard. All the peace Issama had composed himself with shattered. He shifted, cried out, but couldn't move. Not only had he lost too much blood, but several of Togochi's men stood guard around him.

"No! My children!" Issama screamed, and his shrill pleas bounced off the walls of the valley. "They are innocent."

Togochi reached the door, opening it slowly, and growled over his shoulder. "Nothing you have created is innocent."

As he stepped inside, Issama's screams shattered the sky.

Togochi stepped over the threshold. Two boys, younger than his own sons, clung to each other, crying on the far side of the ger. Issama's blood coated Togochi's clothing, and he knew how it must look to them. What sort of trauma would his own sons suffer under similar circumstances?

Siker sat on the bed, glaring at Togochi with pure hatred.

"You look at me as if this were my fault," Togochi said, closing the door behind him, "when I have just freed you from a man who claimed you when he had no right."

Siker pressed her lips into a thin line, then raised her chin stubbornly. Silence greeted him.

"You will see, in time, that this is best for you all," Togochi said. "We leave for the Khan's camp in the morning."

Siker spit at him, but it fell far short. Togochi sighed. Siker clearly had no intention of speaking to him. He left her with her sons in the ger under armed guard for the night.

Dochigen lingered near the door of the ger, holding a sword as he examined it in the dying light of day. "This is a nice blade," he commented. "Mind if I keep it, Togochi?"

Togochi could only shake his head. Dochigen had earned his reward. If Issama's sword was what he wanted, he could have it. The weapon didn't matter to anyone else anymore.

Only one task remained. Togochi thought he would enjoy it, but now wondered if that were true. Issama lay on the ground in a pool of his own blood, unconscious. Or dead. Either way, it didn't matter.

Mandukhai's orders had been specific and clear.

Togochi ripped open Issama's deel to expose his chest. His hand trembled as he pulled his knife from his belt. Carefully, he pressed the blade through skin and muscle, then set to work slicing him open. Issama didn't stir. The trauma and blood loss had taken their toll. Togochi could still feel the ragged, shallow breaths as he pulled the wound open. Then Issama's chest stopped moving.

Togochi plunged his hands into Issama's hot, bloody chest and moved ribs that had already broken when he was dragged back to the camp. As his fingers brushed along the valves connecting the organ to the rest of Issama's body, Togochi swore he felt it beat.

Togochi's jaw twitched. He pulled the heart out and cut it free.

Someone brought a small, colorful clay pot to Togochi. Cold and fighting off the revulsion in his body, Togochi dropped the heart into it and closed the lid.

Issama would no longer be the Khan's problem.

CHAPTER THIRTY-SEVEN

A Widow's Grief

ORDOS BASIN – GREAT KHAN'S CAMP – SPRING 1480

Dayan sat on the edge of Nemeku's bed, his knees bouncing anxiously as his cousin sat cross-legged on the floor with enough patience for both of them. This get-together after Dayan finished his duties for the day had become routine. A few of the men Dayan had bonded with on his campaign joined them, Jangi and Belku among them. The others he had already sent away on other tasks. Dayan knew his cousin had watched him slowly come undone day by day.

Orghana always welcomed them graciously and was eager to remain to serve when necessary, or leave if they didn't want her looming around the ger. Dayan certainly appreciated her consideration. He had grown fond of her, and trusted her no matter what Mandukhai thought.

Two weeks had passed since Dayan had given Mandukhai space to make her own choice. While the days had passed quickly with more work than they could hope to finish, Dayan's nights had been restless. That Great Fist of anxiety he had conquered while on campaign with Unebolod slowly seeped back into his life night by night.

Tonight, Dayan couldn't stop the weight of his guilt from crushing him. Unebolod was dead because of him, which also meant Dayan was responsible for the death of Mandukhai's happiness.

"You need to let this go, Dayan," Nemeku said, and not for the first time. He offered a skin of *airag*. Dayan waved the drink off. The last thing he needed right now was *airag*. "There was nothing you could have done to change what happened."

Dayan shook his head, leaning forward and pressing his elbows between his knees to control his breathing. What had Goram taught him to get these attacks under control? All the monk's lessons fled like birds from a tree. "I spent weeks wishing he would die. Then he did. And the horrible things I said to him ..." He groaned pitifully, unable to say Unebolod's name aloud. If he couldn't even say it, how did he ever expect Mandukhai to move on?

Belku snorted, taking the *airag* from Nemeku. He leaned against the post holding up the roof as he took a swig, then swiped his sleeve across his mouth and offered it to Jangi.

"You may be chosen by the spirits or maybe divine or whatever other crap men like to spew to make themselves feel better, but you aren't a god, Dayan," Belku said pointedly. "You aren't *that* blessed. You can't wish a man dead and have it just happen."

Dayan shot a dirty glare at Belku. "Can't I? If I wished Ibarai dead, he would be before dark."

Belku crossed his arms and shook his head. "Sure. By one of your men. Not just because you thought it, so it happened. I respect the shit out of you, but you need to get over yourself. Quit blaming yourself for what Ulum did."

Jangi shifted his feet from where he guarded the door. "He's right, Dayan. Unebolod made a choice. Not you."

"But if I hadn't challenged his loyalty, would he have done the same thing?" Dayan asked. His chest ached.

"Yes," Jangi and Belku both said in unison.

Belku smirked at Jangi, then said, "Maybe you said some nasty things. Maybe he did, too. Who cares? It doesn't change who either of you are."

"And that you both wanted the same thing was sure to always drive a wedge between you," Nemeku added.

A call at the door for Belku stunned all of them into silence. Jangi straightened and opened the door, blocking the outsider from sight.

"I have an urgent message for Lord Belku," a man said.

Belku, Dayan, and Nemeku exchanged perplexed glances as Belku edged toward the door.

Dayan glimpsed the young man outside, noting the Chakhar cut of his deel. His heart sank. This couldn't be good.

Belku waved his hand impatiently for the messenger to get on with it.

"My Lord, I'm sorry," the young man stammered. "Your father ..."

Belku's spine stiffened. "How?"

"His heart, my Lord," the messenger said. "I came as quickly as I could on urgent orders. Guden khan is dead, and your brother is positioning himself to steal control of the Chakhar."

Dayan's legs trembled from his own anxiety as he stood, but he marched toward Belku and patted him on the shoulder. "Take your men and go. Secure your position, then come back. We cannot afford to lose the Chakhar now."

Belku nodded. He clasped Dayan's hand to shake, then sank to his knee and bowed his forehead against Dayan's hand. "I pledge to you, Dayan Khan, the loyalty and fealty of the Chakhar, from this breath until our last. We will follow you with salt, gers, horses, and blood. From this day on, my Chakhar are yours, and belong to the Borjigin royal line forevermore."

Raising his gaze to meet Dayan's, Belku kissed the ring on Dayan's hand. The oath meant more than Dayan could express, but unless Belku wrestled the position of tribal khan from his brother, the oath was meaningless. "Go, Belku khan, with the blessing of the Great Khan and the Eternal Blue Sky."

Belku stood and darted out the door, disappearing through the crowd milling through the thoroughfare. Only the messenger followed on his heels.

"Do you think he will make it in time?" Nemeku asked, joining Dayan in the doorway.

"He has to."

Dayan's breath caught in his throat as he spotted another figure moving through the crowd straight for him.

Mandukhai.

Nemeku shrank out of sight. He was still angry with her for doubting him and Orghana. Dayan had tried to smooth out Nemeku's ruffled feathers, but his cousin was stubborn. Every muscle in Dayan's body froze. He wanted to go to her, to close the door on her, to run away.

"I've been looking for you," Mandukhai huffed.

"Why?" Dayan asked, his tone a touch cold.

Mandukhai jerked to a stop a few feet away. "Ordag just returned."

Dayan straightened. He had sent Ordag and Altan to find Legusi. Had they done so already? Or had Legusi attacked? "What about Altan?"

"She is riding in with Legusi," Mandukhai replied. "They will be here soon."

Dayan cast a glance at Nemeku. His cousin nodded and waved him along, hiding inside the door. Something struck Dayan, though, and he grabbed Nemeku's arm.

"Bring Orghana to the gathering tent," Dayan said. "I think we will need her."

Nemeku grimaced, but he nodded.

Dayan darted out the door, forcing Mandukhai to keep up as his longer stride covered more ground faster.

There had not been enough time to summon as many of the Lords as Mandukhai would have liked. Not since she had spent so much time looking for Dayan. *I should have known he would be with Nemeku*. She and Dayan had only spoken in meetings since that kiss in his ger. Dayan would show up for meetings, do what was required of him, then vanish. He had stopped following her, stopped talking to her, stopped looking at her. She found this new distance between them unbearable.

But Unebolod still wormed his way into her thoughts unbidden, and the grief over losing him would crop up at the most inopportune times.

Today, Dayan seemed determined to lose her on the way to the gathering tent. Mandukhai had to jog to keep up.

When they were at last seated and waiting for Legusi's arrival, Mandukhai sank back to catch her breath. Dayan was not even winded.

"You should know, I sent Belku back to the Chakhar with his men," Dayan said.

Mandukhai eyed Dayan, anger rising in her. Why did he always make her angry these days? "We need those—"

"Guden khan is dead." He turned his wolfish eyes on her. "And Belku's brother is trying to steal the title in his absence. I told him to secure his place, then come back. It was that or we risk lose the Chakhar."

Two old khans dead now. First Albeq, now Guden. Korgiz had died a few years ago. She closed her eyes and murmured a prayer for Guden, then reached for Dayan's hand.

Dayan withdrew.

Tears stung Mandukhai's eyes, but she turned her gaze toward the doors and firmed her jaw. What did Dayan expect from her? She could not just slide from one love to another. Certainly not when she had spent nearly half her life in love with Unebolod. Two weeks was insufficient to move past his loss. The problem was, Mandukhai was not sure if a lifetime would be long enough to get over Unebolod. She didn't think she ever would.

"You did the right thing then," she said.

The two sat in silence as a handful of commanders entered the gathering tent and took their usual positions. Right about now, Mandukhai would have welcomed Togochi. She missed him. Hopefully his mission to kill Issama was going well.

Nemeku and Orghana slipped through the door and tried to make themselves invisible near the back of the room, but Mandukhai spotted them the moment they arrived. As did Dayan. He called them closer to the dais, then leaned toward Orghana, whispering something to her. The girl paled, but nodded.

Mandukhai eyed Dayan curiously as he sat back in his throne beside her. *What was that all about?*

The young couple sat on the steps of the dais, off to the side and out of the way, but clearly visible to anyone who approached.

The gathered men whispered among one another, watching Mandukhai and Dayan curiously.

Ordag and Altan led a man into the gathering tent. Legusi, presumably. Mandukhai glanced at Orghana for some sign of recognition, but saw nothing. Legusi recognized her, though. His brows rose and he brightened a little.

Legusi was younger than Mandukhai had expected. She had heard rumors he was young, but he couldn't be even thirty yet. Something about the way he carried himself, like a boy trying to be a man, reminded her of Dayan. Mandukhai winced at herself. She had to stop thinking of Dayan as a boy. They had kissed. He certainly wasn't a boy any longer

"Orghana!" Legusi's voice cracked with relief and he took a few quick strides toward his sister.

"Legusi khan," Mandukhai said, her voice cracking the air like a whip.

He froze and flushed, seeming to remember where he was. After a fleeting glance at his sister, Legusi kneeled at the base of the dais with Ordag and Altan each at a side.

"My Khan," Legusi said, dipping his head toward the floor. "It is true then? Lord Bigirsen is dead? I heard rumors, and your commanders here told me you went on a mission to kill him. But ... my sister ..." He raised his head and gazed at Orghana.

"I killed him myself," Dayan said coldly.

Legusi's body sagged toward the floor in obvious relief. "Please, my lord Khan, we ask you to rule us. I can't take any more of this."

"Rule you?" Dayan's voice lowered dangerously. Mandukhai suppressed the urge to rub away the gooseflesh on her skin. "After your men betrayed their oaths to me and murdered my *orlok* and thousands of my men? After you spent years rebuking our efforts to welcome you into our empire? After you sold your young sister into a life of abuse, knowing what Bigirsen would do to her, just to save your own skin?" With each question, the anger in his voice heated.

Legusi's eyes widened a little more at each accusation. His palms trembled against the wooden floor.

"*Now* you want me to rule you?" Dayan stood and descended the steps.

Mandukhai held her breath. The air in the gathering tent grew tense, stale. Anger radiated off Dayan like a pulsing beacon of wrath. Each time his boot contacted a step, the thump resounded like thunder. Even she trembled. He had never been so fierce before ... so much like Genghis. Was this what it had been like to be in Genghis's presence in such meetings? Mandukhia trembled, but a flush of heat warmed her skin. Her pulse quickened.

Altan and Ordag both took instinctive steps back from Legusi as Dayan approached.

At the last step, Dayan reached down, grabbing Legusi's chin tight enough to pinch the skin. He tilted the Ordos khan's face up as Dayan crouched before him. Mandukhai watched the way Dayan's strong shoulders sloped dangerously and her stomach flipped.

"You are spineless, Legusi," Dayan said. "You bow and spew oaths to any man stronger than you. The Ming. Bigirsen. Issama. You give away that which should be most precious like it is nothing. You, Legusi khan, are a man without courage. I do not need your permission to rule, nor your request. I already do. Whether you see it or not."

Mandukhai wondered if she should do something, but also worried what Dayan might say or do if she spoke up at the wrong time. He had a firm command on the room. It entranced her.

However, Legusi had come to them willingly. He bent his knee without being forced. He gave over his control without question. Whether Dayan was right was irrelevant. Legusi had done what others had done. He recognized their right and offered his support and his men. Not even Belku's father had done that much.

Before Mandukhai could collect herself to act, Orghana stood with Nemeku's aid. She edged toward Dayan, her face as white as the moon.

"My lord Khan, I ask mercy for my brother," Orghana said. Her voice trembled. "Please."

Dayan raised his gaze to Orghana, hard and unflinching.

Mandukhai, however, flinched. A shiver raced down her spine and ignited something deep within.

"Why should I?" Dayan asked.

"Bigirsen was a bully," Orghana said. She sounded so timid speaking in front of this gathering. "He gave my brother two choices. Kneel and submit to him or die. Is that really the choice a powerful leader would give?"

Mandukhai caught the implication clearly enough and bit her lip. Dayan was presenting Legusi with similar choices. She admired the girl's courage.

"What else could my brother do? The only way to protect his people was to do what Bigirsen wanted ... even when it meant giving me to him. But ..." Orghana glanced over her shoulder at Nemeku. "If he hadn't, I would not have met your cousin or started the life I want." Her hands tightened against her stomach. "The family I want. For that, I am eternally grateful."

Mandukhai blanched. Orghana was pregnant? Was it Nemeku's child at all? What if Bigirsen had planted his seed before he died?

"My lord Khan," Orghana continued, crouching beside Dayan. She placed her hand on his arm, easing his grip off Legusi's face. "Sometimes the path to salvation is paved with ugly deeds, but it is the only way forward."

Orghana held Dayan's hands—*he didn't withdraw from her*—and stood, forcing him to his feet as well. Mandukhai felt a flash of jealousy. It was like looking in a mirror on her own younger years.

Dayan flushed and averted his gaze back to Legusi, slipping his hands away. "What value do you have to me, Legusi?"

Legusi had been tense through the entire exchange with his sister, watching her with wide-eyed amazement. Now he perked up, hope blooming on his face. "Mogurkei is gathering power, waiting for Issama before he makes his move. I can help you get close enough to Mogurkei to finish him. He will never accept you as Khan."

"Issama will be dead soon," Dayan announced. "I sent Togochi weeks ago to kill him. Mogurkei has nothing."

"Then you will need to get close to Mogurkei before he realizes that, or he will use all the strength he is gathering to target you," Legusi said. "Not just your men. But you, Dayan Khan. And if he kills you—and he will try with the determination of a starving wolf—he will force your Khatun into his harem. If she refuses, he will torture her into submission."

Mandukhai felt all eyes on her. But her gaze remained fixed on Dayan, unable to look away, transfixed by his command of the situation. The idea of pleasuring Mogurkei in any way made her dinner revolt. What sort of torture would he use?

"That will not happen," Dayan said with absolute certainty. "Prove your value. Help us kill him, and I will reconsider your fate."

Legusi bowed his face to the floor once more.

"This is my only mercy," Dayan said with finality.

Togochi woke before the sun rose fully and stepped out of the ger he had slept in. Before going to sleep, he had searched for fresh clothes. Yesterday, he had been full of cold, hard hatred and hadn't thought twice about the blood on his clothes when he had entered Siker's ger. This morning, after dreaming all night about Jaghan, Geriel, and his own children, Togochi's heart ached. Issama's sons were innocent children. While they would likely grow up to resent him—or even hate him—for killing their father, they were still half-brothers to Dayan Khan.

Eager to get back to the Ordos basin—and hopeful that he would be on time to help end the Ordos resistance—Togochi strapped on his sword and glanced at Issama's second wife, curled up on the floor of the ger. She had attempted climbing into bed with him during the night, but he had refused. Not because he wasn't tempted. She was quite pretty. But because he could not stop thinking about what it had felt like having his hands inside Issama's chest—her husband's chest. That memory would haunt him until his own death. Killing was one thing, but what Togochi had done was so deeply personal and malicious, he could not reconcile the act with himself.

He stepped outside and began waking his men. They needed to prepare to ride out. Traveling back to the Khan's camp the two women and two boys in tow would slow them down. Perhaps doubling their time, depending on how stubborn they were or how poor they were at riding.

Once the men were all moving around camp small, and they had pre-pared a cart for Siker's belongings, he entered her ger.

Siker sat on her bed, wide awake, glaring at him just as she had done the night before. Her two young sons slept on the floor beside her.

Had she truly loved that snake? Togochi could not fathom how any woman could care about a man like Issama. As far as Togochi saw it, he had rescued her from a horrible situation. She should be grateful. And he would reunite her with her long-lost son! She must have expected this day was coming. Hadn't she ever wanted it?

Regardless of how she may have felt in the past, there was no doubt about how Siker felt at that moment. She wore an openly cold, resentful mask. Her arms were crossed over her chest, and her lips set in the straight line. Though she glared at Togochi, he thought that, for a moment, he actually saw grief in her eyes.

The other wife was already up, shuffling out the door with no resistance.

"It's time to go, Siker," Togochi said, waving toward the door. "We have a cart ready for your belongings and horses for you and your sons. Let's go. Mount up."

Siker didn't move. She did little more than blink slowly at him.

"I don't understand," Togochi said. "I know Bayan was hardly perfect, but was he so terrible you welcomed this fate instead? That you prefer it?" He shook his head. How could she? Issama was a monster. She couldn't truly care more for Issama than she could for her own son. Could she?

Siker's chin trembled. Tears spilled down her cheeks, but she still refused to respond.

Why is she crying?

"Dayan Khan is waiting for you," Togochi said, edging toward her to take her arm. "Let's go."

Siker jerked away and pressed her back to the wall. "No."

For a moment, Togochi froze in place, still reaching toward her. *No?* "Why?"

She clenched her jaw.

Two of Togochi's men ducked inside.

"We are ready when you are," one man said.

"Get the boys mounted," Togochi commanded.

"Stop!" Siker lunged forward.

Togochi seized her arm. "Siker, is your son, the Great Khan, of no importance to you at all? Do you truly hold your own people in such contempt?"

The boys woke, rubbing blurry eyes as Togochi's men lifted them from the floor and them carried out the door. "Momma!" One boy cried.

Tears streamed freely down Siker's face now. Togochi could not understand her obstinance. Why did she refuse to go? How could she cry for a man like Issama?

"Why are you weeping over another man?" he demanded. "Over this traitor, our enemy, your *son's* enemy?"

Siker continued to refuse him answers. Not that Togochi was certain those answers would help anything. He clenched his sword hilt in his fist, and she did not fail to notice the frustrated motion. Siker raised her chin defiantly.

"We don't have time for this," Togochi growled. "You are coming along either way."

Still holding her arm in a tight fist, Togochi dragged her toward the door. Siker pulled back, dragged her heels, and refused to comply. By the time he reached the door, she had slid her heels so far forward that her backside nearly dragged on the ground. Not even the cries of her sons calling for her stopped her obstinate behavior.

"Help me!" Togochi snapped through the open door.

Dochigen rushed forward and took Siker's legs. Togochi shifted around and slid his hands under her arms. The two of them lifted her off the floor and out the door. Siker continued squirming in silent protest as they carried her to a horse. It took a few attempts to get her into a saddle. When they finally did, Togochi tied her on so she couldn't cause them further trouble. He would lead her horse.

The other woman sat in her saddle, resigned to her fate, eyeing the eastern horizon as the sun rose.

Something caught Siker's attention and she stopped resisting. Instead, her entire body seized up in the saddle. Tears ran in streams down her cheeks as Togochi bound her wrists together to keep her from trying to escape.

Before he mounted, Togochi followed Siker's horrified stare. She had fixated on Issama's mutilated corpse. Togochi quickly averted his own gaze, unable to look upon his handiwork. Both of the boys cried for their father as they waited atop their own horses. It made Togochi's heart ache for the boys, innocent in all of this. He thought of his own sons. *I should have covered the body from sight, or at least moved it.* The boys would never forget seeing their father's body left to rot with a gaping hole in the chest.

Each horse was led by one of Togochi's men as another rode alongside the boys and the other wife.

As they rode away, Siker's gaze remained locked on Issama's body, left in the open for the animals to consume. And she silently wept for her dead husband in a way he had never seen her do for Bayan.

CHAPTER THIRTY-EIGHT

Something to Gain, Something to Lose

ORDOS BASIN – SPRING 1480

Dayan spent the evening alone in his ger, pacing the rugs and absently fidgeting with the colorful belts around his waist. Nemeku had sent Dayan away, saying Orghana was not feeling well and needed rest. Belku was gone to take over the Chakhar. Jangi posted himself as sentry outside Nemeku's door, ever vigilant. Chakicha was busy adjusting to his new position as khan to his tribe. Of all the men he had grown accustomed to chatting with, all had been sent off on missions or were busy with their own lives. They didn't have time to talk down a seventeen-year-old Khan worried about ... *Everything*, Dayan thought. *I am worried about literally everything. Not just her.*

It had been more than a month now. Forty-six days, to be exact. Forty-six days since he gave Mandukhai the freedom and space to make her own decisions about her future. About him. Forty-six days since they had kissed.

Dayan's lungs tightened, and he fought to pull in each breath. For a moment, he paused, clutching the *uni* pole holding up the roof for support. He closed his eyes. The monk's lessons to control these attacks seemed to have vanished completely from his memory.

I have to focus on something else.

Dayan had sent Legusi to join Huoshai and Esige three weeks ago. It made the most sense to him that Legusi would be a believable ally to Mogurkei if he rode with the Urainkhai who allegedly deserted Dayan and Mandukhai. Sadly, for the ruse to work, it meant Dayan also had to allow Legusi to take his men with him. Could he trust the Ordos khan at all?

Before Legusi left, he had stressed the importance of closing in on Mogurkei's position. Legusi had marked out the remaining Ordos camps on a map, as well as safe passages away from the prying eyes of Mogurkei's scouts. Dayan had refused to move into what could be a trap, so after Legusi left, Dayan had sent out a small contingent of guards who would verify the safe passages were actually safe.

The scouts had been gone for more than a week. Not that they should have returned yet, but he grew increasingly anxious each day as he waited for them to bring news. What if it *had* been a trap, and they were dead?

Dayan focused on his breathing. In. Out ... In. Out ...

Any day now, Huoshai would send word that they were in position to meet Mogurkei. Once Dayan finished off both Issama and Mogurkei, he could finally travel to Karakorum and make the reunification official. They would install him as undisputed Great Khan under the sacred *sulde* of Genghis. *Just like Mandukhai promised*, he thought.

Absently, he wrapped the white belt around his fingers—the white representing his purity. It felt like a noose around his neck instead of a belt around his waist.

He closed his eyes and pressed his lips together. The memory of that kiss lingered fresh, as if he could still feel her lips against his. It haunted his sleep when he managed to get it. The kiss had ignited something deep inside, a longing far stronger than anything he had ever experienced. Pulling away from her was the hardest thing he had ever done. But it was the right thing.

Was it the right thing? he wondered as he opened his eyes. He had given her space, freedom, and time. He had expected it would be at least a couple of weeks, but as a month passed, she still had not come. Each day he worried he had made a grave mistake. *Forty-six days. What if she realized she doesn't want me? What if this time has given her perspective and she will never come to my door? How long do I wait before I accept the inevitable and move on?*

Dayan had been so certain there had been something in that kiss. But with each day that passed, he doubted himself. What did he know? He had kissed no one before. For all he knew, it was normal, or friendly.

Each breath became a struggle. Dayan fumbled with the belts around his waist to loosen them, but his fingers felt numb. His skin tingled. He blinked furiously as dark specks floated in his vision.

Mandukhai waited in the gathering tent for Soke to join her. It had been weeks since Unebolod's death, and no one had taken control of the Khorchin or come forward to make any claim. It filled her with so much sadness that the line of Khasar had died with him. *If only he had listened to me and had children*, she thought, folding her hands in her lap. She had saved the line of Genghis while killing the line of Khasar. The guilt sometimes buried her, amplified by the certainty that—if given another chance—she would not have changed anything.

The line of Genghis still hung on the precipice. Unless Dayan had sons, both lines could still die. This knowledge had brought her toward Dayan's ger earlier in the day. She had struggled to summon the courage to knock on Dayan's door, to talk about the offer he had made her. But fear had frozen her. Had it been too long already? For the first week, she had noticed him lingering near his door any time she passed. He no longer waited.

Instead of knocking on Dayan's door, as she should have done, Mandukhai had headed into the gathering tent to deal with the Khorchin lack of leadership. A few Lords made suitable candidates, but Soke clearly stood out above the rest. Unebolod had trusted Soke for years, and Soke had been loyal and wise. She respected him and he respected her. He deserved this.

The gathering tent door opened. Altan marched in and strode straight toward the dais, stopping at the base. Something about the set of Altan's jaw made Mandukhai nervous. Altan folded her hands together in front of her, anxiously rubbing her fingers over her skin. "Can we talk?"

Curiosity stirred Mandukhai's interest. She had never seen Altan so anxious before. "Of course. What's wrong, Altan?"

The other woman parted her lips, but her words died before spilling out. Instead, Altan released a soft, shaky breath. "I ... my ..." She huffed. "This should not be so hard to admit."

Mandukhai's stomach twisted in knots. Had Altan betrayed her? She respected Altan more than most women—and most men, if Mandukhai was honest. Putting Altan to death for treason would not help her already stressful list of to-dos. "You are making me nervous."

Before Altan could respond, Soke entered, striding toward the dais where he dropped to a knee. "Khatun, you summoned me?"

"Yes, Soke. You can stand." Mandukhai's gaze remained fixed on Altan as the other woman stepped aside to make space for Soke. He rose and clasped his hands behind his back, chin held high. "Altan, do we need to continue this alone?"

Altan glanced at Soke, chewing her lip like a dog chewed a bone. When he met her gaze, she quickly looked away and nodded.

"Very well. This should only take a moment." Mandukhai returned her attention to Soke.

He was roughly the same age as Unebolod, but the devastation the Khorchin suffered over the years wore on him. Gray had wormed its way into his hair at the temples and flecked his beard.

"How have you been, Soke?" she asked, leaning closer and doing her best to show sympathy. "I know you and Unebolod were very close, and I'm afraid I have neglected you since his death." She no longer flinched when she spoke of Unebolod's death aloud, but it still made her heart twist. How long before that pain diminished? Would it ever?

"You and the Khan have been very busy, my Khatun," Soke said evenly, but the corners of his mouth dipped downward.

Altan shuffled, watching the exchange like a curious fox.

"I am so sorry, Soke," Mandukhai said sincerely. "You must hurt as much as the rest of us, if not more, since his death has left the Khorchin without a khan."

Soke cocked his head at this. "We have a Khan."

"You have a Great Khan, but you do not have a tribal khan," Mandukhai corrected. "I need to remedy this."

Soke squared his shoulders. "Mandukhai, I do not think you understand. Unebolod clearly followed you and Dayan Khan. I believe he even told you at one time the Khorchin are not his people, but yours. We have a Khan."

Mandukhai's heart ached. Unebolod had spoken those words, but they had been for her alone. Had Unebolod told Soke the same? How many other Khorchin Lords had he told? *That must be why they have not made a grab for power*, she realized. Tears welled in her eyes. Unebolod had believed in her so faithfully that he had abdicated his own title forever.

"The noble line of Khasar has died, though," Mandukhai said, then winced when she saw the pain on Soke's face. "He stubbornly refused to marry and produced no heirs. Even if you no longer want a khan, you still need a leader."

Altan clicked her tongue and cleared her throat, drawing their eyes toward her.

"What?" Mandukhai snapped.

Altan swallowed and licked her lips. Mandukhai had never seen this woman anxious before. "That ... is not entirely true."

Shock hammered against Mandukhai's chest. What part of her statement had not been true?

Soke mirrored Mandukhai's alarm, which offered her some relief. At least she was not the only one who did not understand.

"I can ..." Altan edged close to Soke. "This is why I came. Can ... Can I show you?"

Without thinking, Mandukhai and Soke followed Altan out of the gathering tent.

Dayan closed his eyes and focused on clearing his mind as Goram had taught him. The Great Fist had a firm hold on him, and Dayan struggled for every breath. *Perhaps I have just accepted the inevitable truth. Nothing I do will ever be good enough for her.*

Regardless of the uncertainty around what Mandukhai wanted from him intimately, he had no doubts what she wanted from him otherwise. Dayan had been promised to the people to become the Whole Khan. Once this campaign ended, he finally would fulfill that promise. *But does it mean anything to me without her?*

Doubts swirled around his mind. Dayan could grasp none of them firmly enough to reason them out. The black spots in his vision swelled. His vision narrowed dangerously. No matter how hard he tried, he could not pull in a breath.

Dayan pushed away from the *uni* pole, trying to reach the chest where he kept the herbs. But his body had grown intensely weak. The Great Fist tightened around his heart and lungs until he could no longer breathe at all. His hand trembled violently as he tugged at the collar of his deel to rip it open, but he was too weak to do much more than loosen it from his neck. As he feebly fumbled with the neck of his deel, his feet tripped over each other and he stumbled forward.

By the time Dayan realized he was falling, it was too late to catch himself. Pain lanced around his skull.

Then nothing.

Mandukhai moved as if in a haze through the camp. Soke said nothing as he walked beside her. The two of them followed Altan past clusters of gers, playing children, warriors fletching arrows. Everyone in camp prepared for the coming fight. Mandukhai hardly noticed as she glided along.

Altan stuck her head in her ger, then stepped away from her home and scanned the surrounding area.

Mandukhai followed her gaze, wondering what was happening. The woman had not said another word to either of them as they crossed the camp. She had not bothered to explain herself further.

At last, Altan's stare settled on something. Mandukhai once more followed her gaze and saw Altan's husband teaching their sons how to use knives. Even children would defend the home. Mandukhai sincerely hoped it never came to that.

Altan pushed out an anxious breath. "I hope you can find it in your heart to forgive me," she said, and her voice trembled. What was Altan so worried about?

Soke's brows pulled together as if calculating something, then he gasped and shot a wide-eyed look of alarm in Altan's direction. "That winter when we came to your camp searching for the *sulde* of Genghis ..."

Altan's eyes flicked nervously to Mandukhai, and she paled considerably as she nodded.

"Did he have any idea?" Soke asked.

Mandukhai frowned, hating how she felt outside of the conversation. What were they talking about?

"No. He had a lot of allies, but also a lot of enemies. I worried about what would happen to Bagasun if anyone learned the truth." Once more, Altan's gaze flicked nervously to Mandukhai.

Mandukhai attempted putting the pieces together, but her mind refused to accept the truth. A deep despair sank in her gut and her gaze locked on nine-year-old Bagasun. The boy focused hard on his target, biting his tongue and shuffling his feet before striking out with lightning-quick reflexes. Focus, strike, shuffle back. Repeatedly. His knife carved up his target, hitting a critical mark each time. Mandukhai's heart clenched in her chest. Her breaths came in brief gasps. Tears welled in her eyes.

Soke and Altan continued their hushed conversation, but Mandukhai heard none of it. She took half a step toward the boy, then froze. At that same moment, Bagasun lowered his knife, squared his skinny shoulders, raised his chin proudly, and adopted a stony warrior's mask.

Mandukhai saw the truth so clearly her knees nearly gave out. She battled to rein in her spinning mind, brushing the tears from her eyes. All those years, she had longed to give Unebolod a son. And now, watching Bagasun, seeing that stony face, there was no doubt who his father was.

"Mandukhai?" Altan's voice trembled as she edged closer.

Unebolod had a son and never knew.

Something else occurred to Mandukhai. The timing.

"You said Bagasun was early, only a week old when you joined me against the Oirat," Mandukhai said, loathing how much her own voice trembled. "If he ... If his father ..." Mandukhai couldn't force the words past her lips, as if using her own voice to call Unebolod Bagasun's father made it any more real than it already was. "That would have been right after he left Mount Burkhan Khaldun."

Altan bit her lip, hugging her arms over her chest like a shield. "I would apologize, but I am not sorry about Bagasun. He is strong, so much like his father."

Mandukhai had a thousand questions, but she could form none of them cohesively. Instead, she stared at the boy.

"Does your husband know?" Soke asked.

"He does ..." Altan's explanation continued, but Mandukhai heard none of it.

All these years, Mandukhai had wanted a child. Now, at thirty-three, her child-bearing days were near an end. She had promised the spirits children, and they had promised it to her as well. Or Genghis had. How desperately she wanted a child. All she wanted was someone to want her the way Unebolod had. Dayan had given her the freedom to have that too late.

A memory from two years ago rushed to the surface, as if her mind forced her to recognize what she had refused to see all along.

Dayan took Mandukhai's hand in his own, sliding his thumb over her skin. "If we are going to die, I can think of no better way to go." He pressed a finger to her lips, silencing her protest. His eyes burned into her very soul.

Mandukhai pressed her hand to her mouth. She had not been waiting for Dayan to be ready. He had been waiting for her. But one thing had always been between them. Unebolod. Mandukhai had pulled away from Dayan because she had hoped she could be with Unebolod. Now she held back because she was bitter that she couldn't. Everything she had ever wanted had been right in front of her all along.

A shaky breath rolled from her lips as she gazed toward Dayan's ger. Not that she could see it from so far away.

"Bagasun has all rights afforded him by his father," she told Altan absently, turning away from them.

Without thinking, her feet carried her away.

"Mandukhai where are you going?" Soke called.

She ignored him, holding the skirt of her deel as she rushed toward Dayan's ger on the other side of camp. People darted out of her way.

I've made a horrible mistake, Dayan. I'm sorry.

As she drew closer to the section of camp where their gers rested beside each other, a flurry of shouts filled the air. Mandukhai drew up short as she noticed a cluster of men wearing the black armor of the Khan's Guard shuffling around his door.

Boke's voice bellowed out orders from inside Dayan's ger. "Find the shaman Khosoichi, now!"

Mandukhai's heart plummeted. "Dayan?" she whimpered, edging closer. Then Mandukhai broke into a sprint. "Dayan!"

Without hesitation, Mandukhai shoved through the growing crowd and ran into Dayan's ger. A red pool of blood dripped from Dayan's storage chest onto the floor, soaking into the rugs. Boke adjusted a pillow under Dayan's head as more blood seeped from a gash across Dayan's hair line.

Mandukhai launched into action, her heart beating erratically in her chest. She ripped a strip of cloth, the first cloth she got her hands on from a stack Ong had left beside the door, and pressed it against the wound. Then she seized Boke's hand and pressed it over the cloth. "Keep pressure on it."

She threw open drawers and chests, scavenging for silver. Dayan's servant, Ong, had already set a bucket of water on the stove and now stoked the fire to life.

The rest of the Khan's Guard edged back out the door.

"What in the name of Tengri happened?" Mandukhai snapped. Tears flowed freely down her face.

"I don't know," Boke said, shame pouring from every word. "He was alone. We heard a crash, and when I opened the door, he was unconscious on the floor. I think he hit his head on the chest, but I don't know why he fell. I have men investigating for foul play, but I don't think anyone else was with him."

Mandukhai fished silver balm out of a drawer. Boke kneeled beside the bed, pressing the cloth against the wound with both hands, focusing intently on his task as if blinking would cost Dayan his life.

Khosoichi rushed into the ger and nudged Boke out of the way. The shaman peeled open Dayan's deel and pressed his ear to Dayan's chest. Mandukhai blinked in alarm at the number of scars on Dayan's chest. When had he earned those?

If Dayan died from this wound, would her oath at the Shrine of the First Queen ten years ago bind her next to Unebolod's son? Tears blurred the edges of her vision. Would she be forever cursed to repeat the same cycle over and over?

It seemed hours had passed before Khosoichi finally stepped back and washed his hands off in the bucket of water, now cooling on the floor beside Mandukhai's feet. She had done her best to assist Khosoichi as calmly as possible, despite the tears that had never stopped streaming down her face.

"Will he ...?" Mandukhai's voice trailed off, unable to finish that question.

Khosoichi frowned. "We have done all we can for him. Only time will tell. Let him rest, my Khatun. He lost a lot of blood. If he wakes, he will live."

Mandukhai sniffled and scrubbed her sleeve across her face to attempt pulling herself together. It was a lame, worthless effort.

Khosoichi gave a final prayer to the High Heavens, then ducked out the door and closed it behind him.

Dayan lay on the bed, his chest still bare. Bandages were bound around his head to keep pressure on the wound Khosoichi had attempted stitching closed with a thread of silk. They had packed it with as much silver balm as they could before bandaging it. The color had drained from Dayan's skin, and his usual youthful glow was gone. The ashen color reminded her of his youth when he first came to her and nearly died of pneumonia.

She could not lose him. He could not die like this. Genghis had promised her a litter of Borjigin children! *But that was years ago. I have waited too long.* Earlier, she had thought the line of Khasar had died and the line of Genghis lived. But the line of Khasar had survived. Would the line of Genghis die instead?

Mandukhai climbed onto the bed and curled up against Dayan's side, watching the rise and fall of his chest, careful to avoid harming him further. She rested her head on his shoulder and placed her hand over his heart. It still thumped in his chest.

Please don't leave me, she prayed, then pressed a tender kiss to his temple.

CHAPTER THIRTY-NINE

A Whispered Plea

On any normal day, Esige would hate having her hair done up like a princess—she much preferred braids—but today the spring air felt more like summer heat. With her hair off her neck, she could feel the cool breeze that blew beneath the canopy.

Huoshai, Legusi, and Arqai argued in hushed voices, constantly glancing over their shoulders as if they expected an ambush. For weeks, Esige and Huoshai had worked as a flawless unit, sharing the same story about how Esige felt betrayed by Dayan and Mandukhai. While most of the Ordos men, like Lord Sayiqan, had bought her story, what scared Esige most was that she began to believe it.

They *had* betrayed her. They had betrayed Unebolod. He had believed Mandukhai would choose him years ago—as had Esige. He had believed Mandukhai wanted the same thing as him—as had Esige. But Dayan had destroyed all that Esige had wanted just by not dying when he should have. Esige loved Mandukhai absolutely, no matter what, but that did not mean she did not live with bitterness in her heart about how matters had turned out.

Arqai once more voiced his discontent with any plan to entrap Mogurkei.

Houshai gritted his teeth, the lines around his mouth tightening. He looked ready to pull out his hair.

"Arqai, I think you forget why you are here," Esige said, drawing all eyes to her.

After meeting her gaze only briefly, Arqai redirected it toward the ground. Ever since he had watched her reaction to receiving Bigirsen's head, he had not leered at her quite as openly. He seemed more afraid of her. Esige appreciated this change immensely. Was this what Mandukhai felt like when the men deferred to her so quickly?

"You are here to strengthen our story and validate our new stance in opposition with the Khan," Esige said, adopting a haughty tone she certainly hoped came across clearly. "Huoshai and I are in charge of this mission. Legusi is here to provide council. You only have to nod and agree with our story. Your job really is not so difficult. I don't see why this is a struggle."

Arqai crossed his arms as he spoke, but looked anywhere but directly at her. "I know Mogurkei very well. He might be hot-headed and cocky, but he isn't a fool."

"His messages seem to indicate otherwise." Esige motioned to the newest one in Legusi's hand.

Unlike Arqai, who constantly chaffed at Esige's nerves, Legusi had been perfectly calm, patient, and often eager to help get this mission completed. When Arqai lost his temper, Legusi smoothed it out with just a few calm words and natural confidence. He made a good khan, even if he didn't see it.

Legusi cleared his throat and offered Esige a small nod of deference, which she also appreciated. "Lady Esige, he will expect a response soon. The longer we delay, the more suspicious Mogurkei will become."

"What are the chances this is a trap?" Huoshai asked.

Legusi sighed, glancing at the message in his hand. Esige watched as his dark eyes scanned the page. Legusi was a handsome man, she supposed, and only a couple of years older than her. He had become khan of the Ordos tribes far too young, but since he took over, the Ordos had both thrived and suffered. The red salt lake massacre happened under his reign. She knew it weighed heavily on his shoulders.

"Mogurkei wouldn't bother trapping us," Arqai said. "If he wanted us gone, we would already be under attack."

Esige shot a dirty look at Arqai.

"I didn't ask you," Huoshai snapped.

"I'm not certain he is wrong, though," Legusi replied.

Esige almost groaned at the way this made Arqai's face shift into a cocky smirk, directed at Huoshai and not her, of course.

"Mogurkei is a man who is never satisfied with what he has," Legusi continued, ignoring the way Huoshai and Arqai glared at one another. "He has control of Ulum's men. We know that for sure now. But that will have given him a taste of power and he will want more. He is arrogant enough to challenge me for it."

Esige tapped her nails on the wooden arm of her carved chair. If Mogurkei thought he could take power from Legusi and rule the Ordos as khan instead, that gave them a unique opportunity.

"Good," she said.

Legusi's jaw slackened as he gaped at her. Even Huoshai's brows knitted together in confusion.

Esige stood and glided toward the three of them. "We will send our response to Mogurkei offering to discuss the condition of the Ordos. You, Legusi, will use your power as khan to challenge him. Let him know that, if he wants to be Ordos khan, he can meet you and prove his superiority."

"What—?" Legusi choked. His hand trembled as he pulled the message from Mogurkei tight against his chest.

"Esige, that's a terrible idea." The words rushed from Huoshai's mouth.

Arqai raised his brows, appearing impressed. "No, it isn't."

She hated that he was the one to agree to this plan. "We will ride to his camp to meet him. He can challenge Legusi for control of the Ordos, but it won't matter. Because we will set the day. We will make the terms. And we will send his location to Mandukhai so that when that day comes, we will all be there to close in on him when he least expects it."

Silence settled. A warm breeze blew through the open space. Somewhere nearby, finches sang a song to one another.

"If I lose ..." Legusi shifted feet. His gaze darted between the three of them anxiously. While he was a good khan, Legusi had gained a reputation as a coward. He had spent his entire khanship bending to the will of stronger men.

"You won't lose," Esige reassured him. "You won't even fight him. We will sweep in and finish him before it comes to that." She swayed toward Legusi, placing a hand on his arm. His muscles twitched under her palm. "If you want to prove your dedication to the Great Khan and his budding empire, this is your chance. Do this. Help us trap and kill Mogurkei, and I will personally speak with Dayan and Mandukhai about your future in their empire."

Legusi swallowed, then gave a stiff nod.

"Good." Esige smiled, then gave Legusi's arm a reassuring squeeze. "Let's send our response then. Two weeks. That will give Mandukhai time to move her forces into place."

Nightmares plagued Togochi's sleep. His hands burned hot, covered in thick blood all the way to his elbows. A beating heart in his palm. Issama sneering at him. *I killed all of your friends*, Issama taunted, mocking him. *That is not my heart, but your own.*

Togochi woke with a start, scrubbing his hands over his arms to clean off the blood. His heart hammered dangerously fast. *I need to wash my hands*, he thought, pushing himself toward the door of the ger.

His men had stopped at another yam station on the way back to the Ordos basin the night before. It was one of the few places with a stream to water the horses.

Togochi was not alone in the ger. Every night, Siker, Qolotai, and the two boys slept near him. He often slept fitfully, afraid of waking with Siker's knife if his heart. Not that she had a knife. His men had taken her weapons.

Having Issama's family so close to him at all times did nothing to help ease Togochi's discomfort. Siker dug in her heels indignantly at every opportunity. Whether it was mounting, guiding her mount, eating, dismounting, or sleeping. She refused to cooperate until he or his men used force.

At the edge of the stream, Togochi watched his breath curl up into the sky as he steadied his breathing. Then he held it and plunged his hands into the cold water. Nights were so cold and days so hot. He could not wait until Mandukhai and Dayan finished their mission in the south and returned to the north, where the weather was more predictable.

A whisper of boots drew his attention to his left.

Qolotai kneeled beside him, watching him with intense interest as he scrubbed at his arms in the icy stream.

"Have you dirtied your arms, my Lord?" she asked. Qolotai's voice was so small compared to Siker. "I could help you clean."

Togochi broke his gaze away and pulled his arms from the water. The chilly night air instantly froze them. He began rubbing them with the sleeves of his deel. Qolotai reached toward him with a long strip of cloth. He flinched away for a moment before realizing her intentions were innocent. She used the cloth to rub down his arms, sending heat back into them.

Togochi watched her work warily. Qolotai said nothing as she warmed his arms and hands.

"Why are you helping me?" he asked. "After what I did, I would expect you to drive a knife in my chest."

"Why?" Qolotai asked. The earnestness of her confusion stunned Togochi.

He fumbled for a moment, unsure how to answer. Was she dim-witted? "Issama was your husband."

Qolotai flinched. She finished wrapping the cloth around his hands to keep them warm. As she did, he noted the tears welling in her eyes.

"I'm sorry," he mumbled.

"I didn't choose him," she whispered. Qolotai sank back and stared across the stream, but her gaze was more distant, as if looking into her own memories. "He ... was bored. I was in the wrong place at the right time." She sniffled and wiped away a few rogue tears. "My father didn't protest at all. He said it was a big step up for the family. But Issama was never a good man. Everything he touched turned to ash." At this, Qolotai sobbed, pressing her face into her trembling hands.

This turn of events bewildered Togochi too much to know how to react at first. Issama had taken this girl simply to entertain himself.

"I'm sorry," he murmured.

An awkwardness settled over him as she continued weeping into her hands. He fidgeted with the cloth wrapped around his hands, examining this strange creature beside him. She couldn't be older than twenty-five. How young was she when Issama claimed her? Togochi's stomach churned.

As he watched her cry, he noticed her belt was missing. He frowned, then looked down at his cloth-wrapped hands. She had taken it off to help him. *Why did I not think of that myself?* he wondered.

Togochi unwrapped the cloth from his warming hands, then leaned toward her to tie it back around her waist. Qolotai mistook his movement for comfort and leaned against him. She pressed her face against his shoulder. Togochi froze once more, arms falling limp at his sides.

"What will happen to us?" she asked, her voice thick with tears. "She is the Khan's mother. I am nothing. I am no one. What will happen to *me*?"

Togochi's heart thudded. What *would* happen to her? He did not know. That would be up to Dayan and Mandukhai. Perhaps they would see some unknown value in keeping her around. Maybe she would make a wife for one of their men. Or, also possibly, she would be viewed as an extra with no value. Maybe that coupled with her relationship to Issama would be enough to condemn her.

His lack of response did nothing to comfort her.

"I would like to die here," she whispered against his chest.

Is she asking me to kill her? I can't. I won't. None of this was her fault. If Issama stole her away and forced her into this life, her only crime was staying with him ... and where else would she have gone?

"It will be fine," Togochi reassured her. He folded his arms around her and rubbed at her back. "I will talk to the Khan and Khatun. They are good people."

"Thank you," she murmured. "I have always admired the Khatun. I tried to help her, years ago, by bringing the *sulde* to Lord Unebolod's men. Issama had it hidden in a cart. But the Ming ... I went back for my daughter ..." A sob caught in her throat.

For a minute, they remained there as she collected herself. Qolotai was the one who had given the *sulde* to Unebolod's men? He remembered Unebolod once telling him of a woman who had helped. She brought them the banner then went back for her daughter. *She wanted to leave Issama years ago*, Togochi realized.

When Togochi attempted withdrawing, Qolotai once more mistook his motives. As they pulled apart, she gazed up at him through her long lashes. The moment he realized what would happen, it was too late. Qolotai pressed a desperate kiss to his lips. At first, he was too stunned and forgot himself. He grabbed her shoulders and edged her away.

"Qolotai, I have two wives waiting for me," he said as gently as he could.

"I have heard stories about you," she said. "If I had a choice, I would much rather be with a man like you than be forced to be with another man like Issama. Please."

Togochi shook his head and stood. He ran his hand along the side of his head anxiously. "Look, Qolotai, you are a beautiful woman, and still very young. I'm sure you can find someone."

She sprang to her feet and took his hand before he could draw it back. "Why do you deny me, then?"

Togochi took a step back as far as he could with her clinging to his hand. "Because my wives are as much a part of this decision as I am. And I won't make it without them."

"Then I will talk to them when we get there!"

How had this gone so far off course? Togochi shook his head, but he had nothing more to say. What could he say? Qolotai was beautiful, by his own admission, and she was willing to talk to Jaghan and Geriel—whom he could not imagine accepting this—and this left him with no real argument any longer.

Togochi huffed. "Fine. Talk to them. But this," he jerked his hand out of hers, "doesn't happen without the blessing of both of my wives and the Khan."

Qolotai paled, but she nodded.

"And if any of them refuse, I won't hear another word of it," he finished. "Understood?"

Again, she nodded.

Togochi started back toward the ger, then paused and glanced back at her. "You shouldn't be out here alone in the dark. Come back to the ger."

She rushed to catch up and match his stride.

Somehow, Togochi knew he had just made a serious mistake.

Mandukhai's sleep had been fitful throughout the night. She often jarred awake at the slightest movement or change. More than once, she had startled awake, convinced that Dayan's heart had stopped beating. By morning, his breathing had become more regular. Mandukhai had lain beside him for far too long, watching the slow, even rise and fall of his chest. More than anything, she wanted him to wake. She would give up everything just to have him give her that soul-piercing stare again.

Duty could not wait any longer. Activity outside the ger increased. Mandukhai heard men talking, though she could not make out most of what they had said. It seemed the camp carried on with business as usual. Something she would have to do as well.

Mandukhai carefully withdrew from Dayan's bed so she didn't jar him too much. Her hip ached from sleeping on it all night, and her shoulder throbbed. She stretched out her limbs before slipping on her boots and giving Dayan one last glance. Then Mandukhai stepped outside.

Boke paced outside the door. The moment she stepped out, he froze, gazing at her hopefully. She could only offer him a weak smile and shake her head. His shoulder sagged. Boke would take this injury personally. Dayan had been under his watch when it happened. Boke likely assumed they would punish him for failing to protect the Khan. Not that there was anything he could have done to prevent it. This was an accident. She would get more details once Dayan woke. And he would wake. He had to.

Mandukhai eased the door closed, then marched toward Boke and placed her hand on his arm. "He is still alive, Boke, and at the moment that is all that matters. Khosoichi said it may be a while before he wakes with how much blood he lost."

"My lady Khatun, if he does not survive—"

"He will."

"But if he doesn't—"

"He will," she insisted. Mandukhai would not have a good man like Boke forfeit his life, even if it was custom. There were few men she could trust wholly. Boke was among that select group.

Boke's jaw twitched, then he nodded tightly. The dark rings around his eyes spoke volumes about how his night had gone as well.

"Get rest. Dayan isn't going anywhere today. But he will need you rested and ready soon enough."

For a moment, as Boke gazed at the closed door, Mandukhai expected him to resist. A few seconds later, Boke nodded. "Please come wake me if anything changes."

"Of course."

With that said, Boke turned and trudged away.

Mandukhai ran her fingers through her hair, pulling it over her shoulder. Then she set back her shoulders and walked to the gathering tent.

The copper pots burned away the cool spring morning air inside the gathering tent. Mandukhai was thankful for the heat. She had not realized how cold her skin had grown during the short walk until she felt the warmth of the fires permeate her skin.

Soke, Altan, Nemeku, Orghana, and Jaghan waited near the dais. All five of them watched Mandukhai approach. Each wore a different mask of worry. Mandukhai knew this moment was critical. She had to show confidence for them even if she felt none herself.

"How is the Khan?" Soke asked the moment Mandukhai took her seat.

"Resting," Mandukhai replied.

The news sent a ripple of relief through all five.

"Down to business then?" Altan asked, not sparing another moment to worry over something they could not control. Once more, Mandukhai admired her fortitude.

"Yes. We need to reassess our plan." Mandukhai settled in her seat. "Have we received word from Esige or Huoshai yet?"

"No," Soke said. "But the scouts have returned and confirmed that the passes Legusi marked out for us are safe to travel."

"Any word from Belku or Kelegei yet?" she asked, setting into her seat on the dais.

"Kelegei is on his way back with the support of both Utagachi and Aglaqu," Altan said. "I suggest we divert them along one of the scouted passes."

Mandukhai considered Altan's suggestion and nodded. It was a good plan. "How many men do Utagachi and Aglaqu bring to us?"

"Ten thousand," Soke said.

Mandukhai raised her brows. "Each?"

"Total."

She deflated. Ten thousand was not nearly enough to change their fortunes yet.

"Do we have any idea what has happened to Ulum's men?" she asked. "The Khan swept up nearly two *tumens* of Ordos warriors on his previous campaign. They cannot have disappeared."

"I received a message from Lord Asha while you were tending to the Khan last night," Soke continued. "Asha has captured some Ordos who fled to Hami looking for Issama. He is holding them for your judgment."

Mandukhai knew Asha could not hold the men for long. "How many?"

"Just shy of two *mingghans*."

Altan snorted. "That's hardly even a dent in their numbers."

Soke nodded. "Some of Ulum's men probably turned to other Ordos Lords when Ulum died, which means we could still end up with the traitors in our midst when the dust settles."

Mandukhai did not appreciate this news. Those Ordos warriors had already turned against Dayan once. How could she trust they would not propagate discord among other Ordos tribes?

"Do we know who they have gone to?" she asked.

Soke shook his head. "Not all of them. But if Ulum and Mogurkei were conspiring together against the Khan, we should assume those men have defected to Mogurkei. That's at least a full *tumen* joining his ranks. If not more."

Mandukhai considered the numbers. It was hardly encouraging, but if Huoshai and Esige succeeded in their mission, she would have superior numbers and the element of surprise.

"Any word from Togochi?" she asked, glancing at Jaghan as the woman fidgeted with her rings.

"None," Soke said. "But his men likely could travel almost as fast as a messenger. He should be back soon."

Until she heard from Esige and Togochi, Mandukhai was blind to the path forward. Was Issama dead? Would Mogurkei fall into a trap? Or had their plans unknowingly come unraveled?

Mandukhai thanked them, then returned to Dayan's ger. When she arrived, Khosoichi kneeled beside the bed, checking the bandage and administering fresh herbs to ward off evil spirits.

As she approached, Khosoichi glanced at her over his shoulder.

"Any change?" she asked.

"He still sleeps, but his wound seems to be improving with no signs of infection," Khosoichi said. "If he recovers, it might take some time before he is himself again. We cannot know until he wakes. Head wounds can be hard to treat. But you should know, if he doesn't wake soon, he may not wake at all."

The news stabbed her heart. "Thank you, Khosoichi."

He bowed his head, then made his way to the door.

Once they were alone, Mandukhai sat on the edge of the bed, brushing dark strands of hair away from Dayan's face as they curled around the bandage. In sleep, the worries of the world washed off his hard face, restoring him to peace. She was not sure she could handle losing him when she only just realized how deep her feelings ran. *He has to wake up.*

For the first time, Mandukhai examined the scars on his chest, shoulders, and arms. He did not have nearly as many as Unebolod had, but they were all fairly new. His muscles had become more defined, probably from months of riding and fighting. Dayan had said little to her about what happened while they were hunting Bigirsen. Or perhaps she had not given him a reason to confide in her. *Have I distanced myself so much from him?* It was no wonder he often appeared pained around her. Each of those scars had been hard-earned, no doubt. What scars had she left on his heart that she could not see? *Nemeku was right. I have spent too long coddling him like a child. It's time I treat him like a man.*

Mandukhai took Dayan's hand in her own, cradling it with great affection. His skin was cold, his palm calloused. She turned his hand over and traced her finger along the callouses created by firing his bow and using his sword. Dayan had not been a boy for some time. She had just refused to see it.

"I don't know if you can hear me," she whispered. She wanted to speak, but didn't want to wake him if he needed more rest. "But I need you to come back to me, Dayan." Her thumb stroked his palm. "You were right. I loved Unebolod. I still do. And if I'm being honest, I don't think I will ever stop loving him. But that does not mean you are second in my heart. I made you wait because I didn't think you were ready. But I was not ready either." A lump swelled in her throat. She struggled to swallow it down. "I was scared. Of hurting him. Of disappointing you. Of rejection. Now, I'm scared I have waited too long."

Mandukhai leaned forward and kissed his forehead. "I *do* love you, Dayan. I need you."

Dayan didn't even twitch.

Mandukhai leaned closer and carefully rested her head against his chest. For several minutes, she lay close to him, listening to his heartbeat.

Dayan stood at the peak of Mount Burkhan Khaldun, the hat of the world. The whole of the Mongol empire spread out below like a vast map. He remembered this dream. He had had this same dream before riding into battle against Bigirsen.

Banners fluttered in the wind. Multicolored pennants bearing the crests of a dozen various tribes. He identified each: Chakhar, Ongud, Urainkhai, Khorchin, Ordos, Oirat, and more. Every Mongol banner—except the Uyghur. Drums beat somewhere in the distance and echoed off the mountains like thunder. Hundreds of thousands of horses raced across the Mongol steppe, riderless and free. Armies ebbed and flowed in mesmerizing patterns from everywhere, all converging in one place.

Karakorum.

A monolith towered from the south, surrounded by stones and blue flags. Dayan remembered this from the other vision. The name he could not read, chiseled into stone. Now, it stood out as boldly as if lit by the sun itself. *Unebolod Noyan.*

Dayan reached toward the Eternal Blue Sky as if he expected to touch it. Just as before, the wolf-head sword of Genghis appeared in his hand, pointed at the cloudless sky. All colors of banner merged, becoming one: a blue banner as light as the sky above his head, bearing the crest of Genghis. Dayan's heart pounded with excitement as all tribes became one. This was the promise Genghis had made Mandukhai. Was this dream an omen of what was to come, or a warning that it hung on the tip of an arrowhead?

"I need you to come back to me ..." Mandukhai's voice came from the air around him. His heart skipped.

He swept his gaze across the map, searching for her among the masses of bodies below.

"I fear I have waited too long," she said. He could hear her clearly, but not see her anywhere. "I *do* love you, Dayan. I need you ..."

I need you, too, he thought, wishing he could find her among the horde, pull her to him, hold her and never again let go.

Dayan leaped down from the mountain in a bound, determined to find her. *I am coming back to you.*

CHAPTER FORTY

Facing Rejection

Mandukhai could not remember a day that had passed so slowly in her entire life. Only this morning, she had met with Soke and the others. Yet each hour that passed dragged on forever as she incessantly checked on Dayan.

None of Khosoichi's reassurances that the Khan was recovering had offered Mandukhai any consolation. The wound was clean and healing. Dayan's color slowly returned. That Khosoichi warned her Dayan had likely suffered a concussion in the fall had not helped matters. It would not be long before they had to ride. Would he be healthy enough? An unconscious Khan could lose the support of his men. How long before the Mongols following Dayan Khan decided he was too weak?

Mandukhai spent as much time as she dared in the ger with Dayan, but the responsibilities of running an empire did not wait. If they didn't hear from Huoshai soon, and if Dayan didn't wake, this entire endeavor was in jeopardy. *And what had happened to Togochi? Shouldn't he be back by now?*

Mandukhai glanced at Dayan as she paced his rugs. A sense of dread swelled in her gut. Instinct told her to postpone moving her men, to call this entire plan to a halt. They had spent months toiling over the original strategy, with the brilliant mind of Unebolod and help of Togochi. Now she had neither, and even Dayan was unconscious and could not offer his own insight. The plans had changed, and she could not wrap her mind around how to proceed in this state of worry.

Boke opened the door and reported Soke waiting outside. Mandukhai smoothed her hands over the skirt of her silk deel and stepped outside.

Soke straightened as she appeared, clutching a paper in his hand. "My Khatun," Soke said. "How is he?"

"The same." She bit her lip. "I'm worried that this will not work, Soke. I'm not sure we can pull off this plan to trap Mogurkei. Every instinct in me is screaming out against this. When have my instincts been wrong?"

Soke stepped closer and gave her arm a reassuring squeeze. "It will work. Your men have been crawling the hills around Legusi's paths for days. Our way forward remains clear. At some point, you will have to trust my abilities. I may not be Unebolod, but I learned a lot from him. Which is exactly why I am standing here now instead of anyone else. Besides, we have word from Huoshai and Esige."

He held the paper out to her. "They have sent us their plan." He grinned.

"What? Why didn't you start with that news?" She accepted the message, skimming it as Soke broke it down in simple terms.

"It's good, Mandukhai," Soke said, sounding impressed. "Mogurkei is angling for Legusi's control over the Ordos. Legusi sent him a challenge. The two will meet near Mogurkei's base camp to resolve the dispute. Then we close in on him when he is exposed and finish him. Huoshai has drawn up a plan."

Mandukhai noted the detailed markings showing where the bulk of Mogurkei's forces camped, what hills provided hidden passage for Mandukhai's forces, and where everyone could close around Mogurkei. As Legusi drew Mogurkei out to challenge him, Mandukhai and Dayan were to ride in and take control of his forces.

"Eight days!" Mandukhai exclaimed when she noted the date Huoshai included in the plans. "Do we have enough time to get all of our warriors into position? Some of them will have to swing wide to close in on the south."

"If we send word to the Three Guards leaders now, yes," Soke said. "They will reach the southern passage here—" He stepped closer and pointed at the map. "—just in time for the trap to close. We have two days to prepare here before we need to ride." Again, he pointed out the three positions of entry Huoshai had marked out. "We can easily get our men into these positions by dawn that day. It will be hard riding, but we can manage as long as we leave the families in our camp here and only take what we need."

"What if Togochi doesn't return on time?" she asked.

Soke stepped back and smirked. "A scout returned just a few minutes ago and reported spotting Togochi's men approaching with a small caravan of prisoners. The Khan's mother among them."

At last, some luck! Mandukhai had worried Togochi had died. Now, it seemed, he would be back before they confronted Mogurkei. Then another terrifying thought struck her.

"What if Dayan doesn't wake in time?" she asked, keeping her voice low and glancing around anxiously to be sure no one else had heard.

"There is only one way this can end, Mandukhai, and we are at that critical moment. There is no going back. We don't need the Khan there to finish Mogurkei. We only need the banners to—"

Soke's gaze slid past her. He jerked back, bowing.

Mandukhai frowned, then spun around to see what caused this reaction.

Dayan stood in the doorway of his ger, leaning against the frame. His skin was pale, and every move made him grimace. His eyes bore into her in a way that made her face heat.

Forgetting about Soke completely, Mandukhai rushed over to the door. She stopped with only inches between them. She wanted to throw her arms around him, but worried about his health. He was awake, which was a relief, but how would his body fare under the circumstances? Khosoichi warned her that too much activity could leave permanent, unknown damage on his mind. He needed rest. He needed to sit or lie down.

For a moment, the two just stared at each other. Then Dayan pushed off the doorframe and stood straight. His good hand slid over her cheek, cradling her face.

"I came back," he said.

Mandukhai's cheek pulsed in his hand. Her heart quickened. Did he hear what she had said to him? "I see that," she breathed. "You should be resting."

"How long was I sleeping?" he asked, still gazing intently at her.

Mandukhai suppressed a shiver of delight. "Only a day."

The corners of his mouth turned downward. His looked past her at Soke. "How long do we have before the battle?"

"Two days before we have to ride out," Soke replied. "Eight before the fight."

"Two days," Dayan muttered. "We have a little time then. Until Togochi returns, I leave the organization of the *tumens* in your hands. Go see to it, Soke."

As Soke bowed and left to carry out Dayan's orders, Mandukhai shook her head. "No. You aren't ready to ride. You need more rest or you could fall from the saddle—or worse."

Dayan appeared slightly amused. "Are you telling me what to do?"

"Don't I always?" she teased.

The way he smiled at her made her stomach flip.

"I have seen it already, Mandukhai," Dayan said. His eyes appeared to drift off, gazing at some distant thing. "From a hilltop, the banners will fall."

Mandukhai wanted to ask what he was talking about, but her thoughts were disrupted as he pulled her against him and kissed her forehead. Instead of asking for details, Mandukhai's skin heated. Her mouth went dry. She snaked her arms around him as well, shivering as her fingertips brushed the bare skin on his back, feeling the muscles she had only recently discovered.

She regretted pulling away from Dayan, but quickly slid her hand into his and gently nudged him inside. He needed to rest. Khosoichi's warning had been clear. If Dayan was not careful, the concussion could leave him with permanent damage.

Dayan had woken with a certainty he had never felt before. The end of this struggle was upon them. He had seen it clearly more than once. And Mandukhai would be there beside him. This knowledge gave him a whole new level of confidence as he allowed her to nudge him inside. She closed the door behind her, and his heart leaped with excitement. Was this the moment he had been waiting for? *It's time to prove I'm the man she deserves and not just the boy she remembers*, he thought.

Emboldened by his newfound confidence, he closed the distance between them. His head throbbed like a war drum, but the heat of her proximity persuaded him to power through the pain. Nothing would stop him now. If they were riding off in two days, he would not waste today.

Mandukhai trembled in his arms. *That is a good thing, right?*

Dayan leaned closer, eager to feel her lips against his and capture this moment. When they met, the kiss was tentative, gentle. Brief.

Mandukhai pulled back, releasing a shaking breath. Her hand slid into his. She backed toward the bed, pulling him with her. Dayan's pulse beat wildly, making his head spin and the drums in his head hammered painfully hard. The wound in his head throbbed but he ignored it as they sat on the edge of his bed together.

This is finally happening, he thought as excitement pulsed through him. Their lips met again. This time, Dayan leaned closer, more resolute. Mandukhai pulled back a little, but he pressed his advance, climbing over her as she laid back, leaving no escape. His head was spinning like mad, but he reveled in the rush...the need.

Some raw animal instinct had taken hold of him. His hand fumbled for her belt, jerking it away, then yanked her deel loose as his tongue plunged deep into her mouth. Mandukhai made a small sound deep in her throat that stoked his fire. Dayan kissed her harder, driving his body down against hers. Her body shifted beneath him. Starving for more, Dayan blazed a trail of ravenous kisses against her jaw and neck.

"Dayan."

The way she breathed his name made a groan climb up his throat. Her palms pressed against his bare chest. His head spun so much he couldn't tell up from down, but his hand had no trouble as it wedged between her legs, pulling at the cloth barrier between them.

"Stop."

He heard the word, but no longer had control of himself. Pure lust took over. His mouth devoured her neck like a staving man as his hand continued to fight its way through the cloth barrier. She squirmed beneath him, squeezing her thighs tighter so his hand couldn't find what it sought between her legs. A whimper climbed up her throat and she and pressed harder against his chest.

"Stop!" Mandukhai barked out the command, shoking him back to reality with the forcefulness of her rejection.

Dayan pulled back, stunned and confused, his head swimming with heat.

Mandukhai scurried back away from him to the edge of the bed, hugging her deel tight around her body as she glared at him. "I do want you, but not like this. I can't tell you why, but I need you to trust me. That did not feel right to me."

His body ached. His head spun wildly. The floor tilted and he was thankful for the bed beneath him to keep him from falling over. *She can't tell me? Or she won't?* The fact that it hadn't felt right to her didn't make him feel any better about her sudden rejection.

Does she have any idea what she does to me? I can't take this. Suddenly, the hammering drums in his head became concussive and his stomach lurched. He closed his eyes and swallowed down whatever his stomach attempted forcing out.

"You need rest," she said.

"I have rested already," he groaned.

By the time he opened his eyes, Mandukhai had set to work mixing tea. He cradled his head in one hand, rubbing at his aching temples. It did nothing to help with the ache pulsing in the rest of his body.

Mandukhai offered him the tea. "Tell me what you saw in your vision."

Dayan's shoulders sagged. "The vision," he said flatly. He didn't want to talk right now. He wanted her to leave.

"The hilltop. The falling banners." Mandukhai perched on the edge of the bed beside him.

The childish part of him wanted to push her off the edge. If she didn't want to share the bed, she couldn't sit on it either. But he knew it was a petulant, childish way to act.

Mandukhai had always been very down to business with everyone. Had she been more tender with Unebolod? Dayan couldn't help the flare of jealousy that surged through him, which only amplified the pain threatening to tear his skull apart. All of his exaltation and clarity from the vision had been smothered. *How childish am I?*

Instead of fighting her, Dayan told her everything.

And before they kissed again, she would tell him why she couldn't do this.

CHAPTER FORTY-ONE

Burning Away the Past

Dayan's servant, Ong, finished wrapping the golden ribbon around the knot of hair on top of Dayan's head, fastening it in place. Unlike most men around him, Dayan had elected not to shave any part of his head until he reached Karakorum. He had hoped that would be with Mandukhai as his wife, but her reaction yesterday had left him disheartened and confused. *I cannot let her distract me today*, he thought as Ong placed a gold circlet around his forehead.

Today, Togochi returned from his campaign, bringing along Dayan's mother. For the first time in his memory, he would meet the woman who had given him life. The woman who had abandoned him to die as a baby. Dayan's stomach writhed. He fidgeted with the rings on his fingers as Ong secured a fox-head fur around his shoulders. How much longer would this take?

Ong stepped back, his laborious gaze sweeping over Dayan. For a moment, Dayan held his breath, hopeful that this process was over. Then Ong once more edged toward him to adjust the furs. *As if they won't slide around as I move anyway*, Dayan thought.

Numerous belts were tied around his waist, as always. They represented every spiritual color. A symbol of his divinity, purity, wisdom, prosperity, and eternity. A round, golden disc embossed with running wolves fastened all five of the silk belts together at his hip. Dayan adjusted the buckle, drawing a frown of disapproval from Ong.

Soon, Togochi would arrive with the Khan's family.

Family. Esige and Nemeku were his cousins. Togochi, his unofficial uncle. Mandukhai was his future—he hoped. These people Togochi brought to his camp were not his family. He did not know them, and they clearly did not care to know him, since they had not tried to reach out to him.

Mandukhai had insisted they dress to impress this woman Dayan couldn't make himself care about. A few years back, he had dreamed of reuniting with Siker, that she would come to him and hold him and be the mother she always should have been. It was a foolish boy's dream. He knew that now. Dayan tempered that hope today, placing a wall around it, stuffing it into a void. Hope was a tool for fools. He was Khan of khans. He could not afford to be a fool.

Ong held up a polished silver disc they used as a mirror. Dayan stared at the hard eyes and stony face of the man reflecting at him. Should he be so cold to Siker? Dayan waved the mirror away and marched out the door.

The trip to the gathering tent was short. Mandukhai had parked the massive cart in front of their gers when she set up this camp. He rounded the edge, passing the giant wheels locked in place with wooden blocks, then climbed the steps. As always, Boke and the rest of Dayan's guards followed him like a long shadow.

The wound in his head was far from healed, and somehow the weight of the fox-head fur pulled on the tense muscles in his neck and made his head throb. He clenched his jaw against the pain. He would not appear weak. The boy his mother had left for dead had been weak. Dayan Khan was not.

Still, as he climbed the steps, he had to rely far too much on the railing for his comfort. As he turned into the gathering tent and marched up the aisle toward his seat, the wound in his head—currently not wrapped in cloth—persistently pulsed with heat. How could an injury to his head make his legs and stomach so weak?

Mandukhai waited on her throne. The sight of her made the Great Fist wrap around his heart and squeeze. He wanted her to release him from her mysterious hold over his heart. He wanted her to open her arms and accept him. These two emotions clashed with each other, and he could not meet her eyes.

"Try to smile when you see her," Mandukhai advised as he settled in his own golden throne beside her.

"Why?"

"Because she is your mother."

Dayan shifted carefully to ease the pain in his head. "No, she isn't."

"Dayan—"

"Leave it be, Mandukhai," Dayan said. He adjusted the buckle and smoothed out the colorful belts.

Mandukhai studied him, but Dayan refused to look at her. Not only did he not want her to see the truth, the pain he attempted covering up, but he couldn't handle looking at her face right now. The way her lips called to him. Those bewitching dark eyes. Her smooth, flawless skin.

Dayan stuffed those thoughts away with the hope he had already smothered, then rested his arms on the armrests of his throne, making sure his rings were clearly visible to anyone who stood before him. Today, he was not a son reunited with his long-lost mother.

Today he was Great Khan.

Mandukhai studied Dayan as they waited, worried over his mental state. Reuniting with his mother could not be easy. He knew Siker left him for dead as a baby. He had grown up without her, knowing that she had not wanted him. It had been hard on him, and a few times she had to comfort him when the truth had haunted him.

Instead of waiting with the hope of a boy who would meet his mother, Dayan sat straight and stiff in his throne like the Great Khan he was. Under any other circumstances, Mandukhai would have envied his strength. But these were not other circumstances. What was he locking away this time?

And how could she ever relieve him of the burden?

Boke announced their arrival moments before Togochi escorted Siker and another woman into the gathering tent. Two young boys trailed alongside Siker, clinging to her hands. Mandukhai's gaze darted to Dayan from the corner of her eyes. Everything in her tensed. Siker had sons. Other sons. With Issama. And she had not abandoned *them*. That truth must have been a dagger to Dayan's heart, but he showed no signs of it.

Dayan studied Siker with absolute indifference.

As the group stopped near the bottom of the dais, Togochi bowed deeply. "My lord Khan, I have killed the one who was envious of you. I have brought the one who birthed you."

"And what of the Khatun's request?" Dayan asked.

Mandukhai blinked in alarm.

Togochi straightened and waved a hand behind him. Dochigen marched forward with a small, colorful, sealed clay jar. He placed it on the bottom step of the dais. Mandukhai didn't have to ask to know what was inside. Issama's heart. Just as she had requested. It remained there, a barrier between Dayan and Siker.

Mandukhai knew she could not leave it there between the two of them. She stood and strode toward it, picking up the jar. It was lighter than she expected. Thankfully, they could not see the contents. She turned and held it out to Torgus, who accepted with a bow and walked away carrying the jar. Siker's gaze followed him—or perhaps the jar. *She must know what is inside.*

Once Torgus entered the storage space hidden in the back of the gathering tent, Siker's gaze swept over Dayan critically.

He smiled politely, but it was clearly not genuine. "Mother." Though he said the word, it sounded hollow and meaningless.

"My son died years ago," Siker said tersely.

The air in the gathering tent seemed to vanish, as if sucked away by some great spirit.

"Well," Dayan said nonchalantly. "I'm glad we have that out of the way."

"Your men butchered my husband," Siker said. The arrogance and disdain were hard to miss.

Mandukhai watched for Dayan's reaction, expecting him to shrink back. Instead, he leaned forward. He rested his arm on his knee.

"Your husband's allies murdered Unebolod on his orders," Dayan said, and there was a dangerous menace in his voice. *"That* man was like a father to me. More of a parent than you ever bothered to be."

Siker shot a knowing look at Mandukhai. "Unebolod would have killed you the moment he had a chance. He has wanted what you have longer than you have been around."

Dayan shook his head. "You know nothing. I gave him a chance. I handed him the knife. He refused. Because he had far more honor than your dead husband."

Dayan had given Unebolod a chance to kill him? Mandukhai hoped she hid her alarm at this development.

"What do you know, *Batu?"* Siker snapped. "Only what that witch has told you." She stabbed a finger at Mandukhai.

Before Mandukhai decided if the comment offended her or not, Dayan straightened once more, glaring at Siker.

"Batu died years ago, abandoned and unloved by his own mother," Dayan snapped back. "And if you call her a witch one more time, I will be sure your punishment is quite painful."

Siker sneered. "You wouldn't hurt me."

But she froze as Dayan's gaze slid past her to the boys. Mandukhai saw the cold calculation in his golden eyes and her own heart seized. *He wouldn't hurt them to punish her, would he?*

"Mandukhai saved me from death," Dayan continued, scowling at Siker. "She cared for me, taught me, and *loved* me. Something you never did."

"She doesn't care about you," Siker said, clear contempt cast in Mandukhai's direction. "She only cares about your bloodline."

The truth of Siker's accusation hurt Mandukhai. Yes, she had taken him in precisely because of his bloodline, because he was the last living heir of Genghis. Mandukhai had never once given Dayan the wrong impression about that. From the start, she had been clear that the precise reason she chose him was because of his heritage. Still, as sensitive as Dayan had been lately about their relationship and Mandukhai's own heart's desire, she did not need Siker reminding him.

"It does not diminish her heart," Dayan said. "Some people cannot choose who they love."

Siker stepped forward. Togochi tensed.

"She has poisoned your mind," Siker hissed.

"If there is any poison in my veins, you left it there years before she found me," Dayan said coldly. He leaned back nonchalantly and flicked a careless wrist toward the door. "We are done. I will give you accommodations befitting your station and space to grieve your dead husband for the rest of your days. Not because I am feeling charitable, but because Mandukhai insisted."

Siker squared her shoulders, shot a deadly glare in Mandukhai's direction, and turned to shepherd her sons out in front of her.

"Leave the boys," Dayan said.

Siker froze, half turning to face Dayan. Terror for her two sons was obvious in the way her eyes bulged.

"Tuya and Ong, will care for the boys as they cared for me," Dayan said. "Because even if you are no longer my mother, they are still my brothers. I will not have you poison their minds against me. Besides, as long as they remain under my supervision, you will be less likely to act out against me."

Mandukhai wanted to reach for Dayan and tell him this was not a good idea. The boys were old enough to remember and might resent him either way. But something told her that nothing would change his mind.

Tuya and Ong edged forward uncertainly, glancing at Mandukhai for guidance. All Mandukhai could do was nod. Disagreeing with Dayan right now would solve nothing and might start a fight. Mandukhai was not prepared to take Siker's side in anything.

"Send them to Lady Jaghan and Geriel for now," Dayan commanded.

The servants each took a boy by the hand and pulled them toward the door. The boys resisted, crying for their mother.

"Please." Siker's lip trembled. "You have already taken my husband. Let me have my sons."

"You should be used to abandoning them by now," Dayan said.

Mandukhai shivered.

Siker turned her pleading gaze on Mandukhai, and tears shimmered in her eyes. *How quickly she turned from resenting me to needing my help.*

"Please don't take my boys," Siker pleaded. Her knees buckled as on of the guards picked up the oldest boy when he resisted leaving. The young boy was no match for a member of the Khan's guard. The men and servants disappeared through the doorway with the boys.

"You will be allowed supervised visits," Dayan said. "I'm not heartless like you. Get her out of here. Send her to Lord Qori with instructions to give her space in his back house. Under guard."

Togochi eyed Mandukhai, his lips set in a grim line. She knew how he felt about children being taken from their parents. He did not like this. But, like Mandukhai, he would not say anything. *He expects me to*, she realized.

Two of the Khan's guards seized Siker's arms and dragged her to her feet, pulling her from the gathering tent as she pleaded and cried for her sons in a way she had likely never done for Dayan. Mandukhai placed her hand on his arm.

Dayan ignored her. "Who is this?" he asked, nodding at the second woman.

The woman dropped to her knees, bowing to the Khan. Her voice trembled. "I beg for your mercy, Great Khan!"

Mandukhai studied the woman. She could not recall ever seeing her before, but she was young. Or at least, younger than Mandukhai by perhaps ten years.

"This is Lady Qolotai," Togochi said. "She was one of Issama's wives."

"How many did he have?" Mandukhai asked.

"Just the two," Togochi said.

What happened to Issama's first wife, Uingen?

Dayan cocked his head as he studied the woman still kneeling with her face to the floor. "Why is she here?"

"I was uncertain what to do with her," Togochi replied. He gazed down at Qolotai.

Is that sympathy? Mandukhai wondered.

"I don't have time for this," Dayan huffed.

"Dayan, she is a victim," Togochi said. "Issama stole her."

"What do you expect me to do with her?" Dayan asked, clearly ready to move on to something else.

Togochi heaved out a sigh that rumbled deep in his chest. His shoulders drew tight, and he stared fixedly at Qolotai. "Let me care for her."

Dayan's brows shot up. Mandukhai couldn't help but reflect his alarm.

"You want her as a wife?" Dayan asked, bewildered.

"Only if Jaghan and Geriel agree," Togochi said carefully. "And if they don't, she can be a servant. But it is better if I keep an eye on her than we allow her to run free and cause trouble. Besides, if Siker's sons are to stay with my wives, it might help them to have a familiar face around."

Mandukhai studied the young woman. Would Jaghan agree? She had her hands full with the boys most days, and she had been very receptive to Geriel when Togochi approached her about his second wife. Would she be interested in sharing him with this woman as well?

"Fine. She is your problem, Togochi." Dayan folded his hands over the arms of his throne, wincing slightly at the movement. "Once you trust her, she can help with the boys."

"Thank you!" Qolotai's voice shook with relief as she rose, assisted by Togochi.

Togochi slid his hand into hers and led her out the door.

Dayan groaned and sagged slightly the moment the two of them were alone.

Mandukhai turned in her seat, taking his hand. "Are you all right?" Her knees touched his.

He closed his eyes. His jaw twitched. "For years, some part of me thought she might regret leaving me." His voice was rough. When he opened his eyes, they shimmered with golden light. "But she never looked back. She started a new family and erased me from her mind completely."

"She never forgot about you," Mandukhai said softly, stroking his hand with her thumb.

"Just let it be, Mandukhai," Dayan said, voice tight with sorrow. "She made herself clear. As far as she is concerned, I died a long time ago. I will see that she is comfortable, because regardless of how either of us feel, she gave birth to me. It ends there."

Mandukhai's heart broke for Dayan. How painful was it to have a parent completely erase you from their life? "Do you want to go for a walk?"

Dayan pulled away and eased himself to his feet. He managed a few steps before he stopped. His shoulders sagged, his back to her. Mandukhai fidgeted with her rings as she waited for him to say or do something.

Several painfully long minutes passed in silence before she stood and glided down the steps toward him. She placed her hand gently on his shoulder. "Dayan?"

He straightened. "I want to show you something."

Dayan stepped away, taking Mandukhai's hand and guiding her along with him.

A week ago, Dayan had been on this ridge and marveled at the beauty of the waterfall, the ribbons of all colors blending together in the mist. Mandukhai protested about halfway there, insisting he shouldn't exert himself this much as he healed. Nevertheless, he persisted, despite the way his head pulsed. Hopefully, by tomorrow, he would feel well enough to ride.

As they climbed the ridge and he breathed in sharp, crisp, painful breaths, he hated how right she had been. But he would not turn back now. They were nearly there.

Boke, Torgus, and a handful of their guards had gone ahead to be sure the area was clear of danger. As Dayan and Mandukhai reached the crest of the ridge, Boke gave Dayan the signal that it was clear. Several of the Khan's guards patrolled the far ridge.

Dayan led Mandukhai to the edge, focusing on keeping his breathing even so she didn't fuss over him.

The sun reached its zenith and reflected off the mist of the waterfall, creating the ribbon of color once more. Mandukhai gasped. Her face lit up with awe as she took in the sight. He wanted to enjoy the view with her, but seeing the pure, uninhibited joy on her face made it impossible to look away.

"This is glorious, Dayan," Mandukhai breathed. "But why did you bring me here?" She turned to him, tearing her gaze away from the spectacular view.

The moment she met his gaze, the Great Fist closed around his heart and squeezed. "Because we don't know what tomorrow will bring." He tore his eyes from her and watched the mist dance. "Because this place gives me peace."

Mandukhai squeezed his hand. "It's okay to be hurt by her rejection."

The fist squeezed tighter. No matter how much he tried to shut out the pain in his heart, Dayan was helpless against the sheer force of it.

"I knew better," he said. He hated how weak he sounded as his voice cracked. A few rogue tears escaped. He gritted his teeth to regain control, to no avail. "I am dead to her. Better to be certain than to wonder."

Mandukhai stepped around to face him. Her thumb stroked his cheek, wiping the tears away. "I'm sorry."

Dayan jerked his head away from her touch. "Don't." He longed for her touch, but right now, his heart couldn't handle it.

"Don't what?" she asked.

Did she move closer, or was she always this close to him? "I can't handle any more rejection today, Mandukhai."

"Rejection?" Her eyes widened, taking in his face. The depth of her gaze made a lump rise in his throat. "Is that what you think?"

Dayan worked his jaw, unsure how to answer as she edged closer to him. "You ... you pushed me away. Yesterday." *Did my voice just become shrill?* He loathed how his body betrayed him.

"Oh Dayan." Mandukhai brushed his cheek so tenderly.

He turned his head away. "Don't do that. It makes me feel so small when you call me that."

Mandukhai pressed gently against him, and it sent a shock through his body. "I was scared." Her arms wound around him.

Dayan's arms hung lamely at his sides. He did not know how to react. Should he hold her? Should he push her away? And why had *she* been scared? "I don't understand."

Mandukhai chewed her lip. "You were so insistent and it ... it brought up memories I thought I had locked away."

"Unebolod," he said flatly, grimacing.

She shook her head vehemently. "No. The last time *anyone* touched me like that it had been ..." Her voice trailed off. Pain flashed in her eyes. "It scared me. I'm terrified of giving myself to anyone. But it doesn't mean I don't want to."

Her gaze fluttered up to him. Deep. Longing. "I love you," she whispered.

He swallowed the lump in his throat, attempting to dislodge it. *No. I cannot handle this. Not today.* "Mandukhai …" He averted his eyes and attempted uncoiling her limbs, but Mandukhai clung to him. He could not escape.

"Look at me, please," she pleaded. She pressed her palm to his cheek, forcing him to obey. "We need to take this slowly. At least at first."

How much more slowly can we go? he thought pitifully.

Sunlight and mist cast around her like a halo of light. Her face glowed. The intoxicating scent of her jasmine oils hypnotized him. Her lips parted slightly. But it was the softness of her dark eyes that drew him in. They captured Dayan, and he could not look away. He didn't want to look away. The flush of her cheeks made his knees weak. Her fingers curled his deel into her fist, holding him against her. He became acutely aware of the increasing force of his heartbeat.

He wanted to kiss her. He *needed* to kiss her. But he could not handle another rejection. Instead, he lingered, a breath from her lips, as heady excitement blended with heart-pounding terror.

But he would suffer this rejection a thousand times if it brought her lips to his. The distance between them was too far. He couldn't stand it any longer. The world around them faded. He moved swiftly, afraid she would pull away again.

But she didn't. Mandukhai returned the kiss, gentle, tender. His arm slid around her waist, crushing her against him, blending their lips together until it made him so dizzy he could no longer breathe. Was this what such a kiss should feel like?

Blinding pain hammered across his skull from the gash along his hair line. Dayan broke away, pressing the heels of his palms against his head. The world spun and darkened. No. This could not be normal.

"I worried about this yesterday, as well," Mandukhai whispered.

He opened his eyes, hating how he winced from the scaring pain. Worry shined in her eyes like stars against the night sky. But he understood now. She hadn't just been scared for herself. She had been scared for him, as well.

Dayan slid his hand along her braided hair, refusing to let her step away from him. "This is not fair," he protested, half grinning at her. "We can make this work. I have waited too long to let a little wound get in the way."

Mandukhai laughed, and the sound was light and lifted his heart. "You could black out."

"A small price to pay."

She laughed again. He swallowed the pain pulsing in his head and smothered her laughter with his lips, hungry for more. There was no way he would let a bump on his head stop him when she seemed so willing.

He tested her lips, tasting them, reveling in the touch and smell and taste of her. Dayan drank her in. When he had his fill of her mouth, his lips burned a trail along her jaw and neck, slow and hungry. Every hitch of her breath fueled his desire, deepened his longing, until the ache of it flushed away the agony from his wound. He eased the folds of her deel loose. His fingers slid along the skin of her collarbone.

"Dayan."

The way she breathed his name sent a fierce need through his core. He groaned against her skin. Her fingers slid along his neck and jaw, making his skin prickle. Dayan raised his lips toward hers, heady excitement surging through him. If he passed out in ecstasy, so be it.

But Mandukhai tilted her head away and nudged him back.

Once more, everything crashed down.

"I don't understand," he said, surprised by how raspy his own voice sounded.

"This isn't the place."

"Why?" His passionate gaze burned into her, projecting all of his yearning toward her. He was certain he saw the same longing in her own eyes. His fingers brushed her flushed cheek.

Mandukhai chewed her lip. He wanted to kiss them again!

"I would rather not do this out in the open, in front of the guards," she whispered.

His heart skipped with excitement. "Then let's go home," he whispered. Dayan pulled back, sliding his hand into hers once more.

Siker was his past. Mandukhai was his future. And he would take any risk to secure that future.

CHAPTER FORTY-TWO

A New Beginning

Everything had been rushed. As they headed back toward camp hand-in-hand, Mandukhai had sent a few of the guards ahead to find Khosoichi and have the gathering tent prepared for the ceremony. Dayan had listened to her give the guards instruction, but his mind was swimming in elation. His entire body had become electric with excitement as he realized what would come next. The walk back had not been not nearly as taxing on his injured head as the walk out to the ridge had been—though it had felt so much longer than he remembered.

When they had reached the door to her ger—situated beside his own—Dayan had been reluctant to release her hand. If he let go, would this all vanish?

"We need to prepare quickly, Dayan," Mandukhai said gently, then slid her hand out of his and disappeared into her ger.

He walked in a daze into his own ger and was immediately assaulted by Ong as the servant stripped him out of his dirty clothes, scrubbed him down, fixed his hair, and slid on a fresh, ceremonial deel—one he had never seen before. *Where did this come from?* he thought as he fingered the embroidered blue wolves along the golden hem.

Ong worked efficiently. It had not taken the servant long to finish his task. The moment he was satisfied, Ong escorted Dayan toward the gathering tent. Dayan's stomach writhed in excitement. For so long, he had been certain this moment would never come. He had worked so hard to prove himself to Mandukhai. Now, as she climbed the gathering tent steps to join him, Dayan wondered if he was even worthy of her.

Tuya had outdone herself preparing Mandukhai. Her jade deel accentuated her chest and smoothed out over her hips. The *boqta* matched the deel, topped with a brilliant blue feather that stood at least another foot up from the tip of the *boqta*. A wealth of jade, silver, and coral hung over her long, loosely braided hair.

Dayan drifted to her, meeting Mandukhai in front of the open doors of the gathering tent as if pulled toward her by some mystical force. She was stunning. Far too much to make him feel worthy of holding her hand, let alone marrying her.

Khosoichi stepped in front of them, sprinkling milk in her direction as a symbol of fertility. When he finished, the shaman spun on his heels and led the two of them deeper into the gathering tent. The number of Lords and Ladies who had gathered on such short notice impressed and intimidated Dayan. He could not even see any of their faces clearly in his current state of elation. His grip on Mandukhai's hand tightened as they followed Khosoichi, who continued sprinkling the mare's milk before them.

With each step, Dayan's heart hammered harder and rose into his throat until all he could do was swallow reflexively.

In the center of the gathering tent, two copper basins large enough to hold his entire body blazed with flaming life. They followed the shaman between the two pots—a ritual of cleansing away their old lives to start the new. Men and women nodded and murmured in approval, making Dayan overly aware of just how many eyes were on him now. *Keep your chin up. Don't embarrass her.*

Khosoichi climbed the dais steps. Dayan prayed his legs wouldn't fail him as he climbed alongside Mandukhai. *Don't trip. Don't trip.* Mandukhai climbed as if floating. An air of grace surrounded her. He stared at her in awe when they reached the top and faced one another. She was perfect. Everything about her.

Dayan spent so much time focusing on keeping his breathing even to avoid another anxiety attack that he moved through the ceremony automatically, without thinking. Before he knew it, Dayan heard Khosoichi recited the marriage blessing of the High Heavens. Dayan didn't need the blessing of the gods. He only needed Mandukhai's.

The crowd roared in approval, stomping feet, clapping hands, and shaking the gathering tent with their thunder.

Mandukhai guided Dayan beside her down the steps and along the path between the copper basin fires. The processional to her ger began.

The crowd followed Dayan and Mandukhai to her ger, where they would consummate their marriage. Then the people would feast and celebrate.

By oath, Mandukhai had bound herself to Dayan years ago, but this would be different. A binding of duty against a binding of body and soul. His skin prickled just thinking about it. Just this morning, he had thought this impossible.

High above, a falcon passed the camp. Its shadow rippled over the ceremony in a manner reminiscent of the *sulde* of Genghis Khan. Dayan gazed up at the winged beast as they reached the ger.

Mandukhai's slender hand pushed open the wooden door. Her other hand tightened around his. Dayan glanced down, his fingers wound around hers. *I can't believe this is happening.* An energy built within, preparing to burst out. His heart pounded with adrenaline, a steady, powerful rhythm that made his aching head swim.

A glance around revealed a sea of faces. Dayan could only recognize a few: Togochi, Jaghan, Nemeku, and Altan. Everyone would be there to watch, he realized. Which also meant everyone knew what was about to happen.

Suddenly, the excitement twisted into a knot of nerves in his stomach. *So much pressure!* Dayan used his thumb to twist the Yuan ring on his finger.

Then Mandukhai took a step forward, encouraging Dayan along with her. He glanced at her, and his heart melted in the warm smile on her face. *I can't believe this is happening*, he thought again.

His heart had never beaten so wildly before in his life. As he crossed the threshold behind her, Dayan turned to close the door. Togochi stood on the other side, grinning at him. The *orlok* winked, then nodded for him to close the door. Dayan swallowed the anxious lump in his throat as the door sealed the two of them in.

Outside, the scratches of fingers against felt repeated over the door. Dayan opened his mouth and let out an anxious breath. *Scratch, scratch.* More people offering their blessing for fertility. This was too much pressure. Everyone would expect him to produce heirs now. Crippling anxiety seeped into his bones, freezing him in place.

Mandukhai stepped around him, placing a hand on his arm. "Are you alright?" Her *boqta* was already gone, as was the beaded headdress she had been wearing. Her hair already hung free around her shoulders. She had even removed her belt already, loosening her deel.

She is so magnificent, he thought. He wanted her. High Heavens, he wanted her! But Dayan couldn't move. Out on the ridge, nothing had stood between them. No one had expected anything of them. It had just been him and her. But this ...

Scratch, scratch.

Mandukhai eased him away from the door. Her palm rested against his cheek, turning his gaze toward her. "It's just you and me."

He glanced at the door as another scratch sounded.

Mandukhai kissed his jaw, drawing him back to her.

"Were you scared?" he asked timidly. "You know ..."

Mandukhai laughed in a gentle, knowing way that eased some of his stress. "Terrified. I delayed as long as I possibly could." She brushed her fingers along his temples, up under the golden circlet he wore. She lifted it off gently, setting it on the table beside the door. "But I didn't want Manduul. I never wanted him." With nimble fingers, she unraveled the ribbon holding his hair up. It fell back, slowly uncurling from the twists Ong had put it up in. Her fingers eased through his hair. "I want you."

Dayan kissed Mandukhai. His wife. This new reality stirred up a sense of relief. She was his, not just because she had given an oath years ago. But because she wanted to be.

"Go slow," she murmured against his lips.

Dayan was in no rush this time. He wanted to savor this moment forever.

Mandukhai and Dayan's marriage ceremony had been so quickly thrown together and brief that Togochi had nearly missed it. Once the door to the ger had closed and he had offered the blessing for fertility, Togochi had slipped off into the growing crowd to avoid the inevitable conversation with Jaghan and Geriel.

How could he ask either woman to accept Qolotai? Did he want them to? Togochi knew he could not avoid the conversation forever.

Celebrations sprang up all around the camp. Between the departure of the warriors in the morning and the final, official union of the Khan and Khatun, hope spread through the people faster than a plague. Tonight, the Khan and Khatun would share a bed and begin producing heirs. Tomorrow, they would leave to finally reunite the Mongols under one banner.

A new beginning was born today.

Togochi had left Qolotai with some of his men to watch over her so he could join the celebration. He spent some time at a wrestling ring, drinking *airag* and gambling on the wrestlers.

Airag made his mind a little slow. After a little while, Togochi groaned, then scrubbed a hand over his face as he realized the terrifying truth. He had to go home. Which meant he had to tell his wives about Qolotai.

After bidding the men goodnight and warning them not to stay up too late drinking, Togochi left to retrieve Qolotai. She asked him no questions as he guided her to Jaghan's ger where he could hear his wives talking inside. He paused outside the door, took a deep breath, then pushed it open.

The inside fell silent as he stepped through. Both women stared at him. Geriel with worry in her eyes. Jaghan in anger. *Not off to a promising start*, he thought.

Jaghan's gaze slid past him as Qolotai followed him in. "Who is this?" Her tone bore malice.

"This is Qolotai," Togochi said. He launched into the story, explaining Qolotai's precarious position, and his promise. When he finished, dead silence filled the ger.

Jaghan fumed in silence, glaring at him. Geriel studied Qolotai curiously.

"Well?" Togochi asked. "You have nothing to say?"

"Oh, I have plenty to say, but I don't think you want to hear any of it," Jaghan seethed. "I take it Dayan agreed, since she is here. What did Mandukhai say?"

Togochi fumbled. He licked his lips, slightly numbed from the *airag*. "Nothing."

"Let me get this straight," Jaghan snapped. "You left here last minute on a mission from the Khan. Killed her husband, and promised to marry her?"

"I didn't—"

"And instead of coming home to reunite with the wives you *already* have," Jaghan pressed on, raising her voice over his, "—you disappear all day with *her*?"

"I wasn't with her!" Togochi waved a hand back toward where Qolotai cowered new the door. "I had to see that Siker was sent off according to the Khan's command, then see to the upcoming battle, then witness their marriage."

"You can't even manage the two wives you have," Jaghan snapped. "You don't need another."

"You didn't have such a problem with Geriel," Togochi said, stabbing a finger at his second wife. "It isn't as if we have not been through this already, Jaghan."

"*We* discussed bringing in another woman," Jaghan said pointedly. "*We* were careful and deliberate. *We* took our time and found someone who would fit into our family. Someone we could trust. Now you want to bring in as stray. *Issama's* stray! I don't know this woman."

Togochi's hands clenched into fists at his sides. He had enough. Qolotai had not told him everything, but he knew enough about her to know that none of this was her fault. "I do. And she has been through a lot, lost a lot, suffered a lot."

"I don't care what she has been through!" Jaghan's indignation rolled off of her in overwhelming waves. "It isn't my problem. This is my ger, and she isn't welcome in it!"

Togochi's jaw twitched. He was not sure if he was more disappointed in Jaghan's response, Geriel's lack or response, or just plain angry that his wife was being unreasonable. "Fine." He turned to Qolotai.

Without another word, Togochi yanked open the door, encouraging Qolotai out with him.

"Where are *you* going, Togochi?" Jaghan snapped.

He froze, turning slowly toward her, then straightened to his full height and glared at Jaghan. "Where do you think? You've made yourself clear. This is *your* ger. I won't leave her out in the cold alone."

Jaghan's eyes grew wider than he had ever seen them before. Her jaw hung open as her words finally failed her.

Qolotai placed a hand on his arm, drawing his gaze down at her. "Please. I did not want to cause a fight. Siker hated me. She wanted me dead. I don't want to be in another situation like that again. You told me they were a part of this decision. We agreed that they would have to agree. Clearly, she doesn't."

"Qolotai—"

"It's all right, Togochi," she said softly.

The two of them stared at one another for several agonizingly long seconds. He could see the pain in Qolotai's eyes. She had suffered so much for no good reason. If she believed her happiness was with him and Jaghan refused her, that made Jaghan cruel. Qolotai deserved a chance at happiness. But he knew she was right. They had an agreement. And he loved Jaghan. If he pushed this issue, he risked alienating Jaghan. Togochi swallowed the lump that lodged in his throat.

On the other side of the ger, his wives hissed back and forth to each other. He couldn't make out anything they said. But before he could take Qolotai out, Jaghan huffed.

"Fine, she can stay until you return from the Ordos attack," Jaghan grumbled. "We will sort all of this out after that. And she sleeps over there." Jaghan stabbed a finger to the other side of the ger, as far from his bed as Qolotai could be. Beside her, Geriel offered Togochi a small smile.

He knew what that smile meant. Geriel was not opposed. She would try to smooth this out while he was away.

Mandukhai basked in the warm comfort of Dayan's embrace, resting her head against his chest and listening to the steadying beat of his heart. She felt a sense of safety she had not felt in a long time. While she had always known she had the loyalty and protection of those around her, this security just felt … different. Like she was no longer alone.

Dayan remained silent as he stared at her and ran his fingers up and down her side. The intensity of his gaze gave Mandukhai a thrill. He always had such soulful eyes, but the way he gazed at her made her was not the same. It was warm, comforting, alluring, and filled with singular desire. She couldn't meet his gaze for long before her cheeks flushed. But when she averted her eyes, she instead found herself staring down his body, at his surprisingly strong arms, muscular chest, the dip of his skin just below his abs around his belly button. Dayan was far more attractive than she had given him credit for. By any right, he could have any woman he wanted both as Khan and as an attractive man.

"When did you know you wanted me?" she asked, suddenly very conscious of her older body—even if she was still fit.

"I've always known," he said.

Mandukhai could hear the rumble in his chest as he spoke. She lifted her head, gazing up at him. *Always?* Dayan's hand slid down her arm. He laced her fingers through his and brought her hand to his lips.

She couldn't help pressing the issue. "But why me? You could have anyone."

Dayan shifted, leaning over Mandukhai and forcing her onto her back. His fingers clenched hers, pressing her hand against the bed. His thumb stroked her temple so tenderly it made her heart ache and her body heat.

"Do you honestly believe there could ever be another woman like you? Fierce. Wise. Merciful. Beautiful." His body hovered over her, radiating heat as his gaze penetrated the depths of her heart and soul. "I don't want anyone. All I want, all I have ever wanted, is you." He leaned closer, his lips lingering a breath from her own. "You are my eternity."

Mandukhai's heart thudded. Dayan's lips captured hers as his body pressed closer. The intensity of the kiss took her breath away. The heat and pressure of his lips against her own. The hunger, desire. His kiss gave validation to his words. She believed him wholly.

When he broke the kiss, both of them were breathing hard, as if coming up for air. Dayan lingered over her, his body brushing lightly against her own.

One thing still hung between them. Something neither of them had dared give voice to, but Mandukhai knew that if she wanted to ever heal the cracks in her soul, she had to bare it completely to Dayan.

"I love you, Dayan," she said, then bit her lip and summoned her courage. "And I appreciate that you gave me the time and space to recover from the loss of Unebolod." She felt his muscles tense under her hands the moment she said his name. "I think ... I needed that to gain perspective. I loved him. I still do."

"Would you have chosen me if he hadn't died?"

His question pierced her heart. She had spent weeks mulling this over, and no matter how she looked at it, she always landed on the same answer. "Yes. I think I was in love with you long before I realized it. But I can't ignore the part he played in my life."

"I don't expect you to," he murmured. "I just needed to know you wanted me for *me*."

Mandukhai slid her hand up his chest, then brushed her fingertips along his jaw. "And now?"

The corner of his mouth twitched up into a grin. "You have thoroughly erased any doubts." His lips trailed along her neck. Mandukhai wrapped her arms around him and pulled him close.

For so long, she was sure she would be forever broken by her past. But just as the wedding fires burned away their past, Dayan's spirit filled in the cracks in her soul. He was, as he had always been, her shield against the world.

Sleep had been heavy and peaceful for the first half of the night. Dayan had never had a night of such serene, unsullied sleep before in his life. When he did wake in the middle of the night, he could not sleep again. Excitement and admiration had him staring at Mandukhai as she slept beside him. The way she breathed in her sleep was rhythmic. Soft breath in through slightly parted lips. Loud breath out. Steady and sure. Confident even in her sleep.

Dayan had no words to describe what last night had been like for him. He wasn't even sure the words existed. If he thought he loved her before, it was nothing compared to the warmth that spread through his chest now.

Moonlight shined through the open smoke hole, casting a pale glow on her bare shoulder and back. He wanted to touch her skin but didn't want to wake her. One of them should sleep.

For another hour, he stared at her as she slept, then watched the way the wind made the white belt flutter from where Mandukhai hung it from a *uni* pole. "You don't need this anymore," she had proclaimed before flinging it over the high pole. Not that he could reach it even if he needed it.

For so long that white belt had felt like a rope tightening around his neck, mocking him, reminding him that he would never have her. Now it hung loose and free.

Dayan eased out of bed, wincing as his head protested. As gentle as Mandukhai had been, there had been no way to avoid keeping the war drums from pounding in his skull. But if he could handle last night, he could handle riding.

It took far too long to find his clothes and dress with limited light. A few times, Mandukhai stirred, and he paused, watching her. Not only did he not want to wake her, but he enjoyed the view enormously. She sighed in her sleep and pulled the furs up to her chin. Dayan frowned, then snuck out the door.

The guards stood at full attention as he stepped out. Dayan held a finger to his lips as he eased the door closed.

"Stay with her," he whispered. "I won't be far."

The two exchanged uneasy looks. Dayan knew better. He would end up with at least one guard. They might respect their Khan, but they feared the wrath of his wife.

My wife. How long before he was used to that? Dayan breathed in the cool spring night air.

He strolled toward the gathering tent. If he couldn't sleep, he might as well get something accomplished.

The camp was quiet even at this late hour—or early; Dayan wasn't sure how far it was until the wolf dawn. Now that one of the heaviest burdens had lifted from Dayan's shoulders, he was more confident in his ability to focus on the road ahead: a completed reunification.

Then *kurultai* at last.

As he reached the steps up to the gathering tent, Dayan spotted his cousin waddling awkwardly with a bucket. Nemeku paused as he passed the gathering tent, grinning at Dayan.

"I think mountains move faster than the two of you," Nemeku teased. He set his bucket down, sloshing some water on the dirt. "How does it feel?"

Dayan's cheeks heated. "Are you asking for details?"

Nemeku chuckled. "No. Just ... I know how hard this wait has been on you. Is it a relief to finally have an answer?"

Was it a relief? A burden had been lifted, but Dayan didn't know if relief was the right word. He rubbed his neck. "I guess so. What are you doing up in the middle of the night?"

"It's hardly the middle of the night," Nemeku replied. "Wolf dawn is only maybe two hours away. Orghana's morning fits are predictable now. I learned pretty quick that it's best to have two buckets ready. One to catch and one to clean."

Dayan's nose curled up in disgust. "She vomits?"

"Happens to a lot of women, apparently," Nemeku said with a shrug. He glanced at the moon then picked up his bucket. "I should get back before she wakes."

"Nemeku!" Dayan called after him.

His cousin paused, half turning back.

"I could use good men in the morning. Can I count on you to ride with me?"

Nemeku's brows shot up. He set the buckets down and rubbed his palms together. "Is Mandukhai on board with that idea?"

"She will be," Dayan said confidently, though he wasn't sure he could convince her. "But I am Khan. And I trust your skills. You have proven yourself both to me and in battle. I would rather finish this with you at my side."

Nemeku considered his answer, then gave a curt nod and picked up his buckets. "Then I will be there."

Dayan grinned and climbed the steps of the gathering tent two at a time. A final review of their plans was in order.

Togochi jolted awake from his nightmare, rushing to a bucket as Issama's warm blood made his arms slick. He plunged his hands into the bucket without thinking, then screamed as searing heat pierced his hands and arms. The bucket had been set on the stove to warm overnight so it would be ready for morning. His scream scared everyone awake. He jerked his arms out of the hot water. His skin pulsed in angry life.

Qolotai was the first to move. She had been sleeping on the far side of the ger, away from his bed by order of Jaghan. Before anyone else reacted, she kneeled in front of him with a stack of cloth. Qolotai murmured soothing sounds as she wrapped his hands and forearms in cool silk. Their eyes met in the darkness, empathy passing between them. She understood his distress like no one else possibly could. She had already been there more than once to help him through it.

Jaghan appeared at his side, nudging Qolotai away. The moment she did, Qolotai dropped her gaze to the floor and retreated to her section of the ger. Togochi wanted to reach for Qolotai, but his arms ached. No words could bridge the divide between them. Instead, he looked down as Jaghan removed one of the silk wrappings and began applying silver balm to his skin. The cold salve eased the pain.

"Why did you do that?" she asked tenderly as she gently rubbed in the silver balm.

He couldn't tell her the truth. What would she think of him if he told her what he had done to Issama? If he told her that the defilement of even his oldest enemy haunted him? Instead, he lied, hating the words even as they slipped past his lips. "I don't know," he mumbled.

As Qolotai slinked back to her blankets on the floor, her sympathetic gaze locked on him.

She understood.

Mandukhai rolled over, reaching for Dayan. Instead, she found his place cold and empty. Her heart sank as disappointment settled in. She had looked forward to waking beside him. Last night, his eyes had glowed with almost supernatural light as they burrowed into her soul. And the words he had whispered, only for her, as he had touched her. For the first time in her life, Mandukhai felt whole ... happy in a way that no one could steal away.

Mandukhai closed her eyes and breathed in his lingering scent from her bed. Juniper and sage, mixed with sweat.

No one had ever made her feel so utterly precious. It had been pure. Intimate. Personal. Binding. Mandukhai could not find the right words to describe how Dayan made her feel.

Where is he?

Once she had dressed and run her fingers through her hair, Mandukhai slid on her boots and headed out the door, brushing her fingers over the white silk belt hanging from the *uni* pole. A girlish smile crept across her face. Dayan had worn that belt for years as a symbol of his purity—and removing it last night had been like binding them to one another.

The night guard stood straight when she emerged.

"Where is the Khan?" she asked.

"He has been in the gathering tent for at least an hour," the guard said.

Mandukhai thanked him and headed toward the tent to join Dayan. The guard trailed along behind her and stationed himself at the bottom of the steps when she climbed.

Dayan stood at the map table with his back to her, arms crossed over his chest. His hair was a mess and his clothes wrinkled. Mandukhai's heart skipped the moment she laid eyes on him. A welcome change.

Dayan reached down and shifted a few of the knights on the map, then pressed his fist against his chin, deep in thought. Mandukhai stepped up beside him, sliding her arm around his waist and kissing his shoulder. This novel sensation of open, honest affection made her stomach flutter. She had never cared for Manduul and had never been able to show open affection toward Unebolod. Everything had always been guarded. Was this what Jaghan felt like with Togochi? Was this what Esige felt like with Huoshai? Mandukhai had experienced nothing like it before.

"What have you been doing?" she asked, examining the map. He had moved several pieces into new positions, all converging on Mogurkei's camp.

"Thinking about the coming fight." Dayan rubbed his chin, frowning at the map. "I have an idea, Mandukhai."

She tensed against him. "We have a plan already. Everything is in motion."

"Not everything." Dayan slid his arm around her and kissed her temple. Mandukhai leaned into his touch. "You've done a brilliant job. But there were too many weak spots in our defenses in the south and west. Clever generals will spot a weakness and exploit it instantly."

Mandukhai recognized those words. It was Unebolod's words coming from his mouth.

"Dayan—"

"Hear me out," he said. "Even if we move in swiftly and take his camp before his warriors can ride out to defend, which is a big if, we cannot allow Legusi to be the one to finish him."

"Why not?" Mandukhai asked.

"Because Mogurkei needs to know exactly who he has lost to," Dayan said. "He needs to see my face. Your face. And we will pass judgement upon him and kill him ourselves."

She shivered at the coldness of his plan. She wanted to cling to Dayan, drag him back to bed, insist that they had better things to do and ignore this ugly business just a little longer. But she also knew he was right.

"This is the part you won't like, though," Dayan continued.

She braced herself.

"Nemeku needs to be at my side."

"Dayan, he is hardly old enough to be married, let alone fight."

"He has already been in battle. And let's not forget I have fought him. He's good."

She sighed. "You trust Nemeku?"

Dayan didn't hesitate. "With my life."

"I can't talk you out of this, can I?" she asked.

Dayan grinned down at her, and his eyes danced with a mischievous light. "Not a chance."

This plan risked everything, and now that Mandukhai knew true happiness, she was not ready to risk losing it. But she had accepted Dayan as her husband, as a man. She had to give him the space to be who Genghis promised him to be. They were partners in this now. For better or worse.

"Tell me your full plan."

Chapter Forty-Three

Earning Faith

Tayiqu walked close to Esige as they made their way around camp. She had taken Tayiqu in years ago, when her father died, and had raised her as best she could. Esige adored the girl but knew that one of these days she would have to arrange a marriage with a suitable Lord. The marriage would not happen until Tayiqu became a woman, but that day approached in just a few short years. Perhaps two. By the time this ugly issue with the Ordos resolved, Tayiqu would turn twelve. Esige could put off the inevitable, but Tayiqu had far too much interest in boys already. The sooner something could be arranged, the better.

"I know you are upset with me, so just say it," Tayiqu sighed, clearly sensing Esige's tension.

"I am not upset," Esige replied calmly. "Huoshai, however, was ready to cut off that boy's hands."

"We were just curious," Tayiqu muttered. "Weren't you ever curious about boys at my age?"

Esige snorted. "I thought all boys were dumb as sheep."

"What about Huoshai?" Tayiqu asked. The tone in her voice suggested she didn't believe Esige at all. "Did you think he was dumb? Because you don't now. I've seen the two of you together."

Just what had Tayiqu seen? "Dumb? No." Esige shook her head. "Arrogant and self-important, yes. He was so full of cocky confidence the first time he spoke to me." A ghost of a smile crept across Esige's face as she remembered the way Huoshai had defended her right to wrestle with the men in front of everyone. When she had told him she wasn't interested, he had shrugged it off like it hadn't matter to him. Clearly it had. "But I fell in love with him because he wasn't like the other dumb boys. He saw me, respected me."

They reached a clearing where hundreds of horses grazed carelessly, unaware that in just two days, they would be ridden into battle. Many of the horses would not survive.

"But Mandukhai Khatun let you choose your husband, right? I won't get that choice." Tayiqu pouted, crossing her arms petulantly over her chest. "I heard what Huoshai said. He wants me arranged."

Esige stopped, stepping in front of Tayiqu. In another year or two, the girl would be just as tall as her. When Esige looked closely, she could see the woman rising to the surface in the way her hips flared and her chest developed. "He only said that because of what he caught you doing. Now he is worried you will do something foolish. We have to ride into battle in just two days, and I need to know that, while we are gone, you will not do anything stupid, that you will be around to help Chimgee watch over the boys."

Chimgee was Huoshai's mother. After Huoshai had killed his father, she had spent nearly a year resentful, but that resentment had melted away as she fell into the role of caretaker for their children. Chimgee adored her grandchildren. But in her forties, she had a hard time keeping up with all of them and often needed Taiyqu's help.

"Obviously I will," Tayiqu rolled her eyes, then planted a hand on her hip. "And I told you. Nothing happened! We didn't even kiss."

"This time." Esige felt bad for the girl. If she had acted this way at that age, Mandukhai surely would have forced a marriage on her as well, to protect her from making a dumb mistake. "But next time, maybe he wants to kiss, too. And if you let him, where does it stop, Tayiqu? And before you even attempt answering me, try to see this from our perspective. We found you with this boy in nothing but your trousers. There are few other places that could go but poorly."

Tayiqu scrunched up her nose. "I know what men and women do, and I am not interested in doing that with Hangai at all." All the disgust melted off Tayiqu's face, and a strange, wistful light shined in her eyes. It made Esige unconformable. Because if it was not Hangai she wanted, who *was* she thinking about at the moment? "I want a man."

Esige nearly choked on air as she breathed in. "A man," she said flatly. "Like who?"

Tayiqu clasped her hands over her heart. "The Khan."

"*Dayan* Khan?" Esige asked, unable to mask the incredulity. Surely she misunderstood something.

Before Esige could even put her thoughts together, the girl began gushing her adoration. "Oh, Esige, he is so handsome. Everything about him is perfect. The way he walks like the earth just belongs to him. His arms, have you seen his arms? They are so strong! What do they feel like? Stone? And his eyes! Oh, I melt every time I see them."

Esige's jaw slackened as the girl rattled off the Khan's perfections, unable to hide her shock. Dayan was that gangly boy who always tripped over himself and walked in Mandukhai's shadow like he wished he could disappear into it.

"... and all my friends agree!" Tayiqu continued, finally losing steam. Esige lost half of what she said.

"*Dayan*. The Khan." Esige couldn't help probing for clarification, as if there could be another Khan.

"Yes." Hope bloomed in Tayiqu's dark eyes. Esige's stomach twisted, knowing that nothing good could come from that look. "Do you think you could arrange it?"

Esige opened her mouth to respond, but nothing came out.

Tayiqu stepped closer and took her hands, clutching them tight. "Please?"

"I don't know, Tayiqu," Esige said slowly, trying to gather her wits. "He and Mandukhai only just married. I ... I don't think they are ready to consider anything else right now. And then, you know, he is already married. You would be a second wife, at best."

She shook her head, her long braid swaying across her straight back. "I don't care if I'm the tenth. And it wouldn't be for a few years anyway, right? At least two years. That gives them plenty of time to enjoy their new marriage."

Esige licked her lips and took a deep breath. "Look, I doubt you are the only girl asking this question, but *if*—and that's a big if—he ever takes another wife, it will probably be for strategic alliances. To strengthen his bond with another tribe. We are already pretty tightly bound to him."

Tayiqu pulled her hands away and her shoulders sagged. Tears welled in her eyes. "Because of you."

Esige flinched at the accusation in Tayiqu's tone. "If you carry on as you have done with this boy, I can guarantee it will never happen. Ever."

Tayiqu swiped her sleeve across her cheek to wipe up tears. "If you can arrange this, I will stop immediately."

"If you stop this immediately, I will see what I can do."

Tayiqu threw herself at Esige, wrapping her arms around her and professing her gratitude.

What did I just do? Esige thought miserably. She hugged Tayiqu fiercely. *This will not end well.*

80 Miles North of Mogurkei's Ordos Camp – Ordos Basin – Spring 1480

Mandukhai rode alongside Dayan as they approached the area scouts had selected for the *tumens* to camp. Dayan looked resplendent on his pale mare in the blazing light of the slowly setting sun. Mandukhai could not help admiring him as they rode. His gold-plated lamellar armor reminded Mandukhai of the scales on a great dragon. Despite the battles he had worn the armor through, the golden plates appeared brand new. His helmet rose to a high point, just like hers did, but the horsehair crest had been bleached white. *All colors and none.* Mandukhai smiled, recalling her vision of Genghis a lifetime ago.

Nearly four days ago, all four *tumens* rode away from the families camped within the basin. Kelegei and Ordag had taken another *tumen* south two days ahead of the rest to circle around Mogurkei's flanks. Mandukhai had left ample warriors to protect the camp. She had worried the Ming would attack as they had done to Bigirsen's family camp nearly ten years ago, but she still regretted leaving so many warriors behind. They needed every able body they could find for the coming fight against Mogurkei. At the insistence of Legusi, Qori, Arqai, and a handful of other commanders, there would be no finishing this without a fight. Mogurkei would never surrender.

Tonight, they would make camp and wait two days for the rest of the generals to move into position all around Mogurkei's camp. Kelegei in the south. Togochi in the west. Huoshai in the east. Dayan and Mandukhai in the north. Mogurkei would be surrounded.

"You are staring," Dayan said softly.

Mandukhai's cheeks heated, and she glanced at the path ahead. But not before catching the smirk and sideways glance from Dayan. Their wedding night may have been Dayan's first time with anyone, but it had felt a little like a first for her as well. She had been with no one else in ten years. Some days, that waiting had been agonizing. Especially when Unebolod had often been only a door away. But she had made a sacred vow when she bound her future to Dayan at the Shrine of the First Queen. To break that vow—for any man—would have ensured she could never find peace in the next life. She would never have *had* a "next life."

No one had touched her since that Oirat kidnapping. Not like Dayan had on their wedding night. Certainly not in any deeply intimate way. It made her feel young and desirable again. Dayan hadn't let her forget it either. He seemed determined to prove just how desirable he thought she was at every opportunity, and he was swiftly gaining confidence. In just a few days, his youth and vitality had renewed her own.

He didn't just prove himself in private, either. Dayan's adjustment to their original plan had been intelligent. Not only had Dayan somehow spotted a potential weakness in their defense and strengthened it, but he knew exactly what it would take to get the Ordos Lords to give up this fight once and for all. Sadly, that required Nemeku's presence.

She glanced back over her shoulder at Nemeku, who rode just as confidently as any of the men. Their gazes met. Nemeku scowled, then averted his gaze sharply. He had not forgiven her for doubting him or his wife. Mandukhai couldn't say she blamed him. She would probably harbor resentment as well. But protecting Dayan and this empire was her priority. She had sacrificed Unebolod for it, and Nemeku was certainly no more important than he had been.

Dayan believed that, as long as the Ordos Lords who resisted him thought there was an alternative to his rule, they would never truly become part of their empire. Issama was dead, which left Nemeku as a potential puppet for their needs. Having Nemeku riding, fighting, and conquering alongside Dayan would show the Lords clearly that the two were united and Nemeku served the Great Khan.

Still, she hated having Nemeku along on the journey. Not because she mistrusted him—she mistrusted everyone around Dayan—but because he was just shy of fifteen now, hardly old enough for battle and already having a family. He should be back at the camp with Orghana. Though she was not terribly far along in her pregnancy yet, she depended on Nemeku.

Will I have a child soon, too, or is it too late for me? Though Dayan had made Mandukhai feel years younger, her body was not. It also brought another terribly hard to face truth to light. Dayan would need other wives. Younger wives. Especially if Mandukhai could not produce at least one heir sooner than later. The idea of sharing him with any other woman made her stomach churn. She was not ready. Not yet.

The sun broke the western horizon, glinting off Dayan's armor and making him shine like a beacon. It was hard not to stare at his straight back, strong jaw, or majesty. It was hard not to notice the way he rode with confidence, or how he wore a stoic mask. Until he glanced at her.

"You're staring again."

Mandukhai averted her eyes once more, patting Dust on the neck. "You look like a Great Khan."

He chuckled. "I *am* a Great Khan."

"Not all Khans fit in the skin," Mandukhai replied. Manduul certainly hadn't. Bayan wouldn't have either. Sometimes Mandukhai had a hard time believing that this man was Bayan's son. While they looked comparable on the surface, the similarities ended there. The two couldn't have been more different.

Dayan shifted in the saddle. Before they left camp, Ong and Tuya had worked together to bind Dayan's torso in several layers of cotton to protect the still-healing arrow wound from the last Ordos attack. The wound had closed weeks ago but still ached sometimes. He didn't complain about discomfort, but in little ways, he revealed the truth. Standing in the stirrups likely eased some of the impact on his side. She would not fuss. He had made it clear he wouldn't listen to her fussing over him like a child anymore. And she certainly didn't see a child anymore.

As they reached the campsite, men dismounted and began setting up. For two days, they would wait here for the others to move into position. On signals from arrows, the attack would begin. This camp rested at the northern mouth of a valley passage between rocky red cliffs. At the other end of the pass, Mogurkei's camp waited, unaware of the danger they were in. Dayan's scouts had hidden ahead to dispatch the men guarding the passage and secure it.

Once they defeated Mogurkei—if they defeated him—Mandukhai could finally put her reorganization and reunification plan into action.

Dayan dismounted and sent two scouts ahead to ensure no one would spot their forces. It was critical that Mogurkei did not suspect their presence. If he worried about attack, he would not ride out to meet Legusi in single combat. They needed him to separate himself from the rest of his camp.

Mandukhai dismounted as well. She slid a hand under Dust's armor along the neck and rubbed down the coat. The stallion snorted in appreciation.

"If this goes wrong," Mandukhai began.

"It won't." Dayan sounded so confident, certain, so much like Unebolod.

"But if it does, and we get separated, leave me behind."

Dayan's jaw slackened. He blinked at her for a moment. "Not a chance."

"Dayan ..." Mandukhai edged closer, running her fingers along his jaw.

He took her hand and kissed it. "We finish this together, or not at all."

"A foolish sentiment."

"Really? I thought it was charming." He smirked, and her stomach flipped. His amusement melted away an instant later, replaced by an inward focus. The corners of his mouth curved downward. He met her gaze with serious intensity. "Mandukhai, I told you two years ago, I can think of no better way to die than at your side. I would rather die a thousand times beside you than live a moment without you. Maybe I was trying to be charming, but I was serious as well. I will never, ever leave you behind to save myself." He edged closer. "Ever."

Dayan leaned in, brushing his lips against hers.

Nemeku gagged. "You two know you aren't alone, right?"

Mandukhai regretted breaking the kiss, but was rewarded with a mischievous grin as Dayan turned his gaze to his cousin. "I could not care less if you watch."

Nemeku's nose wrinkled. "Gross. It's like watching my parents."

Dayan turned his full attention to Nemeku as he took a drink from his skin. "I'm only two years older than you."

"Doesn't matter." Nemeku shook his head.

The comment only reminded Mandukhai of how much older she was than both of them. Nemeku likely *did* see her as a parent as much as he would Esige. The age difference was nothing unheard of. Few ever cared about the age of their partners. Manduul had been even older when Mandukhai married him—and she had been younger than Dayan was now. *I am finally happy, and I won't let anyone else ruin that*, she thought as she walked to the edge of the pass, guiding Dust by the reins.

Mandukhai raised a hand to shield her eyes and squinted into the distance. The pass was wide, but it would take some time to funnel their forces through it and into the battlefield. It would have to be quick, and when Mogurkei was distracted by Legusi.

Dust snorted and bobbed his head, then scraped his hooves across the rocky earth to dig up something for grazing. Mandukhai gave him slack to forage.

"We have been through a lot together, old friend," she said, stroking his braided mane.

Her eyes fell on the saddle and a lump swelled in her throat. She edged closer, tracing her finger along the worn dragons etched into the leather. Years of riding had smoothed out some of the dragon heads, making them harder to see. Mandukhai closed her eyes, dredging up the memory of receiving the horse and saddle. A gift from Manduul, commissioned by Unebolod. He had watched her with such interest and even offered her a partial smile.

These past ten years had given him little reason to smile at her anymore. He buried himself in the work, following her orders and offering her advice, teaching the very boy who had stolen his place. She had been certain they would finish this together. Riding into this final battel without her best strategist made her stomach uneasy. Togochi had proven himself over the years, just as Soke had. And Dayan certainly seemed to have learned a lot from Unebolod. But the absence of such a powerful force could not be overlooked. He thrust himself head-first into his new position to push away his own pain. Just had he had when they lost their child. He never told her as much, but she knew it to be true.

Mandukhai had hurt Unebolod deeply when she chose Dayan instead of him. He had insisted he understood, but the more fervently he had insisted over the years, the more certain she became he did not understand. Not fully.

She opened her eyes, and a few tears rolled down her cheeks. Was it wrong to cry over another man? Unebolod had consumed her for so long. She remembered when he had gone off to gather support for Bayan just before Manduul died. She recalled the passion and conviction in their conversation.

You have taken me, a mighty warrior, and reduced me to a love-struck boy. I am at your mercy. Those words haunted her, as did so many of Unebolod's confessions.

I will light your fire for you. Even if I have to wait until my bones are old. And he had waited. No matter how much she tried, Mandukhai had never convinced him to marry another. He remained, until his last days, at her mercy.

"I did not deserve him, Dust," Mandukhai murmured. "I never did."

The stallion lifted his head and gazed at her from one large eye, then returned to grazing. Was he accusing her or agreeing with her?

"He didn't believe in much." Togochi's sudden appearance startled Mandukhai. "But he believed in you."

Mandukhai scrubbed away her tears with the back of her hand, then sniffed as if it could cover her crying. "I'm not sure I deserved his faith."

Togochi gazed into the pass as if seeking weaknesses or danger. "Unebolod was one of the smartest men I have ever known. He knew exactly what he was doing and why." Togochi's shoulders sagged. Silence fell between them.

Mandukhai wished she could believe Togochi. Unebolod was smart, and he did nothing without considering the ramifications of his actions. But why had he followed her instead of taking what he wanted ... She sighed.

Togochi cleared his throat. "You deserve happiness, Mandukhai. It's what he would have wanted for you, whether or not it was with him. Don't let grief and regret push between you and your husband."

Husband. Mandukhai's brows drew downward before the truth of that word really sank in. For years, she had been unofficially married to Dayan, to his cause. Calling him her husband seemed lacking.

"You know, there were times I had wished that a Khatun could have multiple husbands, just as a Khan can have multiple wives." She laughed at her own foolishness. "I understand why it wouldn't work, but there was always room in my heart for both of them." She lowered her gaze and muttered, "There always will be."

"I understand exactly what you mean. He knew you loved him." Togochi turned away from the pass, pausing beside her. "If he were here right now, he would tell you to stop doubting yourself. He wasn't the one who got us this far. It was you."

As Togochi started away, Mandukhai blurted, "He had a son."

Togochi froze, then turned to face her slowly. Mandukhai's stomach wrenched, but someone else had to know the truth. Even if she didn't want to admit it.

He nodded. "I know your child was his and not Manduul's. It couldn't have been Manduul's. Issama confessed to destroying Manduul's seed before he died."

Mandukhai's cheeks heated. "I … that's not what I'm talking about." *He knew? Why did he say nothing? Will he tell Dayan? Should I? Does it even matter anymore?* Fear made her gut churn in a sickening mass. Her palms sweated. Would Dayan care? "I mean in camp. Altan's oldest son, Bagasun."

Mandukhai could almost see the wheels turning in Togochi's head. Finally, he shook his head. "It doesn't matter anymore. Unebolod's people are yours now, and when we defeat Mogurkei, the Khorchin will be reorganized, along with all the rest. They don't need an heir any longer."

That Unebolod's son was little more than a future warrior did not settle well in Mandukhai's heart. Bagasun deserved more. He deserved everything his father could no longer give him.

Yet Togochi had a point as well. Several times over the past few years, Mandukhai had shared ideas with Togochi and Unebolod regarding how she could establish a new, stable government when they finally unified the tribes under the Great Khan's banner. No one else really knew what she had planned, aside from Unebolod, Togochi, and Dayan. The reorganization would blur former royal lines and establish one—and only one—clear line of succession.

"I will take my men at the wolf dawn," Togochi said. "And we will see each other again in two days. Let's finish what we have started, Mandukhai. For the Khan." Togochi paused, raising his chin. "For Unebolod."

Mandukhai took another moment to watch the pass. Togochi's boots crunched the dry earth, receding until all she could hear were the hushed sounds of the warriors setting up camp. The upcoming fight could cost her army precious lives. Would that be the last conversation she ever had with Togochi? Would either of them survive the coming fight? He had become like a brother to her over the years. She depended on his boundless patience.

I hope to see you again, Togochi. And we will finish this, one way or another. For Unebolod, she thought, then turned and headed back to join the others. She would earn his faith.

In just two days.

CHAPTER FORTY-FOUR

Wolf Dawn

Togochi rose with the wolf dawn, stiffness in his joints from sleeping all night on the ground. His two *tumens* had ridden for nearly two days to reach this pass on the western flank of Mogurkei's camp. Mandukhai and Dayan would lead their two *tumens* in the north. Esige and Huoshai had three *tumens* of warriors in the east, and Kelegei, Ordag, and the Three Guards had one *tumen* in the south. He rubbed his fists into the small of his back as he stretched. The wolf dawn had only just begun, but already his camp stirred as men woke to check saddles and weapons, and to organize into their ranks.

Today, Legusi would draw Mogurkei out of his camp to engage in one-on-one combat for control of the Ordos. While they distracted Mogurkei, the rest of the *tumens* would close in on all sides and force the camp to surrender. The plan was simple and elegant, but Togochi had a lingering sense of doubt.

It almost seemed too easy.

As he had done last night, Togochi rode to the edge of the pass, careful to keep himself out of sight in case anyone in the Ordos camp watched the pass. He sneaked to the rim, watching the Ordos camp that was far too close for his comfort. Just as Unebolod would have done, Togochi had sent men along the ridges the second they arrived to get a closer look at the camp. Most of Togochi's ideas stemmed from one simple question. What would Unebolod do? Asking this question kept Unebolod's voice alive in his mind.

Mogurkei had gathered so many men. That camp was much larger than he had expected. By his best estimation, Mogurkei had two *tumens* of warriors who could begin defensive maneuvers—an equal match to Togochi's own forces.

Last night, he had also sent a couple of scouts to try and probe deeper into the camp, but they had come back reporting little more than the watch positions too far out to get close to camp. All night, Togochi had men on watch with orders to kill any Ordos scouts who came too close to their hiding place. All had been quiet.

Too quiet.

Togochi felt the tension knotting in his shoulder and tried to relax.

Hooves approached from behind. A minute later, Altan and Dochigen reined in beside him.

"You look deeply troubled, Togochi," Dochigen noted. "I'm not used to seeing such consternation on your face. You are supposed to be our beacon of hope."

Togochi froze. *He* was the beacon of hope? Wasn't that Dayan's job? Or Mandukhai's? How had that fallen on Togochi's shoulders? "Mogurkei has been gathering his forces here for a while."

"Why didn't he attack us sooner?" Altan asked. She waved a hand toward the Ordos camp in the distance. "Clearly, that is his intention. Why else would he gather an army?"

"Maybe he had hoped someone else would do it for him," Togochi offered, casting a knowing look at Altan.

"Issama." The open disgust on her face made her thoughts on the dead Uyghur apparent.

Togochi nodded. "He probably has not heard about Issama's death yet. The Khan was right. We had to get rid of Issama first."

Thinking about Issama made Togochi's arms itch and become warm. Compulsion drove him to feel an overwhelming need to clean his arms and hands more than once since he cut out Issama's heart. Qolotai had watched his peculiar behavior in silence several times. The other night, Qolotai's quick response had likely saved him from severe burns. Jaghan's careful administration of the silver balm had healed the minor scalding.

The morning he had left on this mission, he had bid all three women farewell. Jaghan had embraced him and reassured him that she loved him—not that he had any doubt. Geriel had done the same, whispering in his ear, "I will talk to her," before pulling away. He had given her a second, grateful squeeze before he had mounted.

As he had said a final goodbye, Togochi had been itching at his hand unconsciously. Qolotai had noticed. She had stepped forward and placed on hand gently over his to stop him.

"Follow Geriel's lead," he had murmured to Qolotai.

She had dipped her head in agreement and stepped back.

This morning, Togochi knew with certainty that he needed her. They were bound by the same trauma. She understood his pain in ways he could never, ever tell the other two women.

If I survive this, I will make my intentions clear to Jaghan and Geriel, Togochi thought. Hopefully, Geriel would have convinced Jaghan already before then.

"Rally the *tumens*," Togochi called. "It's nearly time."

The exit from the pass was too close to the Ordos camp to leave the security of the passage walls until the battle began or they risked detection. But he would have his men mounted and ready to spill out on the battlefield in seconds.

NORTHERN PARTY – ORDOS BASIN

Mandukhai stretched her hand out as she opened her eyes, but, as usual, found the furs beside her empty. It was something she had quickly grown used to, though it filled her with disappointment every morning. Dayan always lay awake as she drifted off, and he always woke before her—a notorious early-riser. *Does he even sleep?* she wondered as she sat up and took in their small, empty tent.

After sliding into her thick silk deel and boots, Mandukhai ducked outside. The wolf dawn had only just begun fading away the blackness of night. Today, they would finally finish this.

Many of the men were already up and readying for the coming fight. She made her way through the camp, searching for Dayan. Eventually, she found him as he patted Chakicha khan on the shoulder and made his way toward Commander Bagatur. By the time she caught up to Dayan, she only caught the tail end of their conversation.

"… reserve with Utagachi," Dayan said.

Batagur nodded. "Makes sense. I'll start gathering my men." He bowed politely to Mandukhai before shuffling off.

"Did you sleep at all?" she asked.

"Enough." Dayan turned and kissed her forehead. "We should get our armor on and mount."

She nodded. Warmth spread through her as his hand slid down into her own. The two of them strolled back to their small tent together. Few of the men had bothered bringing shelter along for the journey, but Togochi had insisted Mandukhai and Dayan at least have some privacy while they waited for the rest of the *tumens* to move into position all around the Ordos camp.

It took no time to dress for battle. Both had become accustomed to it, and had each other to help. Soon, the two of them stood outside, holding the reins of their mounts as Khosoichi made the ceremonial sacrifice of a lamb and inspected the intestines. He raised them high in victory, smiling at the brilliant purple-blue color as blood rolled down his forearm. Once the sacrifice was completed, he fanned juniper needles and spoke the blessing to the High Heavens. As he finished, Khosoichi stepped forward, his joints popping with age as he anointed the Khan and Khatun with a swipe of lamb's blood across their foreheads.

Mandukhai bit her tongue, worried about the old shaman. Khosoichi had served Manduul for years. She had never considered his age before. But now she saw the leathery wrinkles of old age, the white, coarse hair mixed with silver and black. How old was he now? Sixty? Seventy? What if something happened to him and he could not heal the Khan? They could find someone else to help, but Khosoichi had decades of experience.

"Are you all right?" Dayan whispered, leaning close to her.

"Fine."

"Then you can loosen your grip a little." He shook his hand free of hers.

"Sorry." She had not even realized how tightly she gripped Dayan's hand. "Khosoichi, thank you for the blessing. You should return to camp. We may need you later."

Khosoichi uncurled his hunched back. "I am where I need to be. And here I shall remain."

"There is no shame in admitting your age," Mandukhai said kindly. "You need to look after yourself."

He shook his head stubbornly. "I look after our divine rulers, and so the High Heavens look after me."

"As it did for Getei?" Dayan asked. His words were laced with a deep sorrow. Getei had died protecting Dayan's life, just as Unebolod had.

"Getei died doing exactly what the High Heavens expected of him," Khosoichi replied evenly. "Protecting our Great Khan. He knew his fate long before it came to pass. We both saw it in our visions. It was the reason he went with our Khan on that campaign instead of me. Where and when his fate would happen, we did not know, but we both knew he needed to remain at the Khan's side."

"And your fate?" Mandukhai asked.

"Is here." The absolute conviction of Khosoichi's words drew a sad smile from her.

"Very well. At least stay in the pass in case we need you," she said. "There is no need for you to ride into battle. Where would we be if you died?"

"Exactly where you are meant to be," Khosoichi said matter-of-factly.

She blinked in alarm. What did he mean by that? Before she could ask for clarification, the old shaman shuffled away.

Dayan nudged Mandukhai's shoulder before he climbed into the saddle. She mounted Dust, running her fingers absently over the worn dragons.

Dayan turned his white mare to face the warriors gathered around them at the northern mouth of the pass that would lead to the Ordos camp. They stretched into the northern horizon on horseback. Two full *tumens* of warriors ready to ride in the Khan's name, to die for their cause. At the head of the group, Soke, Chakicha, Bagatur, and one of the Ordos Lords sat on horseback, prepared to direct the *tumens*.

"The days of Genghis are upon us," Dayan called out. "We have lost a lot to get us to this moment. Friends. Family. Lovers."

The words pierced Mandukhai's soul, as if Dayan added the last bit just for her. But the way the men responded, stirring anxiously in their saddles, nodding in agreement, bolstered her faith in the coming fight.

"Today, we honor their memory," he continued. "Today, we prove they did not die in vain. Today, we show the oathbreakers our true faces!" Some warriors voiced their assent. Dayan barreled on. "All of us are bound to the will of the High Heavens. All of us have a role to play. As we are crushed in the heat of battle, I vow to you now to live or die at your sides. This is the hour of the wolves, and today we fight. In the years, decades, centuries from now, our people will speak of this day as the day we stood together. The day we mended our fractured empire once and for all. Shed your blood with me, brothers of the united Mongol Nation!"

A chorus of cheers rose in the deep blue light of the wolf dawn. Spears and bows pumped in the air. Mandukhai's own heart beat faster as Dayan's words moved her. She gazed at him, fully in his element, and marveled that this was the same boy she had rescued, the same man she had married.

"There is only one thing left to do," Dayan called out above the noise, his voice cutting through the cheers. The warriors fell silent, eager to hear their Khan's words. "Claim our victory!"

The men released a cheer as one.

"Who is with me?"

The cheers lifted even higher into the sky. For a moment, Mandukhai worried that the noise could be heard in the Ordos camp. But her fear dissolved the moment Dayan raised his sword and spun his mare around, leading the *tumens* into the pass. She watched him for a moment, breathless, before joining.

EASTERN PARTY – ORDOS BASIN

Esige struggled to control her nerves as she waited beside Huoshai and Legusi. Shortly after dawn, Mogurkei and Legusi would meet on the open field to the east of Mogurkei's camp. According to the agreement, both sides could bring only a hundred men as an honor guard. Huoshai had hand-selected the hundred, a mixture of Urainkhai and Ordos men to avoid raising Mogurkei's suspicions. Per Dayan's orders, the Ordos could only carry swords for close combat and no bows or arrows. He still worried about the Ordos betraying their oaths.

Just over the hill at their backs, a full *tumen* of Urainkhai warriors—along with nearly twice as many of Legusi's and Arqai's Ordos combined—waited for the horn to signal the attack. Then, they would ride in and crush the Ordos while Mogurkei was distracted and distanced from his men. Dayan had sent orders to capture but not kill Mogurkei.

The saddle creaked as Esige shifted. Huoshai glanced at her, frowning. The two of them had a bitter fight the previous night. He had wanted her to stay behind, to wait in the camp like all the other women. He had insisted she wasn't safe out here, that she would be a distraction to him. But Esige wasn't safe anywhere if this didn't work, and she could handle herself just fine. Besides, her so-called bitterness toward Mandukhai and Dayan after Unebolod's death was one of the reasons Mogurkei had agreed to this. He wanted control of the Ordos. He also wanted to make allies of the powerful Urainkhai.

"It's not too late," Huoshai murmured.

Esige tightened her grip on the reins. "To apologize? I agree. And I will accept it any time."

Huoshai hefted a sigh that sounded more like a growl to Esige. The two once more fell silent as they waited. Legusi cast the two of them worried glances.

Huoshai had made one good point last night. And only one. If they both died today, their children would be without parents. Esige had left them with Chimgee and Tayiqu. The two of them were more than capable of caring for the children. They would be in good hands should anything happen. And Mandukhai would never allow Esige's children to fall into poverty. If Esige died today, Mandukhai would take them in. Just as Mandukhai had taken in her, Borogchin, Nemeku, and Dayan. Esige straightened. Mandukhai had not given birth to children, but she certainly created her own family.

I don't want to do this with him angry with me, Esige thought, glancing at her husband. If she died, she did not want him living with regret. And if he died, she did not want her last words to be in anger. But the moment Esige considered apologizing, he edged his mount closer to hers, staring straight ahead; a subtle sign that he thought she needed his protection. Her jaw twitched. He would apologize before she would.

"Here he comes," Huoshai announced, then nudged his mare forward at a canter.

Esige rode beside him, heart pounding in her chest in rhythm with the thunder of hooves. She glanced up at the Urainkhai and Ordos banners fluttering in the air beside Huoshai. Her heart swelled. She adored her husband and was terribly proud of the man he had become.

"I still love you," she said, hoping her forward gaze appeared distant or nonchalant. She would accept either.

"Is that an apology?" Huoshai asked. The amusement in his tone made her blood boil.

"No."

He snorted. They carried on in silence toward Mogurkei and his men, still hundreds of yards away. "I love you, too," he said at last.

Esige smiled, then traced her fingers subconsciously over the bow Unebolod had given her eight years ago when he passed through the Urainkhai territory to return the *sulde* to Mandukhai. Huoshai had joked that Unebolod only encouraged her behavior, but he had said it with affection. He had known a bow would never change who she was fundamentally.

The bow was a fine piece of the same style as the one Unebolod had given Mandukhai years ago. The arms were sturdy, but easily bent to her will when she drew back. The horn handle had molded to her hand over the years. She adored this bow. The engraved dancing rabbits along the arms brushed her fingertips, and her heart ached. Losing Unebolod had been like losing a father. Esige had never known her own father, Manduul's half-brother, and Manduul had hardly been a caring father-figure in her life. But she had adored Unebolod, and he had adored her as well. She missed him so much it hurt just to think about him.

Mandukhai had better be right about you, Dayan, Esige thought bitterly. If Unebolod had died protecting Dayan, and that boy was not everything Mandukhai had promised, Esige truly would resent the two of them. This charade would be a reality.

CHAPTER FORTY-FIVE

Fire in the Sky

Huoshai signaled for the men to halt fifty yards from where Mogurkei had stopped his own men. The hill at their backs sheltered three *tumens* of Urainkhai and Ordos warriors following Huoshi's command. On his signal, they would close in and cut Mogurkei off from the rest of his camp. The sun crept up slowly over the hill, casting long shadows across the dry ground. Esige reined in beside Huoshai and they both turned attention to Legusi. The Ordos khan sat rigid in his saddle, eyes fixed on Mogurkei. His concern was obvious.

"Remember what we discussed," Huoshai said. "Stick to the plan. Stall as long as possible, and everything should be fine."

"Should." Legusi snorted. He muttered something under his breath before dismounting and tossing the reins to one of his own men.

Several of Legusi's Ordos guards shifted uncomfortably in their saddles. Esige took little solace from their concern for their khan. They doubted his ability to fight Mogurkei, or to stall him. Even if Legusi died, Mogurkei would still suffer defeat. By the time he could kill Legusi, it would be too late to stop Mandukhai and Dayan from taking control of Mogurkei's camp. Not that Esige wanted Legusi to die. In their brief time together, she had grown fond of him. Unlike Arqai, Legusi was a logical and patient man.

"I'm still worried about Arqai," Esige said softly to her husband.

"If you had stayed behind, you wouldn't have to worry because he would be too terrified of you to try anything," Huoshai replied.

Esige ground her teeth, biting off a sharp retort. It seemed Huoshai would use every opportunity to chaff at her nerves until she broke. *He should know better by now*, she thought.

Legusi and Mogurkei approached one another on foot.

"I will be honest," Mogurkei said. "I thought you wouldn't have the nerve to show up." He breathed in the air as if savoring it. "This is stacking up to be a glorious day."

Legusi stopped in a defensive position, hand on the hilt of his sword. "Perhaps. But not for you. You understand I cannot allow you to live. To take control of the Ordos from me, you must kill me. And if I win, I cannot have you stirring up rebellion. One of us will die today."

"Then I hope you have said your goodbyes."

Esige tightened her grip on the reins. Why were men so insufferably arrogant about their fighting skills?

Huoshai cleared his throat, drawing Mogurkei's attention. Legusi did not avert his gaze from his foe. "My Lords, I want to be clear. I know we agreed to this fight, but I still think it would be better if we worked together to free ourselves from Dayan Khan first. If we are to stop the Khan, we need all able-bodied men. So I must ask, is this fight truly necessary now, or can it wait until we have completed this tenuous alliance?"

Legusi's shoulders visibly relaxed. For a moment, Esige thought the two Ordos Lords would actually stand down. But Mogurkei's eyes instead landed on her. The corner of his mouth twitched upward.

"You were Mandukhai's ward," Mogurkei said. "Why should I believe anything that comes from either of you?" His hand rested on the hilt of his sword, and she didn't doubt he could draw it in an instant.

Esige edged closer. Huoshai hissed at her to stay back, but she ignored him. She only rode a few feet. "Lord Mogurkei, you are right. I *was* her ward. Ten years ago. Since I left her care, our relationship has been strained. I have loathed everything Dayan has done since the moment he arrived in my life. But the worst of all was that Unebolod sacrificed himself for that boy. Dayan doesn't deserve that kind of loyalty. I lost the only father I have ever known because of them. There are no words for the bitterness that seeds in the heart."

Mogurkei sneered at her. "Which is exactly why I should not trust a word that drips from your venomous mouth, girl. Because if you resent that runt of a boy for his part in Unebolod's death, what do you think of me?" He strode arrogantly closer, keeping a wary eye on Legusi. "Because I am the one who organized the attack that should have killed the Khan. Instead, it killed Unebolod. All the better, as far as Issama and I are concerned. Unebolod never would have stepped aside, no matter what happened to the boy."

Despite her best attempts to remain calm, Esige could feel the heat rising in her face. Her jaw tightened painfully. Her fingers edged toward her belt. She could just end this now. Dayan's orders be damned. Mogurkei didn't deserve a single breath in his lungs.

Huoshai trotted up beside her and took her hand as her fingertips brushed the knife handle. He raised her hand and pressed it to his lips. "My wife does not blame you. She blames Ulum and the Khan."

"Issama is dead," Legusi blurted. "So if you were counting on his help, you will be disappointed."

Mogurkei's face fell. He took a step back, studying each of them in turns as if attempting to ferret out a lie.

"Dayan Khan sent his *orlok*, Togochi, to finish Issama," Huoshai said confirmed. "Word has it, Togochi returned with Issama's heart in a jar just a little over a week ago."

Mogurkei shook his head. "No. I received a message just four weeks ago that Issama was prepared to take over Hami and gather reinforcements to come to my aid."

"A lot can change in that time," Huoshai said. "I assure you, he is very dead."

Mogurkei's jaw twitched. He pulled his sword, swinging it at Legusi's neck. Esige yelped, guiding her mount further from the two men. Legusi responded just as quickly, raising his own sword in defense and shoving Mogurkei away. As the two were distracted, Huoshai gave a subtle signal. The Urainkhai banners pulled back from the Ordos—the sign the rest of the Khan's forces would be waiting for.

Now, all the Khan's forces would close in on the camp to capture it.

I hope Dayan lets me kill this Lord, Esige thought, glaring at Mogurkei as he and Legusi danced around one another.

NORTHERN TUMEN

Under the veil of the wolf dawn, Mandukhai and Dayan had led their two *tumens* through the pass and out the other side. The warriors spilled out quietly along the cliffs, using the deep, long shadows for cover. Even as the sun rose, the angle of sunlight against the cliffs cast a shadow over her waiting army. She did not want to attack the camp or harm the women and children there. Her *tumens* would close in on the camp from all directions while Mogurkei was distracted in the east, hopefully ending resistance before it began by capturing the camp. Huoshai and Esige could capture Mogurkei. Then they could end this for good.

In the distance, so far off Mandukhai had to squint to see, a hundred horsemen rode behind the yellow Ordos banner. An equal force of Urainkhai crossed the expanse, their banner fluttering red like blood across the sky. When Legusi had engaged Mogurkei in combat, the Urainkhai banners would pull back to signal the distraction.

"There," Soke said, pointing east.

Mandukhai could just make out the Urainkhai banners pulling back. "It's time."

The signal arrow rippled down the line. It would continue circling around the camp north to west to south. Her forces would know it was time to close in and capture the camp. Mandukhai glimpsed an arrow with a red ribbon arching through the sky far to the west. It only lasted a moment before the arrow disappeared. Had she not been watching for it, she would have missed it entirely.

With the signal, the *tumens* began a slow approach, bows raised to kill any scouts or watchmen who might raise alarms.

Dayan watched the advance slowly unfold with remarkable calm. This was his moment, and he knew it. He studied the way his men rode forward. He would not lose this fight when he was so close to completing Mandukhai's vision. He would not lose Mandukhai, either. Not when he only just married her.

A few Ordos scouts fell from saddles as Dayan's bowmen killed them. He remained composed, watching with detachment. His gaze slid past the advance lines toward the camp itself. Among the maze of gers, he spotted something. A line of long poles angled against the sky. It took a moment to realize what he had spied.

"Dayan," Nemeku said, a tremor in his own voice as he saw the same thing.

Mogurkei concealed lines of trebuchets among the gers. Those had not been there on any of the other scouting missions. Mogurkei had hidden them, somehow. But now they angled back against the sky, primed and ready to fire. Dayan's gaze swept west, following the line of sight...

...Right at the pass Togochi's *tumens* would pour out from.

WESTERN TUMENS

Altan smacked Togochi's arm and pointed toward the north. "There it is!"

The signal.

Mogurkei was fighting Legusi. It was time to move in.

Togochi spread the call to his men. In seconds, warriors poured out of the western pass as the signal arrow fired toward the *tumens* waiting in the south. Togochi waited beside the exit from the pass, allowing Dochigen and Altan to lead the charge.

A horn sounded. Togochi's gaze swept the horizon. It was too soon to sound the alarms. Who was sounding their horn?

Shouts from his own southern flank rose high in the air. Togochi edged his way closer to the southern side of the pass and stood in the stirrups for a clearer view over heads.

In the distance, thousands of Ordos warriors poured out of the southern edge of camp, spilling out in all directions in a mass of chaos. But their target was clear to him. The southern *tumen* was their weakest line. Somehow, Mogurkei knew that already and had launched a full-scale attack on the Khan's southern *tumen*.

Kelegei didn't have nearly enough men to fight off that force. *Where are the Ordos we are supposed to have backing him up?* There was no time to contemplate the potential betrayal. Without support, Kelegei's southern *tumen* would be crushed.

"Rally to the south!" Togochi shouted over the distant clash of steel, thump of hooves, and punch of arrows.

Something cracked loud from the Ordos camp. Togochi jumped in his saddle at the sudden sound.

Blazing fire streamed across the sky. Too late, he realized the danger. More than half of his men were still in the pass. He raised the horn to his lips to call for retreat before the pass could crumble on his warriors. The blast of the horn cut out as the thunderous boom of the fireball contacted the upper wall of the pass. Enormous rocks broke off and tumbled in a flaming mass toward his men.

Toward him.

NORTHERN TUMENS

Ordos warriors spilled out from the eastern edge of camp like ants from an anthill, racing directly toward their northern forces. Mandukhai could not understand why Dayan had sat there in the saddle, unmoving as his *tumens* fell under attack. She called to him, trying to get him to snap out of his trance, and he had ignored her completely. Arrows fell around them, and she did her best to use her shield to block them from both herself and Dayan.

And then he broke out his spell, shouting commands as he charged ahead. Something caught his attention beyond their skirmish.

Dayan whipped his mare into action. She lunged forward eagerly, racing toward the open field where his men churned in chaos.

"Sound the horn!" Dayan commanded.

"It's too early!" Soke called back over the rising thunder of hooves.

The element of surprise had been spoiled. Mogurkei had expected them.

"It's too late!" Dayan snapped.

Dayan rode as fast as his mare could carry him, never slowing. Nemcku was half a heartbeat behind him.

Mandukhai raced Dust after Dayan, trying to make herself as small as possible to reduce the target. When she neared him and opened her mouth to call out, the sound of her own voice strangled as she watched the balls of fire race across the sky and slam into the mouth of the valley. A thunderous crash ripped across the sky a moment after the impact.

Togochi!

EASTERN TUMENS

Legusi and Mogurkei remained locked in combat. Both had sustained injuries, but nothing fatal. Blood seeped from Mogurkei's side where Legusi had penetrated armor. Likewise, Legusi had a bloodied arm from an unexpected blow. Esige watched the two in fascination as they grunted and sweat with each thrust and parry.

Beside her, Huoshai remained fixed in his saddle, watching everything with his hand on his bow. He could kill a man from well over a hundred yards off. Esige was certain Huoshai would kill Mogurkei if he attempted any moves toward her.

Her stare glided past Huoshai toward the north. Dust clouds rose in the air. The ground rumbled. Her stomach sank. The Khan was leading a charge westward—away from her location. *He is supposed to come kill Mogurkei!*

Something was very wrong. "Huoshai," she hissed, nodding toward the north.

The set of his brows told Esige everything she needed to know. The plan was changing. Her heart hammered, picking up speed.

"Now, Huoshai," Esige hissed at him.

"Not yet," he snapped.

She shifted anxiously. They needed to signal their own warriors over the hill.

A great creak in the distance drew Esige's attention past the fight. Balls of fire flew out of the Ordos camp toward the western pass, their tails whipping like angry dragons.

"Now!" Mogurkei roared. He whipped a knife from his belt and thrust it at Legusi's neck. A mad, desperate wrestling match began between the two men.

Then Mogurkei's men charged toward their own.

Huoshai fired at Mogurkei faster than Esige had ever seen him fire before. The arrow pierced through Mogurkei's hand. Even as it punched the Ordos Lord's skin, forcing Mogurkei to drop his knife, Huoshai blew the horn around his neck. New banners unfurled as the Urainkhai banners dropped to the ground. The soaring golden eagle against a blue sky.

The Great Khan's banners.

Soon, the Urainkhai and Ordos would ride over the hills to join the fight. Any second now.

A great crack of thunder ripped across the sky. Horses startled as a burst of flames erupted to the west. Plumes of smoke and dust rose into the sky. But Esige could still see what happened clearly. The Ordos had fired at the pass where Togochi's *tumens* were entering the fray. Boulders rolled down the hillside, deafening even from so far away.

It's too late. Our plan is shot!

The Ordos guard closed in around Mogurkei. Esige snapped back to her own situation as Mogurkei leaped onto his mare. He swung away. Her heart sank, thumping all the way down in the pits of her stomach. The hundred guards Legusi had brought along locked in vicious combat with Mogurkei's guards as the Ordos Lord made his escape with only a handful to protect him.

Legusi lay on the ground, clutching his side. Panic climbed up Esige's throat. As Huoshai fought alongside his men, Esige jumped from the saddle and kneeled beside Legusi, inspecting the wound.

"It's fine," Legusi said. But sweat beaded on his forehead.

"I'm taking it out." Esige didn't give him a chance to protest before pulling the knife from the wound. Either he would die quicker or she could dress the wound. Regardless, they had to resolve this quickly.

All around them, men fell from saddles, too distracted by the other mounted warriors to care about the two of them.

Legusi grimaced as she pulled the knife out. It caught on something along the way and she tensed, her breath catching. Then threads of silk ripped on the blade's edge. She ran her hand over the silk, then pried it wider open with her fingers, brushing cold skin. When she pulled her hand out of the small hole, only a bit of blood had smeared on her finger. She grimaced and stood, pulling him to his feet.

"You're fine," she said impatiently. "The knife caught on silk."

Legusi grimaced, examining the hole himself.

"Get on your horse. We have to fight. Where are our men?" Esige spun around, gathering her reins.

None of the Urainkhai *tumen* had raced to their rescue. But on the hilltop in the east, she spotted arrows flying as another crack of thunder raced across the sky.

Huoshai sounded his horn again, calling for their guards to follow him. Esige leaped into the saddle and kicked her stallion into action. The two of them raced side-by-side toward the hills where the Urainkhai warriors had been waiting.

After cresting the hill, Esige yanked her stallion to a halt and gasped.

"Arqai," Huoshai growled as he realized the sickening truth.

The Urainkhai and Legusi's Ordos warriors fought the men Arqai commanded in a chaotic mass. Arqai had betrayed them. He had broken his sacred vow. *I will cut his throat myself!* Esige thought.

Her gaze swept the battlefield. A flash of yellow horsehair streamed out from a helmet. Esige unhooked her bow and began firing arrows at any Ordos unfortunate enough to get in her way. But her path was obvious. She only had one true target.

Arqai would die by her hands. She had warned him, and now he would feel her wrath.

"Esige!" Huoshai shouted. He cursed as he plunged his mare into action, racing after her.

Wind lashed Esige's face. Her made-up hair bounced and fell free, whipping behind her. Along with the rest of the Urainkhai men, Esige unhooked her bow from the saddle, drew back. Breath in. Hold. Hooves up. Release. She focused on every arrow just like Unebolod taught her, firing into the backs of the startled Ordos warriors.

Unlike the warriors, she wore no helmet. Her armor was minimal, mostly because Huoshai had kept her from actual battle. She never had need of so much armor before today. Considering how much Huoshai had resisted her coming along, she was surprised he hadn't insisted she wear more armor—or at least a helmet.

Horses toppled, throwing riders to the ground beneath the barrage of oncoming hooves. Esige guided with her knees as Unebolod taught her, holding tight when her stallion jumped over a fallen horse.

As the battle in the eastern *tumens* raged, Esige closed in on Arqai, surrounded by his guards armed only with swords. Huoshai had already rallied the Urainkhai warriors with Legusi's help, and now their *tumens* formed a ring around the attacking Ordos, firing arrows against men who only had been allowed swords.

Arqai spotted Esige as she closed in on him. His eyes bulged. "On the right!" he called out to his guards.

Too late.

Esige's blood was up. She calculated her chances with the bow and knew she could only take out one or two more guards. Without hesitation, she fired her arrows to make a hole, kicking off her boots to free up her feet. As the dead guards fell from their horses, she pulled her feet up under her, pressing her balance against the saddle until she was in a crouch, holding on to the horse for dear life.

Her stallion jerked to a stop, but she used the momentum to run from her saddle, across the horse belonging to the dead guard.

Arqai hollered in alarm.

She drew her knives from her belt, clutching one in each fist as she launched through the air at him. More arrows fired past her, providing cover. Some met their mark, dropping more of Arqai's guards. A few glanced off armor.

Instinctively, Arqai raised his arms to block her attack. Instead, he caught her as she hammered into him. The impact jarred her entire body. She thrust her blades toward his neck, seeking flesh on either side. The two of them bounced off one of the horses before tumbling to the ground. Arqai grasped at his neck with one hand as the other wrapped around Esige's throat. She gasped for breath, desperately digging the knives into his flesh and twisting until his hand went slack. His body fell against her.

"Esige!" Huoshai's voice cried out from somewhere distant.

She gasped for breath, certain she would die here beneath Arqai as the ring of Ordos attackers and horses closed around her. They would both be trampled together.

"Esige!" Huoshai screamed.

She closed her eyes. Her head drummed like horse hooves. She opened her mouth to try calling back to Huoshai, but nothing came from her lips. Just pulling in a breath with Arqai's massive weight pressing against her chest made her lungs collapse. A horn sounded to the west. Esige tried to see what was happening, but she couldn't focus on anything except what was directly around her. Chaos. Death. A press of bodies.

The surrounding horses stamped impatient hooves, yearning to break out of the attack. *Huoshai!* She called out, but her voice sounded only in her head. Nothing came from her lips. *I'm sorry.*

Something hammered against her head.

NORTHERN TUMENS

Somehow, everything had quickly gone wrong. Dayan's carefully plotted capture of the Ordos descended into chaos as the Ordos poured from the camp. He watched with calm detachment, analyzing everything. As everyone else burst into a flurry of activity, Dayan focused on his breathing. The calm settled over him swiftly. Years of practice had prepared him for this moment.

"We need to destroy those trebuchets," he called out.

Chakicha nodded. "On it!" With a few sharp blasts to signal to his men, a group of two thousand warriors broke off from the *tumens*. The two *mingghans* raced toward the section of camp where the trebuchets continued their fiery assault on the western pass. Chakicha led the charge.

"Cover them!" Dayan shouted.

Bagatur swiftly moved his men to obey the Khan's command. His five thousand warriors rode after Chakicha, focusing their arrows on the Ordos attackers attempting to cut off Chakicha's *mingghans*.

But concentrating even a fraction of their firepower to guarding Chakicha's warriors left Dayan's own flanks exposed. "Nemeku, take your men to cover our flank."

Without a word, Nemeku and Jangi angled away, calling out to their warriors to follow.

Dayan stood in the stirrups, heedless of the arrows that zipped past him as if some supernatural force protected him.

"Soke!" Dayan barked.

The Khorchin general galloped up beside him.

"Take your warriors to reinforce Togochi's western flank. We can't let it weaken. If they need help, sound the horn and we will send what we can spare."

Soke grimaced. "You will be exposed."

"We already are! Go."

Mandukhai appeared beside Dayan. "That doesn't leave us with enough men to defend ourselves."

Dayan knew she was right. They had quickly gone from twenty thousand to only five thousand, but they would have help. Dayan glanced eastward. "Huoshai and Esige should come over that hill any second to reinforce us from the east. We will be fine."

A horn sounded from the distance, long and low. Mandukhai and Dayan both froze as their remaining warriors turned their charge against the men pouring from camp.

"It's coming from the north," Mandukhai breathed in a panic.

Impossible. Dayan's stomach sank. His confidence faltered. How could Mogurkei have men on the other side of the northern pass? They had scouted the area relentlessly!

But there was no denying it as the horn sounded again. Mogurkei had reinforcements.

And they were closing in behind his position.

WESTERN TUMENS

Togochi blinked, limping to his feet. But his eyes couldn't focus on anything through the burning haze and rock dust floating in the air. Every other minute, another ball of flames struck the mouth of the pass, forcing his feet out from under him as he stumbled along. One arm hung limp at his side, dislocated, he was sure. During one of the attacks, he lost his horse. Whether it was dead or just run off, he wasn't sure. It was hard to even recall how it had happened. But his weapons were on the saddle.

Screams of agony filled the air. Men called out for help or death. Horses squealed.

He searched the haze for his mount, his weapons, but could find nothing more than the crushed remains of his men.

Something wrapped around his ankle. Togochi stumbled to the ground and kicked out in alarm before he realized it was one of his men.

"Help. Please." Tears streamed down the man's temples. Blood poured from a gash on his head.

But the rest of his body was pinned beneath fallen boulders. Togochi could do nothing for him but kill him quickly.

"I'm sorry," he whimpered as he pulled his knife from his boot.

"NO!"

The protest cut out as Togochi sliced the man's throat. Better to die quickly than slowly.

The blood coated his hands. He fell back, dropping the knife on the ground. Anxiety crept up his chest. He fought off sobs as he rubbed dirt on his hands to try and remove the blood. Was the blood even real or just in his mind?

Another fireball slammed into the passage. Togochi yelped, stumbling away from the falling debris.

The pass was closed. His *tumens* were cut off. He had no horse. No weapons. Realizing he had dropped his knife, Togochi scanned the ground but came up empty. How far had he moved from the knife? He couldn't see the man he had just killed any longer.

I'm a dead man, he thought pitifully as he continued stumbling through the haze, seeking anything to save himself. A horse squealed and raced past. He tried reaching for the reins but it moved too quickly.

Togochi had no clue which direction he stumbled along. The sun burned in the sky, but he couldn't discern a direction through the dust floating in the air. He coughed as he inhaled a mouthful it.

Distant shouts rang out. He shuffled toward them, not knowing if they were friend or foe.

The air cleared enough for him to spot a mass of mounted warriors. One voice rang out clear and loud over the din.

"Altan," he croaked. Togochi cleared his throat and spat debris on the ground. He summoned all the strength his lungs could muster. "Altan!"

"Togochi!" she called back, spinning around.

A moment later, she raced toward him on horseback, diving at him from her saddle and flinging her arms around him with enough force to throw him off balance.

"Am I ever glad to see you." She stepped back, tutting as she examined him. "We thought…"

"Me too. How many do we have?"

Altan yanked a skin of *airag* from her mount and offered it to him. Togochi rinsed and spit, then took a generous gulp.

"Not nearly enough," she said. "Dochigen said only about a fourth of his men made it through. I have about that many again."

"Ibarai's men?" Togochi asked, worried that he had been part of this attack.

Altan shook her head. "We don't know. At the moment, we assume he is dead. We haven't seen any of his men."

Dead, or he held his men back, Togochi thought bitterly. The attack on the pass had reduced his twenty thousand to perhaps eight thousand, at best.

"From what we have gathered so far, Kelegei and his men were flanked in the south and are under attack as well," Altan said. She snapped her fingers at a passing warrior and commanded him off his horse, then held the reins out to Togochi. "Arqai's Ordos warriors have turned against us, too. As far as we can tell, anyway. We haven't heard anything from Huoshai."

Togochi's stomach sank. "The Khan?"

"Alive for now," she replied. "His forces are splitting up. Mogurkei had more men than we expected hiding both in the camp and in the wings."

"How many more?"

She shook her head. "It's hard to say. We estimated twenty thousand in the camp, but I expect with the reinforcements that number is almost doubled."

Togochi nodded. If the Ordos turned against Mandukhai and Dayan, their nine *tumens* would be reduced to four, maybe five. Mogurkei's would have increased from two *tumens* to at least an equal force. With those trebuchets in play, this could be a losing battle.

"The pass is useless now," he said. "Anyone not through is dead, dying, or not coming this way. Send Dochigen south to reinforce Kelegei. We ride for the Khan." Eight thousand of his own forces now down to six.

"Fine." Altan nodded toward his limp arm. "But first we need to reset your shoulder."

"And I need a weapon."

CHAPTER FORTY-SIX

Winner Takes All

Bells rang in Esige's ears as she blinked slowly. Her vision was blurred as she came around. A great weight pressed down on her body. She couldn't move, couldn't breathe. The ringing slowly faded, replaced by muffled shouts of men in combat, steel against steel, thundering hooves, screaming horses. Her eyes slowly focused on the dead body on top of her. A scream for help climbed up her throat as she summoned all the breath she had left.

Then she saw him. A shadowy figure looming over her. For a second, relief washed over her. *Huoshai!* But he raised his sword over her, aiming for her neck. Esige cried out and feebly raised her arms to block, helpless on the ground. How had she ended up here?

A spray of blood bathed her face. Then another. But no blow fell.

She dared to peer out from behind her arms as Huoshai yanked his sword out of the warrior's body. He whipped the blood off. He put a boot against the body on top of her—Arqai, she remembered now—and howled as he pushed the dead weight off her. Esige breathed in a great lungful of air, putrid with the metallic tang of blood and death, but glorious all the same. Huoshai seized her arm, pulling her to her feet. Esige's head swam. For just a moment, her vision darkened. She fell against him, thankful for his powerful arm wrapped protectively around her.

Esige glanced around, pressing her cheek against his shoulder. A ring of Urainkhai guards closed around them. A sob caught in her throat.

"I'm sorry," she whimpered against his shoulder.

He held her close with one arm, the sword in the other hand, ready for a fight. Huoshai trembled against her—or was that her trembling?—and he kissed the top of her head.

"Me, too," he murmured close to her ear.

The response both startled and relieved her. She had expected him to say something like *I told you so*. Or *See, I was right*.

"Is it over yet?" she asked.

A distant call made every fiber of Esige's body tense. A horn of warning. Followed by the far-off shouts of the Khan's commanders in the northern field. "Reinforcements!"

"No," Huoshai said. "It's only just beginning. Esige, please. I beg you. Go back to camp."

Esige tried to pull away, but Huoshai held her fast against him. Did he truly think she would leave when Mandukhai was in danger? "No. I'm here. You need me. I'm a good bowman. Almost as good as you."

"You nearly died."

"I didn't, though." Esige peeled his hand away from her and escaped his grasp. His fingers tightened on hers. She faced him, her expression thunderous, set with determination. "You told me you would never cage me. You promised."

He deflated, too stunned to respond. Esige seized the moment to change the topic.

"What about Arqai's men?" Esige asked.

"Legusi is rallying them to him," Huoshai said, slowly picking up his shattered pieces as he spoke. Their guards handed over reins for fresh mounts. "It might take him a bit to organize them and stamp out their resistance, but he will come to our aid."

"Then let's go save the Khan and Khatun," Esige said. She took her reins and swung into the saddle.

Huoshai mounted as well. With a call from his horn, the Urainkhai turned like a great wave to face the north.

NORTHERN TUMENS

Mandukhai and Dayan worked in tandem, rallying what remained of their *tumens*—now down to only five thousand as others scattered to obey the Khan's commands. Mandukhai watched their men shift formation with a few blasts from Dayan's horn. She sat atop Dust, alongside Dayan, in the eye of a great storm of war. Boke and Torgus commanded their guards in a ring around them.

An equal force of Ordos raced toward their position from camp. Were that the worst they faced, Mandukhai's heartbeat may have remained a touch steadier. But twice as many spilled out of the mouth of the pass they had used just this morning to enter the battlefield. An endless flood of Ordos with bows ready for attack. Fear clenched Mandukhai's chest tight. Her back went rigid. Her nostrils flared. Her heartbeat thrashed in her ears.

A hand fell over hers, easing her death grip on the reins. Mandukhai jumped, meeting Dayan's gaze.

"Stay close to me," he said, usually calm under the circumstances.

Numb, she shook her head.

He tightened his hand on hers. "Mandukhai. This is it. This is the promise of Genghis fulfilled. Today. Don't lose faith now."

Tears shimmered in her eyes. Arrows penetrated the first lines of their men. She swallowed the swelling lump in her throat and gave him a small nod of agreement. For a moment, she held his hand tight, drawing from his courage.

Then she let go and unhooked her bow, ready to fire. *Tengri, if this is your will, protect us!*

She let out a slow breath to calm her frayed nerves.

Dayan gave her a brief nod of encouragement.

She pulled in a great breathful of air and bellowed, "For the Khan!"

The cry echoed around their meager army of five thousand. Warriors raced outward in a ring, attempting to force back the oncoming Ordos. Mandukhai rode beside Dayan, firing her bow with careful, practiced ease. Sixty arrows in each box. If she was careful with their use, she could take out nearly as many enemies.

Horses snorted as they galloped forward. The lines crashed together like thunder. Men at the front, their own Ordos warriors, hacked at the enemy while Mandukhai's men fired arrows over their heads and into the enemy Ordos lines. The ragged charge shattered against the Ordos. Men fell from saddles on both sides. Horses crushed those unfortunate souls who had not died before hitting the ground. Warriors on both sides raised shields to block arrows. Mandukhai cursed. What remained of their lines was broken apart by bolting horses, riders either lolling in the saddle or trampled under hooves.

As the lines collapsed around them, Mandukhai gave up her bow for her sword, hacking and cutting at any foes who came too near, always trying to check Dayan. The gap between them grew wider with each heartbeat.

Torgus called out commands to her guards, closing their ranks tighter around Mandukhai.

A call of warning came from behind. Mandukhai spun Dust around as an Ordos cavalry crushed into what remained of their rearguard, using lances and swords to cut down anything in their path.

"Dayan!" Mandukhai called out in warning.

But when she looked back, the crushing lines had formed a wall of bodies and horses all across the battlefield. She could no longer see the Khan or his plumed helmet.

Blood splattered across her chest as one of her guards killed an attacker. Mandukhai closed her mouth, tasting blood. Not her own, she was sure.

All around her, bodies of warriors fell on both sides. Everything moved so quickly, she worried she might accidentally swing at one of her own men in a panicked attempt to save herself.

Mandukhai glanced at the sun, realizing that her guard had somehow turned and now faced the southeast. The Urainkhai horn bellowed from the distance. Ordos around her closed tighter as others called out the warning of another charge from the east. *Huoshai!* She breathed in relief, but knew this battle was far from over.

With a rally cry, Mandukhai led a charge east, hoping to force the Ordos into the oncoming Urainkhai lines.

As they charged their mounts, the Ordos continued buzzing around them like flies eager for a feast. An arrow punched through the helmet of one of her guards. He tumbled from his saddle, trampled underfoot as they carried on the charge. Mandukhai tried to calculate how many men followed her, but could not discern their numbers with so many men around. More of her guards fell.

An arrow whistled across the sky. She didn't recognize the signal, but the surrounding Ordos shifted course. Suddenly, the enemies who had charged alongside her forces, picking off her men, turned their attention inward. Mandukhai swung her sword as one of them raced straight at her.

She didn't wait to see if she managed a kill before hacking away in another direction.

So many blades twirled around her, a chaos of steel and blood. One by one, her guards fell.

"Mandukhai, we need to get back to the other lines," Torgus called, drawing up beside her.

"The Urainkhai are coming. We must be closer to them than our own forces by now."

Another of her men tumbled from the saddle. Torgus fired his bow, riding alongside her. Dust's hooves caught on the body as it fell in her stallion's path. At the same moment, Torgus reached for Mandukhai. His fingers, slick with blood, slid off her armor before he could get a grip, but it was enough to pull her to the side as an Ordos blade glanced off her armor.

Dust tumbled.

Torgus screamed for her.

Mandukhai sensed her death as she fell from the saddle, prepared to be trampled.

But the Ordos had stopped their charge toward her. Dust squealed and kicked his legs feebly. Mandukhai struck the ground with enough force to knock all the breath from her lungs. She gasped for air, clawed her way toward her sword. It had skittered across the ground.

Her hand slipped in a pool of blood. She raised a shaking hand to stare at the red. Then her gaze fell on Dust. He heaved a breath, then fell still.

"No!" Mandukhai cried, crawling toward her horse. Red blood bathed his white coat.

Torgus stood over Mandukhai, firing his bow until he ran out of arrows.

The Ordos closed in a tighter ring.

She wailed, pressing her face to Dust's braided mane. The last breathing piece of Unebolod she had to cling to.

Torgus grunted and stumbled back, slipping on the bloody ground. He caught his balance awkwardly, then another arrow punched into his chest with enough force to send his body spinning.

Mandukhai raised her eyes in time to see him collapse to the ground, clinging to his sword even in death.

Someone stomped toward her from behind and slammed his boot against her helmet. It tumbled to the ground. He repeated before she could react, knocking Mandukhai out cold.

Togochi watched helplessly as the Ordos gutted the Khan's lines. He could not ride fast enough to their aid. Worse than watching the Ordos decimate the Khan's forces was seeing thousands of their own warriors racing in his direction. Togochi released a fierce growl of frustration. What were they doing abandoning the Khan?

Soke rode at the head of the oncoming warriors. *I will gut him if either of them dies!*

"Where are the rest of your men?" Soke hollered as he rode closer.

"Stuck or dead," Togochi snapped. "Why are you headed this way? The Khan needs your warriors!"

Soke glanced back and frowned. "Where did they all come from?"

Togochi raced past Soke. He didn't care where they came from. Togochi had every intention of sending them back.

Another line of men, directed by Chakicha, fired arrows toward the camp. Black clouds of smoke billowed into the sky as trebuchets burned.

Togochi knew he had only moments to change the course of this fight. "Altan! Take your warriors along the western flank of those Ordos and do everything you can to scatter them! Chakicha!" The young khan glanced over his shoulder. "Forget your fire here. Swing north around the Ordos there." Togochi stabbed his finger toward the reinforcements still pouring out of the northern pass. "Soke, you have the best archers. Take ground here, cover the flanks there and pick off any Ordos who attempt escaping."

The generals scattered to carry out his commands. Togochi raised his new bow high and turned to face his men. "Men, to me! Break swords. Shatter shields. Take no prisoners. For the Khan!"

His remaining men cried out fiercely, their voices cracking in the sky. "For the Khan!"

NORTHERN TUMENS

As he charged through the battle, Dayan felt arrows zip past him in the air. He leaned close to his mount to avoid getting hit.

Dayan hadn't flinched when the fireballs erupted against the western valley where his men waited. Togochi and Altan guided those warriors. He had to have faith that those two could avoid disaster. His only goal right now was to hold out until Urainkhai reinforcements could sweep in.

The Ordos continued their press inward, killing without mercy. Dayan glanced over his shoulder, expecting to see Mandukhai glued to his side. But she was gone. Dayan's heart stopped. He yanked his mare to a halt, spinning as his warriors surged around him, uncertain what to do next.

"Where is Mandukhai?" Dayan asked Boke.

The guard paled as he searched the group, peering over heads. An arrow near-missed his helmet. Boke ducked down and shook his head, grim-faced. He already had several wounds sustained from protecting Dayan. It showed his grit that he could fight with so many.

Dayan cursed under his breath. He called for his men to spread out in bow formation, but they could hardly shift their lines under the press of thousands of Ordos riders. The lines collapsed tighter around him. Before he could ride within two hundred yards, his forces were crushed together. Nemeku and Jangi continued fighting at their flank, but even they were pressed close enough for Dayan to see his cousin in the fray.

An Ordos warrior broke through the line, ramming his lance against Dayan's armor. The impact sent a searing heat through his core. He flew from his saddle and hit the ground. His helmet rang against his skull. Dayan blinked, stumbling to his feet and grasping at the first weapon he could get his hands on. The lancer fell with an arrow through his eye.

A horn sounded in the east. *The Urainkhai! What took them so long?*

Dayan fired more fiercely than he had ever done before, determined to break a hole in the line of Ordos warriors. He just needed a horse to reach the other side and he could get to her! She had to be there somewhere. But he was outnumbered. Warriors fell to arrows all around him. His arms ached from battle.

Boke called out to Dayan, and he raised hopeful eyes. His guardsman had dismounted and now fought at his back. Nemeku rushed toward them on horseback, trampling a few Ordos who had broken through the lines on foot. He leaped from his saddle and joined Dayan, along with Jangi. The four of them moved as a unit, but even with their own men around them, there were too many enemy Ordos.

"Dayan, look out!" Nemeku shouted. He lunged at Dayan, thrusting him aside as a horse broke through the line.

Dayan's heart hammered at the near miss. The two exchanged momentary smiles of relief. But the moment was spoiled quickly. Jangi leaped in front of the two of them, then fell to his knees. An arrow had punched through his armor. Dayan and Nemeku both spun around. Nemeku cried out to Jangi—his lifelong guardian—but the warrior thrust his sword upward in a final act of defiance. The blade penetrated the chest of a charging Ordos enemy. Both men tumbled to the ground, staring at the sky with lifeless eyes.

"No!" Nemeku knelt over Jangi. Tears streamed down his cheeks. But instead of paling, Nemeku's face turned red with rage. "Jangi! Get up!"

"Nemeku, he's gone," Dayan said, gently placing a hand on his cousin's shoulder while keep an eye on the battle raging around them.

More horns sounded. Dayan scanned the area around them. Ordos began to scatter. Togochi broken through the lines of Ordos with his own warriors. Disappointment rushed through Dayan. Though he was thankful to see his *orlok* alive, Togochi was not Mandukhai.

"Where is Mandukhai?" Togochi asked the second he reined in beside Dayan.

Dayan shook his head. "I don't know." His gaze swept the chaos as the Ordos pulled back. "She has to be near somewhere. She was right beside me." Terror seized his chest. The Great Fist clenched his insides tight. His gaze swept the ground, worried he would find her trampled under hooves. But her bright armor didn't shine. He couldn't see her helmet anywhere. "She has to be somewhere."

By the time Dayan raised his eyes, Togochi had already taken command and broken what remained of Dayan's men into dozens of arrowtip formations.

"We had better find her then," Togochi said. He tossed the reins of Dayan's mare to him.

Dayan nodded curtly and climbed stiffly into the saddle. With a cry of command, the new formations shot out toward the surging Ordos like bolts from a bow.

EASTERN TUMENS

Esige rode alongside Huoshai, watching as the Khan's forces broke apart under the press of Ordos warriors. They raced as fast as they dared. Huoshai's first line of warriors cut into an Ordos *mingghan*, slicing anything in their way. Esige felt a great press against her chest as if something had knocked the wind out of her. It was only the compression of the Urainkhai in battle, but it made it harder for her to focus. Anxiety pressed down on her. She could fight just fine, but after what happened with Arqai, terror threatened to wash over her. Esige's breath came in brief gasps as blood sprayed in all directions and bodies fell under hooves.

It was all she could do to stay in her saddle. Her head spun. She reached for an arrow to defend herself but came up empty. The box had come loose somewhere in the fray. She had no arrows. Only a sword, which she knew she had not practiced with nearly enough.

"Where are they going?" Huoshai asked one of his commanders as he stabbed his sword toward a *jagan* of a hundred Ordos who broke off from the rest and raced back toward camp.

The commander shrugged. "Should I follow?"

"No," Huoshai replied. "The Khan and Khatun need our reinforcements."

"I can go scout it out," Esige offered, hoping to get away from battle.

Huoshai shook his head. "Not a chance. You stick with me."

Esige resented his need to protect her, but also couldn't blame him. She had never felt so small.

With a few quick commands, Huoshai sent the Urainkhai into horn formation. They would wrap around the Ordos and smother them.

And hopefully Legusi would show up with the remaining Ordos under his command.

ORDOS CAMP

Mandukhai groaned as she woke. Pain pulsed through her head. She lifted her hands to inspect the tender wound on her head, only to realize her wrists and ankles were bound. She lay on a bed inside a ger. Panic rose in her throat. She tugged at the horsehair rope, trying to loosen it. The rope chaffed at her skin, cutting into her flesh the more she struggled.

"Calm down," an impatient male voice said from beside her.

Mandukhai turned her head to find an older man casually cutting a pear and biting into the juicy flesh as if a battle were not raging hundreds of yards outside of his camp. She could still hear the horns of war and thunder of hooves. Only one man could be so arrogant to enjoy fruit so casually while his men died.

"Mogurkei," she said, sitting up as best she could on the bed. Mandukhai rested her back against the ger wall. "You have already lost. This will end poorly."

"Have I lost, though?" he asked, raising a bushy eyebrow. He smirked. "My men have the Khan surrounded. He will be dead soon, if he isn't already." He shrugged as if the death of her husband were a casual, careless thing. "My forces are outmaneuvering your own. And I have you here, in my bed, right where you belong. Seems like I am winning, from where I sit."

Mandukhai sneered. "Qori was right about you. As was Ibarai. You will not see your own defeat until the blade slices your throat."

Once again, he shrugged. "Death is the only true form of defeat. And if you trust Ibarai, you're a fool."

"You have no allies left," Mandukhai snapped. "They are all either mine or dead."

"Oh. You're right." Mogurkei dropped his arms to his knees and nodded thoughtfully. But his tone dripped with sarcasm. If she had her hands free, she would have slapped him. "That must be why Arqai's men turned against yours. Or why Ulum's men flocked to me and not you when your lover killed him."

Her face heated at even the implication of Unebolod. "His death was your plan, wasn't it?"

Mogurkei set down his knife close enough that, if she dove for it, she might get her hands on it. But he was smart enough to know that. He was testing her. "I wish I could take credit for Unebolod's downfall. I suppose I can, in a way. It was my men who launched the attack that led to his death. But the plan was Issama's."

"Issama is dead."

"I know." Again, he shrugged. Mandukhai wanted to take a hammer to his massive shoulders. "Doesn't matter. I would have killed him once he finished his task, anyway. No doubt he would have tried to kill me once it was all done. Can't trust men like him. So thanks. You did me a favor there."

Mandukhai attempted putting the pieces together. Somehow, she had to gain leverage in this conversation. A hard thing to do with both her hands and ankles bound. "Issama made you certain promises. Let me guess. He would ensure we killed Bigirsen. Then you kill the Khan and his *orloks*... What about me?"

Mogurkei shifted from his stool onto the edge of the bed. The way his gaze crawled over her made Mandukhai's skin prickle in terror. Thankfully, she was still in her armor. "Why kill a creature like you? Such a waste." He grabbed her jaw painfully tight in his big hand. "I know exactly what to do with a woman like you."

He leaned closer. In horror, Mandukhai realized he was about to kiss her. She clamped her jaw tight and rammed her head into his nose. Mogurkei reeled back, clutching his bleeding nose in both hands. Before Mandukhai could take a moment to smirk in smug satisfaction, he backhanded her. For a second, the pain blinded Mandukhai. She could taste blood in her mouth from where her lips split. He grabbed a cloth and pressed it to his nose.

"Bitch. You will learn. First, your husband has to die." He stood, snatching his knife up. "Your men won't know what to do. They will look to you, and I will take you in the Shrine of Genghis. Then it will all be over."

The Shrine of Genghis? Mandukhai snorted. "No one has seen his shrine in nearly a hundred years. And even if you knew where it was, simply taking me there wouldn't be enough."

Mogurkei tipped his head back, clutching his knife in his fist once more. Satisfied that his nosebleed had stopped, he leaned close enough for her to smell the stink of *airag* on his putrid breath. "Are you certain of that? Or perhaps my father and grandfathers did not want others to know of it." His bloody fingers caressed her cheek. She jerked away from the touch. "And I didn't say I would take you *to* the shrine. I said I would take *you* in the shrine."

Numbness spread through Mandukhai's limbs as the terrible truth sank in. His horrific plan could actually work. Without an heir of Genghis,

Mogurkei would have proven himself more powerful than any of the other Lords. If he consummated a union with her inside the Shrine of Genghis, the men might actually accept his legitimacy. All he needed was Dayan's death.

"Get the fight out of your system now, because when the time comes tonight, there will be nothing more to fight." Mogurkei pulled back, brushing his thumb over her lips.

A series of horns blasted in the distance, drawing both of their gazes toward the door. Sharp. Quick. Three times. Four. A smile crept across Mandukhai's lips. She knew the sound of that horn. It reminded her of her childhood. Of her father.

The Ongud. *Boragan has come to fight!* she thought as elation spread through her.

"That's the sound of your defeat," she said with vehemence, "and your death."

Northern Tumens

Despite Togochi's clever tactics, Dayan fought helplessly as his men fell all around them. It was only a matter of time. Somehow, Mogurkei had summoned somewhere near fifty thousand warriors to his banners. Dayan had come into this fight with nearly a hundred thousand men spread around the camp. Between the Ordos who had turned against them and the men lost in the western pass and the battle itself, Dayan's forces had taken a critical blow.

He closed his eyes for a moment as he calculated, wiping sweat and blood from his brow. He had perhaps only forty thousand at his disposal—and that was including the Urainkhai still fighting their way toward him. He had half that around him now.

Dayan's shoulders protested movement, but he could not stop. He still hadn't found Mandukhai.

Forty. Forty thousand. We are outnumbered and trapped.

This was how the Ordos operated, Dayan realized. An enemy broke through the line and fired at him. Dayan ducked behind the shield—though it was probably more arrows than shield at this point. Once more, he swung his sword. It skipped off armor.

"Dayan, we need to retreat," Togochi said after fending off an attacker. "Back to the Urainkhai camp."

"No!" Dayan roared. He kicked his mare, but she had nowhere to move. "She's out here somewhere."

"Dayan—"

"I said no! I won't leave without her!" Fury burned in his veins. What had happened to her?

A horn sounded in a series of sharp, quick blasts. Ordos command arrows flew through the air. Dayan watched the soaring ribbons of color.

"What is happening?" he asked in a panic.

Togochi stood in his stirrups as the surrounding Ordos began pulling back. "They're retreating."

"What?" Dayan stood as well, craning his neck to see over the heads and horses.

The Ordos line broke and headed south.

Thousands of horsemen crested the distant hills. Another horn sounded. Banners fluttered on the hilltops.

Ordos. Ongud. Chakhar. A few others from smaller tribes Mandukhai and Dayan had left in the east to cover the supply routes.

Now, their *tumens* charged over the hilltop and crashed into the fleeing Ordos with deadly force.

Dayan's own men cheered and whooped in victory and relief. The Chakhar led the charge of reinforcements as they swept across the remaining Ordos, eliminating further resistance.

Togochi sounded his own horn beside Dayan. In seconds, their remaining forces closed the gap behind the fleeing Ordos, pinching them between two walls of men.

A group of horsemen rode down the hills straight for Dayan. Boke moved into position head of Dayan, but the Khan was not worried. In fact, he relaxed in his saddle.

"Dayan Khan!" Belku called out as he drew near.

Dayan would have grinned were he not so worried about Mandukhai. "Belku. Are we ever happy to see you." He had sent Belku back to secure his place as Chakhar khan when his father had died months ago. It seemed he was not only successful, but he brought more warriors to fight for Dayan.

"I brought reinforcements," Belku said, waving toward the other tribal leaders behind him.

Lords Qori, Boragan, and Unige's young son, Alag, bowed in their saddles.

"He was quite persuasive," Qori said, smirking at Belku. "I don't think any of us stood a chance to resist his arguments."

"Well, we are relieved to have you here," Togochi said. "It was getting pretty grim."

"Where is the Khatun?" Belku asked. "I expected her to be here based on what we were told back at your camp."

Dayan's face fell. He scanned the abandoned battlefield. Devastation seized his insides, twisting them in a sickening mass as the truth pressed down on him. If she lived, she would have joined him by now. Grief creeped up his throat. He blinked furiously to keep from crying in front of the men.

Qori cleared his throat and turned to one of his commanders. "Organize as many men as we can spare. Search for Mandukhai Khatun. No one sleeps until we find her."

"We need to find Mogurkei," Togochi said. "No matter our own losses, we still have to be certain this is finished."

Dayan shot a dirty look at him. The *orlok* was placing the Ordos Lord ahead of the Khantun's life? Togochi quickly averted his gaze, but not before Dayan saw the tears in his eyes as well.

Nemeku's hand fell on Dayan's shoulder. "I will help you search."

The group broke apart, picking their way through the field of bodies as the rest of the reinforcement warriors finished the battle. Dayan rode stiffly, only dimly aware of his own injuries. It didn't seem he had suffered anything too serious. *Unless she is dead*, he thought, swallowing the swelling lump in his throat.

Crows began circling high above, casting shadows. A few dipped down out of the sky to pick at corpses before the living came to shoo them away. Dayan prayed none of the crows had a chance to pick at her yet.

"Over here!" A distant shout drew Dayan's attention. He raced his mare toward the call.

A trail of dead guards littered the ground, all in the black armor of the Khatun's Guard. *No. No, no, no!* Panic clenched Dayan's chest. He struggled for each breath. The world spun.

"Her horse," Altan said, standing over the bloodied white stallion.

Dayan slid from his saddle and stumbled toward Dust. She had loved this horse. There was no mistaking the bloodied golden plated armor or the dragon saddle. Her bow was still hooked to the saddle, sticking up in the air. Dayan's nostrils flared as he fought off the sobs fighting to break free. The longer he resisted, the quicker his pulse raced. Dayan began hyperventilating as the Great Fist tightened around his heart, his lungs, his entire insides more painfully than ever before. His vision darkened in panic. Suddenly, the crowd around them felt too close, too tight. He couldn't get air.

"Where ..." Dayan croaked, fighting off the vomit climbing up his throat. "She isn't ..." His entire body trembled, though he wasn't sure if it was grief or rage. "Where is she?" The words burst out of him like fire.

Without her, he had nothing ... he *was* nothing.

No one around him moved. No one spoke. Their silence only fueled the anger building within.

"Kill them," he said, his voice hollow even to his own ears. "All of them."

"We're working on it, my lord Khan," Belku said, referring to the way their forces finished off the resisting Ordos.

Dayan lunged at the Chakhar khan in his saddle and seized a fistful of deel, jerking Belku toward him. "No. Not the men. *All* of them." If he couldn't have his family, the Ordos would not either. "Women. Children. Animals. *All of them!*"

Nemeku edged closer. The gentleness of his touch did nothing to soothe Dayan's soul as he slowly burned up inside out. "Dayan, you are angry. We all are. But we don't know what has happened to her yet. This is a horse. It isn't her." He gently pried Dayan's fingers loose from Belku's deel.

Belku's face had gone ghostly pale.

"Keep looking," Nemeku said. He gave Belku a small head nod away from them.

Dayan dragged ragged breaths in, struggling for each one. Heat had flooded his entire body. *I truly am burning alive.*

"We will find her," Nemeku said softly. "Breathe."

"I can't ... I ..." The wall threatened to break down. If it did, Dayan knew he would fall apart there on the battlefield in front of everyone.

A voice called his name, screamed at him from far away. He closed his eyes. *I'm hearing things now.*

"Look out!" Qori threw himself at Dayan, tackling him to the ground.

Arrows thumped into the ground where Dayan had been standing.

Boke seized Qori, kneeling on his chest with a blade pressed against Qori's throat.

"I saved his life, you idiot!" Qori snapped. He pointed south.

Everyone stared at the arrows.

Dayan heard his name again and stood, turning his attention south.

Near the camp, a modest group of onlookers gathered around a small cluster of riders. Perhaps ten men in total.

And at the head of the group, Mandukhai sat on a horse with someone behind her. Dayan leaped on his horse without thinking. He raced toward her while Boke and the others called after him.

"Stop!" Mandukhai screamed.

A series of arrows flew straight for him. Dayan ducked low to the horse but didn't slow. His focus was singular. If the visions were to be believed, his rise was the will of Tengri. Dayan could not fall. He would not die this day. He rode with the protect of the High Heavens around him.

I will finish him and complete the promise Genghis made.

Hooves thundered behind him. Dayan didn't look back. He didn't dare as he raced for Mandukhai. Once close enough, Dayan noticed the knife Mogurkei held to her throat as he hid behind her body from Dayan's own archers. Dayan's men picked off Mogurkei's. Still, he didn't slow down.

"Any closer and I kill her!" Mogurkei snapped. To prove his point, he pressed the blade tight enough to draw a bead of blood from her neck.

Pure hate pulsed in Dayan's body, drowning out all else.

Worried that he would lose her, Dayan jerked the reins. His mare skidded to a halt. Instinctively, he reached for his bow and arrows, but there was nothing. Thankfully, Mogurkei didn't have any more archers to fire at him any longer.

"What do you want?" Dayan snapped.

"You. Or your life, that is."

Dayan's jaw twitched. His fevered stare fixed on the Ordos Lord. How could he respond to that?

"Dayan, don't! He will kill you and take me anyway!" Mandukhai blurted.

Mogurkei yanked on a fistful of her hair, leaning close to her neck. Incensed, Dayan's nostrils flared like an angry bull. He had to get Mogurkei away from her somehow. And Dayan could only think of one reason Mogurkei would go to all this trouble. He didn't just want independence like the other Ordos had claimed. He wanted to be Great Khan. He wanted all the power he could seize.

"Fine." Dayan dismounted. He knew what he had to do.

Mogurkei blinked. "What?" He clearly did not know how to respond to Dayan's behavior.

"Let's settle this, Mogurkei." Dayan pulled out his sword and stepped into the space between their lines. "You and me. Winner takes all."

"Dayan," Togochi hissed from behind him. "We lost thousands of men today. There is no way anyone will accept him if you lose."

"I won't lose." Dayan rolled his shoulders, then neck. "Let's go, Mogurkei. Last man standing. If you are so certain you are better equipped for this job, take it."

The surrounding crowd swiftly grew as they heard Dayan's challenge. It dwarfed the crowd he had when he fought Unebolod and Nemeku combined.

Mogurkei tied Mandukhai to the saddle. Dayan's eyelid twitched in rage.

Silence settled over everything. Even the crows stopped squawking. As Mogurkei found his footing, Dayan closed his eyes and took a deep breath. In. Out. In. Out. His raging pulse slowed to a steady thrum. He could hear the breeze. The banners snapping against poles. The snort of horses. Dayan's fingers slid alone the yellow ribbon tied to his sword.

Use all of your assets, Unebolod had lectured him countless times. *Not just speed and strength.*

Mogurkei's boots scuffed against the rocky earth as he lunged into action, clearly expecting Dayan to be a weaker, inexperienced fighter. Dayan stepped to the side, dodging the attack. He raised his sword in a sweeping arc that met something solid, then ground against metal. Dayan opened his eyes as he stepped around Mogurkei. A serene mask of calm smoothed Dayan's features.

Mogurkei moved quick and smooth with his sword. He knew what he was doing. That first attack had been a test. Now he knew Dayan was not a child, but a real competitor. The two men locked in a dance. The more they shuffled, the more Mogurkei's movements became more desperate. Dayan straightened and slid a hand into his own belt behind his back.

"Arrogant prick," Mogurkei muttered.

Again, Unebolod's voice rose to the surface. *Every sense is your ally.*

Dayan centered himself as Goram the monk had taught him years ago. He listened to the way Mogurkei's boots moved over the ground. He watched the subtle tells that gave away Mogurkei's next attack, just like Unebolod had taught him. Sweat rolled down Dayan's spine beneath the silk and armor.

Mogurkei charged him again like an angry ox, all attack and no finesse. His sword scraped across Dayan's armor. Dayan raised his own blade and hammered a blow into Mogurkei's sword arm hard enough to stick in the armor and meet flesh beneath. To his credit, Mogurkei only grunted and gritted his teeth. Dayan yanked the sword free.

The two once more swung and parried. High swings. Leg sweeps. Dayan danced through all of it much like he had countless times with Unebolod over the years. The longer they fought, the more Dayan wore Mogurkei down. Dayan's shoulders burned in agony from a day of hard exertion, but he reveled in the pain and fueled it into his focus.

In a rage, Mogurkei kicked dirt up into Dayan's face, then lunged forward. Dayan snapped his eyes closed and focused on the sounds of movement instead. The scrape of his boots on the ground. The distance between him and Mogurkei. Where Mogurkei moved next. *Men will not fight fair, especially once they have you alone*, Unebolod had taught him. At the time, Dayan had assumed he would never be allowed to fight anyone, let alone on his own. Now he was deeply grateful for Unebolod's harsh training.

The air around Dayan moved across his exposed skin just a fraction of a second before he heard the whoosh of the sword blade slicing the air. He sensed the movement of the blade down in an arc toward his neck.

Dayan moved smooth and graceful, spinning around Mogurkei's attack. The dirt remained in his eyes, but it didn't hinder his other senses. As Mogurkei followed through on the attack, Dayan seized Mogurkei's sword arm in his free hand and twisted it behind the Ordos Lord. Mogurkei attempted resisting, but he was a step behind Dayan. Before he could react, Dayan already brought his own sword up and sliced it across flesh.

Afraid that opening his eyes before this fight was truly over would irritate them and distract him, Dayan held his position, using his senses to be certain the fight was over.

Warm blood poured down his arm, followed by the familiar gurgling sounds of death. Dayan released the body. A second later, he heard it thump against the ground.

Dayan stepped back, blinking to try removing the dirt from his eyes.

"Dayan!" Mandukhai's cry drew him around sharply.

A moment later, she collided with him, throwing her arms around him. Dayan sank against her in relief, blinking furiously to clear his vision. Someone must have cut her free from the saddle.

"Dayan Khan!" The cheer rose all around them and rippled outward.

Dayan buried his face against Mandukhai's neck, breathing her in. Having her in his arms made everything right again. He pulled back and brushed his palm over her cheek, leaving a streak of blood across her already dirty face. "We aren't done yet, are we?" he asked, and his voice cracked over the words.

"I'm tired," Mandukhai muttered.

Dayan half laughed, half choked on a sob. Even in his own ears, he sounded delirious. "We don't sleep when there's work to be done," he said, almost giddy now as he threw her own lesson back in her face.

Mandukhai nodded and pulled back. She turned to face the surrounding crowd. As she did, Mandukhai had all the bearing of a queen.

No. Not a queen, Dayan realized as he stared at her, edging close to her shoulder. That word insufficiently described her majesty. *An empress.*

CHAPTER FORTY-SEVEN

The Sacred Shrine of Genghis

Mandukhai had just finished setting up her ger in the new Ordos camp when Esige knocked on the door. Several days had passed since the battle. Men were still out searching the dead before early spring warmth could cause too much bloating. The cost had been huge. They had lost good men. She'd lost Dust.

"Mandukhai?" Esige called as she ducked through the door. Her voice quivered slightly, which concerned Mandukhai. Esige was always so confident. "Can we talk?"

Mandukhai straightened on the bed, where she had been carefully cleaning her armor and checking for repairs. "Of course. What's wrong, Esige?"

Agitated, Esige rubbed her hands together and chewed her lip, pacing a few quick steps before spinning back the other way. Her clipped strides only intensified Mandukhai's growing dread. She rose and edged toward the woman, taking Esige's trembling hands in her own. "You can tell me anything. You know that, right?"

Esige stopped, nodding sharply.

"What is it, then?"

"Okay." Esige took a deep breath. Then her words came out in a rush. "I wouldn't do this, except I promised Tayiqu and I'm really not comfortable asking but I need to arrange something for her before she does something stupid and, well, she has made herself quite plain that she is only interested in one person."

"Calm down." Mandukhai pulled Esige to a bench and eased her down. "I can't follow. What is it she wants?"

Esige opened her mouth, then snapped it shut again several times. Her cheeks reddened. "Dayan," she blurted.

Mandukhai jerked back. Her heart stopped beating altogether and for a moment she couldn't breathe. "What?"

"I'm sorry." Esige dipped her head, staring at her hands. "I told her—promised her I would ask if there was any possibility. And I know your marriage is still new and he probably has better political prospects if he were to even consider it but she wouldn't be ready for a couple years still, which gives the two of you plenty of time, and I don't know why I am making a case in her defense." Esige took another deep breath and raised tremulous eyes to meet Mandukhai's. "I promised. If you refuse, I don't blame you. But at least I can say I did my part."

Mandukhai's head spun. Her cheeks heated. All she wanted was a bit of peace and happiness now that the worst was over. But already, women were knocking on her door, eager to be Dayan's next wife. Mandukhai knew this was inevitable. And if Esige was asking now, it would only be a matter of time before some of the Lords came asking the same for their daughters. Esige was right. It was not just a matter of what she wanted, but of political alliances. They could strengthen their hold on some of their weakest links through marriage to the Khan. *I only just married him! I'm not ready to share.*

"It's okay, Mandukhai," Esige said. "I understand. I can't imagine considering sharing Huoshai with another woman. Especially not so soon after we were married. It's okay to be a little selfish and want him to yourself for a while."

For a while...

Mandukhai folded her trembling hands together. "You are right, Esige. This is inevitable. But I am not ready yet. And he deserves a say in the matter. Right now, there is no way he will consider it." She couldn't look at the other woman, instead gazing at her hands. Her palms began sweating. "I'm not saying never. Just ... not now. Can we come back to this in the future?"

"Of course." Esige leaned closer and hugged Mandukhai. "I will just let her know you didn't refuse outright. Hopefully, that will hold her off longer."

The two pulled apart as the door opened. Dayan stepped in, grinning from one ear to the next. Mandukhai's heart lifted seeing him so happy, but it also crushed her soul knowing these proposals were not a thing she could ignore forever.

"Hi Esige," Dayan said, giving her a small nod before dismissing her presence completely. "Mandukhai, I have something for you."

Curious, trembling still from the conversation with Esige, Mandukhai rose from the bench, her gaze sweeping over his hands.

"Come out here." Dayan stepped backward through the door, motioning for her to follow.

Swallowing her fear, Mandukhai ducked out after him.

Warm sunshine blasted her face. Spring was in full swing. The grass was greener by the day and nearby trees sprouted buds. Their victory felt more like a new beginning with the new season.

Boke and what remained of their guards loomed nearby. Mandukhai nodded to Boke in greeting as Dayan reached back and grabbed the reins of a horse. He edged the mount toward her.

"I know you loved Dust," Dayan said, stroking the black snout of the stallion as it bucked its head. "I hope this offers some consolation." He held the reins out, sliding them into her hand.

Mandukhai stared at the beast in awe. The stallion's hair was as dark as night. One big, black eye regarded her with understanding—or perhaps resignation. She had hundreds of horses now, but Dust had been different.

Dayan loomed at her shoulder as she ran her hand along the horse's neck. "What do you think? I wanted to get you a new one and spent days searching. But the moment I saw this boy, I knew he was special."

Grief clenched her stomach, twisting in knots as she noticed the saddle. Her saddle. Someone had found it and collected it for her. Unebolod had chosen her last stallion. It had only been a matter of time before Dust died of age. Mandukhai supposed it was fitting to have a younger stallion from her younger husband. Another special gift. Tears rolled down Mandukhai's cheeks.

Dayan stepped around her, frowning. "Is it not... Do you not like him?"

Overwhelmed with love and grief, Mandukhai threw her arms around Dayan and held him close, pressing her cheek into his shoulder. "He's perfect," she murmured against his deel.

Dayan offered an affectionate squeeze, then stroked her hair and tilted back. His lips brushed her forehead. She leaned against Dayan, reveling in this moment just a little longer as the stallion dipped his head to graze on the spotty green grass.

"I will call him Faith," she said, remembering Unebolod's last words to her, as well as the motivation that had driven her toward Dayan in the first place. Faith had brought her here. It was only fitting that it would carry her away.

"Dayan!" Nemeku called out, waving a hand at them as he darted around men and women milling about nearby. "Mandukhai! I found it!"

He stopped in front of them, flush from exertion and excitement. "I found the shrine!"

In the center of the Ordos camp, surrounded by hundreds of gers, rested a low cart supporting the white-felt walls and roof of the Shrine of Genghis. If bringing the last of the Ordos under her banner—Dayan's banner—had been a pinnacle moment in her life, it was nothing compared to the sure victory of standing before this old shrine. The white felt had blue trim and ornamentation, a reflection of the eternal blue sky above them all. No banners fluttered around the shrine. It rested, utterly nondescript amidst so many other gers.

Warmth radiated out through Mandukhai's body. Her heart thrummed to the beat of some unheard drum. Her entire body quivered as she struggled to keep the pure elation from releasing as her gaze remained fixed straight ahead of her. Anxious, she took one shuffling step forward. Then another.

They had followed an eager Nemeku through camp to this place. Now, she could hardly believe her eyes.

Mandukhai dared another step toward the shrine, pressing her palms against her hips to keep her hands from shaking violently. Sweat coated her hands. She tried to wipe it away, but it did little good. *I can't believe this is here*, she thought. *Mogurkei was telling the truth!*

A few steps back, Dayan remained rooted in place, as if he had become one with the earth. Mandukhai reached back, beaming at him, then frowned when she saw the look on his face. Her euphoria crashed down.

Hundreds of men crowded in behind the Khan and Khatun, watching to see what they would do. The most senior members of the military were closest, staring at the Shrine of Genghis in open awe. Many had likely never seen it before. The shrine was a thing of stories, lost in time, much as the Shrine of the First Queen had been.

Yet here it rested. In the middle of the Ordos camp. As if it had always been around.

As if it had been waiting for her.

Though all the commanders and generals gazed at the shrine in awe, Dayan stared at it in fear. He swayed slightly on his feet. The color had drained from his face and neck, all previous excitement vanished. He hunched slightly, leaning back away from the shrine as if it were a dangerous beast.

Mandukhai's heart ached to see such terror on his face. What was he afraid of? She glided over and stood in front of him, filling his vision.

Dayan blinked slowly as his focus shifted to her.

She dried her palm on her deel, then reached up and pressed it to his cheek. "We have done it, Dayan," she whispered, only for him. "All colors and none. The tribes. The *sulde*. The shrines. There is no doubt any longer. No one to stand in our way."

Dayan swallowed and nodded stiffly. He rested his hand on her arm. For a moment, he just stared at her. But she could not tell what he was feeling. Scared, happy, worried, weak, strong. It was impossible to discern. She knew him better than anyone, yet could not read him as she always could read Unebolod. How she wished she could read his thoughts!

Mandukhai pulled back and took his hand. "Come. Let's pay homage at the sacred shrine."

But when she stepped forward, pulling his hand, Dayan still didn't move. She turned back, frowning.

"No."

That one word ripped at her heart. "Why?"

Dayan pulled her back to him, as if afraid of taking another step, no matter how small, toward the shrine. "If I climb those steps ..." He let out a shaky breath before continuing. "I will have installed myself, once and for all."

Mandukhai smothered a smile. "That is the idea."

"You said Esen installed himself without *kurultai*," Dayan said. "The people hung him from a tree."

"Esen was not chosen by divine right," Mandukhai replied. "Nor was he an heir of Genghis. *Kurultai* is pointless. Look behind you!" She waved past his shoulder. "You are already Great Khan, chosen by these leaders."

Dayan glanced at the crowd gathered at his back. But when he met her gaze, she knew without a doubt that she would never change his mind.

"I will do this right," he said. "You planned my installment before. We will do it again." Dayan pulled her closer, wrapping his arm around her. "We have reasons to celebrate."

Mandukhai's heart skipped in delight at the way he stared down at her. So much had happened in the last few days. So much had changed. She wanted him to kiss her as he had last night. Slow. Gentle. Eager. He leaned down. She tilted her head back, hungry for his kiss. But his lips pressed to her forehead. Then he withdrew from her and turned to face the crowd.

"Spread the word!" Dayan said, his voice carrying with far more strength than he had shown her just a minute before. "We are now keepers of the sacred shrines and bearers of the *sulde* of Genghis!"

Cheers erupted from the horde. The sound was like thunder. Some warriors pumped their fists, bows, or swords into the sky.

"Celebrate this victory, brothers," Dayan continued. "Enjoy a year of prosperity. And if in one year, you still see us as worthy, then we will meet again next summer, in the heart of these southern hills, near the greens of Lake Dai. On that day, I submit myself to your selection!"

The cheers grew even louder, echoing across the flat plains of the Ordos basin, deafening in Mandukhai's ears. In that cheer, she heard the glorious chants heralding their Khan and Khatun. The power of Genghis Khan.

The gathering tent had arrived early in the morning following the discovery of the Shrine of Genghis. It had immediately become a hub of activity the moment the blocks were placed around the wheels. Togochi observed everything as calmly as he could. His wives would arrive soon as well. For now, he had work to do.

Scribes carried messages back and forth through the door, where messengers would ride out of camp to carry the words of their Khatun across the empire. Soon enough, everyone would know Dayan and Mandukhai had succeeded in united all tribes under one banner ... and that *kurultai* would be only a little over a year away. Not that Togochi could imagine anyone daring to stand up against Dayan any longer.

For an hour, Mandukhai had gone over the finer details of her reunification plan with Togochi, Dayan, and a handful of other highly-ranked Lords. He had to admit, her vision was ambitious.

Togochi stood beside the table next to Soke, hands folded behind his back. "This is an elaborate plan, Mandukhai."

"I know." Her eyes shined with excitement. Not a hint of doubt lingered in her any longer. He had never seen her so radiant ... so glowing.

"What is wrong with the government Genghis created?" Soke asked.

Togochi figured a few of these Lords would resist. While Mandukhai was not breaking traditions all together, she certainly was reforging the wheel that bound them together.

Mandukhai snorted and raised her brows at Soke. "Is that a serious question? He showed us how we could unite under one banner, but not how to *keep* ourselves unified. He showed us wealth the likes of which our people had never seen before, but that very wealth led to greed. His sons and grandsons settled in cities and built palaces, but could not see the whole of the empire from their walls. We cannot repeat the mistakes of the past."

Dayan stood stiffly at Mandukhai's side, arms folded over his chest. He had hardly said a word as she explained the plan to reorganize the tribes after *kurultai*. Not that he had disagreed with her. What little input Dayan offered had been agreeable. *I don't know why I would expect anything else from him*, Togochi thought. Dayan and Mandukhai had always worked as a unit. It had only become more flawless since their marriage.

"So, you think that by reorganizing *all* the tribes, you can accomplish what Genghis did not?" Soke asked. "I don't mean to second guess you. Your wisdom has gotten us this far. But Genghis also mixed tribes, yet we still broke off and went our own way."

Mandukhai bit her lip. "Genghis reorganized. That is true. And he created new *khanates* for the tribes, with a central overlord to oversee all the people in those individual areas. But those men had sons and grandsons. Soon they had all thought themselves as powerful and worthy as the *jinong*. They called themselves khans and ruled as khans do. When it came time to choose a new Great Khan, why should any one of those men be more worthy than any other? Do you see the flaw in the system?"

Togochi's thick brows drew together as he considered her words. He saw the flaw now. Those khans ruled themselves and didn't need others to rule over them. It broke the system apart again.

Dayan shrugged. "I do."

Togochi nodded as well.

A small smile played across Mandukhai's lips. "The problem, Soke, is that when you have many khans, how can you determine who is the worthy Great Khan?" She shook her head. "That system of lineage and legitimacy was deeply flawed."

"So how does reorganizing the tribes fix that?" Togochi asked.

"It doesn't." Mandukhai smiled again when she saw his obvious confusion wrinkling his forehead. "That is a simple matter of reunification and national pride. A single tribe alone can attempt seizing power. But with many tribes together, it is like the bundle of arrows."

"Many cannot be broken," Togochi said as it dawned on him. "So these left and right wings will comprise of three unified mega tribes, with a khan to rule them and a Great Khan over them?"

"A council of elders. For now." Again, she nodded. "We are one people. Everyone should be able to move freely all around our realm as they desire. No worries about territorial borders or tribal feuds. We will be a coalition of unity."

The handful of men around the table glanced at one another. Togochi found their calculation amusing. He could see they were wondering who those council elders would be, and if it would be any of them.

"So how do we not end up right back where we started, then?" Belku asked.

"Royal titles will only belong to the royal family," Mandukhai explained. "Lesser men have seized those titles and used them to exert their own power, making Great Khans little more than a puppet."

"You mean like Manduul," Togochi said, irritated by the inference. Manduul may have been a bit dim at times, but he was also still close to Togochi's heart. They had a bond that Togochi knew no one else really understood. *Except maybe Unebolod*, Togochi thought. How was he the only one of the three of them still breathing?

"I mean men like Bigirsen or Issama, who thought they could seize power to gain the right to rule us all," Mandukhai corrected calmly. "Each wing will have the governing body, as we discussed already, but only Borjigin royals can hold the title of Great Khan. The highest-ranking son will become the *jinong*, and the only member of the family eligible to become

Great Khan. The rest will be royal lords. Their children will not. Only the Great Khan's children will ever be royal lords again."

Boragan cleared his throat and rubbed his beard, frowning at the map Mandukhai had marked out with new tribal lines. "So we never get to choose a Great Khan again? No more *kurultai*?" He shook his head. "No one will accept that."

Togochi bit his lip. The Ongud khan had a point. He watched Mandukhai as she considered her answer.

"*Kurultai* still exists," she said calmly, offering Boragan a sweet smile. "It will just not be exactly the same as it was before. The *jinong* will be chosen from among the Great Khan's sons."

Dayan shifted slightly, glancing from the corner of his eyes at the men around him. At the moment, he had no sons, which proved a problem with their plan.

Mandukhai pressed on as if she didn't notice his discomfort. "When the time comes, he will present himself to the Lords at *kurultai*."

"And if they don't agree to his rule?" Boragan asked.

"Then they had better have a very good argument against him, as well as another candidate from among the Great Khan's sons," Mandukhai said calmly. "Because *only* the royal line can hold the office. Otherwise we risk falling into chaos again. Gentlemen, we are not seeking expansion or war. We only want stability. For as long as we can create it."

Everyone fell silent, digesting the information Mandukhai just shared with them. Togochi understood the plan well enough. It secured the legacy of Genghis Khan's line, assuming Dayan and Mandukhai had sons. She had made it clear, as had Dayan, at the start of this meeting that only her sons would inherit. Any sons he had with future wives would hold titles of importance, but not the right to the khanship. Unless Mandukhai produced no sons. Then Dayan would select a son from among those he did have.

Togochi bit his lip again, considering the plan. As long as the two of them had support, it would work. Judging by the men around this table, Togochi felt certain they had the support they needed. All Dayan needed was a victory at *kurultai*.

At last, Togochi broke the silence. "This is ambitious, but I would never bet against you." He smiled at Mandukhai, then scrubbed at his neck. "I had better head home. My wives and I have a long conversation ahead of us."

Togochi said goodbye and trickled out the door with the other Lords. No one spoke. It made it hard for Togochi to guess their reactions to Mandukhai's reunification plan.

As he stepped down the stairs of the gathering tent cart, Togochi spotted Jaghan and Geriel. His sons trailed along behind his wives, and at the rear of the group, Qolotai held the hands of Siker's sons.

Dochigen slapped Togochi playfully on the shoulder and leaned close to whisper, "Good luck," before slinking away.

The boys ran at Togochi, throwing their arms around him. Togochi hugged them back. He picked up his daughter and kissed her cheek. She squealed and kicked in protest teasingly. As he set her down, Jaghan stopped in front of him, hands folded demurely in her sleeves. Togochi held his breath.

"You made it back," she said coolly.

"Did you doubt me?" Togochi teased. He was not about to tell her that he almost didn't make it back. A few feet further back and he would have been crushed under falling boulders when the first volley had hit the passage.

She smirked. "No."

Geriel smiled warmly at Togochi as she held their two-year-old daughter on her hip. Togochi grinned at her, and she wiggled her brows at him, then stepped aside to make space for Qolotai. She kept her eyes downcast, as if uncertain she had any right to even look at him. It broke his heart and his grin slipped.

"I had some time to think," he said.

Jaghan cut him off. "Before you say more, I need you to understand how hard this is for me. From the moment I met you, you were my everything. And I know I was the one who suggested bringing Geriel into our marriage, but my reasons were practical. I didn't want to share you with anyone."

Togochi opened his mouth to tell her that he still adored her as much as he did the day he met her. He would have been lost without her. But she held up a hand to cut him off.

"Let me finish, Togochi." Jaghan squared her shoulders. "I feared that sharing you with another woman would mean you would love me less, or desire me less. Obviously that was not the case. But that fear still exists. So when you came home with another woman, it terrified me. And the reasons for bringing her into our family were no longer practical as they had been with Geriel. I can't stomach the idea of you wanting another woman more than me."

Togochi stepped closer, sliding his hands along her arms. Then he kissed her forehead. "It is not more or less, Jagahn. It's just ... different. I am connected to you in ways I could never connect with anyone else. The same goes for Geriel." His gaze slipped to the timid women staring at the ground with burning interest. "And Qolotai."

Jaghan sighed and leaned against him. The kids darted off to play, but Siker's sons continued clinging to Qolotai's side.

"I understand that now," Jaghan said. "Just as Mandukhai had a different kind of love for Unebolod and Dayan. I have seen her around Dayan since they married. It is not less love than she had for Unebolod. It's just ..."

Togochi waited a moment, then finished for her. "Different."

Jaghan nodded. "But I still need time to get to know her before it becomes official."

Togochi slid an arm around Jaghan and rubbed her back. His gaze fell on Qolotai. "Can you agree to that? A period of adjustment?"

Qolotai lifted her gaze for the first time. At her shoulder, Geriel grinned from ear to ear. Clearly she had no problem with Qolotai. Hope bloomed in Qolotai's eyes as she met his gaze. She nodded.

"A bride-price," Qolotai agreed, nodding. "It seems reasonable. But where will I stay?"

Togochi smiled. "We will take care of that. Everything will be fine, now."

All three women stepped closer to him and Togochi held them, reveling in this moment. How had he become the lucky one?

Dayan propped his chin on his fist, lips drawing into a thin line. He had sunk into one of the chairs as Mandukhai finished up her work, impatient. Did she never stop working? He drummed the fingers on his other hand against the arm of the chair in boredom. More than anything else, he just wanted to get her home. Alone.

"Can't this wait until tomorrow?" Dayan asked with a dramatic sigh.

"We will have a lot of tomorrows," Mandukhai replied evenly. "But only one today. Some of this work cannot wait."

He knew there was more work to do, but they had to have time alone at some point.

Mandukhai closed her eyes and pressed her fists into the tabletop. Dayan frowned as he watched her draw in measured breaths. *She is still worried that someone will oppose us,* he realized.

Dayan stood and gently grabbed her arms to turn her away from the table. Her eyes opened, gleaming like jewels in the light from the torches. His heart skipped and he wound his arms around her, holding her tight against him. He kissed her cheek, then his lips moved down to her neck. Heat surged through him.

"Tomorrow will become today," he murmured against her skin. "This can wait." His hand slid along her arm. "Those heirs won't make themselves."

"Dayan ..." Though Mandukhai had meant to protest, the way she breathed his name only intensified that yearning growing in him. He captured her lips and pulled the papers from her hands, dropping them back on the tabletop. Then he took her hand and placed it against his own back. She had spent too much of her life running, hiding, planning. Those days were behind her now, and he had to be sure she understood that. He *needed* her to. She no longer had anything to run from or toward. Nothing to hide from.

But she had him, and he had her.

Mandukhai's fingers pressed into the fabric of his deel, into his back, holding him as tight against her as she could, her back to the table. He nearly moaned in delight at the touch. His desire made his head spin. A stack of papers slid to the floor. Buddhas and Knights fled across the map as the long shadows of the Khan and Khatun cast over the world. Dayan pressed against her. Slow. Hungry. Eager.

"*You* are today," Dayan murmured against her neck as his fingers worked her deel loose. He reveled in the feel of her skin against his fingertips. "And tomorrow ..." The deel fell open as he tugged her belt free. "You are eternity."

CHAPTER FORTY-EIGHT

Kurultai

The land around Lake Dai was fertile, fed by a stream that flowed from the Khingan Mountains to the east. It made for good hunting grounds because they were more likely to find game here.

Tomorrow would be the most important day in Dayan's life. To release pent-up energy before the long day ahead of him, Dayan had gone hunting with Nemeku, Boke, Chakicha, and Belku. These four had become his closest friends—if he could call Boke a friend more than an irksome guard.

By mid-day, Dayan dismounted to stretch his limbs. A hot summer breeze caressed his skin. Dayan closed his eyes and tilted his head toward the Eternal Blue Sky. How much his life had changed since spring last year. He was truly, deeply happy, a completely novel sensation for him. And tomorrow, they would make him finally, officially Great Khan.

Tomorrow belonged to his people. All the days after, he knew Mandukhai had a pile of responsibilities waiting for him. Today belonged to him.

"Dayan," Boke hissed.

"Give me a minute in peace, Boke," Dayan mumbled.

"A messenger."

Dayan opened his eyes and sighed. *So much for hunting in peace.* He shielded his eyes from the sun as he squinted toward the rider. It didn't take long to recognize Togochi's hunched form.

Togochi stopped a few feet away and dismounted. His lips set in a dour line. Dayan inwardly groaned. *He's getting grumpier as he ages.*

"Can't I just have one day to—"

"Siker is dead," Togochi interrupted.

Dayan froze in shock, unsure if he heard Togochi right at first, then unsure how he should feel about the news. Siker never had spoken to him, never had responded to any messages sent to her estate on Qori's grounds. She never had seemed to care that he existed, and he wasn't sure that it mattered to him.

But she *was* his mother. By birth, at the very least. One thing he was now more certain of than ever before was that he did not understand Siker. How could a parent *ever* abandon their child, then not care about them upon finding that child had survived? He shuddered.

"I'm sorry, Dayan," Togochi said, sympathy dripping from his voice. He edged closer, placing a hand on his shoulder.

Dayan shook himself from his shock. "What happened? I sent Kelegei to retrieve her for tomorrow." Mandukhai had insisted on Siker being present for the festivities. Dayan really didn't care if Siker was there at all. He had sent for her to appease his wife.

"Qori says his wife had been keeping a close eye on her of late," Togochi replied. He paled and, unless Dayan misunderstood, his shoulders sagged. "She has been overcome with grief for some time now and Qori's wife worried about her."

"And?"

Togochi pulled in a deep breath as if bracing himself for Dayan's anger. "She drowned herself in the pond."

Dayan's pulse slowed. His heart ached. This woman who should have been his mother would rather grieve over his enemy's death and kill herself than reconcile with him.

"Are you all right, Dayan?" Togochi asked.

The others in his hunting party had crowded closer. Dayan felt tears burn in his eyes. *I won't shed tears over a woman who never loved me.* Instead, he swallowed hard, cleared his throat, and nodded.

"It's fine. Thanks for telling me. Be sure Mandukhai knows I will be back after dark. But I will be back tonight."

Togochi backed up and bowed stiffly, clearly not convinced, but he said nothing. A moment later, he rode off.

"Dayan ..." Nemeku said as he edged up beside him. "It's okay to be upset. As horrible as he was, I still miss my father sometimes."

Pain and grief for Siker had no place in his heart. Dayan turned abruptly to his friends. "Let's hunt!"

Esige leaned over the two infants nestled in her bed as she pinned up her hair. Both boys slept soundly, peacefully. She knew that would not last. At nearly six months old, neither slept for long. Her oldest son, Emeeltoorson, recently ten, sat on the floor beside the bed, peering at the twins as he picked at the rug in boredom.

"Why do I have to watch them?" he pouted.

"This is an important day," Esige said patiently, making her way over to her chest of jewels to fetch the rings and bracelets she would wear for the occasion. "The most important day our people have seen in over two hundred years. It is only until we are ready for the ceremony."

"Why can't the guards do it? I wanted to play with the other boys." Emeeltoorson peered at the twins again and stuck out his tongue. "Torudur and Babaqai set up a special game for us kids to play. I want to join them."

Esige slid the last bracelet on and adjusted her rings. Satisfied, she marched over to the bed, placed a hand on each of the twins, then crouched in front of her son. Togochi's boys were on the cusp of manhood now, and the youngest was far too interested in Tayiqu. To the girl's credit, she remained true to her word, waiting to see if Dayan would ever consider her as a wife. Esige highly doubted it would happen, but she didn't want to let the poor girl down. "Do you know what an honor it is to watch over them? And you won't be alone. Grandmother and Tayiqu will be here to help any moment."

Emeeltoorson gagged as if just the thought of Tayiqu disgusted him. "All she does is talk about boys."

Esige brushed a kiss over her son's forehead. "I need you to be on your best behavior and remember that these two are the future of our nation. Do you understand how important that is?"

He frowned and slouched, resuming his picking at the rug. "Yes," he grumbled.

"Grandmother and Tayiqu will be here soon," Esige reassured him. "Just leave them be for now."

He sighed dramatically. "Fine. But what if they wake up and start crying before grandmother gets here? I'm not wiping their dirty butts."

Esige only smiled at her son as she slipped out the door.

The guards eyed her suspiciously as she stepped out, then they stared at the closed door. Mandukhai had insisted on a dozen guards, as if the twins would crawl away or disappear. She was overly worried about the boys. The guards knew, at least, to allow Tayiqu and Chimgee, Huoshai's mother, to enter. Esige doubted anyone else would be allowed within ten yards of the ger.

Esige strolled toward the Shrine of Genghis to check on last-minute adjustments to the day's events. The air thrummed with excitement and energy everywhere as she walked along the thoroughfares. Even so early in the morning, just into the wolf dawn, everyone was awake and moving. The scent of cooking meat and boiling stews filled the air, overpowering anything else. Esige breathed it in.

Horsemen had been selected for the honor guard and divided into two groups. One would wear white to represent peace and enlightenment. The other would wear black to represent strength and war. Both were necessary parts of any powerful empire. The horses would match the colors of the men riding them.

Cattle and sheep had been assembled over the past few days in sets of nine—a sacred number. This morning, Esige checked the mass of animals and spoke briefly with the cattle masters in charge of the animals.

"Everything is in order, my Lady," the head cattle master reassured her. "We are prepared for the sacrifices."

Esige thanked him and moved on toward the gathering tent where the procession would begin.

Half a lifetime of work would culminate today. Mandukhai could not help feeling anxious about this as Dayan helped her—quite unnecessarily—climb onto her white horse. This was a mare, and in no way even close to a replacement for Dust. But the two of them would ride white mares today as a symbol of the birth of a new empire.

It had taken all morning to prepare for this ceremony, and Mandukhai hated how the deel pressed against her stomach just enough to cause her discomfort but not enough to force alterations on the clothing just yet.

After years of worrying about having children, or if she ever would, the High Heavens had blessed her, just as Genghis had promised. It had not taken long for her first pregnancy to begin after she and Dayan officially married. They had often discussed whether she had already been with child during that final battle against Mogurkei. Dayan, as eager and virile as ever, had not wasted time after the twins were born before he planted another seed.

Dayan mounted beside her, and Tayiqu and the wet-nurse approached, each holding a child.

Ulusbolod squirmed as the wet-nurse passed him up to Mandukhai, but the moment she pulled him close, he stopped and smiled at her. It lifted her heart and warmed her soul as surely as if the sun shined on her.

Tayiqu passed Torobolod—first born of the two boys—up to Dayan. Mandukhai noticed the smile Dayan flashed at Tayiqu, and the way Tayiqu dipped her head and blushed. It seemed ridiculous to be jealous of anyone when he had been so focused on Mandukhai for so long. But she knew it could not last forever. Tayiqu was thirteen now, and blossoming into a beautiful young woman—not to mention her interest in Dayan was never masked.

Mandukhai looked away. Nothing had been mentioned to him more than a year after Esige brought it up. Mandukhai could not avoid the conversation forever. As the Great Khan, he would need other wives to produce as many sons as possible. Not that any sons from any other women would ever hold the title as long as her own sons lived.

Mandukhai smiled at Ulusbolod, stroking his cheek tenderly as they waited. For so long, she had worried about giving the nation the heirs it needed. And in one pregnancy, she had given it two.

In the distance, drummers pounded on kettledrums. The sound made her heart jump and drew her attention back to the path ahead. *This is it*, she thought, casting a brief glance at Dayan. He grinned at her only for a moment, then adopted a stoic mask and fixed his gaze dead ahead. In those brief glimpses, she saw his youth and vitality. It made her love him even more.

They had chosen an honor guard of a thousand warriors for this event. Five hundred warriors in black armor on black horses rode alongside five hundred warriors in white armor on white horses. All of them led the way, making a path forward for their Khan and Khatun.

Mandukhai and Dayan rode beside each other, toward the waiting mass of Mongols. White horsehair banners waved in the wind ahead of them and behind. But far ahead of the processional, Soke rode at the head of the party bearing the black *sulde* of Genghis Khan—an honor that should have belonged to Unebolod. Beside Soke, Bagasun rode on his own horse. The boy didn't fully understand why he had been given this position. One day, he would.

The closer they drew to the event grounds before the sacred shrines, the louder the drumming became. The moment the heralds spotted the Khan and Khatun, they sounded the five-foot-long brass horns, heralding the arrival of the leaders of the Mongol Nation. Mandukhai sat as straight as she could in her saddle, but the slight swelling of her belly and the nearly six-month-old boy in her arms made it hard to appear dignified.

On either side of the wide thoroughfare, white canopies covered the Lords and Ladies gathered there, separated by tribe for the last time ever. The colorful banners of each tribe fluttered on the breeze, the sound of their flapping swallowed by the horns and the swell of the beat on the kettledrums.

There would be no oaths given this day. All the Lords and Ladies present had already given their oath to the Khan and Khatun. Instead, once Dayan climbed the steps and approached the Shrine of Genghis, they would step forward and place their banners around him as a show of support. Not that any present would dare to oppose either of them at this point.

Mandukhai glanced at Dayan, cradling Torobolod close to his chest. His wolf-like eyes remained fixed dead ahead. On the fluttering horsehairs of the *sulde* of Genghis. Soke had planted the pole of the banner in a holder at the doorway to the sacred shrine.

When they reached the end of the road, Dayan held Torobolod out to Mandukhai and dismounted. Tuya and Ong rushed over to Mandukhai and took each of the children so she could dismount as well. Dayan had wanted to leave the boys out of the ceremony, but Mandukhai had insisted they be part of it. The arrival of two boys was a clear sign that the supremacy of the line of Genghis was returning. People needed to see that for themselves.

The couple entered the shrine, and the drums and horns immediately ceased. Mandukhai and Dayan approached the shrine's inside, lit the incense and lamps they had delivered the day before, and offered prayers to the high Heavens for blessings from the Eternal Blue Sky.

When they emerged, Dayan marched to the edge of the platform. Mandukhai sat in the cushioned chair beside the door. This pregnancy was more exhausting than the previous, and she found standing for long periods of time tedious.

"Ten years ago," Dayan said, reciting the speech Mandukhai had forced him to memorize, "the Mongol people were fractured, divisive, wounded. The line of Genghis Khan had seemed to come to an end. The people had forgotten his teachings. Outsiders exerted their authority over our people and our lands. When the Mongol Nation faced its darkest days in centuries..." He paused, glancing back at Mandukhai. "... one person stood before the Shrine of the First Queen and bound herself by sacred oath to the High Heavens."

Mandukhai's lips parted in alarm. Dayan had moved off their planned speech. *What is he doing?*

"Mandukhai the Wise, Empress of the Jade Realm, was born that day."

Empress? She wished he would stick to what they had planned, or they risked losing face when these Lords had gathered to support him, not her. He had joked in private about her being an empress of this new empire, but never publicly. It could delegitimize his position to give her accolades.

Dayan continued, oblivious to her worry, or ignoring it. She wasn't certain which. "She rescued me, a broken and dying boy, the last heir of Genghis Khan. She healed me, mind, body, and soul. She showed compassion and tenderness to those who needed it most, rescuing children who otherwise would have faced a cruel life. For the sake of the Mongol Nation, she forfeited her own happiness. She held the dead vision of Genghis in her loving hands and breathed new life into it. Just as she did for many of you. Just as she did for me."

Mandukhai's gaze swept the crowd, worried about this level of praise. To her surprise, the Lords and commanders all nodded in agreement, gathered at the head of the crowd in their flapping canvas canopies. A lump swelled in her throat. She knew the men had respected her over the years. But this ... to be praised and acknowledged at *kurultai* ... it was something no other women in the history of their empire had ever received.

"We stand here today, under the blessed Eternal Blue Sky, in the presence of the embodiment of the Earth Mother herself," Dayan continued. "If the Khan is the hat of the world, the Khatun is the mother of life."

Tears pricked in Mandukhai's eyes. No one in her life—not even Unebolod—had ever offered her so much praise. As she gazed at her husband, Mandukhai fell in love with him all over again.

"For the past eleven years, some of you have followed Mandukhai the Wise, your Khatun," he said. "Over time, you all had faith in her vision. You supported her sacred vow to me. Today, we gather so that you can choose me, as you chose her years ago. And together, we will form a stronger, more unified Mongol Empire. We will protect our borders, protect our families, and grow as one nation. For one arrow alone can be broken, but together, we are strong."

Dayan paused, and the crowd picked up on the cue, calling out in unison, "So said Genghis."

"I submit myself, my noble Lords," Dayan proclaimed. "As your Great Khan, as the heir of Genghis ... as the Emperor of this reborn realm."

Soke was first to approach, carrying the Khorchin banner with Bagasun—Unebolod's only son. The two bowed deeply at the bottom of the platform and planted the pole of the banner into the ground. Each of the Lords and commanders from the Khorchin tribe followed, touching the pole, then they bowed to Dayan before returning to their canvas canopy.

Togochi led the Khorlod next. After he planted the pole beside the Khorchin banner, Togochi placed his fist over his heart as he bowed to Dayan. The rest of the Khorlod followed his lead.

One by one, the lesser khans and Lords marched forward, placed their banners in the line, and bowed to the Great Khan. Kharchin. Urainkhai. Chakhar. Ongud. Tabun. Oirat. Jalair. The procession took more than an hour as all forty-four tribes added their colors to the line.

All colors. And none.

Ulusbolod squawked and squirmed throughout the procession, but Torobolod watched the fluttering colors in fascination as he sucked on his fist. Mandukhai reached down to the basket holding the twins and offered her hand to Ulusbolod. He reached up, fumbling to grab hold, yanking on her pinky. After a few minutes, his squawks became happy coos.

When the last banner had been planted into the ground, the crowd erupted into cheers.

Khosoichi stepped forward as the crowd celebrated. He sprinkled mare's milk around Dayan, then into the earth, and tossed some toward the sky. He fanned jasmine in the air around Dayan, sanctifying him as Great Khan. By the time he finished, the crowd quieted.

Khosoichi cleared his throat and called out loudly and clearly for all to hear. "So says Dayan Khan, heir of Genghis, divine son of the Eternal Blue Sky, ruler of the Mongol Nation, Emperor of the Jade Realm. May he always remember that it is necessary to accept hard and inconvenient advice, to punish bad people with merciless law, to protect his subjects with kindness, and to strive after a good name which is honored everywhere!"

Dayan bowed to the old shaman and turned his attention back to the crowd. "We have restored the fractured empire," Dayan proclaimed. His proclamation was met with cheers. He waited a moment before pressing on. "But our work is not yet done. Now, we must become one tribe, one nation, under one rule, under the Eternal Blue Sky ... forever."

Once more, the crowd erupted into cheers. So many voice raised in unity as they chanted for their new Great Khan reached high into the blue sky. Mandukhai felt a sense of peace wash over her.

"Today, we celebrate our new nation," Dayan said. "Tomorrow, we rebuild it. We will become the Khalkha—the shield against outside enemies. A support for your precious life. A blade toward those who come. Our one tribe will be a shield against the world."

Dayan's heart hammered in excitement and fear as he finished his speech. Hopefully Mandukhai would not be too angry with him about the first part, but he could not go forward without recognizing the sacrifices she made to get him to this point. He turned to gaze at her while the crowd cheered.

Mandukhai had risen from her seat, approaching him with a child on each hip. She positively beamed with pride and love in a way that made her skin seem to glow. His stomach flipped and a surge of desire coursed through him, as it often did when he looked at her. They both knew that this announcement would likely result in a need for further marital alliances—other Lords would want to become part of the Great Khan's family by marrying off their daughters to him—but he was not ready to share his heart with anyone else. Not yet. Nor could he ever imagine loving any other woman nearly as much as he loved Mandukhai. He had meant every word he said today. This day was hers as much as it was his. Perhaps more so.

Mandukhai rounded the front of the platform and eased down to a knee, bowing her head to him. Dayan hated it. Nothing about it felt right.

Then, much to his own alarm, the rest of the gathering followed her lead. Hundreds of Mongol Lords. Thousands of men and women beyond. A sea of bodies as far as he could see fell to their knees in a wave moving outward, like ripples in water.

Mandukhai rose after a minute, and as she climbed the steps of the platform to join him, Dayan's heart stilled.

This was it.

His vision.

The promise of Genghis fulfilled.

Epilogue
Compassion and Passion

Every part of Mandukhai's body ached every time she moved. Her body showed the signs of age with wrinkles on the front and back of her hands, thick, coarse gray hair braided down her back, and deep lines of crow's feet and wrinkles around her eyes and mouth. How Dayan still found her attractive, she could not understand. How much had she aged since he left to go south? Would he still find her attractive when he returned?

Despite the aches in her body, every morning she rose to perform her offerings to the earth mother. This morning, as she stepped into the courtyard of their small palace, Mandukhai's pulse quickened from the exertion. The bucket of milk was too heavy. She wanted to set it down. But if she failed, even one day, she could lose even more than she had already lost. This offering protected her family—her husband and sons.

Five years had passed since the messenger had arrived in her capital along the banks of the Kherlen River. Four years had passed since she said farewell to her husband and sons. The memory of that day still ached like a fresh wound.

Ulusbolod had gone south ten years ago on Mandukhai and Dayan's orders to help some leaders who were struggling with trade and invasion. Ulusbolod was supposed to install himself as *jinong* at the Shrine of Genghis far to the south, on Dayan's orders. The shrine had been in the care of the Left Wing Chakhar Banner—one of seven banners under the Great Khan, each led by one of her seven sons.

But a man named Irbag had blocked Ulusbolod at the sacred shrine, insisting that Ulusbolod owed him horses for those that one of Ulusbolod's men had stolen. It had turned into a confrontation. Ulusbolod had died on the steps of the shrine. His wife had fled with their son out of fear for the young boy's life.

Tears blurred Mandukhai's vision as she set the bucket on the ground and gazed south. Ulusbolod had been incredibly intelligent, a clear choice between her first set of twins to become Dayan's successor. But he also had a bit of his grandfather in him—impulsive and sometimes reckless.

Mandukhai dipped her ladle in the bucket of milk slowly. Her back creaked with the movement. So many years of riding into battle on horseback had caught up to her. At sixty-two, she could hardly ride any longer. After Faith died of old age, Mandukhai had insisted she didn't need a special new horse. Any from her herds would do. Riding was just too difficult lately. When Dayan had gathered the rest of her sons to avenge Ulusbolod, she had been unable to go along.

She closed her eyes. A tear rolled down her cheek. She pulled in a slow, steadying breath.

Some part of her knew that day she had said goodbye to her husband for the last time. She was old and frail now, and he was only in his forties with so much left to accomplish. When she had sniffed the cheeks of her other six sons, Mandukhai had refused the second cheek.

"I will sniff the other when you return to me," she had told each.

I should have sniffed the other, old fool, she thought.

Mandukhai slowly opened her eyes and sprinkled the milk in offering, just as she had done every morning since they departed.

Dayan had two other wives now—Tayiqu and Kusi. Though he loved them all, he showed special attention to Mandukhai that often made her worry the other wives would become jealous. Where the other two only had one or two children with him, Mandukhai had eight. And her sons would inherit the khanship when the others would not. The two women much younger than Mandukhai as well, and more capable of taking care of him in ways she no longer could. Still, when he said goodbye, the pain in his eyes had been all for her. Somehow, he had sensed, in that moment, that he would never see her again. She wished she had accepted that as well.

"You are my eternity," he had whispered in her ear as he hugged her close, reciting the sacred vow he had saved only for her. Dayan had placed a tender kiss on her lips and pulled away from her for the last time, taking an army with him.

The fight in the south had turned into a revolt between Legusi, Ibarai, and a few former Ordos khans who had for decades been loyal. The aggression and theft had soured them. Dayan had spent the next three years extinguishing their revolt. *I'm sorry, my dear, precious empress, but I do not know when I can return to you. I fear if I leave too soon, all my work here will be undone.* That had been his last message to her. She counted the days until she received another.

Mandukhai did not live in the small palace alone. When Dayan had left with the men, their daughter, Toroltu, and her husband Bagasun had moved into the palace with their two boys. The highlight of Mandukhai's lonely days was talking to her daughter and watching her grandsons.

In honor of Unebolod's sacrifice and everything he had done for Mandukhai, Dayan, and the Mongol nation, his tribe had been the only one allowed to maintain their independent identity when Mandukhai and Dayan reorganized the tribes into the Right and Left Wings. His son, Bagasun, had received an honorable position as Unebolod's only son and heir. Not to mention his marriage to the only daughter of the Great Khan and Khatun. Mandukhai sometimes imagined that her grandsons looked like her own children with Unebolod might have. They certainly had his spirit.

As happy as Mandukhai had been with Dayan, some part of her heart still pulled her toward Unebolod. Dayan knew it. He had accepted it, and had even reassured Mandukhai that he understood after he had married Tayiqu. "I love you both in ways I cannot explain," he had told Mandukhai, "and in ways that are very different as well. I understand the pain you must have held in your heart for so long."

Mandukhai smiled softly to herself as she picked up the bucket to return inside. How she wished she could be twenty years younger and just as fit and strong as Dayan! His confession and acceptance of her lingering feelings for Unebolod had transformed into something else completely, a deeper understanding of each other. It had also resulted in her third and final set of twin boys. She had given herself fully to her compassionate love and restored the fractured empire. Though the new empire still had its problems, Mandukhai trusted it was in capable hands.

Only the one who carries the spirit can reunite the One Nation. Only he of my bone will have the might to hold it. Those words offered Mandukhai some comfort still. Genghis had made her that promise so long ago. Along with the promise that she would birth a pack of wolves. The second, she had done, and so she had to have faith that Dayan was the bones of Genghis, strong enough to hold together the nation she built for him.

"Mother what are you doing?" Toroltu gasped, rushing over to her side. Mandukhai envied her youth and speed. Running like that would exhaust her now.

Bagasun heard Toroltu's call and marched over from their chambers across the courtyard, taking the bucket from her. Toroltu slid her arm around Mandukhai's waist to escort her.

"I'm not an invalid," Mandukhai insisted, but even she heard the exhaustion in her voice.

"Let's get you to bed," Toroltu said soothingly. "You need rest."

"When I was your age, I conquered the Oirat without a helmet," Mandukhai said tersely. "I can handle myself just fine."

"I know, Mother."

The boys burst out of their rooms and raced across the courtyard, laughing and playing with sticks. Mandukhai paused to watch them, remembering when their mother had done the same with her brothers. Toroltu had grown tough as the only daughter among seven sons. But there was a tenderness to her as well.

Toroltu eased Mandukhai down onto the bed. "I will go fetch you some tea and breakfast."

Bagasun towered beside the door, his arms cross over his massive chest. He reminded Mandukhai so much of his father that sometimes it hurt to look at him, while other times she could not look away. As Toroltu slipped out the door, he followed, placing his hand on the small of her back affectionately.

Mandukhai lay on the bed, waiting for them to return. They were right. She just needed a nap. She rested her head on the pillow, smiling at the old white silk belt wrapped around the beam over her head. Dayan had put it there before he left, a reminder of their promises to one another.

She closed her eyes. "I have done all I can do."

She allowed her mind to drift back to younger years full of passion, desire, danger ... Dayan's devotion and complete adoration. Unebolod's faith and strength. Even after all these years, she still loved them both fiercely. A peace settled over her.

Mandukhai stood on a familiar path. Before her, the Mother Tree remained formidable against the rising sun, as if daring the world to challenge it. *This must be a dream,* she thought as she reached out to run her fingers along a glowing yellow ribbon hanging from a branch. As she reached out, she noticed the wrinkles of age no longer marred her hand. The callouses from years of archery and sword fighting had vanished without a trace.

Hundreds of blue ribbons hung from the branches of the tree, making the yellow ribbon stand out boldly against the rest. It drew her in, fascinated her. It reminded her of the yellow ribbon Unebolod had tied around his hilt.

"You have done well." The familiar voice of Genghis drew her attention away from the tree. He stood at her shoulder, just as awe-inspiring as he had been the first time she laid eyes on him. "I knew I chose well."

Mandukhai kneeled before him. Genghis wrapped a powerful hand around her arm, pulling her back to her feet.

"You no longer kneel to me, Empress," he said. His golden eyes glowed, reminding her of Dayan. How she longed to see him again. "We have given you an honor no woman has received."

"What honor is that, Great Khan?"

"A place among the spirits of the Great Khans."

Mandukhai blinked. Did that mean ...? "How much longer do I have?" she asked. If she would die soon, she would spend her last days seeking Dayan and her sons. She would attempt finding him just to feel him hold her one more time.

Genghis cocked his head, regarding her like a bird of prey. "You are here already." He waved toward the world around them. The spirit world she had walked with him before.

As understanding weighed down on her, Mandukhai's heart ached. *I am dead already.* Poor Toroltu would return with breakfast to find her mother dead!

Mandukhai glanced over her shoulder as if her past, her life, waited just behind her. "But Dayan ..."

Genghis nodded and began walking down the mountain, away from the Mother Tree. "You raised him well, taught him well, loved him well. He will not forget what you sacrificed for him. It will lead him to greater things, to control over Beijing, Hami, Turfan ..."

As he said it, Mandukhai could see Dayan in her mind's eye as if watching his through a mist. He looked resplendent in his armor, taking on the world. She reached out as if she could touch him but knew he was not there. It filled her with disappointment.

"Your sons Barsubolod and Arsubolod will challenge each other," Genghis continued.

Again, as he spoke, she could almost see the confrontation and division. It broke her heart. Everything she had worked so hard to build was at risk!

"But unlike my own sons, yours will come to a peaceful agreement in honor of their father and the empire you built for them."

The two men embraced, nodding in amicable agreement. Her sons. They were so handsome! So strong.

"And when they pass on, Ulusbolod's son, Anda Altan, will become Great Khan. Through your grandson, the Mongol Nation will reach a golden age, as his name promises."

As Genghis continued, Mandukhai saw it all. Her chest clenched and breath caught in her lungs as she saw the empire rise, the treaties signed, the foundation of a great city.

"He will become the Golden Khan, forge treaties with the Ming and Tibet, and one of his own great-grandsons will become the fourth Dalai Lama. Altan Khan will establish the Blue City in your honor, just north of Lake Dai and not far from where Dayan Khan stood before my shrine."

Then she saw, shining through a haze of fog, a statue of brilliant white ... of her.

Genghis turned to her. "Your legacy, my legacy, is secure."

Mandukhai's knees grew weak as she watched it all unfold through the fog. Tears rolled down her cheeks unchecked as Genghis laid the fate of her family at her feet. It was everything she could have wanted, everything she had dreamed. Mandukhai had given up her deepest heart's desire to restore the fractured empire, and she had seen some results for herself. But hearing Genghis confirm the security of everything she fought so hard to build overwhelmed her. Seeing it gave her a new sense of satisfaction ... of peace and awe. *She* did all of that. She laid the groundwork for greater things.

"Dayan," Mandukhai breathed, attempting to see him as Genghis had shown her everything else.

He placed a hand on her shoulder. "Don't. He will be along in time. And when he arrives, you will be here to welcome him."

Genghis raised his hand between them, drawing her gaze toward what he held. A heart. "You gave your heart, your purpose to me. You have upheld your promises." He stretched his hand toward her chest, pressing the heart through her skin, muscles, ribs. It did not hurt. Why would it when she was already dead? "It is now yours to give once more."

Mandukhai brushed a trembling hand over her chest where his hand had been a moment before. No traces of blood marred her clothing.

Genghis turned and strode away from her.

Mandukhai raised her hand, helpless to stop him. What would she do now? She turned and found herself standing at the base of the hill where her favorite old birch tree clung to life. And there, beneath the branches, Unebolod waited. Mandukhai closed the distance in a few steps, marveling at how he had not aged a day since she last saw him. He wore the same armor she remembered him wearing that day he approached her beside Manduul's pyre, and white fur lined the edges.

"It took you long enough," he teased. "We have been waiting."

Just the sound of his voice made Mandukhai's heart leap with joy. "Building an empire was no small task."

She had almost forgotten how dark his eyes were, like pools of night sky. Yet his face was softer than she remembered.

"So I've been told." He stroked her cheek. "I told you I would wait."

Unebolod tipped her chin up and brushed his lips over hers, testing them as he had that first time they had kissed so long ago. Everything inside of her alighted at that moment. No worrying about who might see them or what it might mean. No barriers between them any longer. For as long as she could, Mandukhai clung to him, reveling in the kiss, the feel of him. Then guilt turned her stomach. Should she be so eager to kiss Unebolod when she had spent a lifetime in love with another man?

"It's okay," Unebolod reassured her. "Here, we can all be together. No concern for who might see us. Nothing holding us back. When his time comes, he can join us as well. Right now, I have someone I want you to meet. And someone eager to see you."

Mandukhai supposed he had a point. This was the afterlife. She could make whatever she wanted of it.

Unebolod slid his arm around her and the two walked away from the tree together. If she could not be with Dayan, Mandukhai would be happy here in these arms.

And when he did arrive, she would be there to welcome him into their new life.

Thank you for reading the Fractured Empire Saga! If you enjoyed the book, please leave a review. Reviews can help influence other po-

tential readers' buying decisions, which is critical for indie authors like me.

Want to learn how Dayan's father survived his own childhood and met Siker? Scan the code to download the free prequel, Prosperous Eternity.

Historical Notes

For roughly ten years after Mandukhai renamed Batu and made him Dayan Khan, she dedicated her time to raising him to be strong enough to hold the title she had thrust upon him. Details on what exactly happened are sketchy, but we do know that she taught him how to lead and how to fight. She also spent time carefully forging alliances with other Mongol Lords so that, when the time came, she would have a stronger hold over the nation.

While history doesn't exactly say that she did not want to use brutal force to achieve her goals, her more passive approach to ruling for these ten years makes it clear to me that she had hoped to lose as few lives as possible. Since little of note happens during this time around her, I thought it best to skip past these years and get to the part we all wanted to see—her dream fulfilled.

One thing we know for certain is that Mandukhai had hoped the Ming would deal with Bigirsen for her. I don't believe she feared him, but I think she had a healthy respect for what he was capable of and had hoped to avoid confrontation. It is also true that she did not know the extent of Issama's scheming. I am certain she suspected something was amiss with him, but she had no actual evidence for decades.

Dayan was notoriously well-guarded and sheltered. Mandukhai had intended to take no risks in raising and protecting him for as long as she could. As the last true heir of Genghis, he was their last hope at renewing the strength of the line and she would not take risks with his life.

The story about Tulugen and the hot soup is, in fact, based on historical records. It is written about in some detail in *The Mongol Chronicle of Altan Tobci*. Tulugen saw this deception on Bigirsen's part as a deep betrayal. It cost Bigirsen some of the last threads of strength he still clung to. Tulugen vowed, "Until the day I die, I shall never forget this hate." The story became quite famous across the empire. It brought Tulugen to Mandukhai and Dayan and not only solidified their alliance, but it gave Mandukhai vital information she needed about Bigirsen's whereabouts.

The campaign against Bigirsen was the first time Dayan led a mission without Mandukhai looming over his shoulder. He took with him "the Chakhar and Tumed, and assembled them to set out against Bigirsen." The fight against Bigirsen happened in this book much as it did historically. Dayan's forces snuck up on Bigirsen's camp. He put his helmet on someone else and fled for his life. When they caught him, they killed him without mercy. According to Altan Tobci, "It is said that salt grew at the place where he was killed." Bigirsen and Borogchin's son, Nemeku, had been with his father at the time and placed a curse on his father's head, just as he does in the book.

Dayan saw this campaign against Bigirsen as his bride price. While he and Mandukhai had been formally married since she named him at the Shrine of the First Queen, they had not lived as a married couple (for what I hope are obvious reasons). Killing Bigirsen proved, in Dayan's eyes, his worthiness to take that next step. They took that final step in 1480 when he was seventeen and she was thirty-three.

The death of Issama did not actually happen until 1484. He had been forced back into hiding on the edge of uninhabitable desert, licking his wounds and surely trying to recover from a lifetime of plans going up in smoke. Mandukhai knew that if Issama lived, he could still undo all of her hard work. For Dayan, the reason to go after Issama was more personal. His mother had been married to Issama for years by this point. Perhaps he hoped to reunite with his long-lost mother, or perhaps Mandukhai had forced his hand. Either way, Dayan sent a group of 200 men, with Togochi leading the way, to hunt down and kill Issama, then bring Siker back to the Great Khan's camp.

I drew out Issama's death a little for the sake of the story. In reality, it happened much as it did in the book. Togochi's men charged in. Siker prepared Issama's horse so he could investigate. By the time he realized it was an enemy, it was too late. Issama was killed with a single arrow on horseback—an ending not nearly dramatic enough for a villain such as him in the books.

I added the bit about the heart in the jar to show Mandukhai's hatred for what Issama had done to her. However, the way Siker reacts to Togochi is also recorded by Altan Tobci. She refused to cooperate with Togochi, and refused to speak to Togochi. When she was at last reunited with Dayan, the reunion did not go as Dayan likely hoped. Siker had become cold and distant, and had refused to reconcile with her son. Dayan placed her in the care of another where she could live out her days in comfort. Instead, Siker drowned herself in her grief over losing Issama. What exactly happened to her sons from Issama is not written, except that she was separated from them.

Issama's other wife, Qolotai, married Togochi. Why she so willingly went along with him is hard to say. Perhaps she had no other choice and had been forced into the marriage. Perhaps she had been unhappy with Issama and saw this as an opportunity for a fresh start.

The taming of the Ordos tribes in the south was actually much more complicated than I wrote it to be in this book. Some eagerly fell under Dayan's banner. Others resisted. The actual process took a few years. I condensed it down to make it easier to follow and more manageable along the timeline. She did cross the Huang Ho River in the winter before the ice melted. The bridge did not actually exist. The only way to cross was on rafts, boats, or ice. But the bridge presented me with an opportunity to introduce a few other plot elements.

While many parts of the Great Wall existed long before Mandukhai's time, the slowly growing strength she developed, as well as the aggression from men like Bigirsen, worried the Ming. The Emperor's court was divided by its own internal strife and they did not have the strength or resources to start a war against Bigirsen or Mandukhai. Instead, they began expanding the Great Wall to block out Mandukhai's slowly growing army and protect themselves a little longer. This period of expansion was quite extensive. Over 700 more miles of wall were added during this period of unrest.

I wanted to discuss the fate of Unebolod because I am quite certain many people will be unhappy with his death. What exactly happened to him is unclear. He served Mandukhai and Dayan devotedly. He died in service to the empire. Little is written about him during this period. If he was going to die, I needed his death to mean something. What better way for a hero to die than saving his Khan and cementing his absolute loyalty to the couple? It is the hardest death I have ever written.

The Mongol people believe Mandukhai loved Unebolod until her own death, which made their sacrifice even more sacred in the eyes of the people. They loved each other devoutly but sacrificed their happiness together for the sake of the Nation. There is even a Mongol symphony written dedicated to the everlasting love and sacrifice of Mandukhai and Unebolod. This does not mean Mandukhai did not love Dayan. We are all capable of loving more than one person.

I know there are a lot of names to follow in this book, but all of them are based on actual historical figures. Mogurkei was a final holdout who resisted Mandukhai and Dayan's reign. Defeating him meant moving that last piece on the chessboard into checkmate. For a little while, there was peace in the south among Mongols until the incident with Mandukhai's son, Ulusbolod. This created a revolt that finally separated Mandukhai and Dayan. He left on campaign to stamp out the revolt. She remained behind and died before he could return. The nature of her death is a mystery. Some say she was killed. Some say she died in peace waiting for the men she loved. Just like Genghis, her tomb is hidden, but there is a stone grave monument dedicated to her.

During their marriage, Mandukhai and Dayan had eight children together: twins Ulusbolod and Torobolod; twins Barsubolod and Arsubolod; daughter Toroltu; twins Ochirbolod and Aljubolod; and son Arabolod. While he had at least two other wives that we know of, and only two children with each of them, his love and loyalty remained with Mandukhai until his own death. Their reform reshaped the future of the Mongol nation, from the reunification to the creation of the Left and Right Wing tumeds. Their government lasted far longer than the one Genghis built. To this day, they still considered her a hero to the Mongol people almost as much as Genghis himself. The city of Hohhot was established in her honor, and an extensive park in the city—Mandukhai Park—now features a pure white statue of her. As Genghis stated in the epilogue of this book, her legacy was secured.

There is so much more to learn about Mandukhai than I could ever contain in the historical notes of the story. I highly recommend doing your own research about Mandukhai (also Manduhai) the Wise and Dayan Khan. I also recommend reading Jack Weatherford's book, *The Secret History of the Mongol Queens*. It is fascinating and well worth the read.

Acknowledgements

Writing this series was emotionally taxing, but I believe the final results do some justice to the legacy of Mandukhai the Wise. I feel that, first and foremost, I need to give a huge thanks to Mandukhai, Dayan, Unebolod, and the cast of historical figures that made this series possible in the first place. Without Mandukhai, this story would not even exist. I only hope that I have done justice to the legacy she deserves.

To the people of Mongolia, I hope I have given strength and beauty to one of the most powerful women in your history. Mandukhai is one of the most amazing women I have ever learned about and a true credit to the history of your Nation. Thank you for giving me this chance. While the story is historical fiction, I aimed to add nuggets of truth to her background and life. If I have made some misstep in culture, please accept my most heartfelt apology. It was not intentional.

I also wanted to thank my husband for his incredible patience as I shirked my real-life responsibilities to complete this series. I know it was hard, and I appreciate you giving me the space to do this. To my kids, thank you for your enthusiasm when I rambled on about Mongolia, Mandukhai, Dayan, Unebolod... and pretty much everything that frustrated me during the writing process. Your hugs made all the difference some days!

To my editor, Sunny, thank you for your patience and guidance. All your extra work has helped shape this into something realistic and fantastic. And to my cover designer, Kat. These covers look *amazing*!

Thank you to my family and friends who encouraged me even when I was an emotional wreck or perhaps (more realistically) completely absent from life.

To my fellow writers at the SPWG: this series exists as it does in large part because of your honesty, advice, and dedication to helping me meet tough deadlines. I cannot thank you all enough for sticking it out with me, even when I seemed unbearable!

To my Advance Readers: I appreciate your dedication to reading my book, as well as your patience when I have made obvious mistakes in the advance copies. I hope you continue to read and enjoy my books for years to come!

A special shout-out to my Patreon patrons who continue to support me and my crazy work: Tyson. Publishing a book is about more than just writing. It requires editing, cover design, marketing, and a whole slew of other expenses that can quickly add up. Being a Patron helps relieve some of that burden from my shoulders. Your support makes a difference!

And of course, to my readers. I hope you enjoyed reading this epic saga as much as I loved writing it. Saying goodbye to these characters is one of the hardest things I have done. They have grown near and dear to my heart, and I don't think I will ever forget them. I only hope I have made you feel the same.

If you enjoyed the book, I encourage you to leave an honest review. Even just clicking on the star rating makes a difference for small, indie authors like me. It's our own form of social proof, and the more places you can leave that proof, the better it is for me and for other potential readers.

BOOKS BY STARR Z. DAVIES

<u>Divica Stormborn Chronicles</u>
Stormvalor
Stormveil
Stormcrown
<u>Divica War of Two Crowns</u>
Volume 1: Darkness Falls
<u>Powers Series</u>
Ordinary
Unique
(extra)ordinary
Superior
<u>Powers Origins</u>
Miller: Origin
Enid: Origin
Celeste: Origin
<u>Powers Legacy</u>
Powers Legacy: The Prequel
Desolation
Infiltration
Insurrection
Invasion
<u>Fractured Empire Saga</u>
Daughter of the Yellow Dragon
Lords of the Black Banner
Mother of the Blue Wolf
Empress of the Jade Realm
Prosperous Eternity
<u>Stand-Alone Stories</u>
Stones: A Steampunk Short Story

About Starr Z. Davies

STARR Z. DAVIES is an award-winning author of over 20 tales that span dystopian realms, epic fantasies, and echoes of forgotten histories. Dubbed the "Character Assassin," she weaves stories where heroes are tested by fire—both emotional and physical.

From her woodland home in northern Wisconsin, she crafts worlds while surrounded by her greatest allies: a supportive husband, two imaginative children, and a curious menagerie of robotic pets. When not conjuring new adventures, she dabbles in home enchantments, swims like a siren, battles through video game quests, and devours books like ancient tomes of power.

If you want to become friends with Starr, dark chocolate, Doctor Who, Parks & Rec, The Office, and the MCU are all fantastic ways into her heart. That or a love for fantasy books by indie authors.

Learn more about Starr and her books.

Keep up with Starr by signing up for her newsletter.

Want to be part of her community? Follow Starr on social media.